THE CONSTANT
TOWER

THE CONSTANT TOWER

TOWER

CAROLE McDONNELL

WILDSIDE PRESS

For my mother, my husband, and my sons.

Thanks to Becky Kyle, Jessica Butler Fry, Marvin Katzoff, for reading, critiquing and supporting this novel.

Thanks to Carla Coupe, John Betancourt, and Wildside Press for publishing me.

Published by Wildside Press LLC.
www.wildsidebooks.com

And I said to the man who stood at the gate of the year: "Give me a light that I may tread safely into the unknown." And he replied: "Go out into the darkness and put your hand into the Hand of God. That shall be to you better than light and safer than a known way."

—Minnie Louise Haskins

I was blind, but now I see.

John 9:25

THE CONSTANT TOWER

The Beautiful One from my clan, is dead.
The day takes us.
If to forest, no rain.
If to desert, no sun.
For he was rain and sun,
A cloud bringing all my comfort.
In our Permanent Home, the gathered clans greet him.
'His words were daggers, brave and swift,' they sing.
'His heart was kind and noble.
In the world of the living, distress.
But for us, joy.
The day turns,
His longhouse searches for him. But he is safe here in our home.'

—Psal's elegy on the death of his friend, Ephan.

CHAPTER 1

THE STUDIER OF WORLDS

Now my prince, in my former rendition, I spoke of Ephan's deeds. Then you asked me to tell the tale again, and this time to tell you Psal's story. I will play my part. But you must play your part as well. For you it is given the task of forgetting all you have heard of the previous tale and to keep your heart and mind on Psal. Can you do this?

Inside the Nahas longhouse, see then: Psal. A boy of about fifteen. A prince too, like yourself, a studier of worlds for his clan. But primarily, a boy.

He had risen early before the moons waned and, as usual, was thinking of his sweetheart Princess Cassia, the daughter of Chief Tsbosso, his father's great enemy. For six months, King Nahas had forbidden the marriage. Confused, longing for Cassia, Psal knew only this: he breathed easier and walked more joyfully when among the Peacock Clan, the clan to which the gentle, lovely Cassia belonged.

"How wonderfully the Peacock women use twigs to frame their faces!" he extolled. "And how elegant the decorated shells in their hair! They're such simple and natural beauties. Don't you think so? Unlike our women who use pretense and distance so our warriors will prize them! Aren't the women of the Peacock Clans charming in their naturalness?"

Ephan's apricot-colored eyes peered at him through thick locks of white hair. "Breasts and tightly woven hemp skirts *do* have a *natural* effect. But she was very bold that sweetheart of yours, wasn't she? For all that 'simplicity' of hers."

"Cassia is a chief's daughter. Tsbosso's daughter! Why shouldn't she be bold in letting me know she wanted me?" He spoke in a conspiratorial whisper. "She allowed me to kiss her the last time we met."

"Yes, you told me. Several times." Ephan picked up the gray parchments used to track towers. "But she didn't allow you to lie with her, did she?"

"A chief's daughter can't just lie with anyone."

"If this girl wants a lover whose features are like those of her own people, the Firstborn son of King Nahas is not just 'anyone.'"

Footsteps light and soft—a woman's—hurrying down the corridor momentarily pushed thoughts of his beloved away. They stopped outside the keening room. The intricately-embroidered curtained screen in the doorway was pushed aside. Psal looked up from his parchments, outside his daydream: Narena—the midwife of the longhouse—entered. She stood peering down at Ephan, her adopted son, and at Psal, the studiers of the royal longhouse.

"Betri's time has come." She pushed her thick, unkempt, graying hair from her face.

"Why tell us of this?" Psal asked her. "*You're* the midwife."

Even if Psal was only a studier, he was Firstborn of the clan; Narena should've showed him due respect, but she answered curtly. "The birthing's difficult, and Chief Studier Dannal is asleep." She looked from Psal to Ephan, then back to Psal again.

Dannal was not asleep, of course; the old studier's listlessness and stained teeth were only two of the telltale signs that the Tomah pharma had enslaved him.

"Boys," Narena said. "Hurry! Which one will it be?"

Ephan lifted the parchments—pale hands over paler hair—and waved Psal toward the door. "I'm tracking towers. This one's mind is on love. Let *him* bring new life into the world."

* * * *

Bright morning; the moons fled. Psal clutched a newborn boy in the hollow of his left arm. The infant's palate was cleft, the nose split in two.

With his right hand, Psal attempted to ward off Cyrt—a chief captain, his father's close kinsman. A jagged scar on Cyrt's right cheek proclaimed the warrior's bravery in a past skirmish with a Peacock Clan, but now such bravery vaunted itself against an innocent child. Cyrt turned to the others; some gesture unseen by Psal caused laughter to fill the longhouse. Dagger drawn, Cyrt wheeled about to look at Psal again. Smirking, he tossed the weapon from left hand to right. Back and forth, the blade flashed rhythmically, like oil lanterns flickering in the morning light.

Tears trailed down Psal's cheek. *Again, Cyrt's relentless teasing.* The ten years away from his clan studying with the Master of the Wintersea should have given him a thicker skin.

Nevertheless. He turned to his father. "King Nahas, Father. Queen Hinis, Mother. Allow the child to live."

King Nahas stood near the hearth; his face ruddied and shamed by his son's weakness. Near a window, Queen Hinis—regal and cold she was—threw Psal a scornful look. The boy sunk into himself. "Firstborn," the queen asked, "will you grow teats and feed it?"

"I expect he will," Cyrt said, and the queen smiled.

His back against the wall, Psal clutched the child with both hands now. "The other clans, Great Queen. Such damaged little ones…they allow to live. Mother, this one will live. This one *should* live."

He could give no valid reason for wanting the child to be spared. Certainly a vague hope of the child's future usefulness was not enough to disdain the Wheel clan's age-old edict. Male children born ill, damaged, or deformed were killed. Mercy generally did not triumph over the cruel tradition. Psal's father—nature-blessed Nahas, chief of the Nahas longhouse, king of all the Wheel Clans—had mercifully allowed Psal to live.

Yet once again, Psal told himself, *the error of that mercy is being shown to all.*

Psal pushed past shame. "They will not think you weak, Father. Nahas, this child might prove valuable to our clan. As I have, Father. Am I not valuable, Father?" Tears clouded his sight as he waited for the king's answer. "Am I not loved, Father?" He wiped his eyes with his forearm and pointed to his clubfoot, the mark of his ignominy. He lifted the twisted shriveled left leg, a thing he always hid. "I have lived, Nahas, and have proven myself. Am I not a competent studier, Father, deft in all tongues, skillful in all natural lore including tower science?"

The child in his arms gasped for air, a half-hearted fitful cry, hurting its own cause. Yet it must have desired life for it turned its head from Cyrt's dagger and buried its face in Psal's black studier's tunic as it grasped his thumb.

The king spoke to Cyrt and not to his Firstborn, his voice impatient, but not—unlike Hinis—cold. "Cyrt, take the child."

Darkness as Psal closed his eyes. Darkness as he pressed his back against the wall, wishing it would swallow both himself and the child. Light again when he lifted his eyelids and looked on Narena. Narena—she who eyed all damaged children with a shudder—glared at him in silent scorn, and Betri...now clutched...now asked, "Studier, can you not see the child is suffering?"

"Firstborn, you shame your father. Be more of a man." Although gentle and playful toward healthy children, Cyrt never showed mercy to Damaged Ones. Only Ephan had somehow earned his begrudging respect. He spoke now to Ephan, who had hurried down from the rampart. "King's Favorite, tell the Firstborn, this isn't a battle he'll win."

"Cloud," Psal begged Ephan. "Plead for me. Plead with your mother. Tell her *you* have lived, *you* have thrived these fifteen years." He held his breath, hoping Ephan—King's Favorite—would help his cause.

Ephan leaned forward, whispered in Psal's right ear, "Well did our old master nickname you 'Storm,' for you blow both good and bad away. Look now, did they not grant you time to use soothing pharma to kill the child? More than that you did not ask. Little though that mercy was, you should have taken it. Now morning docks in this unexplored region, our studier tasks await us, and the child still lives. Let Cyrt take it outside."

Ephan held a warning finger before Cyrt's face, spoke as if he, a studier, was a warrior's equal. "But, Warrior, take care you kill the babe quickly and mercifully." Ephan reached for the newborn, but Psal clutched it tighter.

"Let me send it from this world," Psal pleaded. "I'll use pharma to soothe it softly and swiftly into a painless death. Please, I will. I will."

The hands of his fellow studier gently pulled the child from his own tightly clenched fingers; the newborn was turned over to Cyrt. Psal leaned against the wall, his arms empty. Once again, he lost the battle against traditional "good sense."

The child's cries faded as Cyrt carried it from the longhouse. Throughout the gathering room, women, children, warriors—even the other three studiers—stared at Psal. Psal took several deep breaths. He placed his empty hand on his left leg. *What will the others see when they look at me? A petulant ghost dragging its lame leg away in defeat.* He glanced at the hearth, then at the Residential Corridor to the left of the gathering room. No escape there. Other warriors had awakened and were walking toward the hearth. He looked in the opposite direction, the passageway known as the Chief's Corridor. *There*, past the Chief Studier's room with its glut of pharma, past the royal chambers, past the grain storerooms, the armories and the ice rooms with fermented meat, the solitude of the stables awaited him. *There*, on the farthest edge of the longhouse, he could chew himself into oblivion on Tomah bark. He could be bowed and cowed by sleep. In dreams, he could forget his ignominy.

Except, he reminded himself, a Tomah-wracked body was not a body a studier should have. *And a Firstborn should not hide his grief in enslaving pharma. I am still Firstborn of the Wheel Clan. Even so, wouldn't it be better to be cast into the fearsome night rather than live with this people?*

He stood unmoving until all eyes but Ephan's turned elsewhere. Then, rejecting Ephan's outstretched hand, he followed his friend toward the Chief's Corridor.

"Cloud," he asked Ephan as the din of the gathering room faded. "Why am I not more accepting of my fate? As a Firstborn, I should be brave. As a studier, I should unflinchingly toss myself into the embrace of the unmaking night as if we were lovers. But here I am. Studier and Firstborn. Both and neither."

Ephan drew a long breath. "Unfortunately, it is an uncommon predicament."

Psal wiped his snotty nose and tear-wet face. "I know it. I know it. And here I stand, being so much and so little, stinking up Nahas' longhouse."

"A small stink, not a great one." Ephan walked into one of the studiers' rooms and waited for Psal to enter.

"Why must you joke? I'm telling you my heart."

Ephan turned, smiled his broken smile. "You had me pondering smells that could stink up a three-hundred-chamber longhouse. I could not help but joke. But do not fear. Perhaps you will do great unsmelly things yet. Only, do not attempt to change things now. Wait until you're a chief. Why battle alone? And so publicly?"

"I didn't battle alone. The child was on my side!"

"How exasperating you are!"

Away from the hearth, Psal considered how his father had ignored him. He forced confidence into his voice. "Nahas, come here! We must speak! Now!"

In the dimly-lit corridor, several young girls on ladders were uncovering the shutters in the ceiling windows while others switched on the roof's sun crystals or extinguished candles. Ephan, the girls, and three women carrying grain from the storage rooms all gave Psal warning looks. He challenged all with a Firstborn's haughty frown and waited at the entrance of the king's chamber for Nahas to approach.

When the king entered his royal quarters, he walked past Psal. "Firstborn," he said with unconcealed impatience. "If you're here to tell me of the new region, speak on. But if I am to be confounded and assaulted by one of your tantrums—"

"You did not honor me as Firstborn, Father." Half-remembering the pose and attitude of some long-dead warrior, Psal tried to make his body—blasted like a weed in a heavy storm—imitate strength. "You should have."

"Firstborn"—the king walked to an unshuttered window and leaned against it, his back to Psal—"I had hoped your training as a studier would change the propensities of your heart. But your anger against your own people is still too great."

Psal crossed his arm. "If I hate my own people, then you should allow me to leave."

"That old discussion again." The king peered into the slowly-emerging terrain. "Firstborn, you've keened us into a thicket. Was there no better place for the longhouse to anchor?"

"The region is full of rocks, lakes, and thick forests, Nahas." Aware that he was still standing in the doorway, Psal tentatively placed his right foot into his father's room, then dragged the left one inside also. "The tower could find no sparser…No, Nahas, I will not allow you to leave the conversation unfinished."

Nahas rubbed his forehead and turned from the window. He stared at Psal as if pondering the strange creature he had spawned. Then he looked outside again and pointed to a tall, looming structure outside. "It looks like an ancient temple. I suppose you and Ephan will want to explore the ruins. But first things first. Soil samples, and mapping...."

Psal bit his bottom lip. "Father, about Cassia—"

"You wanted the girl because she wanted you." Nahas was not looking at him. "That was her greatest virtue. Not her only virtue, of course, but it was the virtue you most admired because you're a boy who hungers for love. A king's son should not be ruled by such heart hunger. Such emotions show a diseased mind, something far worse than a diseased body."

"The Peacock Clan does not disdain my 'diseased' body." Psal grasped his father's arm and yanked hard. "Or my diseased mind! Cassia does not. The Peacock Clans honors all people, whatever their illnesses. They do not kill their—"

"Enough!" The king pulled his hand away, raised a clenched right fist.

Psal flinched. The dull ache in his hip pleaded for soothing pharma, but now his body betrayed him, trembling. He winced. Showing his pain shamed him, but either Nahas had not seen it or had mercifully decided to ignore it.

The king's arms, freckled and tanned, relaxed. It gestured at the world beyond the window. His voice was soft again, patient. "The knowledge of keening is our wealth, Firstborn. Our tower science has helped us survive. We own much. Food, fertile regions, lakes, seashores. You believe a marriage between you and Cassia will end the skirmishes—at least with Tsbosso's clan. But can you not understand? I cannot let a studier marry into the clan of our enemies. Would you not allow your wife to seduce away our secrets?"

"No, Father. I would not."

"See, that is where we differ," the king said. "Truly, I think that within ten days of marrying into their clan, you would betray us."

"And why would I do that, Nahas?"

"To help Tsbosso defeat other Peacock Clan chiefs," the king said. "Because you are too eager to please any who claim to love you, Firstborn. The Peacock Clans—strong as they are—are disorganized and always warring among themselves. Who can count the number of their chiefs? And Tsbosso, your friend, is the wiliest of them. Even now, the friendship between you and that scheming chief troubles me. When you have proven yourself capable of honoring our clan's laws, I will consider allowing you to marry Tsbosso's daughter. In the meantime, if you need a woman, visit the comfort women as Ephan and the others do. The conversation is ended."

Psal looked about the king's chamber to hide his hurt. His gaze fell on a red linen cap lying on his parents' sleeping mat. Similar to the leather caps worn by Wheel Clan warriors and studiers, this cap was worn by chiefs' sons on ceremonial occasions. It was unusual to have both a studier and a prince's cap, but Psal's own red cap rested on a shelf in the Firstborn's Chamber, a room he rarely visited. He assessed his father: the close-cropped auburn hair, the muscular arms, the strong body. *How grievous that one so nature-blessed should be so unlucky to bear a son with my cursed form. And yet...he allowed me to live.*

"Nahas, if I find a girl from our clan who loves me in spite of my infirmity—or because she thinks I might someday become a chief—any marriage would be an unhappy one. Even if the girl loved me, she would tease me relentle—"

"Or you would think she teased."

"Whatever the cause, we would not be happy. This is how these things go."

"Is that *how those things go*?" The king walked from the window and placed his hand on his door. "Firstborn, sometimes you speak like an old man, sometimes like a little child, sometimes both. You are neither. Now, hurry. The dawn is breaking and you have much exploration to do."

Stung by his father's words, Psal blurted out. "Nahas, one day I will leave you, and with that leaving I will leave all that you value."

"You speak your heart's intentions too freely," the king answered. "Should I trust you to keep our secrets, when you cannot keep your own?"

Psal didn't answer.

"And one thing more, Firstborn. You may enter anytime, of course. You're my son. And you *are* Firstborn. But think twice if you open my door only to challenge me."

Head bowed, jaw tight, Psal limped from his father's chamber past the keening room toward the studier room. In other clans, the position of studier of worlds was inherited or earned. Or it was cast like a mantle onto the shoulder of some intelligent child by communal vote, and that child would be taught all the lore, tongues, and beliefs of one of Odun-ao's great clans. Not so the Wheel Clan. They chose damaged boys to be studiers. Such children were expected to be grateful. The Master of the Wintersea had taught his students that they were ghosts, and that being a ghost was an honorable thing: 'A studier is dead while he lives,' the old teacher had said. 'Because, though damaged, he has been spared death, which others think was his rightful due. Thus, he is a ghost, an intermediary between all clans, a mediator between the living and the dead, the

Creator and the created, the organic and the inorganic world. A citizen of all the tribes.' *We are not kings of the earth. We are its very dust.*

He entered the studier room, where he found Ephan sorting through a basket of pharma jars.

Swiveling on his stool, Ephan settled two circular crystals held together with a little wire frame on his nose, then strapped a large dagger to his right thigh and placed a slingshot and several empty jars onto the cart. "That certainly ended well."

Psal limped past him. "If you cannot console me, be quiet. Or speak of other matters."

"This is a watery region. Emon plants should be abundant." Emon, the Studier's Herb. So called because studiers with painful illnesses, like Psal, often reeked of it.

"I suppose so," Psal answered. Where was Cassia today? What was she doing?

He sat on a low, wheeled bed, made comfortable with cushions, that Ephan had designed and built for him. Grumbling, he rolled toward Ephan, who now stood beside the parchment-cluttered shelf. Ephan lifted a brown clay jar containing a sticky white balm that protected those afflicted with the Wheel Clan disease against the sun, and Psal tried to think of exploration, discoveries and soil samples—such things that delighted studiers and bored warriors. He found no joy except when he thought of Cassia.

Ephan opened two more clay jars containing pharma against the venom of reptiles and insects. He rubbing his hands with these ointments, then passed the jars to Psal.

Through the window, the new terrain grew more distinct. The unmaking night was over.

Psal touched his nose, so very like his father's, a nose like a sloping mountainside. Unlike his father and the rest of the Wheel Clan, Psal was not pale-skinned. Nor was he dark like those from his mother's Macaw clan. His skin was honey-colored, and long black hair circled his head in a tangle of loose curls. Not that his clan brothers cared about such matters, but it was another thing that differentiated Psal. Psal caught Ephan's gaze and grimaced. He dropped his hand, then leaned on his right elbow, facing Ephan.

"Cloud," he asked, glancing at his woven blanket. Would it hold all his meager belongings? "Would you think me weak if I escaped our clan and married Cassia?"

"I? I would think you cruel for leaving me behind to be punished by Nahas. Even if I was entirely ignorant of your flight, I would suffer greatly for your deceit."

"But, your suffering aside, would you hate me? I would not like you to hate me."

"I would still love you. Hunted man though you would be. Responsible for war though you would be. I suppose I would worry for you, but I would not worry long."

"Why not?"

"Because, Wayward One, Nahas would drag you back to us. If you wish to be free, why not flee to your mother's clan? Your uncle Chief Bukko is a good man, and you—a peace child—would be honored among them. And *they* would allow you to marry Cassia."

Live with his mother's mealy-mouthed clan? Psal's stomach turned. "I've seen their studiers. Lazy, satisfied, smug. Exploration doesn't interest them."

"True, true. As the clan, so the studier—as they say."

Ironic, considering the studiers of this clan. Psal could hear water nearby. The water spoke of stillness: probably a lake. He heard echoes also, with his studier's hearing, and the wings of bats inside a cave. He groaned. "The walls of this longhouse are eating away our souls."

"Walls have no teeth." Ephan lifted his hands and let half the parchments rain down on Psal's head. "And you don't believe in souls. Nahas rebuked you privately just now. A mercy. And he gave you ten days to betray us. His confidence in you grows. There was a time he'd have given you a whole day. I, myself, am also prone to helping others, but I would hold out more than ten days."

Psal picked up a stylus, wet with blue ink and threw it at Ephan who caught it, laughing. Ephan walked to the window, a wide smile brightened his face. If Psal hadn't always insisted on getting a good night's sleep, Ephan would've stayed up all night watching the regions melt into each other. From Psal's youth he had felt as derelict as the Ruined Lost Cities, crumbling away like a rock beaten continually under a hammer, or like flowing waters wearing away a stone. He pushed away the sharp pain burning through his left hip and stood.

"Father spared me because my mother was grieving for a husband and he for a brother. Killing me would've been one more grief. When he found you, crawling naked and weak and damaged in the desert, that cunning one said, 'these two ghosts will live and grow together. Then no one will consider me weak for saving my damaged son.'"

"Sounds like a thought that would come to Nahas." Ephan walked to the tower stairwell. "We need Rangi too, and more Tomah for Dannal. Although…perhaps we should not let him have more of what enslaves him…."

Psal picked up the boots the women had made for him and stared glumly at the misshapen left foot. "Have you ever wondered what our lives would have been had we been born among the cliff-dwellers or among those who live in the caverns?"

"To live a life huddled in caves is not for you. Nor are you one to remain rooted forever. Cave dwellers are homebodies, always fearful lest the night catch them far from home. Those who live inside cliffs are no better." He pointed through the window. "Nor can I see you living in huts or in tents, under poles and reindeer pelt. In a longhouse, your soul can roam free and you have a clan to protect you. What could be better? Look, look at this new region. Do you wish to know what I saw as I stood on the rampart?"

"I hardly care."

"Ah, but you do! You *do* care!" Gaal's voice.

Tall and stocky with the olive skin and deep-set dark green eyes of the Grassrope Clan, Gaal was the Chief Steward of all Wheel Clan lands. He pushed aside the curtained screen.

"Firstborn," he said, entering, "Cyrt had almost begun to like you... well, not 'like' exactly. But—"

"If Cyrt is as he is, why are you his friend?"

"Firstborn, a warrior offered me his friendship. Should I—a steward—reject it?" Gaal tousled Psal's hair.

Psal pulled away "You are not as friendless as you think. Your fighting and mediation skills are so excellent that all respect you and accord you benefits few stewards enjoyed."

"True, Firstborn, but all are aware that my mother—and not my father—was of the Wheel Clan. It is a curse I must bear." Gaal moved to the window and squeezed Ephan's shoulder. "Cloud, tell me of this new region."

Ephan grabbed two black leather caps from a basket and threw one to Psal. "There's a lake," he said. "But shrub and vines clutter the path to it. Best to walk. The horses couldn't get through. And what do you think is below that clear blue water? An overwhelmed city from ancient times!"

Psal doubted Ephan saw all he claimed. Like all those with the Wheel Clan disease, Ephan's eyes were weak. But Ephan's keen sense of smell and sharp hearing were helpful in hiding his eyes' weakness.

"But tell me," Gaal said, "you saw no clan markings when you stood on the rampart?"

"None," Ephan answered. "No other clan has claimed this lost region. And I heard no other clan tower in any nearby region."

"Firstborn, are you still pouting?" Gaal glanced back at Psal. "Look now, the craftsmen and stewards have created such marvels for your convenience. The royal longhouse is unlike all others! Stools that are tables at one moment or steps and beds the next. Such love your father has for you! You wish to become a chief, do you not? Prove yourself mature. Then you shall not have to accept the place your damaged body assigned to you at birth."

Assigned to him? Had he not accepted the fact that his perfectly-formed, nature-blessed younger brother Netophah would be king? Why should he have to prove himself to be a chief?

"How differently you speak when you're complaining about the Wheel Clan women who refuse to marry you!"

Gaal flinched as if hit. Pricked by guilt, Psal watched the not-quite-warrior leave.

"The day has only begun and already I have been pummeled with rebukes and speeches," he said after Gaal was gone.

"You steadfastly refused Gaal's offer of friendship. And why insult him? He's honorable enough. Separated from the warriors, we of the lesser castes—warriors, stewards, studiers, and farmers—often befriend each other. And steward though he is, Gaal is a better warrior than those with Wheel Clan fathers. You should—"

"Our chief steward is Father's closest friend, Cloud. I have no intention of taking aid from the enemy's camp."

Ephan pulled the brim of his cap low over his face and threw a bow, several arrows, and about twenty small pouches into Psal's studier's sack. He gathered all the parchments and threw them on the council table. Then, lifting the intricately-carved walking staff which Chief Tsbosso, king of the largest Peacock Clan had given to the Studier-Firstborn, Ephan said, "I have no desire to chart endless towers today. Storm, let us venture forth and explore this world."

* * * *

All day the studiers surveyed, collected, and made notations. Deyn, Lan, Broqh, and Kwin—young warriors who had befriended them—remained at their side aiding them. As second moon climbed high in the sky, after Nahas' warriors had hunted, the fires were set. When third moon began to rise, Psal and Ephan climbed to the tower to study the controlled blaze.

See then: Psal and Ephan. Silent, both peering through spyglasses. The double moonlight usually turned the night sky from pale indigo to dull gray. But now, the distant sky glowed like torches: red, white, yellow. Nearby, the smoke mocked the day, misting the forest with bright grays and dull blues. Around the longhouse, the fire flickered and crackled. From the northwest, the terrified howlings of wild cats, from the northeast, the hoof beats of stampeding animals, echoing in the sky the cawing of fleeing birds.

Trouble grew inside the longhouse; First Night had gone. Second Night was come. Psal's young sisters had not yet returned. In the gloom, there was no glimpse of the lost girls' yellow tunics.

"Cloud." Psal noted the fatigued jitteriness of Ephan's eyes. "Are you sure the count is right?"

"I am not blind." Ephan climbed into the watchtower, the rounded spire of the tower. "I've told you already. Four hundred and eighty-six. All are inside except your sisters." His tone calmed. "Psal, the fires are far away. The girls are wise enou—"

"Nine and six year-old girls are not wise, Cloud. Earlier, when you spoke to Father—"

"No, they haven't crept in through any window or any of the lesser doors."

Psal sighed, caught between anger and worry. *What if the fire outpaces my sisters? What if the night outpaces them? Nahas will send warriors to search for them, but the advancing night! Even if we anchor the longhouse tonight in this region, the night....* He leaned against the watchtower, then paced the rampart. He strained his ears. "Do you hear that?"

"The sound of a child crying. But it is not the voice of either of your sisters."

Netophah, golden-haired, nature-blessed, raced up the tower stairs. He tugged at his brother's arm. "Firstborn, Father says Lan is the fastest of us. Lan will search for our sisters. We can wait no longer."

In the gathering room, Lan—fleet Lan, wild Lan—stood at the threshold of the longhouse's main entrance. Twenty years old, well-favored, slender, black-haired Lan was the child of a studier. Psal's friend, he had been allowed inside the studiers' ghostly circle. Smoke billowed past him into the gathering room as all awaited the king's command.

Chief Studier Dannal approached Lan. Aged, his body blighted by enslavement to Tomah and the Wheel Clan disease, he placed a hand covered with cancerous sores on Cyrt's shoulder and spoke to Lan.

"Lan is swift, but—even if he finds them—how would the little ones fare, hungry and night-tossed without a studier's help? Ephan's knowledge will guide all the lost home."

True. Lan knew more about towers than the other warriors, but he was not a studier. A studier could hear the barely audible songs of towers and regions, as well as the heartbeats of spoiled little girls lost in a blazing forest.

"I will return again with the king's daughters safe at my side," Ephan said, but Lan remained at the door.

Psal grasped Ephan's hand. "I will accompany Cloud."

Ephan glanced at Psal's deformed leg. "You'll delay—"

"I will not."

Psal's two young brothers at her side, Hinis hurried toward Ephan. Fear for her own daughter and for Netophah's sister lined her face. She hastily removed the leather cloaken from Lan's shoulder and placed it across Ephan's. Folded and strapped to the shoulder, the cloaken—when unrolled—was large enough to cover three large warriors—or two slender studiers and two careless little girls—and would prevent the night from separating them. "Bring my daughters home," she commanded.

Out the studiers ran, the longhouse fast-fading behind them, second night riding hard at their heels. Psal's weak muscles complained; his left leg and thigh hurt. Emon pharma, powerful though it was, only dulled his pain. Now, as he ran into the smoke, his lungs screamed in pain. Yet, he had to run. Then, a cry so small only a studier could hear it. As one, both turned eastward.

Ephan ran fast, faster, toward the cry. Second night and fire swirled about him, dust and smoke hid him from Psal's sight. Psal hobbled behind, cursing his wretched leg, strengthening his heart against anticipated grief. Then he heard the girls' voices issuing from a smoky clearing beyond a fiery thicket. The flames crackled all around. Past the blaze and into the clearing, Ephan ran. Out he came again, the fire licking at his heels, the girls in his arms coughing.

"Give Ria to me," Psal said. Tears and smoke burned his eyes.

Ephan pushed Psal's arm away. "I can carry both."

Not in this smoke! Not with this fire! Not with the unmaking night fast approaching. "Give her to me!"

Another cry sounded from within the fire. A baby's wail.

"The newborn? Is it still alive? Cyrt promised mercy!"

Ephan grasped Psal's hand. "Hurry! Away!"

Psal shook off Ephan's hold, ran into clearing. The child lay gasping amidst the brush. Psal lifted his dagger, held it high above the child's struggling chest. He could not strike. Out he came again, the blaze nearer. "Ephan! Please! Be merciful! Kill it for me."

Ephan's mouth dropped open.

"You should have killed it when you found it!" Psal shouted.

"The fire rages!" Ephan yelled.

"Where is your mercy? Like Cyrt, you would allow it to burn in this fire!"

Ephan placed Tanti on the ground. Hasting, silent, he raced back to the infant, knife drawn. A moment passed. Ria leaped onto Psal's back. The child's wailing stopped. Ephan scrambled from the smoke, wiped his bloodied dagger against his tunic and returned it to its sheath. Immediately, Tanti climbed into Ephan's arms.

Suddenly, strength and power flowed through Psal's damaged body. How fast he ran—and without pain! As if the wind bore him along. How fleet his feet! As if tower music pulled them in its wake. Like arrows shot forth from a bow, they flew from that forest, the darkening smoke pursuing.

At the longhouse, Psal's youngest brother greeted him. "I watched from the rampart, Firstborn! How fast you ran!"

"As fast as any other." The next to the youngest shouted, leaping as children do.

"Faster! If I had not seen it, I would not have believed it!"

Psal, too, could not believe it. He laughed, blushed when his father smiled. His mother smiled also. A smile not wide enough to remove the memory of her disdain, yet this rare tiny thing lifted Psal's heart.

He set his sister on her feet. "I should've let the Voca find you," he shouted. "They keen for abandoned towers and lost little girls like you!" He pointed through a window to the rising moons. "Did you not hear Lan's horn?" The girls glanced at each other—guilt and relief on their faces. Fear as well. His heart softened, his voice too. "I teased."

His sister threw her arms around his shoulder, kissed his neck. "We didn't want the child to die alone."

Tanti burst into tears. Her he did not tease. Because she was Netophah's sister. Because she was a little thing who could not bear being teased. He only squeezed her shoulder gently.

Cyrt sat near the hearth, eating of a wild boar caught earlier. Psal limped toward him.

"Why was the child made to linger?" He shoved Cyrt. "Even the animals and the fire did not wish to harm the child." He turned to the others. "Only you, members of its own clan...." He caught his mother's gaze, closed his mouth. Whatever glory gained by finding his sisters, he had now lost again.

CHAPTER 2

JOURNEYING TOWARD THE TRUCE FESTIVAL

Like all keening rooms, the one in the royal longhouse enclosed the tower's base. The tower, its door, its internal stone staircase winding upward, the watchtower in its spire—all were Psal's sanctuary. Except for those days when Nahas, his chief captains—Lebo, Seagen, Cyrt—and his stewards entered it for council meetings. As they did now.

The king leaned his elbows on the oval council table. "This harvest festival comes just in time. All this squabbling about regions. Raids committed by the Peacock Clans, burnt fields, looted longhouses, wounded stewards."

"A lasting truce with the Peacock Clans is possible." Gaal stood to the left of the tower door. "We lost much in the past year. Our stewards battle more often than they plant, and when they do plant and sow, the harvest is stolen by Peacock Clans. We stewards fight as well as any true Wheel Clan warrior. But…to defend one's self all day against enemy longhouses knowing help cannot come until the next morning…it is a hard thing. Tsbosso and the other chiefs use their domestication science to steal our livestock and raid our orchards. And we answer them with words? Nahas, the Peacock Clans do not fear our words."

Lebo, the oldest of Nahas' warrior, drew his fingers through his cropped gray hair. "As things are, we're on the verge of a war. I fear war even more than the neutral clans fear it."

"There must be something we can give to the Peacock Clans." Gaal spoke to Nahas but gave Psal a sly wink. "A peace marriage, perhaps?"

"Gaal," Nahas answered, "do not give the boy foolish hopes. Although Tsbosso is much-honored among the Peacock Clans, one truce marriage would not suffice. The Peacock sub-clans are too numerous, scattered, and cantankerous."

"The truce with the Voca has held these sixteen years," Cyrt said. "If we—"

"Truce or not," Lebo said, "when that vindictive queen presented us with the peace child, the seal of the truce between her clan and ours, I trembled at her coldness. Pale as the snow, she is. And lovely. But the blood in her veins is like the icy floes of the Wintersea. And just as unpredictable."

"Ezbel's anger is misplaced," Cyrt's adopted brother Seagen, Dannal's son, said. He winked at the king then tousled Ephan's hair. "A good man between her legs and she'll lose her anger."

"That I cannot say," Nahas said. "But I doubt Tsbosso wants a good man between his legs."

That elicited much laughter from all but Gaal. He spoke solemnly as he looked at the tower crystals in their sockets, "How many new discoveries, culled from their own observances, and improved upon the teachings of their old masters, have our studiers made! And yet, we must wait until morning to aid an attacked longhouse!" He stood in front of the primary keening tree, which was called the Lesser Light, and spoke to it. "Lesser Light, you who steer this tower, and you other keening trees as well, can you not share your secret with us? Is it so difficult? Why so silent? Can you not reveal more of yourself to your stewards and your studiers?"

The two keening trees that tracked Wheel Clan towers, the two others that charted towers from other clans, and the two that sent and received messages—all remained resolutely silent.

"Plead with them all you want," Cyrt said. "These towers are a secretive clan."

Gaal continued toward the final keening tree—the eighth tree, called by all Odunao clans *The Greater Light*. Its sockets empty without crystals, it stood behind the Lesser Light in the traditional place assigned it by the Creator. "Greater Light, perhaps you have some secret to tell us." He turned to Psal. "Is this tree as useless as some say, Firstborn?"

"It is," Psal said. "I keep it here because it is a concession to the old superstition…and because the towers complain when I remove it."

But his thoughts were not on towers or even on the skirmishes and raided longhouses. All his heart's thoughts were on Tsbosso's beautiful daughter and their meeting at the festival.

* * * *

Psal woke earlier than usual, and in a good mood. His eyes had opened upon the twinkling blue crystal in the socket of the Lesser Light keening branch: the longhouse had fully materialized at the festival region. Ephan wasn't in the room, probably sorting specimens or grinding pharma. Or perhaps Chief Studier Dannal had foisted some new burden on him. Psal looked at the parchment at his feet. *Tracking towers and annotating parchments. And all the while, my beloved Cassia awaits.*

He limped to the window, pulled the woolen curtains aside and opened the shutter. Outside lay sandy desert, gathered longhouses, the Great Mesa, and a ruined city. The sooner he finished his duties, the sooner he could wash the stale Emon from his body and race outside to the spontaneous city of longhouses and the ancient edifices on the desert plain and see Cassia.

To those trained to hear them, tower songs sounded like tinkling bells or like rams' horns or like wind blowing through the reeds, like drums great or small. Unlike the restrained songs of the Wheel Clan towers, Peacock Clan towers sounded of rhythmic drumming—wild and sultry, like Tsbosso's daughter. *So many towers! A delightful cacophony.* But among the varied songs of the scattered clans, a song from a dying, possibly uninhabited, tower. Psal could not place it. *Perhaps Ephan can.*

* * * *

"It certainly sounds night-tossed, doesn't it?" Ephan's face reflected Psal's curiosity. "Sounds like a Waymaker clan tower. It doesn't sound abandoned though. But we were planning on going to the Mesa." He glanced at Psal's leg. "Are you able to make both journeys?"

Psal considered the day's challenge: to speak with his beloved and embrace her, to translate treaties for his father, to travel to the Mesa, to explore the possibly-abandoned tower, to return and lie in his beloved's arms until the third moon rose and night forced them to part. *It can be done!* He picked up a spyglass from a nearby shelf. "I'm not as weak as others think. Or, Nahas would've sent me off to a steward longhouse long years ago. We should claim this tower before others do. Our stewards can repair it. And Nahas would be pleased that we found it."

Just then Netophah appeared at the door wearing a brown tunic and brown leggings.

"So you wear warrior's clothes now?" Ephan remarked.

Netophah smoothed his tunic and smiled. "I'm too big for yellow."

Psal turned to his brother. "Why are you here, birthright-stealer?"

"I heard you speaking just now. I wish to wander with you today. May I?"

"Spying on me for Father?"

Netophah's eyes widened. "Why would I do that?"

Psal glared at Netophah until the shamed boy lowered his head and left the room.

CHAPTER 3
CHIEF TSBOSSO

Through their communal echo-location, the towers of King Nahas' royal longhouse, the tower Queen Hinis and the women would use to feast with the Peacock Clan women, and Tsbosso's two Peacock Clan towers spontaneously created a closed feasting hall. All other longhouses—Wheel Clan, Peacock Clan and the great clans—spread out around them in all directions.

In his annals, Psal wrote:

In forty-nine ruined cities of Odunao, the truce festivals.
And in the Eastern Ruined City, sixty-seven Peacock longhouses,
Seventy-eight Wheel Clan longhouses.

Netophah's mother's clan was there.
White-haired, eyes like the crescent moon, the Waymaker clans—
    a good, gentle, wise people.
But scattered—unwilling to grasp and hold, looking only toward
    The Permanent Home.
They lived as nomads, taming regions then moving on.

The Grassrope clans—dark-haired and sallow. A filthy, loutish,
    selfish, grasping clan.
Stout from gobbling, with desperate hungry greedy eyes.

Hinis' people—the Macaw clan, a people skilled in survival.
Hinis greeted her brother, Bukko, loading their baskets with fine
    rarities;
All these clans lived in peace with the Wheel Clan.

Then the great and noble Peacock Clans!
Expert, their mastery of animal science.
Out of Tsbosso's longhouse came lions and reptiles, as docile as
    lambs.

Of all the great clans, only the all-female Voca was absent.
But who was surprised at that? The Voca hated all male-ruled
    clans,
From within the Wheel Clan, Ezbel the Voca Queen was born.

She hated them above all clans.

The smaller clans also feasted.
For one day, equal to the great tribes.

And in the distance, the Great Eastern Ruined City and the Great
  Mesa stood
Reminding all of the ancient time when night spoke of permanence and all the clans were one.

Freed from the duty of translating for his father, Psal clasped his staff and searched for Cassia among the festive crowds. Mark you how gracious, how charming, how exuberant the young prince was when not among his own clan. How he leaped on that withered leg and scampered about with joy! *I have forgotten what I am: a prince, forgotten my own peace. Surrounded by other clans, I find myself again.* Now, girls from the Waymaker Clans stroked his face; women and men from the Grassrope clans flirted with him, running their fingers through his flowing dark curls; Peacock Clan girls flitted past, flirting in their dyed buckskin skirts, their faces painted like butterflies or virginal white; warriors and studiers from clans large and small bowed as they passed him, warriors and studiers from other Wheel Clan longhouses, pointed at him: That is the Firstborn of the Wheel Clan!

But where was Cassia? She should be with the unmarried girls, flirting with young men, teasing old warriors, showing off her beauty. Finding her should not be so difficult. At last Psal saw her, but she walked among the married Peacock women. Her face was no longer covered in white clay but with red. The roundness of her stomach could not be mistaken. Still, hope was securely lodged in the boy's heart as he raced toward her. She half-smiled when their eyes met and walked toward him, glancing around her.

"Why are you here, among these married…" A marriage tattoo on her cheek. *Even if she has married someone since the last time we met, it is possible her husband has died.*

Cassia carried a large wooden bowl. She placed it atop a broken stone column. The bowl of steaming Yisin grain wobbled, but did not fall.

Psal's heartstrings tightened. Could you not have waited for me? "So you're another man's wife now?"

"I have wanted to see you…to explain," she said in the Wheel Clan tongue and kissed his cheek tenderly. "But Father has kept me from you all these moons. When you sent messages to the towers, he did not tell me. And all this morning he ordered me to stay with the married women." Tears trailed through the clay on her brown cheeks. "A chief's son from the Full Blossom Peacock Clan gave Father much pharma science for me. I pleaded and begged but—"

"But you promised."

"My father broke my pledge, Psallo. Not I. My heart continues to desire only you."

"Does he…your new husband…beat you?"

More tears flowed. "No more or less than is expected. But I must warn you—" She stopped speaking suddenly and trembled like a child caught in a forbidden act.

Psal turned. Old Chief Tsbosso strode toward them. Cassia lifted her grain bowl and disappeared into the throng of married Peacock Clan women.

Psal's head throbbed. "Are the truce negotiations finished already?" he asked when the old man stood before him. *Why have you forced her to marry one who beats her, one she does not love?* He reached out and straightened the mantle slipping from the old man's shoulders.

Tsbosso's gnarled fingers pinched Psal playfully on the right ear. "Many clans seek treaties with your father. Small things first, then important things. And you, my boy?" Tsbosso stroked the staff he had given Psal. "Has this helped you? You lean on it like a prince born among my people."

"The others deem me weak when I use it. But it is often necessary to lean upon it."

"You must use it, my boy! Your tender heart, you cannot help. The body, however, can be trained to stand straight and strong. You don't want to look puny, do you?"

Psal nodded. *He's pretending not to see my anger or his daughter's heartbreak, because he knows he's the cause of it.*

They walked toward Tsbosso's longhouse and sat on the ground near its main entrance. Together, they looked out at the festival, talking of this and that, of ancient lore and new discoveries, of illness and health, of the cruel judgments made by unkind uncaring hearts, of clans and traditions.

The old man scratched his head. "I've warned your father more times than I can remember that sending apprentice studiers off to roam the world with disgruntled old masters is a dangerous practice. No, no, that kind of thing never comes to any good. And the Master of the Wintersea? The bitterest of Wheel Clan studiers? No, I knew it would not work. And have I not been proven right? But who can tell Nahas anything?"

"Indeed," Psal said. *Like Nahas, none can tell you anything either.*

"Come now, my boy! You look like a cliff-dweller who has just realized night has fallen and he's two leagues from home." He gestured widely. "We're at a festival. Beautiful girls abound, and you're a king's son. Now, this old man needs your help to get up."

Psal stood and helped the chief rise.

On his feet again, the old man said, "My boy, she is eight years older than you are, and she has a temper as bad as yours. Living with her would've led to one fight after another."

"I liked her temper. I liked everything about her. More than that Full Blossom Clan chief's son could."

He waited for the old chief's rebuke, but whether because Psal was a king's son or because Psal was a particular favorite, Tsbosso ignored the outburst. Instead, the old man pointed. "Your friend has always liked old women."

Psal turned. Ephan stood beside a tree shyly watching Tzaddi, Tsbosso's oldest daughter. A beautiful woman, but ill-treated by her father for some past trespass, she stood next to Poh, Tsbosso's oldest son and Psal's childhood friend. Psal frowned. Cassia probably had such a husband, tall, with a body strong as a tree, nature-blessed and healthy.

"Brother Psallo," Poh called as he walked past. "My other self, my twin."

Psal tried to smile.

Tsbosso slapped Psal on the shoulder. "What do you think of marrying my youngest girl, the one we call 'Moonlight'?"

Psal's mouth fell open. "Moonlight?" he echoed. "She's a jewel."

"A jewel indeed!" Tsbosso said. "As out of reach as the elusive moonlight. But not out of reach for you, Wheel Clan Firstborn."

Lovely, good, and wise was Moonlight. But his heart did not sing for her. "I don't want her. Why do you offer her?"

"These skirmishes must stop, my boy. Or our clans will destroy each other."

"Let the matter rest," Psal said. "Make me less important in your eyes. Betroth Moonlight to Netophah if you wish to prevent skirmishes between our people. They're of the same age."

"I know that Nahas disdains the thought of letting his studiers marry outside his clan. But peace must be attained. Tell me, if Netophah were to marry my daughter, what part of your tower science is Nahas willing to share? Would the king teach us how to keen towers from afar?"

Psal shook his head. "Great Chief, Father will not give you tower science. No, not even if Netophah becomes your son. And as for far-off keening, if you knew that skill you would vie with us for uninhabited and abandoned towers. Ask for some of our oil regions. We have much oil. A small price to pay for an alliance."

"Would he show us how to use false notes to disguise our tower songs?" the Chief asked.

Psal chuckled. "I do not wish to rebuke the chief of a great clan, but why persist in asking for tower science? Great Chief, speaking to Nahas of towers will come to no good."

"But, my boy, consider," Tsbosso pressed. "Today, my youngest son and several warriors must remain with our women in their longhouse as they journey to feast with your women. All across Odunao, as your women and our women meet to feast, my poor warriors are bound to stay with our women. Why? Because someone has to keen our women home. It is a *great* bother. But if we knew how to keen from afar...."

"If you taught your women how to keen towers, as we teach ours, you wouldn't have this *great* bother. Great Chief, your ability to charm fierce beasts interests Nahas. Offer him that. But no talk of towers, please! Yesterday, we found a new region. Fertile, with lakes and meadows. We burned the forest, but did little more. Wild animals still roam free. Since we haven't labored on it, Father may give it to you. Yes, I think he would. He, too, is tired of these skirmishes."

"Well then, I will not ask of tower science. But you send me such sad tower songs, about how lonely you are among your own people. Tell me, if you married one of my daughters, would Nahas allow you to live primarily in our longhouse? If you were Tsbosso's son-in-law, none would dare mock you, even if you lived among your own people."

"Even after marriage I will continue to live with my clan. Father thinks I'm weak, you see, and ready to betray him."

Tsbosso looked appropriately shocked. "Oh, how unfairly that man treats you! You are *not* weak." He glanced at a table where Cyrt, Gaal, and Nahas feasted. "Think of it, Psallo. A marriage into a clan that respects you! Unimpeded explorations! The respect of being the Father of a peace child. Perhaps chief of your own longhouse. I must help your father see clearly."

"Forget me and my sorrows, Great Chief. For our people's sake, make Netophah your son-in-law. My heart is still with Cassia." Psal bowed then walked over to Ephan.

"Ask the woman to lie with you," he told Ephan, "or stop staring at her."

"I'll have better luck exploring the abandoned tower than exploring that beauty." Ephan gave a wistful sigh. "So will Cassia allow you to lie with her again? I haven't seen her as yet."

"Cassia's been given away."

"Bad luck. I know you loved her."

"I did, yes. I will always love her." Psal pointed at the remains of the ancient aqueduct rising high above the dusty road leading to the Great Mesa. "The abandoned tower first. Then the Ruined City, then the Mesa...."

Ephan was still looking at Tzaddi. Psal hoped Tsbosso's daughter would favor his friend.

"She is a lovely one, isn't she?" Psal said. "She seems to like you as well."

Ephan blushed, turned toward the ancient gate. He had prepared a small, wheeled cart with supplies, and they set off on their journey.

They had not gone far from the feast grounds when Psal turned to see Netophah following them.

"Return home!" Psal yelled back at him. They pelted him with stones and twigs but he continued following them.

Thus, the three sons of King Nahas walked toward the abandoned tower—the tall, puny, and peevish Firstborn, the too-pretty albino found-ling, and the well-favored, nature-blessed heir of all Wheel Clan lands.

CHAPTER 4

THE VOCA

Persistent sand fleas and the sun's heat assaulted the boys as they journeyed past ancient stone archways depicting male athletes engaging in sexual acts, past the ruins of brothels where the tiny bones of aborted children littered the long-dried up sewers, past the faded chipped wreckages of fertility temples. In their younger days, the studiers had wondered at the stability and constancy of those ancient edifices. Older now, they understood no more than they did when they traveled with the Wintersea Master. They now contented themselves with the words he always used when faced with some incomprehensible planetary cipher: *There are more things in the universe that can be understood with even my great mind, boys.*

They traveled until the stone road lost itself to the desert. All the while they collected such things that interested only studiers. About halfway in their journey, they saw vultures circling over sparse bush. There, amid scavenging ravens, a woman's rotting body lay clothed in a blue tunic—the common dress of Falconer women. The woman had the features of different clans. Maggots swarmed in her ripped-open womb. Psal looked about. There was no boy corpse anywhere nearby, but that meant little. A living newborn boy would've been borne away by the night. A girl would be nursed in the arms of the Voca chief.

"Is it...the Voca?" Netophah asked, hiding behind Psal.

"Of course, the Voca! No other clan rips children from their mothers' wombs." Psal turned about, his back to the body. "I sincerely hope you will not force the Principles on me and make me bury this woman."

Ephan grimaced. The thought had probably been in his mind. He surveyed the sandy desert, at the sparse plants. "The Voca tower song still echoes throughout the region."

"Where?" Netophah's fingers dug into Psal's arm. "Where? I don't hear it."

"You're not a studier," Ephan said. "Listen. It has a sweetness to it. The sound of honey or very sweet nectar. Can you hear it now?"

"Honey has a sound?" Netophah sniffed at the air.

Psal rolled his eyes. "You're no use at all. Sniff with your ears, not with your nose!"

Netophah wriggled his nose. "I don't hear anything." He looked backward toward the leagues of red sand that lay behind them. "Maybe we should go back."

"Farewell." Ephan poked at something in the body's open cavity with a small twig. "Who knows when we will meet each other again?"

"Alone?"

"You're Nahas' son, Netophah. The truce will protect you." Ephan knelt beside the body. "Storm, come and see. She's a beautiful specimen." He gathered several maggots into a clay jar. "I'm finished. Storm, you can turn around now." His head bowed, he spoke a prayer they had learned from a studier in the Waymaker clan.

The vestige of age-old superstitions, Psal thought but did not rebuke his friend.

They continued on and reached the abandoned longhouse when the sun was high in the sky. The tower had materialized inside a large boulder—an error indicating a damaged tower. The right side of its longhouse had been shattered by the rock on which it had floundered.

The original builders of the towers—thought to be men, gods, or spirits, depending which clan lore one believed—often reveled in creative fancies, making towers of various shapes and of brick, colored stones, metals, or wood, often painted or decorated with precious gems. Seventy men standing side-by-side could encircle this tower, and its height was like that of an evergreen. It was round like most, and its watchtower at the topmost spire perfectly squared. The rampart was extended along the roof—a sign that a large Waymaker clan had once inhabited it.

Psal shaded his eyes. "The tower's song is faint, but it's reparable."

The longhouse door swung back on its broken hinges at Ephan's touch and bricks in the nearby wall crumbled under his hand. On the wall opposite the door, three long parallel lines—markings of the Lake Waymaker Clan—flowed like a winding river past drawings of flowers, beasts, seeds and berries. The warm peppery scent of Naro spice permeated everything.

Ephan shook the dust from his hand. "If Nahas makes you a chief, our stewards could make this a longhouse suitable for you. Claim it for your own."

Psal entered the gathering room with his dagger drawn. No squawk of bird or lowing of animal echoed through the longhouse. Yet…. "Do you hear that?" he asked Ephan. "The tower pulses, as if faint life…are you sure no one's within?" He leaned his staff against a nearby wall and called out in the primary Waymaker dialect. "Is anyone here?"

No answer. He tried again, using a Peacock dialect. Again, no answer. Once more he spoke. This time in the Wheel Clan language, the last of the three universal languages. Still no answer. He whispered to Ephan. "Someone hides within. Do you hear?"

Dagger drawn, Ephan walked down the left-hand hall toward the sleeping quarters, while Psal limped toward the storerooms, Netophah behind him.

"Come quickly!" Ephan called out.

Psal and Netophah raced to the sleeping rooms. Ephan held a skeletal boy—no more than three years—in his arms. A slightly older girl in a hemp tunic stained with excrement clung to Ephan's arm. Their eyes were slanted like those of the Waymaker Clan, Netophah's people.

"Is no mother with them?" Psal sheathed his dagger.

"None. Another child lies in the back. Near death." Psal began walking in that direction but Ephan stopped him. "It's best not to see that one."

Psal paused, then nodded.

"These little ones are too young to care for themselves," Ephan continued. "And the tower's broken. Another night's keen and the longhouse will be completely destroyed. It'll end up in the middle of an ocean or on the edge of a cliff probably."

"And there's the Voca," Netophah added.

All three looked at each other in silence. Yes, there was the Voca.

"Father won't take the boy," Psal said.

"They're from a Waymaker clan," Netophah said, eyeing the boy with pity in his voice and eyes. "As a peace child from a Waymaker Clan, *I* can plead with Father to take—"

Psal opened his studier's pouch. "We'll call Lan." He limped toward the longhouse's keening room. "I'll ask him to bring a cart to carry these foundlings. The clans are all gathered. Someone will surely take them."

The keening room contained only one upright keening tree, the useless one common to all keening rooms, the one superstitiously called The Greater Light. The main keening tree, the Lesser Light, had fallen. Crystals were broken, wrongly aligned, or in the wrong settings. But Psal and Ephan were worthy studiers. With the few tools they carried, they managed—moving crystals here, aligning others there, chipping there— to make the tower chirp, even if they could not make it sing.

* * * *

Lan arrived, dragging a wheeled cart filled with bowls of Naro juice and roasted Yisin grain.

"You took a long time coming." Psal carefully settled the girl into the larger cart, propping her head upon a blanket.

"It's a long way!" Lan snapped. "And Nahas bartered away all our horses! To the Grassrope clan. Filthy pigs! You're lucky I came." He peered at the sun. "I will never forgive you for leaving me at Nahas' mercy. Dannal got engrossed in discussing failing towers with some Waymaker chief and wandered off! I was left with Seagen to negotiate truces and pledges. And Seagen, of course, refused to do anything that 'reeked of studier duty.' *His* words, not mine. Oh, what an infernal language that Peacock tongue is! Side-teeth clicks, front teeth clicks, throat clicks! Back teeth click! My jaws still ache! And Nahas—who knows the Great Languages well enough—seemed determined to—" He stopped speaking and stared sadly at the listless babe Psal carried. "Do you think he'll live?"

"He might."

Lan took grain between his thumb and middle finger and placed it gently in the older boy's mouth but he gave the children mildly despairing looks. "Tsbosso wanted you for his daughter. Moonlight. Not the one you've been pining for."

"Moonlight?" Psal ground his teeth. Hadn't he told Tsbosso to marry Moonlight to Netophah instead? Hadn't he begged Tsbosso to leave him out of the truce talks?

"But the price the old man asked for her!" Lan said. "Some of our tower science! Nahas turned him down, of course. Even for such a beauty, it's too dangerous a price to pay."

Ephan tossed away the dead rodents on their cart and placed the older boy on it. As for the babe, Psal could not leave it, dying though it was. They placed it in its sister's hands.

Lan picked up Psal's staff and thrust it into the firstborn's hand. "Firstborn, how the old man pleaded for you! With tears! As if all the world depended on it. Gaal, too, championed your cause, declaring that a marriage between both clans might lead to a joining of both clans. Nahas seemed almost at the point of relenting, but then…" His words trailed off as he glared at Netophah.

"But then?" Psal pressed.

"Nahas wanted Moonlight to marry that nature-blessed one instead. Well, he doesn't trust you, does he?"

"As a child, I *slept* in Chief Tsbosso's longhouse. I *hunted* with him. Yet I have never betrayed Nahas. But this king of yours insists on distrusting me."

Psal remained silent as they began their return journey, musing on the mixed motives of the wily old chief and on his father's wariness. Then, he felt Netophah's hand on his arm.

"Look, Firstborn!" Netophah shouted.

Emerging in the red desert—in the middle of the day under the day-moon: a longhouse was materializing along their path. Such a thing did not happen. Many studiers—or warriors under an enemy's blast—had tried to keen longhouses before the third moon rose. They had failed, the towers balking at a daytime keen. But there it was, a one-story long-house with the typical Falconer "wings" on either side, keening in broad daylight.

Lan dropped the handle of the cart he was pulling. "A Falconer long-house joined to a tower which carries Peacock Clan memories. Other echoes as well. Do I hear correctly?"

"The small windows in the wing, and the tower at the leftmost front of the longhouse, declare it to be a Voca modification of a Falconer long-house," Ephan said, "but the tower's song also has Peacock rhythms running through it."

"Which is it, then? Voca or Falconer?" Psal asked Ephan. "Or perhaps a Peacock Clan?"

Ephan grasped his dagger. "If any in the Falconer clan had learned the daytime keen, they would have told us! And I know of no other—" He edged closer. "If the Peacock Clans have discovered the daykeen, the Wheel Clan will soon bow to their strength!"

The shimmering longhouse, a pulsating half-visible wisp of brick and wood, barred them from the feasters in the far distance. The keen progressed steadily and Psal approached awestruck. The longhouse fully materialized at last, and when its main entrance door opened, a slender woman appeared. Psal could not tell whether age or illness stooped her, but she walked slowly, like a warrior wounded from many battles. Her pale tan trousers matched her tunic, but a yellow scarf covered her gray hair, which flowed down her back like a snowy rivulet. She seemed to be of mixed Waymaker-Grassrope parentage, and she descended the exter-nal steps of her longhouse with majestic but determined slowness. Five young women with features from various clans followed her, their lances or swords raised high.

Psal limped toward the chief. *The Voca Wheel Clan truce will hold, but what of these children? She shall not have them.*

When he stood before her, the Voca chief placed her long whalebone sword against his left thigh. "Where are you taking my children?"

"Great Chief, I am Psal. Firstborn son of Nahas and a studier for the Wheel Clan. We found these children alone. I ask therefore of your gra-cious mercies that—"

"Indeed? The son of King Nahas?" The Voca Chief eyed the Way-maker clan children in the same way a victim of theft would gaze on her rediscovered stolen property. "I'm Chief Tamira. We've keened for these young ones, bringing their longhouse here. Why do you take what is ours?"

Lan drew his knife. "No doubt it was you who deprived them of their mother. Why then should we reward...."

The warrior nearest Chief Tamira lunged forward and stood between Lan and her chief. "One more step, boy," she said. "And you die."

Chief Tamira touched the warrior's shoulder and the girl lowered her lance. "We claim the girl, Warrior. Only the girl."

Netophah stepped in front of the small cart he pulled. "We won't let you have her!"

The Voca chief tossed him a disdainful glance and spoke to Psal. "Prince Psal, your return journey is long and the place of male feasting is far away. We are many. If we killed you, who would know?"

"Chief Tamira, you would not kill us or break the truce," Psal answered. "And the children are ours. *We* found them. They now are Wheel Clan property."

The chief reached for the girl but the child clutched at Netophah's arm.

"She does not wish to be separated from her brothers," Ephan said.

Netophah added. "If you want recompense, Nahas will give you much for them. I give you my solemn word."

The Voca Chief ignored him, walking toward Ephan. "You must be Ephan, the one they call 'Cloud?' Nahas' Little Favorite? I have heard 'Storm and Cloud always go together.'" She glanced at Lan and Netophah. "And who are these?"

"The older is Lan, a warrior of our clan," Ephan said. "The other is Netophah, heir of all the Wheel Clans."

Chief Tamira's eyes sparkled, her voice rippled with laughter. "So I am in the presence of a future king? Is that why you spoke so boldly to a Voca chief, Little Arrogant One?" She turned to Psal. "And you have accepted this loss of your birth-right, Prince Psal?"

"I consider myself honored to be a studier."

"Indeed? Does the Wheel Clan still say 'Women, towers, studiers—all frail things that attempt to manipulate?'"

Psal frowned. "I have heard it said."

"I'm sure you have. Well, perhaps little Netophah's reign will be more enlightened." She gestured for Psal to walk with her. "Studier-Firstborn, the truce between Nahas' clan and ours forbids our taking *your* young ones. It says nothing about young ones from other clans. Or does Nahas still want to extend his dominion and care to all clans, regardless of their desires?"

"Great Chief Tamira," Ephan called. She turned and smiled so lovingly at him he stammered. "I know it is within the hearts of women to have mercy. Be merciful to us this once and do not separate the children. Let us keep them."

"Nahas will refuse the boy, Little Favorite."

"True, Great Chief, but Tsbosso or one of the other chiefs will accept them."

"King's Little Favorite." She walked to Ephan. When she stood before him, she stroked his cheek so gently she might have been his mother. "Good words. Respectful words. But if you don't give us the girl, the boy will be killed. Now. Bleeding at your feet." She whistled toward her longhouse. From within it came seventy or more young women with daggers drawn. "Would you rather he die than give the girl to your enemy?"

"But you are not our enemy," Netophah said. "You're our ally now."

But Ephan shook his head. "It has to be done." He lifted the weeping girl and carried her to the arms of the Voca chief, who gently bore her away.

The girl stretched her hands toward her brothers. Her screams echoed through the empty desert. The Voca chief whispered in her ear but her words did not staunch the child's tears.

"Who knows when we will meet each other again?" Tamira said, and entered her longhouse. Its doors closed behind her.

As the Voca Chief's dwelling slowly dissolved, the Wheel Clan boys fell silent. Their silence lasted until they reached the place of scorched bones, where the skeletons of children sacrificed centuries before were like black dust on the red sand. There Netophah started laughing, clapping his hands.

"Certainly, we need our hearts lifted as well," Lan said. "Not that anything you say is ever worth hearing."

Netophah gasped in laughter, catching his breath. "First, Psal said… he said, it was an honor to be a studier. An honor. I almost laughed."

"And why didn't you?"

"Because Father has taught me not to show my heart easily, of course. I'm the prince of all the Wheel Clans, after all."

Lan groaned. "And the second?"

"The Voca chief called Ephan 'Little Favorite.'" Netophah's face slyly hinted at adult secrets, leered. "I've heard our warriors call him that. But to think…even the Voca believe Ephan is Father's lover."

Lan pushed Netophah to the ground. "To think Nahas took away the Firstborn's honor and gave it to an idiot like you!"

Netophah picked himself up and brushed sand from his tunic. "You asked me why I laughed. I told you. So, why hit me? And some of our warriors say Father treats Ephan with a special favor. Even for an adopted son."

Once again, Lan pushed Netophah to the ground. "He is the king's adopted son, Netophah. True, adopting foundlings and orphans are common in our clan, but the king's heart seems as bound to Ephan as he is to you. Therefore, be silent, Birthright-stealer!"

Netophah clambered up and shoved Lan, his head buried in Lan's chest, his arms flailing.

"Don't push me!" he shouted. "I'm the future king of this clan."

That declaration only succeeded in getting him knocked down again, this time with the additional ignominy of being pressed into the sand by Lan's right boot. But Ephan lifted him to his feet.

"When I was a boy," Ephan said, "I met the Voca Queen. I was very young, much younger than Tanti. It was some days before Psal and I were sent off to study with our Master. Nahas and his captains stood at my side, the queen opposite us. I remember she had the illness of our clan, my own illness, and had covered herself in a shawl to protect her skin from the sun. I don't remember what they spoke of. I was a child and they spoke of adult matters, cryptically, as adults often do. But she looked kindly on me and I sensed she liked me. I sensed it then and I sense it now. Perhaps because I seemed so sickly and so like a little girl. Although I have not seen her since that day, whenever I chance to happen upon a Voca chief, they call me 'Nahas' Little Prince' or 'Nahas' Favorite.' As for being Nahas' favorite, Nahas loves women…as far as I know. As far as we all know. Nor am I his lover. But ignorant fools are always presumptuous, and you—well-favored, blessed by nature birthright stealer who thinks he's the Creator's gift to the world—why should someone as perfect as you not mock as you do?"

Tears welled in Netophah's gray-green eyes; he was young then and he hadn't the skill to argue with a studier, especially one he had angered. The rebuke silenced him for the remainder of the journey.

At the feast, Psal brought the foundling boys to Tsbosso, who received the children as a gift from his gods. But Tsbosso had something else in mind. "Lie with my daughter until the night comes." He lifted a friendly warning finger to Psal. "Only, do not go too far. I know you understand what I mean."

"But I don't want—"

"My boy, a new love will push an old one away. When I told Moonlight she could have her sister's former sweetheart, she was troubled.

You can understand why. They're sisters. But I told her it was all for the best."

Psal shrugged, frowned, said nothing.

The white oval clay daubed on Moonlight's face contrasted with her dark brown skin, glowing golden in the twilight. Her hemp skirt dyed in bloodroot swung at her waist like tall grasses. A jasper stone necklace hung between her bare breasts like the moon between twin towers.

She should not be called 'Moonlight,' She is the beauty of the sunset.

"I loved one who does not love me," she said as they lay in the red desert sand. "He was a young chieftain from the Waymaker Clan. Today he told me he desires another. My heart is breaking under the hammer of this news. I fear I will remain unloved all my life."

"It cannot be that you could be unloved!" Psal wiped her tears away. "All men in all the clans know of your beauty and your goodness."

Her smile was so sad that Psal's heart went out to her. So they played together, within Tsbosso's prescribed bounds. He fondled her breasts and she caressed him, but his heart remained with his old sweetheart Cassia. All the while, the girl begged him to marry her, to leave his clan immediately and join hers. Such utter despair in her voice and eyes. If Psal had not feared to hurt Cassia, he would have taken her and married into Tsbosso's clan.

As the third moon grew brighter, the feasting and dancing drew to its close. Psal rose from the ground, closed his trousers, and tightened his belt and tunic.

"Life is many days," he told her, "and the Wheel Clan has a long unforgiving memory. Moreover, it's too soon for me to marry. I still love your sister. In the days to come I will grow to love you. Do not weep."

"What if the days bring you someone else to love?" She wrung her hands.

"I am not one whom many wish to marry," Psal said. "And I have a faithful, very uncomplicated heart. I love those who love me. I will wait for you. But we must wait until Nahas relents, and even after we marry, I cannot live with your father in your longhouse. When the daymoon eclipses—it's not too far away, the lunar eclipse!—Cassia will have her baby in her arms. She'll have grown to love her husband by then, and her heart will not grieve to see us together."

Moonlight adjusted her clothing. "No, no, Firstborn, you must love me now and live among us now."

He lifted her and glanced at her stomach. "Or has your lover left you with a child?"

The girl looked at him, eyes wide. She shook her head vehemently.

"I'm sorry. I didn't mean to impugn your virtue. I only…it's just that…you seem so desperate to be married to me. It's quite new to me to be so wanted."

"I'm a virgin still."

"That doesn't matter to me." He hugged her waist and began leading her toward Tsbosso's longhouse. "Even if you were pregnant, I would've taken the unborn child as my own."

She clutched his arm. "It's only that I'm so unloved."

Have I seen her emotion correctly? Ah, me! I've become like Nahas. Does she not seem to wish that she had lied about a pregnancy? Psal kissed her forehead. "You have one who loves you now. One who will love you. Only, don't be so desperate and don't marry the next warrior who asks for you." He led Moonlight to her father and said to the old man, "I'll be faithful to her until we meet."

Her fingers tightened, painful around his. "Marry me now, Psallo. Please! Your father will forgive it in time."

"He will not," Psal said, and the girl left weeping. Left alone, Psal spoke to the old man.

"Great Chief," he said, "have no fear. I will prove my worth to Father and—give me six months! One hundred and fifty days!—you will have this alliance with our clan. But, Great Chief, forgive me for adding sorrow to sorrow, but there is a thing I must tell you."

The old man's mind seemed elsewhere. "Nothing you say could bring me sorrow, my boy."

"Chief Tsbosso, today, as we returned from the abandoned tower, I met a chief of the Voca clan."

"The Voca?" Worry and surprise mixed on Tsbosso's face. "Here? But our towers didn't hear them this morning. Nor have I seen—"

"They came at midday. They left at midday."

"Left? What do you mean 'left?'"

"Have you heard anomalies when tracking towers? Towers seeming to be there, then…not being there at all."

"Yes. In the past few months several…but—"

"The Voca have discovered how to keen *by day.*"

Amazement now. "In the daytime? The daykeen?"

"I saw it with my own eyes. I wonder. Do you think the daymoon figures in their—"

"How clever those bitter women are! They have attacked us forty or more times since the Great Eclipse. Legions of Voca warriors attacking our exploratory longhouses! Our men killed. Our women given the choice of living with them or losing their girl children. Few of our people have escaped. And now this!"

"Indeed, Chief. I have often thought you should form an alliance with them."

The chief waved a dismissive hand. "We make no truces with women."

Psal sighed. He looked past the old man's left shoulder into the darkness. Was Cassia still about? All he saw were mats and tables being gathered up and carried into longhouses, women from different clans calling small children indoors, Wheel Clan warriors from different longhouses speaking to the Wheel Clan king. "I've forgotten to congratulate you on the future birth of your grand-child. May it be a boy."

"It shall be."

"In the meantime, I will ask my mother to beg Nahas to let me marry Moonlight. Moonlight is wise. She will know how to befriend Mother as they feast together. No doubt, this time next year, I shall be your son and peace will rule between our peoples." Nevertheless, he offered the traditional farewell common to all clans. "Who knows if we shall see each other again?"

Tsbosso turned his gaze away, toward the longhouse the Peacock women would be using to meet the Wheel Clan women. "Perhaps our children will meet."

"Or, perhaps my children will be your grandchildren," Psal answered, laughing.

Psal hurried to the Hinis tower, dodging the scurrying Wheel clan women. His mother stood among an assortment of blankets, carts, and foods prepared for the traditional two-day Feasts of Women. Psal limped toward her.

"I'm busy, Psal," she said, before he could speak.

"I know, Mother. Hinis. Queen Hinis. I will not keep you long. I only wanted to...."

Her dark brown eyes dared him to continue. A pile of blankets teetered. She gestured to a young girl, a foundling, who looked shyly up at Psal until Hinis pushed both of them aside.

"Psal," his mother snapped, "why are you always underfoot? And where are those sisters of yours? Why are they alw—"

"My sisters are well, Mother." He had seen them earlier. He clung to her as she hastened to the door. "It's only...Mother...if I were Tsbosso's son-in-law, Mother, Queen Hinis...Mother."

Hinis stood in the entrance, twining the end of her braids absentmindedly and craning her neck as she peered into the darkness. "Psal, the girl you wanted is married. Pregnant too. And this Moonlight which Tsbosso so wanted to give you...I find her too subtle for you. Is your heart so weak that you love Cassia at one moment then tumble to Moonlight the next?"

Psal looked down at her feet. "Moonlight and I don't love each other yet. But…but…love will come. But, but, but, now, we wish to comfort each other."

"No doubt there is much in your life you need to be comforted about." She called to his brothers playing outside with their father. "Go and find your sisters." Then turned to Psal. "How gullible you are to trust that deceitful old man!"

"Nevertheless, Mother, consider helping me. With a woman of my own, I wouldn't be entirely underfoot. To shame you, I mean. And the skirmishes with the Peacock Clan would stop, Mother. Truly, Mother, they would."

The queen stared at him, said nothing.

His sisters soon appeared with his brothers. They dragged a heavily-laden wheeled cart, the girls pushing it from behind, the boys pulling it in front. Queen Hinis gestured them toward the open door. "That the daughters of King Nahas should go about the longhouses begging for sweets! Have you no sense of decorum?"

The girls kissed Psal and dragged their sweet-loaded carts past him. He stepped down from the longhouse and Hinis closed the door behind her.

CHAPTER 5

THE HOPE

The Voca daytime keen was a wonder, not something that a curious studier—even one with a broken heart—could put in the back of his mind for too long. Psal noted the discovery in his tower charts and in his annals. When Chief Studier Dannal awoke from his Tomah stupor, he would have to be told. The disappearing tower anomaly had been explained. Now the old man could focus on his other obsession: failing towers.

Psal heard footsteps near his door and looked up from his wheeled cot to see Nahas standing in the doorway.

"Father! I've been waiting for you." He pushed aside the pain in his hip, back, and thigh and rose to his feet. "What news I have! What news I have!"

Nahas eyed the engraved staff Tsbosso had given his son. "What were you speaking of today, you and Tsbosso?"

"Father, the Voca have—"

"Why is he so insistent about your marrying one of his daughters?"

Psal pushed his father's restraining arm aside and walked toward a woven basket filled with parchments. "Could we speak of Tsbosso another time, Father? There is—"

The king squeezed his forehead. "Is it true? You told him your own people mock you? Firstborn, are you such a child that you complain to your Father's enemies about a little teasing?"

"It is not a *little* teasing, Nahas! It is endless cruelty and mean-spiritedness toward those you consider weak. And I do not wish to speak of it now!"

Psal tried to quell the shaking of his trembling body, tried to push past his fear. "Father, when Hinis returns from her meeting with the Peacock Clan women, we will speak of Tsbosso's daughter. But for now… Father, Nahas…I must tell you. The Voca have learned how to keen in the daytime. I have seen it. Ephan, Lan, and Netophah as well! With our own eyes."

The king's face paled. "But…it is not possible."

Psal relaxed now that the king's anger seemed turned away.

"With my own eyes, Father," Psal panted. "There have been some discrepancies in our charts. Towers being one place in the morning and then appearing in some other place later in the same day. And not only did our listening branches report this, but other clans as well. Yet none of our studiers dreamed it was a daytime keen. The Voca use so many disguising harmonies and...."

"They've hidden their skill well." Nahas paced the length of the room. "And yet! For the Voca to have such knowledge! Committed as they are to their superstition!"

"What superstition?"

Nahas shook his head as if shaking away a dream. "The Voca Queen dreams of finding the legendary Constant Tower."

Psal tried unsuccessfully not to laugh. "She believes the old myth? And does she believe in Samat as well?"

The king laughed. "She probably thinks I am Samat. And the Wheel Clan the domain of all the evil dead. But the king of the Unfleshed Ones is not her particular concern. The Constant Tower is. Indeed, the Tower consumes all Ezbel's thoughts. I pray she never finds it."

"Why does she want to find it?"

"She believes that in the old days, before the clans were separated and developed their own beliefs, peace reigned."

Psal shrugged. "The ruins tell a different story."

"True, but Ezbel believes that with the help of the Constant Tower the night will no longer unmake us, and the clans will be reunited under one ruler."

"Reuniting all Odunao's clans is not likely, Father."

"If likeliness mattered to Ezbel, she would not have discovered the daytime keen."

True. "But that some three outcasts would find a Constant Tower and change the night? That is not likely, Father." Psal knelt slowly and began gathering the parchments on the floor. Pain shot up his leg and back but he stifled his groans in the king's presence.

"The myth mentions one outcast, a damaged one, a female." The king said. "Ah yes, ah yes. You're correct. Yes, in one Waymaker version of the prophecy, it is three. But in another,"—the king squinted, frowned— "it is a longhouse of lost ones."

"And in the larger Grassrope Clans, it is one outcast, a Firstborn. Father, there are so many prophecies. If they are all true, we are faced with a Creator who is either confused or who delights in puzzles."

"I have given up puzzling out the Creator," Nahas quipped. "But Ezbel...well...she must be studied. A woman who believes the prophecy speaks of one who is outcast—"

Psal burst out laughing. "One like herself? Father, do not waste your thoughts on deluded women. There is no Constant Tower." Then, proud to show himself wise to his father, he added, "True, some towers seem constant, but they are not. They move slightly. Instead of materializing across the planet or twenty leagues or one league away, they move perhaps a few paces to the right or left. They lack an adventurous spirit. Nor do any of them have the ability to keen all towers or to change the night."

Nahas slapped Psal playfully on the arm. "It is strange to speak about such things with you, Firstborn. Ephan usually has to endure my ramblings. You must think me quite mad."

"I like to hear you speak, Father," Psal said. "And I already know you're quite mad."

"Have you told Dannal of the Voca discovery?"

"Not yet, Father. He's making notations on the Dama seed."

"Ah!" the king sighed. "Hopefully, it is one seed he will not smoke or chew. Well then! When he's finished 'making notations,' tell him. The teaching masters and the other studiers throughout our clan must be told as well. You might as well tell King Renn. He obviously doesn't know or he would have told us. Our clan has survived because we value knowledge, and our knowledge surpasses the knowledge of all other clans. If the Voca have discovered the daykeen, we can as well."

"Father," Psal said, "perhaps we could simply…ask the Voca."

The king looked at him as if he had lost his mind. "And why would they tell us? They may be our allies, but they are not so stupid as to share their secret with us. And, if they did share the secret of the daytime keen with us, what might they require? Longhouses? Regions? Our first-born daughters? No, it is best if we discover the secret ourselves. And after we discover those secrets, we will keep our secrets to ourselves and we will owe no clan anything."

"But, Father, the Wheel Clan has destroyed itself by being so secretive." Psal kept his voice level, his tone calm. "Shouldn't we learn to share our wisdom? Our people are so rule-bound, so careful, that we've lost all our humanity. Forbidding all but warriors to bear children. Is it a wonder Ezbel rebelled? And truly, our damaged women are better off with the Voca. If we and the Peacock Clan would share our knowledge, become one clan…we would not have to—"

"A studier's dream, Psal. True, my father—and his father—were excessive in many ways." The king drew a long breath. "But the Peacock Clans.…True, there are some aspects of tower science they could teach us, and some we could teach them. But they are not united. An alliance with Tsbosso's clan would not prevent other scattered Peacock Clans from attacking our fields. In another generation, we will know all the Peacock Clans know and more. With our knowledge and theirs, we will then be able to increase our population and these harsh laws will be removed. But for now, if the Wheel Clan is to survive, it is necessary that our male children be born healthy." Nahas walked into the passageway. "Now, philosophical debates aside, let us join our kinsmen in the gathering room. You and Ephan have returned from your travels with the Wintersea master. You're one of us now. Don't stand so far from your brothers."

Psal followed Nahas to the door and into the gathering room. Near the hearth, young boys were listening to Donie, Dannal's wife. She had indulged her passion for solitariness by staying in the longhouse rather than attending the two-day feast with the Peacock women. She and Ephan were now relating the lore and annals of both clans to the boys.

Ah, Psal thought, *these people who are not my people.* His heart felt strangely light. Being the mother of Tsbosso's son-in-law was not a small thing; his ambitious mother would like that. *Perhaps I will forget Cassia.* Emboldened by hope, Psal smiled within himself and listened to Ephan.

"The Peacock Clans believe in a Creator who made the world from light and sound," Ephan was saying. "But this Creator grew angry when we humans chose to do evil. He wanted to destroy us completely and to remake the world. But after thinking very deeply, he decided to allow the world and light to exist during the day, but at night he would unmake those humans who were not inside a shelter. In this way, humans would always know that they were in danger of being unmade. And perhaps, through this, they would learn to seek the One who would bring them to their Permanent Home."

Ephan loved children; they loved him. The children liked Psal as well, but they called Ephan, Donie, or Cyrt when night fell. Then, in the morning, with Cyrt or Ephan at their side, they would peer through the longhouse windows and try to guess the features of the slowly emerging landscape. Psal imagined playing the same games with the children in Tsbosso's longhouse on those days he and his future wife would visit his father in law, and his heart grew more light and joyful. He would not leave the Wheel Clan, but he would be part of another family. A family who would love him and accept him as he was.

CHAPTER 6

BROKEN PETALS

Both Psal and Ephan heard the Hinis tower arrive, but unlike Ephan, Psal did not rush out to greet his mother like a foolish child. He busied himself with soil samples, with charting towers, and with Dannal's latest linguistics notations—a confused work of which the Chief Studier was unduly proud, but which clearly showed his enslavement to Tomah.

Outside, the marsh herons flew and young Wheel Clan boys gathered cattails and tall meadow grasses to kindle the morning fire. Peering through the keening room window past low-hanging vines and thorny brush, Psal sat surrounded by stones, leaves, shells, parchments. Ephan and the women were a long time returning. Perhaps the Peacock Clan's fermented honey had made them merry and they had decided to bathe in the lake. But the birds in the marsh did not complain about drunken women bathers. And what of Ephan's absence? How long did it take to pick silly flowers for one's cold-hearted adoptive mother?

Listening was a honed skill. A good studier could hear a leaf fluttering beside its neighbor, but Psal could tell why it did so. Animal, bird, leaf song, lingering raindrop, solitary insect on a slender stalk—he could discern all. He could even tell why one grain of sand at the water's edge echoed differently from another.

He listened to the Hinis tower song. Something was muted, as if the rhythms of many hearts had stopped. Indeed, the rocks in the forest were singing death, and the conversation of the birds was of blood. He stood, a groan escaping his lips. A strange rhythm coursed through the woodlands, alternating between coldness and heat, echoing in his spirit like a panic; he breathed deeply. He limped into the passageway and called his father, Chief Studier Dannal, and the other captains to the gathering room. Certainly, his heart must be wrong. Certainly, his senses were playing him false.

"Has Ephan returned?" he asked, when all stood before him near the hearth.

Mion, a studier born with the Wheel Clan disease, answered, "Ephan dawdles when walking alone."

"When you were in the watchtower…did you see the women walking outside the longhouse?" Psal asked him.

"No," Mion answered, "The doors were closed."

"Closed?" The king's face mirrored Psal's fear. "The sun is almost high in the sky. Our women are not like Grassrope women, who lie about till day is half-spent."

Soon, the Wheel Clan warriors were running through the thorny woods toward the Hinis longhouse.

Psal, too, ran, Tsbosso's staff aiding him. The wind raced, scenting the morning breeze with blood. Yes, even the forest leaves fluttered, weighed down by blood-heavy air. In the distance, through the creeping vines: Ephan, sitting outside the Hinis tower's main entrance, red wild flowers at his feet, yellow vines in his hand. All but Nahas stopped when they saw him, but Ephan stared into the distance—through pale blond hair, through the arriving warriors, into an unseen world far beyond. The king touched Ephan's shoulder, time lagged. The king walked past him toward the entrance of the Hinis longhouse. Then, time, rhythm, and metre shrank.

The king placed his foot on the threshold of the longhouse door and called for Ria and Tanti. No laughter of sisters, mothers, daughters, wives. No hurried clatter of sandal, no tiny footsteps running on the wooden floor. The king moved, but some great force seemed to weight his heel; he stood near the threshold, his dagger dropped from his hand onto the longhouse floor.

For Psal too, time had returned. In an instant, he caught up to his father. He grasped Nahas' arm. The other warriors, Lan, and Netophah pushed past them into the longhouse. The king pushed Psal away, re-sumed his slow steps. Psal remained outside. Pale tears on Ephan's face and shaking hands. A sudden wail issued from inside the longhouse. Then all was still again.

Psal described the scene in his annals.

'Oh Lowlands, lowlands, oh!
What did those warriors see?
Oh, highlands, highlands.
What can I describe to you?
Only the warriors of the Wheel Clan
Wide-eyed with horrified wonder.
Only a bright morning filled with darkness
and a longhouse turned into a tomb.'

The odor of blood met Psal at the longhouse door and like the war-riors, it pushed past him, racing into the mid-morning sunlight. The light peeked in at the bloody corpse of Lan's mother and at the foundling girl who had looked so shyly on Psal. All else lay in semi-shade, the windows still shuttered.

Blond-haired Kwin, Netophah's closest friend, had flung open the shutters and was calling for his mother and sisters when Psal found Nahas kneeling beside Hinis' bloodied body. Psal had often heard their acrimonious disputes; he had not thought his parents loved each other. But now his father's sobs echoed through the longhouse, accompanied by the tramp of the warriors' boots on the sticky floor.

Psal approached Nahas slowly, and bent over his mother. She had no face. Congealed blood blanketed his little brothers. When he had last seen them, his sisters had seemed like tiny flowers in their yellow tunics. Now they lay near his mother like broken reeds. Psal's body trembled, and he could not stop its shaking. A hand touched his shoulder; he turned: weeping, Netophah stared past Hinis' body to where Tanti lay.

Kneeling in his mother's blood, Psal touched Hinis' head. He moved his hand to her arm, half-detached from her body, and slowly intertwined his fingers with hers. In his annals he wrote:

> "I thought: 'I am alone now.
> In a clan that does not accept me.'
> I thought, 'My brothers and my sisters are dead now,
> and—of all here—
> only they and Ephan loved me.'
> I thought: 'My Father will say to me:
> Your friend has killed your mother, your sisters, and your broth-
> ers.'
> I thought: 'My friend betrayed me once when he took my woman
> from me,
> Betrayed me twice when he killed my sisters and my brothers.
> He will not live to betray me a third time.'
> I thought: 'I cannot leave the Wheel Clan.
> I cannot go to my true home.
> Those in my true home have betrayed me and killed my queen.'
> And all at once, it struck me: 'I have lost my mother.'"

He looked up through tear-blurred eyes and let his mother's hand drop to the floor. He walked outside where he gently, absently, tousled Ephan's white hair. Both sat in silence, the bright sun streaming down on them, until the warriors left the longhouse.

When the warriors returned to the Nahas longhouse, the young boys raced toward them. "Where are our mothers?" they asked. "Where are our sisters?"

No answer came from the warriors; no need. The children saw their blood-stained hands. All that day, the comfort women and Donie, the Chief Studier's wife, wept for their lost daughters, mothers, and sisters.

Donie lay in her room with her husband and her sons, Seagen and Cyrt, and lamented long into the night that her beautiful daughters and daughter-in-law were dead. From that moment, the Wheel Clan called her Rain, because she wept, saying, "My tears will fall like rain forever."

* * * *

Throughout the day, the studiers heard tower song after tower song with the same news. In a single day, under Tsbosso's command, the loosely-aligned Peacock Clans had massacred the women of eight hundred and seventy-one Wheel Clan longhouses. Psal did not tell the number of the murdered, but historians say some seventy-five thousand had been slaughtered—nearly all Wheel Clan woman and girl children. Another has stated that half the Wheel Clan population lay murdered at the feet of the other half.

Nahas ordered his chiefs to keen their longhouses and their dead to the Wheel Clan burial region known as the Meadows. At sunrise, longhouses filled the land. Such spontaneous cities were often formed during times of celebration and grief, this dawn brought only the mournful wail of pipes. Atop the rampart, Psal stood with his father, Ephan, and Netophah and beheld all the devastation his friend's treachery had caused. All about them, in all directions, the bodies of dead women and children awaiting burial littered the ground.

Nahas commanded a war council. The great chiefs stood at his side upon the royal rampart. Chief Ronen, Chief Ruan, Chief Ilbis too, and the great woman warrior Hayla who had inherited her father's chiefdom. Many more. Retribution and warfare began the next day.

Inside his chamber, Nahas called Psal, Ephan, and Netophah to him. The king spoke, choking on his sobs. "Look to your brother, Netophah," he said. "Guide him. Because he has no heart for his people. Look to your friend, Ephan. Guide him. Your friend knows only the workings of towers, not the working of evil in evil human hearts. Both of you, keep him safe from himself or he will destroy himself and his people."

Psal bowed to his father and hurried out.

When they were in their bedchamber, Ephan spoke, his words slurred by Rangi. "If one had told me Tsbosso would allow Samat to usurp his reason, I would not have believed him."

The Master of the Wintersea had taught his students about both wisdom and foolishness. As far as the Firstborn was concerned, evil came from within men's hearts, not from some invisible spiritual entity, and at another time he would have challenged Ephan's belief in Samat. But, on that day, Ephan's words found an echo inside Psal.

He answered, "What is 'reason?' It fails us always. It failed me. For had I used heart-sense instead of reasoning, I would have seen the old man's scheming from afar. It is my own fault that all these innocents across Odunao have lost their lives. I should have heard the girl's heart and married her, should have...." Self-recrimination and sobbing overwhelmed his words and he lay on the floor and wept.

"Are you entirely to blame?" Ephan asked. "He sent Tzaddi to me after we returned. The very one I had longed for. In the meadow, I lay with her, amazed that one so beautiful, so regal, would lie with me. And yet, as I think back, I see clearly that the old chief was trying to seduce me as well, and was planning to betray us and to kill our mothers. So I was as foolish, as unreasonable, as you."

Psal walked to the window where Tsbosso's staff leaned. Geometric engravings carved on it marked events in their friendship, oaths of loyalty, and even private jokes. Before that day, Psal had imagined the Peacock Clan his haven, and Tsbosso's longhouse his true home. But now—tears blurred that memory. He pushed the thought away and raised the staff high. He tried to break the staff—his heart also—tried to push away all hope of escaping the Wheel Clan royal longhouse. Three times he tried to break it. But the thing was made of hard wood and even harder memories; it would not break. He unsheathed his dagger and tried to hack it in two.

But Ephan took the staff from him. "Better to break the owner of this staff than the staff itself. Put aside all tears."

PART II

THE ENCOUNTER WITH THE IDEN PEACOCK CLAN

CHAPTER 7

AN UNEXPECTED TOWER

During the next two years, the war waged on. Warfare, congenital illnesses, and Tomah had exacerbated the illness—and claimed the lives—of many studiers. Many, like Mion, were dispersed from their home sub-clans. Only Psal and Ephan remained in the royal longhouse. Fewer in number, the studiers' duties narrowed to tending the wounded, tracking towers, and war communications. The Wintersea Master, too, had died, but not the wanderlust he had poured into the spirits of his charges. Those fires remained alive within Psal, along with his love for Cassia and his desire to prove himself worthy of becoming a chief.

When the war began, each Wheel Clan longhouse warred against the Peacock sub-clan that had devastated it. But as longhouse after longhouse became decimated or destroyed in battle, many Wheel Clan longhouses merged. Moreover, many Peacock sub-clans not part of the original treachery allied themselves with Tsbosso. War flourished and so plagued Odunao that the neutral Falconer, Macaw, Grassrope, and Waymaker clans continually attempted to effect a truce between the warring clans; but to no avail.

It happened then that one day, in the second month of the year, the Qerys longhouse was engaged in a battle with the powerful Full Blossom Peacock longhouse, the Peacock sub-clan Cassia had married into. Throughout that day and sleepless night, as the royal longhouse keened toward a home region, and as the studiers tended to warriors newly rescued from Chief Orian's longhouse, Psal's mind was set on these two towers. He sent more queries to Renan, the Qerys studier, than to all other battling longhouses. In the morning, when most of the Wheel Clan towers sang victory or rest, the Qerys tower was faint. Moreover, its tower song was undirected and the tower itself had missed its home port, docking instead in a nearby region.

Pacing, weary from sleeplessness, Psal climbed the tower staircase to the rampart to see if Renan or any warrior of the Qerys had sent a smoke signal but no smoke darkened the horizon. *The Qerys has landed in a valley. The lack of smoke doesn't necessarily mean all are dead. Caverns abound there. If they remained there, protected from the night—but they need pharma.*

He looked out over the burial grounds in the far distance. The air was redolent with the aroma of orchard fruits, the scent of the lake, and the odor of burned flesh from pyre burnings. In the near orchards, nets swayed under the trees catching fruit windfall. The lovely Waterfall home region had become a place to bury chiefs and burn corpses.

Psal turned his face to the east, listened. *The tower wails of itself; No one directs it. Does Renan yet live?* Faint though the Qerys tower was, he heard it. Its tower music was fading fast. *Perhaps Lan could reach them. He's swift. Using the horses in the longhouse and in the home field corrals? Too far a journey, though. Even the fastest horse will not return before the third moon reaches its height. And, what do our warriors know of mixing pharma? Perhaps Ephan...but Ephan's been working all night. And Cassia, Cassia. Your tower weeps.*

Psal closed his eyes and listened. An unexpected tower song arose. He descended the stair again. *Why do we not know how to keen in the daytime? We will have to wait for night to keen the Qerys to a home region.*

"Daris!" he called.

The boy appeared at the door, his yellow tunic stained with blood. Pale, white-haired, eight-year-old Daris was the son of the comfort woman Lyrenna and had been born with the Wheel Clan's evil. Had not war prevented it, he would've been a studier, learning from one of the old masters.

"Chief Studier," he said, "Ephan says he's already told you all he knows. Therefore if you've called me to relay your question about the Qerys and the Full Blossom, he will not answer it. He also says—"

"Tell him to come now."

The boy wiped his bloody hand on his tunic. "He won't."

Psal shouted in the corridor. "Cloud! I've heard another tower. Come now!"

"He has an answer for that as well."

"Don't you have duties to attend to? Garlic and fig poultices to make?"

"Already made. I was about to take inventory of our pharma after leaving the sick room."

"Oh? Well, then...do the inventory. And after...try to sleep."

The child frowned. "Are Chief Orian's rescued warriors to live with us?"

"It seems so. Nahas has his reasons, I suppose."

"Orian is hard to endure, is he not?"

"Quite hard to endure." Psal raised his voice. "Cloud! Have you not heard me?"

Moments later, Ephan appeared, his tunic also stained with blood. He leaned against a nearby wall as if the wall alone could hold him up.

"Did you hear this other tower?" Psal picked up a spyglass from a nearby shelf.

"I have."

"Remember the day I thought I charted a Falconer tower and it turned out to be a Peacock tower. Could it be…I was wondering…maybe Cassia's tower added some false notes to their own song. The Peacock Clans have been experimenting with coded and musical interference—"

"While it is true that the Peacock Clans have learned some tricks from the Mockingbird clans, it is not a Peacock tower. Truly, Storm, is this why you've called me?"

Psal pointed to the forest. "Then, a night-tossed tower's nearby. Several different rhythms, but primarily Peacock rhythms."

"Sleeplessness has made you wary. The Peacock Clans are not 'upon' us ready to strike. Now, may I return to my sick room?"

"You've taken Rangi," Psal observed. "You're always nasty when its influence begins to wane. Even if it helps you bear your duties better, you must avoid it. Daris imitates us and—"

"I have not enslaved myself to Rangi. But you.…" Ephan took a deep breath. "You exasperate me, Storm. All night and morning you have been agitated worrying for Cassia. If Nahas suspected.…"

"My only concern is this stray Peacock tower in our fields," Psal defended himself.

"Give me the parchment." Ephan slowly slid down the wall to sit. A gray parchment that tracked the warring Peacock Towers lay near, but he reached for a blue one and a yellow chart that noted changes in level two tower songs. "As I expected. It's a night-tossed tower that has happened upon our fields." He looked back and forth between the two parchments, then dipped his stylus in the jar of red dye and made a correction on a blue parchment. "Its song's a cross-pollination. Towers are good students. Always learning. Even when they're damaged. It's been here and there and has created a lovely song along the way. But no, not a warring Peacock tower."

True, towers often modified their songs, tuned them to other towers they crossed paths with, or to human dwellers, or to regions. They were always adding strange variations. The tendency of damaged towers to transform their tunes made tracking them difficult.

"Mostly Peacock rhythms, though?" Psal's ivory dagger leaned against a large thatched basket. He picked it up. "The towers are their own clan. They would rather avoid each other than meet while some dispute still persists. So why is this tower here? It should not be *here* in Wheel Clan lands."

Ephan hauled himself to his feet and walked toward the door. "Why pay attention to level two night-tossed Peacock towers? No one cares about them. And since the war began, few communicate with them. They're useless in war."

Lan entered, rubbing his eyes. "Watchmen," he asked, "what of the night?"

"The Qerys tower lies fainting at the end of this region," Psal told him. "And—contrary to all common sense—a strange Peacock tower has arrived in our fields."

"The Qerys?" Lan frowned. "Shall I go to them?"

"You and Deyn, perhaps. If the king allows."

Lan walked to the window. "As for this Peacock tower, warring towers avoid each other unless a skirmish is planned. So, unless it's one of Tsbosso's tricks, it's probably night-tossed."

Ephan sorted through the parchments scattered on the floor, then picked up the blue one that tracked the level three towers, those well-maintained towers whose inhabitants had little or no tower science. He then studied the tracks of the abandoned and failing level four towers.

"They are indeed night-tossed." He pointed to a tiny speck. "Orphaned from the Peacock Clan. They're hardly worthy of the Peacock name. They probably aren't even aware we're at war. There's no indication they've encountered any of the great Peacock Clans or any of its allies since this damned war began."

"And yet," Lan said, "Tsbosso is so wily...."

Ephan stifled a yawn. "It's difficult to give a tower a false history. The Peacock Clans are not that clever. No Peacock towers are missing or unaccounted for, are they? Therefore, we will tell Nahas to let these night-tossed orphans glean today in our fields while we burn our dead. When night comes, they will be glad to be rid of our corpses and pyres." He stumbled toward his hallway. "It really is quite a lovely song! Their tower's core rhythm is wholly swallowed up by other tunes. It flows gently, unrestrained. Even with the drumming undertones."

Psal pushed aside the embroidered cotton screen and limped into the hallway, but he returned immediately. "Convincing Wheel Clan warriors to allow a stray Peacock Clan to glean in our field? Their very presence...here...on a day we are burning our dead? Cyrt and Seagen's son was burned here. Lebo's son. How can I ask them to spare—"

Ephan groaned. He took a spyglass from a straw basket. "Upstairs!"

"Nahas isn't cruel," Lan said. "He will not kill innocents. And, look, it is possible these night-tossed aren't of the Peacock Clan at all. Perhaps some other clan found this tower and now inhabit it. Perhaps this is all useless worry."

"I had not thought of that," Psal said.

* * * *

On the tower's rampart, Psal and Ephan searched the forests and the home fields for the green-brown tunics of Peacock Clan warriors. They saw none. The unexpected tower lacked the grandeur and sophistication of Tsbosso's longhouse or any of the larger Peacock Clanhouses. Like all smaller Peacock Clanhouses, its tower was built at one corner and attached to a rectangular dwelling. Two stories tall, the top story was built like a wooden cage that served as both a keep for their animals and an open-roofed rampart. The longhouse front wall bore the oval-eye markings of the Peacock Clans, as well as the painted vertical and perpendicular lines, swirled arcs and half-circles of the Macaw clan. Brown-skinned men and women stood in front of their longhouse building a fire and looking out at the Wheel Clan fields.

Psal lowered his spyglass. "A Peacock Clan. I counted one hundred and thirty-nine in all. Men, women, and children. No doubt others are inside, but even so…it's a small longhouse. They aren't allied to my uncle Bukko's longhouse, but still…a Macaw marking."

"And you're our Macaw peace child," Ephan added. "And the Wheel Clan's chief studier. It's done, then. Nahas will—"

"Nahas will say, 'In a war, a warrior does not choose which enemy to kill.'" Lan shaded his eyes with his hand. "They're from the Peacock Clan. Their longhouse is small but not small enough. Innocent or not, they will not be spared."

"How cynical you are!" Ephan said.

"Not cynical at all, but I know Nahas."

"Storm, ask Nahas to spare them nevertheless," Ephan said. "What harm can these do to us? Or, are you still thinking of inheriting the kingship?"

Lan shook Ephan's shoulder. "As a king's Firstborn son, it is his right! And if he does not become king, he should at least be made a chief over his own longhouse."

"Let Netophah rule the Wheel Clans." Psal leaned against the rampart wall. "Netophah has the mind and the heart to be a king. I'm a studier. The world is my kingdom. But, yes, I do desire to be chief of my own longhouse. So the king's respect matters to me. If I ask Nahas to spare an unallied innocent Peacock Clan, won't he think me weak? Nahas has forgiven my trust in Tsbosso. But…to remind him of my foolish youthful mistakes?"

"Fools do not become chiefs. And the king's memory is persistent." Lan sighed. "This is my counsel. Search out the king's thoughts. See what his orders are concerning the Qerys. The ride to their stricken long-house is far, but it is not arduous. If Nahas hurries to send pharma to the Qerys sub-clan today he has forgiven Qerys's attempt to usurp the rule. But if he shows no care and seems to perhaps wish that all in the Qerys succumb to their injuries, then his anger is hot within him and neither will these innocents have mercy."

"How terrifying you are at times, Lan!" Ephan squinted into the sun, then turned toward the tower stairs. "Yet you have spoken wisely. However, Storm, do not let innocents die in order to get your chiefdom." He glanced at Psal who lingered behind. "Come, Foolish Chief!"

* * * *

Downstairs, the warriors—about four hundred in all—awaited Psal in the gathering room. The longhouse population had changed much since the war began. Death had claimed many. Others, maimed, had been transferred to steward longhouses to guard farmers and stewards from Peacock attacks. New faces had come to the royal longhouse. Warriors, women, and children from destroyed longhouses, adopted children, foundlings. Women from the Macaw, Waymaker, Falconer, Grassrope clans, other Wheel Clan longhouses, and foundling women from mixed clans had married into the clan before the neutral clans forbade the marriages. About seventy new wives in all. There were children also, born from the new marriages, babes who played in the shadow of their treacherously-killed sisters.

Psal approached the hearth and surveyed the chief captains and the warriors standing to the left and right of his father. Broqh and Kwin, Gaal and Cyrt, Seagen and Lebo, Lan and Deyn.

Lan, Kwin, Broqh, and Deyn were his friends; they would support his decision. Cyrt and Seagen would not; they still grieved for the wife they had shared. Lebo would be gentle even if he disagreed with him. Gaal, because many of his fellow stewards had been killed, would cry for vengeance. Chief Orian, lately rescued after a bloody battle with the Bright Sun Peacock Clan, longed for blood. The other warriors in the longhouse, although the king's kinsmen, generally remained silent. Then there was Netophah and Nahas.

"The Qerys tower is faint," Psal started. "But it still sings of human life. It's on the northern edge of our region. Too far for riders to go and return by third moon. Too far to carry the wounded. One of our warriors could ride there with pharma. Lan, perhaps, he has some knowledge of healing."

"What was the last word from Renan?" Lebo asked.

"That the battle was hard-won, that Chief Qerys was slain, and Qerys' son Antun was now chief."

A smile flickered on the king's face. "Qerys is dead, you say?"

Psal ignored his father's apparent pleasure that the attempted usurper was dead. "Perhaps that's why the tower has grown faint. Because it grieves for the old chief or the studier or both."

"Tonight keen the Qerys tower to join us here," the king said.

"But Lan and Ephan could bring them pharma," Psal said, "Even now, they—"

The king interrupted him. "The women of the Qerys understand how to bind up their wounded. Ephan and Lan need not ride to them."

Seagen whispered in the king's ear. Nahas nodded then continued. "We heard another tower somewhere in the forest. Seagen says it sounds like a Peacock tower."

Ephan handed the king a parchment. "Yes," he said, "we were about to mention that."

Nahas studied the charts then gestured to Netophah to approach. Psal hoped his brother would ally himself with him. Ruddy, well-liked, tall, the heir of all the Wheel Clans was hard for Psal to decipher at times.

"They're harmless, Father," Psal said. "A night-tossed mixed clan."

"As you can see," Lan pointed at the parchment. "In the past they made controlled journeys to the thirty Peacock homelands. Then some ten to fifteen years ago, they apparently lost their knowledge of keening. For some reason, their tower—perhaps because it fears arguments—has kept itself reclusive, purposely avoiding encounters with other towers."

"Probably wounded by some disagreement within the longhouse," Ephan said.

"As happens with these Peacock Clans," Lebo said.

"I doubt they're entirely Peacock Clan now," Ephan said. "It's probable that other clans and foundlings have joined themselves to them." He looked at Psal, and raised his left eyebrow.

"They seem to be allied to a Macaw clan," Psal added quickly.

"Are they markings of a Macaw longhouse allied to us?" Gaal asked.

"Not any Macaw clan we know," Psal admitted, "but the longhouse itself seems unimportant. Too small for—"

"You show your weakness, Firstborn," Cyrt said. "The Peacock Clans have murdered *our* innocents. Seagen and I have lost a son and you demand they be spared?"

"Demand?" *I have not demanded at all.*

Orian, who had been in the royal longhouse for only two days but who already had begun to try Psal's patience, now spoke. "I also have lost a son, my Rask. Killed by the Sky Peacock warriors. His body burned in the Eagle's Nest pyres! Moreover, two days ago, I engaged the Bright Sun Peacock sub-clan in battle. Who has not seen the corpses of his own kinsmen? You have not asked my opinion, Nahas. Nevertheless, I will give it. And I will speak in words plain enough for all to hear. Kill them. All the Wheel Clan will hear of your weakness if you spare these people."

"All the neutral clans will hear of his cruelty if he murders them," Ephan countered. "It will be rumored among their towers. Already the great clans have rebuked both the Peacock Clans and the Wheel Clan for this war. Why add further—"

Netophah raised his hand: a gracious hand, a fair hand, yet marked and bruised by war. "Father, if the Firstborn is right and these strangers are unallied to the warring Peacock Clans, they *should* be spared. If they're a small clan, what can they do?"

"Much!" Gaal said. "Have you not seen how the Peacock Clans have rallied other unallied tribes? These outcasts may have been set to ensnare us."

"If they're night-tossed, they should not die," Netophah said. "We will do what we do with all night-tossed towers who cross our path. We will ally ourselves to them and repair their damaged tower. But we will not teach this unallied people any tower science. No, not so much as how to keen." He turned to his brother and winked. "What say you to that compromise, Firstborn?"

"I like it very much," Psal said. "An alliance with them could not harm us."

"A marriage alliance, perhaps." Ephan approached the king. "Especially since the neutral clans have forbidden their women from marrying into our clans. Some of these Peacock women are undoubtedly unmarried and will be pleased to marry into our clan. And to meet so many men from one longhouse at once would be agreeable to them. They would consider it fortunate that many of their sisters could marry into the same longhouse. In addition, fourteen is a Peacock girl's marriageable age. Younger than our tradition, but Nahas would be ready to overlook that. Do you not think so, Adopted Father?"

The king laughed. "Ephan, you were born to persuade."

"Inter-marriage with our enemies?" Cyrt shook his head. "Nahas, your dead father would laugh to hear this."

"I'll make my decision after we've spoken with this lost clan." Nahas gestured toward the longhouse entrance. "War whistles will signal my decision. I and our warriors will journey toward this tower. Have our women prepare a feast."

"Father," Psal began, but Nahas raised his hand.

For a moment, Nahas seemed to study him like an alchemist examining an unknown ore, searching out its value. When Psal was younger he had believed the searching out would one day end, but he knew better now: Nahas was permanently ill at ease with his damaged son.

The faint rhythmic drumming of Cassia's tower continued, but Psal pushed its song from his mind. He could not think of Cassia now, he had to save the Peacock Clan innocents.

CHAPTER 8
MAHARAI

See now: Maharai, fifteen years old but short for her age, with tiny black braids around a thin, plain, dark brown face, scrawny legs, tiny breasts, and round buttocks. She was not beautiful like Tolika, Gidea's daughter, the slender beauty whom Lan and Deyn loved, and about whom many great songs were sung. Neither was she voluptuous like her mother, the round-faced, large-hipped Ktwala. If Maharai had been a beauty, Psal would not have fallen in love with her. She was plain, but plainness isn't unattractiveness. She had an attraction that stemmed from greatness of spirit.

From inside the Iden Peacock longhouse, she heard her mother Ktwala calling the clan to gather. Out she ran into the morning and waited as Ktwala descended the rickety external stairs of their wandering tower.

When the clan assembled, Ktwala spoke in this manner: "In all the directions, all I see are fenced fields and animals kept and guarded. In the distance are two longhouses. My brothers, some great clan owns these lands. Whether they are fierce or friendly, I do not know. But as I looked, I saw pyres and corpses."

Iden, Maharai's grandfather, pulled his grandson Ouis near. "Corpses? Such wanderings we've endured! Such trials! And now, fenced lands and pyres! What will become of us?" He grasped Ktwala's hand. "Daughter, did you see any markings?"

"A large circle with lines." Ktwala squatted and made a mark like the spokes of a wheel as Maharai looked on. Her face shone as if she and the sun were one. "Father! Can it be?"

Chief Iden put his hand to his mouth. "It *is* the Wheel Clan," he said, and looked about the meadow shaking his head. "A noble clan! And yet…corpses?"

Nunu, fat, bent and graying, clasped her hands before her wrinkled face. "It's two years since we've encountered them. In the past we met them often, do you remember?"

The lovely Gidea nodded. "Always those meetings were joyful. Often they helped us, but of late our tower has avoided them, their longhouses, and their fields."

"Perhaps…" Nunu scratched her gray head. "Did any hear the sound of a weeping tower last night?"

All denied.

"I heard it." Nunu frowned. "Strange that old ears should hear such things. Perhaps that tower pulled us here, into Wheel Clan lands. Strange, is it not, that corpses should abound in this place?"

Iden pushed his granddaughter toward the main entrance of their longhouse. "Hurry, Maharai. Fetch Jion. He'll tell us what to do."

Maharai ran inside to the old studier's room. Jion lay half-asleep on his mat, his smelly feet sprawling outside of his blanket. A bottle of fermented Yisin grain alcohol lay beside him.

"Jion, Old Studier, come."

"Why must I come?" He made no move to rise. "What is there to see that I have not yet seen? Let an old man rest!"

"Grandfather is worried. Something about the Wheel Clan and corpses."

"Corpses? Well…Perhaps. The Wheel Clan is quite fierce." Immediately, he grasped a large basket filled with clothing. Rummaging through it, he at last found a tunic. He turned it this way and that, then mumbled, "No, no. This is not impressive enough. Not to meet the Wheel Clan."

Maharai placed her hand on her thin waist and watched as he threw his reeking clothing to the floor. "How you do preen! You must have been quite vain when you were young!"

Jion dug into another basket, threw tunics here and there until he found one, perfect, intricately woven. "This will do nicely." He held the spotless tunic before his gaunt body. "Have I not told you about the Wheel Clan?" He frowned. "You and the rest of our women will have to cover up."

"Why? I'm already covered."

He took her hand. "At least the older women should cover themselves."

"What are you going on about?"

"Wheel Clan men have lustful hearts, Little Spider. And while it's acceptable to walk among our men with breasts covered only by stones, shells, twigs, and necklaces, for the Wheel Clan, it is not so."

"Are they the outlaw longhouses you warned us of?"

"The Wheel Clan are more organized about raping. And they are not outlaws, are they?"

"Rape?" Maharai placed her tiny hands on her breasts. Whenever Gidea's son bullied her, he threatened to cast her into the night where outcast men carried off solitary girls and raped them. Were these they? "They might steal me?"

"They don't have enough women!" He pointed to his boots and directed her to carry them for him. "I told you all this but, of course, you weren't listening."

"What happened to their women?" she asked, taking his boots and following quickly behind him.

"They killed them all, of course. Not purposely, however. The Wheel Clan do not believe in having many children, you see. At least, that is what they believed in the old days. 'The fewer children, the more precious, the less likely for children to starve or to become lost.' That's what they used to say. Land and resources, land and resources. That's all the Wheel Clan think of."

He stopped at the main entrance door and waited as she pushed his feet into his boots. "The pharma they give their women prevent unnecessary unwanted children. It makes the mothers sickly. Some die. Thus, they kill their women."

She tapped his left knee and stood up. He stamped both feet several times. "Also, one woman has two husbands. That solves two problems, you see. And not everyone can marry."

"I don't think I like the Wheel Clan."

"Little Spider, you have nothing to fear. Nor does Ktwala, with you around. Aren't you our own Little Spider who catches everyone in her web? Do you think the Wheel Clan could ever deceive you? Just try to look ugly. Which will be very hard for you to do. But you can manage. I've seen you in your foul moods. You look quite ugly then."

Maharai felt a little—but not entirely—better.

They exited the longhouse to find Ktwala still excited and Chief Iden still wearing that worried frown. Solemnly and with great pomp, Jion took the clan's spyglass and climbed the tower stairs. When he descended he declared, even more solemnly. "It *is* the Wheel Clan!"

Ktwala pulled her father's wringing hands apart. "Oh, Father, Father, they will repair our tower and teach us their tower science! Oh, Jion, do you think they will help us? Shall we visit them or they us? But to which of the longhouses shall we go? The one in the middle of the orchard, where men plough? Or the other on the edge of it? But…should we visit when they are burying their dead?"

"Why visit them if they will steal our women?" Maharai asked, not at all pleased with where the day was heading.

No one listened to her. Whenever the Iden Clan encountered other longhouses—even solitary tent-dwellers or the night-tossed—hospitality abounded. They joyfully took in all they met and their clan had almost doubled in size since the day, sixteen years ago, when internal war broke out inside their longhouse. The brightness of this particular day, however, outshone all others, because today they had happened upon a Wheel Clan longhouse.

True to the old man's words, by the time the sun reached high, a procession of pale-skinned men approached. Their leader was tall and dressed in a tan tunic. He wore a brown leather half-cloak like the other warriors, but unlike the others, he also wore a flowing brown woolen mantle with a pattern that reminded her of the Macaw clan markings on the Iden longhouse. He had straight, dark red hair cut short, and a graying beard, much redder and brighter than the hair on his head. He walked simply, as any other man would, without pomp and arrogance and he winked and smiled shyly at her as her father used to do.

Three boys stood beside the king. One, a honey-skinned boy dressed in black, had abundant loosely-curled black hair that tumbled over his forehead as if swept by a windstorm. He limped as he walked. *Strange that he carries a staff strapped to his back instead of walking with it,* Maharai thought. Another child, white as a summer cloud, walked with the lame boy. This child had a girlish face and also wore black. *The child must be a boy; it is wearing boy's clothing.* He wore something perched on his nose that covered his eyes, a piece of wood in which glass crystals were affixed. The third boy did not wear black like the other two. He walked like one who owned all the corralled fields. He had gold-red hair and slanted eyes that seemed to wish to own her as well.

Indeed, the eyes of the Wheel Clan men roamed the bodies of all the women. Gidea and Tolika seemed especially prized. However, the Wheel Clan chief kept his gaze on Ktwala, who shyly looked at him in return. The older girls and women had followed Jion's advice and wore hemp dresses.

"We little ones should have 'covered up' as well," Maharai whispered to her mother, holding her hands before her breasts which were decorated with beads and shells. She tugged at her mother's dress. "And even though you are 'covered up' that chief is still looking at you."

Her mother pinched her arm, told her to be quiet, and kept grinning like a young girl at the Wheel Clan Chief.

After the Iden hospitality dance, the lame honey-skinned boy removed the long staff from his back. With it, he drew a spoked wheel on the ground, then spoke to Jion in a strange Peacock Clan dialect. Studier to studier they spoke and both the lame boy and the pale ghost kept their gaze focused on Old Jion's lips. Then, after long conversing, the honey-skinned boy bowed low and turned to Chief Iden.

"I am Psal, Chief Studier and Firstborn son of King Nahas;" he said, surprising Maharai by speaking the Iden language as if born to it. "And this: Netophah, his son, Heir of all Wheel Clan lands. And this: Ephan, Studier and Adopted Son of King Nahas. And this: Nahas, Chief of the Nahas longhouse, King of all the Peoples of the Wheel."

The red-haired chief who had been smiling at Ktwala stepped forward. "I am honored that the night brought you to our fields, Great Chief Iden." He did not pronounce the words as well as the honey-skinned studier. "And you too, Ktwala, Chief's Daughter."

"If you speak our language," Maharai asked Nahas, "why didn't you just speak to begin with?"

Her mother pulled her aside, pinched her surreptitiously, and said, "Enough, little troublemaker."

Maharai felt like kicking Ktwala. "Do you want to be stolen, Mother?" she whispered.

Ktwala walked back to the Wheel Clan, bowed. "Great King," she said, "we're happy when others speak our tongue, even if they speak it badly."

"Only our studiers fully understand your language," the king said. "The wrong word, the wrong gesture, can cause true meaning to be missed."

"I would not have the King of the Wheel Clan misunderstand my heart's meaning."

Annoyed with her mother, Maharai approached the pale one. "Are you a boy or a girl? Or are you this clan's guardian spirit? Why are you so white?"

"You ask too many questions," the honey-skinned boy shouted at her. "It's rude."

She retorted, "And why do you smell like that? Like old men. Like herbs and pharma. Are you sick?"

A blush covered the face of the honey-skinned studier; the large loose curls cascading over his forehead could not hide the shamed eyes.

I have hurt his heart, Maharai thought. *I should not have.* Not knowing how to retract her question, she turned to Nahas: "Where are your women? Why aren't they here? Old Jion says a Wheel Clan chief can have many wives. Is that why you're here? To steal our women. We won't let you, you know! These sons of yours? Why don't they look like you, or like each other?"

"My children are peace children, Girlie," the king said. "Born from marriage alliances. Different tribes, different mothers, different alliances."

Her mother pushed her aside. "Great King, be assured, we will touch nothing in your orchards or fenced fields."

"All that I have is yours," the king replied. "I have ordered my stewards to help you."

"How can I repay the kindness of the great King Nahas?" Ktwala asked.

"Noble Ktwala," the king answered, "your presence in our longhouse is payment enough. Even now, our women prepare a feast for you. Til then, your women may glean in our orchards and your warriors may hunt in our forests."

"We may be night-tossed," Ktwala answered, "but we're a hardy people and have much food. Let us repay you for your kindness. Let us prepare a feast for you, and let us not intrude upon the burial of your noble dead."

"We will not take what little you have." The king took Ktwala's hand in his, kissed her fingertips, then said, "After our stewards and warriors have burned our dead, they will find some respite in hunting with your noble clan. But now, I must speak to my captains. Wait here until I return. Then you and I will go to the meadow and talk."

Maharai watched as he and some of his warriors walked to a nearby hill while the younger Wheel Clan boys remained and played with the Iden children.

"Their chief wants to lie with you in the meadow," she said. "And that ghost boy wishes to lie with Gidea. I know that look. Remember when we lost Corrie to that warrior from the Preying Bird Clan? Aren't you worried he'll try to steal you away?"

"I would not mind him stealing me away." Ktwala giggled. "And stop being so mouthy. Am I not allowed some joy in my life? Your father is dead, and I am still alive. And look, they are a noble and kind people. They may give us some of their tower science."

"And those two over there!" Maharai nodded in the direction of two young warriors who stood nearby, one dark-haired and slender, the other pale-haired and slightly stockier. "Their eyes are eating up our poor To-lika."

"Tolika's eyes are eating them up as well."

"I don't like these Wheel Clan men."

"Better a Wheel Clan husband." She laughed. "Or husbands. Than the harsh men of our clan."

Maharai only knew the harshness of Gidea's son. "Are Peacock Clan men all harsh, Mother?"

"Have you not seen? You're only fifteen now, but soon you'll understand such things. All men do not treat their wives as disdainfully as our men do. How lucky you have been not to meet any Peacock Clan men these past two years! They surely would have taken you from me."

Maharai walked toward the two warriors. Smiling, bowing, she told them her objections to their lustful gazes, told them all her heart because she doubted they understood her. The pale-haired warrior gestured that he did not understand. The dark-haired warrior said nothing. When she finished speaking, she began walking away but the dark-haired warrior called out to her.

"My name is Lan, not 'stupid pale-skinned luster' and I understood all you said just now."

She swallowed hard. "Did you?"

He shrugged. "I did."

CHAPTER 9

THE WAR COUNCIL ON THE NEARBY HILL

Atop the nearby hill, Psal waited for his father to speak.

"I like this woman Ktwala and her clan," the king said to Gaal and his captains. "No doubt some of you have also noticed the beauty of these Iden women."

"That we have," Seagen answered. "They're all lovely."

"Well," Lebo said, "not all. But the lovely ones are lovely."

The king laughed. "In the days of my Father, we stole such women. As many as we desired. In the past, I forbade it. But now…Tsbosso's treachery, the edict of the neutral clans, and these years of war—well, we can hardly put down our weapons and go about seeking wives, can we? And the lack of women in our longhouses has caused turmoil."

"But earlier.…" Psal tried to push away his growing fear. "You spoke of an alliance?"

"I cannot afford to leave their brothers alive."

Psal looked down the hill at the Iden children playing with the Wheel Clan boys near a fire. The small boys in loincloths, their buttocks bare; the girls in hemp or buckskin skirts and beaded necklaces. His heart went out to them. "This is a small, small, small people, Nahas."

"Not small enough." Nahas looked down at Ktwala who stood speaking with Ephan.

"Put away your frowning, Chief Studier," Orian said. "I'll admit, I feared the consequences of your birth. Many thought Nahas had gone mad when he allowed you to live. Later, when word of your petulance was sung among our towers and we understood that we had a mad prince on our hands, we feared your weakness would influence our good king. And now you are Chief Studier for all our clan. Nevertheless I trust our king's strength. When you rescued us from our longhouse, I saw a young man who seemed to have a good head on his shoulders, not the pitiful boy I had feared, but—"

"I care little for your fears, Orian." Psal turned to Nahas. "I challenge the king because I see no logic in his decision. Why make unwanted enemies? Why not create new allies? Why must we murder innocents to take women?"

"With the arrival of Orian's men, the number in our longhouse has increased," the king answered. "Many died when Orian's longhouse was burned. Wives, comfort women, daughters. Women are a necessity."

"But," Psal stammered. "You promised an alliance."

"Strays and unallied they may be," Seagen said, "But do you think a Peacock sub-clan will keep a covenant with us in time of war? Even a marriage alliance?"

"If we taught them how to keen…just a little, they would not betray us," Psal said. "Their women would be living with us. Why would they betray the alliance? Remember, also, that in the old times, kidnapped women would put bitterness aside because they knew their men remained alive. But if we kill the Iden men, these women…."

"Father," Netophah said, and all eyes turned to the Wheel Clan heir. "The Firstborn's counsel is wise. The Iden men would not betray us if their women lived among us. If we ally ourselves to them honorably, will we not benefit? Let us repair their tower, give them new keening trees, if they need any, some keening crystals. The Firstborn is well able to prevent their tower from hearing or meeting other Peacock towers."

"You will dishonor our dead if you spare them," Cyrt said, his eyes challenging Nahas. "And what will the Qerys longhouse and the others say of such sparing? Or have you forgotten that battle?"

Nahas looked up. The sky treacherously blue, the air fresh, the wind lovely. "No, I have not forgotten." He took a deep breath, coughed. "The warriors of both clans will hunt together."

"Father, they are hardly 'warriors!'" Psal snapped.

"When night comes," Nahas said, "all the males from both clans will feast together in the Iden longhouse. We'll kill them there. Then we will send their tower to our stewards. The Iden women will not know of it. Rain is a wise woman. She will convince them their warriors are still alive even though they themselves have been kidnapped."

"I will not allow it," Psal insisted.

"Rain will inform them that we're at war with the Peacock Clans and that their Iden brothers were spared because of their marriage to our warriors," Nahas continued as though Psal had not spoken. "The Iden women will understand the implication."

"Wheel Clan heir," Psal said, grasping Netophah's shoulder. "Brother, you should not allow it."

"Firstborn," Netophah replied, "Father rules our clan and his will is our will, even when it is not our will. Our king understands warfare. Perhaps he's right and these Iden would have joined the Peacock alliance in time."

Words useless, brotherly pleading useless, Psal turned toward the bottom of the hill where the Iden men were gathering the tools Nahas' warriors had brought them, unaware the gifted knives and axes would soon be used to slay them. They laughed with Wheel Clan warriors, strapped their pouches to their sides, readied themselves to hunt, unaware they were Wheel Clan prey.

The Iden girls, lithe and graceful, innocent, were carrying baskets of grain on their heads, their contribution to the planned feast. They sang loudly, dancing as they walked, their hemp or grass skirts swinging around them:

> *We have met strangers who are friends*
> *We have met family from afar*
> *Daily the world spins*
> *Daily it turns*
> *And today it has brought us to you.*

Nahas called to five Wheel Clan youths standing at the entrance of the Iden longhouse, then pointed to the Iden boys. "The fish in the lake are abundant now. Bring pole hooks." He turned to his captains again. "The Iden male children must be killed also."

"The little ones as well?" Cyrt and Psal spoke at once.

"Why kill the children, Nahas?" Cyrt continued. "Yes, the adult warriors must be killed but let the night take the little ones. We should not be as that treacherous clan and murder little ones."

"Truly, this treachery offends me as well," the king answered, sighing. "But caves abound in this region. Today, the young ones will surely search the place out and discover them. If we kill their fathers in the field, will they not know? Will they not hide within those caves and remain in this region? Will they not gather against our own stewards? If we kill their fathers in the Iden longhouse, will they not know soon enough?"

"You speak wisely," Cyrt responded. "Yet, I wish it was not so."

The king continued. "Every male three years and older must be killed. Wait until the second moon rises, when the Iden men are well drunk and celebrate the hunt. Do nothing until you hear my whistle. We attack... only when I'm at your side."

Psal began walking away from the group. "Father, the Orian wounded await me in our longhouse. Let me be far from this cruelty."

"Stay here, Firstborn. You must fight with us. You and Ephan both." Nahas shaded his eyes from the yellow-white midday sun as they walked downhill toward two trees. "Firstborn, you wear both the studier's cap and the prince's cap. A chief must learn to kill...even if he has taken a studier's vow."

At the bottom of the hill, Ktwala approached and the king, smiling, took her hand. Together they walked toward the eastern meadow. Nearby Netophah spoke to Lan and Ephan, then he and Kwin led Maharai away, together with the Iden boys toward the western caverns. Fuming, Psal walked to Lan and Ephan.

"So they will kill the children in the cave?" Ephan said. "What Netophah spoke just now, that the king has commanded these innocents be killed…it is difficult to believe. I cannot—"

"He means for *me* to kill, Cloud, not you."

"The air crackles," Ephan said, looking about ominously. "Do you hear it?" He smiled, a sad smile. "These Peacock children are always dancing."

Psal looked in the direction Ephan pointed. A little girl no older than three tugged at Maharai's skirt and was swept into Maharai's arms. They danced together, swaying round and round, as Maharai's grass skirt swung around her tiny waist. Beside them stood Netophah.

"The heir stalks the daughter as the king stalks the mother," Ephan said. "To love and to deceive all at once. It is a thing to learn, I suppose, if one chooses to become a chief."

* * * *

In the far meadow, Nahas and Ktwala lay naked at each other's side. Ktwala had asked him the reason for the corpses. He had told her of the war, how the women in all the Wheel Clan, including his children, had been slaughtered in one treacherous day. But the name of his enemy he would not speak.

Ktwala had wept to hear his tale. "A hard and long task, burying one's dead," she had said. And she had told him of her life and had answered his unasked question about the marriage tattoo.

"My husband lost his footing in one of the cold climes. He has gone to The Permanent Place."

That morning Ktwala had dreamed a dream full of foreboding, a dream in which a great wheel rolled into the longhouse and crushed it. One of her brothers had dreamed of the Iden women marrying men from another clan. Her father's interpretations had piled warning upon warning. How wrong they all had been! Each day brought surprises, of course. Fears as well. But Ktwala had not expected the pleasure of a sudden love. And now she had to steel her heart to lose the very love the day had brought. It had been years since she felt both the joy—and the fear of losing—love. Yet, if the day had to take Nahas, it could leave her with some good: some improvement in the clan's tower science.

"When night comes, my Tender Friend," she said to Nahas, "we'll be lost to each other forever."

"We need not lose each other." He played with her graying hair, played with it as if it were not graying, and as if she was still young. "I lost one whom I thought time would never replace. I had not thought I would ever love another."

"Not lose each other?" she asked. "Do you mean…you will…that our towers will meet again. Yes, yes. Do return to me. When our long-house warred against itself, my father's brother took all the elders with him and all our knowledge—tower science, herbal knowledge, all other knowledge too—and left us bereft of all wisdom. Family as well. We have not met our brothers again in more than ten years. And always those we meet, we never meet again. Who would have thought Odunao was so large?"

"Surely not all your wisdom was lost?" His eyes—sky blue and sky bright—examined her face. "Did I not see the old studier, Jion by name? Does he not know how to keen?"

"He was no true studier. And what he once knew he has forgotten." Her fingers found the juncture of his thighs, wet, moist. A mass of red hair, darkly-bright like the sunset. "We do remember a few things."

He burst out laughing. "I am glad of it."

"I never knew a Peacock Clan woman could make a Wheel Clan king laugh so hard."

"Nor I," he said, and she giggled, like a young girl, surprised at love, surprised at being thought a beautiful woman again "I do not laugh as easily as I once did. But you, Ktwala, you could make a Wheel Clan king do anything."

Naked, she climbed atop his body. His fingers played on her cheek, gently stroked her, from her neck to her stomach. She remembered her husband. He had been a good man, a satisfactory lover, a patient father. But he had gone to The Permanent Place and now her body rejoiced at the tender touch of a king whose hair was like the sunset in a winter sky, gray streaks against red.

"You're silent," she said, feeling his warmth inside her. "You're thinking of your dead wife."

"No, *you're* thinking of my dead wife."

"My dead husband was a very jealous man. If he were alive and found me here with you, he would cut off your…head."

"I'm glad, then, that he is not here to cut off my…head."

Laughing, she tugged at the curly hair between his legs.

"Woman," he shouted, laughing. "you don't need to hurt me. I am quite ready to do your will. But you are talking at the most inopportune time. Do you always talk so much?"

She intertwined her finger in his. "Everyone accuses me of talking too much."

"Well, we must change that."

"The Ever-Present One knows I cannot change my talkativeness. Many have tried."

"You believe in The Silent One?" His words almost pitied her.

The Silent One. That's their name for the Ever-Present One. She saw his pity, pitied him his unbelief. "I have heard you in the Wheel Clan are distant from the Ever-Present One, that you don't believe in the Unfleshed Ones either."

"Samat? And spirits who roam the world seeking to live in human bodies? No, I do not believe."

"Tender Friend," she began, but his kiss cut off her words. *How warm his lips!*

He touched her breasts, pressing her nipples with his thumbs. "Forgive me. I didn't aim to mock. Of late, I always seem to mock those I love. It's only…my people don't think about the Silent One. Not generally. Bleeding, on the edge of a dagger, perhaps, but not generally. The Ever-Present One has always been silent to me. The Silent One was not silent to my father, but his beliefs were his own. Mine are mine. His belief made him weak at times, cruel at others."

"He has been praised by many."

Nahas looked past her toward the treetops. "Only the strong praised him."

"Is it true that you kill your imperfect male children? We Peacock people would rather live crowded in a longhouse or add new rooms rather…than deprive a child of life. We love all children, no matter how sickly they are."

"It's a necessity. We have had to survive. And yet, I am not as cruel as my father was."

He lay on the grass, stroking her breasts, and Ktwala—naturally curious and not one to stop talking once she started asked, "Would your Father have spared your son's life?"

"Ktwala, how bold you are!" Nahas stared at her in wide-eyed admiration. "No, my father would not have spared my sons' lives."

"Sons?" she asked. "How many damaged sons have you sired?"

Nahas laughed. "One day I shall tell you, but now…to the joyful task at hand."

"How happy life must be for you, Nahas! Visiting women from region to region, and not committing your love to any!"

"Ktwala, I have no women waiting for me anywhere." He pulled her close, bent her toward him. "Indeed, I am lying here, your servant, waiting for you. And only you."

CHAPTER 10

SUDDEN LOVE

The Wheel Clan boys carried torches, the Iden children sang. Inside the cave, the loamy ground under Maharai's feet unsettled her. She feared the dark and the dark monsters that croaked, creaked, and clicked under the muddy water. Raising Eala higher up on her shoulder, she resolved to show no fear. The king's son, Netophah, walked at her side. She had not liked him at first. She had had to tune her ears to his mangling of her language, but he had spoken so sweetly to her, asking her to be "compassionate" toward him and to speak slowly, and his eyes had been so gentle as they walked together. She no longer believed the Wheel Clan wanted to steal either herself or her sisters.

"We play here," he said. "Here and elsewhere. You see?"

"I can see better now, yes." She drew out the words, spoke the same thought again in different words, that he might understand her. "My eyes can see in the dark now."

Something slimy crept near her sandals. The shadows and laughter of the Wheel Clan and Iden children moved and echoed along the walls.

"Stay here." Netophah squeezed her hand. "I go, I return." He disappeared further into the cavern before she could protest.

Maharai stroked the whimpering child's back and swayed slowly, comforting it. In the darkness, she saw Netophah's figure—already, she recognized it—returning, carrying two poles: One pole ended with a knife-like hook, the other attached to a net.

"The net catch small fish," he said when he reached her. "The hook large ones." He drew his face closer to Eala's. "Do you want nursing, Eala? Milk? Maharai to nurse you?"

Unsure if Netophah had intentionally joked or had used the wrong word, Maharai said, "I can't nurse her."

"I know." He laughed, then touched her breasts. "They very tiny breasts."

She moved the child upward to block his arm. Still, she liked him. "They'll grow when I get bigger." A defense, a promise.

He moved his mouth closer to hers. "Promise? No, no, they won't grow. Always the same size."

She turned the conversation from her breasts. "You gave my brothers only nets. No hooks?"

"Girlie," Netophah attempted to touch her breast again. Again, she quickly blocked him. "Hooks dangerous," he said. "Father say keep Iden brothers safe. Our new allies not accidental pierce selves, each other. Why cannot I you touch you? I see you want."

She did not say that she had allowed Gidea's hateful son to touch her because he had bullied her often, did not say he had opened his trousers before her and forced her to kneel before him and…"Mother says men should not touch me there."

"I not a man." He kissed her cheek and his hand traced a gentle line along her neck. "We same age."

She liked his arrogance, liked him because he was handsome and his body slender and well-built and because he liked her. She wondered if she should allow him to kiss her—just once. It would be nice to be kissed by one who was handsome and young and who loved her. But Little Eala was in her arms and it would all be so clumsy. Yet she allowed it. She leaned toward him and his lips touched hers. Her body trembled. Warmth course through her veins. She felt a throbbing in her vagina. Only joy, and none of the fear and disgust she often felt when Gidea's son forced her to suck and suck. She didn't feel the passing of the time, such joy she had with Netophah.

* * * *

Two sharp whistles pierced the quiet fields. Voices called out to Nahas from the bottom of the hill. Nahas raised himself onto his elbow and looked toward the Iden longhouse. His demeanor grew serious, distant as if he suddenly remembered he was a king. Ktwala sat up, followed the king's gaze. Three men—two in the brown Wheel Clan short leather cloak, the other in green.

"Your subjects call you." She handed him his tunic, looked about for her own clothing.

"They're two of my captains." Nahas took the tunic, rose from the grass. "Lebo and Orian. The third is Gaal, steward over all these fields and all the fields of the Wheel Clan, my dearest friend."

"That one doesn't wear brown."

"Among my people, the son belongs to its father's clan. One such as Gaal with a foreign father can only be a farmer or a steward. He wears the clothing of stewards. Yet, he is—like all my stewards—as good a fighter as any." He raised his right hand and signaled the steward who nodded. "And of all my warriors, he rests closest to my heart. Ktwala, my warriors await me. There is much for me to do."

"It has been years since I lay with a man," she said, laughing. "Except Ouis. I had forgotten how grievous parting was. If I could, I would lie here with you til third moon came."

She dressed hastily, aware that his eyes admired her body, but sad they were to part. "Already I long for you," she said. "Til the day when our towers meet again?"

"We will be apart for only a little while."

"How long does it take to learn tower songs and the songs of far regions?" she asked.

"The day is far spent." His voice accused. "My people journeyed here to honor our dead. A hard and long task. Yet I have spent the day lying here with you. And now you speak of towers?"

"I grieve for your dead, Nahas. Forgive me. I only…unless you seek us out, you will be lost to me. Long ago, the men in my longhouse warred against each other. When peace could not be restored, it was decided another longhouse should be built and the sub-clan divided. Those who left took all our keening knowledge with them. Help us, Nahas. Don't leave us at the night's will."

The king's eyes searched hers. "And what science will you give us in return?"

Her right hand indicated the orchards, then the corralled fields. "What can I give a Wheel Clan king?" She wrapped her arms around him, kissed his lips. "Be not so distant, Nahas, and trust my love for you."

His voice was distant, his eyes—sky blue and sky bright—full of suspicion. "You speak of love and tower science in the same breath?"

"Do you think I gave you my body as payment for your lore? I did not."

He shrugged, frowned. "It seems I've mistaken a barter for love."

How wary and suspicious the Wheel Clan king is! Hurt, she kneeled at the king's feet, spoke boldly. "I would not have lain with you if I did not love you, Nahas! King or not, your heart has found its place in mine. But, my people are the world's dust, tossed where the night flings us. This is why I ask that you make our paths and journeys straight, that you make our lives as orderly as yours."

"Your people charm and bend animal hearts to their will," he answered. "Teach us this skill, and we will teach you to keen. But not all our tower lore."

He speaks like one bargaining at a marketplace. Ktwala watched the wind play with the topmost branches of the far-off trees. "Skill for skill, yes. But song for song as well. For the songs of pleasant regions, we'll teach you the songs of water reptiles. For the chords that make crystals hone homeward, we will teach you whale songs. And our people are strong. You are no victim of a bad bargain. Ally yourselves to us and we will help you battle your enemies."

"Are you such good warriors?" he asked.

Such wariness in his voice. Should one so powerful seem so afraid? "Not good at all. But we are well able to learn."

He lifted her from her knees. "You plead well for your people, Ktwala. Fear not. I will teach your people tower science, enough that our longhouses may routinely meet." His finger stroked the nape of her neck. "Only, you must live with me. Marry me and be my queen."

Leaping into the king's arms, Ktwala threw her arms around his neck and covered his face with kisses. His hands on her large buttocks and thighs, the king laughed, steadying himself as he carried her down the sloping meadow.

"It is good to see the Wheel Clan king laugh," Ktwala said. "You almost made me fear you."

From the bottom of the steep hillside, a young warrior ran toward them.

"That warrior's name is Lan," Nahas said. "He knows the Peacock tongue." He placed Ktwala's feet on the grassy ground. "He will report this new alliance and our marriage to the women of my people. Rain, an honored elder among our clan, will acquaint you with our ways. All this night my warriors will remain in your longhouse and teach your brothers tower science. In the morning, we men will return. Then, you and I will be wed." He winked. "Officially."

"My children, King Nahas? What of them? May they stay with me or must they stay with my father's clan? Will they be as your own people? Ouis' father is not of your clan. Will he be a warrior? Will he be your son?"

Nahas answered, "Ouis will be as my sons are."

She flung her arms around his neck.

Nahas pointed to the orchard at the bottom of the hill. "Wait there while I speak with Lan."

All around her, the ripening fruit filled her senses. How fruity-sweet their fragrance!

On the slope of the hill, the king and his warrior spoke, hands and body agitated as if some quarrel had risen up between them. Then the boy grew silent, his shoulders slumped. He walked sullenly toward Ktwala. She followed him but he did not speak to her. Near the longhouse, Prince Psal met him. A moment only the boys spoke, then Psal limped up the hill to his father. Then father and son seemed to argue, hands and heads shaking, pushing. Moments later, the studier hobbled down the hillside. When he drew near Ktwala, he did not look at her, but turned his face toward the ground and pushed past her into the longhouse.

Have I offended this great people on the day they bury their dead? Ktwala asked herself. *To lay here in the meadow with Nahas? Is that why this warrior and this prince rage at their king?*

* * * *

When darkness fell, Maharai heard Lan's voice calling to her and Ouis from the cave's entrance.

"I come, Lan," she said and picked up Little Eala who sat on a rock her feet dangling in the dark water.

When Maharai and Eala arrived at the cave entrance, Lan stood in the half-light, a worried expression on his face. "Where's your brother?" he asked her.

"Swimming and fishing with the others."

"Call him. The king commands you and your brother to remain with your mother in our longhouse," Lan said then spoke to Netophah in the Wheel Clan language.

After Maharai called him, Ouis came running up, wet and holding a net with a small brown fish with no eyes.

"Can I stay and play a little longer?" he asked, looking from Netophah to Lan. "Our new Wheel Clan brothers are teaching us to use these nets." He shivered from the cave's dampness. "Please, let me stay a little longer?"

"Nahas and your mother are to be married," Lan said. "Our women wish to meet you."

"Married?" The little boy grinned at his sister. "We're getting a new father?"

"And you will live among us," Lan added.

Quick marriages were commonplace—especially in night-tossed longhouses—when there was no certainty of longhouses meeting again. Ktwala's sudden marriage didn't surprise Maharai. Her trust in the Wheel Clan had grown since morning, and she was glad the Wheel Clan king was taking Ouis and her along. Still, she didn't want to be without the rest of her sisters. "Are any of my kinswomen coming with us?" she asked Lan. "Will I see my grandfather again?"

"Yes," Lan said. "Other women will come with you."

"I saw the way your eyes ate up Tolika. Tolika is coming as well? Gidea won't like that."

"They will not be far from each other," he said. "Both longhouses will be bound together."

Maharai clapped her hand. "You're a very organized people," she said to Lan.

"More than you know," he answered and walked outside. "Come."

She called for the other boys to come but Netophah rested his hands gently on her shoulder, warm hands wet with the blood of fish he had recently hooked. "The girls come our longhouse, meet our women. The boys, with our warriors, the men's feast. Travel tonight, all men. Travel tonight, all women. Tomorrow all together, meet again."

"Ah!" she said. "I'll see you tomorrow? And don't worry. You'll learn our language soon now that you're my brother. I'll teach you."

They stepped outside the cave under a sky that had gone blue-gray and she walked with Lan toward the Wheel Clan longhouse, admiring its watchtower and its ramparts encircling the longhouse watchtower.

* * * *

Inside the gathering room of the royal longhouse, the Iden and Wheel Clan women feasted. The Iden longhouse always smelled of animal dung and urine, but blood, pharma, sweat, and the odor of corpses pervaded the Nahas longhouse. Even the aroma of sizzling hot spices, fermented meats, honey beverages could not blow away the odor of death. Old Jion had told her of the great Peacock chief's longhouse, a chief named Tsbosso, whose longhouse had ebony carvings and walls covered with animal skin. She couldn't imagine it being any lovelier than the interior of a Wheel Clan longhouse, the home of a great king who was to become her father. She placed Eala in her mother's lap and looked around the gathering room in amazement.

Jion had called the Wheel Clan "the masters of the lathe." But Maharai had never imagined the perfection and charm that now shone in the Nahas longhouse. The low-lying steps near the hearth on which the women sat: the pegs, grooves, and carvings of decorative bone, ivory, wood, and polished crystal placed neatly in shelves; the woolen hangings; etched trays; wheeled toys; and the tiny swinging cots in which the Wheel Clan babies slept so peacefully.

Lan introduced her to an older woman with long, graying red hair. The woman was sitting beside Ktwala and all the other women surrounded them. "Her name is Donie. We call her 'Rain,' in our language. She is much-honored among us." Lan pointed to a woman with crescent-shaped eyes sitting to Rain's right. She seemed about the same age of Gidea. "That is Satima, a Waymaker foundling married into our clan. She speaks your language. She will also help you understand our clan."

"Your men don't look like your women," Maharai observed. "Did you steal all these women? And where are your old mothers, and your old fathers? Why is Rain the only old one I see? Does the Wheel Clan kill their old ones to preserve food?"

Lan blinked. "Are you serious?"

"I am."

"These women all married into our clan at the beginning of the war. As for the old ones, they live in steward longhouses far from trouble."

"They're sent away from their home longhouses?"

He squeezed her shoulder gently. "Maharai, I have duties to attend to. Rain will explain all." He bowed then walked down the corridor to the left.

The old woman had a pale face and kind green eyes. *I like her,* Maharai thought. *But why is this particular old one still here? Shouldn't she have been sent away like the others? But perhaps she's the king's mother and he did not wish to send away his mother.*

* * * *

Psal was waiting for his patient—a young warrior rescued from the Orian longhouse—to wake from pharma-induced sleep when Lan entered.

"Firstborn," Lan said, "the king demands you and Ephan battle by my side."

"Am I a warrior?" Psal asked. "No, I am not. I will not. The king cannot insist that studiers battle." A small hearth had been built into the sick rooms as well and now Psal lay his surgical knife on the rectangular white stone in the middle of the red coals. The blood on the knife sizzled away. "Am I—a studier—to harm others? No! I will not do it."

"A chief should learn to harm others, Firstborn."

"Take my part, Lan, or cease speaking with me."

Lan did not immediately answer. He stood near the Studier's Hearth, staring at the embers. Then, like the glowing stone, his face lit up. "Firstborn, I have an idea. Can you not use the ancient covenant to protect this people?"

Psal grimaced. The Principles always gave him a headache. The Master of the Wintersea had given his students so many possible interpretations of the Creator's Principles of Reconciliation that Psal hardly knew what they meant. The fact that the spiritual laws hadn't allowed for a Firstborn not being heir of a clan didn't exactly make him respect them. "There is nothing in the seven principles about studiers learning to kill."

"Doesn't it declare that if a Firstborn marries into a clan, the clan cannot be harmed?"

Lan's interpretation of the Principles was always exasperatingly muddled. And now—studier's son that he was—he was reciting them. They rolled from his tongue like a scroll:

To those who would be holy, hear the laws of the Creator:

Let not Samat usurp your pleasures and your sorrows. Guard the doors of your heart against his wiles. Do not allow him to overtake your senses or rule your mind. The Malevolent One lies near and far, in small matters and in large. He roams the world like a roaring lion seeking whom he may devour. Therefore, hear the Creator's laws and do them:

If you find a night-tossed child, you must by no means leave it bereft but you will take the child into your home and rear it as one of your sons and daughters. You shall in no wise allow Samat to allow you to ignore the poor and the outcast. If you find a foundling marked as outcast, feed him and do not search out the nature of his crimes. Nevertheless, let him not enter your longhouse that his guilt does not defile you. If you meet the poor, you shall give to them all they ask of you, whether thing living or non-living, whether thing tangible or intangible. For the Creator's eye is upon the orphan and the outcast, and the poor are Children of the Creator as you are;

If you fight your enemy and he falls weak at your feet, you shall in no wise leave him bound at nightfall, no not to living, dead, or non-living thing. You shall in no wise allow Samat to lead you to sin. You shall in any case provide your enemy shelter and leave his feet, torso, and hands unbound. If you fight your enemy and capture his house, and find foundling and the night-tossed living with him, you shall in no wise harm the foundling; the night-tossed is not your enemy. If you find a corpse unburied, you shall in all wise, bury it and not leave the dead uncovered. If you desire to kill, refrain from killing. Nevertheless, if you fight your enemy and he dies, you will cover his body that the land may not be polluted; Your enemy is the Child of the Creator, as you are;

If at any time, the night brings you to a place where you find your enemy's landmark, you shall in no wise remove it, for other clans are Children of the Creator as you are. You shall in no wise allow Samat to convince you otherwise. If the night tosses you to an unclaimed place, you may reclaim the land by fire, water, or axe. But only that which you can reclaim in a single day shall be yours. All that fire, water, and axe have not claimed within each day shall not be included within your landmark. The land, fire, water and even your strength belong to the Creator and it is He who creates each day and apportions your lot;

You shall in no wise lie with or marry a woman born in the same longhouse as you. Whether your longhouse contains ten or ten thousand, she is your sister, and your daughter, and your aunt, and your mother. If at anytime you war and find among your enemy's clan a woman your heart longs for, you shall take the woman but for her sake, you shall spare those in her longhouse. You shall ally yourself to them, or you will destroy their crystals that their tower be night-tossed. But you shall not in any wise slay her kinsmen, for your children will be her children and they will rise up against you. The woman shall grieve forty-nine days. Then you shall take her to your bed; If the day brings you a woman, living alone without a clan, if she has no child and desires one, you will give her a child. Nevertheless, in no wise shall you force her to lie with you. Nor will you refuse her request to lie with her. If you desire another man's woman, refrain from taking her. If you desire another woman's man, refrain from seducing him. The man and the woman are Children of the Creator, as you are;

If the night brings you to a fertile place and the animals of that region threaten to over-run you, you shall in no wise kill one kind of animal and let all others roam free. You will study the numbers and the kinds, then you will apportion and kill. For the Creator has set one kind of animal against another that all Odunao will live in harmony;

The Firstborn of your clan shall be unto you as the Greater Light. You will bring all disputes and grievances to him and he will resolve them. The law from his mouth will be like the law from the Creator's mouth. If there arises among you, one who disobeys the Firstborn, that one shall be cut off from the people. You shall not kill that disobedient one but you shall make him outcast because he has disobeyed the Firstborn who is your Greater Light. If there arises one among you who willfully and continually murders, then the Firstborn—the Heir of your clan—shall mark such a one and judge him, for all judgment has been given to the Firstborn, the Heir of your clan. You shall not kill the murderer but you will send him into the cold dark climes or cast him into the night that his Creator might unmake him.

"Are you thinking of the enemy marriage Principle? or the Principle concerning Firstborns?" Psal asked when Lan had finished. "When I met him on the hill just now, I spoke of both principles. He would not heed my counsel either."

The young warrior sleepily opened his eyes. Psal stroked his patient's forehead.

"Aythan, you have awakened in time for today's so-called battle. But, resist the urge to maim and kill until your arm heals. And today you will miss a most ignoble battle." Kneeling, he helped the boy sit up. "See, now it is all over."

Aythan nodded and while Lan warned the boy against looking at his arm and nursing any ideas of wasting away in a steward longhouse, Psal called for Satima. She came running immediately.

Empty-handed. "Didn't I tell you to bring water and cloths?"

"Firstborn, I forgot."

"Of course you forgot," Psal sneered. "You're too busy laying a trap for innocents. Does it satisfy your soul to scheme? You were not born among us, Satima. You were a foundling, rescued and wedded. Why then do you delight in returning vengeance to those who have not personally hurt you?"

"Firstborn!" She lifted her fingers to her mouth and peered nervously toward the gathering room. "Lower your voice. What if they understand you?"

"Then I would raise my voice even higher. Get me water to wash in. Now!"

She muttered some inaudible defense, hurried past the gathering room, then returned later with a basket of cloth in one hand and a bucket of water in the other.

"Where's Daris?" he asked.

"I don't know, Firstborn."

"Find him!"

She dropped the bucket and basket and hastened away, tripping in the hallway in her attempt to escape Psal's wrath. He watched her struggle to get up. *You and the rest of these Wheel Clan women are much too pleased with your treachery.* He washed his hands, doused the sick room hearth, then walked with Lan into the keening room where Ephan waited for him. Daris had arrived, and was chewing a piece of grilled honey-comb with bee larva.

"Daris, where were you just now?"

"With the warriors, Chief Studier."

"You left your mother's side?" He slapped Daris hard against the left ear. "You're a studier. You should not stoop to cruelty and deception." The redness on the child's cheek and the boy's tears brought Psal back to his senses. "I'm sorry, Daris. I shouldn't have hit you."

"I'm sorry I wasn't a good studier, Chief Studier." Daris hastened, crying, from the room.

"Go to your mother, Daris," Ephan said. "You're becoming like Na-has, Storm. Striking those who anger you. The child is still young. He yearns to be like the others."

"He's a studier, he can't be like the others." Psal turned to the tower. "And you, when you realized their tower was coming to a Wheel Clan region, why did you not warn it?"

"The listening tower of the Iden branch lacks crystals," Ephan said.

"Don't excuse it!" Psal shouted.

A war whistle sounded. If the Peacock women visiting the Nahas longhouse heard it, they probably thought that in the distance a bird struggled in a water-logged nest. Or that seabirds skated on waves of some far-off river, or night-birds were welcoming the second moon atop high-hanging branches.

"Is there nothing that can dissuade you from this integrity of yours?" Lan asked, walking toward the corridor.

"Nothing."

Lan bowed and left.

"We cannot remain here long." Ephan entered the base of the tower and began taking several keening crystals from a shelf and putting them inside his studier's pouch. "Even if we do not kill, we should be beside our warriors. As a kind of—"

"Compromise?"

"Not compromise. More like…well, I suppose I really don't know. Today I've found myself thinking about the old master and what he said as we journeyed with him night-tossed."

"He said many things. About women. About valor. Nobility. The stupid Principles."

"True, he was rarely quiet. But, I was thinking of what he said on the day he named us. You argued with him when he called you 'Coming Storm.'" He exited the tower's base, looked at the crystals in his hands, frowned. "These will suffice."

"And did you like the stupid name he gave you? 'Cloud?'"

"I understood it to be the right name so I accepted it. We are often unmoored, or tossed, or in danger of drifting, you and I. Our names suit us. You surely didn't want to be called Rocky or Sandy or some such thing, did you? But, do you remember what he asked us on that day?"

"It's all a blur."

"He asked, 'What do you love, and is your life worth that love?'"

"Ah yes, I *do* remember."

"How did you answer him?"

"I said I loved the Wheel Clan, and that my life was worth that love."

Ephan lifted his studier's sack. "Can you love our people still? I find no honor in this. And yet, they are my people, who found and fed me. I must stay at their side. All this day as we traveled back and forth, bringing them keening poles, branches, and crystals—did you see how hopeful and happy the Iden looked?"

"They called us their saviors."

"And now, we kill. And yet, if we refuse, what will we say when Nahas challenges us?"

CHAPTER 11

THE FEAST BETWEEN THE WHEEL CLAN AND THE IDEN WOMEN

Rain was speaking in a Peacock dialect Maharai found easy enough to understand but her discourse was on the war, and Maharai had no interest in war. She only wished to know which of her unmarried sisters would join her and Ktwala in the Wheel Clan.

The beautiful Gidea was already married. Nunu was too old, but she loved Ktwala and might accompany them if Maharai begged very hard. *I will cry and pretend to lose my breath,* Maharai thought. Then Nunu will leave Grandfather's side and come with us. Gidea would grieve to be separated from Tolika, but Lan had assured Maharai that the Wheel Clan's tower science was so great, both longhouses would frequently meet.

Only when the conversation turned to marriage did Maharai tune her ear to listen.

"Why should warriors not share a woman?" Rain defended the Wheel Clan against Gidea's worry. "Our women are few, our little ones happy and well-fed. Warriors are worthy of wives. They reclaim land from the forest and from wild animals. If it weren't for our warriors, what would happen to the Wheel Clan?"

Maharai tugged at Rain's hem. "What if the king tires of my mother?" she asked Rain. "Will he marry someone else he loves better? And what will happen to Mother when he no longer likes her? Will he send her uncovered into the night as Chief Kalli did to his first wife, and his sixth wife, and his twelfth?"

"You know Peacock Clan history well," Rain said.

"Old Jion taught me."

"Well, then, know this. Nahas has a good heart. Not a weak heart, mind you, but a good one. He will not harm your mother. I will tell you how good your future father's heart is. Sometimes he has even allowed non-warriors to marry."

Maharai didn't think that was particularly good.

"If the women are past the age of child-bearing, and if a man wants her." Rain offered Maharai a round wooden platter filled with small red fruits and fermented salted meats.

The platter's engraving elicited a gasp of delight from Ktwala who immediately praised it.

"Soon, you Iden women will learn this craft also," Rain said. "You're our queen now."

"What happened to the king's other wives?" Maharai asked. "Did they die in the war? Or did he tire of them and give them to others? And how many did he have and who did he love better? He has two sons and an adopted son but I see no wives."

"Ruanna was a primary wife," Rain said. "She belonged to Nahas alone. He loved her greatly. She was Netophah's mother. Hinis was the wife he shared with his brother. Psal was the child of that bound three."

"So Psal may not be Nahas' son?" Ktwala asked. "He might be the son of Nahas' brother?"

Rain straightened her back. "That hardly matters, but you will understand our ways soon. This is how the matter went. Ruanna could not bear little ones at first. In the meantime, Nahas and his brother had made an alliance with a Macaw clan and both men married Hinis. After Psal's birth, Ruanna became pregnant with Netophah. After Netophah, Tanti. Then Ruanna died. A terrible, sudden death. Then Nahas' brother, Psal's other father, died. Then Nahas' other brother died. Only Nahas alone of his five brothers survived. Those were terrible times, but with Hinis' help, Nahas retained his kingship of all the Wheel Clan. Because of Hinis, Nahas rules many of the fertile regions of Odunao. And what chief in our clan or any clan can wrest it out of his hands?"

Maharai frowned. "Mother, don't marry into this family that has such bad luck."

"We will bring them better luck," her mother said. "And enough of your questions."

"Hinis and four of the king's children are all dead," Rain said. "Killed at the beginning of the war."

"Who do you war against?" Gidea asked. "You speak of the war but you do not tell us who your enemies are."

"An evil scattered clan," Satima said.

"That is what you said before," Gidea responded. "Has this evil clan no name?"

"They have a name but we do not speak it. Among our people, to speak the name of our enemy is to empower them."

"Ah," Ktwala said.

But Maharai said, "Old Jion never told me about this particular belief of yours."

"Did Old Jion know all the wisdom and beliefs of the Wheel Clan?"

"He said he did," Maharai answered.

"Our Nahas wants peace during the rest of his reign," Satima said. "A complicated, scheming power-hungry woman would be burdensome.

Give him a simple woman with simple joys, one who will sleep at his side and help his mind to rest, and our king is happy."

"My mother is very simple," Maharai said, and smiled because her mother's sweet simplicity had been apparent to the king.

Once more the conversation began to turn to war; Maharai stood up. She tugged at her mother's braid. "Mother, I wish to see what the men in our longhouse are doing." True, but she also wanted to see Netophah, whose gentle soft touch continually played in her mind.

Rain answered before Ktwala could. "The people of our clan also believe that when clans become allies, the men of both clans should be left alone to understand each other. The women, also, should learn each other's ways. This is also the belief of your own clan, is it not?"

"True," Ktwala agreed. "I remember the old days. Before the elders in our longhouse argued and left us night-tossed. We would visit a Ruined City in the Grassy Plains. There our women would feast with Wheel Clan women. How we would laugh and sing into the night free from the world of men!"

"Those days are long gone." Rain glanced at Maharai. "Girlie, stay here."

No, I don't like this old woman at all. Psal was in one of the corridors. She had heard his voice earlier. Lan had also walked in that direction. She looked at Ouis who sat on his mother's lap. "Rain, if I can't go outside, may I explore your longhouse? Since I'll be living in it?"

Permission given, Maharai strolled toward the corridor on the left. *I will explore one corridor,* she told herself, *then I'll return to the gathering room, and walk down the other.* The smell of pharma and death grew stronger. She entered a large room where warriors on blood-stained sleeping mats stared unblinking at the ceiling. She had seen death before and understood that the warriors were preparing to die so she smiled down at them, and stroked or kissed their foreheads. In the next room, a smaller one, a young warrior lay half-awake, one of his arms missing.

"You have only one arm?" she asked him in the Peacock language.

Surprisingly, he understood her. "Psal removed it."

She kissed his cheek. "One arm is as good as two if you practice well. Don't worry."

He smiled and she rose, bade him goodbye, and continued walking down the passageway.

With the exceptions of Netophah's and the king's chamber, the Wheel Clan used painted or embossed curtained screens instead of doors. Behind one of screens, Maharai heard Psal's voice. Tip-toeing toward it, she peered over it into a room where metals, stones, gems, tools, bottles, clay jars, and parchments cluttered shelves and baskets. Inside were the two studiers she had seen earlier. Psal was lying with his back on a wheeled mat, his dagger on the ground by his side. His trousers were pulled up to his knee and he was rubbing his leg, a strange shriveled thing. The pale girlish studier stood in front of a window looking out at the darkening night. They turned to her as she entered and exchanged surprised glances.

"Girlie, are you lost?" Psal asked in the Peacock language.

"Only little children get lost. Does your leg hurt?"

He picked up his dagger and sheathed it. "Girlie, I understand that you Peacocks are an inquisitive people, but—"

As he struggled to get up, she held her hand over his unruly black curls and ran her fingers through them until he pushed her hand away. The other studier, whose name she couldn't remember, held an open clay container which smelled like the odor that lingered around Psal.

"We're brother and sister now," she said to Psal. "Yes, yes, we are! You and I and Ouis and Netophah. We're brothers and sisters."

The boys glanced at each other, and the pale studier approached Psal with the cup.

She examined the pale studier. "I suppose you're our brother as well, since you're the king's adopted son. What did they call you?"

"Ephan."

"Oh, yes! Oh, yes! Ephan!"

They looked at her in silence, and she suspected they considered her a nuisance. She grabbed the clay cup from Ephan and looked inside it. "Should I rub my brother's leg with this?"

"It's Emon bark soup," Ephan said.

Maharai held the cup before Psal's face. "Drink it all up. Now!"

Psal's staff was leaning against a window. She pressed the cup into Psal's hand then walked toward the staff and lifted it. "Oh, how heavy! And…Peacock markings! It says here…the great Chief Tsbosso gave it to you. I've heard of him. Old Jion says he's our kinsman. Well, actually, our kinsman's kinsman's kinsman's kinsman." She bent toward him, whispered slyly. "We aren't supposed to like him, though. Some ancient grudge or other."

Ephan reached for the walking stick, but instead, she swung it like a club, dashing across the room battling an invisible warrior and overturning the baskets and jars in her path. After an extensive battle with the unseen-yet-now-conquered warrior, she said to Psal, "Old Jion says our warriors take herbs to make them lose their minds when they fight. It must be wonderful to lose one's mind and fight with all one's heart, recklessly, cruelly." Again, she swung the staff. This time much too near Psal's head. "Is that what that is? A brew to make one cruel? Old Jion says the Wheel Clan has become a victim of its own concoctions. Is that true?"

Psal stood up. Immediately she stood at his side, her arm around his waist. "If you used your staff, you wouldn't be in such pain. Your staff must carry you, not you it." She pointed to the concoction in his hand. "I will not move until you drink."

He quickly finished the drink, then pushed her toward the door. "Leave now."

She did not leave. She watched as he put on a pair of strange-looking boots. "Where is your hospitality?" she asked. "Show your sister your granaries and your animals. Everything! I wish to see everything."

Ephan said something in the Wheel Clan tongue and Psal nodded. Maharai walked into the hallway and peeked into the adjoining room. It contained twelve large poles like lamp stands.

"Ah!" she said, "This is what a keening room should look like! Old Jion always told me…but to see the crystals all lit! What new things this day brings!"

"Girlie," Psal said, rising. "We have…."

"Ah, yes! I know! You have to join the warriors. Let them wait. The third moon is not yet high. Or will you stay here to keen the women? But Old Jion says Wheel Clan women can keen towers without men." She grasped his hand tightly, looked into his eyes the way she always did whenever she wanted something from her doting grandfather, smiled. She studied Psal's face; Ephan's agitated sighing proved she had caught Psal's will and could bend it however she wished. *I will be able to command Ephan soon enough.*

"Yes," Psal said. "I suppose the moon is not yet high."

"Tell me about keening, then."

"Keening involves much." Psal began explaining keening in so leisurely and intricate manner that Ephan started pacing.

"Ephan," Maharai said, "Adopted Brother. Don't be so worried. The feast will wait. There will be boar meat and fruits for all."

Ephan laughed.

"One has to know how to shape the crystals," Psal said, "to know their symmetries and counterparts, the angles and positions of the sockets, the carats, how to make different tones, and how to receive music. It isn't a thing easily learned."

"I'd like to enter. May I?" Maharai asked, then stepped into the keening room.

Psal followed after her and pointed toward the tower base. "That's our tower. Inside are the twelve keening trees. The ones outside are spares.

For longhouses we encounter. They like to be lit, too. Just to be involved. Sometimes they help us perform very complicated keens."

"Even from here?"

"Oh, they don't mind. They're near to the tower, even in here. They know how cramped it gets under the tower stairs with all those branches, trees, crystals, and parchments inside. But when there's a council meeting, we return them inside to the base of the tower."

Ephan was laughing and looking at Psal with his mouth opened.

"Don't worry"—Maharai walked toward the tower's base—"I won't hurt the crystals."

A sharp whistle sounded outside the keening room window, like that of a large waterfowl. Ephan took Psal's arm, pulling him. Psal yanked his hand free and led Maharai into the base of the tower. However, as she entered, a little girl dressed very much like herself approached from a small inner room. Maharai extended her hand toward the girl who extended hers also. But unexpectedly, the girl stopped at the tiny doorway. Maharai approached the room, but found she was separated from the girl by a clear impenetrable invisible door. The strange girl looked as perturbed as Maharai felt. It was apparent the tiny little thing was trapped inside.

"Let her out," Maharai pleaded, and pounded the impenetrable doorway. "Whatever she's done, she's sorry to have done it."

"Look behind it." Psal pointed at the shiny door.

Maharai looked behind the tiny door. "There is no behind it. Where is she?" She faced the tiny doorway again and peered into it. The trapped girl had returned. "Is it a window to some other place?" she asked.

"It's a crystal," Psal said. "A very large one. Polished and placed in a wooden box. When we keen, we often use it to set the lights of the crystals. We must look into the mirrors to see the image of the Greater Light."

"And the girl?"

"An image of yourself."

"An image? You've trapped my soul?" Suddenly afraid, she ran toward the studiers and attempted to push past them. "Why did you take it?" she yelled.

Psal pushed her toward the trapped soul. As he did this, his own soul also appeared in the crystal, as trapped as she was. He lifted his hand and the Psal inside the stone mimicked his gesture.

Maharai stood there long, staring at the other Maharai and the other Psal. "Why did you trap your soul with mine?" she asked. "Who can free us now?"

"This is no magic," Ephan called out from where he stood in the hallway. "You've seen lakes, have you not? This is what we call a 'mirror.' In addition to helping us keen, it shows us how others see us."

She had seen herself in lakes before; but never this clearly. *So this is what I look like?* she thought, and smiled at her beauty and how kind her face was. She would have stayed there a very long while except that Ephan grasped her by the hand and led her back into the hallway.

Again, he whispered something in the Wheel Clan language, his gestures even more urgent. Once more, Psal ignored his adopted brother. This time, however, his face was calmer, as if the former anxiety no longer oppressed him.

"This passageway is called the chief's hallway." Psal smiled at Ephan as if daring his friend to challenge him. "Here, we have the keening room, the three studier rooms, the chief's chambers, the chief's family's room, the storage rooms, the sick rooms, the pharma rooms, the granaries, the weapons, and on the other side, our horses." He slapped Ephan playfully on the back and pointed toward the hearth. "The other passageway is called the residential hallway. Warriors and their wives and families sleep down there. Three hundred rooms. Usually two warriors and a woman for each room. Sometimes more, sometimes less. Depending on rescues. The children sleep in their own rooms. Do you want to see that hallway as well?"

They walked past the gathering room to the other side of the longhouse into the residential hallway, passing room after room, of differing sizes, containing one, two, or more beds. They walked past the squatting places with their wooden bottomless toilets to the hall's end where some eighteen women lived, separated into five rooms. Most appeared malformed, bent and frail, or sickly. One or two had bruised faces as if they had been beaten. Some had pale skin with pale hair like Ephan's. The women lay in beds or sat on chairs, or on the floor staring out past Maharai with sunken and morose eyes. Three held small children. One child—a pale boy with pale white hair—approached Psal with his head bowed. Maharai listened as Psal whispered something in the Wheel Clan language which elicited a smile from the boy who returned to the woman's lap.

"Who are these?" Maharai asked Psal.

"Comfort women."

"Whom do they comfort?"

"Men," he said. "Boys."

She sucked at her teeth, trying to understand. "And must they comfort? What if they don't want to comfort anyone?"

"I suppose those who have brothers in our longhouse—who would avenge them—could refuse to comfort."

"Who comforts them?" she asked.

"Rangi comforts them," Ephan said. "Tomah comforts them."

"I don't know what Rangi or Tomah are," she said, "but the one who looks normal—that pale beautiful one—men must love being comforted by her?"

"That one is Lyrenna," Psal said. "She has an ugly disposition. But yes, they do like her body. That little one with her is her son."

Ktwala's voice echoed through the longhouse calling out to Maharai.

Maharai asked Psal, and looked down the corridor at her mother. "Old Jion says your people don't like those whom the Creator badly-made. He says you allow the badly-made girls to live but kill the badly-made boys. Still, look…you're badly-made and you're alive!" Her mother called again and Maharai rolled her eyes. "Mother probably thinks I'm shaming her somewhere. Be safe, my brothers."

She ran toward the gathering room where Gidea was weeping about losing both her daughter and Ktwala at once.

"The separation has occurred too suddenly," Gidea was saying. "I did not wake this morning expecting to be bereft of my daughter. And, although you Wheel Clan sisters assure us that both towers will meet frequently, I must be sure Lan and Deyn are not cruel husbands who will beat my daughter. Therefore, we Iden Peacock women will return to our longhouse. Tomorrow we will show you Iden hospitality. Then we will schedule the courtship intervals. The Iden men must examine the Wheel Clan warriors properly."

Gidea stopped speaking momentarily as Ephan and Psal walked through the gathering room into the night. Satima took the opportunity to speak.

"This is a rare night, Sister. A night when we women can laugh and sport among ourselves without listening to men talk of war. And courtship rituals during a time of war? My Iden sisters, this is not practical."

Ktwala tried to make peace. "Gidea," she said, "let the men fend for themselves tonight and see women's worth. Perhaps Rain will agree to the courtship interval. Even in a time of war. And yet I do believe your daughter's husbands are as honorable as my Nahas."

But Gidea rose from her seat, dragged Ouis from Ktwala's lap. "My sister, you're letting your heart—and that other thing—rule your mind." She turned to Satima and Rain. "I only speak my heart. Don't be insulted. What mother would not worry for her daughter?"

So, the Iden women rose as one—Ktwala apologizing profusely for Gidea's behavior—and forsook the exotic Wheel Clan dainties and fermented meats. They bade the Wheel Clan women goodbye. "Who knows if we shall see each other again?"

And—despite Rain's protestations—went out into the night.

CHAPTER 12

THE SLAUGHTER OF THE IDEN

As the Iden women neared their longhouse, Maharai recognized the markings of their domesticated animals grazing in the darkness. "Isn't that Ghali?" she asked, pointing to her pet lamb.

"It is!" Gidea looked about, pouting. "Our men are useless! We leave for half a day and they allow the animals to escape! And now…with the third moon, there is little time to call them back home."

"Why fear?" Ktwala spun around on her heels and made a gesture that took in all the Wheel Clan lands. "Sisters, we're in Wheel Clan lands. The Wheel Clan, *our* ally, will anchor our longhouse here. Tomorrow our flutes will call our animals home again."

In the distance, near the entrance of the Iden longhouse three Wheel Clan warriors stood looking out toward the forest. Maharai asked, "Shall the Wheel Clan warriors stay in our longhouse tonight? How shall we sleep with men boasting of their kills?"

Gidea laughed. "Oh wondrous our new life will be!"

The aged Nunu dance and sang,

> *"New life for us now.*
> *New life for our women.*
> *New life for Ktwala.*
> *New life for the Iden Clan.*
> *The Wheel Clan has conquered the night."*

They continued homeward, singing, Ouis racing ahead, overtaking Psal and Ephan who lingered along the way. Maharai hurried after him. Then a hand from behind a bush snared her foot. In the dark, Jion's voice, an almost inaudible whisper:

"Little Spider, we are entrapped."

"Old Jion!" Laughter as she kicked at the bush, chiding. "Hiding in the grass? Come, come, drunken one! Tonight the Wheel Clan warriors, our new allies, will teach you to keen our tower! And you lie there—"

She bent low and her voice left: Old Jion's face was bloodied. He lifted himself slightly, then fell into the grass again.

"We…should not have trusted them," Jion said. "Our brothers…murdered."

Maharai could only reach those women who were close to her. She called them. They quickly gathered round. Terror struck, they held onto each other. Old Jion was lying in his blood. Meanwhile, the Wheel Clan warriors, already alerted by their singing, peered into the darkness.

"Ktwala," Gidea whispered, "your new husband's clan has destroyed us all."

Maharai knelt beside the old man, held him close. "Old Jion, hold to life." But where was Ouis? She stood to her feet, looked about. Past leaves, past boulder, no sight of her brother.

"Escape." Jion's voice frail, his tone futile, his eyes already looking past Maharai into the other world. "They want to steal you. Escape. Into rocks and caverns. Or be scattered."

The women looked about at each other. Nunu was too old to run fast, other women carried small children. One was pregnant. The rest were little girls too young or too fearful to escape the Wheel Clan warriors who were almost upon them.

Words spoken in the Peacock dialect but tinged with the Wheel Clan accent called out.

"Your warriors are conquered but young boys are safe inside." A scarred warrior approached them. "Attempt to flee, and they will die. Return with me and your children will live."

Unseen by the Wheel Clan, on the right side of the longhouse, Ouis' small arms made a stabbing gesture to his throat: All inside are dead. All.

The women trailed behind the Wheel Clan warriors, but some—urged on by Gidea—tried to escape. Some to the Wheel Clan fields, some to the hiding places in the Iden storerooms on the right of the longhouse where Ouis stood beckoning. But more Wheel Clan warriors appeared. The women fleeing were immediately overtaken. All but four were captured. Only Ktwala, Janda, Delo, and Maharai would join Ouis inside the secret entrance.

* * * *

Janda and Delo fled to the hidden compartments in the Salt room, the nearest to the secret entrance. Shaking, weeping, Maharai allowed her mother to push her inside the tiny wall of the granary.

"Don't cry"—Ktwala's whisper sounded even more distant in the dark room.—"All will be well. We will be well."

Ouis was hastily hidden in the wall opposite Maharai's. In the darkness, Ktwala's hands warned her: *Stay here. Keep yourself covered. Don't leave until I come for you. Don't worry for me. I'll find a place to hide.* Such animated, desperate gesturings. There were no hiding places nearby, none. Ktwala slipped out of sight, leaving Maharai struggling to stop her frightened panting. Both her breath and her body rebelled against her control. Flushed with fear, she tried to convince herself her mother was safe and determined to wait. Then footsteps approached her hiding place. She tensed. The door in her wall opened and Ouis stood before her, weeping.

"Why didn't you stay hidden?" she chided and reached for him.

He began to speak but the room was flooded with torch-light. Strong hands grabbed both her and Ouis and dragged them into their gathering room. There, the bloodied bodies of her slain clansmen lay, dying or dead. Her grandfather's nearly headless body lay crumpled near their useless keening room. Gidea and the Iden women stood weeping. Janda and Delo as well. Maharai searched the faces of her sister. Her mother's face: not seen.

The king didn't look at her long. He was speaking in the language of the Wheel Clan to the studiers who seemed to be defending something, someone, themselves—Maharai didn't know. A loud blow across Psal's face needed no translation. Psal stumbled backward and fell to the ground as the king, with bloody hands, beckoned to Netophah at the entrance. Flanked by two warriors, Netophah approached and pushed Ouis to the ground. The king shook the pain of hitting Psal out of his hand, and turned to Maharai.

"Where's your mother?" He asked her in her own tongue. He looked down the hallway to the room where Maharai had been found. "Ktwala is here in this longhouse, is she not? In one of the secret compartments you Peacock people are so adept at creating?"

Maharai trembled as children do when they're afraid or cold, and shook her head so vigorously only a fool would have believed her.

The king signaled the torch-bearers, spoke words the girl did not understand, then spoke to her again. "Don't worry, I won't burn the longhouse over your mother. But I *will* find her. Do you understand me?" He beckoned to Lan who immediately drew near, then he faced Maharai again. "Girlie, I asked this warrior to separate you and your brother from the male little ones. Why did you not listen to him?"

She could not speak.

"Your brother's death is your own fault, do you understand? Sparing the life of a male enemy is something we Wheel clan warriors never do. I have appointed death to all Iden men found in your longhouse, yet I was willing to spare him. You understand that now I cannot allow your brother to live?"

She flung herself at his feet. The king pushed her away and Lan held her firmly by the shoulder.

"If you kill him, Nahas," she shouted. "I will kill you."

The king gestured to Netophah. How gently Netophah had touched her in the cave! But no such gentleness was found now when the golden-haired, crescent-eyed prince pushed Ouis to the ground. At this, many of the Peacock women turned their faces, weeping. But Gidea, beautiful and fierce, did not turn away. Nor did the old and broken Nunu, or the beautiful and passionate Tolika. And not Maharai. Gidea kicked hard against the two warriors who held her tight. Nunu wept, her gaze set on the bodies of her sons, grandsons, nephews, and her brother Iden.

King Nahas lifted his bloodied dagger, aimed to strike Ouis. But Psal grasped his father's hand, shouting words Maharai didn't understand. Raging at first, then kneeling and begging, he stood between Nahas and Ouis, his arms outstretched. Then Ephan also approached the king, pleading as well. Nahas listened in silence. Alternating or simultaneously, the studiers spoke.

When King Nahas answered them, he seemed to argue, question, challenge, defend.

Maharai and the Iden women watched the verbal battle intently, the third moon rising. Then the king spoke a word and Ephan stepped backward, suddenly silent.

Psal, however, continued pleading, his voice growing shrill and shaky and echoing through the Iden longhouse. Even when the king raised his hand and two tall warriors pushed him aside, Psal would not be quiet. Shouting, the king pushed Psal and he turned on his bad leg and fell to the ground. King Nahas uttered another word. Psal grew silent.

The lame prince looked helplessly at Ephan, then at Maharai, then at the Iden women. He didn't look at Ouis. The king spoke again and Prince Psal raised himself from the bloody floor and opened the Iden doors. Maharai knew then that all was lost.

How beautiful the Wheel Clan language! The king's words were bright as light, tinkling like water, but Maharai knew them to be heavy, dark, blood-filled words. The king then called Ephan. Ephan bowed to the king then raced toward the granaries where her mother hid unseen.

Now to Ouis' death.

Sharp blades can slit a throat clean through with one stroke. Ouis did not die quickly, as storytellers who sing praises to swift blades and to pale-skinned warriors would have you believe. Not for me such songs of so-called glorious battles. I've seen too much of dark death, and the death of dark peoples to sing songs that praise war. Let white-skinned storytellers exult in blood-letting.

Ouis lay on the ground, his hand clutching his neck, his mouth seeking breath, his pleading eyes turned to his sister. Netophah's dagger hacked at him as butchers hack at livestock. When he died, he was like meat drained of blood. Lan's strong hands held Maharai tight. She grasped them and bit deep. Lan winced, slapped her hard across the face, and she felt herself flying toward the bloody longhouse wall. There, fallen, her face and back aching, she watched helpless as Netophah kicked her brother's hand from the bleeding gashed neck. Then the Wheel Clan heir knelt beside Ouis and took his own blood-stained dagger and cleanly ripped the boy's throat open.

In her annals, Maharai said she must have shrieked to see this murder, because Tolika later told her she had done just that. However, Maharai writes that if sound or shriek escaped her mouth she did not know, because death had touched her before it touched her brother. It must have, for she had grown numb as she watched his death throes and could neither speak nor breathe.

* * * *

Through the plaited bamboo lid in the little inner storeroom, Ktwala peered. Through the latticework of the barrel's cover, she saw: the red daubed ceiling of her destroyed longhouse. She heard: the death agonies of her betrayed clansmen—their horror echoed from its walls. Around her, the smell of spices mixed with blood. Her body trembled, she stilled herself. Inside the barley container, tears washed her face. She stopped the sob from rising from her throat.

Loving words, she thought, *deceiving words. And yet...his heart seemed true.*

In the near distance: booted footsteps trampled the floors of the Peacock longhouse; her brothers' voices fading, surprised to find themselves suddenly outside of life; the quick rip of human flesh.

In Ktwala's mind: Ancient stories of prevailing warriors. Triumphant tales told by Peacock Clan studiers of worlds: *Blood-soaked enemies their braided hair split from their split skulls.* In her heart: Nahas loving words, deceiving caresses. *Your children will be as my children.* Ktwala's mind reeled.

Near the barrel, a Wheel Clan warrior was speaking in her language. She drew her breath slowly, quelled her body's inner trembling. A carved wooden club lay between her cramped legs. She thought: *Why do I sit here safely hidden?* But sense stayed her hands; she did not rise. Barley fell from between her fingers. *I must live and avenge my destroyed clan.*

In the gathering room, Nahas shouted in the tongue of the Peacock Clan: "Iden women, you did not know we warred against your Peacock Clans. Nevertheless, your brothers must die. And you cannot go free. Iden women, tell where Chief Iden's daughter hides."

Ktwala's heart pleaded: "My sisters, my aunts, my daughters, do not betray me." The Peacock women heard her heart and remained silent.

And Gidea said, "Ktwala raced toward the large cliff. She jumped into the river."

Nahas' voice: "We will anchor here tonight. If her body is in the river, it will rise up again."

Away, fading: the weeping voices, the commanding voices. Away, drifting: dying voices within the longhouse. Yet, nearing: footsteps. And soon someone leaned against the locked container, blocked light.

Ktwala heard: two voices speaking in the Wheel Clan tongue. Through the latticework of the barrel's cover, Ktwala saw: pale hands touching the top of the container, twisting.

She held her breath; the cover lifted, light broke in. From above, the face of the pretty pale studier looked down upon her, his eyes and mouth wide open, surprise in his eyes.

A male voice called him from behind: "Ephan!"

Ephan looked up, away from Ktwala. His eyes squinted toward the unseen speaker. He turned again to Ktwala, smiled in wonderment. Ktwala's eyes pleaded. Ephan stared at her, silent. He pushed his long white hair behind his shoulder and replaced the container's cover. The footfalls of the warriors trailed away.

* * * *

Furious, angry, his leg and hip aching, Psal attempted to keep pace with the rising third moon and the Wheel Clan warriors. He felt like one awakening from a Rangi-induced dream. He wished to wake from guilt, from atrocity, from the sense that he had failed utterly to save a good and innocent people. But as he looked around him in the dark forest, the Iden women were bound, struggling, kicking, biting, weeping. It was no nightmare. The home region suddenly seemed harder to navigate and the royal longhouse painfully far away. Before him, Nahas dragged the screaming Maharai by her right arm. In the lead, Kwin struggled with Nunu. Cyrt, Deyn, and Lan struggled with the bound Tolika and Gidea. Behind Psal, the rest of the warriors dragged the other Iden women.

The royal longhouse warriors—intent only on subduing the women and hurrying homeward—were mostly silent, speaking only intermittently to threaten. But Orian seemed unable to stop speaking and railing against Nahas. That Wheel Clan warriors should treat the Iden women as sisters of a marriage alliance! That Nahas should not take the Iden tower! That Nahas should allow the hidden Ktwala to remain inside! He went on and on, annoying Psal more and more as he spoke.

When they arrived at the doors of the royal longhouse, Nahas spoke at last. To Psal, Netophah, Gaal, and his chief captains while the other Wheel Clan warriors took the bound Iden women—all but Maharai—inside.

The king held Maharai firmly, even as she kicked him and bit his right hand.

"Firstborn," the king said. "You, too, Cloud—you're to keen Ktwala's tower to follow in our wake. And to keen the Qerys to join us at the home region."

"If that one's child is a boy," Orian said, looking at a bound pregnant woman being pushed into the longhouse, "it should be killed."

Psal caught Orian's gaze. "If the unborn child is a boy," he said, "I have determined it will become a steward in our clan. Furthermore, these Iden women must be allowed forty-nine days to grieve for their brothers."

Orian stared at Psal in the torch light, spoke to Nahas. "My king, in the old days, kidnapped women quickly forgot their lost clans and were quickly bedded. Why should we treat these enemy captives with the honor and respect due to women of nobler clans?"

"Orian," Nahas said, "I have had your fill of advising me."

But Cyrt grasped Orian by the collar. "Enough! I am tired. I desire sleep. Not your rambling about the golden days of the old king's rule. Continue and you will find yourself anchored in the dark climes. I will personally see to it."

"Orian," Lebo said, "our Nahas still remembers the old strife when Wheel sub-clans fought each other. But few here are honorable enough to speak of it. You are not of the king's sub-clan. Nor were you reared in the royal longhouse. Nor were you part of the king's marriage tribe. You might try to remember that."

Orian lowered his head. "I did not wish to dishonor Nahas."

A tiny rivulet of tears streamed in the white clay on Maharai's face. Psal forced himself not to look at it. "Nahas, Ktwala is a chief's daughter and intelligent. If she is in the tower as we believe, she will not leave it. She knows the Wheel Clan does not easily cast aside towers. And if I set her tower to follow in our wake, she will see the pattern and know her tower is not truly night-tossed. I have listened to the Iden tower and it desires to enter the cold climes soon. If it follows its desired path, it will. But we battle the Peacock Clans in clement region Therefore—"

Ephan interrupted him. "Nahas, this sudden love of yours...consider...the morning may have been full of loves, but hatred swallowed the night. This woman whom you say you love, for whom you keep an oath to her sisters, tomorrow search the tower and find her. Or, are you fearful of looking her in the face? Are you fearful of being shamed in the woman's eyes?"

How bold this King's Favorite is! And how patient this king toward him! Psal awaited the king's response.

But Netophah answered for the king, "Father wills to break Ktwala's will," he said. "And remember your place, Ephan. Favorite you may be, but do not think too highly of yourself. If you would rebuke the king, rebuke him privately."

"Truly, Ephan," Lebo said, "if you had questioned the old king as you now question his son, you would not live to see the next day."

"I have not finished speaking." Netophah touched Lebo's shoulder. "As you already know, Ephan, Peacock Clan women fear isolation. If Ktwala travels alone, her heart will be broken and remade toward her new clan."

Ephan persisted. "But if she travels alone—"

"The Voca will not touch one in our wake," Nahas answered impatiently.

"That was not my worry," Ephan said. "Outlaw longhouses abound. Many of them without towers. Therefore they cannot be tracked."

"Psallo, Ephan"—Maharai spoke suddenly—"I wish to see my mother."

Netophah glanced at her, but spoke to Ephan. "Chief Bukko is Psal's near kinsman and a trustworthy ally. Let our studiers send a message to his tower with the Iden harmonies. He will befriend her. There is no need to tell the Voca. They will see our wake and understand she is under the protection of our truce."

The meadows were already tainted with bloodshed and treachery and the double moonlight had grayed the sky. Blood red clouds streaked above the Nahas longhouse. As Psal entered the royal longhouse, his own tower raged at him because of the Wheel Clan treachery.

CHAPTER 13

STUDIER'S GAME

Psal pushed past the Wheel Clan women into the studier's room and immediately began vomiting. Daris picked up the nearest chamber pot—a clay one from the sick room already half-filled with blood and urine. An unfortunate choice, which only added to Psal's nausea. Psal retched once, twice, hoped the vomiting would stop. It didn't. His body could not stop shuddering or cramping or forcing acrid liquid up his throat.

Ephan hurried to the rampart, but even after the final horns had blown, he lingered there. Then the third moon rose to full height, he descended. He positioned the torch in its place and asked Daris if the Iden women had been securely locked away in the holding cells.

"They're in the chambers near my mother and the other comfort women," Daris said. "Kwin guards them."

Ephan's eyes met Psal's. "Kwin will be gentle to them."

"They're weeping and calling us murderers and betrayers," Daris said. "Better—"

"You understood them?" Ephan asked.

"In war, one understands words like 'murder' and 'betray' quite easily," the child answered, and glanced at Psal.

"Even so. Well-learned." Ephan put his hand on Psal's shoulder. "Don't blame yourself, Storm. Nahas didn't listen to me either."

Psal's stomach heaved again and he grabbed the half-full chamber pot. The blow he had received from his father had brought blood to his nostrils. Blood mixed with salty mucus still trickled down his lips and into the pot. He swallowed hard against something rising in his chest.

"I'm not the Firstborn. Obviously." Ephan removed a pouch filled with ground white seeds from his studier's sack. "But as a studier, and his adopted son, I should have been heard."

"Everything is always so obvious to you," Psal said, "living as you do in the clouds. And no! No Rangi."

Ephan popped one seed from the pouch into his mouth. "The Rangi is not for me but for you."

"Did you really think you would persuade Nahas by mentioning Samat's Unfleshed Ones?"

"I saw them, Storm. We are their tools, mindlessly led, used at their will."

"Not now," Psal said, his voice, throat, and stomach wary.

"Later then?" Ephan asked, almost pleaded.

No, not later either. The debate with Nahas, the cries of the murdered male children—Psal's ears had grown tired of words and of hearing. Only one thing he cared to hear: Cassia's night-tossed, half-destroyed tower. "Yes," he said. "Later."

The curtained screen of the studier's room was being pulled aside: Lan. He glanced sideways down the passageway then entered.

"Firstborn," he said, looking askance at the chamber pot. "Your brothers await you near the hearth. And do not fear. Strange as it may seem, your pleas touched their hearts, struck deep. You challenged the king's action as a true studier." He gave Ephan a playful push. "And this one's talk about the Unfleshed Ones....Who knew our brothers had such guilt and superstition in them?"

"Guilt," Ephan remarked. "But they murdered anyway."

Lan wrenched the chamber pot from Psal's hands. "We are at war, brothers. Yet, although few will say it—we know we should not have murdered innocents. But if you continue here, vomiting and weeping and dulling yourselves with pharma, you will lose your winnings. The Studier's game must be played well. Speak now, and you will be able to protect the Iden women from more harm."

"I was not weeping," Psal lied.

"You were," Daris said. "See, there. A tear."

Lan gave the chamber pot to Daris. "Take this away." He eyed Ephan's Rangi pouch. "Ephan, no more Rangi. Not seed, not bark. Your attempts at temporary oblivion will only prove permanent if you continue. Dull your mind with the writing of dead kings."

"I can hear the Full Blossom Tower." Lan closed his eyes, listened closer. "So, that's why you sit here weeping? Because Chief Qerys has destroyed Cassia's tower? Silly me, I thought it was guilt." Lan frowned. "We're at war, Firstborn. Consider your Cassia lucky. Chief Qerys could have burned the longhouse thoroughly and entirely. Or perhaps he could have keened it to some desert where he could rape your sweetheart and the other women. Have you considered that all day the Full Blossom women have been free to leave their broken longhouse? Do they not have free will? Surely, we no longer have control over their lives. The tower is faint but it is not dead. Its denizens are alive. Chief Qerys was merciful to allow it to fly free." Lan nodded to some unseen someone in the corridor, then lowered his voice. "Perhaps the Voca will find and save them. Many Peacock Clan women would rather live among the Voca than return to their husbands. Whatever happens, these women have received more mercy than our mothers did."

Ephan placed another Rangi seed in his hand, then seemed to think better of it and returned the pharma to his sack.

Lan edged toward the keening room door, looked up and down the hallway, then returned.

"Firstborn, I know you. Do nothing stupid. Cassia is married and has forgotten you." He placed one arm each about the studiers' shoulders and directed them toward the corridor. "If some ill-thought-out plan about saving Cassia dances in your minds...remove it at once. You are not as wise or as safe as you think you are. Do nothing stupid to purge your guilt. Especially, Firstborn, do nothing to destroy your chance at becoming a chief one day. The king awaits us. The Qerys as well. And there are the Orian wounded in our sick rooms to attend to. Can you two not behave like true warriors?"

His attempt to push them forward failed and Psal did not move. Lan took a deep breath. Removing his arm from Ephan's shoulder, he took his knife from its sheath on his thigh. The whalebone blade with its shell-encrusted ivory hilt was now within a hand's breadth from Psal's face. "Beware, Firstborn!" he said. "Enough of this obstinacy! Listen to me. Have I ever failed you? No, I have not. I've saved your life and honor more than once."

"Even so," Daris said, "that gives you no right to order about the Chief Studier and Firstborn of our clan."

Lan gave Daris a stern look and the child immediately lowered his head.

Lan re-sheathed his dagger and once more placed one arm around Psal's shoulder and the other around Ephan's. "They await you! If you do not enter the gathering room by yourselves, I will drag you there myself." Saying that, he pushed both studiers into the corridor.

* * * *

Maharai stood near the king, crying and wringing her bound hands in such a wretchedly pitiful manner Psal immediately wanted to free her. But loosing the hemp cords would only annoy Nahas, and Nahas was already annoyed.

"Latch the entrance," Psal called to Deyn. "Let us put this ignoble day behind us."

But Maharai screamed as the heavy latch fell, shouting, "Murderers! Betrayers!"—echoing the chants of the Iden women in the residential area. Maharai's panicked shrieks elicited a warning look from Nahas. In response, she struck him under his chin with her bound hands. The king flinched, then gently, almost as if she were Tanti or Ria, told her in the Peacock tongue that he would lose his patience if she continued her willfulness. She spat in his face and ran to the entrance and attempted to lift its heavy latch. That earned her a blow to her shoulder, delivered by Cyrt.

"Already, your error shows itself," Orian said. "Nahas, I implore you. Let these women be scattered among our sub-clans. This is what your father would do."

"Psallo!" Maharai knelt before Psal. "Open the door. I know you have a good heart. My sisters and I, we saw how you pleaded for us. Do not let my mother die alone. Let me go to my mother."

"That will not happen," Nahas said in the Peacock language. "Learn to live without your mother. For now."

"If I learn to live without her, my life would be unhappy," she said. "I don't want an unhappy life."

Nahas spoke to Psal in the Wheel Clan language. "Firstborn, have you made the Iden tower's song a priority?"

"You didn't answer our question about the cold climes," Psal said.

"Let her go to the cold climes but later than usual." Netophah spoke from his post at a nearby window. "And return her to warmth early. As for the wake, let it be a loose wake. She should not enter any region when a skirmish is planned, and not meet with any Peacock or Wheel Clan longhouses. She should understand soon enough."

Psal pondered the coldly-calculated heart of rulers: *A man who loves a woman would not allow her to enter the cold climes alone, but these kings and chieftains—*

"Why do you smirk, Firstborn?" Nahas interrupted Psal's musing.

"Smirk, Father?" Psal shifted his weight to his stronger leg. "I didn't smirk."

"Ah, but you did."

"I was unaware of it." Psal responded. He squeezed Maharai's hand then wiped her tears away. "No one will hurt you here. You and your sisters are our people now."

"Nahas," Ephan said. He was looking at Maharai in that inscrutable way he had. "You are king of a fierce clan and fierceness in a Wheel Clan queen is a necessity. But…have you considered that this separation from Ktwala will affect you as well?"

The king didn't answer Ephan's question. He only wrenched Maharai's hand from the Firstborn's tunic and began dragging her down the corridor.

CHAPTER 14

A NEW PEOPLE

The king stopped at the room diagonally across from the keening room, the chamber that Psal had said once belonged to his sisters, the one traditionally assigned to the daughters of chiefs and kings. He released his grasp and pointed to a low-lying bed. "If you want anything, the studiers will get it for you."

He turned to leave but she raced after him and hit him hard on his back.

He wheeled around, eyed her steadily. "Maharai means 'Agreement,' does it not?" He lifted her by the waist and held her dangling above the wooden floor. "But you're not being 'agreeable,' are you?"

She struggled against the strong hands and bit him hard on his right forearm. He winced but retained his hold, carrying her to the sleeping mat where he gently lowered her onto the bed. Then he sat on the floor, his back to her, his clasped hands covering his face. Sweat glistened on his neck and blood matted his graying, dark red hair. Something that looked like fat mixed with blood was splattered on the right side of his graying beard.

"You're the leader of your sisters now, Maharai," he said, then rubbed his bitten forearm.

The king's hair, cut short, was not much longer than Maharai's small fingers. She grasped what little she could and tugged hard. He spun around, and grabbed her hands. When his fingernails dug deep into her wrist, she released her grip.

He spoke firmly, not raising his voice. "Do you want to add to your mother's grief by dying?" His blue eyes peered into her dark brown ones. *How could his eyes hold no guilt?* "Do you want your mother to find your corpse on a hillside tomorrow? I am well able to do that."

No, she did not want that. She fell backward on her bed.

He threw a woolen blanket over her bent, beaten shoulders. "Perhaps you *are* 'agreeable.'"

It took almost all her energy to speak. She lifted the edge of the woven sleeping mat on which she sat and distractedly looked at its gay colors: yellow, red, and blue. "We Iden didn't kill anyone." She spoke more to herself than to Nahas. "My brother, my grandfather, Old Jion, no one killed anyone. You should have asked the Ever-Present One before you killed us. He would've told you we Iden are good. Then you would not have killed us."

The king punched the wall with his fist. "Has the Ever-Present One saved you from me? The Everywhere One who should have saved my children and your brothers was off pissing somewhere or sleeping. Or maybe he is non-existent and my anger has no target." He walked toward the hallway. "Let me hear no more about the Silent One."

She rose from the mat, raced toward him and grasped his arm. "Nahas," she pleaded, kneeling, then placed her hands on his trousers, above his crotch, began unlacing his clothing. "Nahas, for my mother, I will…I will—"

The king's mouth fell open. Momentary confusion flickered on his face, then comprehension and, shock. For a moment he seemed unable to speak, unable to move. Then he pushed her away and left the room.

She hurried after him but a large guard—the same one who had hit her when she tried to unlatch the door—caught her in the corridor and held her head under his massive arms. Nahas entered his chamber without turning to look at her.

Earlier, she had walked these very halls with a new brother. Now, her sisters were imprisoned on the other side of the longhouse, her mother was alone in the Iden longhouse, and she was alone in a room across from the king who had ordered her clan's destruction. Her eyes were red from weeping.

* * * *

Inside the keening room, Psal was having trouble getting the rebellious Lesser Light to obey him. Already, he had replaced three crystals on one of its keening branches. He waited for the replacement crystals to glow. *I beg of you. Even a flicker.* Nothing happened. Behind him, Ephan sat atop the council table chewing a sliver of Rangi bark.

Psal glanced at the gourd in Ephan's hand. "Why do you not help me?"

"Is my conscience any less bound to it than yours? Neither of us believe the battle to be honorable."

Psal sighed, groaned. "Mark you, do not take that for more than two days."

Ephan nodded and continued chewing.

Psal glared at the stubborn keening branch. "I attempted to stop the murder of the Iden! Why…." A thought. "Cloud, if we could save the Full Blossom women—"

Ephan spoke groggily. He climbed down from the table but obviously feeling the drug's calming effect, he stumbled and had to lean on a nearby wall. "You call me mad because I saw the Unfleshed Ones, yet, you're trying to save our enemies' women. The Peacock Clan may hear of it. Have you considered that? Won't they consider us foolish?" He took another sliver of Rangi bark from the gourd, popped it into his mouth and closed his eyes. "I won't even imagine what Nahas would do...." He stopped short.

Psal waited for him to resume, but Ephan sat arching his eyebrow.

"Yes?" Psal prodded.

"I've forgotten what I was going to say."

"Of course you have." Psal limped to a basket of blue crystals, rectangular and newly cut by the stewards. "If we were to save Cassia as an appeasement for killing innocents, the keening trees might—"

"Find another way to appease them." Ephan was slurring his words badly. Psal was tempted to knock the gourd from his hand. "Uhm," Ephan continued, "someone...inside our longhouse...Seagen, Gaal, maybe. Or outside of it...Mion perhaps...will deduce..."

"Wheel Clan Studiers hear many faint towers after battles," Psal whispered. "And keep your voice low. They hear towers going nighttossed, but they don't assume treachery."

Ephan shook his head vehemently, or as vehemently as a studier under the influence of Rangi could.

"Yes, yes, yes." Psal approached Ephan and manually caused his friend to nod agreement. "Only once, that's all. And the thing will only be known between us two. Orian's studier is wounded and enslaved to Rangi and Tomah. He couldn't hear an eagle's cry if the eagle was standing in front of him. Seagen is not paying attention to anything. He and Cyrt will be too full of ale. And...well, Gaal will be angry but he won't betray me. He's still trying to befriend me. And...Nahas only looks at our parchments during war councils. And he only concerns himself with future battles. Mion won't betray us. He's too attached to you."

Ephan laughed, a drowsy laugh, and walked toward the keening branch on wobbly feet. "I see you've figured it all out already. But what of Lan? He's convinced you want to do something stupid. And Seagen... don't forget Seagen. He's the son of a studier as well."

"You worry too much."

Ephan removed another piece of bark from the gourd in his shaking hands but returned it to the container after Psal frowned. Although Ephan eyes usually got jittery when he was tired, he looked calmer now, less agitated. He bent to look at the branch they used to keen towers from afar. "I suppose we could. I've always liked Cassia."

"I thought it was her sister you liked."

"Yes." Slurred. "Her, too. Tzaddi is lovely."

"We'll have to hurry. Their longhouse won't make it another night, and who knows where the night will fling them?" Psal replaced several crystals and waited for the branches to respond. Nothing. "We are going to save Cassia," he whispered to the keening stands firmly. He closed his eyes, imagined Cassia, imagined the Iden tower, imagined Tsbosso's home region, then sent the images to the tower. The tower flickered, understanding. "And this will be our secret. You will tell no other studier. I'm sure you towers won't betray my secret to humans."

Then the tower allowed itself to sing.

"Ay me!" Ephan said, "it is done, then."

So, in addition to anchoring the Iden and Nahas towers to the region and keening the Qerys to meet them in the morning, Psal keened the Full Blossom Peacock tower to Samat's home region. The nightly tower communications about war councils, deaths, lost or destroyed longhouses over, the pharma mixed and ground, the wounded warriors from the Orian longhouse tended to, Psal and Ephan lay in bed waiting for sleep. Momentarily, Psal pondered taking Rangi, but thought better of it.

As they lay on their mats, Ephan said, "Sleep, when it comes, will not remove what I've seen."

"Our minds will put such cruelty away," Psal answered. "They always do."

"This is a different kind of cruelty. I saw the Unfleshed Ones again. With my soul's eye. Storm, if you saw, if you saw, if you saw. There was one, standing beside Gaal. He had talons which stuck straight through Gaal's heart and back. I knew its name. I suddenly seemed to know it." Ephan stared into the darkness. "It turned and looked at me and when it—he—I understood why Gaal is the way he is."

"Ah!" Psal said. "Well, that is good to know."

"It's like a dance," Ephan said, his words slurred from drowsiness. "The way the Unfleshed Ones…tune our lives. They tune us, life, evil… as we tune towers. It is all…so planned."

"Ah," Psal said again. "At least some beings in this world are organized."

"Be patient with me, Storm. Just a little. Hear me. Just a little. When one sees such things…ancient, intelligent, evil…one must speak."

"I'm allowing you to speak, am I not?" Psal covered his shoulder with his blanket.

"But you aren't truly *listening*."

"Oh, must you whine? I *am* listening, Cloud. Sleepy though I am. Odd though you are."

"I saw that although we humans are evil…that these Unfleshed Ones also…use our evil. It was as the old master said. They push us from our path, they use our anger, and our pain. They use the times, nature, the... we are their *tools* against the Creator, Storm. Their tools to attain their own pleasure. I saw one, a red one...red as murder...enter Cyrt. I saw him make Cyrt his home. Why was he red, I wonder? Why do you think he was red, Psal? I wish I knew. And his body...it was not symmetrical, but lopsided and twisting. Why do you think that was so? Why should his limbs be asymmetrical?"

"I cannot tell." Psal hoped sleep would overtake Ephan soon. "I didn't see him. Perhaps he was mentally unbalanced, as you are."

"You're not being serious. Are we not supposed to examine, to study, to analyze?" was Ephan's confused reply. "That his body should be...I wish...I wish I had not seen...could not see."

Psal tried not to sound impatient. "Not something one already half-blind should wish. Ephan, the day has been difficult....Tomorrow, perhaps. Could we discuss these visions tomorrow?"

"We're studiers...." Ephan said, then suddenly with great awe, added, "Storm, I saw such things! Do I wish to see...the Unfleshed Ones? Storm, do you think they could make us—us studiers—do such evil things as well? Could we be their tools as well?"

"We're human," Psal answered. "I'm sure we could be influenced. But we are aware of their devices, are we not? The old master has taught us how to guard our hearts from such beings."

"So, you guard your heart against beings you don't believe in?"

Psal looked up at the ceiling. "I suppose I see them as symbols of vices, metaphors for evil traits, not as actual Unfleshed Ones."

"They are actual, though. I do not want to see. I wish not to see." Ephan continued speaking in barely audible mutterings. Then sleep and Rangi took his words away. Psal fell asleep also, dreaming not of the Unfleshed Ones but of Cassia.

* * * *

Afraid, Ktwala squatted, unmoving. She heard: bodies, writhing and dying on the bloodied longhouse floor. They called out. She could not move. The dying moans faded away. Long, long, she sat there, fearful. Third moon reached its height; the heat of the day left. She thought, *Should I throw myself out into the night?* But afraid of the unmaking, she chose to stay. And night took her longhouse away. All through the gray night, she wept.

Morning came. No dream-sharing, no drumming of calabash. No dance to welcome the day and the new region. No family teasing. Still afraid, she touched the barrel's cover, pushed it and climbed out.

Barefooted, her heels became sticky with blood. The first bodies she saw: Gidea's sons. Her heart numbed.

The new region was a land neither pleasant nor harsh, but it was one she would remember forever. She did not ascend the tower, to search for other towers, to see if wild animals lodged nearby ready to eat human carcasses. But all day she dragged bodies out of the bloody longhouse. Only twice did she stop to question her strange work. Only once she said, "Let me leave this longhouse, go out into the world, and allow the coming night to take me away." That was when she saw her son's corpse, bloodied and ripped and torn. She looked, unable to grieve, promised her dead brothers she would retrieve their wives, sisters, and daughters. She paused long. Then she lifted Ouis' arm and pulled his body through the door. Her father she buried. Her son she buried. The others she piled high. All day, all day, she dragged and carried. Until all the corpses—young and old, male and some female—were outside. Night came again and she re-entered the longhouse. Fatigued, she slept at last and dreamed.

In the dream, a strange clan appeared at her longhouse. Clothed in black, their faces hooded, they said, "You called us? You wished to take the living ones away."

"No, I called you to help me remove the dead."

They turned their hooded faces to each other, then to her. "So, you will not come with us?" one asked her, consternation in his voice.

"No," she answered, "I will remain here."

She woke after that. Too early. Long, long, she stayed awake and watched the new region appear while the old ones with all its unburied memories slowly faded away.

* * * *

While morning was still gray, Maharai heard footsteps scurrying up and down the hallways. Morning and light had come. All around her, the longhouse was waking. Women were carrying ladders and opening rooftop windows. Yisin grain was being roasted and boiled. But no communal drumming called to her. Old Jion wasn't drunk and singing to himself in his chamber. Neither were her grandfather, Ouis, or her mother nagging her to wake and explore the new day.

It was King Nahas, his two sons, and the adopted ghostly studier who aimed to rouse her. They stood together, only in their trousers, looking as if they had just risen from bed.

"Are you awake, Girlie?" the king asked.

Looking past the king, she spoke to Psal. "Psallo, I want my mother."

"These three will teach you and your sisters our ways," the king said.

A small boy peeked in through the door. *About Ouis' age.* He entered and sat beside her.

"Girlie," Netophah said, defiling her language. "You our people now."

"Psallo," she pleaded.

"Push away fear," Psal said.

Ephan placed three small reddish-brown seeds in her hands. "Chew on these and calm yourself."

Feeling his pity, she clenched his arm. "Ephan, my mother." But then Netophah approached, and her body began shaking with anger and rage.

"Your people bad. Raid us," Netophah said. "Many days. Many moons. Our farms and regions. We not retaliate. Although being put to grief. Again and again, they raid us. Tsbosso and the Threshing Floor Clan sudden make war on us. Destroy our people. Kill my sisters and two brothers. No longer, your people. You our people."

The king walked to a nearby window. "Girlie, your women are yet alive. If we deceived you, we used the deception the Peacock Clan taught us. It was your people who started this trouble."

"Do you wish to sit with your sisters?" Ephan asked her.

"Yes, Ephan."

"Then do what is necessary." Ephan gently stroked her face. "Learn the ways of our people, calm your sisters, and you will gain our respect and your freedom. Can you promise me that?"

"I will, Ephan. I will."

The promise obtained, all left, except Netophah.

"Expedient," he said. "No want kill Ouis. Nor grandfather chief. Young boys not forgive. Ouis avenged himself would have, when older. And, know, Father try save him. If Ktwala stay in longhouse ours where was, your brother not die." He knelt beside her on her bed.

She edged away from him. Her breath was trapped between her chest and her throat, unable to go either up or down. Her tears refused to fall.

"Ephan and Psal help you we understand," Netophah continued. "We kind people. They studiers, priests of our people. Teachers. Our Psal… he prince our people…he both, yes. Studier and Prince…a royal priest… not usual for my people…but good…he understand both…he make you understand why necessary my people kill your people." He wiped tears from her face. "No tears. Tears not mar beautiful face."

When Netophah finished speaking, a male voice outside the room called her name.

"Cyrt it is." Netophah unlatched the door. "Help you. Helper you. You need walk inside, you need walk outside, he guarder you. Father not want you run. Cyrt guarder you 'til you our people."

The warrior who had bound Gidea's hands, who had spoken so gently to Gidea, was now Maharai's guard. At the far end of the longhouse, her sisters were shouting a Peacock victory chant. The sound of their angry voices made her weepy. She walked into the hallway. "I want to be with my sisters," she told the guard.

Netophah stood up, shook his head. "No, not see them. Not now." He glanced at her hemp skirt and beads. "Not wear Peacock pantsing! Wear Wheel Clan pantsing!"

"I don't want to wear the Wheel Clan clothes!" she shouted.

"Then be so." Netophah lifted his hands in appeasement. "Be so."

She walked back to her room and looked through her window. Something about the landscape felt strange. She continued peering out at it. At last she understood: *The same trees and meadows from yesterday? I have seen all this before. So this is what Old Jion meant by "home regions" and "recognizing home fields?"* She searched the distance for her mother's longhouse but saw nothing. She slid down to the bed. But how shall I escape? The room was full of many goat-hair blankets, of differing colors. She walked to a pile and picked up as many blankets as she could hold. These she took and built blanket fortresses around her bed, surrounding her on its three exposed sides until she heard footsteps and looked up to see Ephan carrying a tray of food.

He placed the tray on a small wheeled table near a shelf, then pushed it toward her. He glanced askance at her fortress, said, "They're looking for your mother."

"Yes, yes, you must find my mother!"

Once again, his apricot eyes seemed to pity her; he indicated the tray. "Now, you must eat."

Offering her a pronged utensil, he described what was set before her: salted boar meat, fermented vegetables, spiced boar's blood broth, and snake's skin fried and crispy. Five small gourds contained the flavorings the Wheel Clan loved—salty, sweet, fermented, sour, and peppery.

It was a burden to eat, an impossibility. The food was unappetizing. *Who drinks boar's blood or eats snakes?* Besides, tears had taken up residence in her throat and nothing was powerful enough to dislodge them. "I can't eat."

He gently opened her hand and rested the utensil on her palm. "I know you Peacock people don't eat what we Wheel Clan eat. But you are *our* people now and you must eat what we eat."

She threw the utensil at him. "Why should I eat with those who have killed my people?"

"Girlie, I am *feeding* you. Your people are the people who *feed* you."

"Don't feed me, then! Ghost girl!" She hurled the tray at him. The grain, the broth, the spices mixed on the floor with the mud he had tracked in with his sandals.

He left the room, shouting, "Eat from the floor! I'm not cleaning it up."

"Ghost girl!" She spat the words down the corridor. She raced back into her room and grabbed the chamber pot and hurried into the hallway only to find Psal standing at the studier's door, looking at her. She considered throwing the urine on Psal because he was near at hand, but a mixture of friendship, pity, and something else stayed her hand. He squinted at her, eyebrows arched—she had seen that look before—as if he was trying to make sense of something incomprehensible.

He gave her a chiding look. "I don't think you want to do that."

Angry, she returned to her room and used her feet to grind the tossed grain and mud into the rug on her floor. "I will never eat. I will die first."

"After a day or two, you will eat." Psal entered her room, stood in the doorway. "I myself have tried not eating, and I will warn you. The longer one continues not eating, the more humiliating it is when one finally gives in to hunger. Apologize to Ephan. He's kind and good. He won't mock you if you tell him you regret your words." He rocked several times on his good leg then looked down at his left one. "I went without eating for seven days once. Then I had to plead with Nahas for food. In front of everyone. Can you imagine? I, a Firstborn, forced to humiliate myself before my clan? The king asked me, 'Firstborn, are you so weak that mere hunger makes you come begging for food from your enemy?' It was very hard to bear. I would not want you to be similarly humiliated."

"Psallo, my mother....I worry for her."

"I can do nothing about your mother at this time. If she remained in your longhouse, she will do well. Perhaps Nahas will keen for her tower. But if she is lost, what can be done? You like children, do you not? It might be Father will allow you to play with our little ones...if you do not fight his will. Maharai, I advise you to take our Father seriously. He has the patience of kings, which is quite dangerous. Of course, he will not kill you. You're his wife's daughter. But he will, perhaps, do such things that you will wish he had killed you. Trust me, little sister, I know what I say."

"Psallo, you're a studier. You speak to the Creator and He tells you all things. Please, give my sisters and me a longhouse and release us. I know you can do this. The Creator will tell you we will not harm you. Did he not tell you how weak we were?"

Psal smiled, shook his head slowly. "It is not true that you would not harm us. If you were given a longhouse, and if you were to encounter a Peacock Clan, you would seek to join the Peacock alliance and avenge yourself against us."

"I wouldn't war against you, Psallo."

"Ah, but you would," he said, gently, as if they were true siblings, as if his brother had not killed hers.

He called to the pale little boy she had seen earlier and told him something in the Wheel Clan language. The boy listened then left.

"Daris will ask Ephan to feed you. Now, when Ephan returns, do not throw your food on the ground again. Even if you do not wish to eat it, food is not a resource one should waste."

He walked outside, leaving her alone. She looked about the room, weeping. *How often have I wished to be free from the torment of Gidea's son, to be free from being night-tossed, and now how I wish I had never wished.*

CHAPTER 15

THE STUDIERS' HOPE

It was still morning, the sun barely risen. In the brightening gray, the fire-damaged Qerys was still materializing opposite the Nahas longhouse. The odor of burnt wood seeped into Psal's nostrils. The Qerys longhouse clung to its tower like a fire-singed bird's nest falling away from a tree branch.

A slow keen, Psal drummed his fingers on the window sill and drew a deep breath. *All I need! A stubborn, spiteful, rebellious tower.*

"Daris!"

The boy came running in, carrying Psal's studier's pouch.

"Where's Cloud?" Psal asked.

The child handed Psal the sack, which Psal lay on the sill.

"Daris, it is good you respect Cloud, but beware of his talk of the Unfleshed Ones and Samat, the Great Destroyer of lives. There are no such things as Samat or Unfleshed Ones."

The boy frowned, wrinkling his face. "Would the Master of the Wintersea say that?"

Psal lifted a studier's tunic from a clothes basket. "He could be confusing. He was rather a cryptic old man…but he was…rational."

"I'll believe what Ephan believes. He's wiser than you in such matters."

"One can be noble and good without being superstitious like our mad studier." Psal sniffed the tunic, frowned, then proceeded to dress himself.

"Cloud hasn't gone mad. He truly sees the Unfleshed Ones."

Psal smiled, pitying Daris. "Tell Cloud if he believes the Ever-Present One has caused him to see the underpinnings of the world, then he should be strong and commit himself to seeing them instead of fearfully allowing them to disrupt his sleep." He finished lacing the straps of his tunic and looked out the window again. "Orian's warriors are burying their comrades. And now the Qerys clan. Ah, me. All this death."

"Chief Qerys is from the Hokkan sub-clan, is he not?" Daris asked.

"He is. Why do you ask? Has Ephan been teaching you the ancestries?"

"No, but…was it not Chief Hokkan who recently sent word to the stewards claiming one of the free towers?"

"The very same."

"I have heard it is Chief Qerys' habit to leave Peacock women in burning longhouses? Chief Studier of our clan, does he do it as an act of mercy or of torture? Do you know?"

"I am not privy to Chief Qerys' thoughts," Psal answered. "It seems strange that they do not save the women and scatter them to different longhouses or send them night-tossed into the night as other victorious longhouses do. But it is the habit of the Hokkan sub-clans to be inscrutable." *My Cassia, my Cassia. What has this evil clan done to your tower?* His heart tightened. *Stay your mind on the situation at hand.* "Inundated by chiefs and warriors from two arrogant longhouses! And the corpses of those Iden warriors we slew outside their longhouse also litter the ground." *Even now, poor Ktwala, you're surrounded by dead kinsmen.* He tousled the boy's hair. "Daily, you're surrounded by death. Not a thing for one so young."

Daris walked past Psal to study the crystals on the keening trees. "I'm strong, Chief Studier."

"I didn't say you weren't strong. I said you were *young*." Psal spoke with increased tenderness. "You're free to be a child. That is what I meant to say. Do you understand?"

The boy's eyes widened. "I did not know that, Chief Studier."

"You may run to your mother if sickness and death and the sick rooms overwhelm you. You comfort Lyrenna much."

Daris looked relieved. "Thank you, Chief Studier."

"Learn to play. However, not today and not outside. Remain indoors or with the farmers. Or, stay with your mother. One thing only I ask of you." He lifted a neatly folded white parchment from the council table.

Daris gave him a huge smile. "I know what it is, Chief Studier."

"You do? And what is it?"

"You want me to heat water. For cooking and to cleanse the wounds. I should also ask the stewards in the longhouse for more platters, bowls, cups, and gourds because new warriors now abide with us. Also, I am to grind pharma, and put the centipedes in fermented Yisin liquid to counteract the Peacock dagger venom. I should also crush more scorpions to rub on the limbs of paralyzed soldiers and arrange for the stewards to transport them and their belongings to the steward longhouses. But I am not to grind Dovi and Tomah, and I must not remove the venom gland from the snake in the Chief Studier room."

Psal heard Ephan laughing just outside the door. "Daris," Ephan said, entering. "Perhaps the Chief Studier doesn't want you to do so much."

"I am well able to do so much, Cloud," Daris answered. "I'm off now. To prepare cauterizing fires and hot stones in the sick rooms."

Psal straightened Daris' studier's cap, one he himself had worn when he traveled as a young boy with the old Master. "I will add two chores more."

"What, Chief Studier?" Daris asked.

"The first. Tell Satima to make you a little studier's cloak."

"Truly?" Daris grinned so wide, and Psal might have laughed if the child hadn't looked so pleased.

"Truly, Little Studier! And the second. Take this parchment and give it to the steward named Jarid. No other eye should see it."

"None other will, Chief Studier." Daris took the parchment and left, shouting to the women near the hearth that he had become a real studier.

Psal lifted his studier's pouch from the window sill and threw it over his shoulder. He looked at Ephan, who was squeezing his forehead as if trying to hold his head together.

"You stay too often with Father," he said. "You're beginning to be his mirror."

Ephan smiled. "Do I?"

"Yes," he said. "You act very like him sometimes. Look at yourself, holding your forehead! Nahas does that as well. When he thinks the world is falling all around him."

"When he is worried, he gets headaches."

"The secrets you two share! And, what has caused you a headache now? The girl's not eating? Let Daris feed her. A true compromise. You both will win."

"No, the girl was not on my mind. I…your rescuing the Peacock women, Firstborn. It's only…beware your schemes against Nahas."

Psal grinned, pulled on his shoes. "If I scheme—and I do not say that I do—surely the King's Favorite will protect me." He limped into the corridor and was almost jolted back by the loud chants of the Iden women. He spoke to Maharai who stood at the door. "Can such women walk freely in our longhouse? Soon—when you are more like us—you and they will walk as freely as any in the Wheel Clan."

* * * *

The Qerys was typical of all Wheel Clan longhouses, and thus less accessible than the royal longhouse, which had been adapted by the crafts and skills of the Wheel Clan for the comfort for a king's studier son. The exertion of climbing the entrance stairs of the Qerys made Psal's hip ache. Moreover, to preserve its waning energy, the failing tower had stopped converting the sun's rays into light and heat. Before Psal's eyes grew accustomed to the darkness, he was repeatedly stumbling over corpses or wounded warriors,

As he neared the keening room, he glimpsed a hunched-back man in studier's black lying on his stomach. "Brother Renan?" he called and hurried along the corridor toward the prone man.

"I am here." The Qerys studier raised his right hand, shoulder, and torso only momentarily, then fell back weakly to the ground.

"Brother Renan." Psal knelt beside the studier.

Renan's dazed green eyes looked toward the gathering room, past Psal, unfocused. Blood streamed from his eyes, nose, and ears—a sign of Dovi poisoning. An empty gourd near the studier's feet smelled strongly of the fatal herb. The odor of Tomah permeated the dying man's flesh. He appeared to be about thirty, younger than Psal had imagined when they communicated through the towers.

"You bleed? You took Dovi?"

Renan lifted himself slowly. "Forgive me, Firstborn-Damaged One."

Psal cradled the studier's head in his lap. "You who wrote such bold, beautiful, tower music…you willfully took Dovi?"

The Qerys studier lifted his hand; his fingers slowly wove themselves through the too-long black curls that covered Psal's forehead. "I had not thought I would die in the arms of our Mad Prince."

Our Mad Prince. Psal had first heard the appellation after his return to the royal longhouse. It was generally used when others thought him elsewhere; only Cyrt had been bold enough to hurl the words directly at him. Over time he had grown indifferent to the title's power to wound him. Now, however, Renan spoke it lovingly, almost as if it was a blessing.

"Renan, what is the name your master gave you?" Psal asked, looking toward the keening trees within the base of the tower. "You told me once he called you 'Mist.' Am I right? Yet, you do not use it?"

"Yes. That was the name the old man gave me."

"A kindly name," Psal said. "He thought you a gentle influence, then? He named you well. You have gently touched the lives of many."

Blood trailed from Renan's lips. "I am an inconsequential thing fated to fade away."

"I doubt that was the old master's meaning. Your master was my master as well. The Master of the Wintersea. He was bitter, perhaps, but not unkind."

Footsteps approached and stopped immediately behind Psal, who turned to see a warrior dressed in the tartan of a Qerys chieftain. The man was about thirty, perhaps older. Slender, nature-blessed like Nahas, with neck-length blond hair. He wore a leather belt carved with the markings of the Hokkan chiefs. It took Psal a moment to recognize the warrior as Chief Qerys' son, Antun. He had seen Antun before but had ignored him as he generally ignored all Wheel Clan chiefs, especially those in the arrogant Hokkan sub-clans.

"Firstborn." Antun pointed toward the gathering room in great agitation. "My sister's son. He needs your help."

"Renan, being a studier like myself, is my higher concern."

"Firstborn!" Antun snapped, then calmed, clasping his hands. "Come now and help. My sister's son. My son now, for he is all I have left of my close kinsmen because my father and brothers lie slain. Please, help me, Studier Firstborn."

Psal twisted as he sat, his hip aching, and again turned to Antun. Climbing the unaccustomed stairs and walking the rail-less Chieftain's corridor of the Qerys longhouse had already taxed his hip and leg. The fact that Antun was now pressuring him—even if gently—to leave a dying studier and help his young nephew only brought more discomfort.

"The boy cannot be saved here," Psal said. "I will tend to him when he's in my sick room."

"But, Firstborn, Chief Studier. If you could—"

"I will return soon," Psal told the dying studier. After, propping Renan against the keening room wall, he limped to the gathering room where the child lay moaning on the floor in a half-sleep. *Grievous, grievous. About Daris' age.* The boy's forearm hung from his elbow, half-detached by a Peacock warrior's machete, wrapped by a bloody cloth. Psal bent over the child and smelled the bandaged forearm.

"Renan has already neutralized the Peacock Clan venom," he said. "But the blood loss…."

"Studier-Firstborn," Antun pleaded, "he must not die."

Psal called to Kwin, who was helping Ephan lift a wounded warrior onto a pallet. "Kwin, take this lad to my sick room. Tell Daris to give him Rangi sweetened with honey. No more than twenty small leaves. Tell him to prepare the amputation knives. I'll be there shortly. If you cannot find Daris, ask Lan or Seagan to do it."

"Can you not attend to him now?" Antun pleaded.

"All warriors must be removed from a damaged longhouse before treatment of any one warrior begins." Psal walked toward Renan and prepared for an onslaught of verbal or physical bullying from an indignant Hokkan chieftain. "Those are Wheel Clan traditions."

But the young chieftain only said, "This child—my sister's child, now my child—must not die."

Psal hid his surprise, spoke softly, tenderly. "And I must attend to Renan. That is a studier tradition. We studiers have no clans and belong to all clans. Yet, we are our own clan. I will not let a studier die alone."

Again he knelt beside Renan and leaned the studier's head upon his own shoulder. "Taking Tomah and Dovi is no way for a sweet, refreshing mist to die."

The studier's sad eyes struggled to stay open. "No, Studier- Firstborn, it is not." Renan's voice sounded weaker and he gurgled as he spoke. "Knowledge of your existence has softened my own. You're one of the glories of the Wheel Clan."

"Foolish words, Renan." Psal wiped the new flow of blood from Renan's mouth. "I'm hardly glorious."

"Many studiers have desired to see the day when one of the damaged ones rules over our people." He coughed and blood mixed with mucus flowed from his mouth. "Many times I've dreamed of a Wheel Clan longhouse filled with others like ourselves, ruled by you, the Firstborn of the Damaged ones, the captain of our royal priesthood. There we would live in peace, called out from our clan to be our own great people. There, we would not always be tempted by Samat to free ourselves from this life." Renan's blood-stained hands grasped at Psal's studier's tunic. "You must become a chief. You were born a damaged Firstborn for a reason. You were created to help other studiers. You are fated to change all the Wheel Clan's cruel ways. It might be you will bring peace to all of Odunao, not only to Wheel Clan studiers. Firstborn-Studier, don't let Samat, the Destroyer of Lives, swerve you from your destiny. That lying thief is relentless, but you…you must be stubborn as well." His bleeding eyes stared at Psal intensely. "Promise me."

"I promise you I shall be quite stubborn," Psal said, pitying the man's Tomah delusions.

"Good." Renan gently loosened his grip on Psal's collar. His last words. Psal continued beside him, as the studier faded in and out of consciousness.

"Tomah blasted his mind, Firstborn," Antun said with a humility unexpected from a Hokkan sub-clan chief. "Forgive me. I didn't understand until too late its stronghold on him."

Forgive you? "I'm sure he hid it well. Tomah-addicted studiers are adept at such deceptions."

"He could neither live with nor without it. I often told him that you had endured much and you had not allowed Samat to tempt you with that evil pharma."

"You should not have told him that," Psal answered. "You did not know if your words were true."

Antun lowered his head. "Forgive me, Firstborn. I thought it for the best. And now—all the good I have heard of you, Studier-Firstborn, is nothing compared to what I now see. Perhaps if you had been here to encourage him."

He spoke twice of forgiveness? The Mad Prince of the Wheel Clan found himself speechless. He remained so until Renan died, then he tenderly lay the studier's head on the floor and stood. He walked into the keening room. All but one of the keening trees lay in stubborn darkness; only the listening tree allowed its crystals to shine. "How despondent these keening trees are!" he said, more to himself than to Antun.

"Their souls were knit closely with Renan's. When he lost his will to live, they lost theirs as well. I tried to coax them back to life but I'm afraid they find me a poor substitute for their beloved Mist."

"True," Psal said, "they are often very willful. It seems they have now chosen to live listening to the lives of others instead of having lives of their own."

* * * *

The aroma from fruit trees waiting to be harvested mixed with the odor of corpses as Psal and Antun walked toward the royal longhouse.

"Antun"—Psal wiped the perspiration from his face with his right hand, sticky with Renan's blood—"tell me about the Peacock longhouse you battled. The Full Blossom Tower, was it? You Qerys warriors seem to have a habit of damaging but not utterly annihilating Peacock longhouses."

"Their men were all dead or dying, Firstborn Studier."

"You knew that for a fact?"

"The tower spoke only of female life."

"Still, they're our enemies. Their women helped to kill our women. Why did you not ensure their deaths? Why allow our enemies to go free?"

Antun lowered his voice. "Father always...I...I didn't wish to burn women and little ones alive. I thought to let the night do its own evil. Their tower was very much damaged, Firstborn. Believe me that I have not betrayed Nahas or our brothers."

Chanting from the Peacock women in the royal longhouse rose above the songs of the wind and the cicadas. Psal spoke louder above their din. "When you say the longhouse was damaged, what do you mean?"

Antun looked toward the royal longhouse. He turned once again to the Firstborn, seemed to study him. "Are those Peacock Clan women in your tower?" he asked. "Taken by your warriors as prizes?"

"Your warriors could have raped and taken the Peacock women. Why didn't you?"

"Our longhouse was too destroyed for us to take them."

"Do not speak so subtly, Chief Antun. Nahas hates such subtlety and I have little time for it. There were other times when your longhouse was not so destroyed. Why didn't you take the women during those times?"

"The work of raping and capturing, then separating the women is one my dead father, Chief Qerys, did not like."

"You call rape 'work?' You and your warriors do not pursue for the 'Warrior's Prize,' then?"

"I do not like such doings."

"To exempt one's self from raping women? Interesting." Psal stood. "In many ways, your father and mine are alike. The taking of the Warrior's Prize is a rare occurrence in the royal longhouse as well. Partly because we rarely battle, except against the great chiefs, and partly because the tradition offends Father. He allows his warriors to do what they will, of course. But since the war began, when the warrior's prize has been offered to Nahas and Netophah…they have refused it."

"So you do not rebuke me, Firstborn?"

"I do not rebuke you. I simply sought to understand your own motivations, because there are many in our longhouses who consider it their due."

"And yet"—Antun indicated the royal longhouse—"you have collected these women and kept them together in your longhouse?"

"These wailing women were captured yesterday. A marriage covenant exists between Nahas and Ktwala, a woman of the Iden Peacock Clan. When our warriors finish the salvaging of your longhouse, they will search for Ktwala's body…if she is dead."

Antun laughed, with surprise, yet without scorn. "A strange kind of marriage covenant, Firstborn. I have heard often that Nahas knows when to show mercy and when to show his ferocity. But is it not strange that he should keep a covenant with the sisters of a possibly dead wife?"

"If you remain long with us, you will see things even stranger than this." Psal stepped into the royal longhouse entrance. "But we were speaking of the Full Blossom tower. The longhouse will no doubt be destroyed but the tower—what were its dimensions? Even if the women did not please you, did you not think of perhaps capturing the tower?"

When Antun stepped into the royal longhouse, the same surprise that often appeared on the faces of visiting chiefs now showed on his. He stood in the doorway silently perusing the royal longhouse gathering room. No entrance steps but a gradual incline upward, low-lying tables, railings along the walls. He bowed slowly. "I have heard of your Father's love for you, Firstborn. Now I see it with my own eyes."

Psal shrugged. "We were speaking of the width and length and height of the tower."

"Yes, yes, the tower." Antun continued looking at the gathering room with amazement. "It was five-sided, made of bricks but some wood as well. Quite beautiful. When we breached the longhouse, their studier fought bravely to defend it. It was average-sized—about fourteen paces across, with a large winding stairwell, very wide and high."

"How many women do you think could fit inside the base of tower and its stairwell when the longhouse falls away?"

"One hundred perhaps. Surely not all the women and children in a Peacock longhouse. Unless a Peacock longhouse finds them, they will be lost, of course. The Peacock chiefs still haven't taught their women how to keen, as far as I know. And the Peacock Clans have not discovered the ability to keen lost towers from afar. So, unless the Ever-Present One helps them, there's no hope."

Psal turned toward his sick room. "You sound as if you wish the Peacock women well?"

Antun's smile hinted at a conspiracy between them. "Perhaps I do."

* * * *

Inside the sick room, Antun kneeled at the boy's side, his body hiding the knife in Psal's hand from the boy's sleepy view. Psal tried to focus on the task at hand—removing the arm. As he pulled his basket of tools nearer and pushed the cauterizing stone's red edge deeper into the fire, Netophah entered.

"Chief Antun," Netophah said, "Nahas requires that you remain within this longhouse until another is made. If you wish, you may merge your longhouse with another of our clans. Are there any sub-clans you wish to join?"

"It is not something I've had time to ponder, Wheel Clan Heir." Antun bowed to Netophah.

"There are those who think of such things." Netophah sounded officious, almost cold.

Not his usual way, Psal thought. Although he always thought it best to ignore power struggles, in this case, because he had begun to like Antun, he said, "In my experience mergings of clans never work. Even in war, our warriors can think of nothing better than to compare and compete against each other. And chiefs are often loath to give up their privileges. It is best if Chief Antun have his own longhouse."

"Firstborn," Antun replied, "privileges matter little to me."

Netophah and Psal exchanged glances. "Still," Netophah said, "as the only living son of Chief Qerys, the privileges of chief are yours now that your father is dead. Father will honor you as chief while you remain in the royal longhouse. Your voice will be honored in war councils above our captains, and any women we find along the way—or whose husbands have died—will be yours if you want them. The main problem, however, is that you have no studier. No doubt you will ask why Nahas simply doesn't give up one of his studiers—"

Antun spoke with restrained exasperation. "The request was not in my mind, Wheel Clan Heir."

"Perhaps it was not," Netophah said, "but it has often been in the mind of other chiefs. I tell you now what I have told them. True studiers are rare these days. Ephan and Psal cannot be separated from the royal longhouse because when not engaged in battle, the royal longhouse rescues damaged longhouses. The wounded need quick tending. Only one studier—"

"As I said," Antun said, with a hint of impatience, "these matters were not on my mind. And truly, I have no great desire to order people about. As for women, my wife was killed on the same day as the king's dear wife. My heart doesn't long to replace her."

Psal found himself liking Antun more and more. *With chiefs like Antun,* he thought, *I could well like this clan of mine.*

* * * *

After the amputation, Psal entered the keening room where he found Lan pacing.

"Firstborn!" Lan caught Psal by the collar of his tunic and thrust him into the tower's stairwell. Psal managed to cover his face with his hands but Lan gave him a powerful blow to the stomach that left him feeling that the wind had been knocked out of him.

The commotion brought Ephan running from one of the sick rooms. Ephan now became Lan's new target.

"You allowed it?" Lan shouted and immediately pushed Ephan up against the wall near the doorway.

Ephan had enough sense to gesture to Lan to lower his voice. "The Rangi allowed it,"

Lan whispered, "I cannot kill the Rangi."

Ephan frowned at Psal who was clutching his stomach in the stairwell. *Your fault,* he mouthed. "Could you, please, put me down, Lan?"

"If you don't protect this one from himself, who will?" Lan asked.

Antun, Netophah, Kwin, and two warriors unknown to Psal who wore tunics with the Orian sub-clan pattern, peered into the keening room.

"Studier, is all well?" one warrior—red-haired, slender, and nature-blessed—asked, eyeing Lan curiously.

"All is well." Ephan gestured impatiently. "Be on your way. Be on your way!"

The warriors bowed and continued down the corridor. Netophah shook his head impatiently and returned to his council with the king, but Antun remained.

"Firstborn Studier," Antun said, his gaze on Psal's bleeding nose. "Is all truly well?"

"I'm quite all right, Chief Antun," Psal answered.

"Ah," Antun said, but did not leave. "I might be more comforted if that warrior removed his hands from your friend's throat."

Lan let his hand drop and Ephan stumbled to his feet.

"Well, then," Antun said, leaving. "I'll be on my way."

After Antun had gone, Lan kept his voice low. "Idiots! Seagen can track towers also. Have you forgotten that? He hears them if they're near. Why did you—"

"He doesn't know one tower from another," Psal whispered, rising from the stairs. He ran toward Lan. "And so what if he hears them? He won't assume it's a Peacock tower being sent home. He's not as knowledgeable as we are. And Nahas and his captains are too busy to look at our parchments."

"Gaal? Gaal looks at our parchments. Gaal can discern towers."

"Gaal will not—"

Lan closed his eyes. "I cannot believe it. Two studiers who do stupid things relying on other people to be even more stupid? Did you learn this stupidity with the Wintersea Master?" He picked up Psal's staff. "I'm going to burn this offensive thing. It has clouded your mind, Firstb—"

"Give it to me!" Psal pushed Lan aside and struggled to retrieve the staff.

But Lan held it firmly at either end and was attempting to break it against his right knee. "Firstborn! The girl is no longer yours. Nor is Tsbosso your friend. Break the staff, just as the friendship and the love are broken."

Psal made a grab for the staff. "It is not meant to be broken."

"Lan," Ephan said, "don't break your hand trying to break this 'not meant to be broken' staff of his." He extended his hand and Lan reluctantly gave it to him. He placed it against the window again. "You who don't believe in destiny or spirits, you believe the staff has a fate? Well then, it must have a destiny."

Lan walked toward the door. "Burn it! I will kill you the next time. Both of you. Do you understand?"

Kill us? That Psal doubted. However much he frustrated Lan, Lan was his friend and could not remain angry with him for too long. "There will be no next time," he promised Lan.

"Make a pact with me, then, Firstborn," Lan whispered in an ancient Falconer language his father had taught him. "I shall keep this thing secret, and you will save no more Peacock women."

So the pact was made.

As night fell, Psal tried to keen the Qerys tower to a home region in the northern mountains. It rebelled against him. It had not failed, entirely, but with the exception of sending a message song relaying the deaths of Renan and the warriors of the Qerys, it stuck stubbornly to its isolation and for several nights refused to speak or to be told what to do.

PART III

STRATEGIES AND COUNTER-STRATEGIES

CHAPTER 16

THE MERGED CLANS

Some mornings, Ktwala heard longhouses in the distance. But she never ventured forth to meet any. Grief made it difficult to rise from bed. She never reached for the ancient spyglass which was always near at hand. She never ascended her tower, never peered into the directions. Sleep fled, adding to her grief no respite in dreams.

Thirteen days after the murder of her clan, she woke to the smell of death. The odor wafted through the mud walls and shuttered windows, soaked her hair, skin, and blanket. She looked through the window: the air was dark with flies, the ground crawled with maggots. Countless Peacock Clan warriors lay where they had fallen dead. Empty eyes stared out past her, surprised at their sudden entry into their Permanent Home. She stumbled back, startled. Her heart raced. She had arrived in a region of corpses. She hurried from her bed to the main entrance door, bolted it tight and sat nauseated, weeping with terror and grief.

Next morning, she arrived outside a corralled field with Wheel Clan markings. She saw no longhouse. Whether one lay in another direction, she did not know. But she smelled burning flesh as on the day the Wheel Clan had murdered her brothers. She steeled herself to walk across the corridor to a room on the longhouse's other side. Through a window, she saw smoldering pyres with burning Wheel Clan corpses on them. *But is this not the very same region where I lay with Nahas?* She walked to her gathering room and paced, wondering if any would come or if she should venture outside. No one came; neither did she leave the longhouse. Then third moon took her away.

The next day the freshness of fruit trees awakened her. But she was ill, nauseated. *Grief and blood has sickened me.* But, truth dawning suddenly, *Pregnant? That murderer's child?* She had lain with no others. Her pregnancies had been painful, harrowing. She had miscarried two children. Her own life had almost been lost when Ouis was born. *I am old now, my sisters taken. And I am alone.*

She climbed the outside tower stairs up to her rampart. In the distance, a longhouse with Wheel Clan markings stood beside a watermill. Stewards were carrying large sacks. Fearing, she remained in the longhouse. At midday, footsteps approached.

A voice called out to her: "Ktwala, Queen of the Wheel Clans."

She walked to the window where she saw a red-haired young man with a scarred face and a twisted arm. He greeted her with a low bow.

A Wheel Clan steward? "You bow? Do people who disobey the Creator's Principles—and murder the families of those they marry—bow?"

"I will admit, it is not our usual habit. To murder innocents, I mean. Not bowing. I am Jarid, born in the Hokkan Wheel sub-clan of a Wheel Clan woman and a Falconer Clan man, chief steward of the Deep Tundra longhouse." He stepped aside and indicated a wheeled cart on which several baskets lay overflowing with tubers and grains, fermented meats, honeycombs, and salts. "The king has determined that at such time when you arrive at our longhouses—whether the longhouse contains a steward or no—food shall be provided for you."

"Your king has already glutted me with corpses," she said. "Tell him I will not eat his food. Neither will I will be queen of so harsh and treacherous a people."

"Even so, I have a message unto you, Queen Ktwala." He retrieved a white parchment from inside his tunic.

She began to latch the window. "I will not read it."

"This message is not from the king but from the Firstborn. It is at great risk that he wrote it and even greater risk that I bring it to you. Should you not hear the words of our honorable Firstborn?" He lay the parchment on the window sill. "He speaks of your daughter."

She took the parchment, opened it and saw the following words written in the formal language of the Peacock Clan:

> *To Ktwala, Great Queen of the Wheel Clans, my mother, and the wife of my Father King Nahas. From Psal, your son. Greetings. First, know this: Your daughter lives. She is lodged in the royal corridor and is now sister to me. The king aims to turn her heart to her new clan, and I suspect mother and daughter will not meet again until both hearts are changed. I beg your forgiveness. Because of my great unworthiness, your people were destroyed. My accustomed petulance prevented my brothers from receiving my counsel. Therefore, Mother, let not their crime be laid to the charge of my people. The sin is wholly mine.*
>
> *Know this now: Unworthy as I am, I am yet able to free you. Weak and insolent towers litter our world. I am able to keen one from afar and to present you safe in one of the Peacock Clan home regions before Nahas is aware of your flight. Or you may remain in this longhouse if you wish to be reunited with your daughter. You have no other choices. Know this: the king is determined to break your will. Mother, I am sorry for this. Often has my father attempted to break my own will. I should not like to see you stand broken before him. Speak the word only, and this good steward will inform me of your wish.*

She finished reading. *I cannot blame you for your father's crimes, Psallo. What power do little boys have against the will of their fathers?*

"What is your response to the Firstborn?" Jarid asked.

"I will remain here, Jarid. Why should I be free when my sisters are enslaved? And would the king not know his son had betrayed him by freeing me?"

"In freedom, you could fight, Ktwala. Unlatch the entrance and let us speak freely."

She opened the door to him. "Jarid, does your king know his son and his steward plot against him? Would Nahas not kill you if he discovered this treachery?"

"Nahas does not easily kill, King's Wife. Although, he *would* put me in the dark climes." He gestured toward heavy-fruited trees. "We stewards guard and plant all these. All this is ours, and yet not ours. Why should I not help a Firstborn who understands our lot? But, Great Queen, consider carefully what the Firstborn has said. He is well able to free you."

Ktwala grasped the folded parchment tightly. "Tell the Firstborn I am glad I have an ally and ask whether he could hide me safely in some tower where neither the king nor his enemies could find me until he can bring my sisters and my daughter to me. If he cannot do this, I will abide here in this tower. Tell him that my daughter is wise and he will find her a true ally if he gains her trust."

"Even so?"

"Even so."

"There is something else, My Queen. A message from the king. I must speak it because he requires an answer."

"Say on."

"The king has asked you to consider the death of your people a necessary act of war. An expedience that was required. He desires that you turn all your thoughts to understanding why he chose that particular action. Then, if you understand his heart, that he is not bloodthirsty, he requires that you consent to return to the royal longhouse as his wife and the leader of your sisters. What is your answer?"

"Tell the king he should have told me of the war as we lay in the meadow. He should have trusted my people."

She nodded to Jarid and closed the longhouse door. Jarid left, but the wheeled cart laden with food remained.

Throughout the day, she considered life with a Peacock sub-clan but not life among the Wheel Clan. *If I live among my own people, I would not be alone. I would have the comfort of sisters. I could rejoice when my brothers vanquished the Wheel Clan in battles, or comfort them in defeat. Yet, I have no desire to see battles, and the men from the Peacock Clan are harsh to women. If I say I am unmarried, will they not force me to marry one of their warriors? And who knows if he will be kind-hearted? But if I say I am the wife of the Wheel Clan king, what might the consequence be?*

Before third moon rose, the steward returned again on horseback, and asked again of her decision. "The Second Dusk has arrived," he said, "and I have told the king your words. His tower returns this answer merely: 'Ktwala, do you not understand war?' I have told the Firstborn your message and his tower has returned this answer. 'Mother, if you do not wish to join the Peacock Clan, I will send you to King Renn of the Falconer Clan, a most noble and a neutral king. However I cannot set you adrift to permanently wander inside a dying longhouse. Outlaw longhouses abound. And, if they find you alone, they will do you great harm. Neither can I return your sisters or your daughter to you. Doing so would cause my father to be ridiculed within his own clan and his longhouse. The king would not forgive me for such an action.'"

"Then I shall remain here. That is my answer to them both."

The next day, nauseated, she woke with the dawn and willed herself to rise from bed. She sniffed the air and smelled water. Not death and cadavers, not life and corralled fields. She looked through the window. A meadow and grasslands. In the far distance a longhouse, too far away for her to fear its inhabitants. A river slowly-flowing in a valley. In the dry grasslands, she lifted her flute to her lips. A lion's roar answered her; an eagle as well. All three returned to the longhouse, the lion like a trained dog at her feet.

At midday as she cast her fish net in the river, hoof beats. Her lion afield, her eagle aloft, she hurried up the hill to the longhouse door. The hoof beats stopped. Hasting, arriving at her tower, she found the rider waiting: Nahas.

"Ktwala." The king stood at the threshold of her door, barring her entrance. His eyes were full of admiration and longing for her. He extended his hand, like a lover pleading. "I have come to make you understand."

Words could not come. She stared at him in disbelief. *Why has he come? Does he truly expect me to understand?*

"My wife," he said, drawing near, "your brothers would have betrayed me."

She shook her head. "No, they would not have."

The king rubbed his forehead with his thumb and forefinger. "Whether they would or would not, the thing is done."

"Yes, it is done. My son killed, my daughter stolen. Murder is done. Now, return my daughter to me. Return my sisters to me. Then set us all adrift, far from men and their wars."

"That I cannot do."

Her angry shout echoed along the hillside and through the valley. "Why can you not? Why can you not, Nahas? Are you suddenly so powerless? You were not so powerless when you killed my son."

His words remained calm. "My warriors are set on the women, as my heart is set on you. If I were to release them now, I would seem to be a king who regrets his actions. Such seeming I cannot afford. Therefore, Ktwala, ask me some other recompense for your dead son."

How calmly he speaks! Has he no capacity to hear my heart? "Return my daughter to me, Nahas!" she shouted. "What do I care about kings and their seeming?"

The king's eyes pleaded with her. His arms reached out, awaiting her touch. "My love, my love, I hear your heart. But much depends on seeming. I must not seem to regret my action."

When she did not take his hand, he drew back, shaking his head repeatedly. He covered his eyes with his hands and for a long while stood with his back turned to her. Silence as they stood there, motionless, like etchings on an ancient Falconer manuscript. Then, seeming to rouse himself, he walked to his horse.

Will he leave already? Has he no heart for anger?

"You are still too overwhelmed with emotions," the king said, answering her thoughts. "We will meet again when you are able to think. When you see this life clearly, tell my stewards and they will relay your message to me."

Ktwala watched in disbelief as he led his horse toward the distant longhouse. "How inhuman you kings are!"

He did not return answer to her, he only struck at his horse and sped it across the fields.

Throughout the day, Ktwala considered the king's words. *Perhaps I should have agreed to return with him,* she thought. *I would not be his wife, but there I would be with my sisters and my daughter. Within the longhouse, I might have persuaded him to set us adrift.*

She waited for the king to return but he did not. The next day her longhouse arrived at a region of sand. Sand and nothing else. Regret and despair battled in her heart. She thought, *Why has that cruel king brought me here? Has he decided to free me? But if I am now free, how will I return to my daughter and my sisters?* The day after she awoke in the same region. *How vindictive this Wheel Clan king is! Has the king determined to anchor me in this place because I spurned him?*

But the next day she was surrounded by Peacock corpses. The day after—burning flesh and pyres. The next—a fertile land with a longhouse and a windmill. No steward worked in the longhouse, but food baskets awaited her on a circular table. The next four days—pleasant fields and a river shore. Then once again, Peacock corpses and pyres. At last she understood. *So this will be the pattern of my new life. The Wheel Clan controls my journey.*

Yet the Wheel Clan king could not control all. One morning a towerless hut with a mixed-race clan appeared near her longhouse. *Three men, five women, many children.* She watched them through her window as they dug tubers from a Wheel Clan field. *How fearful it is to be alone,* she told herself. *I must repair the internal stairs of my tower that I might reach the rampart from within instead of venturing outside on the external stair! In early morning, I could see what evil awaits me from within the safety of my tower. How many years my brothers allowed it to fall to ruin saying, 'The tower and the room within it are good only to store food.'*

Wary, she leaned against her window, and blew on her flute. No lions in the region. But several eagles rested on her rampart. In the watering hole, hippos. *Those Nunu could tame.* In the clearing, in the trees, snakes. *Those Gidea could tame.* Ktwala felt her aloneness. She locked the doors and with lance and dagger in hand, waited for night to come.

At the beginning of the third month of the year, a month after the murder of the Iden boys, Ktwala awoke to the laughter of children, like water rippling. She peered through the window. Five women, of various clans, stood outside her longhouse door. Some forty children, all girls, played in the field, another sixteen, with bow and arrow nearby, stood behind them.

The lion at her side, flute in hand, Ktwala opened her door.

"I am Alora, chief of this longhouse. We are the Voca. Are there many with you?" A slender woman, tall, and green of eye walked toward her.

Ktwala remembered Old Jion's warnings:

> *Like honey the Voca are when few in number;*
> *Like snakes they are when they scheme;*
> *Like hungry lionesses when they encounter small prey.*

The lion rose from its rest and stood before Ktwala. In response, Alora beckoned to two warriors, women of the Peacock Clan. They stepped forward, lifted their flutes to their lips, played softly.

"Many are with me," Ktwala answered. *The Unfleshed Ones, my dead brothers are here with me.*

"From our rampart we looked," the Voca Chief said. "But our spy-glasses saw no one. None until you exited your longhouse. You say you are many, yet your tower speaks of no other voice within. Do you, a woman, speak falsely to other women? You are not a man, that you should lie."

"The many are the dead who are with me. I only am escaped alone to speak for the Iden."

Chief Alora sidestepped the lion. "And how came you to be alone? Where are your people?"

Ktwala answered, telling her all her heart, how Nahas had seemed to love, then had slaughtered all, leaving her alone with the child inside her.

"So you will have a child?" the woman asked. "We're well-met, then. For we Voca can care for you. I know this Nahas. He is our Great Queen's great enemy. Yet she loved him once and made an alliance with his clan. When the king hears of your child—for no doubt his stewards will tell him when it becomes apparent—you will be deprived of peace. And no one, no not even your calmed lion, will be able to help you."

"Chief Alora, I've forgotten what peace is."

"Men destroy all peace," Chief Alora said. "Always they war and destroy families and the land, which is the dear mother of us all. But we Voca are no longer victims of men and their wars. The ways of men are passing away. Stay with us. Let your heart be healed. Be free from men and their ways."

The chief then told of marauding men who would destroy Ktwala and her child. But Ktwala looked at the children dancing among the fields and rocks and thought, *Why are there no male children present?* She answered the Voca chief, "I will stay here, where the blood of my dead brothers protect me."

"Are you so weak that you sit here trusting your dead brothers' blood to protect you? You shame women by your weakness, Ktwala."

"Are you—who has ripped the unborn from their mothers' wombs, and who has never borne children—belittling my grief, Chief Alora? My grief is too large and wide to be judged by one who easily murders."

The Voca Chief smiled, stroked Ktwala's cheek. "Perhaps when I return you will think differently of me."

So, until the sun rose high in the sky, Chief Alora stayed at Ktwala's side, telling her of the Voca, how that many had been reared in the Voca clan from birth but others—especially women of the Peacock Clan, had joined of their own accord. The first Voca Queen, Alora said, was born in the Falconer clan and her lover was a woman of the Black Water Grass-rope clan. They had ruled one longhouse only, but then Queen Ezbel arose, one born damaged in the Wheel Clan. It was she who had made the clan great. "And, one day, when the Constant Tower is found, Ezbel will rule the world and bring peace to it."

"Indeed?" Ktwala said. "I can imagine a woman ruling the world, and I can imagine one like Ezbel ruling it. For all those who aim to rule the world are cruel."

Chief Alora rose. "I bid you farewell, Ktwala. Who knows when we will meet each other again?"

So, night fell and the Voca left Ktwala, promising to return to help with the birth of her child.

* * * *

Twenty-five days after the Iden women were captured, Nahas added Iden markings to the royal longhouse's outside wall. When the Iden women heard of it, they responded with bitter chants that echoed over the crackling smoke of the pyres.

On top of the rampart, Psal listened with agitation. "These women are driving me mad," he said to his fellow studiers.

Ephan shrugged.

"It's the infighting of the three sub-clans that bothers me more," Daris said. "And Nahas says nothing. Are kings always so inscrutable? Or is it an adult trait? Can you not speak to Nahas about it, Chief Studier?"

Ephan looked up from his parchments. "I would not recommend it."

But Psal said, "I've been thinking of speaking to Nahas a good while now."

He descended the tower stair, and walked into the corridor toward the king's chamber. Leaning against the king's doorpost, he waited for permission to enter. The king glanced up from his war reports, nodded to Netophah who was seated opposite him, but said nothing.

This waiting to be permitted to enter. Ephan—King's Favorite—would not wait. Why, then, do I always fear entering? He has not forbidden me...and yet... Psal put his right foot forward then slowly dragged his left foot into the chamber.

"The reports from Chief Maldon are distressing." The king lifted one particular parchment, re-read it, then thrust it away from him. "He delights in describing his blood lust. What? Does he think his cruelty impresses me?"

"Perhaps, Father," Psal said. "He does seem to delight in vaunting his bloody deeds."

Nahas sighed. "And yet, he was faithful to my father when Qerys sought to take the rule. And he has been faithful to me. One must endure one's allies. But, tell me, Firstborn, why have you entered? Do you wish to keen for new pharma or is this merely a paternal visitation?"

"'Paternal visitation,'" Psal echoed and laughed. "I like your wit, Father."

"Such as it is."

"I have come, Father," Psal said, "because the warriors of each sub-clan refuse to honor the captains and chiefs of the other clans."

"Why should that matter, Firstborn," Netophah asked, "if all honor Father?"

"True, Wheel Clan Heir, but...have you seen? Gaal, Cyrt, and Sea-gen—they seek to make the king inaccessible to Orian's and Antun's warriors. Cyrt has even declared that any warrior who wishes to speak to Nahas must ask permission of him first."

Nahas and Netophah laughed. "Has he?" the king asked.

"His actions amuse you, Father?" Psal asked.

"Firstborn, you must learn to laugh." The king leaned back on his chair.

"I am not entirely without humor, Father. But, it is all so troublesome. The Iden women chanting, Orian bewailing the days of yore. And, you... you allow it."

"How do I allow it?" the king asked, smiling.

"By your silence, Father."

"Is my silence such a formidable thing, Firstborn?"

Netophah walked to the door and closed it. "Father, I understand what the Firstborn means. Those reared in the royal longhouse understand your silences. Those who have just now entered our longhouse—Orian, Antun, and their warriors—they don't know what to make of it. They assume all manner of things. I've heard it said by some—who did not know I stood nearby—that befriending you is like shadow play. With the lights off. In the dark climes."

Psal looked admiringly on his brother. *And how freely, they joke together.* "Antun's crew, Father. They keep to themselves like strangers, like outcasts."

"Perhaps Antun thinks himself superior to these petty wars," Netophah said.

Psal shook his head. "Pride is not in him. I believe, because his father Qerys warred against our grandfather, Antun is wary of you, Father. Therefore, if you could, maybe...perhaps, befriend him." From the corner of his eye, Psal saw Netophah grimace. *What have I done now?* Psal prepared for the king's verbal assault.

"Befriend him?" Nahas buried his head in his palms. "How consistent you are, Firstborn! Always befriending my enemies."

Enemies? This king always gorges me with my flaws. Psal turned to leave. "I entered only to remind you that I rule all things *within* this longhouse. *You* rule the Clan and its sub-clans."

"These three sub-clans *are* within the longhouse now, Firstborn."

Psal nodded in his brother's direction. "Let Netophah judge between them."

"It is not Netophah's judgment I wish to judge, but yours," Nahas retorted. "When their forty-nine days of grief are finished, I trust you will release the Iden women to our warriors?"

With the subtlest movement of his eyebrow, Netophah warned Psal do everything the king wished.

But Psal said, "I will not release them until their hearts are healed, however long—"

Netophah's exasperated groan cut the Firstborn's word short.

"You've chosen an odd battle," the king said, "forbidding our warriors to take the women."

"I didn't choose the battle, Father. I merely hold to the traditions of our clan."

"Chiefs and studiers share the same traditions," Nahas said. "but a studier's life is free from politics and warfare. What will you choose to be in our clan? Studier or Chief?"

"A Firstborn should not give up what is clearly his," Netophah said. "And a studier—"

"He cannot be both studier and chief, Netophah! One thing more, Firstborn." The king searched among the reports on his table. "Ah, yes!" He lifted two parchments, one in his right hand and the other in his left. "What do you see on the back of these reports?"

Netophah started laughing.

The left parchment had an image Psal recognized immediately. A drawing of the buttocks of a plump, dark-skinned woman; Ephan was always drawing naked women. "I shall warn him, Father." He stepped closer to see the other, then slowed his steps when he saw his own handwriting as the king read Psal's poem aloud:

> *From where he sits*
> *in our Permanent Home*
> *on the edges of the river*
> *looking on our shore,*
> *Ouis understands.*
> *Bright is his joy now!*
> *Why am I still troubled?*
> *What does that sin matter now?*

(This is where the famous saying on Odunao comes from: "How weak am I that this sin should taunt me even now?")

But as the king read, no one was pondering posterity.

"It is a month since the battle." Nahas threw the parchment at Psal's feet. "And you're so guilt-struck you write of the afterlife? I thought you were an unbeliever."

"Maharai's room lies opposite the Firstborn's." Netophah took hold of Psal's hand and was already leading him out the king's chamber. "Her sobbing…for her mother or Ouis…it is like a continual heavy dripping from a leaky roof or like water wearing the tiles away. It bothers *me*. For a studier, taught to hear the smallest of sounds, such weeping—"

The king waved them both toward the door. "The Firstborn should learn to push such things from his mind. Or, if he cannot wrest the thought from his heart, he should learn to keep them private. A chief's thoughts should not be etched on the back of tracking parchments for all to see."

Rebuked, Psal bowed and left the king.

CHAPTER 17
HOME REGIONS

Psal stepped into the corridor, annoyed that he had now officially been charged with overseeing the three sub-clans. *If I had not asked, I might not have been charged with this unpleasantness. Or...was the duty already mine? If so, why did this subtle king not tell me?* Voices in Maharai's room intruded on his thoughts: Lan, Deyn, and Tolika.

The night before he had returned women from a shattered Peacock tower to Samat's home region. *Our longhouse did not battle them. And I keened them two days after their battle with Chief Hayla. Lan will not suspect.* He walked to Maharai's doorway. *And yet, perhaps I should cease saving these Peacock women. One should not press one's luck. Lan can be as suspicious as Nahas. And if he brings Tolika...here...opposite the keening room....*

Maharai and her guests were sitting on her sleeping mat. Netophah, who had followed Psal out the king's chamber, stood with him at her door. *Ah, Netophah, I pity your poor love-struck heart. Your eyes plead to me for help. But what can I do for you, Brother? Maharai is not like Tolika. Even before the so-called battle, Tolika was already won. But Maharai has seen your hands murder her brother. She will be harder to win.*

Lan and Deyn rose to their feet as the Firstborn and the Wheel Clan Heir entered. Tolika blushed. *Her eyes are sunk from weeping. Still, they no longer look out past me into some distant lost world. With two suitors, she has begun to forget her own people. Soon, she will join the Wheel Clan. But when will the other Iden women follow? How long?*

Maharai ran to Psal. Her hands clasped, she spoke in the Peacock tongue, asked him what she always asked. "You will look for my mother's longhouse today, Psallo? You can hear her tower, you hear all towers."

"If the tower still sings, he can hear it," Netophah said.

Maharai turned her back to Netophah. "Firstborn, Lan and Deyn brought Tolika to visit me. But, if they could bring sisters—"

"I don't think they wish to bring the others," Psal said.

Maharai frowned. "Tolika shouldn't be coddling the enemy. Gidea won't like it. None of my sisters would."

'Coddle the enemy.' Psal thought. *How interesting this new sister of mine is!*

"We no longer your enemies," Netophah said.

"That reminds me." Tolika lifted a bowl of dried red mud that lay on one of Maharai's shelves and started smearing it on her arms and face. It was part of the Peacock tradition to grieve by refusing to bathe or by throwing mud and dirt on themselves when their guards brought them outside to the Wheel Clan lakes. After that, they steadfastly refused to bathe.

Has she brought the mud here specifically for this purpose? And do both her husbands permit this deception? These Iden women are not only intent on holding on to their sorrow but they delight in making themselves undesirable to my Wheel Clan brothers. "Tolika, why continue this pretense?" Psal asked. "Indeed, why return to your mother? She has no power over you. Live with your husbands."

She smeared mud on her neck and her braid while Lan covered her breasts and back. "That I cannot do, Firstborn," she said.

"We promised among ourselves that the consummation would not take place until the Iden women could accept the marriage," Lan said.

"Firstborn"—Deyn scooped the remaining mud from the bowl—"did you know your decree would be the cause of such games?"

"I confess, I did not."

It is because she has no strength of soul. If Maharai loved one of our warriors, she would not hide it from her Iden sisters. "So, your mother continues to think you spend the nights with Maharai?" he asked Tolika.

Tolika bent her mud-streaked face toward Deyn for a kiss, giggled as Lan squeezed her bare breast over the Peacock dress. "Firstborn, truly, I do visit Maharai."

"Only for a short time," Maharai complained.

"But, tell me," Tolika asked, "why is she forbidden to visit her sisters?"

"Even a Firstborn cannot break a king's decrees. But does it not bother you that you and your sisters smell so horribly?"

"I am ready to return to my cell." Tolika walked past Psal, her two suitors at her side.

The foolishness I have been made to bear! "Maharai, will you be as your sisters as well? Wearing the Peacock clothing you were captured in?"

"I will be like my sisters in all things," she answered.

"If you continue wearing your clothing, I would recommend bathing." Leaving her, he pushed Netophah aside and spoke in the Wheel Clan language. "Wheel Clan heir, set your heart on the daughter of that Waymaker Chief. She likes you, doesn't she? But forget Maharai and any of these Iden girls. They will not forget Ouis' murder."

* * * *

Anticipation was a large part of being night-tossed, but that old life was gone. Maharai fell back onto her woolen mat, bored at returning to a familiar region. *The Waterfall home region today. Tonight we keen to the Eagle's Nest home region. Tomorrow a battle, the day after burnings and burials, the day after...a war council, I think. The day after that, the meeting with the Deep Tundra stewards and chief.*

A voice called from outside her window. She rose, peered out and recognized a Wheel Clan steward, one of many who had befriended her.

"Little Princess," he said, "the meadow flowers are taller, the fruits have gone from green to gold, new herb gardens have been planted. Meet me by the watermill. You know the one. We're gathering fruit for Chief Hokkan's longhouse. You like that, don't you?"

She nodded. "I will meet you soon. After Ephan tells me the names of Wheel Clan chiefs."

"Ah," he said, "a colorful bunch. Come when you're finished."

"I must bathe today," she said. "In the lake. Psallo told me to."

"Good, good. A princess should not reek, should she?"

The steward left and Maharai waited for Daris to arrive with her food and for Ephan to come and teach her. *I walk more freely in the home fields than in the royal longhouse,* she told herself. *Cyrt's purpose is really to guard me against meeting my sisters. They want to take all my memory away.*

* * * *

Ktwala woke to find two longhouses facing hers. Their markings: the Macaw Clan. Peering through the window, she watched the spontaneous marketplace burst forth on the desert sand.

She had no wish to arise, but by the rise of the daymoon, the drumming and the sound of human footsteps called her into the sunlight. She commanded her lion to roam free but to return at nightfall, then she walked into the Macaw clan market where women carrying large bowls on their head, backs, or in their hands, and warriors hauling animal flesh all greeted her in the Peacock tongue. *How happy my now-destroyed people would be to meet these people!*

A man—thin, dark-brown skin with a turban of shells and gems, of about sixty years—wearing a chief's mantle around his slender shoulders approached her.

"My name is Bukko," he said. "Chief of the Bukko Macaw longhouse. That other is the Karis Macaw longhouse. And what do your clansmen call you?"

Ktwala forced herself to speak. "They called me Ktwala."

"'Called you?'" He sniffed the air, held his hand to his nose. "Yes, yes, the scent of blood lingers around your clothing and your longhouse. Were they slaughtered, then? Are you the only one saved alive? Was it the Voca?"

"A Wheel Clan longhouse betrayed us. My daughter and sisters were stolen. My brothers and son, killed."

"'Betrayed,' you say? I do not understand. How can there be betrayal when the Wheel Clan and Peacock Clan are at war?"

"We did not know they were at war. We befriended them."

"Ah, I see. So the Wheel Clan used the same ploy the Peacock Clan used against them? My daughter, the Peacock Clans killed the little ones and women of the Wheel Clan in a single day. A treacherous scheming conspiracy. Yet, you say your daughter and sisters were stolen? The Wheel Clan chief showed you great mercy."

'A great mercy?' What was their war to us? We were unallied and night-tossed. "Brother, do not ask me to understand the cruelty of my enemy."

He nodded. "Look now, it is good we've met. The markings on your longhouse show you're allied to a Macaw clan. So, I am your brother indeed. Come now, leave this grief and solitariness and live with us."

"I cannot. My people lived and died here."

"But, Sister, their lives are over now. Think of us as your own people and live with us. Do not let grief take your life away."

My own people are the Iden. "I will not die. The child within me, although it is Nahas' child, it will live also." *We will live to keep the name of the Iden clan alive.*

The chief's eyebrow arched. "Nahas' child, you say?" He frowned. "King Nahas? Of the Wheel Clan? So it was he who attacked your clan? And you are sure…it is his child?"

"Yes. His. All these years since my husband died, I lay with no other."

"So, are you the wife of the Wheel Clan king?"

"His wife, yes. Our women were set to celebrate it. But what does that matter? During the third month, we would prepare ourselves, taking animal skins from the baskets and salting meat together. Now all those happy days are lost."

"Sister, your sisters still live! That great and noble Wheel Clan king has spared them."

He sings my enemy's praises. He refuses to hear my heart. Ktwala turned to leave. "Chief Bukko, I must return to my longhouse and commune with myself about my own grief because you do not see the world as I see it and you hurt my heart by dismissing and belittling my sorrows.

I see now the truth of what the Voca said, that men see the world with different eyes than women do."

"The Voca?" Lines of worry appeared on Bukko's face. "Have you met the Voca?"

"I have."

"An evil, unrelenting, bitter clan. Great is their tower science, greater still their evil. Sister, I hope you did not tell the Voca of this unborn child?"

"I did."

"My girl, you should not have done that. You have destroyed your life." He glanced at her stomach. "Did you tell them of the time of life?"

"I did, for they asked." *Has a month come and gone already? Is it truly twenty-five days since my son died?*

"This, too, my girl, you should not have done."

"They spoke of a truce between the Voca and the Wheel Clan. It is Nahas' child. I felt myself safe."

"Oh, my girl, Ezbel honors the letter of the law only, not the spirit of it. You are not in a Wheel Clan *longhouse!* These Voca! Their own male children, they kill. If they find women alone, they keen for them to gather them to their clan. Like hawks they swoop down. Their talons grasp the unborn child. And if your child is born, they will take it. And if your child is unborn, they will take it. A boy they will kill, a girl they will steal. And, living or dead, you will rest alone. Empty stomach, empty arms. Once only did their queen show mercy. In days past, when Nahas saved a pale boy child. But at all other times she has been most merciless."

So, I must fear women as well? Ktwala's heart tightened, but she hid her fear well. "That women should grow cruel does not surprise me. I have lived long in the world."

He sighed as if she was a young spoiled child. "Long have I lived also, and I have seen that the days are evil. Other women have forgiven those who raped them or slaughtered their husbands and little ones. Yes—for your own happiness—learn to forgive."

"Old man," Ktwala said, turning away, "you are full of counsel for one who has not suffered as I have."

He nodded and bade her farewell. "Who knows if we shall see each other again?"

But he returned some time later as she sat crossed-legged in front of her longhouse. With him walked a pale-skinned, limping, club-footed boy of about eight years.

"Take this boy with you," Bukko said. "The Principles declare we should give you a child. We call him 'Lian.' He cannot speak. He was found half-alive nursing at his mother's corpse. The Voca Clan."

"A gift from the Creator." Ktwala looked at the child who smiled shyly up at her. "But why tear him from his new mothers? And they from him?"

"My heart tells me he belongs with you. The tattoo on his hand declares his mother was from the Preying Bird clan. A clan of mixed peoples. A good people, very learned in the languages of the great clans. Their people had no truce with the Voca. Keep him safe."

"I will receive him into my heart," she answered.

"Good, good," he said, then added, "We will see you again in the future. My women are worried for you, and you will need a midwife."

"I will rejoice to see you again," she said a traditional, but not heart-felt, response.

Inside, the longhouse, Ktwala spoke to her new son. "Remove your Macaw clothing. You're part of the Iden clan now. Do you understand? You are my son."

He nodded.

She dressed her new son in Ouis' clothing. The clothes hung loosely on his body. "You may go outside and play and feast with the Macaw Clan. Silent though you be, bid your farewell to your brothers and mothers. Then return here with me."

This he did. Then as second moon rose, the Bukko Macaw clan approached Ktwala's longhouse with red clay. Around the front of her door, they painted a symbol: a vertical line intersected by a horizontal one. A symbol older than time, it was understood by all the clans of Odunao that the longhouse and all inside it were under the protection of a great king and that no outcast should harm any within it.

Night fell, the lion returned to Ktwala's door. Through the window, Lian looked. Terrified, he clung to Ktwala's dress. "The men in my clan do not know this science," she told him. "It is the secret power of Peacock Clan women. Our only power. But you I will teach." She placed the flute on his lips, put her fingers on the third, fourth, and ninth holes, taught him the tune to soothe lions. "This lion will already heed you, because it is ours already. But you are not skilled as yet to call any others." She taught him what image should rest in his mind as he played. He blew, the lion entered and lay at his feet. Then the studiers' keen flung Ktwala and Lian to one place, while the Macaw studiers took their longhouses elsewhere.

That night in a dream Ktwala walked through a spontaneous market-place created by the meeting of many clans. The wares were many but she had nothing to barter with and none of the market's goods tempted her. At last, she arrived at a vendor from an unknown clan, a clan of mixed peoples from all the clans and tribes of Odunao. One called out to her: "I counsel you," he said, "to buy from me salve for your eyes that you may see." That she felt inclined to buy. She searched her market sack, and having nothing to barter for the ointment, she made to pass it by. But the seller pressed it on her. She took the salve and immediately woke up.

Two days later, the longhouse arrived in a field of corpses. Lian knelt on Ktwala's bed, gazed out the window. His terrified screams echoed through the longhouse. She caressed him, held him close to her chest. He stared through the window silent, unspeaking, urinating where he sat.

"My son," Ktwala said to him, "This is the path my longhouse treads. Tomorrow when you rise, you must not look out the windows. If you wish to remain with me, this will be your life. If you wish for peace, I will return you to Chief Bukko's longhouse when our longhouses meet again. Or, if you wish, I will ask the Firstborn of the Wheel Clan to place you in one of his steward longhouses."

The boy nodded, clung to her tunic, pointed at her face.

"You have determined to stay with me?"

He nodded.

"Brave boy. Well, then, each day, when morning comes, don't look outside until I tell you to."

The boy swallowed hard, then nodded and trembled.

* * * *

"Firstborn!" Nahas' agitated voice called Psal to his chambers.

Psal came running in. "Yes, Father?"

The king closed the door behind Psal. "Ktwala is pregnant."

"Indeed?" Psal said. "I had not heard—"

"Your uncle told the stewards, and the stewards have informed me."

And why did Bukko not relay this news through the towers? Why hide the news from me and dishonor me? "I thought her past the age of child-bearing. And the child is yours? You're sure of it?"

The king paced his room. "Yes. The child must live. If Netophah should die—"

"Indeed," Psal said. "Quite true. A king should have more than one son in perfect health if he is to ensure his dynasty."

"Are you being sarcastic, Firstborn?"

"No, Father. I stated an obvious fact. So...shall we send warriors to Ktwala and compel her to live in the royal longhouse?"

"Do you wish me to be ridiculed, Firstborn? Can you not see it? A pregnant Peacock Clan wife cursing at me in my own longhouse."

"That would be problematical…although…I doubt you would be ridiculed. Well…perhaps Orian would—"

Nahas thrust his fist into the wall. "The woman is unrelenting. Perhaps, a long visit in the cold climes would help her see clearly. When her tower readies itself to go to enter the cold climes, send her to the harshest regions."

Psal raised his eyebrows. "Do you truly wish to do that? To a pregnant woman?"

"Do not question me, Firstborn," the king snarled. "Do what I have ordered you to do."

"As you wish, Father." Psal bowed to the king and left.

* * * *

Some days later, on the first day of the fourth month, Psal stood on the rampart awaiting a scheduled skirmish. Peacock warriors chanted their battle songs, and Wheel Clan warriors chanted theirs. In the midst of the meadows, a tumbledown hut, its rounded walls half-broken, lop-sided, swayed; one more tossed night and it would crumble. Those who inhabited it were a pale-skinned, haggard group, consisting of four women and one man. They sat on the edge of the meadow near the lake shore holding a roughly-built wooden cloaken and looking perplexed.

When Ephan walked up the stairwell, Psal said to him, "The night has tossed these strangers into the midst of our battle. How cruel this Creator of yours is! A studier would say that we should repair that nonexistent one's errors and bring them into our longhouse. What would a chief say?"

"A Wheel Clan chief?" Netophah asked from the tower's stairwell.

"Yes." Psal turned to see Netophah and Lan at the top of the stairs. "A Wheel Clan chief?"

"I have no answer," Ephan said. "Having mixed Dovi all morning to swathe our warrior's swords, I have little to say about the Creator's cruelty."

"Keep your mind on important matters. Not those night-tossed ones." Netophah studied the Peacock ranks, sighed. "Chief Minook's warriors."

"Yet again," Lan added. "But his Valiant Ones are almost all dead. His young warriors are useless. Who would think so noble a warrior as Minook, whose mind and heart were set on agriculture and who knew nothing of warfare, would join Tsbosso's alliance?"

"They need resources," Psal said, "resources we've stolen and hoarded, if we're to be honest."

"Firstborn," Netophah warned, "you must learn to keep your opinions to yourself. Especially today when Father has declared you are the rampart captain."

Psal's mouth fell open. "I'm no captain to direct a battle."

"True, but Broqh will be at your command." Netophah pointed to a group of ten or twelve Peacock warriors holding clubs, daggers, and lances. "See there! They've placed those with daggers beside others carrying slingshots, and horsemen beside those carrying swords."

"A confused strategy showing their inexperience." Lan slapped Psal's right shoulder. "This will be no hard battle. And you, a studier-chief, will be credited with the victory."

"They haven't prepared themselves against our siege balls, battering rams, or fire arrows," Netophah went on. "They believed the false tower message you sent that we wouldn't use siege balls on such terrain."

"Their tower sang of youth and extreme age," Psal said. "But how inexperienced the little ones seem and how defeated the remaining old ones appear!"

"Firstborn," Lan chided, "let not your heart pity them. Think only of the victory. A studier's deceptive song and a chief's commands. All will sing your praises. Therefore, Firstborn, prove you weren't born to care only for the weak and listen to far off towers."

Psal shrugged. "Be not so joyful. I have not yet accomplished this cheap victory over young, untried boys."

"Look," Netophah said, "the king has given you Cyrt to command the fire archers below, and Broqh upon the rampart. Kwin will be your runner. He has made victory easy for you. Why be insulted because Father gave you an easy win?"

The wind blew across the rampart, rustling Netophah's gold-red hair, reminding Psal of the statues in the Ancient Ruined City. Perfect in form and facial feature, perfect in spirit and emotion. Always in good humor, always sensible. "You understand Chief Minook's strategies?" Netophah asked.

"Such as I've heard through the towers and what I know from war councils."

"Chief Ronen has said Minook prefers to stay near his longhouse entrance," Lan said. "Today, this day, you will guide Broqh's arrow to its new home in Minook's heart."

"Orian has also fought this sub-clan once before," Netophah said. "He says the younger Minook warriors prefer fighting in tall grasses. The older ones are skilled at fighting in water. They will run towards the south there, and near the lake there, where the night-tossed are sitting."

Lan looked over the countryside, a place of boulders, dense shrub, and trees. "Cyrt says it's best if we burn the grasses everywhere they might run." He looked at the sky, then at Ephan. "What say you of the winds? Should we use fire arrows?"

"Fire shields for our warriors perhaps?"

"Lan." Netophah pointed to a boulder near the river and another smaller one in the tall grasses. "There and there should be your posts. You will see the Firstborn's directions clearly but you will be out in the open. Broqh's arrows will be your shield. Ephan, are you able to work in the sick rooms alone?"

"I am well able, Wheel Clan Heir."

"You seem…different." Netophah studied Ephan's face, wrinkled his forehead.

"Different? How?"

"When I spoke of the winds, you did not mention the Unfleshed Ones. You often take the opportunity to—"

"I no longer see them or hear them," Ephan answered.

Psal laughed. "You sound as if you miss them."

"I cannot tell if I miss them or not. Certainly, seeing Samat and his evil clan is not a thing I would wish on any. And yet—my eyesight as bad as it is—and my inability to see physical things clearly, it is perhaps a shame that I asked the Creator to close my inner eye."

"You think the Creator truly took the gift away?" Psal asked.

"To battle then." Netophah called out, interrupting their conversation. "Lan. Let us leave these studiers who—I need not remind them—should keep their minds on battling humans and not on battles with the Unfleshed Ones."

Lan and Netophah hurried down the stairs, leaving Psal to remark, "I should not resent him, I know. But, does he not look and sound like a true Firstborn?"

"Perfection can be galling, yes." Ephan shaded his pale eyes from the bright morning son. He looked toward the group of night-tossed and grimaced. "Storm, promise me you will do nothing to endanger yourself in the king's eyes."

"Pondering my quick defeat in an unlosable battle, Cloud?"

"No. Pondering the hut-dwellers and hoping you will not speak to Nahas about them."

"No doubt—after sitting there all day, watching both our clans bash each other's heads in—these night-tossed will rejoice to join one of our clans."

Footsteps climbed the tower stairs behind them. They turned to see Broqh, his quiver on his shoulder. He walked toward the high walls of the east side of the rampart, peered in the distance toward the two boulders, then squatted on the ground. "If those night-tossed ones are wise, they will show no preference for either longhouse, not giving water or aid to any fallen warrior of any side."

"The night-tossed are always self-serving," Ephan said. "I only hope Storm knows to serve himself well."

"Indeed," Broqh said. "But I doubt your hope will ever be fulfilled. But heed your fellow studier, Firstborn. If these night-tossed seek refuge with us, Wheel Clan traditions will not allow the man to enter. You have already won several victories since your decree about the Iden women. The newborn Peacock Clan boy, for instance, has been allowed to live. The small Iden girls are not caged with their mothers but are allowed to play with Wheel Clan children. Therefore, care not for the old man. Why push?"

"Broqh, you only encourage him by reminding him of his victories," Ephan said, then descended the tower stairwell.

A drumbeat from a Minook warrior and a long sharp note on a Wheel Clan horn and the battling began.

* * * *

That day, Psal proved himself. He guided Broqh's arrow to lodge in Chief Minook's heart, and under his command, ten Peacock Clan captains were slain. But when Lan, Netophah, and Kwin joined him on the rampart, he could not command his eyes to stop fixating on their bloodied tunics. *Have I done all this?* he asked himself. *I have no heart for bloody victories.*

"Well-fought, Netophah," Psal said. "Several times I feared for you. But here you stand, bloodied but well."

"Brother, your good-wishes strengthened me. And yet, how weary I am!" Netophah pointed at one of the night-tossed women as he leaned over the rampart.

The battle ended, the night-tossed stood amid the carnage while warriors from both longhouses carried away wounded. They did not move to any specific longhouse but argued among themselves, pointing first at one longhouse, then the other.

"These night-tossed women are good gifts for our warriors after battle, if they choose to come to us," Netophah continued. "All four. Even that old one, gray enough for our Ephan. He likes those sad, old beauties."

"The young one would suit you, Wheel Clan Heir," Kwin said.

"You know where my heart rests," Netophah answered.

"A shaky kind of rest," Kwin replied. "Maharai will never like you."

"Cyrt will demand the women be given only to the king's warriors," Lan said. "The battle outside the longhouse finished, the battle inside begins. Because—do I not speak the truth?—Orian will argue that all in the king's longhouse are the king's warriors. But a bribe could turn Cyrt's heart toward you. Obviously. Why battle him?"

"Let us speak privately." Psal led Lan away from Netophah and Kwin to the eastern edge of the rampart. "Giving foundlings to either Orian or Cyrt? The thought nauseates me. Do not—"

"Your nausea aside, Firstborn, it is best to throw the foundlings to them. Sacrifice the strangers to bring yourself peace."

Psal frowned. "You have lived with Nahas too long."

"Indeed, his talent for expedience does taint all who encounter him. But, Firstborn, consider this. Towers are failing, enemies outside war against us, enemies caged and bound within our own longhouse taunt us, yet our kinsmen war among themselves. Truly, I am tired of it. Why not seize an opportunity to bring peace?"

A sudden thought. "You have not told Tolika the Wheel Clan secret, have you?"

Lan looked confused. "What secret?"

"The secret all but the Iden women know, that Ktwala's tower follows in our wake?"

"No, Firstborn. Love has no power to compel me to foolishness." He gave Psal a sly look. "Unlike its power over you."

Psal understood. "I saved Cassia's tower once. Why charge me with lovesickness?"

"Because, Firstborn, I cannot believe that you have not saved other Peacock women since then. It is the way with humans, if they succeed at some illegal scheme, to continue in them." Lan leaned on the rampart wall. "Although I have no proof and I have studiously set my ears not to listen, whenever I hear Peacock towers grieving because its women are lost…at those times Firstborn, I fear you will do something quite stupid."

"So that's why you linger near the keening room after certain battles?"

"Firstborn, Nahas would not approve."

"Are you threatening me, Lan?"

Lan laughed. "Now, *you* sound like Nahas. No, I merely worry for you. My presence has deterred some of your actions, I believe. But, not all, has it? I doubt your body could endure a month in the dark climes, even with Ephan at your side."

"But Nahas will not find out, will he?" Psal looked out into the darkness, called to the outcast women. "Foundlings, choose who you will align yourself to. Why stand there wavering between two camps?"

The strangers looked at each other, gestured in hand signals that they did not understand his words. He spoke to them again, using all the languages of the great clans. Again, they said they did not understand. He spoke then in the language of several cave-dwelling tribes. At last, the gray-haired woman answered him in the language of the Eastern Cave Dwellers. She grasped a younger girl by the arm and ran into the Wheel Clan longhouse. Another woman rushed toward the Peacock longhouse and was allowed in. The remaining man and woman stood alone holding the tattered cloaken.

Behind Psal, footsteps climbed to the rampart. Psal returned to the top of the tower stair to see Nahas ascending.

"Why do you waver?" Psal shouted to the remaining night-tossed. "Hurry to the Peacock longhouse. They will accept you both."

They did not move and soon the latch of the Peacock longhouse entrance door fell heavy, locked. They now had only three choices: to return to their damaged hut, to trust themselves to the cloaken, or to plead with the Wheel Clan.

"The woman may enter," Nahas said to Psal. "The man must stay outside."

In the graying twilight of the two moons, Netophah nodded almost imperceptibly, so small a movement only a brother would notice: *It is no use,* the gesture warned; *Father will not allow it.*

Psal shouted to the woman. "Why did you not enter the Peacock longhouse?"

She answered in the language of the eastern cave-dwellers, although some of her words were partly cobbled from the Falconer, Waymaker languages. "I hate them. Yet, I also know the traditions of you Wheel Clan. This man is my husband but even so, I will marry one of your warriors, if you will allow my husband to remain with me. Why should I leave my man to battle the night alone?"

"The moon rises." Nahas walked toward the stairwell. "Take the count of our warriors and attend to the wounded. Tell the woman to return to her hut."

After his father had gone, Psal bade the woman and her husband farewell: "Who knows if we shall see each other again?"

Then he called Lan and Kwin, "Go now. I will do what this king of ours demands, but I will not allow these people to suffer. Have Aythan, Deyn, and Daris collect some of our reindeer pelts. Nine or ten, large enough to sew into a tent. Six wooden poles also. Yes, yes, and bone needles. Give them to these outcasts. Tomorrow, if their hut endures and if it throws them to a pleasant region, they can sew themselves a new home. And—in case it does not—hurry to the storage rooms and bring them one of our better cloakens."

Lan did as the Firstborn requested.

All the while, the king watched, unspeaking. Later, as Psal tended to the wounded, his father called him aside. "Come to my chamber when you're finished."

Psal plunged his hand into a bucket of warm water filled with Dama seeds, then quickly limped after the king, blood and pharma dripping from his hands. "I'm coming, Father. I'm almost finished."

"You did well just now, Firstborn. A true compromise by one who is both a Firstborn and Studier."

The king's smile was so loving, so paternal that Psal blushed. He savored the rare praise, grinning from ear to ear. "Pleasing you pleases me, Father," he said and wiped his bloody hands on his tunic.

Nahas pointed to the two night-tossed women sitting by themselves near the hearth. "Firstborn, you will—of course—give one of these foundling women to Cyrt and the other to Orian."

Psal's heart fell. The moment of reconciliation had been short-lived. "Father, Cyrt…he rages. And no one knows why. And when he's drunk, Father…no. I cannot. And Orian, he is no better with his talk of the ancient ways. Why, he'd abuse a wife as men in the Peacock Clan do."

"See clearly, Firstborn. The other warriors will not challenge Cyrt if he wants one of the women. The women will remain unchosen. Not a good thing. Not a safe thing. They will have no protector, or worse, they will be turned into comfort women. Should they suffer because you do not wish to appease your enemy? As for Orian—"

"Father," Psal said, "the foundlings have no kinsman here to protect them if their husband abuses them."

"No doubt these foundlings can take care of themselves." Nahas opened a pitcher, found it empty and frowned. "Nevertheless, as foundlings, their gratitude will make them do what is required of them. Hasn't Satima grown to love and accept our ways? Now go. You have a few days to make your decision. Make the right one."

"I do not have a *few* days, Father. The Principles, Father."

Nahas gave him a questioning look. "You and these confounded Principles you do not believe in, Firstborn. It is well past forty-nine days and you have not released the Iden women to your brothers. And now this? Are you not tired of your own unhappiness? Or do you delight in filling your path with obstacles?"

"You're the one who puts obstacles in my path, Nahas." His hip and leg aching because of the day's long standing, Psal leaned against a nearby wall. "It's as if you want me to stumble."

"Do you truly believe that, Firstborn?" Nahas sounded surprised; Nahas rarely sounded surprised.

Psal rubbed his hip. "Yes, Father, I do truly believe that."

"You believe that I wish you to stumble?" Nahas asked again.

"Perhaps you only wish to make me better than I am," Psal conceded. "Yet you don't understand my cause, you belittle my cause, and all Netophah's actions go unquestioned."

"Because all Netophah's actions are right, Firstborn." The matter-of-factness of the king's reply wounded Psal more than the pain in his leg and hip.

"Other chief's sons are not the king's son," Nahas continued. "Nor were they born damaged. When you become chief, none will be able to grasp it from your hand. To be thought undeserving of a chiefdom is to risk mutiny. Or do you not remember how my father and Qerys battled for the rule?"

"How can I forget it, Father? You speak of it always. Yet should a studier hone cruelty?"

"Perhaps a studier should not, but a Firstborn should."

"Enough." Psal limped out of the king's chamber. He entered the pharma room where Daris sat grinding Emon. "Call the foundling women to my room."

The child took off running and Psal went to the smaller of the studier rooms where he lay on his wheeled cot.

"Are all Wheel Clan longhouses like this one?" the older one, a dark-haired, graying beauty asked him in her language as Daris led her into the room. "It's very...interesting." She was the straightforward, bold one.

But the younger one, her blotchy face flushing in concern, asked, "Are you ill?"

"I am well." Psal pushed her hands away. "Sit and speak to me. If you're to join our clan, I must know about your journeys. Certain matters must be attended to quickly."

While Liorin, the younger one, sat beside Psal's bed looking about at the messy little room, the older one, Yvo, sat on a stool and did most of the talking. But she coughed often, and often looked at him through her graying brown hair as if awaiting a rebuke. She reminded Psal of himself, defensive, strong-willed, and petulant; he liked her instantly. *Either the perfect wife for Cyrt. Or not.* When Liorin was not looking around the room, she kept her blotchy pale face turned to the ground. Psal believed less than half of what Yvo said.

"It is understandable that you choose to lie," he said, after she finished speaking. "Only your hiding of the truth must not harm my people."

Yvo attempted to stifle a cough with her hand. "But why should we lie to you?"

"Yvo," he said firmly, "your breath smells like forest leaves, and you cough often. I have seen this illness before in the lungs of cave dwellers. Your illness is infectious. Is that not the reason your chief turned you out? Bats also shared the caves with you, didn't they?" He looked at Liorin who immediately lowered her face. "Liorin, did your people cultivate honeybees?"

Tears welled in Liorin's eyes. She spoke, almost whispering. "We had hives outside our cave, but—"

"Your breath smells sickly-sweet. The Wheel Clan has pharma for both your illnesses. Nor will I send you away as your clan did. For your part, tell no one here of your illnesses, even after you're cured. Father will not consider you damaged, but the fear of bearing damaged children...it is always present in some minds. You cave-dwellers are prone to...well, filthy unclean things live in those caves. Bats, reptiles. Gorek pharma will purge you. Bring the contents of your chamber pot to me every morning for me to examine it." He presented the women with a clay jar full of mulched Gorek bark. Liorin grimaced but Yvo took the pharma jar, opened it and chewed a piece of bark boldly.

"I could mix it with Mirta berries to make it more palatable," he said, liking Yvo more and more. "But even then, the bitterness lingers."

Yvo answered him, "Bitterness is not new to me."

Psal laughed. "After you've grieved for your family, you may enter our clan."

"Enter your clan?" Yvo looked about her. "What do you mean 'enter?' You mean marriage, right? Or you want us to be your servants?"

"Our Wheel Clan longhouse does not enslave foundlings. We've found that the towers dislike it. So you will marry one of Father's warriors." Psal called to Daris who entered, carrying a mortar and pestle and smelling of Rangi. "Bring Deyn."

The boy left and Psal continued. "It's best that you marry. Safest."

When Deyn appeared in the doorway, Psal told the women, "This young warrior is Deyn. He will lead you to your holding room. Don't be afraid. I will find you good husbands. Or you will find yourselves good husbands. In the meantime, my fellow studier Cloud and the young one you saw earlier will teach you our language. Do you understand all I've said to you?"

The women nodded, but when Yvo stood up, she gave him an exaggerated bow. "That warrior bowed to you," she said. "And you said 'Father' when you spoke of the chief of this longhouse. Are you the Firstborn here? A future chief?"

"That is something I must decide on," he answered.

* * * *

But when morning came, just as the sun had risen, Gaal, Lan, and Netophah entered the keening room. They stood, looking down on Psal with their hands folded.

"Has something happened?" he asked, looking at the group from under his forearm.

"Get up, Firstborn." Lan kicked his mat. "We're here to open your eyes."

Psal looked past the feet of the group at Ephan who was pulling his blankets over his head. He tapped Ephan's elbow. "Our warriors are not greatly wounded. Today was to be a day of rest, but now...do you see this great company that has come to open my eyes?"

Ephan opened one eye then the other, looked up at the group then through the window. "I see," he said.

Gaal knelt on the floor beside Psal. Psal sat up in bed. A shooting pain streaked through his hip. He reached for a nearby jar of Emon paste, opened the jar and began rubbing his hip with the pharma.

"Tell me first, Gaal," he asked, "whose cause is this, truly? Cyrt's or yours?"

"I seek a wife for myself, and Cyrt wants a wife as well."

"Cyrt does not wish to lower himself to beg a damaged one for a wife?"

"He doesn't understand why you have such enmity against him," Gaal said. "Firstborn, I know you do not share the prejudices of our clan."

"Indeed I do not," Psal answered. "And I would rather give a woman to a steward than to a warrior. But...to give one to both you and Cyrt?"

"He's as good as any of our warriors," Netophah chimed in. "None of the king's warriors will challenge him for one of the women."

"True, they will not." He scooped out more pharma and smeared his upper thigh. "But I will deny you."

"But why?" Gaal asked.

"I understand each man has his own sexual tastes, but I will not put a foundling girl into your hands. Or Cyrt's, for that matter. The comfort women are often in pain after you have lain with them, and Cyrt's rages are inexplicable." He looked at Netophah and Lan. "Wait until the Peacock women have finished their mourning and choose one of them. The Peacock women will have their sisters to defend them against you and Cyrt. And have I not seen? Both you and Cyrt want Gidea. Wait for her and forget the foundlings."

Gaal answered, "But all know Ephan wants her and you are Ephan's friend."

"The day calls," Ephan said suddenly and rose from the bed. He grabbed his crumpled tunic from the floor and began dressing hurriedly. In an instant, barefoot and dressed only in his tunic and undergarments, Ephan had rushed past the group into the corridor.

"Firstborn, you are unaware of the good I've done for you," Gaal pressed.

"You've done me good?" Psal picked up his tunic at the foot of the bed. He sniffed it, looked about the room. "Indeed? When?"

"When you returned from the Wintersea Master," Gaal answered, "your father inquired of me what should be done with a Studier-First-born. I said, 'As Nahas rules the clan, let the Firstborn rule the king's longhouse. In that way, you would be honored among our warriors above all studiers, and the king could try you to see if you would become a worthy chief of our clan.' Firstborn, it was I who gave you this power and privilege in the royal longhouse."

"Ah," Psal said, "I see. This is news indeed."

"Father has told me this very thing," Netophah said.

Psal pulled his tunic over his head. Smiling, he bowed exaggeratedly low to his brother.

Netophah responded, "There is no talking to this one."

"Firstborn," Gaal continued, "consider also that I have covered many of your deceptions, and allowed them to go unnoticed."

Psal was tempted to ask what those deceptions were but thought it best not to know.

"I will not live an owed life, Gaal," he said. "I'm glad you informed me of my debt. I will repay it. But I will not be told how to repay it. You will get a wife, Gaal, but not a foundling who cannot protect herself against you. It must be one of the Peacock women. If you and Cyrt wish to woo Gidea, I will not challenge the match. Although it bothers me that he should get another wife to abuse when other warriors have not had their chance to abuse even one."

The crystal on the Lesser Light keening tree flickered. Psal took a deep breath, sent the keening trees this question: *Do you not see that I am trying to understand? I have not spoken against my conscience.* "I cannot give them one of the foundling women. The tower might not like it."

Netophah gestured Lan aside. "Firstborn, tell them to consider. Deyn is your friend, and known to be cruel to women. But because Lan is also Tolika's husband, Deyn does not harm her. They have accepted Deyn's marriage because *you* accept it. Tell the towers if one foundling chooses

Cyrt, you will let kinder warriors be the second husbands. Don't infect the towers with your scruples, your fears, or your bitterness."

I will try to understand. Psal rose from the mat. "Enough now, Netophah. You're the one infecting the towers by relegating me to 'marriage-maker.' No doubt your mother would feel vindicated because her son has taken the kingship from me."

"You're being sarcastic in a very childish way, Firstborn," Netophah said. "When you speak like this, I cannot take offense even if I wished to. What does it matter that your mother killed mine? Your mother is your mother, and you are yourself. It is because I love you that I ask you to see clearly. Is that so difficult a thing?"

Psal limped to the window. *I will try to compromise. Father will see that I am not petulant.* Outside, Ephan was teaching Maharai and little Eala how to ride the two-wheeled pedaled contraption he had recently invented. "I will see what I can do," he said. "But I will not disregard the wishes of the foundling women. Now, be off with you. You have conquered me and opened my eyes." He almost laughed at himself, at his sudden willingness to please. *Have I truly matured? Have I outgrown my bitterness against this clan?*

"Do you mean it, Firstborn?" Gaal asked.

"Go and attempt to win the women, Gaal. If they will have either you or Cyrt, I will not challenge you."

The crystal on the Lesser Light stopped its flickering and grew steady again. Lan looked at Psal, grinning. A wide smile played on Netophah's face. Gaal bowed, threw his steward cap in the hair and caught it. He hurried from the room, almost bumping into Daris who was coming in from the hallway.

"Why is everyone smiling?" Daris walked toward a basket on a shelf. "What wonderful news have I missed?"

Psal squeezed Daris' shoulder. "They think I've become a true mature Firstborn."

"Good news indeed!" Daris picked up the basket then started toward the entrance. But Netophah stopped him.

"Why does Ephan make such useless things?" Netophah asked and lifted a small wooden mouse from the basket.

"The Wheel Clan Heir is jealous," Psal slapped his brother's shoulder playfully.

"Why should I be jealous of Ephan?" Netophah asked. "I'm a Wheel Clan prince."

"Because he's Maharai's friend," Daris said. "Because they're always together."

"I am no Grassrope clansman to indulge in that petty emotion. I only wonder why he should waste his time with such useless toys when our wounded warriors and pregnant women are in need of him."

"Ephan has battled death all night," Daris said. "Why judge him because he makes inventions to keep himself from going mad? Besides, we children like riding on it, and his inventions are never useless. Hasn't he made chairs for our paralyzed warriors to move about in? Have you seen these?" From the basket, he removed three carved wooden wheeled mice, all wheeled but different from each other, painted in red, yellow, and green. He put them on the window sill in front of Netophah.

"A studier making toys in time of war?" Netophah asked. This time his jealousy was even more apparent.

Lan called Ephan down the hill to the window. "Ephan, come and explain your mice to this jealous one!"

Ephan arrived and grinning shyly, pointed to the yellow ones. "These are the simplest ones," he said. "For the children. To play with in the field. The yellow makes them easier to find."

"And this one?" Lan indicated a red one about the size of his hand.

"That's the fire-mouse." Ephan's face beamed as it always did whenever he explained one of his inventions. "One winds it by using that little spring there. I have to work on making it move slower though. Now if it moves too fast, it falls over."

"Why do you call it the 'fire-mouse?'" Gaal asked from the doorway.

"You've returned?" Psal asked. "I thought you would be pursuing your courtship."

Gaal nodded toward the door where Cyrt stood. "Cyrt did not believe me when I said the Firstborn had granted him one of the foundlings."

Cyrt asked, "Is it true, Firstborn?"

"It is true, Captain. If you're able to win her. And to win the towers."

Cyrt smiled at him, bowed.

This newfound feeling of acceptance. Should I allow myself to be swayed by it?

"See there," Psal thought it best to focus on the mice. "It's hollow inside. We can fill its insides with tinder. Or put candles there. The mice will be sent into thickets. An easy way to burn through jungles."

At the window, Ephan smiled apologetically. "I haven't perfected them yet. They tip over on rocky terrain. They can travel well over grass though."

"And this green one?" Gaal asked, placing a green mouse in his palm.

"That's a tower mouse. Those are hollow as well. I was thinking they could hold tiny keening crystals. We would send them into Peacock towers after battles. You know…when both sets of warriors are keening away. They would find a crack in the tower, climb it maybe. Then they'd send messages back to the tower that sent them. I've made it green, which was a stupid mistake. I think they should be brown. So they can hide themselves better in the crannies of the Peacock tower wall."

"They look quite lifelike," Cyrt said and grinned at Ephan. "I won't find any of these crawling around in the storage room, will I?"

"I'm trying to make them wiggle their noses," Ephan joked. "So, Storm, is this great enlightenment council finished?"

"It is," Psal answered. *I will try to understand. I will try to please Father.*

"Then give the wounded their pharma, and come out quickly. How warm the lake is!" Ephan smiled his half-smile at Netophah, a smile subtly mixed with triumph. "A day for studiers and captive princesses to bathe together."

After all but Daris had left the room, Netophah spoke to Psal. "Brother, Firstborn. I want to speak of something close to my heart."

"You have a heart?" Psal feigned surprise. "This day brings many new wonders."

"Yes, Brother, I do have a heart. And it longs to speak the Peacock language well."

"So you can better explain your love to Maharai?" Daris asked. Netophah pushed Daris away but Daris continued. "It's obvious you love her. You enter her room in the morning and the night. We can hardly eat without you bothering us. But I will tell you. You cut her brother's neck. She will never love you."

"No, she will not," Psal agreed. "Brother, I do not get involved in failing ventures. Unless it's my own particular failing venture. I cannot help you. You may ask Ephan if you wish."

"Ephan won't help you either," Daris said. "We're practical, we studiers. Ask Kwin. He's your friend and he knows the Peacock language well. He also believes in lost causes."

Netophah called out the window as Ephan returned. But after he had given his request to Ephan, Ephan also rejected him. He left the room, calling for Kwin.

"I am glad to see you attempting to please the king," Ephan said. "I know it was not easy for you."

"Yes," Psal said, "It was not easy. Not easy at all, considering how vilely Cyrt treats us Damaged Ones."

* * * *

After visiting the sick room, and before he bathed in the lake, Psal decided to go to the residential hallway to speak with the foundling women. On his way, he stopped at the room occupied by Lan's eimi, where he found Tolika putting dirt and mud on her face for her return to her mother's cell, while Deyn kissed her about the neck and hugged her waist.

"Deyn," he asked in the Wheel Clan language, "do you…hurt this girl when you two lie together?"

"Has Lan accused me?"

"Lan has not accused you. It's only…I know your ways."

Deyn hugged Tolika close. "No, Firstborn, I do not harm her."

"The old desire to harm women doesn't afflict you anymore?" Psal asked.

"It continues to stalk me, Firstborn. But when such perverse images come to my mind, I go to the comfort women."

"Is that the right and good thing to do? Some of the comfort women carry diseases, brought by warriors from other sub-clans. Why bring such diseases to your wife?"

"I am careful, Firstborn."

Psal nodded. "Indeed? And why should the comfort women be harmed? Are they not worthy of your kindness as well?" He rubbed his forehead. "Do not let my towers lose hope in either you or me."

"I will not cause you to sin against your conscience and the Lesser Light, Firstborn."

Psal left and continued toward the cell with the foundling women. Several warriors from the three sub-clans stood outside their cells examining them as farmers and stewards examined ripe fruit.

"Tell me," Psal asked the women, "What man of these would you marry?"

"No man can best me," Yvo said. "I would be happy with any." She indicated her friend lying on the sleeping mat, her face to the wall. "But Liorin needs a kind man. She lived with a tent-family before she arrived at our cave. Eleven people in all. The older son wanted her, but the chief beat her often. She's afraid to marry."

Psal squatted on the floor near their bed. "I promise she'll be given to a good man."

"There's one already who likes her."

"So soon?" Psal smiled, pushed away the pain in his thigh. "You know his name?"

"Young. Your age maybe, or older. Dark eyes. Brown-haired. Braided long to his waist."

"Broqh?" Psal asked, recognizing his friend who wore his hair in the Falconer fashion.

"Yes, yes, his name is Broqh. He brings her little gifts and she shines like the sun when he arrives."

Psal burst out laughing. "A sudden love, indeed. Just arrived and already receiving gifts?"

"He came last night. Twice. This morning. Twice. He wanted to know what she wished to eat. He brought a tray. All kinds of dainties. And she picked what she wanted."

"Broqh is a worthy warrior. Too young perhaps to get a wife if an older warrior wants her. But he is my good friend, and our warriors like him. I will bring them together. She will have to marry another warrior as well. Does she understand that?"

"She does."

"Good. I desire that she consider three others as well."

"We will—"

"There is another here who might want one of you. Not a chief yet, but one greatly honored among our people. Cyrt, by name."

"But he's not a true chief yet?"

"Not yet."

"Then I don't want him."

"There is another. Gaal, by name. The King's Friend. Consider him as well."

"I will. But you will not force us?"

"I will not force you. There is a third. Orian. A true chief, but he has lost his longhouse. Would you have him?"

"Is he good to look at?"

"I have not considered it."

"If you have to consider it, he's probably not so good to look at."

Psal smiled, liking her even more. "Indeed." *If only she could like Ephan!*

He left the longhouse and spent much of the day with the stewards. Just before the second moon rose, he decided to journey to a dense patch of woods where Emon and Rangi bloomed profusely. The lake was beyond a dense forest and as he walked there, Cyrt accosted him.

"Firstborn," Cyrt said, bowing low. The scent of fermented ale issued out of his mouth. "I am glad this war between us has ended."

"It was not I who warred against you, Cyrt."

Cyrt laughed. "Perhaps we warred against each other, Firstborn. But, yes, I have never liked you or your kind. You studiers weaken our clan, and you're an arrogant lot, not knowing your place. Yet, men grow and mature, do we not? I have grown to like you. Even though you were Hinis' son. Because you are the king's son. So, Firstborn"—Cyrt grasped Psal's arm firmly—"I rejoice that you are attempting to like me as well."

'Grown to like me?' No, he tolerates me. "I rejoice as well. And which of the women do you want? You must court them, and do all that boasting you warriors are so good at."

"I will try, Firstborn." He put his arms around Psal's shoulder. "And yet, what does it matter if she likes me or not? You will give her to me even so, won't you? What are love matches in a time of war?"

"I will not force them," Psal said. "But…tell me, if the foundlings reject you…if you win Gidea, would you allow yourself to be joined in a marriage with Ephan? You both like her."

The disgusted look on Cyrt's face was answer enough. "I know we all have much to learn, but that I could not abide. To share a wife with a damaged one? Never."

He shudders in disgust. Even though Chief Studier Dannal adopted him. Hurt, Psal pushed Cyrt aside. Old memories returned; he thought of days when as a child he longed unsuccessfully for Cyrt to carry him shoulder high as he had carried other children. *But I was damaged and he would not touch me.* All his new-found respect for his clan left, and all his petulance returned. *I am wrong to compromise with this people.* "Do we disgust you so much?" he retorted. "Well, then, you cannot have Gidea or the foundlings! Why should they desire a fat and balding one such as you? Even if I was not Hinis' son, even if Ruanna gave birth to me, you would have killed me in her womb."

Cyrt laughed. "So your petulance remains? As my dislike against your kind remains."

"Let us part before this truce fails completely."

"Remember, you live among your people now, Firstborn. Not with the Wintersea Master or among studiers who have nothing better to do each day than to philosophize."

"You would have me dead and not here to taint your great clan!" *How weak I am! Weeping like a child because this drunk rejects me.* "Why should I reward one who hates my kind?"

Psal turned to leave. But Cyrt's hand was on his back, pushing him. Psal fell, stumbling, to the ground. Instantly, Cyrt was atop him, pressing the Firstborn's head into the mud.

Psal did not cry out. No one was nearby. *This present humiliation will end soon.* He would go to his room and whine to Ephan like a little child. He struggled to get up. But Cyrt's fury continued; burning pain, dull numbness as Cyrt rained blows upon him. Footsteps hurriedly approached: Gaal racing through the dense wood toward them.

"What is this you've done?" Gaal asked. He looked about the wood warily. "Cyrt, it is death to attack the Firstborn. Even you will not go unpunished."

"Why did the Creator fill the world with these inferior things?"

"But this morning...." Gaal extended his right hand to Psal. "Peace was almost....Firstborn, whatever the disagreement, it is over now. Nahas need not know of this. Cyrt, the child is too ashamed of his weakness to tell Nahas. And he has shown himself ready to befriend the warriors of his clan? Is that not true, Firstborn? Up then, Firstborn."

Psal tried to rise but Cyrt kicked Psal to the ground. "Why," he asked, "should we have a damaged one as our Firstborn?"

"Not this old discussion," Gaal said. "I an sick of your hatred for weak and damaged ones."

Cyrt removed his dagger from its sheath on his thigh.

"Warrior...." The fear in Gaal's voice worried Psal. He attempted to grasp for something—a stone, a branch—but stone, branch, royal longhouse and steward longhouse were all far in the distance, far from his reach. But suddenly, in the flash of a moment, the sharp edge of Cyrt's knife in his side.

Cyrt lifted the dagger again. "Such imperfect ones are like infections that must be rooted out." Four times the dagger struck.

But the Chief Steward, the king's friend, one of Nahas' best fighters, stood still, as if horror and fear mired his steps. Only when Cyrt placed his hands around Psal's neck did Gaal seem to come back to his senses.

"No," Gaal whispered, holding Cyrt's hand. "If you kill him, his corpse will remain here. And it will be easily seen that a man harmed him. Nahas will suspect one of his warriors. No doubt you. Wound him only, that the night will take him elsewhere." Gaal turned from Psal's pleading face and vomited. He wiped his mouth, returned, paced. "His tunic. Rip his tunic. As an animal would rip it. Let his blood soak into it. Bring it to Nahas, as evidence of his death."

"Wise counsel, Steward," Cyrt said. "You've saved me from my hastiness."

"'Wise counsel?'" Gaal asked, anger edging his words. "Speak not of my wisdom. The morning brought hope and now....Why did you harm the child? The king's heart will break if his son is not—"

Psal did not hear the rest of Gaal's words. Another knife blow pierced his side. *How I am loathed!* Warm blood flowed from this new wound into the mud. Psal felt his head lifted, then dropped hard against the ground. *Dying because I am...inferior...an abomination...inferior.*

Cyrt lifted a boulder, threw it fiercely against Psal's twisted leg. "How that abomination disgusts me! How it makes my skin crawl! That such a one should be the Firstborn of our clan. Since his birth, he has weakened us." Cyrt's fist struck Psal across the face, hard. "The king might endure you but no, Damaged One, I do not." Mud and blood flooded Psal's mouth and nose. All the while, Gaal did nothing.

They dragged Psal's wounded body under a thick brush. Then, as third moon rose, they slowly walked away.

At first, as he watched their boots retreat, all was silence, although not a studier's silence; birds cawed near the lake, insects twittered, leaves fluttered, jostled by the wind. Then the grayness of the two rising moons. In the gray, creatures: corpse green, slime brown, and gray. Not the gray of the moonlight, but a gray like the ashen corpses burnt on pyres. The clan of the Unfleshed Ones. They approached Psal, peered down at him, argued among themselves in a language he did not understand. Yet he understood. He sensed they feared him, or rather they feared some great deed he would do. They argued among themselves, then the smallest of them—but by no means the most powerless—laid wraithlike hands on Psal and pushed hard against his back, as if Psal's body was a long-house it intended to enter. Dulled, yet declaring his right to his body, Psal willed his soul and body to close against the thing. It fled him, and entered Cyrt's body which gave it ready access. As the Unfleshed spirit sealed itself inside Cyrt's body, Psal faded into unconsciousness.

* * * *

Psal woke in his own sick room. With the waking came the memory of the assault. Yet, he felt strangely distant, separated from the dull pain in his body, his limbs heavy. *Rangi*, he thought. *Someone has given me pain-easing Rangi.* A few scattered voices, several shadows, dull wisps of candlelight passed the open door. Ephan and Daris were talking in a nearby sick room. *Ephan...Ephan...if I call out? Don't panic. Don't weep.* He took a deep breath. *Rangi, let not your peace wane. Cyrt or Gaal?* He steeled himself.

But Ephan and Daris entered. Ephan's wide smile, Daris's worried frown as they kneeled over him, lifted his spirit.

"You're awake?" Ephan brought the candle close to Psal's face.

Psal looked through the blur of candlelight and stray tears. "How was I found?"

"Third moon rose to its height and you were not here." Ephan helped Psal sit upright on the mat, moved the candle to the left of Psal's face. "No, no, don't turn your head." Psal complied and Ephan moved the candle to Psal's right. "Look right." Again, Psal complied. "Good, good. Then Cyrt and Gaal found your torn tunic. Nahas sent Kwin and Lan to search for you. Lan found you and brought you here, carrying you on his shoulders."

"I owe Lan much."

Daris shook a warning finger in front of Psal's face. "How could you, a studier, be so stupid to let a night-tossed outcast attack you in your own home region?"

"An outcast? Is that what happened?" Psal blinked twice to push away the blurry vision. "Daris, you've worked hard. But little studiers need their sleep. Go now and stay with your mother or sleep with the young children."

"I wish to stay here."

"The Chief Studier is right, Daris," Ephan said. "It's time you were in bed. Besides, haven't you noticed that the warriors don't bother your mother when you're with her? You're your mother's protection. Now, do what the Chief Studier says. A true studier obeys his master without questioning. Moreover, there is much work tomorrow. Or aren't you interested in choosing swords from our foundry?"

The child grinned, liking swords, and left.

Psal gestured that Ephan pull the screen door. "It was no outcast, but Cyrt and Gaal," he said, speaking in the ancient Waymaker language.

"Nahas should be told," Ephan answered in that same language. He grasped his dagger, but Psal held him back.

"Let none else know. Not my brother, not my rescuer, not the little one."

"But—"

"Should I tell the king I was called an 'abomination?'" Psal struggled to stand but his body was still heavy under the Rangi's influence.

"The king has heard you called worse." Ephan resheathed his dagger. "Nahas might surprise you."

"He will not. I know already what he will say. 'Firstborn, if you had not been so peevish, you would have long ago won your brothers' respect.'"

"Storm, they tried to *murder* you. This is no mere—"

"I said no. I will not tell him. I had forgotten how loathed we were."

"So your would-be slayers will go free?"

"While the war rages, yes. But, they will not remain forever unpunished."

Anger, outrage flashed across Ephan's face. Then he smiled so suddenly and so strangely that Psal wondered at it.

"Why do you smile?" Psal asked.

"You are very much like the king," Ephan said. "Nahas also is not one who returns retribution immediately. You yourself know it. Until they are punished, the guilty ones in our longhouse do not sleep easy. They chew their meat absent-mindedly, one eye on their platter and the other on Cyrt or the king. They wonder always if they're truly forgiven, or if some sudden punishment awaits. And now…to see you do the same thing."

Psal smiled bitterly. "So this ill-born abomination has a chief's heart in spite of itself?"

"Storm.…" Ephan put the candle on the floor. "Yet, even now, you are not safe." He walked to a nearby window, clenched his fist and stared out into the darkness. "What a fool I was! You should have seen it. Day and night they were often at your side. I thought them overwhelmed with worry for you."

"Day and night?" Psal asked. "How long have I slept?"

"Four days."

"Four days? Was I so badly hurt?"

"At the point of death. We thought we lost you. *I* thought *I* lost you. Even with the Rangi, you slept fitfully. You seemed to grow better. Then suddenly you fell into a deep sleep and.…" His voice trailed off.

Psal nodded. "Rangi poisoning. My body was heavy when I woke. It is heavy even now. Like one recovering from over-indulgence."

Ephan ran to the door. "Even as you were recovering, they tried to kill you. Will they not try again? Will they not assume you will charge them to Nahas?"

"Come near and don't look so bewildered. Let me hold on to your shoulder. Help this 'abomination' to rise."

Ephan placed Psal's arm around his own shoulder and helped him to stand. "You are no abomination to me. Promise me this shame will not persuade you to commit self-slaughter."

"My life is all I have now. And in the language of the ancient Way-maker Clan, which is as true a language as any, I promise you. This infection will thrive in spite of my enemies."

Ephan's shoulder visibly relaxed. "I believe you. So, I will tell our brothers that you have recovered? I will say you have no memory of what befell you. The effect of Rangi on the mind of one born damaged has caused such troubles before. I will say that all these misfortunes combined to harm your memory."

"Ah," Psal said, "so something good can come from being born damaged?"

"Cyrt would readily believe such stories. Gaal is more subtle."

"Gaal will choose to believe it," Psal said. "Because he is aware of his cowardice."

"You must appear as one who has forgotten. Fear shows itself, anger shows itself." Ephan took a gourd of Rangi seeds from a nearby shelf and offered it to Psal. "Take this."

Still unsteady, Psal tried to feel the floor under his feet. He still could not. "I have no need of it," he said and pushed the container away.

Ephan pressed the gourd into Psal's hand. "Take it! If not to be calm, at least to appear calm." So Psal took it.

* * * *

Psal's knee and wounds mended slowly, but the Rangi and Ephan were faithful. Ephan gave out that Psal was unable to comprehend much of what was spoken to him. The war councils, generally held in the keening room, were moved to the king's chamber to prevent the Firstborn being disturbed. All the longhouse troubled itself because of the Firstborn's illness. As for the vision of the Unfleshed Ones, Psal dismissed it and the fear of it; he was a rational boy and expert in putting aside all that challenged that rationality. A trick of the mind, he thought, and no more.

Thus, Psal was free to slowly pull himself out of his desolations. His duty torn from him, Ephan charting towers and sending and receiving messages, Psal stayed in the keening room and coaxed his heart to prepare to meet Cyrt and Gaal. Such freedom from care was unsettling for a studier and he determined to busy his mind. He read through the annals of the Wheel Clan kings, the medical lore of the Preying Bird and Mockingbird clans, and because they lay at hand, the Book of Life of the Waymaker and Falconer Clans.

Then one night he chanced to hear an abandoned tower. The region in which the royal longhouse now docked lay near several Falconer home regions. The Falconer clan's peculiar tradition of anchoring longhouses semi-permanently in home regions, leaving only on the fiftieth day for one night-tossed day, then returning and repeating the forty-nine day anchor seemed a good place to start. Although King Renn was his friend, Psal considered this Fiftieth Day tradition—which was rooted in superstitions about a coming New Day when all on Odunao would be freed from the old day—ridiculous.

But since the war began, the Wheel clan had not consistently tracked non-combatant, neutral, faint, and abandoned towers. Having nothing to do, Psal resolved to chart them and, after searching about the keening room, he found the Falconer scrolls—mold-covered, foul-smelling, but still legible—under a pharma basket. These he took and lay on his wheeled bed, listening for Falconer towers.

Six Falconer towers lay to the north, fifteen to the east, four to the south, and twenty on the mountains of the west. *There should be more,* Psal thought. *Should I analyze each tower's history or send a message to King Renn asking for an explanation? He's always forthcoming about such matters. But Seagen might hear, and will he not wonder why the*

Firstborn is muddling through Falconer songs when Rangi is suppos-edly teeming through his brain? So he merely charted the active towers and noted which ones had gone almost mute or had disappeared entirely from the map. The next day, the royal longhouse traveled to a region of low grasses and cool streams. Once again, Psal listened to Falconer Tow-ers heard; once again, he heard fewer towers than expected. For thirteen days, he studied Falconer towers, wondering if some of their towers had failed or if Renn was indulging yet another of his strange inventions. Then a thought struck him. The Peacock towers? What if…what if some of them also have failed? What if they were not destroyed as we thought? What if some Peacock Clans merged because of failed towers and not because of lost battles?

He studied the problem a long while and would have studied it longer but one morning Ephan said to him, "Your wounds are healed and your knee is almost mended. But as the pain wanes, your fear rises. I am wearied with doing both your tasks and mine."

Psal looked toward the door, his heart tense. "Do you think I'm afraid? I am neither fearful or ashamed."

"I wouldn't build a tower on so slim a premise."

"Tomorrow, this abomination will face them."

"You must stop using that word. Even if it encourages you to use it as your sword, its sharp edge wounds me."

"I had not thought you were one who would wish to forget how hated we damaged ones are." Psal picked up the gourd of Rangi which lay near his pillow. "Take this. It is not a thing I wish to be enslaved to."

Ephan made it known that the Firstborn's mind had found itself, and that night, all in the longhouse—all but Cyrt and Gaal—came to the keening room to visit him.

Psal's visitors asked the same questions they had often asked when Psal and Ephan would visit the royal longhouse during their sojourn with the Wintersea master: "Do you remember me, Firstborn? Say you have not forgotten me."

"I have not forgotten you nor any in my clan," Psal answered, using the same words his younger self had said.

Yet again, he told himself, *they rejoice to see me. But, never again will this damaged one be fooled by this glut of love.*

The words Cyrt had thrown at him and the fear of being assaulted pricked him continually. Although he worked with Ephan and Daris in the sick room and in the keening room, he never visited the gathering room. At last, Antun visited him.

"Firstborn," Antun asked, "you have said you were your old self again."

"As healthy as one born damaged can be."

"Yet you do not walk the longhouse or eat with us near the hearth?"

"My leg lags behind."

"Command your body and mind, Firstborn. They will obey." Antun picked up Psal's boots. "If you don't challenge that foot of yours, it will weaken your mind in time."

Psal half-smiled. "You sound like one I used to know."

"A friend, I hope." Antun gathered Psal's leg braces and staff.

"Tsbosso, the chief of the Peacock Threshing Floor Clan."

"I have heard he was your friend, that you were betrothed to his daughter. It's a grievous thing that he betrayed you." He kneeled and lifted Psal's left foot into the boot, pushing Psal's hand aside. "No, Firstborn, it is my honor to help you."

I need no help, Psal thought, but allowed Antun to push his foot further into the boot. "I am used to betrayals. From inside and outside this longhouse. But the girl was not yet betrothed to me." He looked toward the window. "We've arrived in one of our pleasant home regions."

"All home regions are pleasant, Firstborn." Antun stood up. "But, yes, this is one of the most pleasant." His pale eyes searched Psal's face. "Nothing but low-lying grasses here. One can walk freely without fear."

"Speak plainly, Antun. Do you think I fear something or someone?"

"No, Firstborn. I spoke generally." He walked toward the door. "Yet if I did not speak generally, if I spoke plainly, will you not rage at me?"

I suppose I must go into the gathering room now that Antun has challenged me to it. "I will not rage, Chief Antun."

"Your friend has told your kinsmen that night-tossed outlaws waylaid you."

Psal rested his weight on Tsbosso's staff. "And you do not believe him?"

"I will believe what I am asked to believe, Firstborn." He paused, looked at the floor, at windows, but not at Psal. "But there is a word—"

"Speak, Antun. Never fear to speak your heart to me."

"I will speak all my heart, Firstborn." Antun took a deep breath. "I find myself continually amazed at your father's patience with you. If I had not seen your actions—and his mercy toward it—with my own eyes, I would not have believed it."

"Antun," Psal said, raising his voice, "if you and I are to be friends, you will not call my father's attitude toward me 'mercy.'"

Antun bowed. "As you wish, Firstborn."

Psal softened. "Being born an abomination, I shame Nahas. It is not mercy but pity he feels. But why speak of it now?"

"I only wondered...."

"Wondered what?" Psal's eyes dared Antun to continue.

"I wondered if perhaps others here in the longhouse might have tried to kill you."

"Because I am a blight on their clan, you mean? Or because I've denied them the women?"

Antun nodded slowly. "Both or one or the other…or…."

"None here has tried to kill me. If they wish me dead, they fear Nahas too much to kill me."

"They know Nahas loves you, Firstborn. And they love you as well." Antun walked to the window and looked out onto the terrain. "When I was younger, I saw Nahas at a festival. My uncle said, 'That is Nahas, our kinsman and our king. His father and yours battled for the rule of our great clan.' I watched your father in awe, amazed at how humanly he walked. I suppose I expected him to walk as many of our chiefs walk… arrogantly, cruelly…but he did not. When I heard he had spared his own son, I was pleased that our clan had such a merciful king. Since then, I have spoken to many studiers who are glad of your life, Firstborn. There-fore, do not imagine enemies roundabout. I—"

"I did not give you permission to speak to me about my life," Psal interrupted him. "And do not tell me I am loved when I know I am not."

In the silence that followed, as Antun held Psal's gaze, only the din of the wailing Peacock women was heard.

"Firstborn," Antun said, "you gave me permission to speak from my heart. Be satisfied that any word from my mouth will not harm you as other words from our clan have. True, our people view damaged ones as an evil to spurn, and indeed Renan was often badly treated even though my men knew I would punish them for abusing him. But know this, Firstborn, your illness has caused many of your brothers to spare their own damaged ones. I meant only…if you were to reconcile yourself to—"

Psal moved toward the door. "Should I reconcile myself to men who mocked and belittled me? I attempted a truce and I was grimly rewarded for it. No! No! To reconcile is to allow them to triumph over me. I will not do it."

"Is it so painful to have others triumph over you, Firstborn?"

"Yes, Chief Antun, it is. Quite painful. Should I live as a grateful abomination who walks around like one who is sorry for his damaged life?"

"I suppose not, Firstborn. But one thing more." Antun bowed low. "To assume that I am like those who have insulted you, to assume others will mock you as these have…do you not think that you have put your future friends inside an incredibly harsh prison? To assume the worst of everyone you meet? It is a world where every stranger can be judged and everyone can be bound—and can never be released—because of what one or two others have done. Do not presume to know my heart, Firstborn. See me only as I am."

"Forgive me, my anger," Psal said, touched by Antun's words. "I should not have raged at you. If we're still friends, you will allow me to lean on your arm as I enter the gathering room."

Antun offered Psal his arm. "It would be my honor, Firstborn."

When Psal limped into the gathering room, he was greeted like one risen from the dead. Even Orian cheered to see him enter.

Cyrt and Gaal approached him as he sat at the king's table. Gaal spoke first, studying his eyes. "Firstborn, it is good to see you walk among us."

"I am quite well." Psal lifted the tunic to show the wound at his side.

"Ephan is truly skilled," Cyrt said.

"Quite skilled," Psal answered, and moved aside to give Gaal room to sit.

"And you remember nothing of the one who attacked you?" Cyrt asked.

"Nothing."

"A pity you did not wound him," Gaal said. Then added, "But perhaps you have. Who knows?"

"Who knows?" Psal answered.

Cyrt and Gaal looked at each other, then at Psal. If they thought he deceived them, they did not show it. But after many more days they seemed to believe he had indeed forgotten all, and this was easy enough to believe, for in those days, many believed many false things about frail minds.

CHAPTER 18
THE WAR WITHIN AND WITHOUT

The wars within and without the longhouse continued; the war within Psal's heart as well. He had found a new skill, that of pretense. Formerly, the idea of hiding his heart would have seemed dishonest, or a succumbing to humiliation. He wrote in his annals, *Now I understand the advantages of pretense. In addition to keeping me alive, it allows me to preserve my pride. Yet, deception is a killing thing because I walk among people who scorn me and I must pretend maturity as well as ignorance. The longhouse has become even more constricting.*

His body, too, enclosed him. Since the attack, it had become uncontrollable, shaking, trembling always; and muscle aches, fever, and nausea continually assailed him. He went about his work, sickly and feverish, his weakness apparent to all.

But early one morning, at the beginning of the fifth month, as he reclined on his wheeled bed updating parchments and charts, a shriek echoed through the dark longhouse. Some moments later, Satima and Daris pushed aside the embroidered curtain of the keening room screen.

"It's Deyn," Satima said. "He's been attacked."

Daris tugged at Psal's tunic. "Come now, Chief Studier! Now!"

"Where's Ephan?"

"Busy! Come!"

Psal struggled to his feet. Daris thrust two nearby pharma baskets into his hands, then pushed Psal into the corridor. They walked past the gathering room into the residential hallway where about twenty women including Rain stood outside of Lan and Deyn's room. Inside the room near a window, Tolika stood with Maharai.

"The wound was not made to kill." Rain's eyes signaled: Tolika is the cause of this.

Psal entered and knelt beside Deyn's bloody bed. "Who did this, Deyn? Was it Tolika?" He turned to Daris. "Bring me a candle."

Deyn shook his head. "No, Firstborn."

Psal shook Deyn's shoulder. "My friend, you must tell the truth. Do you understand?"

"The pain is hard to bear, Psal."

"You will be well," Daris said.

Deyn glanced at Tolika who stood near the window, Maharai's arms around Tolika's waist, then at Ephan who entered carrying a clay jar and a torch. Together Ephan and Psal found the source of the wound. Deyn's testicles hung from his body by a small string of flesh.

"More light reveals greater troubles," Ephan said. "Deyn, you must force yourself to swallow a very strong infusion of Gorek. It will remove any infection you received from the dagger." He slowly lifted Deyn's head to allow him to drink from the jar. Deyn swallowed, grimacing at the pharma's bitterness.

Taking the gourd of Rangi seeds from the pharma basket, Psal counted thirty large seeds and handed them to Daris. "Set these to boil and bring some Emon paste as well." Daris took them and ran outside to the hearth.

"Don't the wounded warriors need you, Cloud?" Psal asked.

"I did not think you would be able to...." Ephan began.

"I am well able to heal my friend."

"Enough of this gawking!" Netophah's voice. "The Chief Studier doesn't need eyes watching his every move. Return to your beds."

The group dispersed, leaving Netophah, Maharai, Tolika, and the three studiers.

"I feared this," Ephan said. "Deyn, why did you not heed Lan's warning? To harm your wife is to harm his wife as well. Or are you too foolish to understand that?"

Psal looked at Deyn, then at Tolika. *Lan, yes. How had I missed the obvious?* "Ephan, I am well able to do this alone."

Still Ephan did not leave.

Daris returned with the soupy Emon paste. Psal poured half on the wound and the other he gave to Deyn to drink.

"We can re-attach the sack," he said. "But—"

"You won't be able to have sex with a woman in the future," Ephan interjected. "But don't worry. You won't have the urge to."

Psal gave Ephan a chiding look.

"Well, it's true," Ephan defended himself. "And Daris, bring threads and knives, stones. And find Lan. Make sure the dagger he brings is his own, not another man's."

Daris took off running.

"I am well able to do my studier's duty," Psal said to Ephan. "You need not remind me how to investigate."

Ephan nodded. "I'll leave, then." He walked outside, leaving Psal at Deyn's side.

Daris returned with a pharma basket full of surgical tools and with stones he had heated in the hearth. But Lan was not with him.

The needle burnt hot between Psal's fingers as he spoke to Deyn. "Now, are you sure you feel nothing?"

"Nothing, Studier." He paused. "I feel nothing. Is it true?"

Psal squinted as he threaded the hot needle. "Is what true?"

"What Ephan said. That I will not have any urge for women?"

"Be of good cheer. Lan could've done greater harm. It is Lan who did this, is it not?" Looking behind him at Tolika whose apparent indifference to her husband's hurt was sending chills down his spine, Psal had a new thought. "Or was it Tolika?"

Deyn's voice was almost inaudible. "Neither, Firstborn."

"Ah! I don't think that is quite true." Psal took the clay jar of Rangi water from Daris. "And you know I cannot take your word for it." Psal willed his hands to stop their shaking. "We'll begin."

As Deyn succumbed to a numbed drowsiness, Psal set to work. He had almost finished sewing up the wound and removing the rest of the sack when Lan arrived, Kwin at his side. He walked to Tolika. She greeted him with a kiss but kept her eyes on Deyn.

"One in your eimi is wounded and you disappear?" Psal asked, finishing up the stitches.

"I was in Kwin's room. Tonight was Deyn's night to be with Tolika."

"I don't quite believe that. You must have heard the ruckus. Everyone else did." Psal stood up, rubbed his leg, then extended his hand. "Or were you asking Kwin to plead for you to Netophah? Give me your dagger."

Lan reluctantly placed the dagger in Psal's hand.

"It's wet. Was there any reason why you chose to wash your dagger?"

"None, Firstborn."

"I thought a perfect eimi had been created," Psal said. "You're kinsmen. You both like each other and the girl. So, why this? Why now?"

"He told you?" Lan asked.

"No. Your kinsman has been faithful to you."

"It was done in anger, Firstborn," Lan said. "I regretted it immediately."

Psal glanced at Tolika. "Your wife doesn't seem to regret it."

"I warned him, Firstborn. Four times. Tolika is a shy little thing and—"

"She is no shy little thing," Netophah shouted from where he stood.

"He lay with her, Firstborn. Despite the promise. What if she were to become pregnant? Why should her mother or sisters shun her?"

"Indeed. And yet, to castrate your friend? You're both from the same sub-clan, kinsman to Ronen. Why should Tolika matter?"

"I didn't wish to hurt him, Firstborn. My two hearts struggled against each other."

"And this was their compromise?" Netophah asked.

"I'm sorry, Wheel Clan Heir." Lan turned to Netophah. "I've sinned by allowing Samat to use my anger to cause harm. But, one wish—"

"I already know," Netophah said. "You want me to preserve Tolika?"

"I do, Wheel Clan Heir. I do not say to deceive your father, but—" He looked from Netophah to Psal.

Netophah sighed. "Of course you're saying to deceive Father. At other times, I would gladly deceive Father to protect you. But to deceive him for a woman? A woman not of our clan? A crafty one, at that? Speak truly. Who did it? You or Tolika?"

"I did," Lan said.

Netophah looked at Kwin. "Friend, did he confess to you? Did Tolika do this?"

"Wheel Clan Heir," Kwin answered. "That I cannot say. Only, plead for them both."

Psal placed Lan's dagger on the window sill. "Netophah, bring your dagger."

Netophah ran down the hallway, past the hearth, and into the King's Corridor to retrieve his knife from his room. Meanwhile, Psal removed a jar from the basket and poured some of the liquid inside it upon Lan's knife. When Netophah returned, Psal poured the same potion on Netophah's dagger, then lay it beside Lan's. Soon, flies appeared, tiny white flecks in the darkness. They swarmed and lit on Lan's dagger.

"There's blood on your weapon, Lan," Psal shook the flies from Lan's knife and returned it to Lan. "I hoped in vain for another outcome. I will not use centipede to ascertain whether it is human blood or not. It is Deyn's blood, no doubt. And yet I do not believe you would harm your friend. Nor do I believe you gave Tolika your dagger. I think she took it from you when you were unaware."

He walked to Tolika and proceeded to pour a sweet-smelling oil on her hand, but as he did so, Lan called out to him. "Firstborn, don't."

"But the Firstborn must know if her hands touched the hilt of your dagger," Netophah said.

"Let the matter rest," Lan said.

"But the others will say that—" Daris began.

"Without adequate proof, she will be safe." Lan looked at Netophah. "Will she not be safe, Wheel Clan Heir?"

Netophah retrieved his dagger from the sill. "If you declare that you wounded your friend, Father will ask, 'Why did you not fight him in daylight in front of the warriors?' He will consider this vengeance petty and mean-spirited, something only the Peacock Clan or Grassrope outcasts would do."

Lan held Tolika's hand. "Deyn should not have forced her."

"A weak defense to save the girl's life," Netophah said.

"Lan," Psal said. "I have allowed you to keep your dagger. Because you said your anger has already cooled. Don't make me appear foolish by murdering your kinsman in his sleep."

"Do you truly believe him guilty?" Netophah asked, frowning.

"Let it be as he said," Psal replied. "But Lan, make your defense ready. Father hates liars even more than he hates those who allow women to rule them." He approached Maharai. "Tell your cousin that she belongs to the Wheel Clan now and she should not live with her mother or with her sisters since she has no mind of her own. Tell her I believe she was the one who wounded Deyn, and not Lan. But for her sake, we will say otherwise." He removed a woolen cloth from a nearby shelf and wiped his hand.

"You must protect her, Firstborn," Lan said. "She has lost brothers, Firstborn. At our hands."

Psal glanced at Deyn, who slept fitfully. "She has now gained a brother."

* * * *

At midday as Psal sat on the rampart decoding war reports sent through the towers, he heard sandal clatter hasting up the stairs. He turned to see Satima.

"Firstborn," she yelled, "you must do something! The royal longhouse is in an uproar and you sit here doing nothing. Have you not heard?"

"I have heard, Satima, but I tuned my mind to ignore it."

Her crescent eyes glared at him. "So? You have determined that Tolika's lie should go unchallenged? Those…those…hateful Iden women are declaring Tolika was cruelly raped! She was not! You and I and all here know she was not." She wagged her finger in Psal's face. "Those of us who understand the Peacock language remonstrated with them. 'Tolika was willingly married,' we told them. 'The girl has been deceiving her people these three months,' we said."

"Yes, I heard. Your voices were equally loud." Psal looked down at a report, smiled to himself at Mion's skilled encryption, and waved Satima downstairs.

She made no move to leave. "Firstborn, the longhouse is your domain. Are you content to just sit there?"

"How I wish sometimes we had not rescued you!" Psal said. "Your character is strong, true. And you have certainly won Rain's heart. But you often forget your place. Rain may honor you. But I am Firstborn here. Do not order me about!"

Her eyes filled with hurt tears. When she spoke again, she said, "You do not see how this affects you, do you, Firstborn? You do not see that I care for my new clan as deeply as I care for you, its Firstborn and my first friend." She wiped her eyes. "Well, let me explain. Tolika was rejected by the Iden women for her deceit—"

Softened by her tears, Psal thought it best to pretend indifference. "About time."

"In her effort to prove her lie, that she was not married at all, Tolika told her sisters that it was she, not Lan, who castrated Deyn."

"Interesting."

"It is not *interesting*, Firstborn. The girl has no conscience and should be punished. All are saying she should be made outcast. Not I alone, but all. Orian says your decrees are injurious to the Wheel Clan at large. The warriors are now demanding all the women—the foundlings and the Iden women—be immediately released to them. You did not keep me imprisoned for three months, did you?"

"No, I did not. But you knew who you wanted, and they wanted you. Bad choices, for they both died. So—"

"Even so I have much respect here. And I love you, Firstborn. I do not like to hear Orian insulting you. Moreover, Nahas has sent me to ask if you intend to sit here cocooned in the watchtower."

Psal sighed. "Tell him, it is a tempting thought. This is a peaceful place. But, return, find Kwin. Have him bring the Foundling women to the Chief Studier's room."

* * * *

"Which of my kinsmen have you chosen?" Psal asked the women when they arrived.

"Antun and Broqh," Yvo said. "Broqh for Liorin and the young chief for me. These warriors have been kind to us."

"None others of my kinsmen showed you kindness? Gaal and Cyrt?"

"They were kind but we don't want them." Yvo folded her arms before her.

"Ah. I see."

"Antun, every morning he greets us. Then, he greets the quarreling dark woman. Then the pale and deformed women. Then he leaves. Always, every morning. A noble heart, that one. And a body a woman would want to hold." Her eyes gleamed with anticipation. "This Antun is a chief, isn't he? I've seen the others bow to him as he passes. I would very much like to belong to a chief. They get a large portion of the clan's goods, don't they? More than the warrior's share?"

"Liorin, you cannot have Broqh only. Another may want you." Psal turned to Kwin. "Tell our brothers to meet me near the hearth."

* * * *

In the gathering room, Psal called Antun to his side. "Antun, you have no longhouse, but you're still a chief. Take the older of the foundling woman as your wife."

"I'm honored, Firstborn," Antun said, awkwardly. "But others more worthy—"

"She'll be happy with you." Psal placed Yvo's hand inside Antun's. Then he spoke to Broqh. "Broqh, I've heard you want Liorin. And she wants you as well."

Broqh blushed, stepped forward. "Why should ones as young and untried as we take a girl? Give her to Cyrt, Firstborn."

Cyrt took the younger girl's hand. "She will be mine and Gaal's."

Near the entrance to the King's Corridor, Netophah gestured to Psal to give the girl to Cyrt.

But Psal placed the girl's right hand in Broqh's and called Kwin to their side. "Take her," he said. "Although you're young, Broqh is the Firstborn's friend and Kwin is the friend of the Wheel Clan Heir. None would harm you."

"Even so, Firstborn," Broqh answered. "Let Cyrt have her. Let her be a sister to me."

Psal tried not to raise his voice. "You have friends here who are worthy of a wife. Lebo, for instance. None will challenge a bound three made up of you and Lebo."

But Lebo said, "The girl is not to my liking."

Standing near the hearth, Ephan laughed. "It is Cyrt that is not to your liking, is it not, Lebo?"

"The Wheel Clan men refusing women? This is a strange thing!" Psal shouted to Nahas who was standing at the juncture of the king's hallway and the gathering room. "Your warriors are sheep, Nahas."

"A moment, Firstborn," Nahas called to Psal. Those in the gathering room stepped aside to let Psal pass.

"Why keep her from Cyrt?" the king asked, when Psal stood before him. "He has the allegiance of his comrades. And one day he will be a chief."

"She is a tender little thing who will wilt if touched by an unkind man."

"You underestimate our women, Firstborn. Why do you think they will not protect her?"

"I will not put her in a bad marriage on the mere wisp of a hope."

"Is there some other matter between you and Cyrt, Firstborn? I thought you and he had been reconciled to each other."

"Were we?" Psal asked. "I do not remember it. I have forgotten much since my wounding." *And remembered much as well.*

"Then let us ignore the forgotten past," Nahas said. "Think only of the present. Begin a new truce with Cyrt. Give him the girl. You will show yourself mature and your brothers will grow to trust you. Didn't the old master teach you never to swerve from your path for the sake of a small battle?"

"To the girl it is no small battle, Nahas. And I have decided I do not need my brothers' love." Psal limped back to the hearth where Cyrt stood, holding Liorin—who did indeed look like a bruised reed—by the wrist.

There, he pried Liorin's hand from Cyrt's and dragged her toward Antun. He thrust her at Antun. "Antun, here, have this one as well."

Cyrt bowed low to Psal, then walked away. Nahas said nothing—which, Psal knew, could only mean trouble.

* * * *

The next day, the royal longhouse docked at the Eagle's Nest home region for a war council. When night fell, just before the third moon was at its height, Nahas gathered the Iden girls between five and thirteen years of age and divided them up among the ten longhouses present. The night took the girls away. Their daughters removed, the Iden women raged more furiously. Angry, Psal responded by rendering his decision on Tolika: Lan, Deyn, and Tolika would remain together; Lan and Tolika would not be punished. The king then called Psal to his chamber.

"Firstborn," he said, "for my every action, you have a faulty response."

"You should not have sent the little girls away. But you were spiteful and petty for Cyrt's sake."

"And Tolika's punishment? When you gathered us together, I thought you would deliver your judgment."

"The Iden women have lost their daughters. Why should they lose Tolika as well? You should not—"

"Firstborn, you often forget yourself. I will not always wink at your petulance." The king walked to a small table and began pouring ale from a pitcher into a goblet. "The girl admits her guilt. And Cyrt should—"

"I do not like Cyrt." Psal knocked the pitcher from his father's hand. "True, he is a near kinsman, but why is he so close at hand? Do you wish to watch his every movement as you watch Orian's? Is that why? Do you use Cyrt the way one uses a dull tool? Is there some family secret I do not know? Is that it? Whatever the king's reasons they no longer interest me because this king has chosen not to tell me his heart. I will not waste tears or time attempting to understand what you so willingly and carefully hide from me."

"Is this where your anger stems from? You think I have not shared my heart with you?"

"Because I am the only one you do *not* share your heart with, Nahas." Psal kicked the pitcher and turned toward the door and shouted at the top of his voice. "As for the Iden Peacock women, they are our sisters, allied to us through your wife Ktwala, whom you are presently torturing. They will be treated as women married into or born into our clan. I will not force them to marry our brothers. And, Nahas, I am the Firstborn. You may be king of this clan, but you were never a Firstborn. In this thing, you have to obey me. You did not hearken to my voice when I argued against murdering the Iden men. But in this thing—this thing! this thing!—you will obey me." With that, he left the king's presence.

* * * *

On days free from corpses, pyres, and Wheel Clan stewards, Ktwala would walk outside with Lian at her side. But one day, her side and back aching, she said to Lian, "I cannot walk anymore. Your brother dislikes it."

Lian would walk forever if he could. But he nodded and kissed her pregnant belly.

Ktwala returned to her longhouse and closed the entrance door behind her. She sat in the empty gathering room, rubbing her legs and trying to catch her breath. In the farthest reaches of the longhouse, she heard footsteps. They tramped toward her. Soon—wearing buckskin breeches and a ripped tunic, with damp black hair falling over his shoulders—a man appeared. His swarthy skin was covered with scratches as if he had tramped through briars. He held a small gourd of salted insects from her storage rooms and was chewing on dried berries.

Her brothers' wooden lances lay on the floor, but Ktwala did not reach for them. She only eyed the man in silence, and gestured to Lian to stand near her.

The stranger lifted his hands, dirty and reddened by the berries. *So he has no weapons?* Ktwala rose slowly, the child at her knee. She took a lance from the floor. The stranger flinched, drew a dagger from a leather pouch hidden in his buckskin boots. *Liar.* Unfearing, Ktwala pointed to a drawing of Peacock and touched her heart, head and feet.

He nodded, said in a jangling mish-mash of her tongue. "So you're from the Peacock Clan? I thought so."

She made a motion with her hands like a wheel turning, traced a circle on the ground.

The stranger resheathed his dagger. "The Wheel Clan?" he asked. "No, I'm not from the Wheel Clan."

He made a motion, like that of a rope being wound and thrown: the Grassrope clan. A selfish, lawless, thieving clan, known for cruel and perverse sexual acts. Ktwala drew Lian closer. The Grassrope outcast pointed in the direction of the other rooms. "Anyone else here with you?"

"Only the boy."

The stranger tapped his nose. "Tomo."

Ktwala touched her heart: "Ktwala."

Solitary foundlings and outcasts often spoke too much or too little. Tomo spoke much, leaning against her window and rambling on about his solitariness, and of being often unmade by the night. Ktwala listened to him, comprehending most of what he said.

"But," she asked, interrupting him, "why are you lost to the night?"

"I killed my kinsman. My longhouse cast me out. Some enemies one can kill. Others one must learn to live with. Others one must flee. I chose to kill." He lowered his glance, looked slightly ashamed. "I won't kill you. I am no murderer. That one was cruel. That's why I killed him."

Ktwala walked outside with her flute in her sack, Lian beside her. The Grassrope outcast explored the longhouse all day, never once stepping outside of it.

When Ktwala returned, he said, "Ktwala, I've found all the hidden entrances. You can never lock me out."

That night, she warned Lian of the evil done to boys by Grassrope men and slept with a dagger at her side. The next morning she woke to the footsteps of the Grassrope outcast walking to and fro in the longhouse. Smaller steps trailed the heavier ones. The scent of wood, corpses, and smoke filled the air. She walked outside. Afire was the clothing her people had worn. Afire, the male cloaks and tunics of the Peacock Clan. Tomo and Lian were carrying Peacock amulets and charms outside and adding them to the flame. Dead was her lion at the stranger's feet.

"Why have you killed him?" she asked.

"I'm here now. I don't need your Peacock magic to protect myself." He removed some herbs from a pouch he wore around his neck. "Know what this is? It's Dovi. A powerful poison used by the Wheel Clan. I put it in his food and water. I burned your flutes as well."

Ktwala glanced up at her eagle flying above them. The stranger spoke in his jangled mish-mash of tongues. "That one you can keep. But don't try your Peacock tricks again. I don't like feeling threatened in my own longhouse." He looked about the field. "Dead bodies. Dead bodies. This war taints the whole planet."

Ktwala slung her sack across her shoulder. "Lian, let us walk into the far meadow."

She avoided the Grassrope outcast all day, teaching Lian the uses and dangers of the herbs of the field. When they returned, the outcast had emptied the longhouse. Maharai's dresses, Ouis' tunics, lay in the pile of clothing thrown to the ground. Silent, Ktwala entered her usurped longhouse, but when the sun and the daymoon began to wane she walked outside. There she found the outcast had used red clay to cover the external walls with his clan's symbol: birds singing on a grass rope.

"We Grassrope have music science too," he said. "We can kill with our flute music." He sucked at his teeth. "I never learned though. My mother knew how."

Ktwala walked past him, retrieved Maharai's clothing, her husband's tunic, and those of Ouis.

The Grassrope outlaw approached her, swaggering. "This is a Grassrope longhouse now. And I, Tomo, am the clan chief here. Chief Tomo."

She laughed. Was it the first time she had laughed since her son's death? *Grassrope Outcast, you have placed yourself in a Wheel Clan's prison.*

A day of burnt pyres followed.

"How strange this tower is!" Tomo shouted. "Death yesterday and today as well. I can understand if it wishes to visit dead Peacock corpses. Towers are faithful like that. But why visit a Wheel Clan burial ground?"

Ktwala said nothing, and all day, Tomo paced the longhouse like a caged animal. Then, the next day, a home region. Tomo raced down the tower, called out to Ktwala.

"At last the tower has found its senses and has stopped bringing us corpses everyday! What madness? And what blessings it has brought for us. It's Wheel Clan lands. Hurry now. I saw a one-armed man running to meet us, pulling a wheeled cart with three baskets."

When the steward arrived, he called to Ktwala in the Peacock tongue, "My Queen, the King and his Firstborn have sent you food."

Tomo opened the entrance and grasped the handle of the wheeled cart.

The steward looked him up and down. "Ktwala, your tower spoke of a new inhabitant. I had not thought it would be a Grassrope outcast." He held Tomo's gaze. "Stranger, whoever you are, do not touch this woman or you will have built your own pyre. She's a king's wife. And, for your own sake, although the food from our Nahas is good, do not set your heart on it."

"I stay where I want to stay," Tomo answered, looking up from the basket of Wheel Clan delicacies.

"The world is a wide place. Let me not see your face again," the steward replied. He reached inside his tunic and retrieved both a flute and a parchment.

"How did you know my flutes were burned?" Ktwala asked him.

"Your tower told the Firstborn. It missed your music." He handed Ktwala the flute and parchment, then spoke to Tomo. "The night will be more merciful to you than Nahas will be. Look, I have already warned you." Saying this, the steward left.

"A 'Queen?'" Tomo asked. "I am fortunate indeed! 'Nahas?' That's the Wheel Clan king, is it not?" Tomo searched the baskets, opened each bowl of fermented meats, fruit, or grain while Ktwala unrolled the parchment. "And the man? One of your servants, no doubt? What is that message he gave you? So this is how kings punish their wives?"

Ktwala opened the parchment, several strands of curly hair fell from the packet. Her heart leaped. Maharai's hair. She rubbed it gently between her fingers. "The man you saw is a former warrior of the Wheel Clan, wounded now and unable to fight. It would be wise to heed his warning."

"Why should I leave? I have not harmed you. It could be argued that I do the king's bidding and am protecting his wife. Now, you didn't answer the more important question. Why is your man punishing you? Are you the cause of this war?"

She didn't answer him. Her eyes were brimming with tears. Weeping, smiling, she read the Firstborn's message:

To the Great Queen Ktwala, Wife of my father, and my mother. From Psal, your son:

"I remember a day the royal longhouse keened and moored on the Wintersea. There, we harpooned whales, stored blubber, restocked our ice tunnels. I had cut deep into the ice, wielded axe and shovel—my fingers numb, despite the furred gloves. The stewards had requested oil and Nahas had driven the warriors hard: the cold exacerbated the pain in my hip. My leg not good, my body not right, I did not speak of my ordeal. Stalwart silence is expected of studiers. I had sharpened my spear—stone against metal—and had let it fly. I caught nothing, but I kept my heart merry because my mother was at my side. Ephan walked on the land bridge and into the Wintersea, Narena—his adopted mother—at his side. With their arrows, mother and adopted son had aimed. When they lifted their harpoons and struck, sea mammals bowed to their strength. Ephan is not easily deceived. He must have seen, felt, Narena's dislike; yet he lay trophies of the hunt at her feet. But I fumbled. Who would not fail with Hinis at his side? I will do better next time, I told myself. But the Peacock Clan's treachery prevented that. In our Permanent Home, therefore, if such a place exists, I will lay trophies at her feet. But not *here. My new mother, my mother Ktwala, it is no whale I seek to catch. I wish to catch your love. An even greater task—I wish to turn your heart to the king who has destroyed your people. If you will not leave this longhouse, then you must make bitterness outcast. One or the other must go. Who will be your people if you divorce our king? What will you do if all your sisters have married into the Wheel Clan? Forgive, Mother. It is the needful thing. For Nahas is not responsible for this war. I speak as one who has had his will oft broken. I speak as Nahas' son, one eternally dragged in his wake.'*

How strange this boy is, Ktwala thought and smiled that he knew her flutes had been broken. *And yet because of this strangeness he will keep my daughter safe.*

"You laugh and weep at the same time?" Tomo said, and Lian extended a bright red fruit toward her. "It's good to see a queen laugh."

Ktwala refused the fruit but Tomo took it and bit. She pointed to the baskets. "Eat all if you wish. I will have none of Wheel Clan food. As for this war, if you wish to know its origin, ask Bukko, a Macaw chieftain who worries for me and meets my longhouse often. You will meet him soon enough."

Tomo looked about the longhouse. "Do you love this husband of yours? What could you have done to offend him?" He lifted the apple, then tore some flesh from the boar's leg and put it in his mouth. Then he gave some to Lian who also ate. His mouth full, he looked past her, through the window where her eagle flew free. "And yet, to be like a caged animal, fed and tracked. Ah, me! What evil have you done? Can it be…did you perhaps take a lover? You're pregnant, aren't you? It's a small bump, but it's there. Was it your lover's child?"

"I did no evil, Tomo. And I warn you. Follow the steward's advice. You have lived long with the unmaking night. Therefore, stay here until you find a suitable longhouse or hut. Then leave. I would not taunt the Wheel Clan king. He murdered my son. He will not spare you."

He stared at her, silent.

That night, as they sat near the hearth he spoke gently to her. "I am a rough man. An outlaw. I am no king. But I've grown to like you, Ktwala. And I will be good to you." He took her hands in his. "Listen now. I know a little of keening and of crystals. I will free us from this Wheel Clan."

"No one can free himself from the Wheel Clan," Ktwala answered.

"Queen Ktwala," he said, speaking in his mish-mash of her language. "My mind is not filled with lofty thoughts. I do not concern myself with great matters or with things too high for me. But, this one thing I know.

I would not kill the son of my woman. I would not. No matter what she had done to me. And I would not send her alone into the world."

Ktwala rose. "Your words are foolish. Your love for me is foolish. Leave the longhouse. Do you believe the king—who did not spare my son—will spare you?"

Tomo did not leave. The days, corpses, pyres, and stewards rolled by. One morning the crash of broken crystals awoke Ktwala. It came from within the keening room. She entered the room and found Tomo raging, with crystals and branches at his feet.

"I am sick of all this death," he shouted. "And whatever I do, I can not override the keenskills of the Wheel Clan studiers. All the keening branches remain faithful to them." He took Ktwala's hands in his. "Queen Ktwala, let us build ourselves a cloaken of wood and leather and let us cast ourselves out into the night."

Ktwala did not answer him. She slung her sack over her shoulder and she and Lian went outside to gather salt, the eagle flying above her.

Tomo did not leave the longhouse and soon met more Wheel Clan stewards. He met Bukko as well, who also warned him to leave the longhouse. On a night they encountered Bukko, Ktwala dreamed again of a marketplace. Here again, one gave her eye salve. This time, however, she anointed her eyes. The ointment stung and her eyes watered.

* * * *

That morning when she woke, she was in a Wheel Clan burial field. Burning pyres surrounded her longhouse and the air was dense with the ash of the place. It was then her eyes were truly opened. She saw the clan of the Unfleshed Ones, walking among the tribes of Odunao, wreaking havoc and using the hearts and minds of man to advance evil.

As she looked on at the Unfleshed Ones, Tomo spoke to her, "Through the mist and smoke I saw another longhouse with a tower. I saw women walking near it. Can we not seek them out? It might be they will allow us to live with them."

"You, yourself, go. Seek refuge with them. Be safe. But I cannot leave this longhouse."

He frowned. "I will not leave you." He called to Lian. "Boy, one day you must leave your mother's skirts. Come a-hunting with me. Far from these pyres."

After the man and boy left, when the sun was highest in the sky, the Unfleshed Ones faded away. But women arrived at Ktwala's longhouse door. Their chief, a pale woman in buckskin dress and leggings. A tan shawl of woven hemp covered her head and neck. Her hair, white, yet not gray, she seemed a woman of some sixty years, still beautiful.

Sweet-voiced, she spoke to Ktwala. "I am Ezbel, Queen and Chief of this tribe."

When she heard she stood before a queen, Ktwala bowed low. "Long have I lived, meeting only the lowly and the poor. And now within three months, I have met royal ones. Truly, it is hard to feel safe in such powerful company. So, you are the Voca Queen? I am told I should fear you."

Ezbel stood beside Ktwala's fire pit and lifted her long scarf against the sun. "Women should not fear each other. So you are the wake-trapped mother of Nahas' child?"

"Wake-trapped?"

Ezbel tilted her head toward Ktwala's tower. "Yes, it is a wake. About fourteen days."

"A fourteen-day wake?"

"You follow the king's longhouse by fourteen days," Ezbel explained. "Each day you are where Nahas was fourteen days before. But it is not a strict keen. Some days, your tower is allowed to sail freely. Perhaps because the king does not want you to meet the wrong longhouses or to enter dangerous regions."

Ktwala looked about her. "So fourteen days ago the royal longhouse docked here?"

"Most likely. So you loved my Nahas? I loved him once. Who could not love the young Nahas?" The Voca Queen smiled to herself, as if at an old memory. "Who can not hate him now that he's older? He is, perhaps, not as cruel as his father, but he holds to his Father's beliefs." The queen looked in the direction where Tomo now hunted. "But tell me...the man I saw with you earlier, the tall one who climbed your tower, has Nahas sent him here to guard you? Or is he a foundling outcast?"

"Queen Ezbel"—Ktwala leaned against a boulder and held her belly—"Do not deceive me. Do not speak friendly to me here while elsewhere your warriors kill my friend."

"Your friend will not be harmed by me. Nahas will do that. And why should I kill one who protects you and your unborn child?" The Voca Queen approached the entrance of Ktwala's longhouse, looked inside. "A lovely tower song, they've given you. Wise gentle studiers. It's a time of war, yet they allow your tower some freedom. Who are they? Tell me their names, if you know."

Her womb cramping, Ktwala winced as she spoke. "A dark one, Psal, who limps. A pale one, pretty as any girl, Ephan."

Queen Ezbel directed Ktwala to the Iden longhouse steps. "Sit, Ktwala, and rest. So, he has not parted them? I met them when they were young. How timid and pitiful they looked in their black tunics. They were about to be sent off to the Wintersea master. They were not free, but I can free *you*, Ktwala."

"I follow my sisters."

"True, and they follow you."

Ktwala's eyes widened. A thought struck her. *Truly, my sisters do follow me.* "So, Nahas returns to some home regions often?"

"Some more often than others," Ezbel answered.

If my sisters have eyes to see, they will see signs of my own presence when they return again to these home fields.

Night came and the pale queen rose to leave. "Farewell, Ktwala. Who knows if we shall ever see each other again?"

But Ktwala remembered her words; as both longhouses prepared for the unmaking night Ktwala tore a swath from one of Maharai's dresses. This she tied to a tree near one of the pyres. After that, it became her habit—in whatever region she arrived—to tie cloth upon the trees, for she said, "It may be that Maharai and my Iden sisters will see it."

* * * *

Psal could not enter the gathering room without someone shooting some impatient look at him. He had his supporters, of course: several foundling women, the comfort women, some of the Iden women, Chief Antun, and Maharai. These stated that he was Firstborn and if he did not want to punish Tolika and if he wished to protect the foundlings, it was his prerogative. But their encouraging voices were small compared to the rebuke he received from the rest of the longhouse. Hurt, he garrisoned himself within his little corner of the longhouse. He attended no war council and spoke to Nahas only if the king spoke to him. He went from rampart to keening room to studier rooms to sick rooms to pharma rooms and ate his meals in the watchtower which became his stronghold, obsession, and haven. Neither his mind nor his body wandered far from it.

But one morning, as he and Daris studied his track notations and compared them to those from the previous night, he saw that none of the reports from his fellow studiers mentioned the Merad. *Mion is near where the Merad docks. He should know if Chief Merad's longhouse arrived at its destination.* He checked his charts again. Again, Psal asked his fellow studiers to re-do their morning work. This they did. All morning, he compared reports. The Merad was nowhere to be found.

Then Mion, studier now in the Hokkan longhouse, wrote: "The studier on the Maldon answered my query earlier, but now its tower's song grows faint. It has always been reclusive and sullen, but now I fear the Merad is lost and the Maldon is determined to follow its lost cohort into resolute isolation."

Psal answered, "Encrypt a message and relay it to all our studiers that the Merad is lost and we must prepare a rescue. I will notify the king."

"I will be honest with the Firstborn," Mion answered. "I do not want Chief Maldon or any from his sub-clan in our longhouse. I will suggest this to Chief Hokkan. I advise you not to clutter your longhouse with such refuse either."

"As always your suggestions are most wise," Psal responded and ended the encrypted tower communication.

Psal looked up from the note through the windows at the colored swaths hanging from bare tree limbs. They had begun to appear more and more as the longhouse returned to battle grounds, burial grounds, and to their home regions. They swayed like tree moss blown by a gentle wind. "Another day to bury our dead." He turned to Daris. "Remind the stewards to be more diligent in removing these cloths before our longhouse arrives."

"Like a fruit-gatherer collecting ripe fruit." Daris handed him two parchments he had been decoding. "I've decoded the latest news from Bukko and the stewards."

Psal took them, groaned. "Work well done. Be off then. Hopefully, Maharai and the others will not recognize the patterns. I must speak to Ephan and the king."

* * * *

He gathered the parchments and walked down to notify Ephan. As he left the keening room, Maharai called to him, pleading—as usual—to see her sisters.

"I have other matters to attend to," he said, pushing past her.

At his curt reply, her face fell.

He stopped, bowed to her. "Forgive me." A thought struck him just then. "Tell me, Maharai, how well do you write?"

"Old Jion taught me well."

"Tell me, then, what would you write to your mother if she stood before you now?"

"I would tell her not to fear, that we keep her in our hearts, that she should not leave the longhouse and become lost, that we will find her. But why should I write? She will not see it."

"I will send you parchment." He stood at the doorway of the larger sick room. "Write to your mother. Your people understand the smoke language, do they not?"

Her eyes lit up.

"Daris knows the smoke language and understands the way of the winds. When he is finished, I will store your message. You are a princess of our clan now. All princesses write annals. Can you do this for me?"

She hugged his neck, kissing him. He hasted into the sick room smiling in spite of himself.

In the sick room, Ephan was carefully winding a clean linen cloth about Broqh's broken and bloodied arm. Psal had heard of Broqh's fall the day before. Supposedly from a high rock. Psal had found the story suspect. *If Broqh's arm is broken,* he thought, *I'm sure Cyrt is the cause of it.* But he kept his opinion to himself.

"Ephan," he said, entering, "The Merad is lost. And now the Maldon, the longhouse of Merad's uncle, threatens to fail."

Ephan and Broqh stared at him in disbelief. "Lost?" Ephan asked. "Are you sure? Usually, we lose no more than one tower every forty years. Among the scattered clans, perhaps sixty or more are lost in that time period. And of those sixty, twenty or more could be repaired by a good studier." Ephan lifted Broqh's left arm, examined the bandaging. "The last time a Wheel Clan tower threatened to fail was twelve years ago."

"I remember," Broqh said, "I was there. But you were traveling with the Wintersea Master. I was still a child then. How the worried faces of the adults frightened me! I thought the world had come to an end. The gathering of the sub-clans, the dismantling and removal of beds, clothing, food, from the disabled longhouse. The grief when the tower faded into the night. All were saved. It was quite a feat. But, Firstborn, are you truly sure? Perhaps a Peacock Clan destroyed it."

"Last night, the Merad sang victory." Psal showed them the tracking charts. "But today, no one has heard it. Not a whisper, not a groan. A Wheel Clan longhouse now roams the world, hoping chance will bring it to another Wheel Clan longhouse or one of our home regions."

"Odunao is large," Broqh said, looking over Ephan's shoulder at the parchments. "Even now that tower lost in my childhood has not returned to any Wheel Clan region."

"True," Psal said, "and how shall they manage if their tower tosses them into a Peacock home region? And if their angry tower seeks the cold dark side of our planet, our women and children are unlike the denizens anchored in that place. How shall they survive?"

"So you think their tower wills to kill them?" Broqh glanced toward the royal keening room. "But yes, these towers are terrifying in their anger. How often I have found myself fearing them."

"No doubt our anger terrifies the towers as well," Ephan said.

"And yet," Broqh said, "the Merad was a cruel, vicious sub-clan. Ripping open the wombs of pregnant Peacock Clan women. Enslaving foundlings. If their tower rages against them, what can be done?"

"One can only hope it will show them mercy." Psal handed Ephan the genealogical chart.

Ephan quickly perused it. "Their longhouse holds five hundred fierce warriors. A great loss in a time of war. If their tower wanted to rebel against them, it should have waited until the war ended. And their kinsmen are dispersed throughout many Wheel Clan longhouses." He looked up from the charts to Psal. "Those longhouses will not willingly accept the loss."

"They have to accept it. There is no skill or lore to retrieve them. We can turn our efforts only to save the Maldon. It is not an operation to be safely done now during wartime."

"Do you suppose the Voca would help us?" Broqh asked. "They are skilled at detecting even the smallest tower whisper. They keen for lost towers, don't they? Perhaps they know where the Merad rests. They're our allies, ask them. They might help."

"Or they might not help." Ephan handed Broqh a gourd of Emon. "Now, Friend Mine, you're mended. Don't use the arm until I tell you!"

Psal hasted to the keening room and sent a message to the Voca Queen, requesting what help she could give. She returned this answer: We are your allies, not your mothers.

The answer received, Psal and Ephan brought all the news to Nahas.

* * * *

The king looked up from his war charts when Psal entered his chamber. "The madness continues." He indicated the cloth forest of gently wind-swaying ribbons.

"It does, Father." Psal edged closer to the king, then realized his body had begun its shameful shaking. "And more madness besides." He handed Nahas the parchments.

"Are you well, Firstborn?"

"I am well, Father."

"This trembling of yours has worsened. Take heed you do not tire yourself unduly. Find some pharma to cure it. Your continued illness unsettles our warriors."

Psal had forgotten he was shaking. Or, rather, he had become used to it and had forgotten how much his father had not.

"I'm sorry, Father."

The king looked at the messages written in Daris' handwriting first. "'Claims Ktwala and threatens to take her.'" Nahas repeated the words from Bukko's letter. "This Grassrope outcast has gotten bolder, although Bukko and my stewards warn him. Firstborn, I *said* to stop shaking. Can you not learn to hide your illness? Even our women are stronger than you." He leaned back in his chair. "I assume you're here to prevent me, once again, from killing this outcast?"

"Killing the Grassrope outcast would dishonor Ktwala and impugn her with adultery. Also, some might assume the king of the Wheel Clan was jealous, which—as you know—is considered a most loathsome crime among our people."

"Studiers, stewards, and warriors are to defend their king's honor, not judge him."

"Men will judge if given the opportunity, Father."

Nahas smiled a half-smile that looked strangely like Ephan's. "How subtle you are in your subversion, Firstborn."

"We studiers study to be both subtle and subversive, Father. Our lives depend on it."

The king almost chuckled.

Psal went on. "Moreover, possibly because of the Iden women, possibly because we pull the Iden tower in our wake, our tower has developed a protective affection toward those in the Iden longhouse. I cannot harm the Grassrope outcast without bringing trouble on myself. You know how willful and insolent this tower can be when riled. To do so might add to the epidemic of failing towers, Father. I would not wish to make our tower heartsick." Psal held his own shaking hand, pointed toward the other parchments. "But there are other matters this morning. Worse matters."

"You and Ephan have taught it this willfulness," the king said, turning to the other parchments. "It was not so easily riled when my father ruled."

"I doubt we could teach a thousand year old tower anything, Father."

Psal took a deep breath, spoke as his father studied the reports. "Father, none of this is as important to me as failing towers. But know that if you kill the outcast, the tower will know of it. If I whisper it in my bedchamber, a bird of the air will tell the matter. Ktwala would be alone and our tower might suddenly bring her here in our midst when you are not yet prepared to hide your guilt from her."

"The Merad is lost?" A worried frown lined the king's face. "Are you sure?"

"I am quite sure, Father. And the Maldon is failing. And the Voca will not help us."

"Curse those vindictive women! And what do my studiers suggest?"

"It would be useless to attempt to find the Merad, but the Maldon can be saved if we work quickly."

"There are only forty or so skirmishes today." Nahas paced. "I suppose it has to be done. And yet, I do not like this sub-clan."

"Neither does our tower like it."

"Yet they were faithful to my father and have been faithful to me. And, like them or not, a Wheel Clan longhouse cannot be lost. I will receive of its warriors no more than twenty. Warriors with wives and children. So small a number should not taint our warriors too much. Good work, Firstborn."

* * * *

Nahas sent word to all the studiers and chiefs saying, "Our kinsmen in the Merad are lost. It may be that at some unknown time, the day will bring them to one of our longhouses and they will be returned to us. Let those who believe in the Silent One pray for them. He alone can help them. We are able, however, to help the Maldon which even now threatens to fail. To all chiefs who are not preparing for battle or who have not battled in the two previous days, I send this request. If any longhouse is willing to accept Maldon refugees—I do not command this—keen yourself to the desert near the Great Mesa in the Ruined City, which is a neutral place and wide enough to contain all our longhouses. I will keen the Maldon to meet us."

The next morning, thirty-five longhouses keened to the desert. Several Voca longhouses were present as well, but they kept themselves apart, observing merely. The day was spent in dismantlings and separations. Some fifty warriors and their wives were added to the royal longhouse. But not their chief. Instead Psal took all the foundlings Maldon and his warriors had found and enslaved. One of them was a little honey-skinned girl about Maharai's age named Indina, whose body was bruised from whippings her mistress had given her.

Atop the rampart, the king spoke to the gathered Wheel Clan longhouses. "You Maldon warriors will not long be separated from your kinsmen," he promised. "If the studiers cannot help the Maldon reconcile with its tower, our stewards are well able to build you a new home."

But although the gathered studiers tried to coax the Maldon tower to life, it remained resolutely high-minded, suicidal. Accepting defeat, Nahas ordered the studiers to research abandoned, failed, and night-tossed towers. In the royal keening room they sat, listening to towers in the nearby region.

"At the beginning of the war, fourteen failed towers rested in this region." Mion looked about at the studiers' circle. "And now, thirty-three. Is my count correct?"

The studiers answered. "It is correct."

And Ephan added, "Fearfully correct."

Thus while the warriors wept for Chief Merad and their lost kinsmen, and the Maldon longhouse fell away into the night, the studiers in the royal keening room bewailed lost towers, and the world's future.

"Firstborn-Studier," Mion said, "we will do all that is necessary. We are ready to obey you, even if the king considers it mutiny. There are many stewards who will obey you as well. But the war must end. Or the towers will fail and the Wheel Clan will be no more. And then, Firstborn-Studier and King's Favorite, who knows when we will meet each other again?"

* * * *

One morning, blinding light and the scent of snow. Ktwala woke, her arms and feet cold, her fingers and toes numb. Lian was not at her side. She peered through the windows. Outside, snow covered tall evergreens, frozen tundra, and distant boulders. On the field, in the air, white snow prevailed. If the day followed the pattern of other days, a longhouse would be nearby. *But I will not take the Wheel Clan food.* Across the knee-high snow, deer ran. Underneath a frozen lake, fish could be found. She would dig. Tomo would hunt. Tiny footsteps raced to her door. Lian soon stood in her entrance, snow on his shoulders, shivering, shaking and wrapped in a blanket.

"We're in the cold climes," she said. Cold white mist came from her mouth.

Tomo appeared next, snowflakes on his head, a blanket across his shoulders. Both now wearing fur-lined boots. "The stewards should've brought food," he said.

"Why accustom ourselves to their poison?" Ktwala answered.

Tomo said, "If food is given, take it. What do you think, Queen Ktwala? Is your husband warring in the cold climes now? Or did his warriors travel here to catch fish and hunt whale fat?" His fingers traced the broken shutters of the windows. "Cold steals in." He gave her the spyglass. "And yet?"

Ktwala blew on her hands. "And yet?"

"This morning I climbed the tower. I saw no longhouse. Nor for leagues around."

"You saw nothing at all?" Ktwala shrugged. "They have horses. The longhouse might be far away. A steward will ride toward us bringing food. But should an outlaw accustom himself to Wheel Clan bounty?"

Shame flickered on Tomo's face. He left the room, returned with blankets and a spear. "When a man's hungry, he eats. Come, boy!"

Ktwala followed behind them, but they pushed her back.

"What if you fall on the ice?" Tomo asked. "You will lose Nahas' child."

"The child belongs to me, not Nahas."

"Whosoever child it be, I have no studier skills to save an infant born too early. So, sit down and wait for us men to return."

Lian, too, gave her a rebuking frown. She returned to her bed and looked about the empty room.

There was much to do. Blankets and animal skin had to hang in front of windows and over leaky walls. With whalebone needle and spun hemp, she could work and forget her lost children.

That night, Tomo piled blankets upon her and on Lian who lay beside her. "Tomorrow, we will be free from this place," he said, then left her to warm sleep.

That night she dreamed of the Wheel Clan king.

In the dream, the sun had reached its height, and Ktwala stood on her rampart, the spyglass in her hand, as she had done on the day she met Nahas. Jion was at her side. Again, she watched some fifty or more Wheel Clan warriors approach her longhouse with Nahas leading the procession, the Macaw feather markings on his cloak. Again, she noticed that he walked as one who walked as if all times and climes belonged to him. Again she heard herself ask Jion, "Is that their leader?"

But this time, her gaze was fixed on the studiers in their black tunics and leggings. The limping one. The pale one plagued by the Wheel Clan's great evil. In the dream, she studied the boys, loved them as her own son, Ouis. Then she ran downstairs and scrubbed clay from her face—and yet it was not clay but blood, and the water fell from her face like blood rivulets. She saw again the hospitality dance, gifts of fruit and grain and the Peacock warriors atop horses, their reptiles and lions bound by leather ropes. But this time, her brothers themselves were bound.

She saw the honey-colored studier speak again, but now the boy had taken on the appearance of her own dead son:

"I am Psal, Chief Studier and Firstborn son of Nahas. And this: Netophah, his son, Heir of all Wheel Clan lands. And this: Ephan, Studier and Adopted Son of King Nahas. And this: Nahas, Chief of the Nahas longhouse, King of all the Peoples of the Wheel, Your husband, the murderer of all your people."

She remembered how he touched her on the hillside, how a sudden love had risen up between them. And when she woke in the morning, she could feel his kisses on her lips. Her heart struggled against itself: why did it still love the Wheel Clan king?

CHAPTER 19

THE COUNCIL

For several days after the loss of the Merad, the mood was heavy in the royal longhouse. Several steward longhouses were loosed from their moorings to search for the missing Merad but had not found them, and all efforts of rescue were put aside. A Wheel Clan longhouse was lost, and another divided. Separated kinsmen would not meet again unless some fate brought them together. The king called the royal studiers to council in the keening room.

"They are a hardy people," Gaal squeezed the king's shoulder. "Be comforted, Nahas. They will do well, wherever the night brings them."

"And yet," Nahas answered, "to be cast adrift, to lose brothers, fathers, sons because of a spiteful tower."

"The tower kept to its principles," Ephan said. "Or rather, it kept the Creator's Principles. I do not think it was spiteful."

"You saved the Maldon, Nahas." Gaal rose from the table. "You and your studiers. Do not be so cast down."

"A well-coordinated masterful effort," Lebo added.

"It is a rare occurrence, Nahas," Cyrt said. "Never to happen again in our lifetime."

"Not true. Such incidents will happen more and more." Psal directed their attention to the parchments on the table. "The number of failed towers have risen drastically in the past two years. Most of them were already abandoned or insolent, true, but some of them were quite healthy."

"'Happen again,'" Daris echoed. He was sitting on Psal's left as scribe for the council, and nibbling roasted honeycomb crumbs from the platter of dainties Satima had prepared.

"You studiers like dreaming of doomsday," Seagen said. "My father was obsessed with it, continually speaking of the day all towers would fail. It was foolishness! Born of age, his disease, and too much Tomah. The Merad tower failed because Chief Merad murdered the unborn in their mothers' wombs and because he offended the Lesser Light by his extreme brutality to his studier. The same crimes the Maldon seems to have committed. And the tower grieved for its brother. Was that not the consensus of you studiers?"

"The Maldon tower would accept no one else to rule it," Psal said. "No one from the Maldon longhouse. No studier or studier-apprentice from any other longhouse. No woman, no child. It rebelled completely.

This anger, this rage, is growing. Why this suicide covenant between the towers? Why the epidemic of failing towers? And this infection of anger?"

"Many towers have failed through disrepair," Ephan added. "Others pine away because their caretakers were lost or slain. But most have simply lost their will to believe in humanity. Towers are not merely fickle mistresses and studiers their confused lovers. Towers are the heart of the planet and at present all our towers are heartsick because of the war. A studier is the conscience, the Lesser Light of his longhouse. If a studier's conscience is seared and he willingly does evil, or if his longhouse forces him to sin against his conscience, the tower will lose all hope."

"And this war," Psal said. "Even neutral towers are rebelling against the continual fighting. It was understandable that a tower whose original inhabitants were killed might will itself to die, especially if it has remained empty long. But towers belonging to farmhouses and stewards are failing as well, sickening even when they haven't been attacked. Even Falconer, Macaw, Grassrope, and Waymaker towers—neutral towers all—have caught the epidemic."

"They're as sick of the war as I am," Ephan said. "The Merad is only the beginning of the end."

Orian leaned back on his chair. "From of old, our ancestors have spoken of this day of wrath, and as yet, the world has not rebelled against us humans. Young one, keep your head out of prophetic lore and learn to hope. The towers and the world are not angry with us."

"Orian speaks true," Cyrt said. "These doomsday threats and preparations against the end of the world are as old as the world itself."

"Old they may be," Antun said, "but ancient truths aren't necessarily false."

"Stranger"—Cyrt turned to face Antun—"Do you challenge me?"

"I do not challenge," Antun replied. "And I am no stranger. The same blood that runs in your body, in the body of all our people, and in the Firstborn, runs in mine."

"Your father claimed this same blood when he warred against his king," Cyrt retorted.

"I am not my father," Antun answered. "I say only…let the Firstborn speak. He is correct. We have become vicious. No wonder the towers—"

Cyrt laughed. "And you say you are not like Qerys? You speak very much as he did."

His voice was drowned out by the Iden women who had begun their daily victory chants.

We will trample you, Wheel Clan.
Our brothers build home fires in their permanent home

But their spirits burn within us.
Their flame will destroy your tower.
If you roll into our campsite,
You will find yourselves engulfed in flames.

Orian shouted toward the passageway. "Tell those women to be quiet. Their whining grates on my mind."

"'Whining,'" Daris echoed, spelling out the word as he wrote.

Antun rose from his seat. "Nahas, I honor you even if you do not honor me."

Nahas nodded but said nothing.

Antun continued, turning to Psal. "Firstborn, what do you expect us to do about failing towers? How can they be repaired?"

"A true 'failed' tower cannot be repaired," Psal answered. "They are forever lost. One can only coax a reluctant tower into life so many times."

"The towers want to help each other," Ephan said. "They dislike warring against each other. They would rather die than continue living in disharmony. Some, like Orian's tower, have become anti-social. They revive themselves occasionally but suddenly set themselves to fail when stewards begin building longhouses around them."

Orian sputtered. "Are you saying my tower—"

"We need to track all our towers more closely," Ephan said. "We need to track all of Odunao's towers. To examine the epidemic. To see what towers should be quarantined. To watch for our own recalcitrant towers."

"Our studiers are busy," Nahas said. He squeezed his forehead. "But yes, the work is necessary."

"It would not be too difficult to track them," Ephan said. "The studiers throughout our clan would send their information to Storm as they do every night. Except they would track all towers they heard in their regions, not only the Peacock and Wheel Clan towers. And someone here—anyone with a little knowledge of tower science could learn to do it—would gather and interpret all the—"

Nahas looked at Seagen. "Seagen? Are you—"

"I am no real studier," Seagen quickly put in.

Psal immediately agreed. "Let it be Lan."

"Lan it will be."

"On the twenty-first day of the six month," Daris spoke, writing, "Lan becomes studier to track night-tossed towers."

Nahas rose from the table. "In the meantime, let us remind these wayward towers that the war will soon be over. Are you satisfied with that, Firstborn?"

"I am *somewhat* satisfied, Father."

"Somewhat?" Gaal asked, lifting a pitcher of wine from the table. "What else would you desire?"

"That the war might end," Psal answered. "That instead of battling Poh in fifteen days, we would meet with Tsbosso and seek out a way to heal the towers."

"The sixth month is the time of the twins, is it not?" Cyrt said. "When our sun lingers listlessly over our deserts, because of the death of one of his twin sons. Was that not the name the Peacock Clans gave to you and Poh? 'The twins?' Because you played so often together?"

Yes, Tsbosso's household called us that, Psal thought. *I had forgotten the name. Yet Cyrt remembers it?* "I do not remember the name," he answered Cyrt. "I only remember the myth, that the sun was so grieved at the death of one of the twins that he buried him on one side of our planet."

"Oh, I know this myth," Daris said. "The myth of the suffering son and the triumphant son. Both were ill at birth but only one lived. The sun grieved twice as long for his dead son. Two months. Twenty-five days for his own grief, and twenty-five for the grief of his surviving son. But on the fiftieth day, the day of jubilee, he stopped grieving. He never returned to the place where he buried his son. And this is why our sun never goes to the dark cold side of our planet."

"They teach you well," Cyrt said. "You will make a good studier yet. But tell me, Firstborn, will you spend the month grieving for this 'brother' of yours?"

"The Firstborn is well able to put aside old friendships." Netophah rose from the table and walked to the shelf, which contained the basket of mice. "Have you seen Ephan's toys, Father? He contends that he has not perfected them." Netophah pointed at Ephan. "See there, he blushes. But let him explain the workings of his mice."

As Ephan concluded, Gaal said, "Nahas, I wonder if our stewards could combine the red fire mouse and the green mouse?"

"Why should we combine them?" Ephan gathered his mice to the basket as if they were living pets.

"The fire mice could burn down our enemies' longhouses, of course," Gaal said. "One would have to make the timing mechanism better but—"

"I'm not skilled enough," Ephan said, firmly.

"Of course you are skilled, Ephan," Nahas said. "Your ingenuity always amazes me."

That night as Psal lay in bed, he chided Ephan for suggesting that another studier be brought into the keening room to track the failing towers. "Why did you not think before you spoke?" he asked. "What if

Seagen had accepted Father's command? Nahas would discover we have rescued the Peacock women?"

"I *do* wish you would stop rescuing them." Ephan unlaced his tunic. "Lan is quite angry about that."

"True, but he has not betrayed me to Nahas."

"If you continue rescuing them, Lan will be considered complicit." Ephan's gaze was on a shelf where the basket of wooden mice and Maharai's latest parchments to her mother lay.

"Father praised your work today," Psal said. "Did you see his face? He could not have been prouder if you had been his very own son."

Ephan blushed. He picked up the basket of mice and stood looking at his mice for a long time. "I saw. I suspect they were a pleasant diversion. Less worrisome than failing towers." He walked to the window and opened it. "And yet...."

"To bed. How badly our days are spent! Dovi and poultices! Instruments of murder and healing. Being caught between warring chiefs, mealy-mouthed stewards, and angry towers!"

Ephan smiled. Then, one by one, he removed each mouse from the basket and smashed them across the window sill. Then, he threw them into the night.

"A strange thing to do?" Psal said as Ephan returned the empty basket to its shelf.

"My mice were not made for murder."

"Why didn't you tell Father that?"

"He would not have listened, and unlike you, I see no reason to be unduly honest." Ephan removed his tunic and lay on his sleeping mat. Then, "Warn Antun not to challenge Cyrt. It's dangerous."

"Cyrt wouldn't kill a chief," Psal answered.

Ephan laughed. He laughed so loudly and so long that Psal grew ashamed of himself.

"Am I so ignorant?" Psal asked. "Don't make me feel stupid. Why would Cyrt kill Antun? I know Cyrt still remembers how Qerys challenged my grandfather. But even so—"

"Because Nahas will allow Cyrt to kill him," Ephan said, matter-of-factly.

"True. He would allow it. And yet...that Cyrt and Father should still hate Qerys although Qerys is dead. Yet, I cannot hate Poh, my living enemy."

"You lack a warrior's heart."

Psal rose from his bed and entered the gathering room where the Maldon refugees sat drinking with some of Orian's warriors. Antun stood near a window.

"Antun," he said, "I have often heard your footsteps roaming the longhouse while others sleep."

"This upcoming battle oppresses my mind," Antun said. "My blood boils to think we will battle the son of treacherous one who started all this bloodshed."

"Yet you also roam the longhouse on nights when no battles are to be fought."

Antun looked through the window. "At nights, my mind roams and I think always of my dear wife, Ndai, and of Elon, the other warrior in my eimi. Ndai and our daughters were killed in the Peacock Treachery. Elon died of self-slaughter after that. He was a gentle soul, unable to bear much grief. Our son, born damaged, was sent to live among the stewards, but died there of his illness. Only I and my sister's son are left."

"Truly," Psal said, "I am sorry to hear this."

"It is well, Firstborn. They are in a better place. I look forward to the day I also put off this physical cloaken and join them in our Permanent Home. But, I have a question to put to you."

Near the hearth, one of the Maldon refugees was bullying little Indina; Psal raised his hand. "You there! Have I not commanded you to desist? She no longer belongs to you. If you want ale, get it yourself! And…if you hit her once more, you, your wife, and your little ones will be thrown out! That is a Firstborn's promise!" He turned to Antun, shook his head. "The cruelty of these Maldon refugees! I cannot bear it."

Antun nodded. "I have seen. A ruthless bunch."

"You said you had a question. Ask it."

"Yes. Firstborn, Renan thought you were placed on this world for some divine reason by the Ever-Present One. Do you believe that, Firstborn?"

"I remember his ramblings. A strange thing to think, that my life should mean something?"

"Yet it does mean something, Firstborn. For, already, you are of great importance to—and loved by—many."

"To some, perhaps, but not to many."

"Firstborn, Studier-Firstborn, consider how the stewards and studiers love you. They see you as one of their own. Indeed, consider your friends. Lan, the son of a studier. Broqh, the son of a Falconer chieftain. Deyn, the son of a comfort woman. Kwin, the son of a steward. I heard he would have been reared as a steward because his father was not a Wheel Clan warrior, but his father was of great renown, and Nahas relented."

Psal laughed. "So you have been studying my friends? I am honored. And yes, they are an odd assortment." He lowered his voice. "Study my enemies also, for they are your enemies as well. Take heed, especially of Cryt."

"I will, Firstborn."

"But Renan's words were wrong. There is no reason for my existence…except perhaps to make the king's life miserable."

"Ah yes!" Antun said, laughing, "That you do quite well."

* * * *

Ktwala awoke, her toes numb with cold. She looked out. *Are we still in the cold climes?*

The day after that, and the next. No pyres or corpses came, no trace of congealed blood browning to black. Only the empty whiteness of snow: Her heart almost broke. *Perhaps Nahas has freed me.*

On the ninth day of wind and cold, Tomo taunted. "Has this great king anchored his wife to the cold climes? You do not understand men, do you? Can you not see that because the Wheel Clan king cannot win you, he has taken your daughter as his wife?"

Her feet touched the cold longhouse floor. "Nahas would not do it."

"So you know this king? This king who killed your son? Woman, listen to me. You are not so lovely. You are an old woman and your daughter is like you, only younger. Why should he not take her instead?"

"Speak of other matters."

"Queen Ktwala. The king's stewards have not brought food for many days. Nor have we seen corpses."

"Do not call me 'Queen.'"

He spat on the ground. "Your heart still loves the Wheel Clan king. It cannot see his cruelty. I am a man. I know and understand these things."

"It could be his tower is destroyed," Ktwala said. "A destroyed tower cannot control anyone's life."

"The tower of the Wheel Clan king cannot be destroyed." Anger made his face red. "No power outside of the Wheel Clan can destroy the Wheel Clan. Ktwala, can it be—poor as I am—that I have made the king jealous?" He strutted past her bed to the window. "Wheel Clan men don't want their women touched. Maybe, because of me, he's rid himself of you."

She could not help but laugh, even in her fear. "Nahas does not believe I've allowed you to touch me."

"And how do you know this?" Tomo thrust his face toward hers, his chin jutting toward her nose. "Has he sent you news of his love? Is that what those parchments speak of? His love?"

"He sent me news through my dreams." She pushed Tomo aside and walked to her doorway.

"Then you must tell him in dreams that you no longer love him. Do you hear me? Tell him he has destroyed your clan."

The next day, again the cold clime. And the day after. No longhouse, no sign from the Wheel Clan.

Freedom from the Wheel Clan and my daughter lost to me? No, no, it cannot be! Freedom, yet her heart grieved.

Their granary was full; for oil, they had seal fat. And Tomo was a good hunter. As they ate of fish, of winter rodents newly caught, he said, "When you say the Wheel Clan king has not forgotten you, you speak like one imprisoned by love." Tomo's taunting words were like fiery darts.

I do not love Nahas. It is not sane or natural that I love him. What has usurped my heart? Outside, the winds blew hard. The slats and cracks of the Iden-Grassrope longhouse were covered in fur, skin, and blankets. Nevertheless, Ktwala shivered. Not from cold but fear. *Has Nahas separated my daughter from me?*

Tomo wiped his mouth, looked about the longhouse. "Why does your heart insist on living with the dead and forgotten ones? We will build our own people." He pushed his platter toward Lian. "I will raise Lian and this unborn child as my own. I will teach them how to be a true outlaw, far from the rules of men and clans. Think of new things."

Ouis, dead; Maharai, stolen. My people slaughtered. Yet my heart holds to this evil king. Is my heart not mine? Can the heart love in spite of itself? "My children will not learn to attack and rob innocent clans," Ktwala said.

"My mother loved the wild life." He rose and looked through the window. "Loved her outlaw man as well. Yet, she was a good woman. A good woman. She told me many things, told me of the Creator's Principles. Once she told me why animals were not night-tossed. Because they had not rebelled against the Creator. She told me that one day an Outcast would come. He would belong to all clans and to no clan. He will bring a new day and bring us into our Permanent Home. Yes, a good woman brought me into this world and she taught me well."

Ktwala smiled. "I know the Savior will come. He will revive our spirit on the great fiftieth day. Then the world will be as it should be. It was good your mother taught you. And yet…" She turned to face him. "She should not have taught you to rob innocents."

Tomo pulled Lian by the arm. "Boy, go to your bed. Your own bed. As a child I did not flee to my mother's bed when the cold wind blew."

Lian nodded, took off running to his room.

"Ktwala, accept the truth. You're no longer a king's wife. Let us lie together to keep warm. We're man and woman. Strangers. We will not be sinning against the incest taboo. I am unable to stop thinking of you. At first, I feared touching a woman the King of the Wheel Clan loved." He scratched his unkempt black hair, walked toward her and placed his calloused hand on her right breast. "But now that he has forgotten you, why deny ourselves?"

She threw her food to the floor. "If by eating your food, I am your woman, then I will not eat it."

"Another man might have raped you," he said, adding weakly. "I have thought so…that other men might have done that. But I have not."

"I am glad rape has not entered your heart," she said, then went to her room.

That night, as she slept she sensed one entering her chamber. Now, whether awake or asleep—she did not know and the annals do not say— she saw a shining one, beautiful to look upon and full of light standing beside her bed.

"Ktwala," he said, and his voice was both regal and comforting, "Arise."

"Is it you?" she asked.

"I am he. The Ever-Present One."

Ktwala did not immediately speak. It is not everyday one meets the Creator.

"What am I and who is your handmaid that you should visit her?" she asked him.

"I have seen your tears," he said. "I have seen your suffering. And now, hear me, imprisoned wife of Nahas, seek your own freedom. I will protect you." He beckoned to her to rise and she rose from her bed, following. "Throughout Odunao—in longhouses and huts—humans stand my their windows, waiting, waiting. How enslaved you humans are! But I have seen your sorrows and I have come to you with heavy tidings. Your daughter is given away, married to the son of the Wheel Clan king, the prince who slew her brother. She has turned her heart from her people. Therefore, O Ktwala, turn your own eyes away from her. Cast yourself from this longhouse. In that wide world and large, I will care for you."

Then, it seemed two hands covered her eyes. Darkness fell. A light pressure, as if those covering hands rubbed eye salve on her eyes. Then the hands faded and again she could see Samat. She seemed to see inside him, to see past the golden mantle he wore and the glittering white tunic. Her skin crawled.

What did she see? She did not say. But in her annals, she wrote,

> *I thought: So, this is Samat?*
> *Truly?*
> *Is this he that terrified the nations*

And broke the hopes and heart of humanity?
This worm?
This small, small, deceitful thing?

As she finished speaking, the imposter disappeared. She lay in bed, contemplated on all she had seen, sensed, and heard. *Why does Samat wish to free me from Nahas? Why, why, should my life—and this cruel marriage—be important to that Great Deceiving One?*

The next morning as she ate with her new clan, Tomo told her all his heart, how he would care for her and protect her, how he had had many women but Ktwala had made a permanent home for his heart, and how he wanted to live inside her heart but she would not allow it. He spoke so lovingly that even Lian frowned at her.

"I do not wish to be your woman," she told him. "I am wearied with the rule of men."

"Then you will rule this longhouse," Tomo answered. "I will allow you to."

"'Allow me to?'" Ktwala laughed.

"Why laugh?" he asked. "I will be kind to you. I can be kind to a woman. Don't you believe me?"

"Even kind men destroy women's lives," she said. "Especially kind men. For women see their hearts and cannot leave them. A hateful man we would quickly be rid of."

He thrust his face toward hers. "So Nahas is kind?"

She nodded. "Nahas the man is kind. But on the day he murdered my son he was not merely a man. He was King of the Wheel Clan."

After Lian and Tomo left to hunt, Ktwala walked outside into the cold. With spear in hand, she dug beneath the ice for fish, beneath the marshy frozen sand for frozen insects.

But then a wind, cold and cruel, like the slap of an icy hand across her face. The force of it! She crashed to the ground. Another wind, this one greater, with cruel purpose, lifted her. Aloft in the air, her body hung like fruit on an invisible branch. She heard quickly, though no voice spoke, "Yes, I am Samat and you know my will. Do you intend to obey it?"

"Whatever the end, whatever the result, I will never bend to Samat's will," she answered.

She waited, hanging on nothing in the air. In an instant, she felt herself being thrown through the falling hail. Just in time, she clutched her belly, turned in falling. She fell on sand locked in ice. Aching, her back bruised, she could not move but, lying on the ground, watched the gray of the cold climes grow grayer until Tomo and Lian returned.

Tomo chided her, spoke harshly. "So you have fallen on the ice? You who walk in pain even in the longhouse—why walk the ice while pregnant?"

He carried her to the longhouse on his back.

Each day when she attempted to walk—whether through ice-sheathed grassland or ice-slick sandy desert—Samat battled against her. At last Tomo and the boy forced her to remain indoors.

"I am no fool," Tomo said. "We have arrived in Samat's icy world. Remain indoors until the child is born. It is the child he wishes to kill, is it not?"

Now all my freedom is taken away. Not only by the Wheel Clan king, the Grassrope outcast, and the child within her who filled her days and nights with sickness and pain, but by Samat's anger.

A day came when a naked Peacock warrior, battered and bleeding, arrived at Ktwala's longhouse. With cupped hands, he begged for food. She fed him, tended his wounds, covered him with furs and boots. When Tomo returned, he pushed the broken man out into the night. For many days Ktwala would not speak.

One day, the night brought the longhouse to cold salt beaches. Repentant, Tomo allowed Ktwala to walk outside although her salt barrels already overflowed. As she walked, she found the pitiful bodies of night-tossed people who had died in the cold. *I do not like my clan,* she said to herself. *And I do not like the Wheel Clan. But these two are close to my heart: The Creator and the wounded among men. Such is the life of those who have no longhouse to protect them.* Ktwala scooped up salt with frozen hands and returned home, her legs and belly aching, the container heavy on her back. All those days in the cold clime she grieved for the lost old times, for the days before Nahas had pulled her into his wake, when Samat had not made her his target.

CHAPTER 20

THE WARRIOR'S PRIZE

The morning came when the Wheel Clan battled Poh and Psal stood on the rampart. As he awaited the signal for the battle to begin, the strong odor of Emon wafted up the stairs. Supposing a wounded warrior was climbing the tower stairs to join the upcoming battle, he turned to chide. But the climber was Netophah, carrying a bow and three arrows.

Psal limped toward his brother. "Has Nahas called for me?"

"No, but I wished to speak to you."

"Do you need more Dovi for your weapons?" He began walking toward the stairwell. "It's in the usual place, but yes, yes, perhaps…more should be mixed." Then he noticed the bow Netophah held bore his own markings. He had hidden Broqh's bow to prevent his friend from shooting even one arrow until the arm was healed. "Look now, Netophah," he said. "Return my bow to its place. I admire Broqh's valor, but you should not encourage him." He called down the tower, waited for Broqh—as he supposed—to climb up. "Broqh! If you shoot even one arrow before your arm heals, it will be I who breaks the other and not Cyrt."

Footsteps hurried up the stairs and Psal prepared an angry medical tirade against his friend. But it was Lan who stood before him.

"Lan?" Psal asked. "Why stand here? Has Seagen not commanded you to watch from the western cliffs?"

Lan spoke to Netophah. "Haste, before the battle begins and Nahas calls you."

"Hold this!" Netophah thrust an Emon-smeared arrow, slippery and pungent, into Psal's hand. Then he reached for the arrow to take it back again.

But Psal held it firm. "I will not."

Lan wrenched the arrow from Psal's hand and gave it to Netophah, who set it in place on the bow.

Netophah walked to the edge of the rampart and lifted the bow. "The last time we battled Poh, he clothed himself like a common warrior. But you, Ephan and I know his face well, above all the others."

"Yes, the unhappy lot of princes and studiers is to be acquainted with princes and—"

Netophah sent the arrow flying before Psal finished speaking. The arrow sped toward a small group of warriors. Among them, Poh. Tsbosso's son fell backward; three Peacock Warriors rushed to shield their fallen leader.

"Listen," Netophah said.

Below, in the gathering room and outside, in front of their enemy's longhouse, confusion. Who had shot the arrow before the beginning battle signal? But for Psal, no words. Only eyes burning with tears for his childhood friend.

"What a woman you are!" Lan said. "Crying for your friend? Must you weep so easily?"

"They are tears of victory." Netophah smeared the bow from tip to shaft with Emon.

They decidedly were not tears of victory. Psal watched in conflicted grief as Netophah lay the bow on the rampart and Lan placed an Emon-smeared arrow beside it, then dropped another such arrow over the rampart wall. Then Lan produced a cloth smelling of boiled hyssop and thyme and wiped his own and Netophah's hands.

Netophah shook Psal by the shoulder. "Don't stand there looking amazed and astonished. Downstairs, our brothers are asking who was wounded and who shot the arrow." He turned toward the stairs. "It was you who laid Poh low. Do you understand? Not I, not Ephan, not Lan, not Broqh, but you."

Psal grasped Netophah's arm. "No one will believe I would shoot in secret before the—"

Netophah pushed Psal's arm away. "They will believe what they are meant to believe. Brother, your anger at Father, your mercy toward Tolika, your dishonoring of Cyrt, your friendship with Tsbosso…all will be washed away with this victory."

"Hurry!" Lan urged. "Firstborn, I recommend you not stand there like a fool and making yourself a target."

Netophah hurried down the stairs as Psal stared over the rampart at Poh's body, slumped against the wall of the Peacock longhouse.

The Peacock Clan fought valiantly, but Poh's death crushed their spirit. The battle raged on the hillside and in the caves and rivers. When night fell, the routed Peacock warriors fled to their longhouse. The dead Peacock warriors littering the ground and the scarcity of Peacock Clan fire arrows made it evident that Poh's longhouse was near annihilation. The cry of "Torches! Torches!" echoed through the region and both clans lit their fire arrows. One after another, the burning arrows flew, but more arrows flew from the Wheel Clan longhouse than from Poh's. Blazes caught here, there. When night took both longhouses, the remaining dwellers of the Peacock longhouse could be seen attempting to douse their blazing longhouse with buckets of water.

"A great victory!" Lebo said when all had gathered inside after third moon rose. "And the chief's son dead! Success indeed!"

"True, Lebo. When Poh died, they lost heart." Netophah lifted a cup of the celebratory mead. "Speak now, who slew Tsbosso's son? You shall not lose your reward."

"Not I." Gaal unlaced his leather armor. "But I will take the glory if no one else will."

"I, as well." Antun's eyes searched among the fatigued warriors. "Who did the deed?"

All eyes looked about but no warrior claimed the victory.

"Who stood on the rampart?" Nahas asked. "Even before the fray began and all the doors were opened, the killing arrow came from the rampart."

"Speak up!" Netophah looked around. "Who killed Tsbosso's son?"

Nahas turned to Broqh who stood near the residential passageway, Liorin's arm about his waist. "My boy, was it you? But no, you do not know Poh. And your arm is still—" He looked at Ephan who was binding the leg of one of Orian's warriors. "Ephan, my lad, was it you? You shoot well."

Ephan looked up. "At reptiles and big cats, Nahas, but I have a studier's vow."

"A holy vow," Daris said to the king. "Remember, we studiers do not kill."

"Seagen," Nahas said, "fetch me the bows in the archery. All others, bring your weapons before me. A strange thing that one of our Valiant Ones should shy away from honor."

"The Wheel Clan has no such humility," Daris said, laughing, "but let the king honor the bow if he cannot honor the archer."

Nahas laughed as did all the others. "These two will turn you into a true studier yet."

"Perhaps the Valiant One left his bow on the rampart?" Cyrt ran toward the keening room, overtaking Seagen who was walking to the armory.

"None but Psal stood on the rampart, Nahas," Kwin said.

And Orian added, "I doubt he could kill anyone. Certainly not his friend."

Just then, Cyrt descended the rampart with Psal's bow. "The First-born's bow. It smells of Emon." He wiped his hand on his tunic.

The king took the bow and sniffed it. "Indeed, it is. The scent of damaged ones and wounded warriors. And, Broqh, you are sure you did not shoot with the Firstborn's bow?"

Broqh nodded.

Nahas walked to Psal. "Isn't this your bow? Did you shoot the arrow, Firstborn?"

Netophah took the bow and turned it over in his hand. "True, it bears the engravings of the Firstborn, Father."

"My boy, have you done this?" Nahas asked Psal. "Was it truly you?"

Netophah shouted in amazement. "It cannot be, Father! And yet, it seems so."

"Claim your glory, Firstborn!" the king shouted. "Today, you learned to kill a childhood friend. I am honored to have such a son."

"You killed?" Daris asked, looking up at Psal in disbelief.

"I would not think it possible," Gaal offered the Firstborn a glass of fermented honey. "Perhaps the Firstborn has outgrown his youthful madness. Honor the Firstborn, my brothers."

Lifted high on the shoulders of his Wheel Clan brothers, Psal knew himself to be a charlatan. Nor did he imbibe the celebratory drink to enforce the lie.

"You'll be a true chief yet," Lebo said, slapping him on the back.

Psal begged leave to be lowered from their shoulders. "I must attend to the wounded and track towers. I am still a studier with much work to do."

They cheered him as he left and he hastened away to the studier's room where he immediately vomited on the floor. There, he called for Daris and a bucket.

Ephan entered, smelling of Dovi, Rangi, and Emon. He side-stepped the vomit on the floor and said to Psal. "Vomiting is a small price to pay for a lie."

"True," Daris said.

"You know of the deception as well?" Psal asked Daris.

"Lan would not exclude us studiers from the scheme," Daris answered.

"All that talk in the gathering room? It was all pretense?"

Daris grinned. "I pretend well, I think."

"Who else knew of this conspiracy?" Psal asked Ephan, hating the acrid taste in his mouth.

"All who love you," Ephan answered. "Netophah, Lan, Broqh, Kwin, Deyn, Daris, Antun, me. You have many allies in the king's longhouse."

Psal sat down to forget his false victory and to listen to the tower of his retreating enemy. It was then he heard something in the Peacock Clan tower, something he rarely heard. *The Peacock studier—perhaps he's young...perhaps he is panicked. Grieving perhaps—Why has he set course for a Peacock home region where Poh's longhouse will have no ally to help defend it?* Psal sighed. *Fellow studier, it is a bad move.* Psal studied the charts carefully to see if other Peacock towers were keening to there or were anchored there. He found none. *Shall I set to shadow keen?*

The co-ordinances of Nahas' tower were already set and the keening had begun. To change destination once keening had begun in order to pursue or deceive another longhouse was called a shadow keen. Shadow-keening was only understood by a few clans and was rarely done. Towers often balked at such misdirection and often petulantly, spitefully, became night-tossed for several days as if to chide their wayward keeners. If the tower vindictively left them night-tossed, its studier had to allow the tower to drift for a day before getting it on course again. If the Nahas longhouse became lost to the night for a day, little damage would be done. No damaged Wheel Clan tower was calling out for rescue. No battle or war council awaited.

Poh rules a rich region. Second in size to Tsbosso's. If we destroy Poh's longhouse, this region will be ours. Psal grieved for his childhood friend, but a good opportunity had presented itself. He stood up, called the king, Netophah, the captains, Gaal, and Ephan into the keening room and counseled the shadow keen. "We have engaged in battles to destroy warriors and longhouses," he said. "But here is a chance to capture a large region with an expanse large enough for eighty longhouses to meet together. It is no war ploy. The Peacock Clan studier is not thinking properly. Shall we pursue and destroy?"

"Pursue," the king said. "The region will be ours."

After all but Ephan and Kwin left, Kwin said, "It is good that you are showing yourself fierce, and Nahas will see that you are able to pursue your enemy's longhouse and grind it to powder. But, after you have conquered, what will you do when the Warrior's Prize is thrown at you?"

The Warrior's Prize! Psal had forgotten. Rape was expected. Hidden away in the studier's room, Psal did not usually see such depravity. Vanquished women would be passed from one warrior to another. If the warrior wanted to keep his prize, he could. If he didn't want her, she would be killed or made into a comfort woman. The only exception was for Tsbosso's family. Nahas had ruled: nothing but Death awaited them. Psal had not thought of all that. He would think of it all night. The loveliest woman from the defeated Peacock longhouse would be his. Yet he did not want her.

In the middle of the night, as the longhouse keened to Poh's region and one landscape blended into another, Psal lay on his wheeled bed wondering if he should rape in order to show his ability to compromise. All night, the Lesser Light flickered and Psal often found himself holding his breath. When morning was almost come, and he heard footsteps outside his room. The visitor was Antun.

"Enter." Psal began rising to his feet.

"Prepared for victory?" Antun stopped him with a friendly gesture of his right hand and Psal returned to his prone position, his forearm over his face.

After a moment's silence, Antun continued. "It is difficult, one's first rape," he said. "And for a studier....Perhaps now...now that you've killed your friend...peace will rule between you and your father. Take the prize."

"Antun," Psal answered, "peace may will rule but at the price of my conscience. Understand, I have no wish to bring about a revolution among the studiers. Nor do I care about gaining the respect of warriors. My aim is to become a chief and to gain my own longhouse. It is a small wish for a Firstborn, and now because of it I am trapped, and forced to break my vow for a prize I do not want."

"True, studiers are not to do violence against another. But this once—only once, Firstborn! And—"

"Only once?" Psal laughed. "To break an eternal vow 'only once?'"

Antun walked toward the keening trees. "The Warrior's Prize is not a tradition one such as you can easily change. Netophah, perhaps, but not a studier, and not a studier many consider half-mad."

"Are your wives not pleasing to you?" Psal asked hoping to change the conversation. "Many say that's why you walk the longhouse at nights and why you allow Broqh to lie with your wife."

"The women are quite pleasing." Antun stood in front of the Lesser Light, studying it intently. "And yes, Broqh may lie with Liorin whenever he wishes. It is not a thing a Wheel Clan chief should do, but I have given him permission. You will laugh to hear this, but often I think my dear dead wife would be jealous to see me lie with another." Carefully avoiding the crystals and branches of the other lamp stands, he walked behind them and solemnly knelt before the Greater Light, an act Psal considered quite pitiful.

"Do you sometimes seek the Greater Light?" Antun asked. "Or the Constant Tower?"

"The Wintersea Master said the Lesser Light in our hearts is enough." Psal looked out under the arc of his elbow. "We need no external Greater Light to teach us. As for the Constant Tower, studiers argue endlessly about the truth and meaning of it. The legend says that only he who is fated to find it will find it, therefore I have not concerned myself with it."

"Actually"—Antun bowed toward the Greater Light then rose and turned to Psal—"the legend says he who is fated to *recognize and understand its song*. Perhaps it is recognized even now by many but its song is not yet understood. My mother used to tell me a prophecy from her Falconer Clan. 'Outcasts, your feet are stiff and hard to move. But one will bring you movement. You will enter into his Constant Tower, and he will bring you to your Permanent Home.'"

"Ah," Psal said, which seemed answer sufficient enough.

"You humor me." Antun looked about at the stone tiles and wooden frames of the keening room. "And yet, I believe the tower and its song will be recognized and understood by all Odunao soon. Perhaps our reconciliation with the Ever-Present One is near. Renan often said the fullness of time has arrived and the night's power over us will soon be no more."

Psal nodded, non-committal. Some wise studiers believed the night had always been thus, others—equally wise—believed differently. Warriors who pondered the Constant Tower, the Fiftieth Day, and other spiritual matters had learned to discuss such things only with Ephan. Still, warriors died and their wives died; and death often made even the most hardened curious. Seeing life vanishing before them, they wanted to know something of that Permanent Home they would soon enter. It was a studier's arduous duty to speak of such matters. So, Psal reasoned, if grief was responsible for Antun walking the night, he had a duty to listen to him.

"I saw the Constant Tower, awake, with my own eyes,"—Antun spoke shyly, as if ashamed he had brought up a subject he knew his new friend found laughable.

"You saw and recognized the Constant Tower?"

"Yes, Firstborn. I was blessed to recognize it, yes. My men were wearied of war and we had no battle planned for some days, so I told my tower to fly free. We arrived at a path which led to a large clearing with a tower. Of course, when I first approached it, the tower seemed a mound, overgrown with plants. It seemed ancient, ugly, piecemeal. Not whole, not uniform or beautiful in anyway. Some parts seemed human-made and reminiscent of those false towers our ancestors and our modern studiers attempted to build. But Renan told me to look with my heart. I did, and all at once the tower changed before my eyes. What was before only a mound and an accretion of bones suddenly was golden, transparent, sturdy! I felt—no, I *knew!*—the Creator Himself had built it brick by brick. And the more I believed, truly believed, the more the tower took on beauty—an unworldliness, a purity and holiness that only the greatest Builder could have imagined and executed."

The master of the Wintersea had effectively eliminated all possible Constant Towers as pretenders, natural phenomena, and delusions. But

Antun was not a studier and, like all those who were unenlightened about such matters, was prone to superstitions. Psal did not want to laugh, but could not help himself. He snorted.

Antun blushed. "Yes, I know. I dote on a dead wife and dream of towers."

"I didn't mock your grief," Psal answered. "Only your tower. Perhaps you and Renan are the Fated Ones."

"We did not understand its song, Firstborn. Even though, only Renan and I saw the tower. I asked my captains to describe what they saw. As for my men, some saw a broken, a badly-built edifice of planks and weeds. Others a normal looking tower. Others a pile of twigs and weeds. Others…well, a mixture of things: wood mixed with stone and dead men's bones. None saw the same thing, and none saw the tower. And none heard its song either. I heard a song. But when I sang it to Renan, it was not the same song Renan heard. Both were lovely nevertheless. My captains heard nothing. Is that not strange?"

Psal did not think it particularly strange. "I have heard of this strange tower before." He rose from the bed and picked up a clay jar containing juice from a fruit he had recently determined to be safe. The tartness of the juice pleased him and lightened his spirit.

"The co-ordinates are in my memory," Antun continued, much to Psal's annoyance. "It's in one of the Voca homelands."

Psal offered the clay cup to his friend. "Our brothers like sweet things. Drink, and tell me what you think."

Antun took the cup, sipped the beverage, then returned the jar to Psal. "Our brothers will like this stronger. Fermented."

"No doubt," Psal said. "If this is the tower you speak of, many studiers have been challenged by it. It is a curiosity. A trick of light, some say. Others say that gas in the atmosphere produces an effect upon the mind and eyes. Whatever it is, it is entirely natural. Certainly, it is not made by the gods or by one God. It is like the Great Mesa, which plays its part in our past, being—as many suppose—the place where the gods scattered the human race—but it derives its power from human belief and naiveté. Truly, Antun, the Constant Tower is a dreamer's comfort, a myth which is the sum of our longing. I have heard and studied many such 'magical' towers. They are airy dreams. It is best if you think of the Constant Tower as a metaphor, a symbol of our hope for permanence in this world. It looms large in all the creation and afterlife myths of all the clans because we humans often feel the need to settle around a common king and to build cities around a common longhouse. True, each clan remakes the legend to its own needs. But as for being a real tower….No, it does not exist." He pointed at the Greater Light. "As also, that Greater Light—or rather, what it refers to—does not exist."

Antun was silent for a moment. "What if I told you that this strange tower did not move? We watched it several days, and tried to keen it to home regions but morning and night, it remained in the same place. And when I slept in the tower, I awoke in the same region. Several nights." He looked into the passageway, shaking his head. "We saw, also, that all bricks in all towers spoke to this one tower, as the legend speaks, that some of the bricks from the original Constant Tower were duplicated, then scattered and assembled into all towers we know." He walked to the window. "Is that not strange, Firstborn?"

Psal sighed. "Chief Antun, towers have been rebuilt and cobbled together for ages. And all towers speak to each other. It is not strange that certain bricks in certain towers should echo each other. But tell me, when was this research of yours performed? Were you experimenting on towers in a time of war?"

"Before and after the war began, Firstborn."

Psal sighed. Day was dawning and the Peacock women had started their morning chanting. *Soon, Maharai will arrive with her latest "annals" for her mother. I would rather smoke signals than a rape. Failed warrior that I am.* "Tell me, Antun, if the Creator is so good, why has he made humans so evil? And if goodness rules the world, why do the powerful who rule it make such cruel traditions?"

"Such questions only a studier can answer. I'm a warrior. And as a warrior—"

"Then, a question to a warrior. How shall I escape the Warrior's Prize?"

"You are a studier, and wise. Surely you could devise a way. If not, you shall have to rape. Then, after you have had her, drink the grief away."

* * * *

Morning light came and Poh's longhouse—already half-destroyed and weakened by the death of its chief, its valiant warriors, and knowledgeable studiers—was powerless against the Wheel Clan's deadly arrows. The battle ranged in woodlands, caves, swamps, and sand pits, but was finished by midday.

As always, the studiers in Nahas longhouse remained within. But now, as Psal mixed pharma, Gaal entered and placed his sweaty blood-covered arm around Psal's shoulder.

"Ready to become a man, Firstborn?" Gaal asked. He looked down at Ephan, who was surrounded by measuring tools and pharma.

Psal pushed Gaal's hand from his shoulder. "I would've preferred becoming a man in the usual way."

Gaal tousled Ephan's hair. "And you, Cloud, will you not come to see your friend's glory?"

"There are pegs and crutches to be made," Ephan answered, without looking up.

"And the little man?" Gaal bent low and gently pinched Daris' nose. "Will you come and see your master become a warrior?"

"I will not. I am still recovering from seeing my master murder."

"The Firstborn finds himself in like-minded company," Gaal answered. "But now, he must show himself a warrior to his brothers. He must do what men do."

Leading Psal from the Chief Studier's room, Gaal spoke encouraging words, playful banter, hinted at Psal's sexual innocence. "Firstborn, the eyes of all, the eyes of your Father are on you. Don't shame the king by showing a weak heart."

"The king should not allow the shame of others to taint him," Psal answered. As he passed by the keening room, he noted the flickering crystals on the Lesser Light keening tree. "Let my shame be my own."

"This once, put aside your studier's vows and seem to compromise. Put on a false face if you must, like those false legs and false arms Ephan makes for our wounded. If you find falsity unsuccessful, think of the bloodied corpses of your sisters and brothers and remember that these Peacock women snared them. Close your ears to the girl's cries as she closed hers to Tanti's."

Outside, the king approached Psal—the bright sunlight and wet blood reddening his auburn hair even more. "An easy battle, Gaal!" he said. "And the Firstborn is the cause of it."

Gaal wiped blood from his arm. "Tsbosso's son is dead now, Nahas. As your little ones are dead."

Behind Nahas, the Poh longhouse and the wails of women and children inside. The Wheel Clan warriors stood shoulder to shoulder, awaiting Psal.

"Take your prize, Firstborn," The king said.

Cyrt walked toward Psal, whispered in his ear words that were probably meant to stir Psal's manhood but which made Psal shrink from him as from a reeking dunghill. Tears welled up in Psal's eyes. *I am no warrior. Why must I pretend to be?* All the king's warriors were watching him. Although bloodied and tired in victory, Deyn, Broqh, Antun, Kwin, Lebo, and Lan understood him. Yet, even so. Nearby, Netophah leaned against a tree. *The destruction of Poh's longhouse—was that not a Studier's victory?*

From behind the closed entrance door of Poh's longhouse, footsteps dragged, lingered. The door opened and Seagen appeared. He, Orian, and the other captains were pushing the Peacock women through the entrance. Several Wheel Clan warriors exited, carrying small children, about forty in all. Another ninety or more older children followed them crying and holding to their mothers. The boys would be killed, of course. Girl babies would be adopted by childless Wheel Clan women or reared in steward or farming longhouses. The older girls would be raped, then—unless they caught a warrior's fancy—killed. But the loveliest of all would be given to Psal. The procession passed before Psal and at last...the last appeared: a young girl, being led by Seagen and Lebo, weeping with her hand covering her face.

"You killed the leader of their longhouse." Seagen pushed Psal forward. "You've proven yourself a warrior, Firstborn. Take her."

Psal gently pulled the girl's hands from her face. And, behold, the beauty of Poh's longhouse, a warrior's worthy prize: Moonlight.

Psal's breath caught. The girl and the studier stood looking at each other. Her face, grown lovelier and sadder through the years, accused him. The precise accusation, he well understood. Certainly, if he had taken her as his wife, the war would not have occurred; if he had stolen away into her Father's longhouse, all Odunao would be at peace. And now, he had killed her brother.

Behind him Cyrt whispered a joke, cruel in its crudeness. "The studier fears studying a woman. Studier, if you need help in your studies, call your elders." All the while the girl eyed Psal bitterly, her gaze never wavering.

"You'll have to kill her," Lebo whispered. "She's Tsbosso's daughter."

Psal forced himself to breathe. "But I can save her if I can, can't I?" he asked Lebo. "I'm the Firstborn, and we need women in the longhouse."

"It will take much to convince Nahas to save Tsbosso's daughter," Lebo replied.

"I can convince him."

"I do not recommend attempting to, Firstborn." Gaal's eyes roamed the girl's uncovered breast. "She *is* beautiful, isn't she?"

Psal didn't answer. He took the girl's hand and led her toward a flowery meadow atop a high hill. He knew the place well. As a child, he had played there with Poh while Cassia hovered over them like a mother hen.

As they walked, Psal glanced behind him momentarily. He saw Cyrt gesturing to two Maldon warriors carrying children in the breech clouts generally worn by baby boys of the Peacock Clan. The babes were tiny, perhaps no more than six or eight months and the warriors had brought them to Cyrt, placing the children near Cyrt's feet. Psal found the action unsettling and turned to leave, grasping Moonlight's hand tightly. He continued climbing the hill until a woman's piercing scream stopped him and something brown flew past his right shoulder. He looked in the direction of the object's trajectory. At the exact moment, he heard a sickening splatter. One of the children previously at Cyrt's feet lay dashed on rocks on the hill ahead.

He looked down the hill at Cyrt. Cyrt was laughing. Psal stood, amazed. He remembered how Cyrt had pleaded to save the Iden children. It was not like Cyrt to harm children. *War has made us all mad. Or is this the effect of the Maldon warriors? Is he trying to impress them?*

A screaming woman—the child's mother?—struggled with Seagen at the bottom of the hill. Near Cyrt, a warrior from Maldon's sub-clan was holding onto another screaming woman who was reaching for a child in Cyrt's arm while Antun and two of his warriors were trying to pry the child from Cyrt's hands. Two distinct groups of warriors had formed and were facing off against each other—Antun's warriors on the left, and warriors from the other merged sub-clans on the right. *But why does Nahas stand apart, not stopping it?*

The contention grew and became sharper, and all the while Moonlight stood beside Psal in silence. But at last Netophah approached and spoke briefly to Antun and Cyrt. Whatever he said made Antun and his warriors withdraw. Cyrt was left holding the child. Psal's hand went cold. His head swam. It was not the result Psal wanted. Psal wanted the child killed swiftly, beheaded with one of the sharp swords made by the Falconer clan, or given a killing dose of Rangi.

Then Nahas approached Cyrt and took the child. The Maldon game was over. The other children were being taken from their mothers. They would presumably be quickly killed by a Wheel Clan dagger: That was the Wheel Clan way.

Psal continued to the top of the hillside and stopped in a place where a group of flowered shrubs blossomed densely. He absently rubbed his side. His words, spoken in the Wheel Clan language, tumbled from his mouth, a confused jumble. "Lie...here, and Moonlight...you must remove your...all your clothes. The eyes of others, the eyes of others... are...others will wound you."

"Is it true?" She spoke in the Peacock language.

"Is what true?" he asked in her own tongue.

"Was it you who killed my brother?"

"I did not," he answered. "You must undress, Moonlight. Or the others will come."

"Who killed him?" She angrily pushed one of her many braids behind her shoulders.

"Why does it matter? And who killed my sisters?"

"Who killed my brother, Psallo?"

"Netophah killed him. Now hurry—"

"If Netophah killed him, why do they believe you did?"

"Undress!" he shouted, then lowered his voice. "Or the others will… they will…." His words trailed off and he slumped silently to the ground.

In the distance Gaal and the other captains were looking in his direction.

He shouted down to them. "I am well able to do this! Leave me to my fumblings." Once again, he turned to Moonlight. "You must undress," he pleaded. "Or the others will come, and they will take you, and all, all will…lie with you."

The same girl who had allowed him to play with her breasts two years ago now lowered her head and looked at the ground, shame and fear binding her hands.

"You must do it," he said, gritting his teeth.

Slowly her hands touched the richly-embroidered royal Peacock mantle. Hand shaking, she removed it from her shoulders and lay on the grass, naked before him. Her golden-brown body, beautiful as it was, did not excite him. He forced a memory to his mind: the sight of little Tanti and Ria, like broken flowers. But instead of anger and the desire for vengeance, only grief came. He pushed the memory aside.

"I won't hurt you, Moonlight. Only…the others must think that I have lain with you."

The Wheel Clan captains stood afar, the Chief Steward too. *To mark my fumblings, to scorn my tenderness and youth, to lust over the girl.* He wanted to cover Moonlight, to hide her humiliation. The only thing he could think of was to lie on top of her. Kneeling against his aching side—he had been so worried about the prize he had forgotten to take Emon—he slipped down on the grass and made pretense of raping her.

The day was not far gone. If he rose to leave her, others would come. So they lay together. The girl was eerily silent. She stared up at the sky as if no one lay at her side. All the while, all around them the shrieks and wailing of other raped Peacock women echoed along the hillside and in the meadows. Meanwhile Psal's mind raced. He thought of Tolika, of Maharai, of Ktwala, of Cassia, of Gidea, of Tanti, or Ria, of Narena, of his mother, Hinis. He squeezed the girl's hand, but she lay beside him, as the sun moved across the sky, unmoving.

* * * *

When he heard Gaal's voice calling him, the sun was lowering in the sky. He covered the girl with her tunic, and continued staring ahead in angry silence.

"Firstborn," the Chief Steward called, walking toward him on the hillside. "The Poh tower is now being keened to The Great Tundra region for our stewards to tune its crystals to our regions and tower songs." He looked about him. "As for this land, Nahas has determined the Ronen and Hokkan longhouses will guard it."

"Wise choice," Psal said.

"Before you kill this one," Gaal said. "I want a taste of her as well."

Psal's heart raced, his blood boiled in anger, but he purposed to be quiet that his ruse wouldn't be discovered. "There are others you may take. Haven't you had your fill today? Is she not my prize—Tsbosso's daughter?"

Gaal wrinkled his face. "Firstborn, if she is to die, what use if—"

"I'm a chief's son. I will not share my woman with a steward."

A raised eyebrow. "So you will not plead and beg to change your Father's heart? That is unlike you, Firstborn."

"Everything today is unlike me." Psal looked down the hill at the royal longhouse. "I have lost myself today. And yesterday as well. But tomorrow I will regain myself. But as for now, it is best that she die. If Nahas acquiesced to my wish, I would daily see my guilt walking before me in the longhouse, and see my childhood friend being abused as a comfort woman. No, it is best that she die."

Gaal bowed low and walked to Cyrt near the bottom of the hill. They stood talking and looking up at the Studier-Warrior.

The girl remained hard as metal, and Psal found himself becoming angry at her. Her brother had died, true. But so had his siblings. Greedy though the Wheel Clan was and had been, the Wheel Clan had not been the treacherous aggressors. He spoke to her firmly.

"I don't care if you answer me, but—for your own sake—it is best that you do. You have two choices. Only two. Be killed or pretend to be killed. If 'pretense,' then you will be night-tossed."

Terror struck the girl's face. "Night-tossed?" she asked in the Peacock language.

"It is either death or be night-tossed."

"I cannot, cannot. No, no, take me with you. I cannot....But didn't that one say....Can you not keep me with you?" She suddenly seemed helpless, clinging and pulling at his tunic, but he pushed her hands away.

"I cannot take you with me." He remembered the chief's game. Or perhaps it was the studier's game; he wasn't sure. The coldness he pretended seemed to emanate from both. "You're Tsbosso's daughter.

If Nahas allows you to live—which is unlikely—the warriors will rape you, the Wheel Clan women will hate you, and Father will fear your influence among the Iden Peacock women."

"Psallo, who am I to have influence on them?" She sounded weaker now.

"You're Tsbosso's daughter." His hands shaking, he removed a dried brown Rangi leaf from his pocket. "Chew this and you'll sleep while the night unmakes you. But I must wound you a little. Just a little." He pointed under a rib on her right side. "Here."

"No, Psallo!" she shrieked. "I beg you! Do not, do not cut me."

"If I pity you and make a small cut, you will be free," he explained, his royal coldness amazing even himself. "If I do not wound you, others will come and make a larger cut. Do you understand? Do you want to die?"

"I don't want to die, Psallo." She was screaming so loudly, the captains at the bottom of the hill began walking toward them. Psal suspected they feared he would weaken and relent, or that the girl would flee and outpace the lame studier.

"You will not die," he told the girl and raised his hand to halt the approaching captains. "I'm a studier, remember? And if you use the pharma as I direct you, you will live a long life. Now, be silent. Or the others will come."

She stopped crying and said softly. "Thank you, Psallo, for sparing my life."

"My sisters pleaded in much the same way. Yet your brother was not merciful to them." He removed a clay jar of Emon from his studier's pouch. He gave her the last of his batch. "When you awake, wherever you awake, use this to dress your wounds. Do you understand me?"

"I do."

"Don't be afraid," he said gently. "Trust me. You will go into the night unknowing and you will not feel the wound."

The girl took the leaf and chewed, dressing herself as she did so. By the time third moon began to rise, she was asleep. Psal removed his knife, and rubbed its blade into the Emon. He lifted her Chief's Daughter's tunic, pressed the knife against her skin, closed his eyes and cut. The green tunic slowly became suffused with blood. He stood up. She was curled up on the ground as if dead. When Psal saw Gaal approaching, he ran, limping toward him.

"She's dead then?" Gaal asked.

Psal nodded.

"You surprise me. I did not think you would sin against the Lesser Light. Perhaps you're a true child of the Wheel Clan, after all."

The words were faint praise, edged as they obviously were with hurt and anger.

Gaal walked past Psal toward the body and kicked at it. Psal bit his lip and reminded himself to keep silent. From the bottom of the hill, Antun called to Gaal.

"Young chief?" Gaal shouted back.

Antun ran toward them and nodded to the Firstborn. "Chief Steward, let the girl lie where she has fallen. You have not examined other kills, why examine this one?"

Gaal nodded, glanced at Moonlight for a moment, then walked toward the longhouse where Cyrt met him.

That night, as all cheered Psal for finally becoming a warrior, Psal stood afar off from the hearth, watching the night change and hoping the Creator he did not believe in would preserve Moonlight. Later, after he had begged Lan, Ephan, and Netophah to refrain from making him a warrior in the future, he went to one of the studier's storage room and opened a jar of Tomah.

Promising himself it would be the last time, he put a leaf in his mouth. He had no wish to become enslaved to Tomah. Freeing himself from it would be arduous, being enslaved to it would be dishonoring. No, he had no wish to cover the floor with mucus and vomit as other Tomah-enslaved studiers had done. Nor did he want his descendants harmed, for so the ancient lore proclaimed, the forbidden herb would taint his children as well. But that night, he gave himself to Tomah dreams. Perhaps they would bring him to Cassia and to Moonlight, both safely harbored. The effect was almost immediate: a pleasant numbness; colors unseen by human eyes; the heightened music of trees, rocks, and stars; bright and dark beings floating just out of his view.

As he thought on those things and slowly melted from the world, Daris entered the room.

"Chief Studier of the Wheel Clan," the child pleaded. "Tell me you did not kill."

"I did not kill, Daris." Psal spoke out of his stupor.

"But they say the Warrior's Prize is dead."

Psal grinned. "She is alive. We studiers are well able to deceive."

"Tell me your deception, Chief Studier." Daris sat beside him on the bed. "The secret will remain in my heart."

"I know it will."

So, as the child leaned against his side, Psal related how he had deceived the warriors of the Wheel Clan. The boy's conspiratorial laughter helped to push his guilt away and he fell asleep dreaming of Cassia.

CHAPTER 21

ANTUN'S DEATH

The day came when Antun, Psal's friend, died. This is how it happened.

After a battle, night fell and as each group of warriors raced toward their longhouse, Antun fell suddenly like a fish caught unawares in a snare, and in an instant Cyrt was at his side. His warriors bore his body inside and Psal examined the wound, which smelled of Wheel Clan pharma, and whose shape was like that of a Wheel Clan blade. On a blood-soaked bed, his body pin-pricked with blood, Antun lay dying.

"The wound is deep, but you will live," Psal told his wounded friend, knowing his friend must die.

Antun died the next day; his death hidden from him, dying in pharma sleep.

"This is a grief that is hard to bear," Psal whispered to Ephan and Lan that night as they sat beside Antun's corpse. "Yet I must bear it. But Antun didn't fall on his own dagger as I have made the others believe. Antun never bathed his dagger with Dovi. I've never seen him do so."

Ephan added, "Certainly, he never asked for it."

"So?" Psal said. "You see what I see? You understand what I understand? Cyrt is the cause of his death."

"True," Lan said, "a warrior should die honorably. He should not be treacherously murdered by his kinsmen at the close of a battle."

"Let the thing be forgotten, Storm," Ephan said. "You ended his life swiftly and did not make him endure the worst of the Dovi poison. The day will come when you will be chief. In this, if you battle Cyrt, you battle the king. Therefore, keep your anger sheathed, for the king will not grant the Firstborn power to send Cyrt into the dark clime. Who can touch him if Nahas protects him? Or if he protects Nahas? It's all one."

The next morning Psal heard that Cyrt had walked into Antun's chamber and taken the dead chief's weeping wives into his own bed. Psal immediately went to his father's chamber.

"Nahas," he asked, "why have you allowed Cyrt to take the widows?"

"I have decided to make Cyrt chief over Antun's warriors."

"Antun's warriors have no desire to make him their chief. Let them choose from within their own ranks."

"That they may deceive me in the future?"

"Then let Lebo be their chief."

"Cyrt will be their chief," the king said. "And if he wants the widows, let him take them."

"Letting all see Cyrt receive the reward for his crime? I had thought you ruthless, but not stupid."

"Be careful what you say, Firstborn." Nahas raised himself up in his bed and reached for his tunic. "I did not like Qerys. I neither liked nor disliked the son. But I lost two young brothers in that strife."

"You killed Antun for an ancient grudge?"

"Firstborn, I have told you this before. You have too much integrity. Have you not read in our annals that integrity is a wild beast that must be caged?"

"Words spoken by a cynical Grassrope chief, Father. When have I cared for the wisdom of the Grassrope clans?"

"Even so, cage this integrity of yours, if you wish to be a chief. A chief, and a king, cannot long survive with too much integrity. Forget your friend and let Cyrt have the widows."

Psal walked to the door then turned once more to Nahas. "Father, only this once, appear to be my ally. Please, Father, that he may not triumph over me. Take the widows to your own bed."

"One wife is more than enough for me. Ktwala, and Ktwala alone. I am too old to be caught up in intrigue of multiple wives. Let the widows be Cyrt's reward. Now that sly Antun is dead—"

Psal raised his voice. "Antun was not sly, Father."

"It seems your blindness remains."

"Who is blind but he who suspects evil where none exists?"

"The conversation is ended. As your war with Cyrt is ended."

So Psal left, but he could not keep his peace. Some days later when the royal longhouse arrived at the Red Mist home region, just as the third moon began to rise, Psal went to Cyrt's chamber and removed Antun's widows. He also took Autun's sister's son. The women he gave to two Hokkan chiefs and the boy he sent to live with Jarid the steward. When the king saw what Psal had done, he—in turn—declared Cyrt chief over Antun's warriors.

* * * *

Maharai heard of Antun's death in the same way she heard of other deaths: Ephan told her, and she saw the Wheel Clan women washing his corpse. She had seen and heard of other deaths, but she had often seen Psal and Antun speaking in the keening room and it was apparent that Antun's death greatly affected Psal.

"Are you well, Psallo?" she asked, entering the sick room.

"I am quite well." He had poured a sweet-smelling oil into a cup of black powder, and the aroma of it filled the room.

"It grieves me that your friend has died," she said.

"It cannot be helped." He limped into the passageway and called to a little girl dragging a sack of grain from one of the storage rooms. The language in which he spoke was neither the Peacock nor Wheel Clan language and a jealousy arose in Maharai's heart, that the girl and Psal shared a language she did not understand. The girl left the grain sack and took off running toward the hearth.

"Maharai," Psal said, "I have not been properly mindful of you. Losing my friend, I can understand how solitary your life has been. Tolika no longer visits you?"

"No."

"I've asked Indina to call Lan. He will take you to your sisters. From now on, you can visit them anytime you wish. Only, you cannot live with them."

She clapped her hands, surprised at her sudden freedom. She hugged Psal, and when Lan arrived, she grasped Lan's hand and dragged him toward the gathering room.

Maharai found her sisters imprisoned in two chambers, each equivalent in size to the Chief Studier's room. When she entered the nearest of the rooms, those in the cell—about thirty-eight—immediately surrounded her. Their faces were covered with dirt and mud, and the rank smell of unwashed bodies filled her nostrils. "Maharai," they shouted, "how we have longed to see you!"

The remaining children—Eala and the tiny babes who had not been scattered to the other longhouses—they too, pulled on her tunic and hugged her, singing and dancing and little Eala leaped into her arms. Maharai felt like one brought back from the dead as Gidea held her tightly. Through freely-flowing tears, Maharai looked about for fierce, comforting Nunu but could not find her. She walked to the door, spoke to Lan in the Peacock tongue. "Lan, tell the guards to release the rest of my sisters. I want to see them."

"How powerful you've become!" Gidea said to Maharai. "Now you can order the king's warriors about!"

"They want me to learn their ways," Maharai said. "Because I'm Ktwala's daughter. I am to be princess here."

"Indeed? They took our daughters away." A fierce scorn lingered on Gidea's face. "In one way. Or another. But you, you are a princess?"

"If we follow their ways, they will bring your daughters back again. I know it."

"Do you?" Gidea asked. Scorn again. "Are you privy to all their thoughts?"

Why is she so hateful toward me? What have I done? "No, but…they, they think of us as their people. They will not harm us."

Nunu and the rest of the Iden women now came pouring through the door. Nunu the aged and strong, Nunu fat and warm, said, "Child, I hope you have closed your ears to all they tell you. They scheme to make you forget your own people."

"Yes," Maharai agreed, "they often tell me I belong to the Wheel Clan, that I'm no longer of the Peacock Clan."

Gidea pushed Lan's hand from his wife's waist. "And why are you still here? Or must she be guarded even when she visits her sisters?"

"This is my counsel." Lan hugged Tolika again. "Heed it if you will. If you want the girlie to roam freely, don't fill her head with rebellion. It is my counsel." He walked out the door and down the hall.

When he had gone, the Iden women attempted to do just that. This was the song they whispered to Maharai.

> *The Wheel Clan king wants to divide us. He will not.*
> *The Wheel Clan king wants to steal away the hearts of the*
> *Peacock women. He will not.*
> *Instead, the Peacock people will conquer them.*
> *Instead, Maharai will destroy them.*

When they finished singing, Gidea asked Maharai, whispering, "My daughter, can you kill?"

"I can kill Netophah," Maharai answered

"We must kill them all," Gidea said.

"We're few, we Iden," Maharai replied. "How could so few kill so many? And we are not skilled warriors."

"We can kill their valiant ones," Nunu said.

"If you want to kill their valiant ones, why don't you allow them to marry you?" Maharai asked. "Then you can kill them in their beds."

Gidea's eyes smiled admiringly at Maharai. "How clever you are! But you have always been clever. Even as a child you were shrewd and knew how to wrap your grandfather and your mother around your little finger."

"I had considered allowing our women to marry them," Nunu said. "But separated from each other, we would weaken. And we did not have the means to poison them in their sleep. But now, daughter…with your help…we will avenge your brother and all our dear brothers. The studiers are your friends, are they not?"

Maharai nodded.

"And the prince," Gidea asked. "The one who left your brother bleeding on the floor like livestock? Has he befriended you?"

"He is not my friend, but he seeks to be."

"They are knowledgeable in the nature of plants, are they not?" Nunu asked. "Let Psallo share his wisdom with you. Are there not poisons that can bring slow agony upon their victims, yet which do not betray themselves?"

"I suppose so," Maharai answered. "It is a strange thing to ask someone about poisons. And Ephan will tell me that no one talks about poisons unless they wish to poison."

"But you are clever," Gidea said. "And you honor your people. You will not forsake your people as Tolika has?" She glanced at Tolika who sat silent on a nearby mat. "The Ever-Present One made you clever, Maharai. Good at pretense. Therefore, use your body if you must, but do what is necessary. You do want Netophah destroyed, don't you?"

"I do. I do," Maharai answered shaking her head.

"Can you be brave and endure his touch?" Gidea asked.

"I think I can, although it will be difficult."

"Then, go, and use all your mind and body to help your wounded, heart-broken sisters."

"I will try to do as you say," Maharai said. "But you must give me time."

"Do not forget your brother's suffering, Maharai," Gidea said.

* * * *

When she returned to her room, Maharai stood at her doorway, awaiting Netophah. It was his habit to pass by and attempt to speak to her. *I shall have to convince him of my friendship,* she thought. *But will he believe?* As he approached, she looked up at him and smiled.

His face lit up. "Am I forgiven?" he asked her, in his practiced Peacock Clan language.

She edged away from the door, her head bowed. "I do not know if you are forgiven yet. I still see my brother's death before my eyes. But Ephan has explained that your little sisters and brothers were murdered as mine. I will try to understand."

"My heart clung to you, then. And now, even more, since you have lived in our longhouse," Netophah replied, his eyes admiring her face. "Remember how we played in the cave?"

My heart cannot return to the love I had for you in that cave. "I remember," Maharai said and squeezed his hand gently.

Smiling in surprise, he intertwined her fingers in his and walked with her to the entrance of his room.

An embroidered door blocked her entrance, its wooden frame intricately carved, its fabric delicately worked. Netophah pushed the door open and pulled her inside. She found herself in a chamber three times as large as the one given to her. Tidy and neat, it contained several shelves, tables, and baskets. A large window lay opposite the door and several sewed pelts hung on a railing above it reaching to the floor. Beside it, a hinged window. A smaller window lay near the corner. Below it rested a bow, several arrows, a shelf with knives, and leather armor.

"How I have desired to show my heart to you, Maharai!" He knelt before her. "And now The Silent One has granted my heart's wish! Do you understand now? Do you truly understand?"

"I am trying to understand," Maharai answered.

"I love you so much, Maharai. Each morning when I see you, joy rises in my heart. One day I will become Wheel Clan King. Many women want me. But I want you to become my primary wife, above all others."

Maharai kept her gaze on the daggers in the shelf. She imagined striking his neck and face and tearing out his heart. "I would like peace between our people as well," she said.

"Peace will come," he said, "and your mother will be my mother. And you, and Ktwala, will be our queens."

* * * *

Ktwala woke, heard shouted words, "The cold climes are behind us!" Green regions again, the odor of wild cats and marshy woods. Ktwala threw off her blankets, ripped animal fur from the window, turned her round belly toward the sun's heat.

Tomo entered, holding the spyglass. "In the distance, a small tower and a woman. But swampland and reptiles cover the journey. Come now. Let's see what we can see."

Ktwala gathered rope, tools, dried meat. She hid knives about her waist, placed a wooden flute in her pouch and one in the pouch on Lian's back. "The lions can be charmed," she told him. "But perhaps the girl's brothers and husbands wait inside the girls' hut, ready to rape, ready to kill."

"The girl is alone," Tomo insisted. "I saw none else besides her. Because you have lost your daughter—if she will join us—this girl will be a daughter to you."

They walked over hill, past stream, Ktwala charming the wild cats and fierce reptiles with her flute. At last they reached the far tower in a clearing, surrounded by thorn berry bushes.

The girl gathered them in her basket, ate as she gathered. Ktwala blew three notes on her flute. The girl wheeled round to face them, dagger drawn. She shouted in a tongue Ktwala didn't understand. Tomo continued towards her, pointed at Ktwala. Long, long, they stood there, until Lian walked toward her and began eating fruits from her basket. The girl lowered her arm.

The girl could be no more than twenty—bruises covered her face, her eyes bloodied, her nose swollen. Yet the girl's loveliness shone through. All the beautiful women of that time placed together in a row would not have compared to her.

She was from the Waymaker clan, crescent-shaped eyes, pale white hair—a kindly tribe that valued learning. She spoke many tongues perfectly! She spoke in Ktwala's language. When Ktwala heard her own language again, she wept. The girl's name: Sumra. Because she was so beautiful.

She had stumbled in a forest and fallen, she said. Limping back home after dark, the night had caught her outside. Her family tower had faded away. She had found this new tower.

"I have little skill in keening," she said. "But I remember my family's tower song. But see there: The hut breaks from the tower's base. Each day the damage becomes greater. And how will I find my lost parents again?"

"We're alone," Ktwala said. "Only three. Such work as your tower needs cannot be done in one day. Why live alone, then? Why be cast to the night? You know your tower's home song, you say. Teach it to us and to our tower. Perhaps the towers will one day find each other. Come live with us and share your beliefs, knowledge, and love with us."

So the girl came to live with them and the Iden tower clan grew. Ktwala's heart remained unhealed, but no longer numb. She still longed for her daughter, longed also for the Peacock corpses and the Wheel Clan's pyres, which had not returned.

CHAPTER 22

PSAL'S DEFENDER

In the passageway, words flew between Psal and Cyrt like arrows. Yet Netophah would not lift his head from Maharai's lap to let her rise.

"But I wish to see," Maharai's hands played gently with his golden hair. "Why can I not see?"

"Because women should stay out of harm's way when warriors fight." Netophah placed his arm around her neck and drew her closer to kiss.

Maharai pushed against the urge to draw back and allowed his lips to touch hers. "Ephan told me Cyrt took Antun's wives. Then Psal took those wives away and gave them to the Hokkan chiefs. Psal has won the battle, then? Cyrt no longer has the women he stole?"

"Psal has won, yes." Netophah raised himself up, drew his feet together and sat by her side. "But it was a foolish victory. Psal had almost convinced Father of his maturity. But Psal has not learned to pretend well."

"Have you learned to pretend well?" she asked.

"Pretense is necessary," Netophah played with her braid, then showered her face with kisses. "But you I will tell all my heart! I pretend other things. I pretend to like Cyrt, for example. I pretend to like some of my father's rulings. I pretend—"

"Why pretend with Cyrt?"

"I suppose I would worry that he would harm me if he knew I disliked him." Netophah burst out laughing. "I am not as fierce as I should be. I don't think he likes that." He kissed her cheek, turned her face toward his. "I am glad you have chosen to love me again, Maharai. I do love you so much, with all my heart."

Maharai did not love Netophah. His gentle kisses enraged her and his touch disgusted her. *I can no longer endure being touched by the one who murdered my brother. If I cannot kill Netophah, I will have Cyrt do it.*

That night, as Cyrt passed her room, Maharai said to him in the Peacock language. "Netophah told me Psallo triumphed over you, that you lost the women you stole. He says he is weak and you do not like weakness. But he says he does not like you either. Is it true that you think him weak?"

A hurt look came across Cyrt's face. He bowed and left her room. *That should suffice,* she thought. *Cyrt will kill Netophah now.*

But next morning before the sun rose, booted feet approached. An intruder laid siege to Maharai's blanket fortress. Its destroyer was tall and stout and smelled of fermented honey. In the gray: Cyrt stood above her, his knife unsheathed. He kicked the last of her besieged tower over and its walls tumbled to the floor. He glanced at the hallway behind him before kneeling beside her bed and speaking to her in the Peacock tongue.

"Do you think you can insult me, Girlie?" He held his knife to her throat with his right hand, while his left hand loosened the leather lacings of his trouser. "Afraid? I promise you. You'll learn not to open your mouth to me again."

She edged backward, looked past her broken fortress, past the large shoulders and the drunken sneering face. *But you were supposed to kill Netophah.*

"The studiers are upstairs on the rampart," he said, guessing her thoughts. "And Netophah and Nahas…well, they and Gaal have arisen early to speak with the stewards of this region."

"Why harm me? It is Netophah who hates you." Scrambling to her feet, she tried to push past them, but he held her fast. He pushed her backward with the hilt of his dagger and his clenched fist. Backed up against the wall, she could go no further.

"Have you ever heard of 'hitting twice with the same stone?'"

She shook her head. That she did not know. Yet she understood threats. Gidea's son had used them. So as Cyrt pressed his knife's blade against her cheek she did as she had been trained to do and kept silent.

He lay on top of her. *Gidea's son would have done this. Soon enough, he would have done this. Whether in my own longhouse or a stranger's, I am harmed. Marked to be harmed.* She closed her eyes and kept her eyes on the woven patterns on the topmost blanket of her fallen fortress. *The blue threads from top right to bottom left.* The yellow….Searing pain between her legs. Then Cyrt stood up.

He tied the laces of his trousers and stared down at her. "Lift your arms, Girlie," he ordered.

She raised both high above her head. She was not angry. Long ago, when Gidea's eldest son forced her to suck, she was angry. Her only emotion now was sadness, and the fear that some sign invisible to her but bright to cruel men—marked her.

He pushed the dagger under against her right armpit. A sharp piercing pain followed. A tiny droplet of blood spotted its tip. Her armpit burned. The mere act of lifting her hand widened, deepened, the wound.

"A warning," he said. "And did you think to turn me against my prince? Girlie, I have survive the machinations of Queen Hinis, who was shrewder and wiser than you." He re-sheathed the knife, then walked toward the doorway.

Her left hand slowly found the sore place between her thighs. It burned, burning as if a lighted torch had been placed inside her. When she lifted her hand to her eyes, it was covered with blood. *Yes, Gidea's son would have done this soon enough.* Then, smelling, Cyrt's drunken odor on her, she vomited.

CHAPTER 23

WHAT AILS YOU?

When the three studiers descended the rampart, they could hear Maharai weeping in her room.

She grieves again for her mother, Psal told himself and walked into the first sick room. *Netophah will comfort her.*

But Netophah arrived later while Psal and Daris mixed pharma.

"Firstborn," he said, "Maharai will not speak with me. She weeps now and will not allow me to comfort her."

"Have you spoken harsh words to her?"

"No, Firstborn. I told her only what I have told her these ten days. That I loved her and would heal the breach between my people and hers."

"Listen well," Psal said. "She has tried to love you but her heart was not willing. Whether guilt or grief prevents it, she can never truly love you, Netophah."

"Do you not have ears?" Daris said. "Find another girl."

"Attend to your pharma parchments!" Netophah shouted back to Daris. He turned to Psal. "But she seemed to love me."

"Brother, the daughter of the Waymaker King is lovely. And it is sung through the towers that she loves you. After the war, her father will allow a marriage."

"It's Maharai I want."

Psal tapped his brother's cheek. "How deeply I loved Cassia! Brother, you are afflicted with a love you cannot have. Who would have thought that I, the Damaged Firstborn, would pity the nature-blessed Wheel Clan Heir? And yet, I do pity you."

"Wheel Clan Crown Prince," Daris said. "Is love truly necessary? Kings and princes marry for reasons more important than love. But even so, you might learn to love the Waymaker princess in time."

"Truly," Psal said, "if I had known marriage to Moonlight would have spared us this war, I would have married her even without love to bind us together. And did Hinis and Nahas truly love each other?"

Netophah frowned. "That I will not say. But I would prefer to have a love match, a wife who loves me. Brother, she seems to like you. Can you not woo her for me? Or, if she is unwilling to be mine alone, woo her for both of us."

"I do not want her. But leave her alone for a while. I will try to win her for you." He walked into Maharai's room where he found her lying on her mat.

"Girlie," he spoke in the Iden dialect. "You've been crying all morning. And you will not tell the Wheel Clan Heir why. What ails you? Are you afraid to love Netophah?"

"I cannot love Netophah," she said. "I cannot love the Wheel Clan."

"Maharai, the past is finished. We are a longhouse full of grief where all have wounded and have been wounded. All, all, have suffered. Can you try to understand that?"

She looked past Psal toward the corridor. "I will try to understand." she said. "And has Cyrt suffered as well?"

He nodded. "Yes, even that strong one. I do not like to think of it, because I do not wish to pity my enemy. But he, too, has suffered. The son of his marriage died in a battle last year. Can you try to understand that those who have wounded you also bear wounds as well?"

"And yet...Lebo is kind to all," she said. "Has Lebo had a son killed in this war as well?"

"Lebo as well. And Kwin a brother. And Satima a husband. And Daris a brother. But they treat you well, do they not?" He held her head against his chest. "It is a mystery how some retain their kindness. But you, you must not weep. And don't consider yourself a traitor to your people because you do not hate those they hate. Try to give your heart to Netophah. He is a noble youth, and if you marry him, you will be our queen. Would that not be a good thing? Throughout all our longhouses, you could rule our people and protect yours."

Maharai crept backward, pulled her blanket about her shoulders. As she did so, Psal noticed blood on her bed sheets.

"Do you not know what this is?" He pointed to the blood-stained blanket. "This is a thing that happens with women. Did your sisters not have a yearly fertility festival when they sprinkle young women with pollen? Is this the first occurrence with you? Is this why you did not speak to Netophah?"

She looked up at him, then at the door.

"Don't worry. I will not speak of it to him." He stood up. "This blood, it will happen to you every month from now on. It will re-occur until you grow quite old. It means you will be able to have children. That's all I will say about such things. Ask your Iden sisters or, yes, yes, the Wheel Clan women as well, for they are your sisters too. You must remember that. All the women here are now sisters." She winced and he chided himself for his digression. "I'm sorry. You're in pain. It seems to pain some women. But I know the right pharma that will help you."

He returned with a gourd containing several small green berries.

"This is Kepbu," he said, "a berry for women. They're very tart when dried, but very powerful as well. Eat no more than ten, or your tongue and mouth will grow numb. It's a pleasant numbness, but a dangerous one. Too much will cause more blood to flow, and you wouldn't want that. Chew ten in the morning, and before going to bed. That should lessen the pain. Do you understand?"

She nodded and Psal placed the Kepbu into her shaking hands.

"I could give you something more powerful," Psal continued, "but it would harm you as it has harmed so many of our women. You do not wish to be harmed, do you?" He watched as she put a berry in her mouth, then he gently tugged on her braid. "See, it's a pleasant tartness. Sometimes you might even find one which is a little sweeter. So, stop weeping. This is entirely natural. I'll call Rain and have her help you."

In the doorway, he called for Satima, who appeared with little Indina. "Prepare a bath for the king's daughter," he told them.

Soon Indina was rolling a wooden tub toward Maharai's room and Satima was carrying two large buckets full of water. Meanwhile Psal went to the storage room and returned with a red clay jar. When he opened the jar, the room became redolent of the sickly-sweet oil.

"You will take a bath," he told Maharai. "To honor the day. This is what we do with our women. You've become a woman now."

The viscous oil clung to Psal's fingers. He shook his hand vigorously in the water: a disintegrating swirl of red specks circled his wet fingers. "Do you like hot baths?" he asked her. "I like them very much. We have so many hot springs, the Wheel Clan. But...." He indicated that she step into the water. "Today you will use warm water from our hearth."

She slowly sat in the tub, scattering the floating oil specks. More buckets of water were poured on her, warm and comforting, rising to her chin. But the kindness of the Wheel Clan women and the warmth of Psal's hand along her thighs as he scrubbed away the trail of dried blood didn't push the discomfort away.

Outside, Netophah waited for him.

"How like our dead sisters she is!" Psal exclaimed.

Netophah laughed, then smiled, a good-natured, beaming, admiring smile, which Psal always found hard to resist. "I do not think of our sisters when I see her. Perhaps in some small way but…did she say why she closed her heart to me?"

"Look," Psal said, "she's almost half-won. She is trying to understand this war and the lives of our people. She may never allow you in her bed, but she has a kind heart. I have no doubt one day she will give you her friendship. Let her rest peacefully. Gidea has filled her mind with angry thoughts of loyalty. Tomorrow, perhaps, she will return to your former friendship."

Netophah knelt on one knee and touched the hilt of the Firstborn's dagger. "I owe you much, Firstborn."

"Up, up," Psal said, blushing. "The Wheel Clan Heir should not shame himself by being seen bowing to a Damaged One."

"It is no shame for me to bow to the Firstborn of our clan, Psal. And if she chooses to marry you, I will gladly be her second choice. It was evident from the day she entered our longhouse that Father wished to bind her to one of his sons. So, if she wishes to marry you, remember me, Firstborn."

Psal laughed. "I have no desire to marry. But I will continue to press your cause."

* * * *

Psal hurried up to the rampart where Lan was charting neutral and lost towers and Ephan and Daris were peering past the trees at the Cavern Dwellers.

"Do you remember those days when we played in these caverns?" Ephan asked him.

"I remember them well."

Ephan leaned against the watchtower. "Consider, these people might be my own people."

"No, not this people," Daris said. "But I understand your meaning."

"Yes," Ephan said, and straightened Daris' little studier's cap. "I know you understand. But Storm here does not. He has kinsmen in two clans and he cares for neither. I would be happy to find my true people, even if they were of the worst kind." He looked toward the swamps then once more at the cavern dwellers. "Sometimes when I think of my lost mother...."

Daris looked up. "Narena?"

"No, Little One," Ephan answered. "Not Narena. When I say 'my lost mother,' I think of the woman who threw me away."

"Do you think of her often?" Daris asked.

"Quite often. And when I do, I think how grievous it was to be thrown away. I ask myself if she did not love me. At those times, I find myself falling into despair."

Daris' little mouth opened wide with surprise. "I never thought you despaired."

Ephan gently yanked Daris' hair. "Only when I think of my lost mother. Then, to bring my heart up again, I tell myself that my mother did not throw me aside. When I speak to Nahas of this, he tells me that perhaps she loved me, would have loved me, but perhaps the Voca Queen killed her and left me to the night because I was a boy child. All this is probably not true. Nahas often tries to comfort me with his lies. And yet it is comforting, and at times I choose to believe him. Yes, I choose to believe that somewhere out there my mother longs to find me."

"Come now, Ephan!" Psal chided. "All love you here. Much more than they love me."

Ephan gave Daris his spyglass. "See there, this people! These Cavern Dwellers! They have much wisdom, these people. Listen well today to all they say as you gather crystals. And kind hearts too! A good and lovely people! They have little room in which to live…yet they live peaceably and no talk of war ever enters their conversation."

"Peace will come soon." Lan stood and stretched. "After vengeance, peace. But now…no more talk of peace until Tsbosso is dead. And look you, Firstborn, I heard Netophah just now as he spoke to you. I did not mean to listen. I had descended to gather more parchments."

"Ah, you heard the impossible mission he saddled me with?"

"The Wheel Clan Heir is correct." Ephan took the spyglass from Daris and turned again to look at the Cavern Dwellers. "The girl should marry one of the king's sons. It's—"

"But if she will not marry Netophah, and if she loves the Firstborn, why should the Firstborn share her with Netophah?" Lan asked.

Daris wrinkled his brow. "Why do we stand here, marrying off the Firstborn when his heart will always remain with Cassia?"

"True," Lan said, "but even so, if he marry, he should not share any wife, unless absolutely necessary. My father, who was as wise a studier as any, used to say that such arrangements lead to trouble. He said Nahas and his brother feared Hinis's power. Even though they loved her less than their primary wives, they vied with each other to please her. And after all those surprisingly sudden deaths in the line of succession, and Nahas alone surviving—it was apparent that Hinis wanted only Nahas and wanted to be rid of Ruanna. No, it does no one any good to have two chiefs sharing a wife."

"So you think the Chief Studier will become a chief one day?" Daris asked.

"I have no doubt of it. The very tower the Firstborn and the Favorite found on the day of the feast, the tower Chief Tamira keened for, is being specially crafted for a lame prince to rule in. Nahas has allowed no other chief to take it—although many, including Orian, Hokkan, Maldon, have asked for it. Would Nahas do that if he did not intend to make the Firstborn a chief? Therefore Chief Studier, Friend Psal, Firstborn, hold to your rights."

Daris turned to Psal. "I agree, Chief Studier. Have you considered how humbling it will be for you to share a woman with your future king, that perfect nature-blessed brother of yours? I know you do not like humiliation."

Psal listened intently. "I promised Netophah to woo her for himself, for himself only."

"She doesn't want him," Daris said. "She wants you. Do you not want her?"

"She wants me?" Psal stammered.

Lan and Ephan started laughing.

"Am I so blind?" Psal asked.

"You are very blind, Chief Studier," Daris answered. "All see her love for you. The things your searching eyes never see!"

The conversation opened a door in Psal's thoughts. There it was suddenly opened before him: the possibility that he was loved. And for the first time it occurred to him that he could fall in love with Maharai.

CHAPTER 24

A KING'S INDIFFERENCE

Maharai stood beside her sleeping mat as Indina changed her bedding. Rain stood beside her. She didn't want to see Rain. Sometimes, the old woman seemed to treat her as an enemy. She looked past Rain through her window at a clear blue river flowing in the distance. She wanted to go to the river and wash all her sorrows away. But Rain left and she felt alone. She walked to the hallway. *I will visit my sisters,* she thought, but as she walked down the King's Corridor, Cyrt appeared. He stood in the juncture of the gathering room and the corridor. A smirk on his face dared her to pass him, dared her to tell his secret. She turned around and hurried toward her room.

As she stood in front of Psal's room, Cyrt tapped his dagger's hilt.

"I want to see Psallo," she said.

He slowly stepped aside. She peered over the keening room's curtained screen. Psal lay on his stomach, his legs toward the door, parchments scattered all around him on the brightly colored carpet. Containers, jars, baskets, and oddly-shaped instruments filled the shelves that lined the room.

She took a deep breath, pushed the screen aside and stepped inside. Psal looked over his shoulder at her then slowly, almost strenuously, rose to his feet. Cyrt remained in the hallway but he kept watching her, his silence a threat.

"I want to live with my sisters, Psallo." Her voice was halfway between a complaint and an accusation.

Psal rubbed his hip. "Nahas will not allow you to live with them."

Cyrt stepped into the room unasked.

"She no longer needs to be prevented from visiting her sisters," Psal said. "You are no longer needed."

But Cyrt said, speaking to Maharai in the Wheel Clan languange, "Long has Ephan taught you. Why do you insist on speaking our enemy's tongue?"

"What does it matter what language she speaks?" Psal defended Maharai.

"I do not perfectly understand their Iden dialect perfectly," Cyrt retorted. "It troubles me that she—"

Psal turned to Maharai and spoke now in the Iden dialect. "Maharai, now that you can walk the longhouse freely, you should wear the tunics our women wear. Our warriors are preoccupied with women's breasts. Now that you no longer have Cyrt at your side—"

"I heard my name just now!" Cyrt snarled. "You must command her to speak our tongue."

"You might encounter trouble," Psal continued, ignoring Cyrt. "You've seen our longhouse, the many rooms, many corners where warriors might hide. And some…especially the Maldon refugees…might… well, it isn't safe. Ephan told me you have no wish to live with people who trap their farts in wool leggings but.…" He nodded toward the hallway. "Trapping your farts is a small price to pay for safety. Also, if all know that you are Netophah's woman, you will be safe as well."

Maharai's throat tightened. *Safety. Which is safer? To keep this shameful secret? To risk his dagger now? But would he kill me here in front of Psallo? And if I keep silent, will my night not be filled with Cyrt's continuing visits? Is this not the same thing Gidea's son did to me?*

She stepped closer to Psal. Her body shook. *To be Netophah's woman? No. No.* "So, if I put on one of your tunics, I will be safe?" Her voice trembled. "I don't like Cyrt."

Psal squinted, studied her face. He turned, glanced at Cyrt. Silent, he lowered his eyes toward her legs. An angry flush rose on his face and he lurched toward Cyrt, his dagger drawn. Afraid for Psal, Maharai ran to the doorway and shouted for help. Meanwhile, both tumbled to the floor struggling, like coiled serpents in a death battle until Psal's dagger fell from his hand. It lay near their heads and Cyrt kept grasping for it, dragging both himself and Psal nearer the knife. Maharai threw herself on Cyrt's back and struck him with her fist. An ineffectual move. Cyrt easily threw her from his shoulder and grasped Psal's dagger firmly. He lunged at Psal, but the dagger's blade struck the floor. Cyrt lay atop Psal, hitting, punching. Maharai jumped on Cyrt's back and bit his shoulder. He lurched to shake her off and Psal edged away. The fight continued with both clutching at each other's hair, pushing and hitting faces, shoulders and stomachs.

Two young warriors came running. Maharai recognized them as Broqh and Kwin. The attempt to part Psal and Cyrt only dragged the fight into the corridor.

Then the king's voice. "End it! Now!"

Cyrt pushed Psal away and bowed to the king. He wiped his bloody nose while Psal hurled insults at him.

"Firstborn! Be silent!" Nahas shouted. "Cyrt! To my chamber! Now!"

Cyrt followed Nahas immediately, but Psal called for Satima, told her to dress Maharai in the hemp tunic and buckskin leggings of a Wheel Clan woman and to warn the warriors never to touch the king's daughter.

Inside the Chief Studier's room, Psal tried to catch his breath.

"Firstborn!" the king called again.

Psal looked past the partition of the keening room into the corridor. "No," he shouted to Nahas. "I am Firstborn and the Chief Studier of the Wheel Clan. You must come to me!"

He waited. The king did not come. Instead, two warriors from the Orian sub-clan caught hold of him and dragged him into the king's chamber. Nahas stood near his window, blood on his hand. A knife wound—newly-made—stretched from the upper left side of Cyrt's face to the lower right. Psal had seen such wounds before. *The king has marked him. So? Has Cyrt gone too far at last?*

"You push too far, Firstborn." Nahas gestured to the warriors to leave, then closed the door behind them.

"Father...can it be? Do you intend to punish Cyrt in the dark climes?"

Nahas rubbed his forehead. "If I punish him, you will have to join him as well."

"And what have I done? Did I rape her? A girl he knew should not be touched?" He turned to Cyrt, screamed at the top of his lungs. "If you wanted a woman, you should've gone in to the comfort women."

"Silence! Firstborn...." The king paused. "You and Cyrt. Alone together in that forsaken place, you might grow to understand and respect each other." Another pause. "But we're at war. Therefore, this is my decision. Cyrt will no longer be chief over Antun's warriors. When a longhouse is prepared, Lebo will become their chief."

Psal laughed. "How unworthy to be king! How unworthy to be my father!"

Nahas raised his hand. A flash of metal and the sudden sting of a blade. Before Psal knew it, the king's knife had struck. Droplets of blood trickled over Psal's right eyebrow, past his eyelid and nose and onto his left cheek.

"Do not presume, Firstborn." Nahas wiped his dagger and returned it to its sheath.

Now I am as marked as Cyrt is. A marked Firstborn! The wound stung. Several wicker baskets rested on a shelf nearby. Enraged, Psal sent them crashing to the floor. Ground pharma, wine, herbs, inks, and parchments mingled together on the woven mat.

"A childish response," the king said.

"A girl you have claimed as your daughter, Father."

"The girl's unharmed." Nahas walked to the window. "No doubt she suffered worse in her Peacock longhouse. And tell me, should I send away my best warrior in a time of war? Should I make him outcast for something as small as raping a girl? I have marked him. It is enough."

"Yes," Psal sneered. "It is enough. He rapes a girl. He kills a chief. These are small things."

Nahas grasped Psal by his collar and threw him against the floor. "Firstborn, lower your voice. Or do you wish to bring mutiny to my longhouse? Antun died because of you. The girl was violated because of you. Do you not see that?"

"Me, Father?"

"Antun did not want the women. He loved his dead wife. Would he have died if you had given Cyrt a woman?"

Psal's head throbbed. *Yes, I am responsible. And yet, and yet....* "Whether I gave Antun the woman or not, he would have died, Father. Because you wanted him dead."

He stooped and retrieved the contents of the flung baskets. After returning them to the shelf, he bowed to his father. He opened the door, but then a thought: *Is no woman in this longhouse safe then? The young girls?*

"Father"—he touched his wounded face, studied his bloody hands— "Is it possible that Ktwala's daughter is not the only one Cyrt has violated?" His voice sounded weak, almost servile. He did not wish to speak, but...."The Iden women, Father. The foundlings from the Maldon. Little Indina...they—"

"Firstborn." Cyrt wiped away the blood on his face with his right hand. "Am I such a reptile that you accuse me of such things? The girl dishonored me and I...."

Psal pushed at him. "How did she dishonor you?" Psal waited. "Tell me! How?"

"It is not important," Cyrt said.

"How small your soul is if it cannot receive an insult from a little girlie!" Psal snarled.

"Enough!" Nahas said. "As for the little foundling, why should Cyrt not have her if he wishes? Why should any warrior not take her?"

"She is *young*, Father. If one warrior takes her, others will. Why should she be destroyed, spoiled, abused, simply because she is a foundling?"

"Firstborn!" Nahas shouted. "Learn to care about the warriors you wish to rule. Not about women and the weak."

"Well, then. I will consider releasing your poor needful warriors from the terrible bonds I've placed on their lusts. Even so, Cyrt, don't touch Maharai again. Or Indina. And as long as the war continues, make sure no sword or dagger strikes you. If you are struck, be careful that you take no pharma from me." He turned to Nahas. "Nahas, king you may be, my father you may be. But strike me once more and I will kill you."

Nahas burst out laughing. "Firstborn, if you tried to kill me, I would gain much respect for you."

CHAPTER 25

ARE YOU HURT?

When Maharai entered the cell inhabited by her sisters, they stood aloof, perplexed at her Wheel Clan clothing. Gidea—whose scrutinizing eyes missed nothing—asked, "And you walk strangely, with halting steps. Like a girl on the morning after her wedding night? Is it the prince? Have you won his heart?"

Maharai remembered the rage that had flamed through the Iden women's cells when they learned about Tolika's rape.

"It is not the prince," she said. "And I'm only a little hurt."

Gidea circled Maharai like a vulture studying prey. She walked to the entrance of her cell and looked down the corridor. "It is well," she said. "The guard is near the gathering room." She walked back to Maharai. "So, you have become part of their clan now? But you say you have not lain with their prince?" She grasped Maharai's tiny waist with both hands and spun her around. "Tell me you have not sold your virginity, your birthright, and your people for yourself alone."

"I have not sold my soul."

But Nunu said, "It's obvious you have sold it. They have begun giving us more freedom. Leaving our door unlatched and not guarding our doors. Surely, you're the cause of this?"

"They're inviting us to become one of them." Gidea looked at the speechless, sullen Tolika, the symbol of treacherous assimilation. "But we will never become one of them. And did Tolika benefit from the bargain she made? I hope you have not forgotten your people."

Only Milia, who held tiny Eala on her knee, defended Maharai. It was hardly a defense. "Such things happen," she said. "She's young."

"You were always easily deceived by her," Gidea said. "This girl understands more than you imagine."

"Let the child speak!" Nunu said. "If she has not sold her soul, she will tell us."

Maharai heard herself promise the first thing that came to her mind. "Psallo can bring your daughters back. I have asked him, and he has promised he will bring them back to you."

But Gidea said, "So you didn't lie with the Crown Prince? You lay with the lame prince?"

Maharai took a deep breath, glanced at Tolika, who would surely hear about the rape from Lan. "No, I have not lain with him. Cyrt forced me."

Gidea glanced at Nunu, nodding. "That one comes to kneel at my bed often. Him and his friend, Gaal. He tells me continually that he wants me. He raped you?"

"And will the lame prince force you to marry this Cyrt?" Nunu asked.

"No. Psallo doesn't like him. It is entirely my fault I was raped. I said a thing, hoping Cyrt would kill Netophah. But, instead, he raped me. I told him Netophah hated him. I thought he would kill Netophah."

Gidea hugged Maharai's shoulder. "You are young yet. True, you are shrewd and clever. But men are not so easily controlled. You reason like a child, but children do not know the world. In the future, let your older sisters guide you."

"I will, Gidea."

"You have to be subtler, Ktwala's Daughter. But it is a small beginning."

* * * *

That night, Psal stood by the keening room window looking out at the changing landscape. *Humanity is confusion itself. No, it is not in a man to direct his own steps. Yet how arrogant the powerful are—thinking they could know, understand, and control life. And what have I now done? I have promised Father to allow my arrogant kinsmen take grieving Iden women in forced marriages. How foolish have I been!*

He rose from his bed, sent a tower message pleading with his uncle, Chief Bukko, to give some Macaw women to the Wheel Clan warriors, but Bukko rebuffed him as he always did, reminding him of the pact among the neutral clans forbidding any marriage to the Peacock and Wheel Clans until the war ended. At last Psal gave up and lay in bed. As a peace child, he had proven useless…and dangerous to his friends and to those he loved.

As he thought on these things, Maharai entered his room, her small form lit by the gray half-light of the two moons. Seeing her, he thought of Tanti and Ria, his dead sisters.

She touched the Emon-smeared poultice across his nose. "What happened?"

"The king marked me."

"Forgive me. It is my fault."

"It was entirely my own fault, Maharai. But now, go to sleep."

She lay on his mat and her hands held him tight. "Psallo, let me sleep beside you. Let us keep each other safe."

"Nahas has ordered you to sleep in that room in your own bed. Moreover, this is the keening room. I don't want you stumbling around in the dark, brushing against keening branches and breaking crystals. It's enough that we have sick warriors wandering in during the night asking for pharma. When Ephan finishes his task, he will not be happy to find you here." He stroked her shoulders. "Netophah waits for you."

"I do not wish to lie with Netophah."

He sighed, sat up in bed. "Well then. Tonight only." He gathered up his bedding, and walked with her into her room. There, he placed their sleeping mats side by side as she built her blanket fortress.

"You won't leave while I'm sleeping?" she asked, when she had finished restoring her breeched walls.

"That would be deceitful. I'm not a deceiver."

She frowned. "You deceived me once. On the day you became my brother."

"True, but I will never deceive you again."

"I believe you." She smiled and pulled a blanket over his legs and hers, then placed his hand about her shoulder. "And I will not deceive you."

He squeezed her forearm. "My sisters, too, did this. When they were afraid. They held my hands and pulled them around their shoulders as you have done."

"My sisters long to see their daughters. They will trust you if you bring their daughters back. I promised them you would."

He leaned on his elbow and looked down at her. "I cannot bring their daughters back, Maharai. Nahas has ruled th—"

"But you're the Firstborn, and....Are you totally without power, Psallo?" She held his face between her hands. "Are you weak, Psallo? I would not want you to be weak. My mother told me my father was kind, but proud and weak. It is a bad thing, being weak and proud at the same time. Mother says if my father was not proud, our longhouse would not have been lost. Because he did not call upon his Macaw clan for help when our elders took away our keening knowledge. You must not be weak. Promise me."

"No, Maharai, I am not weak." He hugged her neck. "I promise. I will be strong and not do stupid things."

"Psallo, there are so many people in the world. So many who never question themselves…or say 'I was wrong. I should not have done that.'"

"I question myself in all things, Maharai." He gently pushed her toward the sleeping mat. "Now to bed."

That seemed to comfort her and she fell asleep, her hands on his chest.

In the next morning when Psal awoke, he was clutching Maharai close. *Such protective love engulfs my heart!*

He arose and left her room, but Netophah accosted him in the corridor.

"Firstborn," he said. "Last night, as I walked to my room, I looked in and saw you lying in each other's arms. You comfort Maharai well."

"It is not a job I wanted," Psal answered, "But it is mine at present."

"I wish it had been my job. But she will not come to me."

CHAPTER 26

WOVEN TOGETHER

When Maharai saw a cloth tied to a twig, she thought she dreamed; the pattern was very like that used in Iden cloth. She longed to go outside and retrieve it. But the royal longhouse was engaged in a battle and Psal and Ephan were tending to the wounded. At the rise of the third moon, as Psal and Ephan bound the wounds of a warrior, she entered the sick room.

"I have seen a certain cloth," she told him. "It hangs on a low branch. It's from my mother. You must retrieve it. It's her answer to my smoke message."

"It is a common pattern," Psal said. "Many Peacock Clans weave clothing of that kind."

"They're not all the same, Psallo. Old Jion told me that. Every sub-clan knows its own pattern. I know that one. It's ours! Retrieve it for me."

He did, and they returned to the sick room where she continually lifted the cloth to her nose, smelling her mother's scent.

* * * *

When Gidea saw the cloth, she said, "We've fought in this region before. How long ago I do not remember, but this proves Ktwala is not lost, no! That evil king has placed her in one of their longhouses! She follows us. If that lame prince loves you so much, tell him to bring Ktwala to us. Surely, he knows where she is. See, see"—she showed the cloth to the others—"Ktwala fights and awaits us. We must fight as well." Gidea then spoke softy to Ktwala. Of late, Gidea had begun to speak to Ktwala as if Ktwala was at her side. "My dear sister, Ktwala, you allowed your heart to deceive you. But, hear me, these Wheel Clan warriors have anchored your people in the depths of the caves of the earth."

"I can ask Psallo, Gidea," Maharai said. "But I cannot...demand."

"Do you hear that, Ktwala? Your daughter lies with the lame prince but she cannot demand? She has no power with this Psallo you pitied so much."

"It is not easy to demand."

"True." Gidea lowered her voice. "But you can scheme and plead and beg and manipulate? Were those not the skills you used with your mother and grandfather?"

"But…."

Gidea's lips were so close to Maharai's ear, Maharai felt their warmth. Gidea whispered. "And with my son as well?"

Maharai's mouth fell open but she did not defend herself. *But I did not manipulate your son. It was he who forced me.* And then, a realization. *Has she known this all this time? Then why did she not save me from him?*

"If you cannot control the prince," Gidea continued, "can you not hide some of their daggers under your tunic? Can you not take some pharma from their sick rooms? Can you not kill? I thought you said you could."

Nunu's normally sweet round face took on a fierce look. "When you meet Ktwala again, will she not be proud that you have used the studier's love for you to destroy his people?"

"But I don't think Mother would….I don't know if Psallo loves me. And even if I did, I don't have power to make him give me poisons."

"Tolika told me the others treat the lame one with disdain because he has a damaged body," Gidea said. "They say his mind is damaged as well, that he weeps easily and cannot hold his patience. Such a mind, always seeking love, is easily manipulated. And now that you have been raped by this Cyrt, the prince's mind will turn towards you with kindness and pity. It is the way with some damaged boys to pity damaged young girls. Therefore, he has already begun to love you. So, feed and water his disdain for his father. Make it grow like a venomous plant. After that, you will have gained an ally."

Does Gidea not love me? "Psal is a priest of their clan. He cannot kill."

"Make him want to kill." Gidea whispered, winding and unwinding the piece of cloth around her wrist. "Other women have caused men to kill."

Why did she not defend me against her son? "They were more beautiful than I was. Old Jion said so."

"But you pretend innocence well," Gidea said.

"I don't think Psallo thinks I'm innocent." Maharai stretched out her hand to take the cloth, but Gidea held it so tightly, the cloth tore in their hands.

Gidea showed her the cloth now ripped in two. "We are woven together, we Iden women. Don't let them tear you from your people. Now, ask your prince to give us flutes and pipes that we may play the songs of our people."

Maharai left her sisters feeling like one whose eyes had begun to open. *But open to what? I see now, but what is it I see?*

As the night took the royal longhouse away, the king called Ephan and Psal to the keening room.

"A chief's wife should know how to aid her people," the king said as he walked among the branches.

"Do you speak of Maharai, Father?" Psal asked.

"During the recent battle she stood in the gathering room and gave no aid to our people. Ephan, does she not understand that we are her people now? Both of you, continue to teach her our ways or she will make herself noxious to our people. And will she be respected when she marries the Firstborn and Netophah?"

"She does not want to marry Netophah," Psal said.

The king shrugged. "I heard she has found a cloth, tied to one of the trees, a token she swears belongs to her mother."

"How did you hear this?" Ephan asked.

"The warrior whose arm you tended understood her language. If you wish to speak to each other of private matters, be more careful in the future. And—about these cloths—Ktwala is obviously signaling her sisters. If my wife finds comfort in tying cloths to trees, let her tie them. Our stewards need not remove them. But if the Iden women attempt to relay messages to her in the same manner...*those* cloths you will remove. Let Ktwala hear no words from any within this longhouse. I hope this will put an end to your smoke signals."

* * * *

Psal left his father and entered the keening room. He walked toward a basket of parchments, ready to track towers. But Maharai entered his doorway. Again, she begged him to sleep at her side. Again, he relented and found himself in her bed after his day's work was done.

As they lay together, Maharai whispered, "Psallo, my sisters want me to murder you."

"Ah me! And will you?"

"I don't think I will."

"Good. I would not want to be murdered."

"And yet I should kill you," she said. "Because you and Nahas have conspired to hide my mother from me."

"It is not I who stole your mother," he answered, pulling the blanket over his shoulder.

"But you know where she is now."

"You, as well. You knew she hid herself in the Iden longhouse."

"But you know where the Iden longhouse is, don't you?"

"I will not lie to you." He turned on his side. "Therefore, let us not speak of it."

"There's something else."

"Is it worse than your sisters wanting to kill me? This day with its many wounded has already overwhelmed me. I could not endure much more."

"I know you're a powerless prince, but—"

"I'm not as powerless as all that. I am Firstborn, after all. What is this other thing you wish to speak of?"

"My sisters request flutes and pipes."

Psal laughed. "They cannot have them. Do you think I want them to call a herd of elephants or lions down upon us?"

"I did not think...." she began.

"Perhaps you did not. But those sisters of yours are subtle and shrewd. They did not tell you why they wanted the flutes?"

Her voice grew faint. "No."

Psal raised his eyebrow. "Do they trust you?"

Maharai did not speak immediately. "I had not thought they might be deceiving me."

"Best to suspect everyone. Now, is that all? Or is there something else this powerless prince can *not* do for you?"

"Psallo, promise me you will let my sisters and your warriors believe I have not learned the Wheel Clan tongue." She edged closer to Psal. "If I learn your language, my sisters will think our ancestors won't be able to speak to me."

"Ah. We would not want to silence the ancestors, would we? But why shouldn't Father's warriors know? And truly, do you think our people will believe you don't know our language? You've been with us almost five months now, Ephan teaching you. Father is not easily deceived."

"Even so, let me pretend for as long as the war lasts. Many in your clan think we Peacock women are stupid. And many in my clan think I am quite stupid."

"Yes, I have heard it said by some that the Peacock Clan is unable to understand our wisdom. But not all believe this." He kissed her forehead. "Well, then, play the part. But I warn you many will not be convinced, and they will only consider you conniving."

"I will be conniving and convincing, Psallo. Don't worry. And, who knows? Perhaps my pretense will help you as well. One never knows."

Psal gently pinched her nose. "If we are conspiring together, we should tell Ephan of your plan. If he denounces your stupidity, all will believe him."

* * * *

The morning came when the Iden longhouse opened its doors: Warmth outside. A wooded glade. Five Peacock warriors under a cloaken stood before Ktwala. An old man approached, stately, with black skin, and a grievous foul-smelling wound.

"Daughter, my name is Chief Yona. Many nights my warriors and I traveled, the cloaken keeping us together. We saw your longhouse. Though marked with the Grassrope marking, we sensed perhaps some of our own clan lived within it. Are we mistaken?"

Yet, will you choose to take my longhouse from me? "You're not mistaken. Enter."

Those tired Peacock warriors fed on Wheel Clan fermented meats. She tended their wounds while they spoke of their battles with the Wheel Clan.

From his tunic, Chief Yona brought green and yellow crystals. "With these," he said, "I can free you from the wake of this Nahas. We will then return to our home region. Truly, Sister, when the war is over, we will bring your lost daughter to you again."

Ktwala took Tomo aside. "They must not stay with us," she said. "These are men who enter into longhouses as lambs and turn upon their hosts like lions. Hunt with them but separate yourselves early from these warriors. Sumra and I will go gather salt and we will return early to bar the longhouse doors. When you return, go to the hidden window, and the hidden places."

He stroked her braid. "And they might take you from me, even if you're the Wheel Clan's Queen."

"What does that matter? Do you not have a woman now?"

"I want you as well."

Ktwala pushed his hand away. "I cannot go to their home fields. Would he not know the home region where these warriors would take us? If I lived among my people, would war not wage before my very eyes? I've seen enough of war. No, we cannot bind ourselves to these men or attempt to free ourselves from the Wheel Clan's wake."

"So…your will to be free is broken? Nahas has won?"

"My will is not broken," she answered. "But I will not become an object of particular interest to both Nahas and the Peacock Clan."

Ktwala returned to the warriors near her hearth, took a basket in her hand, even though their barrels overflowed with salt. "Salt abounds in this place. We will sift and collect. Tonight we will journey to your home region."

Tomo and Lian hunted with the warriors, while Sumra and Ktwala went to collect salt. This is why to this day when the Odunaons plan a ruse, they say: "We will go and collect salt."

Night fell, and the third moon waxing, Ktwala turned to Sumra, "We must hurry homeward. Night must not find either you or me outside our walls."

But as they hurried, a strange and eerie whirlwind arose. Yes, even though the day had been calm. Touching neither leaf nor branch, animal or bird, rock or fallen log, it blasted the women only, lifting Sumra and throwing her body down to the bottom of the sloping hill. Then it left as suddenly as it had come. At the top of the hill, Ktwala peered through the woods and vines toward the Iden tower. Too far to call for help.

"My legs are wounded," Sumra said. "I cannot lift myself."

"Let me run home," Ktwala answered, "and bring rope from the long-house."

"There is no time to go and return. Stay here and help me, Sister."

A small rope lay in the bottom of Ktwala's basket. One end she tied around her own stomach, the other she staked to a gnarled tree. Four and a half months pregnant, she descended the cliff. At the bottom, she lifted Sumra, tied the rope under their armpits. Her feet against the cliff side, her sister's back to hers, she pushed and climbed. At last, they reached the top.

But the third moon hastened and the girl could neither walk nor be carried quickly by the pregnant Ktwala.

Tears streamed down Sumra's face. "Ktwala, my sister, the time has come for us to part. You must find your lost daughter. Why allow the night to take you? Why let the warriors take the longhouse? If I die here, my husband will meet me again in our Permanent home. But who knows? We are woven together. We might perhaps see the goodness of the Creator in the land of the living."

Ktwala held both hands to her face, wept. She had no cloaken. What use staying with the girl? The night would separate them, whether she stayed or left. Already the moon was near its height; she could delay no longer. "Goodbye, my sister."

Outpacing the rising third moon, she raced homeward. As she entered the house, Tomo and Lian looked out behind her in the darkness. Tomo asked, "Where is Sumra?"

"The Unfleshed Ones and the night conspired to take her," Ktwala answered.

This she said because although evil and chance is common to all, she had surmised that some evil conspired to destroy the clan. For why should Sumra have fallen on the night they planned to deceive the Peacock Clan?

Outside, Chief Yona called out to them: "Open the door, Ktwala."

Lian hurried to the door. Him, too, Ktwala grasped.

"Go to our lost sister," Ktwala told the chief. "Cover her with your cloaken. Let her be one of you."

"Perhaps there is time yet," Tomo said. He grasped a cloaken, then the latch of the door. Ktwala held his hand. He pushed her away.

"Whether we leave the longhouse or not, Sumra is lost to us," Ktwala said. "For she is far from here. The third moon is already high. You cannot go and return here in time. If you leave now, the night will take her in one direction and you in another. And if you open the door, the warriors will overwhelm me."

The betrayed warriors' voices echoed all around. "We are tired of being tossed by the night, our Sister Ktwala. Let us in."

But entrance doors, windows, secret places were locked. Ktwala closed her ears to them. The tower fled that region. As the warriors and the old terrain blurred away, a wail escaped Tomo's lips. Ktwala placed her hands on his shoulder to comfort him. He wheeled around and hit her hard against cheek, knocking her down. Angry, he blamed Ktwala for Sumra's loss. From that day onward, he sought to slay her eagle, until at last Ktwala told the bird to fly free.

Some days later, the longhouse arrived to greenery and mildness. A sack Ktwala lifted, and her flute, and left the longhouse. All morning, she roamed, gathered.

"The Wheel Clan owns too much," she told herself.

Returning, her foot on the threshold of her longhouse, she smelled blood and fat and flesh. Tomo sat with the slain carcass of a boar: "See what I've done. See what I have killed. But none of this is yours. Because you left my wife alone to the night."

Night came, and morning. The warm earth, floral aromas. In all the ten directions, mildness and beauty. The outcast climbed, descended, reported what he saw. Pyres. Ktwala's mouth fell open: they were once again being pulled in the Wheel Clan wake. She would see her unseen daughter again.

Night came. And Ktwala's heart both feared—and wished—to see a steward longhouse. All night she could not sleep. Had they truly returned to Nahas' wake? The next morning she woke to green fields, but found no longhouse. The next day when they docked at a desert—sand and scrub, her heart sank. It should have been a day of corpses, or pyres. The next day, a day of fenced fields. Ktwala did not know what to think.

Tomo descended the tower: "I saw a longhouse, toward the East. Past a forest, a blue lake, and fruit orchards. Toward the west, a flowered meadow."

Ktwala smiled, glad he spoke to her again. The sun rose high, no steward arrived. They had come to a field with an uninhabited longhouse filled with freshly-made food. Did the Wheel Clan king expect her to enter and take? Her basket across her shoulders, the sun shining, she did not take the Wheel Clan's bounty.

In the distance, she saw a mud-built hut. She gathered a small shovel and a bone knife. In Tomo's back pouch, axes and ropes. In the hand of the child, a woven basket which Ktwala filled with wild fruits and tubers. Tomo killed small game. The sun rose higher, beat down. They arrived at the hut. Inside, rusted tools and containers. Crystals too, of all colors and sizes. Tired, fatigued, Ktwala touched her belly; the child inside her stirred. The child at her feet lay outside on the grass.

"This hut can be our home," Tomo said.

She did not answer him. Tomo grasped her hand. "Death, death, and more death. I am tired of my life. Ktwala, love me, and leave that long-house." He kissed her hard against the lips. She pushed him away.

An old memory returned: a day she lay in the grass with the Wheel Clan king. Tomo's hair did not shine red like the sun, but was untamed and dark like the night. His arm was his only power, his humor was of common things. She might have loved him if she had met him first. "I am my enemy's wife," she said. "I cannot love you."

But then she saw…on a nearby hill, a man in the green clothing of a Wheel Clan steward.

"Did you know he stood there?" Ktwala asked the outcast.

"I did."

"Is that why you kissed me? Do you know what you've done?" she asked.

"I've challenged a king. I've taken a gamble. The king has obviously returned you to his wake. But he might not want you if another man has had you."

"Foolish, proud one, you have destroyed your life."

She told herself she should save Tomo. Before third moon rose, she would latch the doors. She did not want another of her clan brothers to die. When second moon rose, the steward arrived at her door with a basket of salted meats. Then, from a pouch slung on his shoulder, he removed a packet of parchments.

"These," he said, "are from your daughter. Kept for you by our noble Firstborn while you journeyed in the cold climes. Speak to no one else of them."

He says nothing of the kiss. Ktwala opened the parchments. Maharai's tiny script. She sat poring over each message, read of the daily chores and sorrows of her daughter. Her heart swelled with joy and hope, and love too yes! love for her son, the Firstborn son of the Wheel Clan.

She looked up at Tomo, who had stood above her wondering. "I crave a plant I saw in the fields," she said. "Near the briar patch at the river. Do you remember it?"

"I remember the briar patch. But not the plant."

"It has yellow fruit with leaves that shine purple in the moonlight. Go and gather it for me for my soul longs for it. I do not know when next I may find it and it is good for the birth of children."

Tomo raced through the door toward the orchard. As soon as he left, quickly, throughout the longhouse, Ktwala closed all doors and windows, all the entrances Tomo knew. Then she sat reading the parchments again and waiting.

He returned, and pushed at the door, knocked hard to batter it down. "Ktwala!"

Lian walked toward the latched door.

"Do not touch it, Lian."

The boy halted. Fear like a sharp edged-knife etched the boy's face; it sliced, too, through Ktwala's heart.

"Ktwala, open to me!"

"Lian, do not touch the door."

"Ktwala!"

Ktwala walked with the child to her room. There, she lay in bed, weeping, resolved, the child also weeping beside her. Outside Tomo's voice echoed. Then all grew silent. Ktwala told herself, "All for the best."

She craved sleep to forget all her forgetting. Night grew gray with the brightness of the second and the third moon. Then, footsteps sounded through the longhouse and neared her bedroom. She sat up to see Tomo standing above her, the plant and its root in his hands. The child woke and climbed into his arms. Tomo stared at Ktwala long, then threw the dirty plant at her. "I will not leave you. Do you hear me? I will never leave you."

He sat beside her, holding his head. She pulled him down beside her on the bed. Yet she did not lie with him. The next day she woke and found the wall near one of the casement windows broken through. "My love for you made me strong," the outcast said.

CHAPTER 27

PUNISHMENT

Ktwala's cloths, the Iden women, Maharai's pleading, even the war faded in importance when Psal considered the immensity of the tower epidemic. But, as he lay on his wheeled bed in the keening room, Tolika appeared in the doorway. The double moonlight streamed from the window onto her face. Even the mud covering her face could not hide her beauty.

He rose to greet her. "Welcome, Tolika. Is there some trouble with your sisters?"

"Firstborn, I have come to plead that you free me from Deyn." She walked toward several low-lying shelves where baskets of all sizes lay in disarray. "Only Deyn."

"I cannot do it. If I were to release you, punishment would have to be exacted in some other way. Would you rather be married to Deyn or to be anchored in the cold climes for two hundred days?"

She removed the cover from one small large bottle whose sides were red-speckled with its former contents. She sniffed the bottle and walked toward him. "Is this a poison?"

"No poisonous pharma there," Psal said. "Nothing but keening ink, jars, and studier tools." He looked at his parchments again. "But now you must go. I have...."

In an instant, Tolika was upon him, thrusting Lan's dagger into his shoulder. She struck several times. Few but deep gashes; blood flowed along his tan tunic and onto the floor. As they struggled among broken jars and scattered pharma, Tolika's beautiful face grew distorted. She continued to strike even when Ephan and Nahas came running in.

Before Psal knew it, Nahas had taken Tolika by the neck and was banging her head against a wall. Once, twice, three times. Blood flowed from her nose, broken teeth, and bruised forehead. Then dragging her by the hair into the gathering room, Nahas ordered Cyrt to open the longhouse's main entrance door.

Psal limped after Nahas, Ephan and Netophah following. An audible gasp rose from among the women near the hearth when they saw Psal's bloodied tunic.

"Cyrt," the king repeated, "open the door."

But Cyrt lingered and soon joined Psal and Ephan in pleading for Tolika. Meanwhile, Tolika's cries had rallied the Iden women. The residential hall echoed with their angry shouts.

Nahas pushed Tolika toward the door, spoke to Cyrt. "Has love for the mother weakened you? Open. The. Door."

"Nahas," Cyrt said, "she is—"

By then Deyn and Lan had entered the room. More pleas assailed the king. Nahas listened to all in silence, his hands tightly grasping Tolika's wrist.

But at last, Rain stood up. "Nahas," she said, "do not forget how treacherous the Peacock Clan was on the day they killed our children. Do not forget that Tolika has caused a noble Wheel Clan youth to harm his friend, his own near-kinsman. Shouldn't the king repair the harm the Firstborn did by forgiving her? Should the king not bring justice to Deyn?"

So Tolika was cast out alone into the night, her weeping voice echoing in the landscape, despite the pleas of her husbands, the Chief Steward, Nahas' Captain, and the studiers. Then Barron, a warrior from Orian's clan, and Aythan, the young warrior from Orian's longhouse whose arm Psal had removed, came running in, struggling with Gidea.

"She was trying to climb through a window, Nahas," Aythan said.

Gidea bit Aythan's arm so fiercely that he threw her to the ground. "Release me to die with my daughter!" she shouted. "Give us a cloaken. You will be well rid of us."

Nahas approached Gidea, his face red with rage. A swift blow across Gidea's face followed, which caused her to fall to the floor. But she was not cast out.

"The Firstborn is a king's son," Cyrt held Gidea close, laid her head against his shoulder. "No one is allowed to harm the Firstborn. I am sorry your daughter had to be made outcast. But it was expedient. Do you understand my words, my love? It was expedient."

* * * *

Psal touched his shoulder and the woolen bandage Ephan had wrapped about his arm. "It is death to kill a Firstborn," he explained to Maharai. "Especially a Firstborn who is a peace child. Father had to send her into the night."

Maharai looked out the window, silent, tears streaming down her face.

"Maharai, my sister, my love. Do not weep, do not weep. You will break my heart with all this weeping."

But only sleep could stop her tears from flowing.

As she lay sleeping, Psal arose and went to the room Deyn and Lan shared. He entered, head bowed. But he did not speak. Their grief was too great. Then, after mourning with them for some time, he left their room. As he walked through the gathering room, Seagen met him.

"Why let yourself be seen comforting one whom Nahas has punished?" Seagen chided.

"Why should it matter whom I comfort?" Psal hastened his steps. "I was the victim of Tolika's crime. And the cause of her being made outcast. Why should I not—"

"How little you understand!" Seagen said. "Firstborn, it matters very much what you are seen doing. At best, you show yourself too much of a studier, too tender-hearted to be the chief of our great clan. At worse, you endanger your friends' lives. If you wish to be a chief, then show the king and all others in the royal longhouse what they long to see. Give your people a thread to hang their hope upon. Wrong decisions have been made." He shook his head as if the world he knew was about to end. "By you, and by Nahas. These Iden women should have been killed or made outcast or scattered among—"

"Enough!" Psal cut him off. "I'm tired of lectures."

Psal walked toward Maharai's room. As he pulled aside the screen door, a chamber pot came hurling towards his head. He managed to dodge it, but its contents spilled onto the wooden floor.

"Maharai," he pleaded, and spoke again of the mandate that any who harmed the Firstborn should be punished. Again she wept and continued weeping until sleep overtook her.

After she fell asleep, Psal rose. *I need pharma to sleep, pharma to soothe my mind.* He entered one of the pharma rooms. Ephan and Daris were mixing pharma for the next day. Under the guise of needing calming pharma for Maharai, he took a jar Rangi and—hiding it under his tunic—a gourd of Tomah as well. He returned to their bed and lay at her side, chewing both barks.

As he chewed, it seemed his thoughts grew clearer and he marveled at the power of Tomah bark. Among the Waymaker Clan, a myth existed that the Creator had forbidden men to touch a particular tree, a tree that would bring great knowledge. According to the old story, humanity's first parents had disobeyed and eaten the forbidden fruit. The plant had opened worlds to them—all the worlds the studiers examined, and much more. Worlds where they saw strange creatures, strange colors, understood wisdom that brought them great enlightenment, euphoria, ecstasy, and despair. The Waymaker Clan were full of such myths. *The Falconer Clan as well. Yet, they respond so differently! The Waymaker Clan say there is no permanent home in this world. The Falconers seek to find it.*

Two different clans, how much better the world would be if they were as one. Truly, if Tomah was not that original forbidden plant, it should have been. Suddenly, the answer comes clear.

Something has to be done. We are two kingdoms in this longhouse, divided among ourselves. The raping must stop. The divisions must stop. Perhaps the time has come for the Iden women to be separated.

He rose again from Maharai's side. The effect of the Tomah was not as calming as it had been when he first started chewing. He was calm, yes, but his emotions bounced from dulled despair to a detached excitement. It seemed to him the only way to return to that calm was to take more Tomah and he hated himself for wanting more. He could smell the hated bark on his breath, and was glad he could. Those who became enslaved to Tomah sometimes developed an inability to smell it, even when they reeked of it. *Ephan will smell it, however.* He opened the window and spat the chewed Tomah bark into the night. Emon was powerful enough to cover the Tomah odor. He rubbed Emon on his face, chest, and wounded shoulder. Once he had smeared himself with the greasy ointment, he called Ephan from the sick room.

"I have a grievous thing to do," he said. "I have no other choice. If we must win the war outside out longhouse, we must win the war inside it. Go now. Gather the Peacock women. And tell Lebo to call our warriors together as well."

Then, because the pharma made him unsteady, he went into the keening room and retrieved his staff. Leaning on it, he entered the gathering room.

PART IV

WAR AND MARRIAGE

CHAPTER 28

MARRIAGES

When all had crowded in the gathering room, Psal spoke to the Peacock women in the Iden dialect. "Sisters, this wailing has lasted long enough. I'm tired of rapes. I'm tired of chants. I'm tired of warfare within our longhouse. What I am about to do, I must do."

The Iden women exchanged nervous glances and huddled together.

"You will have to be separated. Not from our longhouse. But from each other. You will have to marry." Next he spoke to the warriors in the Wheel Clan language. "My brothers, those of you who have no women will have a chance to take one. Choose any you wish, but choose wisely. Those warriors bonded to each other by previous marriages may once again choose the same wife. Or they may choose another friend to share a wife with. I would rather that those who have had no wives be the first to choose but do what you wish. All I want is peace."

Nunu came forward. "You've taken Tolika away and now you force us to marry? We will not do it."

"Tolika tried to kill me," Psal answered her. "Probably at Gidea's request. Do not blame me for that. Now, it is safest for your sisters if you marry. Or do you want more women raped or thrown out?"

"They don't want to be married to Wheel Clan warriors!" she shouted at him, her old eyes fierce.

"My brothers," he said, turning away from her. "There are among these fifty-eight women, women who would make perfect wives for you. No doubt this singing will stop when they're divided."

"Find my daughter," Gidea said, her voice so weak Psal had to fight to prevent himself from pitying her.

"Your daughter is lost to the night," Psal answered.

"They have tower knowledge enough to find her," Nunu said to her Iden sisters. "Let them find her and bring Ktwala back."

"Obviously, you're an ignorant woman who doesn't know tower science," Psal said. "We are not gods. We do not know where she is. She is being unmade by the night. Where the night will toss her, I do not know. Nor do I care." He turned to Ephan. "Speak to them. You understand whiny women better than I do."

But when Ephan attempted to speak to them they pleaded with him, begging loudly. "We will not do it, Ephan! Find Tolika first."

"I will make your choices clear to you." Psal pushed Ephan aside. "You will each be given in marriage to two of our warriors. You have some choice in this matter. You may refuse a warrior, but you cannot refuse all. Therefore, if kind and good men approach you—and most of us are good—accept them."

"I will not do it," Gidea said, her voice thin and fading.

The pain in his shoulder made Psal impatient, the Tomah made him uncaring, the suspicion that worse trouble lay ahead made him ponder expedience. "Do you have any power to make me not do it, Gidea?" He made a sweeping gesture toward all the Peacock women. "Now! Everyone from age fourteen and upward, approach! Now!"

None of the women moved.

"This is how the matter stands," Psal continued. "If you do not choose to be married, you will become a comfort woman. Instead of two men, you will have five hundred. Maybe all in one night. Do you understand that? And when we meet other longhouses, your days and nights will be even busier. If you persist in challenging me, I might even turn you out alone into the night. There are no other choices. Now!" he repeated. "Or do you wish to become comfort women?"

Several women lowered their heads and glanced at Gidea, then stepped forward. The more argumentative ones, like Nunu and Gidea, remained unmoved and unmoving.

Nunu, wrinkled and bent—as if still stooping over the corpses of her husband and sons—shouted, "I will not take a new husband."

"Old woman," Psal snapped, "why do you think one of our warriors would want a toothless hag like you?"

"Nor will I allow any of my sisters to be taken!" She raised her body to its full height and stared him in the face, daring him to challenge her. "We will not marry those who killed our men."

"Truly?" he asked. *Why does she not understand I am trying to protect her sisters?* "Who are you to allow or not allow?"

Behind him, Seagen said, laughing, "Our lame studier is taking on an old woman."

Nahas stood at the corridor's end, studying him.

Psal gestured to Kwin. "Open the main door."

Kwin shook his head, glanced at Lan. But Orian grasped the old woman and threw her out. Nunu's fingers held onto the latch. Lan ran toward her, held the door open that she might re-enter. She squeezed herself inside and clung to Lan's arm as she stood shaking near the threshold.

"Put her outside again and close the door against her, Lan!" Psal shouted.

Lan, his face pale from weeping, held her about the waist, hesitating. "Firstborn," he pleaded, "she is only an old, broken thing. It is not...."

"Put her outside and close the door!" Psal shouted. "Did you not hear me?"

Lan did not move. But Orian drew near and wrenched Lan's hand from the old woman's waist. Once again, and for the last time, the woman was put out and Orian closed the door against her.

A terrified shriek from the corridor made Psal look up. Maharai was running into the gathering room toward one of the windows. She called out into the night and Nunu thrust her arms through the opening. Maharai attempted to pull her inside, but only a wail could squeeze through that opening. Soon, both Nunu and her voice faded away into the night.

"Maharai, it is too late!" Psal said, raising his voice. He turned to the warriors. "Brothers, choose a woman. Take Gidea first. Who will—"

Maharai struck his betraying knee, almost toppling him.

"Go to your room, Maharai," Psal ordered, steadying himself. "To your room, Maharai! I will speak to you later."

She didn't move. She was looking at Ephan.

"Cloud! Take her away."

Ephan took her by the arm but she pushed him away and was soon at Psal's side. She beat his chest and clawed at his face. The pounding exacerbated the wound Tolika had given him earlier. He called Kwin and Broqh who caught her by the waist and shoulder and held her fast.

"She's not a prisoner," he said. "She's Nahas' daughter. Soften your hold, but take her to her room."

After she was dragged, screaming and kicking to her room, Psal—fighting against pain, blood loss, guilt, and Tomah—spoke to the warriors again. The room blurred around him but the matter had to be finished.

But near the door he heard Lan challenging him. "The old woman may have been troublesome, but the Wheel Clan doesn't make bothersome little old ladies outcast."

"I will not have my decisions questioned," Psal retorted, hurt that he was now being challenged by one he had earlier defended. "Now, Brothers, as I said, Gidea will be the first."

Although all were surprised by the Firstborn's anger, Orian, Cyrt, and several chief warriors stepped forward.

Psal spoke to Orian first. "Orian, as a chief, you have the right to choose. But you've chosen a walking firebrand."

"When I lost my wife that night," Orian answered. "I had not thought I would want another to lie beside me. But Gidea is a lovely woman, truly."

But Gidea slapped him hard across the face.

He rubbed his cheek. "This one will push my words back down my throat," Orian said. So Orian, who had fought too many battles within and outside the longhouse, did not want a battle inside his own chambers as well.

Then Cyrt approached. Unlike the others, he did not peruse her like one from the Macaw Clan perusing livestock, or like an outlaw from the Grassrope clan setting his lust on a foundling woman. He gazed tenderly at her.

"I want her," he said, his voice soft, a shy smile wavering on his lips.

"If anyone can tame her," Kwin said, "that noble warrior can."

"You've had wives enough," Psal said.

"Wives taken by divorce and the Peacock treachery," Cyrt said.

"Other chiefs and captains need women as well."

"Why continue nursing some grudge against me?"

Psal stepped aside. "Take her if you wish."

Cyrt took Gidea by the right hand and Seagen took her left. Gidea spat in their faces, fought so valiantly that they dropped her. With a loud thud she tumbled to the floor. Seagen punched her hard across the face. It was perhaps not the thing to do, for in an instant, Gidea had struck Seagen, and they were kicking and hitting and beating at each other, neither relenting.

Gidea stood up and kicked the nearest at hand: Cyrt—a well-placed kick in the groin. Then she grasped Psal's finger and bit Psal hard. His finger ached so much he thought the skin was clean cut through. After studying his finger, he pointed at the main entrance door. She shrank backward and sat on the floor, her chest heaving.

The minor battle ended, Psal thought it best to protect and marry off the remaining Iden women. He placed the girls who were not quite of marriageable age with honorable young warriors who had lost sisters and mothers, commanding them to treat the girls as their sisters. The older women he gave to warriors from all three sub-clans: Orian's, Antun's, and those reared in the royal longhouse. But to the Maldon warriors he gave none, for those warriors were already married. In the end, five or six feisty older Iden women remained unchosen, Gidea among them.

"No one wants you, Gidea," Psal said. "As I warned, a woman who is unwanted and unchosen will become one of our comfort women. You and your sisters will join the other comfort women in the king's longhouse. The others are quite ugly. I suspect you will collect their wages and their customers."

It was then that Psal saw a thing he had not ever dreamed of seeing. Cyrt fell to his knees; kneeling, he touched the hilt of the dagger on Psal's thigh. "Firstborn, I beg you. Give the woman to me. My heart cries out for her. Don't make her a comfort woman." He remained in that position, head bowed, awaiting Psal's answer.

Psal stood in silence, studying the bruised hand that had brought his father so many victories. "She doesn't want you," Psal said. "Have you not seen?"

"I want her nevertheless." Cyrt's head remained bowed.

Cyrt's continued submission made Psal uncomfortable. He was unaccustomed to it. Worse, the other Wheel Clan captains were pleading Cyrt's cause and an uproar even arose among the Wheel Clan women, all begging the Firstborn to give the woman to Cyrt. But Psal pushed Cyrt's hand from his dagger.

Then Gaal stepped forward. His voice low, his demeanor submissive, his face looking toward the ground. "Firstborn," he said, "if you cannot give the woman to Cyrt, give her to me. Remember, I have done you much good. We in the Wheel Clan honor those who have done us good."

"You will give her to Cyrt," Psal spoke equally low. "He is your friend, is he not?"

"We are not bounded together," Gaal answered. "I want her for myself. To protect her. But if you cannot give her to me, I beg you give the woman to Cyrt. For the peace of the longhouse. And for the woman's sake. One so lovely would be greatly abused by having many lovers. Give her to one warrior alone. To Cyrt or to me only."

"And if I give her to you…do you not think he will harm you?" Psal asked.

"He would not harm me, Firstborn. Nahas would not allow it. But the woman, Firstborn. I will protect her."

"I cannot renounce," Psal said. "I have told the women the punishment for not accepting our warriors is to become comfort women. It is the word of a Firstborn. I cannot renounce it."

Gaal smiled. "But, Firstborn, I am no warrior."

"True words, Gaal. Subtle words. But you cannot have her. You will share her with Cyrt and I do not want that." He placed Gidea's hands in Gaal's. "She's yours to do with as you will, but return her to the comfort rooms when you're done. She does not belong to you alone. She belongs to all the men of our longhouse." Gidea fought and kicked against Gaal as he led her to his chamber.

But Psal was not finished yet. After he sent the remaining feisty Iden women to the comfort rooms, he called little Indina to his side.

"The foundling is a tender thing," he said. "I worry that one or more of you will violate her."

"You offend your brothers, Firstborn," Netophah said, looking toward the residential corridor where Gidea's screams echoed.

"Why should the truth offend them?" Psal asked. "I speak the truth. Therefore, it is best the girl be married off. I prefer she stay in this longhouse that I may ensure her safety. Also, the one who marries her must not lie with her until she has reached her sixteenth year. Who wants the girl and who is willing to wait for her?"

Because Indina was a likable and dainty girl, many of the warriors declared they wanted her. Yet Psal found only these five worthy of her: Lebo, Broqh, Lan, Kwin, and Deyn. Kwin had never had a woman of his own. Lebo had lived solitary since his wife died. Lan and the castrated Deyn still loved Tolika. Broqh loved the absent Lirion. Psal made his decision. Kwin, aged nineteen, and Lebo, sixty, were good friends and greatly respected. An eimi consisting of Lebo and Kwin would not be challenged. He ordered them to come forward and told Indina to join them. This the little girl did, standing between her two husbands like an obedient little warrior.

After Psal dismissed everyone, he called Ephan and Lan to the stairwell in the keening room.

"You know I'm unallied and a studier," he told them. "Yet you challenged me in front of the others?"

"Why did you send the old woman into the night uncovered?" Lan asked him, and sat on the steps, his arms folded on his knees. "She won't live long, outcast, alone, aged."

"You reek of Tomah," Ephan said. "It makes not only the body insensitive, but often the heart and soul as well."

"I am not enslaved to Tomah," Psal snapped at him.

"I did not say you were enslaved to it," Ephan raised his voice. "Only that...that...." He walked to the door. "I will not argue with one under the influence of Tomah. Tomorrow we will speak of this."

"Can you two not see that I did it for the good of the Iden women?" Psal shouted. "I had to seem strong."

"A weak way to be strong," Ephan said.

"Should I have allowed an old woman to best me?"

"Is there any virtue in besting an old woman?" Lan retorted. "Or in forcing Gidea and the others to become comfort women?"

"Why did you not give me Gidea?" Ephan asked from the doorway. "I would have taken her."

"To give you the woman would be to seal your death," Psal said.

"Nahas would not allow any to kill his favorite." Netophah's voice. He entered, but Nahas stood outside waiting. "Is this the chief's game you're playing? Using Gidea to create a wedge between Gaal and Cyrt?"

The thought might have been on the edge of Psal's mind but he did not wish to recognize it. He spoke to Ephan alone. "We will speak of this matter tomorrow, when you understand things the way I do."

"But Nahas wants to talk about this 'matter' now," Netophah said.

Psal joined the king and the Wheel Clan Heir in the king's chamber.

"So you sent an old woman into the night?" Nahas asked Psal. The question neither accused nor praised.

"She was a leader among the women," Psal answered. "I had to do it."

"Indeed?" Netophah asked in a non-committal way that annoyed Psal. Psal managed to restrain himself from reminding Netophah that he himself was the Firstborn son.

The king poured some fermented ale from a large pitcher into a narrow goblet. This he gave to Netophah. He poured more of the ale into another goblet. This goblet he gave to Psal. Then he poured some of the ale for himself. Both drank slowly, solemnly, but Psal paced back and forth, his drink untouched.

"Once a chief makes a decision," Netophah said, "he cannot and should not undo it. Nor should he hide away in his room."

"I was not thinking of undoing it. Or of hiding away."

"Truly?" Nahas did not look convinced. "You've hidden away before. And you studiers often think and rethink a matter. Especially studiers who are challenged by their friends."

"Do I *seem* to be rethinking anything? You seem to delight in continually making assumptions about me."

"Drink." Netophah sat on the edge of a chair near his father's royal bed. "It pushes the guilt away."

Psal placed his goblet on a nearby shelf. "I have no guilt."

The king walked to the window and leaned against his elbow as he looked into the night. "You make yourself out to be some great sufferer? Have I not lost two wives and four children?"

"My mother was one of those wives, Nahas. Those children were my siblings."

"All men suffer, Firstborn. You often *seem* to forget that."

"True, Nahas, suffering is common to all men. But I have endured the common afflictions of this life and much more. Multiple afflictions simultaneously! With new ones arising daily. Moreover, I have endured the ignorant judgment of fools who mock what they cannot understand. I am damaged, Father, a creature of taboo, rejected friendless in my own home, and you do not seek to understand." His words ended in a flood of tears.

He had attempted to speak as a studier and as a chief, but the vain attempt ended with his father and brother looking piteously at his trembling treacherous body. He walked out of the room. In the hallway, little Indina was on her knees, a bucket of bloody water at her side, scrubbing his blood from the floor. He called to her and she turned a grateful smile to him, then returned to her cleaning. He thought of Maharai and marveled at the persistence of his need for her. Then—wracked with pain in his legs, waist, and shoulder—he steeled himself for her anger.

CHAPTER 29

WOMEN, STUDIERS, AND TOWERS

Psal's halting steps echoed in the corridor. Maharai waited for him to push the curtained screen aside.

"I'm sorry, Maharai," he said when he entered. "It was necessary. Your sisters would not have fared well. They had to be married."

She edged away, but he held her hand and pulled her toward him.

"And Nunu?" She remained sitting on the mat.

He slowly unlaced his tunic. "Nunu had to be cast out."

As she watched him remove his leggings, Maharai asked herself if she could lie beside someone who had sent old, kind, Nunu into the night.

"Maharai," he said, searching her face. "You must try to understand."

Intent on avoiding his gaze, she looked about the room. Parchments and pharma bottles were scattered about. The chamber was now as much his as hers. When she looked at him again, his tunic lay on the ground near his twisted foot. She glanced upward, from the foot to the bandaged shoulders, then the scarred face. The heavy smell of Emon and the odor of some other strange pharma made her see him again as her weak friend. And yet....

"Ephan and Lan are both angry with me," he said. "Nahas and Netophah as well. Therefore, you must not be angry with me, Maharai."

She looked up at the ceiling, her eyes wet with tears. His hands touched her shoulder and as he lay beside her, he gently tugged her downward. She allowed herself to lie beside him, but didn't look at him. For a long while, they lay together in silence. Try as she could, she could not bring herself to speak. He should not have thrown Nunu into the night or forced Gidea to become a comfort woman.

Psal was stroking her stomach. His lips kissed her shoulder. He had never done such a thing before. There was something different in the way he looked at her, something like the passion she had seen in Nahas' eyes when Nahas first saw her mother. But another emotion was intermixed with that passion: a need, a desperate desire to please her. She began to understand what Gidea meant by "using her body." Yet this knowledge of the "use" of her body had come too late to save either Tolika or Nunu. Psal's sheathed dagger lay near the foot of their bed. She could use the knife: plunging it into his heart. Or she could wait for him to sleep. Or she could use her body as Gidea had advised. But which brother? Psal or

Netophah? She no longer knew which of the two had true power in the longhouse.

She was no fool. If she distanced herself from Psal, the king might give her to Netophah. Netophah had promised she would be his primary wife. How much power would that bring? And when?

And I do not hate Psal as I hate Netophah. "You must leave, Psallo," she said, pushing him off the bed. "Return to your room. Or I will kill you in your sleep if you stay. I know I will."

"Don't hate me, Maharai." He stood up, tarried at the door a very long time, then limped out into the corridor.

After he left, she also rose. Walking past him in the hallway, she stopped at Netophah's chamber.

When he opened the door to her, Netophah asked, "Tell me. Have you come because you want me or because you are angry with the Firstborn?"

She did not answer him.

"I have seen your love for Psal," Netophah continued. "When you walk with me, I do not see that love. But try to love me, Maharai, and I will make you my Primary wife."

"But why should I be a Primary wife?" she asked. "Why should you marry another wife?"

"It is a necessary thing," he said. "A king must have allies and peace children, but if you desire…you could be shared wife to both of us. It is both an honor and a sorrow to be a shared wife of two chiefs. If you become a shared wife…and Psal becomes a chief, you will have to travel from longhouse to longhouse, now staying with his set of wives, now staying with mine, now living among one group of warriors, now living among another. Always you would have power, much power. But primary wives have their own kind of power."

She started weeping. *Should I marry one I hate?*

She walked away with him, the night bringing a demoralized stillness. No longer were chants heard from the Iden women. Since their imprisonment, the Iden women had not been apart. Now—with the exception of the "unruly six" as Daris was calling them—they lay with strange husbands in the residential section.

Maharai found Gidea with the comfort women, surrounded by the rest of her "unruly" sisters. Gidea was lying on a mat with her face turned to the walls. The Iden women now joined themselves with the Wheel Clan comfort women, women who gave them Rangi and Tomah to ease their grief. All sat looking at Maharai.

"My enemy," Gidea said, "your lame prince has killed my daughter."

Maharai answered, "She is not dead. Only, night-tossed."

"So, you've found your strength now?" Gidea asked.

Maharai did not answer her. She only thought of how Gidea's son often forced her and how Gidea knew all along.

* * * *

The next morning, Psal woke to the sound of nothing at all. Ill at ease, he turned in his bed.

Then Ephan said, fear in his voice, "Do you hear that?"

Psal listened. Two Peacock longhouses were materializing in the early morning.

"But," he stammered, dressing hurriedly, "how could they? The Peacock Clan doesn't know how to...."

"They did not bring us here. The tower did! These Peacock warriors are as unprepared for battle as we are. It's because you cast the old woman out. It liked her." Ephan ran frantically, looking at the crystals. The crystal on the listening branch had dimmed. Crystals on all the keening branches flickered, winked, then faded. Psal and Ephan exchanged glances. "This vindictive tower has tossed us into battle with Threshing Floor Clan and one other longhouse. Wake Nahas. Now!"

Psal ran half-naked from the keening room into the king's chamber.

"Father," he gasped out the word. "We must prepare for battle. Now! Listen. Can you hear them? The Threshing Floor longhouse and I think... the Double Eclipse longhouse are outside."

"Outside?" Nahas walked to the window, listened. "But how?"

"And, Father, the crystals in all the sockets on the listening branch have gone black. If any new information is being sent to them, they aren't telling. Nor are they sending any. If...."

"Yes, I know." Nahas grasped his armor, called for Netophah. "But how...."

"The tower is angry with me. Because of the old woman."

"Our towers should be on our side." Nahas walked to the door. "Let these tower understand reality! To destroy us for the sake of an old woman!" His voice echoed through the longhouse as he called Netophah and his warriors to the unplanned battle.

"Will we die?" Daris asked when Psal re-entered the keening room.

Psal shook his head. "We are not entirely out-numbered. The Maldon crew is with us."

"But hasn't Tsbosso also rescued warriors?" Daris asked.

"Are you born to think such confounding thoughts?" Psal sighed. "But you're correct. It is possible Tsbosso has also rescued warriors."

"Stupid tower!" Daris entered the base of the tower and shook his fist at it. "Women, studiers, and towers! All unpredictable! Would you rather be with us warring humans or be anchored in the dark cold climes far from those you love?"

The tower ignored him.

"How vindictive you are!" Daris shouted to the keening branches. "To throw us—outnumbered—into a day-long battle!"

* * * *

Maharai and her Iden sisters watched the battle as they watched all battles. But this time, like Maharai, the Iden women looked out through the windows in the gathering room or their chamber windows.

Whenever Maharai heard her imprisoned Iden sisters, shout "Victory, Victory!" whenever a Wheel Clan warrior fell, her heart was like a leaf floating above a watery torrent. Try as she could, she could not wish the Wheel Clan failure. But neither could she wish the Peacock Clans success. Near her, little Indina wept for the Wheel Clan as if they were her own people. All about the longhouse, Wheel Clan women rushed, carrying pharma, water, weapons. As a daughter of the Peacock Clan, Maharai could not run, would not run, would not aid. Still, when a Wheel Clan warrior was brought inside, wounded, she often found herself on the verge of tears. She was an indecisive, still, shadow.

Aware of Rain's accusing eyes, she grew ashamed. The battle sides inside the longhouse were as clearly drawn as those outside, and as Rain and other Wheel Clan women bound up the wounded, the Iden women— although married—still continued their bitter Peacock war chants, even as their new husbands fought and battled outside. As for Maharai, she stood by herself, belonging to neither group.

When the sun was high in the sky, Rain walked to Maharai's side. The old woman looked her up and down. "Are you of the Wheel Clan or not?" she asked Maharai in the Peacock language. "You're the First-born's woman, aren't you?"

Maharai nodded.

"Then, future Chief's wife," Rain said, "why do you halt between two clans? Choose you this day whom you will serve. This is the first battle we've fought since your sisters married our warriors, but it will not be the last. If your sisters continue their taunting songs, they will be taken from each other and scattered among all our longhouses where they will become comfort wives. If they bear future children, those children will be taken from them. Do you understand my words, Maharai?"

"You're asking them to love those who've killed their sons and husbands," Maharai said.

"Our warriors have chosen to love your sisters although your people killed our women," Rain answered. "If your sisters wish to live, they must change their hearts. I'm sure you can make them understand the situation as you now understand it. Do you understand it?"

"I understand it."

Maharai called the Iden comfort women and the rest of the Iden women into the gathering room. "We're in this longhouse," she began. "We have no other home. We should—"

"Our home is there." Gidea pointed past Maharai's left shoulder at the Double Eclipse Peacock longhouse.

"Why not the Threshing Floor longhouse?" Maharai asked. "Will they not understand what our common enemy did to us?"

"The Threshing Floor longhouse," Moko said, "are a hateful people."

The ancient grudge again, the one the elders never discussed in front of us young ones.

"Our brothers in the Double Eclipse Peacock longhouse will accept us," Milia, Eala's mother said.

"I will grieve to see you go but your unhappiness here will destroy you and the Wheel Clan if you remain. I will plead with Rain to let you leave."

"If they allow us to leave," Gidea asked, "will you stay with this cruel people?"

"I must remain here. Or how shall I be restored to my mother?"

Maharai returned to Rain and the other Wheel Clan women near the hearth, and told them in the Peacock language her sisters' decision.

"If they cannot truly join this clan, let them leave," Rain said. "Things cannot remain as they are."

"But should they venture out into the darkness and trust their lives to this Peacock sub-clan?" Satima asked. "Vicious, cruel, self-serving, this Double Eclipse Peacock Clan is known for nothing but evil."

"There is some ancient grudge with Tsbosso's Threshing Floor clan," Maharai answered. "My sisters will not ask help of them."

"Well, then," Rain looked at the Iden women sitting near the hearth. "The Iden women will suffer if they leave. Satisfaction enough for me."

"But the Double Eclipse Peacock longhouse will not allow them to enter," Satima said. "I have heard of them. Such is their evil they don't follow the great principles the Creator gave the peoples of Odunao."

"Even better," Rain said. "Then these bitter Iden women will be lost to the night."

"But," Satima asked Rain and the others, "would you allow them to remain outside if the Double Eclipse rejects them? Or would you let them return to us?"

"Why should mercy be shown them?" Rain turned to Maharai. "Your sisters may leave if they wish. However...if the Peacock Clan rejects them, they cannot re-enter."

As Maharai relayed the message to her sisters, Gidea's brown eyes grew bright with hope. "Are they truly giving us a choice?" She walked past wounded warriors, and stood by the opened main entrance of the longhouse. "We will take our chances with our own people. If the Double Eclipse sub-clan rejects us, the night will become our husband. Surely the night will not be as cruel as these Wheel Clan men."

"Who else will go with Gidea?" Maharai asked the others.

Two groups slowly emerged. Fifteen Iden women hurried to the longhouse door, but others—either because they had heard about this selfsame wicked Peacock sub-clan or because they hoped to be reunited with their children scattered among the Wheel Clan longhouses—stood with Maharai.

"The decision is made," Maharai said. "Those who remain here, there are wounds to bind up, balms to mix, broken axes to mend. You have chosen to belong to this people, now help their warriors. The rest of you....Farewell. Who knows when we will meet each other again?"

How sad that parting was. Gidea walked through the longhouse door saying, "Do not cry for us, my captive sisters. We will return and destroy these warriors who have destroyed our husbands, brothers, and our sons. We will restore your lost daughters to you."

So Gidea and her sisters went outside and as the battle waged, they sang Peacock victory chants. The histories do not say how the Wheel Clan men reacted to that sight. Perhaps they were too busy fighting to care, perhaps the string of their hearts had not knitted with any of the departing women. But many must have lost their hearts that day, for the Iden women had been so long with them some affection had grown up toward them. By the time the third moon and second night came, the Double Eclipse sub-clan was roundly beaten, but they did not allow the defiant Iden Women to enter their longhouse.

After the corpses of seventeen Wheel Clan warriors were carried inside and piled in the gathering room, the royal longhouse doors were locked. The only people left on the battlefield were Gidea, the Iden women, and dead Peacock Clan warriors.

"Shall I ready the fire arrows?" Kwin asked Netophah.

The king answered him. "Wait."

So they waited. Psal and Ephan had left the keening room and now stood near the hearth. Maharai sensed they would not help, could not help. The eyes of all were on her.

Meanwhile, outside, the Iden women continued their Peacock victory chants but the Double Eclipse longhouse did not greet them as long lost sisters.

Broqh called to the king. "Nahas, the third moon is almost at its height. Should we ready the fire arrows or not?"

"Ready them!" Nahas shouted. "Aim at will."

As Kwin, Broqh, and the rest of the royal archers aimed their fiery arrows at the Peacock longhouse, Maharai grew more afraid.

At last, she shouted to Lan. "Open the door! Open the door! Let my sisters back inside!"

Lan looked to Nahas then to Rain. "What is to be done?" he asked.

"Do you truly wish them to enter?" Nahas asked Maharai. "If you wish it, this longhouse is yours to command. You are the Firstborn's woman, after all."

She nodded. *I have exerted my influence as the Firstborn's woman. I am not as powerless as Gidea thinks.*

The door was opened at her request. The Iden women returned, shamefaced, defeated.

That night Maharai spoke to Gidea and the others. "Don't you see?" she asked them. "We have no one but these people who feed us. Our own clan rejected us."

"They thought we were part of a Wheel Clan ruse," Gidea said. "Or why would you have suddenly ambushed them?"

"We did not ambush them!" Maharai shouted. "Our tower tossed us here!"

"A Wheel Clan tower tossing a longhouse into a battle?" Gidea mocked. "I do not believe it. And it is not *our* tower. This is our enemy's tower."

"Even so," Maharai said. "But *our* people did not receive you willingly, did they?"

"It has been said," Gidea retorted, "that the Double Eclipse Clan is an evil clan. And the Threshing Floor Peacock longhouse are our ancient enemies. Another Peacock longhouse would have accepted us."

* * * *

Psal threw his hands up in the air. "I give up. I give up." Immediately, all the keening crystals shone, as if gloating in their triumph. "Ephan! Daris! Come! We're forgiven!"

"I don't know why you're triumphing over us," Ephan shouted at the keening trees as he entered. "We studiers are on your side. Or have you forgotten?"

"The battle with the Peacock Clans might be over but this tower still wars with us," Psal said. "Neither of its messaging branches are co-operating. We can neither hear nor send tower songs. And who knows where it intends to throw us?"

Daris held a woven basket half-filled with empty pharma gourds and jars. "But Chief Studier," he asked, "is it not strange that the tower brought the Iden women to two Peacock longhouses that would not take them?"

"Perhaps it hit with two stones." Ephan walked back into the sick room, Psal and Daris following. "It rebukes both the Iden women and Psal with one blow."

Ephan nodded toward Netophah, who stood in the corridor with Maharai.

"Is the tower's anger quenched?" Netophah asked.

Psal avoided Maharai's gaze. "Almost."

Netophah bowed and walked away, holding Maharai's hand.

"Your Maharai received much honor today," Daris said. "Everyone is calling her 'The Firstborn's Woman.' Perhaps she will allow you to lie with her tonight?"

"The Firstborn has no power over his woman," Psal answered. "I am still outcast from her bed." He looked longingly in the direction of Maharai's chamber. "For my own health, it would seem. She fears killing me."

* * * *

The first words Psal heard the next morning were Ephan's: "And where are we?"

They were spoken in a slightly slurred manner and the question itself made Psal desire to remain in bed.

But Ephan crawled out from under his covers, rubbed his eyes, and looked out the window. "Remind me not to drink again." He lumbered to the window, went silent, stood long looking out into the lightening gray. "We've materialized in a grassy clearing. Woods too. But a path in the distance. Oh, can it be? Storm, up! Up! Now! Can it be? Is this not…. Yes! I have heard of this place. The Wintersea Master never allowed us to visit it."

Psal did not rise. Why should he? Through no fault or laziness of his own, he had a rare day of rest. The tower was steadfastly, resolutely silent, neither speaking nor listening, nor relaying messages. True, Nahas would be annoyed and would demand the tower behave, but truly on such a day, there was nothing any studier could do. The inhabitants of a rebellious longhouse could only attend to present immediate things, banal matters that did not differentiate between foundling or royal. And as for tired studiers…they could attend the sick, mix pharma or explore.

Explore! Psal sat up on his elbow. Explore. Yes. He would rise from rest, even if rising meant having to endure the king's—hopefully short—tirade. "What place?" he asked Ephan.

"The place of the…you know! The Voca region where men see the strange tower. Ah, ah! You know, Antun…your friend's tower."

"Where all men see different things?"

Ephan grabbed his tunic, then rushed past Psal barely-dressed. He stood in the corridor in his under-garment, calling for Daris.

Daris arrived with the king who made the expected comments. The tirade endured, explanations made—about spiteful towers and the like—the studiers were free to tend to the sick, then venture out.

The tower lay ahead at the end of the path, surrounded in a heavy mist, which made the morning as gray as the pre-dawn. Behind it lay a wide expanse, a desert so wide it could probably hold all the longhouses of all the clans. Yet, because of superstition and unease, no clan but the Voca ever attempted to claim it as a home region. Nevertheless a comforting presence enveloped Psal as he and the two studiers approached the tower. *I was lovingly cared for once,* he heard himself think. *The lost days with the old master. My sisters, my brothers—all loved me! Antun as well.* He did not know why his mind was suddenly filled with the joy of being loved, but he accepted it anyway. Ephan and Daris hurried before him, stopping frequently to wait for him. *Yet even in their impatience, there is love. How deeply they love me! It is the effect of this region. I must read the annals and the lore of this place. Some pharma or herb in the air produces this euphoria.*

They arrived at the tower after a long walk. Psal studied the phenomenon before him. *This is the tower? This accretion of dead men's bones? I see nothing but mortar and twigs resting on untenable foundations, broken branches forming shaky steps.* "Rightly did the Wintersea master describe this tower. It is no tower, merely an accident of nature, an illusion which self-deceived and needy men wish to believe in."

"Do you recognize it?" Ephan asked.

Recognition? Yes. Nostalgic, as well. But why? Can one love and long for a place one has never been? How strange and bizarre this phenomenon! "It is surely a haunted place," he answered, laughed. "Although I do not believe in spirits."

"So you feel it as well?" Daris asked. "As if, as if this place is home?"

"Our Permanent Home?" Psal joked.

"Perhaps," Daris said. "As if it is part of that place, the earthly entrance to it."

"The earthly entrance to the Permanent Place—if such a permanent place exists—is a pyre," Psal said. "And pyres give me no such peace."

"But do you feel the discomfort as well?"

"Studier Cloud, do you see anything? Do you see anything?" Daris looked about, peered through the dim gray. "There are things to see, aren't there?"

"Things?" Psal asked.

"Things," Daris replied. "Things."

Psal looked at the "tower." He turned and looked about, pointed to the sky. "See! The wind, the heat, the mist! They play with the mind."

Ephan turned to leave.

"You leave already?" Psal asked.

"Do you hear that?" Ephan asked.

Psal shook his head.

"I do not like this place," Ephan said. "It asks too much of me."

Psal shrug. "But to return to Father's complaining and the Iden women's grief." He slapped Ephan on the shoulder. "Come now, Friend Cloud. Let us stay and examine this great non-sight, this 'thing' that deludes great men. Tell me now, what do you see? If the lore of this tower is true, you should not see what I see."

Ephan took a deep beaten breath. He squinted, peered deeply into the structure. "It is perhaps…crystal. As though carved from stones taken from the Crystal caverns. Marble as well, with solid pillars."

Psal laughed, wondered at his friend's sanity and failing eyesight.

"It is triune," Ephan continued. "No, no, it has three parts, but three in one. These three hold the structure together. There is one part which has the appearance of a white parchment, white as marble…a parchment built on rock, made of rock."

"Like parchment?" Daris' eyes grew wide. "Can you read what it says?"

"I do not care to read it," Ephan answered.

"Because it doesn't exist?" Psal asked, teasing.

"Because I'm afraid," Ephan answered. "Because I sense…I sense this parchment will tell me of myself, that it is a mirror which will show me the world and myself. And I do not wish to see myself. I am not prepared for it. The rest…a marking over the door."

"You see the door as well?" Daris asked, excitement in his voice.

"I see it. The marking is made of two intersecting lines. Horizontal and vertical. Blood red. The third aspect, the crystal, like a flowing river, reflecting the bloody mark and the parchment."

"Is the door made in the image of a man?" Daris asked.

Ephan nodded. "It is. The man is the door."

Daris laughed and clapped his hand. "So we see the same thing?" He took Psal's hand. "Studier, Firstborn, let us enter into it."

Psal frowned. "I need no little child to lead me into a false tower. And, Cloud, you say you saw all that? You who have sworn off seeing? You see no such thing."

Ephan shrugged. "I see what I see."

"But I see nothing!" Psal did not hide his impatience. "How strange this air is! Have the plants and pharma from this region been studied? The Tomah plant has a near cousin, a kind of moss which—"

"Shall we go?" Ephan turned to leave.

There is terror in his voice, Psal thought. *And yet—he will not admit it—yearning as well.*

Daris grasped Ephan's tunic. "There must be a reason the tower threw us here." He lifted his left foot, held it above the ground, raised his eyebrows. "May I? Should we not...should we not...try to understand why?"

"The tower brought us here because it was being spiteful!" Ephan shook the child's arm away.

Yes, interest, yearning. Yet he will not admit it. And why is he afraid? Would he be more afraid if he saw and heard the spirits as in the old days? "Studier Daris, will you stand there on one foot all day?" Psal asked. "If you wish to approach this mass of...'things' to study it, go. But, I beg you, do not climb it. It is unstable. Despite Ephan's crystals and woods and marbles. If you fall into it, I will have Lyrenna cursing my life."

Daris put his left foot on the ground, took one small step, then another. Then another. His pace quickened as he approached. "It's calling me!" he shouted as he ran.

Ephan and Psal watched at a distance, not venturing nearer. Whether man-made as Ephan surmised or trick of the mind, neither wanted to concern themselves with it.

"He hears it calling him!" Psal snorted. "I hear no song."

"It is calling to me as well." Ephan turned and peered back in the distance toward the longhouse. "The path is clear enough. Why haven't the others come?" He looked about at the woods, green, lush, cool. "It's a pleasant place, and although this is an unexpected journey, our warriors would normally venture forth. Especially after a battle."

"Some are comforting their new wives, no doubt."

"But not all have new wives. And even those who have ventured outside walk far from this place." He turned, glanced at Psal then shouted to the tower, "I resist your call." He called to Daris. "Return! We have finished here!"

In the distance near the tower step, Daris pleaded, "Chief Studier, please allow me! It invites all to come. If we enter the door, all will be safe."

"Daris!" *This region! It's making my studiers mad!* "We must leave at once! Now! I have had enough of this...illogical...'thing.' We have left that prison of a longhouse to explore. Then let us explore."

So Daris turned from the tower and followed his masters, his steps lingering behind them.

The next morning, Psal woke with a dread only the night-tossed understood. He did not know where the night had thrown the longhouse. But when he looked at the keening branches, all its crystals shone bright, and its keening branches sung compliance. The royal longhouse now rested in a region just east of their previous landing.

"I will confess," Ephan said, "I wanted to see if that tower was truly constant. And yet, I still hear it. It is a lovely song for those who can hear it."

Psal sat up in bed, looked at his twisted leg. "Why clutter the mind with useless songs? Look now, here is a region of unexplored land."

"Our tower's forgiveness," Ephan said. "A reconciliatory gift for the trouble it caus—"

His words were interrupted by a shriek from the residential areas. Moments later, Satima came running in. "Firstborn, one of the Iden Women has cut her wrists. She died on the bed of her new husband."

From that day, resignation fell upon the Peacock women. It could not be said that they loved their husbands, but they seemed to decide that life was better than death, and marriage to a Wheel Clan warrior better than continually grieving for dead sons, brothers, and husband.

CHAPTER 30

WINNING FORGIVENESS

"The child should not scramble up the external stairs," Ktwala told Tomo. "They're dangerous to climb, and moreover…why should we have to go outside to survey the land? This is a day when Peacock corpses lay on the field like sand at the seashore. Why venture out? Fix the internal tower stair, for the child follows you everywhere."

Tomo laughed. "When you harangue and nag at me, you remind me of my mother. The child is a boy. Why should he fear climbing? And yet, because you bring back thoughts of my dear mother, I will do it."

All day Tomo hammered and fixed the stair, singing Grassrope songs and telling Lian of his days spent among his outlaw clan. "I needed a good woman," he would sing. "One like my mother who would make me love my life. And my mother, looking down from the Permanent Home, has sent me one."

It was an ancient Grassrope ditty, and Ktwala found herself humming the tune in spite of herself. When Tomo finished restoring the stair, she said to herself, *The men in my longhouse, grieving as they did for their lost brothers, allowed this internal stair to rot. They saw no hope without their knowledgeable brothers, who took all our tower lore. They could not dream. Yet this man dreams. But what does he dream of? Me? I have no wish to be an outlaw's woman.*

The next day, Ktwala climbed the newly-repaired stairs. From her rampart, she saw: in one direction corralled fields and fenced orchards, a vineyard where the favored vine of the Wheel Clan grew, fenced fields with owned animals. In the other direction, pyres. In the far distance, a young man crouched naked. His white hair flowed about his shoulders. With a lance, he pursued a large cat. She descended the tower.

"A young warrior hunts in the distance, pursuing fierce prey. Let us help this young outcast."

"If the boy is a man, he doesn't need our help. If he's strong, he will take you from me. If he needs a woman's help, what use is he? Lian and I go a-hunting."

Flute in hand, the child within her five months, Ktwala hurried through the tall wet grasses. Rain-soaked, the ground sank under her feet; water-laden low-hanging vines snaked along her way. When she stood about twenty paces away, the boy turned to look at her. His gaze flickered—to her right and to her left. He lifted the lance he carried high and shook it threateningly. She stopped. Yet she was not afraid. *I have encountered night-tossed children before; I know their terror.* She put one foot forward. The boy waved the lance. *Yet he makes no attack.* She advanced and saw his face clearly now. Sloe-eyed like the Waymaker Clan. He had a whole left arm only, his right hand withered and stiff at elbow. Those crescent eyes, at once youthful and aged, once more searched the dense woods behind her, as animals do who know themselves prey.

Ktwala pointed to her heart, then touched her lip. "I have come to help you."

She lifted her flute.

The Peacock Clan had many domestication songs. Songs to call animals, songs to keep them at bay, songs to calm them. She blew a sweet melody and the large puma lay subdued in the grass. They raced toward it and the boy struck hard.

The boy's muddy left hand pointed to his chest: "Gillan Waymaker," he said in the Peacock tongue.

She touched her heart: "Ktwala."

They dragged the cat across the grasses. When she was a young woman, she was strong even when pregnant. She was older now.

In front of the Peacock longhouse, Gillan exclaimed, "A Peacock Clan longhouse!"

"It is," Ktwala said. "It was."

He stood long at the door before entering. Then he smiled suddenly and bowed to some unseen other and dragged the dead animal inside.

How that boy's eyes roamed the longhouse walls! He ran to the walls on which Old Jion had written the lore of the scattered clans. He searched until he found a group of circles. He pulled Ktwala's hand toward it: The sign of the Waymaker Clan. Then he spoke to her in her tongue "The Peacock markings outside are half-covered. I hardly knew what I saw."

"As always, you of the Waymaker Clan speak all tongues."

She led him to the room where several woven blankets were stored. "I can make you tunics, woven in the style my husband wore. Waymaker Clan you may be, now you will be from the Peacock Clan."

He dressed himself and together they cut the animal, its blood pooling into the basin Ktwala brought from the storage room. Long without companions, the boy rambled on.

"Many such fields have I seen," he said. "Wheel Clan markings everywhere. I have walked often inside their orchards, Whether attended by farmers in longhouses or left unwatched. They do not mind. They are a good and noble people."

Ktwala said nothing.

"I am often happiest when I find their fruit orchards. Their fields are numerous. Yet what do they leave for the homeless and the night-tossed? In one field, they plant only grain. In another only legumes. In another their beverage vines. In another their pharma or their tubers or their fermenting spices. Lakes, too, and rivers, they claim as their own. As if the Creator made water to be owned! When one's stomach growls for food and all one finds is Dovi. Or Emon. Or caftay beans…one can become disagreeable. Still, something is better than nothing, is it not? Better to eat peppers all day than to be eaten, I say. One goes where the night takes one."

"How came you to be night-tossed, and alone?"

"A sad story, that."

"It is always a sad story."

"We lived in a towerless hut, a large one, well-made. One day, Father found a woman. She was lost and alone in the world and he pitied her. Pity turned to love. But this girl disliked my mother. They fought mornings. They fought when the sun rose high. They fought at double moonrise. The girl was young, willful, and beautiful. I had hoped Father would have given her to me, instead of keeping two women for himself. After many clime changes, we happened upon a little hut without a tower. Not large. Not well-made. When night fell, he told my mother it was her new home. The girl must have forgotten about the grief of her own night-tossed life. She must have…or she would not have forced Father to send Mother away."

"Perhaps she remembered and wanted to hurt your mother," Ktwala said.

"True, perhaps she remembered." A tear fell across his cheek. "She was very like my father, spiteful and unfeeling. And we often wish others to suffer, do we not? However, I did not wish my mother to be outcast and alone. I left Father's longhouse and journeyed with her. Mother died soon after, weeping for her other children. I could not save her and I was left alone."

Ktwala wiped his tears away. "Gillan, live with us. Share your beliefs, your knowledge, and your strength."

He looked about the empty longhouse. "Us?"

"In my journey, a Grassrope man found me."

Gillan's gaze rested momentarily on Ktwala's pregnant belly. "The Grassropes are a jealous people. And I have heard—"

"This one has not been unkind to me. Neither has he harmed or assaulted my son, Lian, a goodly child who does not speak, but who has a kind heart."

"They alone are your people? All others are lost?"

"How old are you, child? I do not wish to tell you hard truths that may hurt your heart."

"Sixteen years, I believe. More or less. And, fear not to tell me your heart. I wept just now but I am not weak. Only…only, it has been so long since one has invited me to live in a home. Even the Wheel Clan has not done so."

"It is of the Wheel Clan I wish to speak. Their king, Nahas, killed my brothers and my son and took the women away. My daughter, too. I was left solitary, grieving."

He eyed her askance. "The Wheel Clan is not known for such cruelties."

"Yet they were cruel to me."

"Do not worry, Mother. The Ever-Present One puts the solitary in families. He has brought me here to be your son. I will help you to find your lost daughter."

"I too believe that the Ever-Present One is with me. Silent though he often is."

When Tomo returned, he looked Gillan up and down. He pulled small reptiles from his pouch, carried them to the carcass room, ordered Ktwala to dismember them.

"And why should I do as you order?" she asked. "Do you own me?"

He mumbled something in the Grassrope language and went outside grumbling, taking Lian with him.

"It is true," Gillan said. "That one is quite jealous. And yet you say, no one owns you? You are not his woman?"

"One owns me, but not this one."

Gillan remained silent. When he spoke, he said only, "I am too young to understand such things."

When the third moon began to rise, all four sat together, salting meat. Gillan and Ktwala spoke together, Lian at their feet; but Tomo fumed, silent.

"When I saw your longhouse I did not wish to come in," Gillan said. "The spirits here cry out for revenge. But they saw I was not their enemy and put their anger aside. I rejoice the spirits of your clansmen allowed me in. I had no wish to walk among pyres until third moon rise."

Tomo stood up, shouted in the Grassrope tongue, "You speak too quickly. Too quickly for me to understand. What is that you said to her? All those words. All those words. Speak nothing here unless I understand it."

Gillan spoke again. In the languages of the Grassrope and Peacock Clans. Every sentence twice, every word doubled.

Tomo snarled, "I do not trust your translations."

A day brought the Iden tower to a place where the corpses of Peacock warriors lay rotting.

"I smell death, Ktwala," Gillan said.

"Death taints Odunao," Ktwala answered, "But it also taints me. On some days you will have no need to climb the tower. One day, we arrive in fertile fields, another day in regions of mauled human bodies. This Wheel Clan king seeks to break my will."

"Perhaps he will not," Tomo said.

"Who knows?" Ktwala said.

"Another lost one," Gillan said, "would choose endless random wanderings rather than this constant reminder of death and life. But I have found a mother again, and I will not leave your side. I have found a brother again, and I will not leave his side. I have found a father again. I will travel always at his side."

* * * *

On the second night of the seventh month as the studiers lay in bed, Ephan said, "How long will this continue? You're a chief's son and you allow the girlie to make you tremble in fear!"

It was true. Psal did tremble in fear. Maharai's anger had steadily grown as Psal's need for her had grown. She walked the longhouse, greatly honored. But it was Netophah who was always at her side.

"Why would she choose me when Netophah walks at her side?" Psal defended himself.

"Consider. Maharai cannot live happily with one who does not know her heart. Netophah lies in bed asleep. But where is she? In the gathering room. With all the other women who hate their husbands. If she loved Netophah, would she leave his side so often? Go to the gathering room and win her. Act like a man and show her clearly the grievous path she has begun to tread."

"But...." Psal stammered. "She treats me so cruelly."

"Because she wishes to kill you, yes. But I doubt she will kill you. Her anger is against you and the Wheel Clan, but she will not kill you. She knows you alone are the one to help her bear her sorrows. Go now and win her, or I will drag you into the gathering room myself."

So Psal rose and entered the gathering room, where he found Maharai leaning against a window and holding little Eala in her arms.

"Will you be happy if you marry Netophah?" he said to her.

She did not answer.

"You will be powerful," he continued, "but is it not terrifying, heart-destroying, to lie beside the one who killed Ouis? Pretense has its rewards, Maharai. It can make you queen of the Wheel Clan. But I know you. I know your rage. What if…what if…one night when you lie beside Netophah, you can bear it no longer? What if you kill the Wheel Clan Prince in his bed? Do you think your Iden sisters will go unpunished? Do you think I would love you if you killed my brother?"

She put little Eala on the ground but did not turn to look at him. Her anger made him love her more. He stood admiring her, then gently tugged her short braids.

"Maharai, even the youngest Wheel Clan child is adept at seeing enemy longhouses in this darkness. But Netophah does not see the viper he nurses in his arms. He doesn't wish to see it. But I see your pretense."

She wheeled about and spoke firmly, clearly, in the Peacock language. "And why do you think I would not kill you?"

"Because of all your enemies, I am the one you love most."

She did not immediately answer. When she did, she said, "Free Gidea. Take her away from Gaal and Cyrt and make her no longer a comfort woman."

"A chief's words are like a rock, unbreakable. I will not allow it to be said that I don't understand the consequences of the commands I give. Consider also. If Gidea is freed, she will endanger both herself and her sisters. And the king's patience is not to be played with."

"What has happened to my mother?" She held his gaze. "If you love me so much, why do you not lead me to her?"

"Maharai, you must trust me. I am the enemy of your enemy. But you must love and marry me."

She raised a scornful brow. "Marry you?"

"The well constellation returns in a month? Did you not say you were born under the well constellation? You'll be of marriageable age." He leaned toward her. "And what if my kinsmen don't love me? It doesn't matter if Maharai is my loving wife."

"If I am to be married off to my enemies, I suppose it's best that it be you."

"But you do love me just a little bit?" he asked.

"A little bit," she answered.

He hugged her shoulder; then kissed her. "With you and Ephan loving me, I can well endure this clan. For your sake, I will be a great chief. And Maharai will be my primary wife."

* * * *

The next morning, after rising from Maharai's side, Psal entered his Father's quarters.

"I have something wonderful to tell you, Father," he blurted out, almost singing.

His father looked up at him smiling. "Joyous news is always welcomed."

"Oh, Father," Psal said. "It is good news." He removed his studier's cap. "Oh, Father, it is an amazing thing! I've found a woman who loves me. The daughter of Ktwala loves me. *Me,* Father!"

"This is old news, Firstborn," the king said, smiling. "I've seen."

"Have you, Father?" Psal said eagerly, almost dancing. "Have you, really?"

"It's obvious you like each other." The king removed two large goblets from a shelf and filled them both to the brim.

"Is it, Father?" Psal blushed and tried to stop the childlike grin that was taking over his face. "Yes, I suppose everyone has seen it."

"You follow behind her like a little lost sheep."

Psal laughed. "I do, Father. I do."

"And who will you share her with?" Nahas asked, offering Psal one of the goblets.

A shared wife? Psal took the goblet but did not drink. "No, no, Father. I don't wish to share her. She's to be mine alone, all mine. My *primary* wife."

Nahas shook his head, and all of Psal's joy fled like ripe figs shaken by a strong wind. "Firstborn, when you walk as one of the chiefs of our people…but…now…you must share—"

"But, Father, you allowed Cyrt to have two wives, and Cyrt was not yet a chief."

"Share her with Netophah. My brother and I married your mother. A suitable enough match."

A suitable match? Rumors still abounds about that eimi. "You're not hearing my heart, Father. I do not want to make her a shared wife. To be in a bound three with Netophah! No, Father! No! When the birthright was originally mine! No, Father. I could not endure it. I will not." The strings of Psal's heart were so taut his chest burned. "Make me a chief now, Father. Give me some great deed to do, some victory to win and then I can take Maharai."

"Firstborn."

"Ephan, then. Let me share her with Ephan."

The king frowned, poured the fermented drink on the ground. "Ephan."

Why not Ephan? Perhaps it is true that….

"Father, if it is true…that Ephan is your own particular 'favorite' and you refuse to share him with another—"

The king chuckled. "He's not my lover, Firstborn. I only wish you to understand. If she loves one more than the other, you might lose a friend. A brother one can never lose."

And yet, Hinis killed your brothers, Father. "All the music in my soul finds an echo in Ephan's, Father. Is that not a good thing? We three will be happy together. We will both be loved, Ephan and I. Netophah she will never love." *And she might kill him in their bed.*

Nahas returned his goblet to the small shelf and took the cup from Psal. "Firstborn, I'm as trapped with you in this longhouse as you are in this clan." The king's voice was coldly patient.

Psal's heart fell.

"Already you and Ephan tend to reclusiveness," the king said. "Will this marriage not create a bound three that cocoons itself away from all others in our clan?"

"I would not hide myself away, Father. I love our people, Nahas. Have I not—in my own little way—honored and helped them?"

"Your deeds were owed to the clan, Firstborn. Nothing more." The king walked to the corridor and called for Netophah.

CHAPTER 31

THE MARRIAGE OF THE KING'S SONS

When Nahas and his sons entered her room, Maharai looked up. Psal.

"Maharai," Netophah began, "I woke alone, to find you absent from my bed. And now Psal—the Firstborn...." He paused. "And now the king tells me...."

She didn't answer him. Neither did she feel any guilt when she heard the hurt in his voice. She extended her hand and Psal limped to her side.

"She is not to be your wife," Psal said.

"Brother." Netophah spoke as if waking from a dream. "Have you conspired against me all this time? Why do you challenge me? Do you not see that I'm willing the share the girl with you?"

"Netophah," Psal retorted, "why will you have one who does not love you?"

Netophah looked at Psal then at Maharai. "But," he began...but his words were dissolved in boyish tears.

"The Firstborn came to me with a request." Nahas spoke to Maharai in the Peacock Clan language. "But I have told him he has only three choices. You may become the primary wife of Netophah, the shared wife of Netophah and Psal, or the shared wife of Psal and Ephan."

"King Nahas," Maharai answered, "I will marry Psal alone."

Nahas tore Maharai from Psal's arms, squeezing her wrists tightly. She had not expected him to be so angry.

"Girlie," the king said, "consider carefully who you will have. Netophah will be king over all Wheel Clan lands. Psal—who has asked for you—was born damaged and might never be a chief. I think you would not want a husband so powerless. Choose Netophah. I, myself, have lived about forty years. At your age, you may consider that very old. But I don't feel old. Youth should listen to the advice of the age. Choose Netophah."

"If you're so old, then die quickly!" Maharai snapped. "But don't force me to marry one I can never love."

Like one hit by an arrow, Netophah lowered himself to the floor. "You do not love me?"

"I do not wish to be the shared wife of the one who killed my brother. I do not wish to be the shared wife of anyone. I will marry Psal alone."

The king spoke, either to Maharai or Netophah, Maharai wasn't sure. "What does love matter?"

"If you become Netophah's primary wife," Psal said, "you will be one of many women, called to his room only when it pleases him."

"Not true!" Netophah rose from the floor, pushed his brother aside. "If Maharai wishes, I will marry her alone."

Can I murder? Can I kill and succeed at it? If I fail to murder Netophah, if I succeed, will I not be cast out into the night as Tolika was?

"Netophah," the king said, "marrying Maharai alone is not an option. A Wheel Clan king cannot have only one wife. Maharai, Psal does not have the right to have a primary wife. He might never gain such a right. Do you understand that? You will always be shared if you marry Psal. But marry Netophah, and he will be the only man to touch you. Come now, Girlie, I thought you more shrewd. If you will not marry Netophah alone, be the shared wife of both my sons."

"Let her marry Ephan and me," Psal said. "If she married Netophah, the Iden women will not respect her."

Maharai took Psal's arm. "I will marry Psallo and Ephan."

"Girlie, you've made a foolish choice. Psal, tell Ephan the news." The king spoke to Netophah, whose face had gone pale with anger. "Be happy for your brother." Then to Maharai. "I suppose you will tell your sisters. I would be quite interested to see how the interested parties accept this."

* * * *

When Ephan heard that he had been married him off, the clay mortar and pestle fell from his hands onto the floor. He paced the floor, walking and turning about as if suddenly lost in the dark clime. "Netophah likes the girl. I don't."

"I would be tied to Netophah for the rest of my life," Psal said.

Ephan picked up the mortar and pestle and the half-pounded tree bark. "He's your brother! You're tied to each other anyway. No! No! I won't accept it." He put the bark in a jar of fermented Yisin liquid and shook it with such anger that the mixture splattered all about him. The room reeked of fermented Rangi bark.

"I have not imprisoned you in the cold dark climes," Psal said. "You're behaving—"

"Did I tell you I wanted a wife, Storm?" Ephan asked.

"No, you want loveless trysts," Psal said. "You want old comfort women who belong to every other warrior. You don't want to open your heart to love."

"Did I tell you I wanted to open my heart to love?" He pressed his index finger into Psal's forehead and pushed hard, causing Psal to stumbled backward. "I. Do. Not. Like. The. Girl." He pushed him again. And again. And again. Until Psal's back was pressed against the wall.

"So these unknown women who toy with you and this unknown, unseen Ever-Present One you often speak to are all you need?" Psal asked.

One more push and Psal's head was trapped between the wall and Ephan's finger.

"They suffice."

"Love for Maharai will give your life meaning," Psal said

"I didn't want my life to have meaning." Ephan released his prisoner. "Do not give it meaning." He walked to a nearby table, rubbing his forehead as he went.

"There's no other I would wish to be bound to," Psal said, following him. "And Father would not allow me to take her for myself. So you were the only choice. Don't you love me? If you love me, you would happily do this thing for me."

"If you love me, you would happily not ask me to do this." Ephan's face softened slightly. "And stop saying I don't love you. You know I love you. But I cannot. I cannot. I have never sought a heart opened to love. I do not wish to be bothered by it now."

Psal studied his friend for a moment, the pale face, the pale hair. "Cloud, are you as bloodless as you often appear to be?"

Ephan stared at him, eyes wide, mouth open. "You're often selfish and cruel when you want something."

"And how cruel you become when someone forces love upon you! And yet, how much time you spent bribing that mother of yours to love you!" Psal limped to the door. "I have always thought that when I become chief, you and I would create a longhouse of freedom and peace, a respite from all the worst of Wheel Clan values, the glory of all our greatest traditions. Perhaps as Renan imagined it. Do you not see that if you and I were bound together with Maharai…we could dismantle this world?"

"You can dismantle the world without me."

Psal had no wish to dismantle the world without Ephan, and he wanted to marry Maharai. So he silenced himself and, for the rest of the day, spoke nothing of marriage or of dismantlings. Whether they met in the sick rooms, the pharma rooms, or the keening room, they talked only of skirmishes, keening, and pharma. Ephan would relent, Psal told himself. Ephan always relented. *Not because Ephan is weak,* he told himself, *but because Ephan loves me and will do anything for me.*

* * * *

"I have a family again," Maharai told Gidea in the comfort women's room. "People whom I own and who own me. I will never lose a family again."

"So you have left your people?" Gidea asked.

"I have not left my people," Maharai answered, "but now Psallo and Ephan are mine."

"How unfortunate! To marry for love when you should have married to kill Netophah."

"One should love one's husband and not seek to murder him. Is it not best that I live with those who seek my good?"

"And we did not think of your good?" Gidea asked.

Maharai bent low, whispered. "When your son forced me, you knew and did not help me. No, Gidea, you meant me no good."

"And you will betray your people because of my son?" Gidea asked.

"I can still murder. If I wish to. But I don't want to marry the one I hate in order to do it."

Maharai stood up and left, but as she entered the gathering room, Netophah approached her. He brought gifts to her: shells, leaves, stones, flowers, perfumes, cloths, and crystals—such silly gifts that lovers find important.

"Even now," he said, "you could choose to marry me. I would be satisfied to be second place in your heart forever."

"I'll marry only Psal."

"When the war is over, your clan will be no more. I will be a great Wheel Clan chieftain by then. I will rule a great region and have a home region of my own. But you already rule my heart, Maharai. What can Psal give to you?"

It is not what Psal can give to me, but what I can give to you. If I married you, you would not live. I could not let you live. She turned from him. "If I married you I would hate myself and hate you. This I cannot do."

He clutched his heart then, as if an arrow had struck him. She hastened her footsteps and continued up the corridor until she reached her room.

* * * *

When Ephan walked into the keening room at nightfall as Psal was preparing to track towers, Psal was sure Ephan had come to his senses at last.

"Uhm...." Ephan stammered. "Your Father...the king...Nahas." He squatted on the ground. "My heart reels, Storm. And my mind....I cannot seem to...."

Historians have always said that the phrase—'my heart reels'—is the most famous declaration of Odunaon history, but when Psal heard it he said, "You certainly look like one with a reeling mind."

Ephan looked up vaguely into Psal's eyes then about the room as if the thoughts flying around his head were too many for him to grasp. "As I stood in front of him. As I stood. In front of the king. Oh…I cannot seem to grasp what Nahas has just revealed to me."

A clay platter filled with pieces of roasted wasp larvae and honeycomb lay on the council table. Psal reached for the clay platter. "Chew on this. What did the king tell you? That you should marry Maharai?"

He waited for Ephan to speak, but Ephan just sat there squeezing his forehead.

"You must not let Nahas' words bother you," Psal prodded, growing curious. "Surely they weren't so harsh? Nahas loves you as if you were his own son."

Ephan laughed. How he laughed. A laughter that was a mixture of bitterness, hurt, and scorn. Psal had never heard the like from Ephan's throat. "I have been so blind," Ephan said. "I want my eyes—my heart—to see all it should see." He studied Psal's face. "No longer will I be willfully blind."

Sighing, Psal endured the visual examination. "The king's words cannot be so wounding. Nor so surprising. Tell me what he said. Come now, Heart-Friend and Adopted Brother, speak! To speak one's mind is to calm it."

"The things I have not seen." Ephan looked past Psal at the room, then back at Psal again, his face a firm resolve. "Our king wills that I do not marry Maharai. So I have decided that I will marry her and we will become a bound three."

"You're marrying her because the king asked you *not* to?"

"I do have a mind of my own, you know." Ephan extended his hand to Psal, who grasped it, and helped him to his feet.

"But you were so against it!" Psal watched as Ephan picked up several tracking parchments. "You should have jumped at the king's command. So, is that why your mind reels? Because you disobeyed your king? Does it hurt you so much to challenge Nahas?"

"I do not wish to speak anymore of this. I am now married. That is all that matters. There were no threats. He said he was disappointed in me. But he will not hurt me. That I know."

"I am grateful to you, Ephan." Psal would have clapped his hand. But his joy was intermixed with guilt. Because he knew he was being selfish, because he should not have forced his friend into the marriage.

"It isn't so bad, is it? To be married? I've not tied you to a crocodile at third moon, have I?"

"She is a *bit* of a crocodile."

"She'll be quite beautiful when she's older," Psal said. "Then you'll like her."

"I probably won't. By then I'll have begun to love very, very, *very* old women."

"True. And, when I'm chief, I'll make you a chief as well…and you can have as many old hags you want."

"To work, then." Ephan walked to the doorway, where he called to Lan and Daris in the gathering room to join him on the rampart.

"You will not tell me why your mind has gone reeling?" Psal asked. "Or shall I ask Father to tell me?"

"*I* will tell you one day. The king has given that duty to me. But I shall not tell you now." He ran up the tower stairwell.

Psal called out, limping slowly behind him. "Cloud, let your heart add Maharai to those it allows itself to love. Look now, we are three. A threefold cord is not quickly broken. That is a good thing, is it not? Maharai will love you as I love you. Our eimi will have many little ones. We will have a clanhouse of our own. Then what will the pitiful esteem of the Wheel Clan matter?"

"You are married?" Lan overtook Psal on the tower stairs. "You and Maharai and Ephan?" He grinned, slapped Psal's shoulder. "Yes, yes, a perfect match. Stupid of me to not have considered the possibility."

* * * *

When Maharai heard that Ephan had agreed, she found her heart strangely warmed. *Is it possible,* she asked herself, *that I love Ephan as well? I have been thinking like a girl from the Peacock Clan, that I could only lie with and love one husband. And yet, how natural it seems that I should love Ephan as well. Have I now developed a Wheel Clan heart?*

"Tonight," she told the studiers, "and from this night onward, and on all nights, my husbands must sleep with me in my room. One on one side of me, and the other on the other side of me."

This they did.

"We should eat our meals in my room also," she said the next morning when the studiers rose early to attend their duties. "Because Gidea and many of my sisters are angry that I have chosen to marry the one I love instead of marrying and killing Netophah."

"But," Psal said, reaching for his tunic, "if I absent myself from the communal table, the king will charge me with petulance."

"I have no desire to eat in the gathering room either." Ephan buttoned his tunic. "To see Nahas ruins my appetite. If the king challenges us, I will bear the blame."

One night as the studiers lay like tower walls on either side of Maharai, Nahas visited their chamber and stood in their doorway.

"Remember you are part of this clan," he told them. "If you are not in the keening room or the studiers room, you hide yourselves away behind Maharai's fortress. Why?"

Ephan raised himself on his elbow. "King Nahas, in other longhouses we damaged ones are not welcomed in the gathering room. Am I not damaged, King Nahas? Why should your nature-blessed ones look on imperfect ones like us? But if it is your wish that we disgust them with our presence, we will promise to eat with them. But, be warned, it is not a promise I intend to perfectly keep."

The king made this reply. "I had not thought you had such venom in you, Ephan."

"What? You did not? Have I been all this time with you and yet you do not know me? You will know me soon hereafter."

Nahas made no reply, but after he left, Psal exclaimed, laughing. "You have left the king speechless! May I never earn *your* anger!"

CHAPTER 32

THE REQUEST FOR A MARRIAGE TRIBE

"A Wheel Clan marriage is like all marriages," Rain told Maharai as they carved boar flesh in the Eagle's Nest home region. "A married woman is like a tower forever drawn in another tower's wake. But, which tower pulls the other? Much power will be in your hands, Maharai. If your husbands are brave, harsh, stupid, or weak, you will suffer the consequences. As for having two husbands, one may benefit you in some ways, the other will benefit you in others. Whatever your affection, it's best that they believe you love them equally and in unique ways. A wise woman has power to rule her eimi. A silly woman will be enslaved by it, or will destroy it."

"I don't think I'll destroy it," Maharai stoked the hearth fire.

"Then why do you allow Ephan to rebel against the king? If they rebel against him, they will fall. And if they fall, you will fall."

A faint smile lingered on Rain's lips as she spoke, so small Maharai might not have caught it. She thought, *Did this Wheel Clan woman smile just now? Even as she urged me to seek my happiness? Is she hoping for the failure of my marriage?* Therefore, to test the old woman, Maharai said, "Ephan is angry with the king and he will not tell us why."

"It is important to speak of such things!" Rain dug her knife deep into the boar's stomach. "Especially since you're marrying two studiers. Why should a husband keep his heart from his wife?"

Yes, yes, she did smile. I will not force my eyes to be blind to it. When I was younger, I saw things as children did. I allowed myself to be deceived. But now, my eyes are open and I have willed myself to see.

"They tell me nothing," Maharai answered. "I know that both my husbands know where my mother's longhouse roams. I know you all know. But no one will tell me. And although my husbands could bring me to my mother if they wished, they have not told me. Even Ephan, although he hates Nahas, has not betrayed the king's secret."

"It is best if you do not know, Little One." Rain directed Maharai to lift the boar's hind legs.

I suspect you know the cause of Ephan's anger. You can not deceive me again, Rain. You smiled and laughed with me then as you do now. I can deceive as well. Skinned, with its throat cut, the boar was held on its side between Maharai and Rain and its blood flowed into the ground. *As Ouis' blood flowed.*

"Do you know," Rain asked, "in the days before this war, the Wheel Clans would gather the newly-married young of our clans and set them adrift in a marital longhouse?" She smiled. "What joyful days they were! Full of anticipation and excitement. The marital longhouse was often built around a tower that had recently been found and repaired. The eimi would travel with six, ten, twenty, fifty other eimi from different longhouses. It was better that way. To avoid the incest taboo, and to create alliances among our sub-clans. Often, the marriage tribe would build the longhouse themselves with the help of a studier and one of the stewards. Oh, those dear, old, peaceful times! After a great celebration, the marriage tribe would leave. If no studier was among them, the longhouse would fly free, but would be keened to return to one of the home regions after the forty-ninth day." Rain pointed to the ground near Maharai's sandals. Maharai looked behind her to see Satima and Moko from the Iden clan. They had cut the throat of a small deer. It was a stray bloody rivulet from this deer that now covered Maharai's foot. She stepped out of the blood's path. *So Moko has forgotten how they killed her father and brother?* Maharai thought.

"When they returned, the marriage tribe would be greeted with festive joy and all would hear of their travels. We would know their strength then. If they liked each other well and were many and strong, they would be the beginning of a new longhouse."

Travel? To leave this longhouse? Perhaps I can convince my husbands to seek my mother. "But since the war, there have been no marriage journeys?"

"Of course not!" said Rain. "None here had marriage tribes. One can't send young warriors out to create new longhouses during a time of war."

Psal should have a marriage journey. "Oh." Maharai stepped aside to avoid another pool of blood. *I will demand it.*

Rain tugged at Maharai's braid. "Don't sound so disappointed. You're marrying the king's son. When the war is over, Nahas will no doubt allow Psal to prove himself with a marriage journey." She seemed momentarily lost in a memory. "My husband and Nahas were all of the same marriage tribe. Lebo, as well. Our marriage tribe consisted of seventeen eimi. And we have never parted."

"But don't you think Psal should have a marriage journey?" Maharai asked, letting the boar's hind leg drop. *If all its lifeblood has not left its body, I do not care. I have spent all morning cutting and skinning. I am sick of it.*

"To let our young ones be attacked by Peacock Clans? If the Peacock towers hear of such a journey, they'll attack you. It's easy to conquer the young, you know." She lifted Maharai's hand and attempted to pull it down toward the boar's left hind leg. Maharai resisted and Rain let the hand go, shrugged. "No, rest here in your own longhouse, among our people. When the war is over, we will return to the ancient ways. Besides, your husbands are the only accomplished studiers left in our longhouse. Would you leave us in Daris' hands?"

A studier's wife. Maharai looked around at the cauldrons about her, sniffed at the odor of seething flesh. *Or should I speak as the wife of a future chief?* "Wasn't your husband a studier?"

"He was."

"So you understand? The royal longhouse should be made to understand the hard lot of studiers."

"Perhaps Nahas would allow you seven days. He'll give you no more."

"Convince him for me," Maharai said.

Rain frowned. "And why should I do that?"

Because you're old and weak and Psal and Ephan will one day have your life in their hands. "Because my husband is a chief."

The old woman stared at her. "How like Hinis you are!"

For Psal's sake, I will be greater than Hinis. "In time, I will make your sons and the sons of your sons—those from your own womb and those you have adopted—chiefs as well. Help me to honor Psal in the eyes of all and you will not regret helping us."

"Cyrt as well?"

"Cyrt as well." *What is his chiefdom to me if my husbands and I have fled this longhouse?*

"I suppose the basics of tower science are known to Nahas and our warriors," the old woman said. "My son, Seagen, learned much from Dannal. But your reasons might not satisfy the king."

"If Psal travels with warriors who respect him as the king's son, Psal will once again consider himself a part of the Wheel Clan. Wouldn't the king want that?"

"How subtle your mind is, Maharai. I find myself fearing it. But yes, you are quite right. Psal must not be so alienated in his mind from his own people. And tell your husbands if they learn to hide their hurt as my husband did, they will do well." She gently stroked Maharai's cheek. "But, let me speak to Nahas first. Return to your room. I see you have no heart for this bloody work."

Maharai thanked the studier's wife, and raced immediately to the larger of the studiers' rooms, where Ephan and Daris mixed pharma and Psal read a pharma parchment. She flapped her hands like a mother hen calling her chicks home.

"Psallo. I've just conceived a plan. Right now. This very moment."

"Ah!" Ephan said, looking up from measuring a potion. "A plan is it? For what reason?"

"She's always full of plans." Daris eyed her Wheel Clan dress askance. "How bloody you are! Can you not bleed an animal without getting its blood all over yourself? Your sisters are—"

"Husbands, if all goes well, we will leave on a marriage journey."

Psal raised his eyebrows, Ephan laughed.

"But it's true. Yes, yes, yes! And Rain will help us."

"Beware Rain's help." Daris cleared his throat.

Maharai pushed him aside and pinched Psal on the shoulder. "Imagine that! A longhouse for ourselves! Just now she has gone to ask Nahas."

Psal rubbed his elbow, stretched. "I wish you had asked me before you decided to ask Nahas."

"Nahas will not allow it." Ephan put the pharma bottle in its place on a nearby shelf. "He does not trust us."

"I am well able to make him trust us," Maharai said. "I have asked for seven days."

"Seven days isn't enough to find a good abandoned tower or even a good hut," Daris whispered, shooing her out of the room. "That is what you want, isn't it? To escape the longhouse? If I suspect you—and I am a mere child—won't Nahas also suspect? Your scheme will not succeed, Maharai."

Forty-nine days, then? I'll ask Nahas for forty-nine days. She sighed. "You only suspect because you are too shrewd for your age. One can find many huts and longhouses in forty-nine days. Psallo, what do you think?"

Psal looked up from his parchments. He had a twinkle in his eyes. "Perhaps…"

"Perhaps?" She looked at him. "Do you…are you beginning to believe?"

"To escape? Perhaps. But even so. To be away from war."

"And to prove yourself able to rule a longhouse! For, no doubt, being the king's son, he would make you chief of the marriage tribe."

"You would leave me alone here?" Daris looked suddenly worried. "Without you? All by myself?"

"If we succeed, I suppose you would be here without us." Ephan touched the wall, slowly moved his finger along it, then looked through the window. "Yet, although I love you, Little One, I would gladly give up our friendship to be free from this longhouse. Since Nahas revealed his heart to me, these walls have begun to eat away my soul. If Psal wishes to try the venture, I will join him. So, then, go and speak to this lying king of ours. Yes, go and see what this Nahas says. And plead well. You know how to plead well."

* * * *

So Maharai went to the king's chamber. Netophah was present as well. She was not sure why. *Did the king seek Netophah's guidance on this matter? Why?* "Father," she said in the Peacock tongue. "I wish to speak to you. Has Rain told you my wish?"

Netophah and the king exchanged what appeared to be conspiratorial glances.

"It has been more than five months now since you entered our long-house," the king said in the Peacock tongue. "Already some of your sisters understand our tongue. Yet you lag behind. Is Ephan not a good teacher?"

"I had determined not to understand it, Father," Maharai answered. "Because I remembered how you killed my brother, and because you took my mother away from me. And I would not listen to Ephan unless he spoke in my own language."

"You were always stubborn," the king said.

"But now, Father, if you grant my request, I will be a true princess of your clan and a true daughter to you."

"Rain has told me your plan," Nahas said. "It seems my son has found himself a thoughtful and strong wife." He turned to Netophah who lingered near the window. "Psal would be honored in the eyes of his brothers, would he not, Netophah? And ruling a marriage longhouse, he would prove his skills as a Wheel Clan chief."

Netophah shrugged.

The king stood up. "You will be sixteen at the time of the lunar eclipse. When the Greater Light and the Lesser Light meet. A good time to consummate this marriage, if you have not already done so."

"No, Father," she answered. "Not yet."

"Present sweetness should remove past bitterness, should it not?" The king began leading her out of the room. "And consummations must be done quickly or your husbands will become your brothers. But be careful that you treat both these boys equally. The one you love more must not know it. Likewise whoever you love less must not know it. It is best to alternate. One night you lie with one and the next night you lie with the other. But now, go. Tell your husbands to ring the news through our towers that we need to find the Firstborn a marriage tribe. A seven day journey?"

Maharai did not move. "A thought occurs to me, Nahas, Father, King. Seven days is not honor enough for my husband. Forty-nine is best."

"And why is seven days not enough?" Netophah snarled, turning around.

"Maharai, we're at war," the king said. "We cannot do without our skilled studiers for forty-nine days."

"You Wheel Clan men know about keening. Lan, Cyrt, and Seagen were raised by studiers. Psal and Ephan have taught Daris much studiers' lore. Rain also knows—"

"See how she enters the king's chamber armed," Netophah said. "She stores facts as archers store arrows. Then she readies her quiver to aim her darts as she sees fit."

"And why should I not store facts?" Maharai snapped back. "Or emotions either? You killed my brother! That is a fact I will never forget. I am not a prince who has been trained to have two minds!"

"Forty-nine days is too much." The king gestured Maharai toward the door.

"You could have chosen to forget it!" Netophah shouted at her. "But you chose not to open your heart. Instead, you stored all your anger, kept it close, lured me, in order to wound me and to break my heart."

"Netophah!" The king hurried to stand between Maharai and Netophah. "The girl did not choose you. Put aside your anger and find yourself another wife. Maharai, I cannot allow my studiers—"

"Let other longhouses rescue your wounded warriors, Father," Maharai said. "Already our longhouse overflows with rescued warriors. Anchor the royal longhouse in one of your home regions and let Wheel Clan chiefs meet you there for war councils. Or spend forty-nine days meeting other chiefs and kings."

Netophah walked toward the door. "The girl has an answer for everything, does she not, Father? Maharai, a fifteen-day journey is enough to give your husbands honor in their own eyes, and in the eyes of those who have forgotten how much we owe to our studiers."

"Psal and Ephan will explore new regions," she countered. "Let it be forty-nine days."

"Maharai, I do not like bargaining," the king said. "Nor do I wish young warriors to be alone and away from their home longhouses during war."

"It is best to make the Firstborn's presence with his marriage tribe a short one," Netophah said. "They will not bear long with him."

"Enough, Netophah!" Behind the king's shoulder, the old day's terrain slowly melted into the night.

"Is it not true what Rain said?" Netophah asked. "That Maharai reminds her of Hinis?"

"For Psal, it's a good thing," Nahas answered. "He needs a strong woman." He turned to Maharai. "Yet don't be too much like his mother. You'll make the boy afraid of you."

"I will remember, Father."

"Forty-nine days, then," the king said and looked at Netophah. "Is the Wheel Clan heir satisfied with that?"

"I am not satisfied." Netophah's face was red with rage.

"Netophah, perhaps it is best if you and the Firstborn spend some time apart."

"But Father!"

"And do not shame me. Truly, I am sick of petulant children. If you cannot remove this base jealousy from your heart, pretend to remove it. Enough. Call Seagen to me."

Netophah glared at Maharai then walked to the door and whistled three times. The tread of heavy boots stopped at the king's door and Seagen entered.

"You wished to see me," he asked Nahas.

"Our studiers will be traveling with their marriage tribe."

"Yes. My mother told me just now. Good fortune and blessings on the match! May the Firstborn's eimi have healthy daughters."

"I receive your blessings," the king answered. "In the meantime, while they're away, you'll be studier for our longhouse."

"My fathers taught me no tower lore," Seagen said, half-scowling. "Nor have I skill to mix pharma should the need arise."

"Enough!" Nahas said. "I trust you. Lan, I do not trust. And would it help your shame if I told you that your mother recommended you?" The king glanced at Maharai. "Are you still here, Daughter?" he asked in the Peacock language.

She nodded.

"Tell Psal I wish to speak to him."

She returned quickly to the studiers and told them, "It is almost done. Only, he wishes to speak to you?"

Psal held Maharai close. "He said that I am to be chief of this tribe?"

"He was too easily convinced." Daris pressed his dagger hard against a particularly hard piece of Gorek bark. "Don't you think so, Chief Studier?"

"If you prove yourself," Maharai said to Psal, "he will make you chief."

"But you don't care about being chief, do you?" Daris said "You wish to escape this clan."

"If I become chief," Psal answered, "we can belong to the Wheel Clan and yet be outside of it. In our very own longhouse, with others who are mocked and jeered at as we have been."

"Whether in the clan or outside of it, I have no desire to continue living in this longhouse with Nahas," Ephan said. "But Daris is right. The king has agreed too easily to Maharai's request."

"And if Rain is involved," Daris said, "I would doubly fear this. Do you truly think the king believes you do not speak our language? Yes, I listened outside the king's door. And my heart tells me you should not believe the king is easily deceived."

"You're too cynical for your years," Maharai told Daris.

"I'm a studier," he answered. "I have read many annals. I know the minds of men. Indeed, I know the minds of kings."

"A Wheel Clan longhouse filled with those like ourselves," Psal said, in childlike glee. "We could breathe freely, walk freely."

"We'll have to endure the warriors the king puts in our marriage tribe," Ephan said. "He will not send us with damaged ones. He will send his best warriors, people worthy of going on this journey, warriors he trusts because of their skill and because they worship our clan. And these warriors who will journey with us will continue their mockery and oppress us. Our longhouse will not be truly ours. Do not think we could escape such warriors. No. Do not think we will have peace if these great nature-blessed ones become part of our longhouse. So tell your heart to stop dreaming of a longhouse full of damaged ones."

Maharai looked at Ephan, speechless. She had never seen him so bitterly angry.

* * * *

"Consider, Cloud," Psal said as they lay in bed one night, "that perhaps I was born for such a time as this, a time of war and failing towers. Perhaps we should not seek to escape the Wheel Clan entirely. Perhaps the world needs those like us."

Ephan looked past Psal to Maharai, then at Psal again. "You who do not believe in the Creator, you who do not believe in the soul—do you now tell us that by virtue of your birth you were born to care and protect all in Odunao?" He shook his head. "Do not betray us, your eimi, because of some dream placed in your head by a dying studier. If we go on this marriage journey, it should be because we wish to escape this clan entirely. We were not born to help the Wheel Clan rule and oversee Odunao."

Nevertheless, Psal could not put the idea away. *A longhouse of damaged ones!* Not until he had spoken did he understand the seed that had lain dormant so long in his heart. It is a true and right purpose. Perhaps not so mystical as Renan proposed, but true nevertheless. A damaged Wheel Clan prince can do much to influence his clan.

Therefore, when the king finally called him to his chamber, Psal spoke thusly:

"Nahas, there are things I must prove to you and to my brothers. I know you want to make me a chief, Father and—"

"Ah, you know that, do you? You have become a volcano of knowledge overnight, Firstborn." The king poured ale from a pitcher then into Psal's cup.

"No, not so much, Father." Psal took the offered cup, sipped. *My Father loves me, I think. How happy I am when I feel his love!* "But I believe you want me to bring true glory to myself. Even if I am damaged. And I know you are concerned with your own honor as well, that men may not blame you for being the sire of a mad son."

"Indeed? Firstborn, it is one thing to deceive your own longhouse brothers who are willfully disposed to honor you, but *seeming to* kill Tsbosso's son from a rampart is not to be compared to living forty-nine days with noble warriors who disdain being ruled by a Damaged Firstborn?"

Paul, swallowed hard, almost choking on the ale, coughed several times. *So the thing is known?* "Who told you my secret, Father? Did Daris tell you?"

"Daris?" The king grinned. "Daris knew of the exploit as well? Clever little studier! No, no, Daris kept your secret. As did all your friends. I know Netophah's mind. Nothing more. And I know how much your friends, especially Lan, love you. I needed no one to tell me."

"But...at the time...you seemed convinced...amazed—"

"Amazed at the success of the ruse, yes." The king walked to his window. "I knew you could not kill your childhood friend, even if that friend is now your enemy."

"Well, then, Father. Does this not show that I must prove myself to you? Let me prove the worth of all studiers and all damaged ones."

The king kept his gaze on the graying dawn and the looming, emerging terrain. "I've often wondered what you did with the girl," he said. "Mere curiosity, I suppose."

"Moonlight?"

"Yes. Moonlight."

"She's dead, Father. I killed her."

The king frowned. "No, Psal, you did not." He sighed. "Are we not friends, you and I? Why should you lie to me?"

"But I *did* kill her, Father. I did."

"You lie to me now because you know you should have killed her. For your sisters' sakes, for your brothers' sakes. For your mother." Nahas sighed. "Nevertheless, unless we meet them again, your treachery to your clan will remain hidden. With hope, she will remain lost or die in a blazing Peacock longhouse."

Psal almost spoke, almost rebuked his father for Moonlight's sake. But he remembered not to swerve from his path. His aim was to create a longhouse of damaged ones, to prove the worth of the damaged.

"I will bring myself true honor this time, Father. The matter of the Warrior's Prize is done. I received glory from it. Much glory, which I have subsequently lost. If I gain glory as chief of a damaged longhouse, I will not burn it away again. Only, let me prove to my kinsman and to you that I am not so weak as they believe."

The king looked at the terrain, seeming to ponder great and small things. "Maharai and Ephan are as good comrades as any," he said at last. "But tell me, why does she hide her knowledge of our tongue?"

"She does not…" Psal began, but thought better of it. "She thinks it best, Father. For my sake."

"I suppose she will succeed with those in your longhouse." Nahas closed his eyes, rubbed his forehead. "They do not know her as we do. Now, as for this longhouse of Damaged Ones, you know who you wish to join you on your journey?"

"I do, Father."

"Write me their names on a parchment, and the names of those who will do their work in their absence. The other chiefs and my captains must give their approval, you understand?"

Psal almost danced with joy. "Yes, Father."

Some days later, Psal sat with his eimi across from the king, Netophah, Cyrt, and the other Mighty Ones. He attempted to explain his reasons for a longhouse full of damaged ones. All the while Nahas kept shaking his head as if he had never heard such folly.

"I must admit," Gaal said, "this marriage tribe you intend to create sounds intriguing. Studiers would understand each other, could plan their exploits better, would be less prone to self-slaughter or becoming enslaved to Tomah—"

"This strange band of companions is more like an outlaw longhouse than a Wheel Clan tribe." Seagen studied the list of damaged ones Psal had requested. "These are the very worst of the Wheel Clan. Failed studiers, sickly damaged ones, contentious stewards, and Tomah-enslaved misfits."

"True, Nahas," Lebo added, "there is no one on this parchment who has not caused trouble in his own longhouse."

"These are people like myself," Ephan defended Psal's list. "And having put us away in our own longhouse, would not the rest of the Wheel Clan be free of our presence and the contention it brings? Do you not wish to be rid of hateful, damaged ones like myself, Nahas?"

"But all contention would be in one powerful longhouse," Netophah countered. "A longhouse ruled by the king's Studier-Firstborn. Do you not see that that might present a problem?"

"Choose easier minds for your marriage tribe," Gaal offered.

Ephan turned, spoke to Netophah, spoke as if they two were alone in the room.

"Netophah, you are nature-blessed and not like us. Therefore, Wheel Clan Heir, keep your opinions to yourself. If Psal's marriage tribe becomes a true longhouse, we will live happily, day by day. We will feel ourselves loved and accepted and will strive to do great things for the Wheel Clan, to prove our worth. Yes, we will be free from you perfect ones. Our tribe will be so content that all our anger will turn to competition and we will outdo all other longhouses for the Wheel Clan's great glory. Is that what you fear, Netophah? That we will show how small and unimportant and frail you nature-blessed ones are?"

Netophah grasped Ephan by the tunic and pushed Ephan's head against the table. "Your argument is with Nahas, Ephan! Do not presume to add me to it." He released Ephan, bowed to the king, and walked through the door.

"Firstborn," the king said after Netophah had gone, "do you still believe as you did in the old days, that you would be more at peace with the Peacock Clan than here with your own people?"

"I do, Father," Psal answered. "I do not say that they are a better people than we are, just that I would be respected among them because they do not treat the damaged with disrespect. This is the very reason why if I were chief—"

"You praise your enemies while we're at war with them?" Nahas asked.

"I do not praise my enemies, Father. I spoke my heart because you asked me to."

Gaal ripped the parchment of names in two. "Firstborn, you must learn not to speak your heart, even when you're asked. You have destroyed your cause."

Both Lebo and Seagen nodded.

"Firstborn," Nahas said, "your becoming chief is in my hand. Yet you spoke your heart to me? In front of my captains? Could you not have lied just now? Could you not have told me what you knew I wanted to hear? Instead you have now given me reasons for rejecting this strange longhouse you say you want. Beware that you do not cause your marriage tribe to dislike you. You will get your marriage tribe, but Gaal and I will choose those who will accompany you. You may leave."

Psal and his eimi rose as one. "Father," Psal said, as they stood in the doorway, "while I'm gone on this journey, do not tell the stewards to kill the stranger from the Grassrope Clan."

The king's face reddened. "Even now, you tell me what to do?"

"Although Ezbel may remain faithful to the truce, Ktwala is heavily pregnant with your child. She does not allow the stewards to help her. Nor will she allow my uncle Bukko to let one of his midwives stay with her. Therefore, let her—"

"Our stewards are well able to take care of her."

"They are well able to murder her friend, you mean." Psal bowed and he and his eimi left.

* * * *

The eclipse arrived and Maharai's sixteenth birthday as well. The royal longhouse tower sang with the news of Psal's marriage, and all the Wheel Clan towers returned their congratulations. Psal's marital longhouse had been anchored in the home region called the Lake Palace. There Psal's eimi celebrated with the sixteen Wheel sub-clans to whom his marriage tribe belonged. Still, after Psal heard the names of the warriors his father had appointed to accompany him, he felt like one already dead.

These are the names of the eight eimi—those appointed by Nahas to be the core of Psal's sub-clan should Psal prove himself a worthy chief. They are recorded in Psal's annals:

> The Lilea eimi: Lilea, eighteen, a chief's daughter from the Waymaker clan; Dez, twenty, the oldest surviving son of Chief Ronen, skilled with the arrow and renowned for killing seventy-three Peacock valiants; Payton, twenty-four, a comfort woman's son, adopted by Chief Ronen after his mother died. He had been lost to the night after battling the Eastern Sea Peacock sub-clan, then after many days had returned to his clan.
>
> The Jodhi eimi: Jodhi, seventeen, a chief's daughter from the Lindru Wheel Clan; Steen, sixteen, a steward's son, skilled in the use of the lathe and the slingshot, with which he killed Peacock raiders; Allian, his twin brother, a talented stone-carver and mason.
>
> The Madora eimi: Madora, twenty, a girl from the Kondeen Wheel Clan; Jeejo, seventeen, fourth son of Chief Hokkan's primary wife, a singer of songs, and storyteller. From horseback, he had slain two hundred Peacock warriors with his lance, and from a rampart he slew other twenty with arrow and bow; Tonn, fifteen, his half-brother. The child of a

Peacock Clan woman married into the Wheel Clan, he had traveled with his mother to the Peacock feast and had lost one arm in the Treachery.

The Thia eimi: Thia, twenty-two, a woman from the Falconer Clan; Galef, seventeen, son of a comfort woman. He killed two of Tsbosso's mighty men with his bare hands. He also went down among the Cavern Dwellers in the snow clime and killed a serpent who threatened them; Richu, eighteen, brother to Dez, the son of a comfort woman who was a favorite of Chief Ronen.

The Sulani eimi: Sulani, thirty-one, a foundling woman born among the Western Mound Dwellers; Warrek, eighteen, a steward but a peace child between the Wheel Clan and one of the larger scattered Grassrope clans, skilled in the making of parchments; Landen, sixteen, brother to Jeejo and son of the shared wife of Chief Hokkan and his brothers.

The Jula eimi: Jula, fifteen, daughter of a comfort woman in Chief Ronen's longhouse; Meeka, twenty, son of a Macaw woman. He struck down one of the Peacock Clan, a giant of a man whose spear was like a weaver's rod. Meeka grasped that warrior's spear and killed him with his own weapon; Danu, seventeen, adopted third son of the great female warrior, Chief Hayla, and rumored to be the Voca peace child.

The Beki eimi: Beki, forty, a woman from the Waymaker Clan; Louk, eighteen, a foundling, adopted by Chief Ronen. From the ramparts in battle, his arrow found and slew three hundred men of the Peacock Clan; Connell, twenty-three, a damaged one whom his father allowed to live, kinsman to Deyn, a studier afflicted with the Wheel Clan's Great Evil.

The Jesska eimi: Jesska, fourteen, a foundling; Rollin, twenty-seven, son of a renowned Wheel Clan female warrior from the Qerys sub-clan; Jin, twenty, a steward's son, skilled in the training and rearing of horses.

You have heard this record before, when I told you all Ephan endured. You have heard of the marriage tribe's journeys to the Crystal Caverns, the Eastern Mountains, and the Wintersea. The warriors, kings, and regions I spoke of that rendition will matter little in this recitation for then I spoke of Ephan—for he is honored as the true hero of the Constant Tower. But this is Psal's story. These, then, are the names you should now remember:

> *Lilea's eimi: Lilea, Dez, Payton.*
> *Jula's eimi: Jula, Meeka, Danu.*
> *Remember also Jeejo, the storyteller.*
> *Galef, the son of a comfort woman.*
> *Steen, a steward's son.*
> *Richu, the son of a comfort woman, and half-brother to Dez.*
> *Connell, kinsman to Deyn and a damaged one.*

I will also tell you Ephan's marriage song. In my earlier recitation, when I spoke of Ephan's adventures, I did not think you would wish to hear of Psal's life as well. So I recited Psal's marriage song, to give Psal his due. Also, it was the lovelier of the two, and it is the song most honored among our people. Now, however, we will hear Ephan's song, a song no less famous, but—you will agree—not a true love song. The tune is long-forgotten but the words run as follows:

> In the days before cities existed, before the night lost its power,
> The great chiefs dreamt of cities built on tower music,
> Locking towers to fertile regions.
> A place of unending abundance, safety, and continual rest,
> A world where none were scattered, where night had no power to
>   separate.
> Music filled the universe then as now.
> Music undergirds it.
> Music sustains human cities and human hearts.
> In the old days, they lived with no greater joy than to fill the air
>   with song.
> Living chords, are what we are.
> The world is made of sounds, sounds unheard and sounds heard.
> But the ear must be trained to hear them
> As the heart is trained to hear the echoes of love.
> Sounds make words and words make worlds.
> Flesh, color, light, stones...All are made of sound.
> My heart is your keening room.
> It is a room filled with hollow reeds, with drums, pipes, and shin-
>   ing many-colored crystals.
> Their rhapsodies sing of regions, like regions of my soul,
> Their variations link towers, as your heart and mine are linked.
> Their chords record histories, like the histories of our people.
> Their harmonies send out messages.
> Their codas sing destinations, the future of our lives.
> Hold your hand above my heart as you would above a drum.
> Touch and feel the world's heartstrings.
> Music, like love, undergirds the world. It upholds the universe.
> Lovely to hear the tower music,
> The sequences, the arrangements, the rhythms, chords, and
>   metres.
> But not to be compared to my sweet One's voice.
> How beautiful you are, my wife!

While Maharai celebrated with the women, Psal and Ephan were called to the rampart of the royal longhouse. From high above the other revelers, Psal's brother and friends urged him to remember the journey's purpose: to prove himself worthy of becoming a chief.

Lan paced the rampart, chuckling to himself. "It is difficult to imagine the Firstborn trying to impress these noble perfections. Yet, we must hope for the impossible, must we not?"

"But some *are* damaged," Broqh said, slapping Psal on the shoulder. "Seek those out, and avoid the perfect ones. That is the only thing to do. And keep your mouth shut."

Daris stood at Psal's right hand, chewing on fried snake skin. "But even studiers cannot evade the Peacock Clans, marauders, and outlaw longhouses—"

"Outlaw longhouses will not attack a Wheel Clan longhouse full of warriors," Psal said, "But perhaps I should carry Tsbosso's staff."

"Do you truly think the Peacock Clan chiefs will honor Tsbosso's staff?" Kwin asked, leaning over the rampart wall.

"They will honor it," Psal said. "Of this I am sure."

Broqh said, "How I envy you! To be free from this war…to journey freely as we did before all this bloodshed began."

"Did the king's best archer say he envied us studiers?" Ephan asked.

"If you knew the name of the Voca peace child," Broqh said, "you could send to that unknown prince. He would ask his cruel mother to watch over you as you joyfully roam."

"It is his own traveling companions he must fear." Netophah walked toward the tower steps. "The Voca will not harm them. But this morning, as I sat among the chiefs, I saw that our Firstborn continues to wear a studier's cap. You may insist on wearing your studier's black, but why wear the cap as well? No, you will only earn mockery." He hurried down the stairs, shouting as he ran. "Brother, you must remove that cap."

"And yet," Lan said, "I do fear that great unknown world. If the Voca could protect you, you would be doubly safe. I've heard that this unknown Voca prince doesn't know Ezbel is his mother. At least, that is what my father told me. Ezbel herself does not wish to make it known."

"And the chief who fathered the boy?" Deyn asked, looking back at them.

"He, as well, wishes the secret to be kept hidden." Lan laughed, his dark hair falling into his eyes. "Try as I can, I cannot imagine any of our chiefs lying with that woman. The thought alone leaves me nauseated."

"I've heard the Voca Queen has something of a heart and loves this son of hers," Broqh said. "It is said she fears all her sins and murders would fall on his head should vengeance be sought against her."

"The man who could lie with such a woman would be envied. He would surely brag of it." Ephan took one of the crispy snake skins from Daris' platter.

"I have heard no bragging," Lan countered.

"Because she ate him alive," Deyn said. "As some spiders do."

"A woman who eats men alive would be passionate indeed," Ephan responded and looked out into the sunset.

"Look who speaks of passion!" Kwin slapped Ephan on the back of the head. "The one whose marriage song was of towers. Towers! Perhaps he is the king's 'favorite,' after all. Perhaps the Voca Queen's son—"

"Kwin! Enough of this talk of the Voca peace child." Netophah's voice. He gave his friend a warning look as he stood on the top tower step, the blue chief's cap in his hand and the chief's mantle thrown about his shoulder. "No talk of Ezbel either. We were discussing the Firstborn's chances of becoming a chief."

"Adopted Brother," Ephan asked, turning angry eyes on Netophah. "Why should we not talk of this 'unknown' peace child?"

"Because there is a proper time to speak of it." Netophah approached Psal and removed the studier's cap from Psal's head and replaced it with the chief's cap. "Although you were born to it, this cap is as yet un-earned. It is a mark of honor that our chiefs are allowing you to wear it."

"Truly, Firstborn"—Although Kwin spoke to Psal, he glanced guilt-ily at Netophah—"This is the first time a Wheel Clan studier has worn a chief's cap."

"I always knew you'd wear a chief's cap," Lan said.

"I always knew he'd have a Peacock Clan wife," Broqh quipped.

Psal immediately removed the chief's cap. He held both caps in his hands, the studier's cap atop the other. "Only sixteen longhouses," he said. "And I a king's son."

"Firstborn," Lan said, looking out into the twilight, "look at this great crowd, all in your honor. Wear the cap and put petulance aside."

"You consider this a great crowd, then?" Psal asked. "I think it not so great."

"Firstborn, it is great enough." Lan held Psal's right cheek between his thumb and forefinger. "Ephan, tell your wife's husband not to speak so openly of his supposed dishonor. If he plays the chieftain's game as he played the studier's game, he will do well."

"Let the Firstborn act in whatever way he wishes," Ephan said. "What should it matter what these nature-blessed perfect ones think of him? The warriors of this cruel clan are nothing to him or to me."

All looked at him in silence, but Netophah said, "The petulance of studiers becomes tiring after a while. You'll dig your own graves if you don't desist. Look, Father has allowed a celebration even though war rages all around. Sixteen longhouses celebrating a marriage in wartime? It is a *great* honor. Should all our ten thousand longhouses forsake battles for the Firstborn's sake?" He pointed to Psal's marriage longhouse. "And look. This longhouse you found on the day you lost Cassia…these two years our father's stewards kept it solely for you, even when chiefs as powerful as Orian and Qerys demanded it. Qerys! who would have been king had not Nahas' father defeated him. Yet Nahas denied the opportunity to appear conciliatory and commanded the stewards to prepare a wonder for you. Is that not respect?"

Daris spoke, crunching a piece of roasted wasp larvae. "True. King Nahas honors our Firstborn-Studier. Studier Cloud, have you not told me that Samat lives to steal, kill, and destroy? Therefore, let him not deceive you or tempt you to destroy yourselves. Put aside your petulance and your anger. Hold fast what you have, that no one take your chiefdom."

"No one will take it, Brother Studier." Psal hugged Daris about the neck. "Not even such nature-blessed ones. We damaged ones will always be outsiders, but I am well able to pretend friendship." He glared at Netophah. "As some others do."

"Listen to the counsel I give you." The Crown Prince threw the chief's mantle over Psal's right shoulder. "Whatever you may think of me. Do not appear weak, or show untoward kindness to any weak ones you encounter. Nature-blessed ones do not easily forget such weakness. Now, the chief's cap, return it to your head."

Psal lifted both caps, then put the chief's cap on. It fit well enough, but his head felt uncomfortable in it; he held the studier's cap tightly in his hand.

CHAPTER 33

THE MARRIAGE JOURNEY

As the other established sub-clans and the royal longhouse faded away into the darkness, Maharai turned to look at the warriors and women in the gathering room of her marriage longhouse.

Already Maharai disliked Dez. He walked as Cyrt walked, like one who owned the world. He did not sit on the floor as the others did, but chose a chair larger and wider than all the others.

Dez's wife, Lilea, was equally distasteful. She sat wrapped in white and wearing useless shoes. Obviously the girl would not be working. Her white arms held Dez's waist and her lips constantly kissed his neck. Dark-haired Payton, the other in her eimi, sat on the floor near their feet, his hands folded on his lap like one at a feast who had been given an empty plate.

"We will become a great Wheel sub-clan." Dez listed the virtues of each warrior in each eimi as if he was a studier annotating historical annals, leaving his own great feats for last. If any had forgotten he was the oldest surviving son of Chief Ronen and had killed valiant Peacock men in one battle, they now remembered. After he finished, he pointed to Danu who sat on the floor directly opposite him. "Even the rumored son of the Voca Queen is in our tribe."

"I am not that woman's son," Danu said, but although he denied, he smiled slyly. He squinted in the darkness. "Being the adopted son of Chief Hayla is difficult enough. But look, they didn't give us enough candles. Or do they expect us to make candles ourselves?"

"Perhaps the chiefs thought we wouldn't need them," Ephan said. "This is a marriage journey, after all."

"True," honey-colored warrior Meeka said, laughing. "But I, for one, do not intend to spend my days frolicking in bed. Even now I am not sleepy. After such a feast, sex is not foremost on the mind. My Macaw mother often says that boisterous marital acts should not be done when one's stomach is full. Aside from the discomfort within one's belly, one never knows what might—"

"Yes, yes," Dez said, "No need to paint the image. We have imagination enough. We thank you, however, for your cautionary advice."

Meeka beckoned to Psal, a familiar gesture that did not offend Maharai because it was so full of friendliness and kindness. "Come, Firstborn. We Wheel Clan sons of Macaw mothers must stick together, unlike these pale ones who become as red as their hair when they stay too long in the sun. I've heard much about you, Studier-Firstborn and am honored—"

"I too have heard much about this Firstborn," Dez said. "Not all good, and not all worthy of honor."

Maharai clenched the window sill and resisted the urge to throw one of the nearby lances through Dez's heart. She had only disliked him before, now she thoroughly loathed him.

Ephan stoked the hearth's fire with the sharp end of a lance. "Let's discover for ourselves who we are. What do the opinions of others outside our longhouse matter?"

Dez countered, "I suppose such wisdom is why the king has made you his 'favorite.'"

"Ephan is his adopted son," Psal said. "Nahas loves him as his son, no more."

Dez laughed, looked from one to the other. "I see now. You studiers fight each other's battles."

But Meeka defended Psal, because they both had Macaw mothers. Soon the lines were drawn. Dez, Payton, Danu, and the rest of the chiefs' sons, as well as the sons of warriors, took the traditional line. Connell, Galef, Meeka, Jeejo, the damaged ones, the sons of comfort women or studiers took Psal's part. Steen and the other stewards' sons remained silent, keeping their opinions to themselves.

As night drew on and Meeka spoke of the Macaw Clan's greatness, Lilea gave a long sigh of exasperation. "So are we to be regaled with stories of the greatness of Macaw women for the entire journey? Certainly if Macaw women were so great, the Firstborn Studier would not have married a woman from the Peacock Clan. But perhaps a lowly Peacock woman was all he could find, since no Wheel Clan woman would have him."

"Women of the Waymaker and Wheel Clan have not interested me," Psal answered her. "I find them mean-spirited, with small minds and even smaller breasts."

"When more Wheel Clan women existed," Dez said, rising to his feet, "large breasts could be found. But now few Wheel Clan women exist, being all murdered by your wife's Peacock Clan."

The words were barely out of Dez's mouth before Ephan's red hot lance was at that arrogant warrior's throat. Steen rose quickly and stood between them. "Let us not begin our journey with wranglings and baitings. We have enemies enough outside without arguing among ourselves." He pointed to Jeejo. "A song, friend." He pushed them apart, then smiled at his wife, Thia. "A song to make women forget their home clans and long for new longhouses with their new husbands."

Jeejo lifted his string lute from the ground and strummed a low note, but Dez said, "At one of the eclipse festivals my father, Chief Ronen, pointed you out, Firstborn. I was a child then, yet I was surprised to see that our king had a damaged son. Do you remember, Richu, how startled we were?"

"It was a long time ago, Brother."

"Since then," Dez went on, "I've heard many say that Nahas showed his weakness and weakened himself by letting you live."

Psal laughed. "I've heard the same."

"I've also heard," Dez continued, "that you two have been damaged companions from birth, born during the same week."

"Not during the same week," Psal said. "Ephan was born some months before I was. But yes, we lay in the same cradle and traveled with the same Master. Is there anything else you wish to tell or ask me?"

"Why did your father, our good king, mark you?" Dez asked, eyeing the scar across Psal's face.

"Brother!" Richu said. "The Firstborn has done you no wrong. Why speak of such matters?"

"I speak from the heart," Dez said. "Should I lie to the Firstborn of our clan?"

"I might recommend it," Steen said, pointing at the lance in Ephan's hand.

"I will answer the question," Psal said. "The king, my father, is fierce. He expects much from his sons, adopted, nature-blessed, or damaged. I challenged him one time too many and he struck me. If I am marked, I am marked for the sake of my clan, because I stood for the truth."

"What was this 'truth?'" Dez asked.

"It is not a truth you would understand. Accept that it was a truth, and because of this truth I was wounded in the house of my friends." Psal called Ephan and Maharai, speaking to them in the language of the Peacock Clan. "To bed, then?"

"Why do you use our enemy's tongue?" Dez asked, his voice almost a snarl.

"My wife does not understand the Wheel Clan tongue," Psal answered. "She will understand the primary Peacock Clan dialect. Speak it if you understand it."

"The Peacock language hurts my tongue and heart," Dez said. "It troubles me to hear it uttered. I was told she has lived in the royal long-house these six months. How is it she does not know our language?"

"That a language has power to hurt!" Psal said. "How frail you warriors are! But, if you will know...my wife sat in her chamber in great grief and sorrow. She saw her brother killed before her eyes. Moreover, her anger is fierce and unrelenting. She steadfastly refused to learn the language of those who oppressed her."

"Indeed?" Dez glanced at Maharai, then spoke under his breath to Lilea. "A well-spoken, well-rehearsed story. But I do not wish to charge the Firstborn of our clan with lying."

But Steen said, "Being a steward's son, I learned the Peacock Clan language before the war. And those here with Peacock Clan or Macaw Clan mothers know it. The way I see it, the Firstborn's wife no longer belongs to that wicked people. She should learn our language, of course. But since she does not as yet know it, we should honor the Firstborn by speaking it. And no doubt it would be beneficial to speak the tongue of the Firstborn's wife." He was a thin, dark-haired boy with an easygoing smile, and had been nervously braiding and unbraiding his wife's long black hair throughout the long, tense night.

Psal managed not to laugh. *Steen, although a warrior, speaks as his steward father speaks, protecting himself, not wishing to offend either warrior or studier.* "Well spoken, Brother. So it is agreed? The Peacock tongue."

"The Peacock Bride obviously rules her eimi." Dez spoke in the Peacock tongue. "But explain…why should a chief share his first wife, a chief who is the king's own Firstborn?"

Maharai answered him. "Know this, Nature-blessed ones. My husband will rule over you as Chief one day. He will also be Chief Studier for all the clan. Ephan, the King's Favorite, will rule your studiers as well. You are away from your longhouses with two studiers to guide and protect you, to heal you and to set you adrift. You should not challenge them. Nor should you persist in hating me. I am the sister-in-law of Netophah, the future king of the Wheel Clans, and I am the daughter-in-law of King Nahas. Consider carefully, therefore, whom you mock. Studiers and princes have long memories."

A long silence followed. Dez stared at her. "Perhaps the Firstborn spoke true. We have a Peacock warrior among us."

"'*Perhaps* the Firstborn spoke true?'" Meeka echoed. "Dez, do you intend to engage in subtle accusations against Wheel Clan studiers? It is not an exploit I recommend."

From that moment, a war rose up between Meeka and Dez. Not because—as was often the case—both wished to become the chief's right hand, but because Dez could not countenance a studier chief and Meeka insisted on honoring a damaged Firstborn.

Ephan walked to the Chief's Corridor, "The Firstborn, Maharai, and I will sleep on this side of the longhouse. We rule this longhouse. It is only right." He pointed to the residential corridor. "All you others… sleep over there."

Meeka nodded. "It is as it should be, King's Favorite."

"Well, then!" Steen slapped Psal heartily on the shoulder. "Firstborn Studier, where will you take us on our journey? Joyous, lush places, I hope!" His body visibly relaxed as the dispute seemed to come to an end. "With white sands, warm skies, and blue seas. Regions of wild fruit and small and large game. That's where I want to go."

"I shall try to aim for pleasant places," Psal said, "but you, being a steward's son, should know that Father will track our journey."

"True words," Steen answered. "The king is like the sun, aware of all things. But we should enjoy ourselves, shouldn't we? They've given us enough food to give us rest but not so much to make us lazy. So we will have to prove ourselves. But is there anything wrong with seeking food in pleasant places?"

Psal leaned against his staff. "Know this, all of you. I will deal justly with all. However, mercy is a chief's prerogative. In other longhouses, warriors rule. Not here. Because Ephan and I are studiers, some of you will think the world has turned upside down." He placed one hand on Steen and the other on Connell. "You will find that in this marriage tribe, stewards, and those born damaged—like Connell, Ephan, Steen, and myself—will be highly esteemed. Therefore, before you begin creating hierarchy among yourselves, before you irk me by telling jokes against those I esteem highly, be aware I lack humor where teasing the weak and cruelty are concerned."

"Firstborn," Payton said, laughing, "you should have said that earlier."

"I did not think it necessary to speak the obvious. I speak it clearly now because I am beginning to see the obvious might not be so obvious. Now, we studiers have keening to attend to. I bid you all good rest."

As he turned to go, Connell also rose from the floor.

"It is your wedding night," Psal halted him. "Take your ease and rest. When you return to your longhouse, you will have much work to do."

"Firstborn," Connell said, "let me work at your side. I have heard that you sat at the feet of the Wintersea Master. As a studier, I would greatly benefit from standing beside you and—"

"If I desire your help, I will call upon you."

The studiers left for the keening room. Most of the marriage tribe retreated to their chambers in the residential corridor, but some remained. As Maharai turned to leave for the Chief's Chamber, she remarked how those in the gathering room sat. The sons of comfort women, stewards, studiers, and out-clan fathers on one side. The sons of warriors on the other.

She nodded to Dez who was stretched out like a king, his head on Lilea's lap, while Payton lay on the floor near their feet. Then, because the conversation was of the strangeness of the longhouse, its chief and its eimi, she thought it best to go to bed.

But after she had lain in her room for sometime, her husbands came to her. They closed the door behind them, held their fingers to their lips.

"You are the 'healthiest of us three,'" Ephan whispered to her, laughing. "Steen's opinion. Although Jeejo did lay aside his reed pipe to say that you were stupid and fierce." He bent closer to her. "A bad combination, he thinks."

"Apparently, you are all the Wheel Clan's Firstborn could get for himself," Psal said. "They imagine Mad Prince Psal will take a lovelier primary wife after he becomes chief—if he becomes a chief."

Maharai looked at them, puzzled.

"Dez and the others," Ephan explained. "They did not live with the Wintersea Master. We who hear far-off towers, can we not hear the treacherous whispers of those the king has set to spy on us?"

"The king has…" her barely-audible voice became a whisper.

"He has ordered them to report all Storm's actions," Ephan said. "That they are to watch us at all times, that we do not cast ourselves onto the night."

"Nahas suspects?" she mouthed. "Daris spoke wisely."

Psal sat on the elegantly-embroidered blanket on the bed the stewards had made. "We have some possible allies," he said. "The sons of stewards, the damaged ones, the studiers. The foundlings as well, but they are often faithful to the clan."

"Count Meeka as an ally as well," Maharai said. "At least against Dez. You've fired up a war between them."

"But what use are allies if all their eyes belong to the king?" Ephan asked, squatting on a woven mat on the floor. "What is more worrisome than traitors in our midst? Bad enough we have a sullen listening branch which refuses to listen for other towers. And now this."

"It is a sullen tower, is it not?" Psal said, nodding.

"It has heard of many deaths," Ephan defended the keening branch. "And it has stayed far from war, at rest in a home region, with no care of its own except for steward gossip. It rebels at being pulled into the fray. Its fear of war…well, it simply refuses to pay attention to anything near or far." His eyes lit up. He stopped speaking, then raced from the room.

Psal and Maharai sat in silence. Then Psal smiled. A few moments later, Ephan re-entered the room.

"How did you do it?" Psal asked.

Ephan clapped his hands. "I reminded it that we had saved its former inhabitants, giving the girl to the Voca and the boy to the Peacock Clan!"

"Only that?" Psal asked.

"Only that. It challenged me, of course, threatened to rebel utterly and entirely. But at last, I promised that I would not seek out news of wars as long as we journey, and that should Psal become a chief, we would become a rescue longhouse and care only for the ill, we would not engage in battle. That—and reminding it of its lost children—seemed to suffice."

"It is a good-hearted little tower," Psal said. "It will keep to its promise if we keep to ours."

"Brother Storm"—Ephan began removing his tunic—"do you remember the many stories of our great ones, the legends of passionate and sudden love?"

"I remember them."

"It could be...that...such passionate love exists, but from my meager experience, it seems lovemaking is a battle against awkwardness, grief, and fear. At least in my experience." He laughed so hard Maharai slapped him on the arm.

"It is a strange sort of wedding night." Ephan rubbed his arm. "Psal is wounded in the hip, my wife is wounded in the heart, and I, myself, am wounded in spirit."

"He rarely speaks," Maharai said, "but when he does, he speaks so strangely. How could you have endured him this long?"

"Because he endures me, I suppose." Psal lay on the bed. "But let's prove him wrong. No doubt we will grow to love each other, and all this talk of wounded lovemaking will be set aside." His fingers slowly unlaced her tunic. "If it is to be done, let us do it."

"Enjoy yourselves, then, but when I fall asleep," Ephan said, "do not wake me with questions about how the thing is done. It is something I have done often, true, but it is not something I am expert in. Nor is it something one can teach."

* * * *

The next morning, Maharai lay naked between two studiers. She wasn't sure what she had expected of sex with Psal. He was gentle, as Netophah had been gentle. But she had not expected the action to cause him so much pain. Her own pain, the rape by Cyrt, had been present as well. She studied Ephan's face. *You were correct. And what pain will you bring to my bed when I lie with you?* She rose and looked out the window, drawn by the aroma of flowers and honey. A region of lush greenery greeted her.

"What pleasant place is this?" she asked her husbands.

"The Majestic Flower home region." Ephan sat up in bed. "It is the region marriage tribes often visit. At least in the old days." He glanced at her breasts, frowned. "Your breasts are very tiny, aren't they?" he said, sounding disappointed.

"They're all you will ever have, so you best begin to like them," Maharai retorted.

"True words," Psal said.

"If we found my mother," Maharai began, "we would—"

"There is nothing we could do if we found your mother." Ephan stood up. "Do you not understand? How can we escape if the nature-blessed ones refuse to let us out of their sight?"

Again, he spoke truly because all that day never once was Psal's eimi left to wander alone. By nightfall, Psal had lost his patience, and when Steen remarked that he wished to anchor in that same place one more night, Psal said, "I promised the king I would explore. That means we are expected to let the tower fly free. And have we all not consulted together to not seem like lazy warriors? But there is something else I wish to speak of. Today, Ephan and I wished to lie in the meadows with our wife. But we were not left alone. We should have been allowed to rest from the rituals of yesterday and the burden of having to form new bonds. Indeed, you all allowed yourselves times of freedom and refreshment but us—*my* eimi—you followed like dogs at the heel."

"We only wished to honor you," Dez responded. "You are, after all, the leaders of our longhouse."

"If you wish to honor them," Maharai retorted, "leave them time to play with their wife!"

The next morning, when Maharai woke, candle-light and shadows flickered across the ceiling. Cold pierced her bones, and she could in no wise warm herself. Nor was there sunlight or any light coming through the window. Only a cold, dreadful darkness closing in about her. Tears came to her eyes; her fingers and toes burned with intense cold: she sat up, grasped Psal's right hand and placed it on her feet.

Outside her door, Dez shouted, banging on their door. "Where have you brought us, Studier?"

"The cold dark clime," Psal calmly called back, rubbing Maharai's toes.

"Why?" Dez cursed as he stumbled against some unseen thing in the hallway.

"We need to pick Dama seeds." Ephan's teeth chattered as he spoke. "They grow in this region."

"You have brought us to a place suited only for murderers and outcasts, a place where the face freezes if one goes outside uncovered, to find seeds?"

"As children, Ephan and I—weak studiers both—anchored here with the Wintersea master for many days. We survived. You will as well. Or are you weaker than studiers?"

"So, that is it? For the mere sake of proving yourselves equal to Wheel Clan warriors, you—"

"Every warrior must learn to fear this realm," Ephan said. "He must fear the chief who can imprison him here and the studier who can anchor him here. And what are your complaints to us, who are both your chiefs and your studiers? We are not like the Voca who know how to keen by day. Therefore today, you must live where the day has sent you. Build a fire in the hearth. Gather wood from the stables. Take small and large logs, and bring the axes from the storeroom. For you will have to venture outdoors to cut wood. I will have no splinters in my longhouse." He laughed, whispered to Maharai, "Am I drunk with power?"

She was too cold to laugh.

"And," he shouted to Dez, "tell your wives to bring blankets from the storage room as well. And candles. For the gathering room. The large ones."

Dez banged even harder on the door.

"Now I understand why princes and chiefs have doors to their rooms," Psal rose and opened the door. "I would suggest you get the wood quickly, Warrior. Cold though it now seems, the heat stored in our roof crystals will disperse soon. It will become much, much, colder."

"The roof crystals will stop working?" Lilea's agitated voice came from the dark hallway. "The Ever-Present One help us! This idiot has brought us here to freeze to death!"

"If we do not learn how to battle the cold today, I shall anchor us here another night."

"He would not dare!" Lilea's voice again. This time she was shouting. "I am a chief's daughter! Connell! Connell! Where is he? Connell!!"

"Connell is well able to keen us away from here," Dez said. "And the rest of us have studied keening." He attempted to calm Lilea. "My love, my love! All will be well."

"It will not be well!" she shouted. "It will not be well! My Father will hear of this! Call the Voca! Now! They must daykeen us this instant, far from this place!"

"Dez," Psal said, "all know keening, but not all are studiers. If you wish to trust your life to your own slender knowledge, go ahead. But I warn you. You do not know song regions. You do not know what tower might be keening to the same area you're keening to, and you are dealing with a very recalcitrant tower. As for the Voca…you are mad if you think they will help us in a matter as small as being stuck in the cold clime. As for Connell, he did not study with our Master. I doubt he can override our keen."

But Ephan said, "If you challenge us, it is mutiny. Now, if you're finished rising up against us, go and tell our brothers that they must chop wood and find Dama seeds. Get dressed. Every true Wheel Clan warrior should know how to forage in this darkness."

"So," Dez asked, "you intend to venture outside to help us cut wood?"

"That I do," Ephan answered. "I am almost blind as it is. The darkness will not challenge me. And the darkness brings much relief from the sun. But this cold will exacerbate the Firstborn's illness. He must stay inside. Be careful, however. Despair is an effect of the region. But don't despair. We weak studiers are well able to keep you strong ones alive."

CHAPTER 34

THE GLEANERS

After Dez left, Ephan said to Psal, "Do you hear weeping voices?"

"I hear them. Women and little ones."

Maharai could hear nothing. She collected more blankets from the basket at the foot of their bed.

"The pale denizens of this region, perhaps?" Ephan said.

"No," Psal answered. "The little ones of the Listening Clan are well-used to this dark cold. And their towers would not weep so. This weeping…the language…its rhythms are those of the Peacock Clan."

The cold jabbed at Maharai, but the thought of little Peacock Clan children weeping from cold and the fearful darkness pricked her heart. "Those poor children…how near are they?"

"Far," Psal said. "We cannot reach them and return in one day. But perhaps the night will take them away, and tomorrow…"

"Don't lie to our wife." Ephan said. "That clan is *anchored* here. Their tower song already has taken on some of the rhythms of this region. The song has a contra-puntal rhythm, as if this tower once had a partner, another tower it traveled closely with. But then…about three, perhaps four days ago…a parting. But…why anchored?"

"As punishment, perhaps," Psal said. "That is often the reason. Some war perhaps…that broke out between the chiefs of both longhouses."

Maharai wrapped herself in a blanket. "But surely you can help them. You're studiers."

"The longhouse and tower seem healthy," Ephan said. "The tower's undamaged, but some of the keening crystals are missing."

"Do they have heating crystals in their roof?" Maharai asked.

"Did you have heating crystals in the Iden tower?" Ephan asked.

She shook her head.

"Roof crystals are tower science known only to the Wheel Clan," Ephan said. He turned to Psal. "I could break their anchor tonight. To-morrow, they will rejoice to find themselves free. and in pleasant places."

"But today," Maharai said, "they have no food."

"It would appear so."

Maharai retrieved the fur-lined boots the Wheel Clan women had given her. "We will bring them food," she said.

"Are you able to walk in this dark cold?" Ephan asked her.

"I am well able," she answered.

"What a wife we have!" Ephan said.

"Come closer, husbands."

Both studiers stood beside her.

"Perhaps this is our chance to escape," she whispered. "Let us travel to this strange tower. The dwellers will no doubt accept us with open arms when we bring food and clothing for their little ones. And if we venture out, the nature-blessed ones will not follow us."

"It is a far journey," Ephan said. "The children can wait one night more without food."

Maharai began crying.

Ephan studied her face in the flickering light. "If only I knew," he said, "why you weep. Do you cry for your mother? For the children? For yourself? Whom do you truly weep for?"

Psal held Maharai about the shoulder. "Cloud, have you become like Nahas, seeing schemes where there are none?"

"Whether I see scheming or not," Ephan answered, "there is no armor against tears. If you are willing to brave the cold, let it be as she wishes."

But when the studiers told the marriage tribe their intention to bring food to the starving children in a far-off longhouse, the others naturally objected.

"You're going into the dark cold to give our food to a Peacock Clan?" Dez bellowed. "Firstborn, are you truly as mad as they say?"

Psal beckoned to Ephan. "What does it matter what these others say?" he said for all to hear. "We are determined to go. The journey to the far-off longhouse is long and if we are to return before third moon, we must leave now."

Wrapped in blankets, Dez and Lilea followed the studiers to the storage rooms. As Psal and Ephan gathering cloaks, gloves, caps, and food, Dez said "You must listen to reason."

Psal answered, "Whether they be an outcast clan, a night-tossed people, or our sworn enemies, their children are hungry."

"I don't believe there is any such tower," Dez finally said. "Have any of us heard it?"

"The tower exists," Steen said. "I'm a steward's son. We are taught to hear such things. Perhaps not as well as the studiers, but I hear the tower as well."

"I hear it," Connell said.

"And the children?" Danu asked.

"I do not hear the children," Galef said, "but I do not doubt they're there. A tower with starving children will call out to the ten directions for food."

Jeejo shivered near the hearth. "It's some ploy to escape us."

"Has someone told you I wished to escape you?" Psal asked.

"Uh…no, Firstborn," Galef stammered. "It's just…"

"You may doubt the words of your future chief," Maharai said. "But whether or not Nahas makes Psal your chief, the Chief Studier of the Wheel Clan will remember that you distrusted him."

"It is dark outside." Danu said. "That is my concern. How will you see in all this great darkness?"

"Don't you know?" Payton said. "They're *studiers*. Their ears and noses can lead the way."

"Indeed they will," Ephan wiggled his nose.

The studiers filled a wheeled cart with blankets and food, and stood at the threshold of the main door.

"I hope you come back." Candle light and the hearth's flame both flickered across Jula's face. "If not, we will have to answer to the king for your loss. And what will we say? 'We allowed the Firstborn to go out into the dark to save some outcast Peacock longhouse?' Nahas will believe it a conspiracy, a story made up by warriors who murdered you."

Psal laughed. "If you murdered me, the king would understand the cause of it."

Dez said, "Nevertheless, we will go with you."

Psal's heart fell. Dez would walk with them, chafing and arguing through the length of the journey, never relenting or turning aside.

"Why will you come?" Psal unlatched the door. "Stay here in the comfort of the longhouse. This is not a place for—"

"For warriors?" Dez gave Maharai a scathing look. "But the 'fierce' girl from the Peacock Clan can walk in this darkness? Do you think so little of your own people?"

Psal pushed the door open. "If you will come, come. But let me hear no whining, and do not try to dissuade us as we go."

* * * *

Dez, Jeejo, Meeka, Payton, Danu, Galef, and Steen journeyed with the studiers while the other warriors and the women—all but Maharai—stayed behind to collect brush. To collect brush and Dama seed. Psal's eimi traveled in silence, each carrying a lantern. Whenever Psal looked back at the warriors, the light from the many lanterns seemed like a ring of fireflies or a circle of faint faraway stars. The darkness may have deterred the warriors, but they continued their dogged following. Often Psal looked at Maharai and when he did, his heart leaped with joy at the queen he had married, a girl who walked in the cold without fear and complaint, even when warriors behind her seemed unable to stop whining.

They walked for much of the afternoon, and although Psal was well-protected against the cold, his body threatened to fail him several times. One moment nausea assaulted him, another time his hip and leg burned like fire. Sometimes his cold body flushed with both chills and fever. Nevertheless, he continued onward. Soon he heard the sound of water flowing underground. *Water lies ahead, under thin ice.* He continued, knowing the water was shallow. Still, the ground that had been slick and hard grew soft, and mealy. At last he stopped and spoke to the others.

"Stay here"—he gave Steen his lantern—"we studiers will continue. Past here you cannot go."

"And why can we not go?" Dez asked.

"We're approaching a great sea," Psal lied. "It is too wide for us to go around it, and too deep to wade. To continue, you will have to swim. The cold is too strong for you and I will not risk your deaths."

"But you will risk your own?" Steen asked. "Perhaps the cart will float. But you won't."

"He's a studier." Maharai took Psal's hand. "And a chief. He knows what he's doing."

"That doesn't mean his mind is chief over this cold," Galef said. "And studying the cold doesn't mean one has conquered it."

"Stay here and build a fire until my eimi and I return," Psal said, his teeth chattering. "But if, peradventure, we don't return, don't stay here long. Return to the longhouse. We have cloakens with us. And we will send you word from the Peacock longhouse that we're well."

"You carried cloakens?" Dez asked. "Why?"

"We will stay," Payton said, "but Maharai must stay with us."

"Why?" Maharai asked.

"If you love your woman, why force her to swim this sea?" Dez asked Ephan. "Turn back. My mind cries out at this foolishness! How foolhardy this journey has been!"

"I will not turn back," Maharai shouted. "I won't."

"Your man is sickly, Maharai," Jeejo said. "Born with a disease that torments and kills. He's damaged! Will you hasten his death simply to feed those strangers?"

Maharai fell silent.

"You shall have to swim," Steen said. "And who knows how much farther in this cold you'll have to walk once you've crossed this great sea? And will you travel in this cold in wet clothes? And then, having warmed yourself by our enemy's fire, will you trust them to allow you to return to us? Come now, Firstborn, do not make me think I have a chief so foolish?"

It was foolish indeed, but Psal said, "We will stay in the strangers' longhouse. Even if they are our enemies, they will acknowledge our kindness to their children. They will not harm us. They understand their own trouble. After we repair their tower, they will allow us to keen their longhouse to some pleasant region where we will reunite with you. Connell will—"

"Did you not say that Connell knows little compared to you?" Dez retorted.

"I have released the anchor," Psal said. "Connell can—"

"Let us return to our longhouse," Ephan suddenly said. "Jeejo speaks the truth. You are too sickly to wade this river."

"Finally, a word that makes sense!" Dez said.

"Perhaps the chief has been testing us," Meeka said. "I have heard of such trials, created by chiefs to test the faithfulness and courage of his tribe. Is that it, my Macaw-Wheel Clan brother?"

Steen turned to Psal. "Is that true, Firstborn? Is this some perverse test?"

Psal was tempted to say it had been a studier-chief's test. To call the journey a joke would have been a lie, however. The lie would make him appear witty and fierce. His father would smile at the lie, even if he suspected the truth. But Psal had a foolish integrity. "It was no test," he answered. "I want to help these people. Tomorrow we will keen this lost longhouse to join us."

In the darkness, someone sighed, and another groaned. Maharai squeezed Psal's hand. He held her close against the pain in his hip and the ridicule erupting around him.

"Pitiful words from the son of a king," Dez continued his triumphant mocking through the journey back.

When they returned, Lilea echoed her husband. It was all she talked about, even as Psal shivered and vomited and ached. That night, Psal and Ephan keened the Peacock longhouse to join them in a pleasant place. They lay in bed with Maharai, and Ephan rubbing Emon paste on Psal's hip, leg, and stomach.

"Storm, today you harmed yourself walking in this cold. A double error. You showed yourself weak and you made yourself weak. Netophah warned you against seeming too kind. Such decisions! If we cannot escape, you will lose your chance to become chief."

"If I lose the chiefdom because of kindness," Psal answered, "then I lose it."

"But will you lose your future and your life?" Ephan asked.

"No," Psal said, "those I would not want to lose."

"Brother Storm, if we do not leave this clan, we will have much to contend with if we fail this journey. Have you not seen? It is obvious Dez wishes to be chief of a longhouse. He is like Cyrt in many ways. Befriend him. Earlier, when he suggested you keep the hearth lit throughout the night, that all would sleep in the gathering room for warmth, you should have agreed."

"Longhouses have burned because of that," Psal said.

Ephan rolled his eyes. "You sound like an old woman. The longhouse would not have burned. Come now, bend the rules a little. No one likes stumbling around in the darkness."

"Should we train our tribe to leave fires untended while we sleep? If the longhouse burns, will we not be all dispersed?"

Cloud groaned. "Find another way to please him, then. Become chief the easy way. These are not the old days when your grandfather and Qerys fought for the clan. Now, it's all about playing the game." He turned to Maharai, "We are one eimi. I will not forsake either of you. If one escapes, all escape. If one stays, all stays. But, my wife, I only wish your husband were more 'agreeable.'"

* * * *

The next morning Maharai woke alone. For a moment, fear struck her, struck deep. Had Psal died overnight from his illness and from the cold? She ran to the keening room, shouting for her husbands. Through the window she could see a green and grassy hillside, but this did not comfort her until she heard Psal calling from the rampart. She climbed the tower stairs. Her husbands were looking at a small tower with a shattered Peacock longhouse attached. Taking Psal's spyglass, she thanked her husbands for keening the Peacock longhouse into their wake. The three watched as a group exited the longhouse.

The Peacock Clan approached Psal's marriage longhouse, their bodies bent submissively, their hands cupped. Thirty or forty of them, the records say. But many scholars believe there were many more, and that Psal hid their true number for his own reasons. Naked all, gaunt all. Men, women, and little ones. A dark brown man with thin skin sagging over protruding bone led them.

Dez held a lance. "If this is some Peacock trick to destroy our marriage tribe I will kill them. I've already ordered our warriors—"

"How could it be a Peacock trick?" Ephan pushed Dez aside. "The Wheel Clan towers told of our marriage journey in riddled rhythm. All Peacock Clans, indeed all clans, know of the marriage but they believe our longhouse contains hundreds. Our tower upholds this riddle, and the Peacock Clans lack the power to discern the truth. Moreover, look at these people. Their skin clings to their bones. Would they starve and set themselves to freeze in the cold dark climes in order to capture us? The Firstborn son of the Wheel Clan king is important, but not so important to freeze one's self in darkness." Ephan took his wife's hand. "These are my wife's sisters, her brothers too. They will become our longhouse's first alliance, this night-tossed Peacock Clan. So, no more talk of attacking them."

Dez turned and started down the stairwell, but Maharai dashed to the entrance door. Outside, the skeletal leader knelt in the mud before the longhouse. Although alive, he smelled like the corpses Maharai had seen.

The man bowed to Psal, then stood, his hands covering his genitals. He approached Maharai, examined her face; tears came to his eyes. "We were once called the Udevi clan," he said. "We traveled always together. Our longhouse and another. But things went badly for us. Udevi died. I, Amar, am now chief."

"How came you to be lost?" Psal spoke the old man's language as if born to it.

"Those in our companion longhouse wanted to join Tsbosso in his war against the Wheel Clan. My brother Udevi and I had no desire to engage in war. The knowledgeable ones in our longhouse, those who understood tower science, joined Tsbosso. Then they cast us into a dark cold place. They took all—weapons, food, clothing. Days came, I know not how many. But what is the day or the night in such a place? We thought we would die there, but suddenly the anchor was broken and we found ourselves here! How happy we were to see your tower."

"Your little ones need to eat," Psal said. "You are among brothers."

Their hollowed eyes came to life again when they saw the grains, fruits, roasted meats in the marriage longhouse.

"My husbands," Maharai whispered, "let us leave with them tonight. Let us hide a cloaken among the food and blankets. We will escape with them and tomorrow, we three can leave their company and, taking the cloaken, find our way in the night."

Psal shook his head. "Father will seek their tower and destroy them, whether or not we're with them."

"And," Ephan added, "Seagen tracks our tower even now. He knows the rhythms of Peacock towers, even half-destroyed ones. Moreover, their longhouse is more damaged than I had suspected, and their keening room lacks adequate crystals. If we repair their tower, these nature-blessed we walk among, and those in the royal longhouse, will be much aggrieved."

"Nahas will understand us rescuing them from the dark cold climes," Psal added. "He will excuse my weakness in feeding them. But we cannot escape with them, and we cannot be seen doing more than is necessary."

"I thought Nahas's opinion no longer mattered to you," she challenged.

"He has power to make me a chief. It matters. If I remain in this longhouse, it matters. But the king has taught me much about compromises. Let us repair their longhouse only. Then we will send these Gleaners to some pleasant forest. That should suffice."

But all day, Maharai complained and begged Psal to leave. "You wish to return to Nahas and become chief," she said, angrily. "You no longer wish to be free or to rescue my mother."

"My wife," Psal answered, "with you and Cloud at my side, I would be happy far from the Wheel Clan. But…let not our new allies be killed. Do you not understand? Now, Ephan and I must speak to this great chief. He has become the first ally of the Psal longhouse. Let me go and bid them farewell."

"I will go with you." Her eyes were on a cloaken leaning against a nearby wall.

"If you go with us," Psal said, "you will try to persuade us to accompany them."

"If you go with us," Ephan added, "Dez will send warriors to accompany us." He winked. "And we would not want that."

Ephan and Psal stayed with Chief Amar until the third moon rose. All the time, Dez paced before the doors. When they returned, Dez accused them of repairing the damaged tower.

The studiers declared they did not repair the tower, but that night as they lay with Maharai, they whispered that Dez's accusations were not entirely false; they had indeed given the Gleaners some tower science and some extra crystals.

"They're quick learners," Psal said. "We have keened them to a pleasant place. Father would expect that. But we have taught them much. We asked only that they allow themselves to be night-tossed for the next forty-nine days and not to use any crystal or tower science we taught them until after the fiftieth. So the king will not track them. Besides, we will be home by then. By then, they will have met—hopefully—other longhouses. If they show up on the charts of any of our studiers, it will be assumed other longhouses helped them and not us."

"But," Ephan said, "the important thing is that it cannot be said that we actually *repaired* their tower. We have only given them knowledge on how to repair it."

"We have cautioned them, however," Psal added, "not to share what we taught them or to visit us again to ask for more tower lore."

"My people are wise," Maharai said, feeling less angry at her husbands. "You teach us a little and we learn from that little. Soon they will understand more than you do."

"I hope so. Or else they'll come looking for me again. And we would not want that, would we?"

"No," Maharai answered, "we want to meet my mother."

CHAPTER 35
ADVENTURES AND CHOICES

Some days into their journey, as Psal worked on tower notations, Ephan stood in the doorway with a plant he had discovered. "How bound to our studier's hopes we are!" he said. "Working while on our marriage journey!"

Psal laughed. "True. For I sit here trying not to hear Peacock towers and continually reminding myself not to send war missives to Father."

"Best not to. One should not break promises to towers, especially rebellious, bitter ones." Ephan removed the round crystals from before his eyes and wiped them with the edge of his tunic, then put them on again. "Yesterday I had to stop myself from sharpening surgical tools."

Psal limped to a stool where his wheeled boots were kept. "This marriage journey has brought back memories of the old joys. And our fellow travellers seem to like being night-tossed as well. Although they will not admit to it."

"Your experiment has brought mixed emotions to all," Ephan answered. "Happy anticipation, dread, and delighted discovery. They're remembering the days before the war as well. As for me, in the royal longhouse the keening room was both our haven and our tomb. It vindicated us and opened other worlds and closed us in. Here, we have found our lost selves again. And yet, I cannot help but think that if we escape our marriage tribe, we would be alone in a hostile world without the support of our great clan." He paused. "And yet I am ready to cast myself out."

"You're as confused as I." Psal laughed. "But all decisions bring conflicting thoughts."

Ephan gently placed the plant on a shelf, then squatted on the carpet in front of Psal. In silence, he helped Psal put on the boots. When the leather latches were drawn tight, he tapped Psal's thigh.

Psal stood, wiggled his toes. "Snug. I do like skating and racing through these halls." The aroma of blood flour and fermented meat filled the air. "The food smells good. Our new sisters are good cooks."

"Except Queen Lilea. That one will not lift her hand except to preen."

Psal laughed. "True, but already this longhouse feels like it will be our true home. I even long to see young ones running up and down the corridors."

"And the stable horses neighing all day."

"Them too. And Daris as well. I will miss his jibes if I do not return. But…if I do return, and am made chief of my own longhouse, I will—"

"Firstborn," Ephan began, then paused. "Firstborn," he repeated, kneeling.

Psal looked down at his friend. "'Firstborn?' Why so formal? How serious you sound! How strangely you behave sometimes!"

"I have something to tell you. But…Firstborn…"

Psal sighed. "Again this word. 'Firstborn?'" He extended the hilt of his dagger. "Well, then, if we are to be formal. Good Studier, what is your request of the Firstborn? Longhouses? Old Women?"

Ephan touched the dagger's hilt. "Firstborn, I have two secrets to tell you."

"Only two? I had imagined many more."

"No, only two. Two that make me fear, anyway."

"Fear what? Me?"

Ephan nodded.

Psal rolled his eyes. "Nonsense. What can I do to the King's Favorite…my favorite as well? Now, on with it. Your first secret. Although I do so hate promises and secrets. They often lead to trouble."

"Storm, you must stop your teasing. This unsaid thing is like a fire in my bones. I must tell you and—"

"Say it, then. I would hate to see you burn to dust before my eyes. Only…I hope I do not live to regret this. Are you sure you cannot keep this secret to yourself? Do I truly need to know?"

"On the day of the battle with the Iden," Ephan said holding Psal's gaze, "I heard the woman Ktwala in the grain container. The studier's talent for hearing, I suppose. And…I…"

"Ah me! That was a stupid thing to do!" Psal exclaimed. He lowered his voice. "Your kindness to Ktwala cost our longhouse much. And much has been added to our keening duties. Continually dragging the Iden longhouse in our wake, communicating with Bukko and the stewards about her daily care, steering the Iden clear of warring Peacock towers…and burdening me with the task of convincing Nahas not to kill her Grassrope male friend…yes, certainly, it has been quite a bother. Ah me! But the world will not end because of it. Certainly I have worse secrets." Psal placed his thumb on Ephan's right hand and tapped gently. "It is well. Your secret is safe, Brother."

Ephan did not release his hold on Psal's dagger.

"Oh, yes," Psal said, "I had forgotten. There is another secret equally unimportant. Truly, you and your scruples! Say it then, quickly. Good cooking, the imperious Lilea, and the new region await us."

He waited for Ephan to speak. But Ephan delayed.

"Is it so very difficult to say?" Psal asked, growing curious. "It cannot be so very bad."

Ephan nodded.

Psal waited. And waited. After, a long pause, Ephan removed his hand from the hilt.

"You will not tell me?" Psal asked.

"Not now."

"But now you've made me curious. I demand you tell me. It will cause no great harm. If I tell you my own Ktwala secrets, will you be emboldened to tell me this second secret?"

"All your secrets, I already know," Ephan said. "But when I gain more courage, I will tell you my great secret, Firstborn."

Psal sheathed the weapon and leaned on his friend's shoulder. "I do not like it when you call me 'Firstborn.' The word puts a distance between us and I do not want that. But mind you, tell me this other secret before you tell Maharai. Or tell us both at once. I don't want to be the last in our bound three to know your heart."

So there was Ephan's secret, untold. But you, my prince, already know what it was. Who knows how matters would have fallen if Ephan had told it then? Perhaps Psal's eimi might have ventured forth earlier and Netophah would not as suffered as he did. But, as it happened, the secret was not told and the journey continued.

Now, it happened that one morning, the marriage tribe rose to find themselves in a dense forest. After climbing the tower, Psal looked through the spyglass and saw a strange people, squat and bent, with strangely-turned feet, people living in a clearing toward the western end of a thick wood.

Their towers—there were sixteen—sang of four regions. "These towers are like singers singing part of a larger communal melody," he told Ephan. "A strange thing, is it not? Not even Falconer towers move in such harmony. And even more strange, the melody is rigid, unchanging. I doubt it has changed in hundreds of years."

"I hear sixteen songs," Ephan said, "yet…in this region, I see only four longhouses."

Psal pointed to the chart he had hastily created for this previously unknown clan. "Look here! There are twelve more towers in three other regions, all singing together. Four distinct groups of four towers traveling nightly among four regions?"

"A closed circuit."

"And only now do they reveal themselves?"

"Only now does our tower reveal them to us, you mean," Ephan said.

Psal nodded. "True. How willful and secretive these towers are! Why do you think our tower has chosen to reveal them now? And why have all the towers on Odunao have colluded to hide this people's song from us all these years!"

"Doesn't one of the ancient prophets state that when the time of the end comes, knowledge shall increase?"

"I try not to study the ancient prophets," Psal said. "They make my mind reel, Secret-keeper. But look here. Each tower group every four days arrives at orchards of fruit, or corralled lands of herded animals, or a woodland forest in the cold climes, or a home by the sea." Psal tapped the chart. "I can hear the echoes of those regions in their song. And look, even now these reclusive towers refuse to speak to our tower."

"Their towers reflect their wishes." Ephan looked about the forest. "And our tower colludes with them. You can't force it. Well, then, since these strangers do not wish to see us, let us ignore them. The eastern edge of the woods is verdant. There's a lake as well, and ancient ruins. We should—"

Psal rose to his feet. "I wish to meet these people. Such tower science they have! Linking their towers together! Such wisdom even the great clans would envy! Could this ability to link not help us when towers fail?"

Ephan shrugged. "This people know one thing and they know it well. Their towers conserve energy by dedicating all their skill and purpose to linking only to each other and only to four regions! But what does it matter to us? Storm, decide once and for all if you wish to return to Nahas or to escape him."

"All I have decided this morning is that I want to understand the tower science of these people. Prepare gifts for them. They will be the second allies of Psal's longhouse."

So having prepared carts and gifts for denizens of that forest, when the sun was high in the sky, Psal and his tribe journeyed to meet them. But the people proved unkind, ugly, and deformed as well. A people of enlarged ears and three-toed hobbling feet, squat and bent. Psal had seen such errors before, often in the caves and cliffs, or as the result of incestuous marriages where lust and solitariness overtook common sense and morality. Such were these, but hateful as well. Limping, spouting undecipherable words, they chased the marriage tribe away with fierce grunts and sharp wooden lances. Psal's tribe hasted away. In the rush, they left their carts and gifts scattered along the way.

"Well, then," Danu said, catching his breath. "If these pitiful ones refuse our friendship, why press it on them?" He broke a small branch from a nearby tree and stripped the smaller twigs from it. "But that we should run from damaged ones who can hardly walk! They threaten us and we run?" He laughed aloud, flushed with humor and the exertion of running.

"They're a small and foolish people," Dez said, but unlike the others, he did not laugh. "Their land is fertile, but they're unworthy of it. We ran from them, but why? Not because they were powerful—they could hardly walk!—but because our chief thought it best!"

"Outnumbered by limping snails!" Jeejo sat on a boulder. He glanced at Psal's feet. "Forgive me, Firstborn. I did not mean to imply—"

"What can stop us from taking their fields?" Dez asked.

"Damaged they may be," Psal said, "a people spoiled by inbreeding. But their land is theirs. We will not take it. And these damaged ones are not foolish. The Wheel Clan can only anchor towers to regions for forty-nine days. And we can link one tower to follow another's wake. But what these people have done! True, they are not permanently anchored in one place but, they link towers to towers and regions to regions…indefinitely! No hand has touched their keening tree. The keening and linking is perpetual. Even the Falconer Clan does not have this knowledge."

"What shall we call these strangers?" Ephan walked behind Maharai and placed his arms around her waist. "Surely we should call them something?"

"What do you wish to call them, Cloud?" Psal asked, still catching his breath.

Ephan kissed Maharai's cheek. "The Sailing Clan would be a good name."

"No, no, the Four Winds Clan." Galef pulled Jeejo to his feet. "Because their longhouses face east, west, north, and south."

"Their longhouses face only each other," Psal said. "They care nothing for any but themselves. And I like the 'Sailing Clan.' They have four ports and the wind blows them home safely. And I'm chief here." So the Sailing Clan it was.

But then Connell said, "But Chief Studier, if the Sailing Clan has such tower science, should we not force them to tell us?"

Psal leaned on his staff and clambered over a tree. "Even if they were friendly, it is not something they seem to know. Their towers do all the work. Perhaps in time past their ancestors tuned their towers and they forgo—"

"What if the Peacock Clan discovers them?" Dez interrupted him. "We did, why won't they?"

Psal nodded. "True. Yet strange. The towers have been trained to reject all other towers. But for reasons I cannot understand, they allowed us to find them."

"Perhaps they wanted our Studier-Firstborn to discover their secret," Meeka said.

Galef tugged Meeka by the right ear. "Flattering the Prince again, Meeka?"

"I see no reason why they should seek me out," Psal said. "Nor do I think the Peacock Clan will find them. But I'll do what I can. I will interweave some masking harmony into the songs of these sixteen towers. It would not change their ways, but it will protect this people from the Peacock Clan and from the Wheel Clan as well."

Ephan grimaced. "The old master used to say 'make one small change and the whole dismantles.' We should not—"

Dez interrupted again. "Nahas should know of this."

"Why should he know of it?" Psal asked.

The others looked at him.

"Each marriage tribe has its secrets," Steen said at last. "But to ask us to betray our king?"

"Speak of it if you wish," Psal continued toward his longhouse. "Nahas doesn't seize lands from small clans, but the war has caused him to make cruel judgments. No doubt Seagen charts our travels. He may or may not see the Sailing Clan in this region. They have disguised themselves all these centuries. I will tell Father of their science but I will not give him the tower song. Why should these people be removed from their land or their towers confiscated?."

So all day, as others walked outside among the fields or stayed inside making love, Psal studied the towers of the Sailing Clan and charted their chords, echoes, rhythms. Always, the answer was just out of reach. Night came and then all at once: *Ah, so that is how the thing is done!* Happy, he raced to his marriage chamber where he found Ephan and Maharai making love. Double joy!

Maharai wrote of this incident in her annals:

> *At nights my bed was my fortress*
> *Flanked by two warriors on either side.*
> *One night, in the double moonlight,*
> *One love lay above me,*
> *His hand stroking my thighs;*
> *The other near the door,*
> *His face surprised and smiling.*
> *My Love said to my love.*
> *How happy I am to see your heart opening to love.*

And this is one of Psal's poems about his own nights with Maharai and his marriage tribe.

The Longhouse is redolent of sex;
I, myself, am perfumed in it.
How, then, can I leave my marriage tribe?

Some speak with me as an equal.
For them, the words from this studier's lips
Are like a Chief's law.
How, then, can I leave my people?"

Maharai and Ephan were like smoldering fire, and lovemaking allowed their restrained fires to blaze brightly. This Psal understood. He pondered their lovemaking with amused fascination. But not envy. He understood that Maharai loved him. Their love was not fire meeting fire, but something more earthy, more full of comfort. Moreover, a body that continually ached and burned and screamed with pain could hardly pause to give itself to passion. Psal walked to a sleeping mat where, not wishing to disturb them, he fell happily asleep.

The next day he told his marriage tribe about his discovery.

"So now that you have discovered it yourself," Dez asked, "you will tell the king how to link towers? Now you don't have to tell him where you discovered it?"

Psal nodded. "I suppose so. But this incident has brought to my mind my good friend, King Renn of the Falconer Clan." King Renn who honored and understood him, King Renn who never found him bewildering. "I have set our towers to keen to the Falconer King's Home region. They are a good people, a strange people. I have much to discuss with him."

* * * *

It was not warriors but a large falcon that greeted Psal's marriage tribe. Psal removed the parchment from the bird's leg.

It read: "The king desires to greet the Firstborn's eimi before he meets the rest of the marriage tribe."

Psal's eimi followed the falcon into a nearby wood.

The Falconer Clan's obsession with rootedness was well-known, but Psal was not prepared for the mounds of dirt piled high, the scaffolds, the poles rising from cavernous pits, the catacombs, the experimental keening trees. He stood over a pit, King Renn by his side, and studied the king's newest project with equal parts awe and worry. Had his royal friend lost his mind? Still, if it was a royal folly, it was a communal folly. From the farmer to the princes to the studiers who rode as equals at the king's side, all were equally obsessed.

"Has any of this actually worked?" Psal asked the king.

"Well, no." King Renn laughed. "Each morning we rise, we study our experiments. Have we created new towers? Have we anchored towers for more than forty-nine days? Have we rooted a tower overnight? No, no, no."

"And what was last night's experiment?" Ephan looked askance at the large pit.

"During the large eclipse, we tried to bind a longhouse to the ground."

"I see no longhouse," Maharai said.

"No, Little Princess, I see none either," Nanookay, the king's studier, said. He walked like a king among kings, such was the honor shown to studiers in the other clans. Nanookay leaned forward. "How deep do you think this hole is, Little Princess?"

Maharai looked into the darkness. "It's very deep."

"It is the depth of five of our towers. Deeper than the edifices at the ancient Ruined City. Yet even when we build and bind, using half a forest to build catacombs, the night still takes our longhouses. Certainly, it's a good experiment for our studiers who often find themselves in far-flung unknown regions, but what shall we do when the towers fail?"

"You think the towers are failing as well?" Ephan asked.

"I know it," Nanookay answered. He smiled as Maharai curiously tugged his long braided hair. "And you, Little Princess, what shall you rule over when you become a chief's wife if no towers and clans exist?"

As they talked of failing towers and of the changed future of all humanity, a heavy weight of responsibility oppressed Psal. *Is there no time left?* Psal thought. *Have we truly come to the time of the end of towers?*

When Psal and his eimi returned to their marriage longhouse, Connell met them, flushed with excitement. "I had not thought to see the home region of the Falconer king. All morning I stood on the rampart looking down at the many scurrying feet, running hither and yon, carrying and dragging boulders and bricks. I must say it puts me in a strange humor to see a clan so industriously obsessed with challenging the night and creating a permanent home for themselves. That they should all share this madness!"

"It's a madness, yes," Psal agreed. "But is it madder than spending two years killing others when towers are failing?"

"Now you talk of failing towers?" Dez asked. "What are we to do with a chief who falls into the great obsessions of studiers?"

"We will anchor here for the next few days," Psal answered. "Unless you all seek adventure?"

"You are our chief," Steen told him. "You should not ask but command. And I wish to remain here. Is it true what I've heard? Do these Falconers truly have no privacy in their longhouses?"

"None at all." Ephan pointed through the window at ten or more Falconer warriors approaching their longhouse. "The Falconer do all things in the open."

"Sexual intercourse, grooming, defecating?" Steen asked, wide-eyed. Psal nodded. "Those and more."

"It's their response to the incest taboo," Ephan said. "In a longhouse without true rooms and true doors, how can evil occur?"

"Or perhaps it is their fundamental belief in honesty and transparency," Connell said.

"That as well," Ephan said.

Psal walked through the door. "My spirit soars when I visit these people. I rejoice at being away from that cursed bloodletting."

"You say they don't believe in secrets?" Dez exchanged a conspiratorial glance with Payton. "Does that mean they tell all their tower secrets?"

"Indeed it does." Psal said. "There is nothing they do not share, and they have not lost by sharing. Connell, if you wish to discover anything about their towers, ask their chief studier, Nanookay."

"While you and the king speak in private?" Lilea's voice accused. "The Wheel Clan and King Nahas does not—"

"The king is a friend of my husband, not his co-conspirator," Maharai snapped. "Why should kings not walk with kings? And if a chief hides his thoughts from those he rules, that does not make him a conspirator. Know your place and stop questioning your chief."

But Psal said, "I have not shared any new tower science with them. As always I honor our king's request. And I need no warrior's wife to tell me my father's traditions. Now, since King Renn has invited us to stay with him, I will keen our longhouse to remain here overnight. If your eyes become overwhelmed with too much seeing—defecating, sexual intercourse and the like—close them."

"I shall keep them open, Firstborn," Connell said.

"I as well," Steen added.

"One thing more," Psal said, "The Falconer tradition demands that all who enter the king's longhouse should not raise their heads higher than the king's. When you enter the longhouse, fall to your knees. Wait to see if the king is on his High Seat. If he is not, continue kneeling. Walk on your knees, if you have to."

"Stand up when he sits down," Jula joked. "Sit when he stands."

"Exactly," Psal said.

After midday, the falcon arrived to lead the marriage tribe to the king's longhouse. As Psal's marriage tribe journeyed to the king, Psal whispered to his eimi, "I will ask Renn his counsel, if I should stay with the Wheel Clan or escape them."

"He won't tell your Father?" Maharai asked.

"He keeps some secrets," Psal answered.

* * * *

Renn sat on his High Seat, his long black hair flowing over his shoulders onto the longhouse floor. He greeted Psal bowing, and allowed Psal's eimi to sit nearest him.

I had not thought myself proud, Psal told himself. *Although I play at pride well enough. But now…to be seen as a prince in the eyes of others! To be privileged to sit at the side of a great king and to speak to him as an equal! I am not so honored in my own longhouse. Even Dez seems perturbed. It is good to see one of the nature-blessed ones appear perturbed. And yet, this honor—a prince is not born for mere honor alone. Is he not also responsible to his people? And I, Firstborn in Odunao's greatest clan, do I not owe my people and all the people on this planet my life?*

After the feast, Psal's eimi journeyed with the king to a nearby hill. There they told the king all their hearts.

When they finished speaking, Renn gave them his counsel. "Although no one can force a prince or a prince's eimi to do something they do not wish to do, I do not recommend leaving your clan. But this is not new to you. As often as you have suggested escaping your clan, I have recommended the opposite. The Wheel Clan demeans its studiers, but a Wheel Clan studier Prince can do much, if he has the ability to endure."

"But the cruel mocking…" Psal objected.

"This tradition of your clans," Renn said, "the marriage journey to make you understand all clans and all the outcasts you meet…do you not think it a noble tradition? Your clan is not entirely evil, Firstborn. And, it seems to me, a marriage with a Peacock woman, will help all the clans heal when the war is over."

"But Netophah is Wheel Clan Heir, and Maharai is married to me."

"I was not thinking of Maharai, but of her mother," Renn answered. "No, Maharai, I do not think you should free your mother from the king's wake. Nor do I think you should encourage your husbands to…" A falcon lit on the king's arm. "Ah, news from far regions."

"This new obsession, King Renn," Psal asked as Renn removed a tiny parchment from the falcon's right leg. "Sending news now by birds? Why not send news through the towers?"

"One day towers will no longer exist," the king said.

"You really do prepare for all contingencies, don't you?" Ephan said, laughing.

"We must. That's why your friend and you must stay where you are, my lad. It is your destinies that you were born studiers. Your people need you. I doubt they think they need you, but they do. The failing towers, the war, your birth, Ktwala's imprisonment. They are all interwoven."

"You see meaning in too many things," Psal retorted. "And even if there is meaning, one can argue that meaning does not imply the Creator's intention."

"True," Renn said, reading the parchment. "The Creator is light and in Him is no darkness at all. I do not think He ordains cruel fate to us in order to achieve some mysterious good. He is all good and all light. Nevertheless, I believe you should not leave your longhouse. Nor should Ktwala leave hers. Unless of course, the Creator tells you—or her—to."

"What is the message you just read?" Ephan asked.

"One of my chiefs is considering building a four-story longhouse." Renn sucked air through his teeth. "It is not a plausible solution, however. Some of our home regions won't be able to produce food for so many people. Certainly his fenced fields won't be able to."

"*It is a stupid* plan," Ephan agreed.

Psal smiled. "Ephan often speaks when he should not. Forgive, Great King. He should not be so bold."

Renn tousled Ephan's hair. "The King's Favorite stands doubly close to royalty. I would not dare challenge one who is my equal."

"Truly, you are a gracious king, King Renn," Psal replied. "And yet, your life…your life as it is now…your life as it may be if all your plans come to success…or if they fail…"

"All my life I have been taught to believe the end of the ages would come in my lifetime. So it is no surprise to me that we live at the end of the time of towers." The king drew a long breath. "But perhaps it is all a myth. Perhaps the night has always been as it is, and the old stories of a once stable night is only something we use to comfort ourselves, like the dream of the afterlife and going to our Permanent Home. And yet…without working towers…should I not prepare our clans to live night-tossed lives? Prince Psal, could we endure such aimless lives? It will be a strange world, an uncontrollable one. Perhaps not a bad one. Just different. No clans, only ever expanding or ever-decreasing isolated longhouses."

As the day ended, Psal's marriage tribe returned to the Falconer royal longhouse. There, Nanookay performed his rendition of the ancient tale of the Savior princes. The story struck deep into Psal's soul. Nanookay was an excellent teller of tales. I cannot accurately reproduce the means and wordings of so excellent a storyteller, but I will try to do my best. Nanookay spoke thusly,

"Once, long, long ago, two princes were born in different longhouses, in different clans. The first prince was well-favored, nature-blessed.

The second had no beauty in him that his people should desire him. The nature-favored prince grew up among his own people in a longhouse filled with the riches of the world. Because he was the king's beloved Firstborn, he was not allowed to be cast about but was spared the miseries of life. Yes, even his eyes were spared. No sick, hungry, ugly, or despairing person was allowed to stand in his presence.

The time came when the young protected prince ventured out of his royal longhouse. There he saw such horrors, his heart broke. He had always imagined that all men lived as he did, without care, full of joy and happiness. How surprised he was to see the diseases that ravaged humankind, and the wracked bodies of starving children. Devastated by all he had seen, he could not eat, he could not drink, he could find no joy in life. He thought long about the world and sought to destroy himself. But one day, as he lay traumatized in his longhouse, sudden enlightenment came to him. The world, he realized, would always be full of sorrow, sickness, and poverty. It could not be helped. Nor could he himself help all the poor in the world. So he resolved to live his life and not grow attached to life's comforts. To live he must not let his heart care too much about the poor or the diseased either. He taught his followers that grief and joy, illness and health, were of no importance, that one should submit to whatever state one was born into.

The other prince, also beloved of his father, was sent out into the world to suffer as one of the common people. At birth, the king gave him to poor people to adopt. He was allowed to hunger, and to work for the little he ate, and to live among a suffering people. Yet, although he lived as one of them, he was despised and rejected by them. Because he was not like them. He was a man of sorrows and acquainted with grief. In time, he came to understand that he was strong because he had been weak, and blessed because he had suffered. He taught his people that sickness, poverty, rejection were evil and that they were to hate evil and to conquer evil by destroying the power of the Unfleshed Ones, that they could heal the sick, and actively fight all the evil that beset humans.

Nanookay ended his tale by turning to Psal. "What prince's philosophy will you accept?"

* * * *

When night came, as Maharai slept, Psal spoke to Ephan in the lushly-decorated room Renn had appointed for the convenience of Psal's marriage tribe.

"I had forgotten the responsibilities of chiefs," he whispered in the old Waymaker language.

"Nanookay and Renn have played you well," Ephan replied, speaking in the ancient language as well. "No doubt the Falconer king knew the story would touch your heart and mind. So now he has turned you against your cause? Do you think Maharai was so easily convinced?"

Psal raised himself from his bed and looked about the makeshift wall Renn had created for his tribe. "I'm born to study the world," Psal said. "The pharma, the animals, the peoples, the lores of all the clans. Not to strut about, mock, or murder. I am more studier than Wheel Clan chief. This marriage journey has brought back some old joys. They say joy leads us to our true path."

"To escape this tribe of ours?"

"To make all Wheel Clan chiefs as we studiers are." He stroked Maharai's back. "Our wife will understand. I hope you will as well. And when I return, I will keen Ktwala's longhouse to join the royal longhouse. I will bring her into our longhouse. Maharai will be happy. And what can the king do? If he challenges me, I shall remind him of what the stewards say, that the pregnancy is difficult for Ktwala. Why should Rain and Satima not care for the king's pregnant wife?"

Ephan answered, "I do not wish to return to the royal longhouse. But I will not leave my eimi, and in all you choose to do—because you are my friend and the Firstborn of my clan—I will obey you."

Psal's heart grew sad. "I wish you would not speak so formally to me. When you speak, I fear I have become your oppressor."

"You have," Ephan answered. "But there is nothing to be done about it."

The next day, Renn gave them parchments of tower lore the Falconer studiers had discovered. Some of this tower science Psal already knew; others delighted his studier's mind. In turn, he shared his discovery about the Sailing Clan. He did not tell Renn he had deciphered the workings of the Sailing Clan tower. Nor did he tell him the regions where the Sailing Clan so cleverly hid themselves.

"But," Renn said, "although they have no power to choose where their towers travel, they are a wise clan, this Sailing Clan. I know you, Young Prince. You have—or you will—decipher the secrets of the Sailing Clan. When your marriage journey is over, consider telling the secret to me. Until then, who knows if we shall see each other again?"

That night, as Psal lay in his own bed, he was in joyous spirits. "Maharai," he asked. "If I could free your mother and cause her to live in the royal longhouse...would you prefer to live with her there? Or would you rather live with her and away from the Wheel Clan?"

"I wish to see my mother," she said. "That is all. Do what is necessary, even if it helps your clan."

* * * *

One day the Iden clan arrived in a place of wild cats and corpses. Gillan, who had been sharpening a lance near the hearth, stood up. "Lian, let's climb the tower to see what this day has brought us."

As a roar sounded in the forest, he climbed the internal stairs, then descended.

"From the rampart, I saw a lost clan, white of skin. Seven men, two women, four children. They have no tower, but their hut is half-destroyed with its roof open to the sky and it is sinking slowing into the swamp. Ferocious cats, reptiles—larger than a man—surround them." He grasped his lance. "Come and let us rescue them."

Tomo looked out a window in the gathering room. "These cats are licking the bones of those Peacock warriors clean," he said. "A human leg in the mouth of that female, a human head in the mouth of the male. And look up there. Reptiles gnawing a man's leg. Well, he's fat enough. Was fat enough. Flesh on him to feed all the reptiles and lions in the region. And he won't mind, will he? Seeing he's dead. No, I will not venture out."

"But should we not deliver those outcasts from the swamp?" Ktwala asked.

Tomo walked away. "What are we against the swamps and the reptiles and the lions?"

But Ktwala raised her flute.

"Are you mad?" Tomo asked. "You see the dead Peacock warriors, do you not? What use was the Peacock domestication science to them?"

"They were men," she said. "Peacock men do not know this science. It is taught by women to their daughters. And even if I did not know this lore, I would try to deliver these people."

Tomo sighed, lifted his lance. "The stupid things you have made me do!"

Outside, Ktwala blew on her flute—different notes. The roar sounded again. Others joined in. Several lions appeared, growling and walking slowly toward Ktwala. The Iden men lifted their spears. Ktwala's tune floated across the dry grasses and through the swamplands. At last, a large lioness, crept out of the brush and bent low before Ktwala. From a short distance, thundering footsteps, heavy and steady approached. Ktwala waited. Three large elephants advanced through the brush. The one walked to Ktwala's right side, the other to her left. The third marched behind the lioness. Other cats nearby flanked the group or walked behind them.

"I never thought I would see the day," Gillan said, carrying Lian on his shoulders.

"Don't speak so soon," Tomo replied. "We haven't returned in safety yet."

But they did return safely. With the strangers who fled their tottering hut and entered the Iden longhouse. The leader, his two wives, his children, and his brothers: all from the Grassrope Clan.

After they had eaten and calmed themselves, their leader said, "Two days ago, at the sun's height. A cruel clan—a woman pale as ice, and cold, took our girls from us. That loss endured, yesterday, our hut materialized under a jagged cliffside. An avalanched tumbled down upon us. And today we arrived in this clime, our home destroyed. Three days of grief! My eyes are dry from weeping."

Tomo said, "Sorrows are often relentless. But live with us and add your strength, knowledge and beliefs to ours."

Ktwala shook her head. "No, you cannot live with us."

All eyes turned to her.

"Mother," Gillan said, "if we are many, we will live in safety, protecting our longhouse."

But Ktwala said, "I will not be outnumbered in my house. Not by a Peacock Clan, Not by a Grassrope Clan."

"But we are so few," the Grassrope leader said. Fear, anger, and gratitude mingled on the faces of the others. "Let us stay with you or we will be scattered with no hope of finding my lost daughters."

"You may stay among us until you have found a new hut," Ktwala answered, "or until a new home can be built for you. But you cannot stay among us, because after you have forgotten your grief, you will cast us out into the night. Not that that would do you any good because this longhouse is guarded by the Wheel Clan and they would kill you if they found me missing. They would surely avenge me. Nevertheless, I would have been cast out. I have fought long to stay here. I will not be cast out of my own house."

The next morning the Iden longhouse arrived in semi-arid desert with no trees or mud to build a new home. The day after that it arrived in a place of corpses where blood mixed with loam and clay.

The Grassrope men asked Tomo, "What is this?"

"Did I not tell you?" Ktwala answered them. "The Wheel Clan guards me."

The day after, they arrived in a place of pyres. The Grassrope men looked at Tomo. "What is this?"

He answered nothing, but Ktwala said, "Have you not heard what I said? The Wheel Clan steers this longhouse."

The day after that, they were in a fertile field where a steward handed them a basket of fruits.

The Grassrope leader said, "Is this the region of the Wheel Clan king?"

Tomo answered him. "The Wheel Clan leader loves this woman. It is he who brought us to the place of corpses, to the place of pyres, and to this place. This is the routine of our lives, and it will be yours as well if you join us."

The Grassrope Chief turned to Ktwala. "A strange sad life indeed." He breathed deeply. "All the world knows the Wheel Clan is a large and noble clan. If they have such power, perhaps they could plead with the Voca to return our daughters to us. I pray you, ask your husband to help us."

Ktwala answered, "I will ask the stewards to build you a home. Some eighty or ninety are anchored in this orchard to guard it. They will build you a dwelling place. But I cannot plead for the return of your daughters. The Voca, like the Wheel Clan, do not return stolen daughters. Farewell, then. Who knows when we will meet each other again?"

For Ktwala's sake, the Wheel Clan agreed to build a new house for the Grassrope foundlings. And once again, Ktwala asked Tomo to leave her side.

"Go," she pleaded. "Be part of their clan."

Again, he would not leave her.

That night the Grassropes remained with the Wheel Clan stewards and stayed there until their new home was built. When Ktwala arrived in that region again, the Grassrope Clan was nowhere to be seen.

* * * *

Around the beginning of the eighth month, two weeks into Psal's marriage, as Psal lay in bed, he heard voices—so low only a studier might hear them—in one of the studiers' rooms. He arose, leaving Ephan, whose hand lay on their wife's left breast, and Maharai asleep in bed. He walked to the Chief's Studier's room. There, he encountered Payton—the third in Lilea and Dez' eimi—and Jula—the wife of Meeka and Danu—hastily clothing themselves.

When she saw Psal, Jula immediately pointed her finger at her adulterous partner and shouted, "He forced me."

"No," Psal said, "I do not think he forced you."

"True, Firstborn, I did not force her." Payton finished lacing his trousers. "We…"

"Why have you done this?" Psal attempted a studier's detachment but his faltering voice failed him. "You've put me in a bad situation. Do you love this woman? Is this the reason you dishonor my longhouse?"

"No, Firstborn. I do not love her. Nor does—it seems—she love me."

Psal pushed back nausea. "Then why do you lie with her?"

"You've seen, Firstborn," Payton answered.

"What have I seen?" Psal asked him.

Payton lowered his head. "Lilea gains pleasure from depriving me."

"You're well-known and greatly honored," Psal said. "Why should she deprive you? Have you offended her in anyway?"

"No, no, Firstborn." Payton hurried to the entrance. "I could not hurt her. But I love her so deeply, and am so weak when in her presence she delights in wounding me."

"Perhaps you should not love her so much." Psal lifted his right hand. "I have not given you permission to leave yet." He turned to the woman. "And why have *you* done this?"

"Lilea mocked me," Jula answered. "She mocks me continually."

"I have seen," Psal replied. "But she mocks everyone."

Jula crossed her arms over her breasts. "But the husbands of others defend them. Mine do not."

His voice softened. "Neither of them?"

"Neither," she sobbed, perhaps in pretense. "Meeka and Dez continually argue. Because of you."

"So you blame me for your incest?"

"Incest, Firstborn?" Payton asked, eyes wide.

"Not exactly, Firstborn."

"Then do not include me in your defense if I am not guilty," Psal said.

"I will be careful, Firstborn. It's only...Meeka wishes to heal the breach with Dez and he urges me to ignore Lilea's insults. And Danu says I am strong enough and can defend myself."

"So you decided to hit twice with the same stone? Wounding Lilea and your husbands with one sin?"

"Yes, Studier-Firstborn,"

Manipulative perhaps. Nevertheless, her words twist my heart. "Jula, you risk much and you dishonor my longhouse by breaking the incest taboo." He reached to touch her shoulder, but withdrew his hand, the taint of the incest taboo clinging too tightly to her. He turned to Payton. "Payton, when our longhouse door closed on the night of our marriages, all women in this tribe—all but your wife—became your sister. All the warriors became your brothers."

"I understand this, Firstborn," Payton answered. "I do not need to be enlightened on the basic teachings of our clan."

Are you so haughty with me? You who sit on the floor by your wife's feet like a puppy? "Do you not? Even so, allow me to bring you light." Psal's voice shook. From anger, from dishonor. "It is not right that you should have your brother's wife! You have betrayed the brothers you're sworn to protect. This too—Jula is a child of a comfort woman, as you are. Whatever one might wish to think, your lineage as well as hers is unknown. She might be your sister! It sickens me that you should do this."

"Firstborn"—Payton's face paled—"forgive me."

"It is not a thing easily forgiven. In the future, know only this: you may lie with anyone outside of this longhouse, and anyone not born in your father's or mother's longhouse. Your wife, if she wishes to risk her life, may lie with anyone outside of this longhouse." Again, he pushed back nausea, swallowed the acrid fluid that had risen in his throat. "But do not taint my longhouse!"

"Forgive me, Firstborn." Payton looked past Psal into the corridor.

"How many damaged children have I seen!" Psal said. "If this thing were done in my father's longhouse, it would mean a sojourn in the cold dark climes. The girl herself might be made into a comfort woman."

At that, Jula wept, perhaps more sincerely.

"Did you not see the Sailing Clan's Evil?" Psal continued. "Have you not read our histories, how—after the Creator destroyed the night—our forefathers created such evil that the Creator had to send us his Principles? What does the Creator demand of you? His principles are not grievous. Nor does he wish to restrain our joy. He wishes only to prevent damaged ones born among us. Yet you, a Wheel Clan warrior, cannot keep your trousers laced!" Psal limped to the room entrance. "Do not look into the hallway while I'm speaking, Payton! What if she has a child? How can the lineage be truly known? Who can that child marry or not marry? I do not wish to give her pharma to prevent the child's birth, nor do I think her husbands wish it. Such pharma is destructive to—"

"Firstborn, no more, no more!" Payton kneeled, touched the Firstborn's damaged knee. "Rebuke me no more, Firstborn Studier, or I shall not recover from this shame."

Psal sighed. *I am berating one who is already a bruised reed.* "Are you a warrior? Yet you weep? Do not weep. We are warriors now, whatever our age. Forgive my anger. I should not have raged against you." He placed his hands on Payton's face and inclined it toward his own. "Truly, I do not believe in the Creator, but I have seen too many ills born from defiance of his laws. Come now, both of you. We must follow this sin to its conclusion."

Psal walked down the passageway, Payton behind him, but the woman lingered.

"What will you do, Firstborn?" Payton asked.

"Come," Psal ordered Jula. "And you, Payton, such fear on the face of one noted for his fearlessness! Do not fear. I shall have to make this sin known. You must forgive me. I've been rebuked publicly enough to hate such public chidings. But rebuked you will have to be. I can soften the hammer's blow, but I must hit. Follow me."

"But why, Firstborn?" Payton asked. "Why must it be known? Or I be...shamed?"

"Because you will lie with her again if you are not," Psal replied.

They walked from the Chief's Corridor into the residential corridor into the room where Dez and Lilea lay, huddled together. Near the sleeping lovers lay a wooden tray filled with clay jars, paints, perfumes, and such baubles that the arrogant daughters of chiefs used to decorate themselves. All of which Psal was tempted to throw on the selfish pair. He tapped Dez's shoulder. Dez looked up from drowsy sleep.

"Firstborn?" He sat up. "What has happened? Has some evil befallen us?"

Psal pointed at Jula, who stood near the threshold of the chamber.

"Why is that one here?" Dez tapped his wife's arm.

"Keep your voice low," Psal commanded.

"Why is that one here?" Dez raised his voice even higher.

Lilea now woke. "Why is that damaged one awaking us?" she asked her husband.

Psal answered, "Rise from your beds. Follow me to the chief's side of the longhouse where only grain and crystals can hear us."

This Lilea agreed to do, but she complained all along the passageway, like a great queen awakened from great dreams of herself. When they arrived at Jula's door, Psal called her husbands also.

In the keening room, Psal said, "These have broken the incest taboo."

Lilea pointed at Payton then at Jula. "With each other?"

"Certainly not with me," Psal answered.

Lilea pushed Payton aside, removed a pearl-encrusted comb from her hair and threw it at Jula. "That one lay with my husband?" she sneered. She raced toward Jula, hands raised, claw-like. Psal stepped between the women. "You, you, daughter of Grassrope whores, you lay with my husband?" Lilea pushed Psal to the floor, then cornered the cringing Jula against the wall until Dez pulled her away.

"Keep your voice low, Lilea," Meeka said, then looked at his wife. "Why should the others hear of our dishonor?"

"The laws of our longhouse have not been established," Psal struggled from the floor. "I had hoped to create the laws of our sub-clan at the end of our journey. I thought that by then I would know which of my father's laws I would keep and which I would cast aside. But, as you can see, my aim has had to change. What, then, is to be done to a woman who betrays her husband and to one who endangers and dishonors his clan?"

"Send the whore into the night," Lilea shouted.

"No, Firstborn," Danu pleaded. "Be merciful to my wife."

"Send her into the cold climes then," Lilea shouted. Spite flickered across her face.

"Be quiet!" Meeka repeated. "Dez, can you not control your wife's tongue?"

"Among most Wheel sub-clans," Psal said, "the crime of one in an eimi is the crime of all. It is a tradition I may adopt as well. But you, you decide. Think carefully. Should the guilty one's eimi be sent to the cold clime as well?"

Lilea was momentarily silent, then she said, glaring at Jula and Payton. "Punish all who are guilty."

"Indeed?" Psal wrinkled his brow. "Well, then. These things cannot be done in the night. All here will have to agree on the laws our longhouse will follow. Tomorrow we will discuss the law but not the particulars. Justice is often not justice when the guilty are known. Is that understood?" He turned to the guilty. "Return to your eimi. And look you, Lilea, be kind to Payton. In the meantime, I will keen an empty tower from one of our home regions. Tomorrow, it will stand before us and if you still insist that the guilty be sent to the cold dark clime, the guilty shall enter it. You understand that we might have to force them to enter it, and that after they have borne their punishment, their crime will be forgotten like a rock thrown into the sea."

All said they understood.

That day, Psal heard a faint tower, of the kind the Wheel Clan often used to imprison wrongdoers in the cold clime and he keened it to meet his longhouse. The next morning the empty longhouse stood opposite Psal's.

"Why have you brought a dying longhouse to us, Chief Studier?" Connell eyed Psal warily. "They're useful only for anchoring. Can it be that it's true? Are you truly trying to escape your clan?"

"If I were to escape my clan," Psal answered, "I would seek out a better tower." He chuckled. "Of course, the tower might not be for my eimi at all. But come to the keening room and I will tell you all."

At the council table, Psal declared, "The time has come to ponder the laws of our future longhouse."

The Great Principles were recited, pondered, debated. As were Wheel Clan traditions, and the traditions of the Great Clans. At last the ordinances for Psal's marriage tribe were decreed. "A marvelous collection of laws," Psal said. "Some more severe than I would wish, some less so. But all agreed upon. As I look upon you nature-blessed, I must confess, you all have made me proud to be your chief."

The tribe touched the hilt of Psal's dagger and vowed allegiance to the Wheel clan and to the Greater Light. After they finished, Psal stood, ready to dismiss them.

But Lilea grasped his hand. "Firstborn, have you not forgotten something?"

"What have I forgotten, Lilea?" Psal asked. *Let the matter rest, Lilea.*

"Shouldn't the guilty be punished?"

"What guilt?" one warrior asked.

Ephan stood and walked to the door. "The trespasses which occurred before the laws were passed are not true trespasses. Where there is no law, there is no sin. Those are the Creator's words."

Lilea stood up, pointed at the newly-written law parchments. "These laws existed among the Wheel Clan from the beginning of time, and our longhouse is a part of the Wheel Clan."

"Well, I don't know if they actually began from the beginning of time," Psal began, but Lilea cut him short.

"Damaged One, the guilty are indeed guilty of this trespass."

"What trespass?" Richu asked, looking about. "Has something happened? Already? Ah me! Who has sinned among us? Is it I, Firstborn?"

And the others all asked, "Is it I?"

"One among us betrayed her husbands," Psal turned to Lilea. "Do you truly want the guilty punished?"

She folded her arms. "Our laws declare it. Three days in the cold dark clime."

How pleased she looks! Curse this woman's petty vindictiveness! "Are all here satisfied that the guilty should be sent to the cold dark clime?" Psal asked.

The others looked about at each other. "It is a harsh thing," Steen said at last. "Having been twice in that evil place—not because I had sinned but because the tower needed some new crystals—I would not send another there."

"Nor I, Firstborn," Galef said.

"Think on it," Psal waved them out the door in the manner of his father.

* * * *

Although the empty longhouse stood with its door opened, none in Psal's tribe entered it. It happened that some hut-dwellers had also been brought to the region that day. They were a friendly, dark-haired, honey-skinned, green-eyed people of mixed Waymaker-Grassrope-Peacock stock. They spent a great part of the day examining both longhouses and the head woman—for a woman was chief of that clan—asked Maharai,

"Why does this tower stand here, opened, with no one entering it?"

"My husbands must punish some warriors today and send them to the cold dark clime," Maharai answered.

"A harsh punishment," the woman answered. "What crime have they done?"

"They trespassed against the incest taboo."

The woman nodded. "Ah, yes. Then it is necessary that they be punished. But tell me, you speak as one of my mother's people, one from a Peacock Clan. Yet you have married the Wheel Clan king's son? Are they not at war?"

"King Nahas, the Wheel Clan king, is my father, but my husband and I will return to change his heart."

"Towers bring trouble." The woman shook her head. "We're content to live without steering our lives. Thus, we are free from wars. Still, I wish you wisdom and favor. May you and your husband help to end this war quickly. Remind the Wheel Clan king also that he does not own the planet. Everywhere we go…Wheel Clan owned fields!" The woman looked about her. "We go hunting. Do you wish to join us? Another flute would be helpful."

"Old Jion taught me to fashion a flute," she told the woman, "but I was taken from my tribe before my mother taught me how to charm animals. She was afraid I would end up being eaten."

"I will teach you." The woman searched until she had found reeds of different sizes. After the flutes were made, the woman blew into it. A roar sounded in the forest. Again, she blew through the reed—different notes—and the roar sounded again. Then Maharai blew on her little reed. The warriors of Psal's longhouse lifted their spears, but the hut dwellers showed no fear. They neither fled nor huddled together. At last, a lioness appeared, roaring and bowing before Maharai.

Seeing this, Maharai burst into tears and ran into the longhouse. *My lost clan,* she thought. *This grief presses at my heart. We Iden were able to charm wild beasts, yet mere humans destroyed us. Shall I seek freedom or should I return to destroy this clan who destroyed my people?*

When First Night rose, the hut-dwellers retired to their hut, but Maharai spoke to her eimi in the Chief's Chamber before Psal called the rest of their tribe together.

"My husbands," she said, "I am in a strait between two longings. Ephan wishes to escape the Wheel Clan entirely. Psal desires that we return to the king's longhouse, find my mother, and destroy this evil Wheel Clan."

"Those are the two choices," Psal agreed.

Ephan turned to Psal. "Storm, the chiefdom is not yet in your hands. If you intend to return to Nahas, do not make Dez your enemy."

Psal answered, "All day Dez and Lilea whispered against Jula and her eimi. They have told the others the particulars of Jula and Payton's sin, although I've warned them against speaking of it. Even now, Jula sits alone, weeping and rejected. And Lilea aims to punish Payton for his sin against her."

"Reject your heart's counsel just this once." Ephan raised his voice. "Befriend your enemy while you're on this journey with him."

"Why should I befriend Dez?" Psal said. "And why should Lilea triumph over Jula?"

"I also do not like Lilea triumphing over me," Maharai said.

Ephan shrugged. "I have given you my counsel," he said. "But what is my counsel when those I love are against me?"

Psal did not answer. *If only I knew why he is so angry at Nahas! Although he will not leave me, he has grown so sullen. It is a hard thing, his simmering anger.* Psal took Maharai by the hand, squeezing it tightly, and brought her into the keening room where his marriage tribe awaited him.

"What is your decision?" he asked his tribe.

"Send Jula into the dark clime," all but Psal's and Jula's eimi said.

"Ah," Psal said, "I see you are aware of Jula's crime. Who told you the crime was Jula's?"

"Indeed, Studier," Connell said, "It was hard for such a thing not to be known."

Galef nodded, glancing at Lilea. "Out of the abundance of the heart, the mouth will speak. And Lilea's heart was much aggrieved. She had to speak."

"Yes, she spoke a great deal." Psal beckoned them to follow him to the empty longhouse.

As the night wind blew through the meadows, Psal's marriage tribe stood in front of the empty longhouse. "Let the eimi of Jula and Lilea enter the longhouse," Psal commanded.

Lilea looked at him, mouth open. The others looked one to another.

"But, Studier, Firstborn," Connell said, "Lilea has done no crime."

"But she has," Psal challenged.

"What is my crime?" Lilea shouted.

"You refused to lie with your husband," Ephan said. "You fomented treachery against your chief. You and your husband created dissension in the longhouse and against the son of the king." He turned to Jula. "As for you, Jula, you know your trespass. And certainly, the crime of adultery cannot be committed by a woman alone. If one in an eimi sins, then all in that eimi must be punished. Both eimis have brought dishonor—and the Creator's wrath—against my Chief's longhouse. One has trespassed and taken his brother's wife. The other has trespassed against his chief. Both shall be punished."

Meeka knelt and touched the ivory hilt of Psal's dagger. "My chief," he said, "this punishment is for the betterment of our tribe and the success of my eimi. I accept it. Truly, I do not wish to return to that dark cold place. Nor do I wish to endure Lilea's whining for three days. But you are my chief and the son of our great king, and the word of the Creator in the mouth of the Firstborn is like the same word in Creator's mouth."

"I have never seen such honor done to me." Psal touched Meeka's hand. "I wish I could do otherwise, but you must go. And do well to love this wife of yours. I do not understand the hearts of women, but the annals say 'a wounded wife is like an unsheathed dagger.' Already Jula has proven it."

Steen and Galef gestured toward Danu. "Firstborn, what if this one is truly the son of the Voca Queen? Will she not be angry to hear her son treated so shamefully?"

"He did not defend his wife," Psal said. "Any true son of Ezbel would defend women and the damaged. Should the news come to her ears, the Voca Queen will honor my actions."

"I will not go!" Dez yelled. "Why should I? I did not sin."

"Is the Wheel Clan's great warrior a coward?" Psal asked.

Insulted, challenged, Dez pushed the Firstborn aside and entered the longhouse. Jula's and Lilea's eimis were then sent into the cold dark climes without food, candle, cloaken, or wood. Three days they stayed there, having to work together, then Psal keened them to return. When Dez returned to Psal's longhouse, he pushed past Psal, causing him to tumble to the ground. But from that day onward, Lilea treated Maharai with the respect due to the wife of a Wheel Clan chief.

* * * *

Ktwala could no longer walk with her clan. It had become difficult for her to even rise from bed. Whenever she stood, her legs and back ached and the ligaments of her womb burned. She remembered her many failed pregnancies. "I will not lose this child," she told her clan. "In less that one hundred days, the child will be here."

Chief Bukko challenged her. "Let my midwives help you."

"I will not."

Gillan pleaded with her. "Let one of the wives of the Wheel Clan stewards help you."

"I will not."

Jarid pleaded with her. "Come to the king's longhouse and let your sisters care for you."

"I will not."

The days of corpses and pyres increased. Fewer now were the days of respite from death. The king seemed determined to terrify her. Bedridden now, she was doubly trapped. By the king's edict and by her own aging pregnant body.

The night also trapped her, because now dreams haunted her and night visions terrified her. The history of the war was continually played before her eyes. In the first, her grandfather's enemy, stood before her, his mantle across his shoulders. "You blame me for this war," he said, "as your grandfather blamed me for the death of Iden's brothers, as the Wheel Clan king blames me."

"Why should you not be blamed?" she asked him. "Always, you deceive and murder to impose your will."

"The past is past, Daughter." He removed his mantle and lay it on the ground before her. At first it lay there, empty, a mere mantle. But then she saw that the home regions of the clans were engraved upon it. "Do you see, Daughter?" he asked her.

She saw. Odunao. Its dark, cold clime was useless but it encompassed half the planet. Bordering the dark climes and the fertile regions were the cold climes, gray, but still touched by the Sun. Then the fertile regions, half of which were owned by the Wheel Clan.

"They own much," she agreed.

Tsbosso responded, "And would own more if I had not battled them."

When she awoke, she thought of old Tsbosso whom she had not seen in ages. She told her new brothers, "The one who stole my grandfather's region and killed my father's brothers came to me in a vision of the night."

"And what did he ask of you?" Gillan asked.

"Only that I see," she answered.

The next night, Nahas came to her dream. "Ktwala," he said, "I want you to see."

"Who am I that you and your enemy come to me asking me to see?" she asked.

"What I do now, you will understand later." He brought her to a Wheel Clan longhouse. "Look within."

She did. On the floor, lay dead and dying Wheel Clan women and children, cut by Tsbosso's machete.

When she woke, she said to her Iden brothers. "How strange it all is! First Samat visits me, then Tsbosso, and now the Wheel Clan king."

"You are very important, it would seem," Gillan said.

"Pregnant women dream such dreams," Tomo dismissed them. "You wish honor and success for your child. That's why you dream such things. For all children are honorable, and all have a great task to do for the Creator."

Ktwala put her hands to her mouth. "And yet, when I was pregnant with Maharai and Ouis and all my lost children, I did not have such dreams."

More dreams came, with more visitors. From the living and the dead. The dead—both Peacock Warrior and Wheel Clan warrior alike—came to show her the details of their death. The living came to bewail the war, the destruction of the planet, and those lost to the power of the night. King or outcast, they all spoke as if Ktwala had power to help them. A stout balding Wheel Clan officer appeared often. Blood smeared his tunic and dripped from the dagger in his hand. A demon, like a python wrapped itself around him, constricting, squeezing away his life. Standing among the Wheel Clan pyres, he never spoke to Ktwala. But she sensed a fury in him, and a sorrow. Oftentimes, when waking from dreams of him, she wanted to comfort him.

Daily the dreams came, and when Ktwala woke, she would say to those around her, "Oh, that this pregnancy was finished with! Then these dreams would end, and I could walk outside—even in corpse-filled fields!"

* * * *

Dez's anger stood in the path of Psal's goal. Thus, when Dez and Jeejo suggested a day of hunting, Ephan commanded the tower to find some pleasant hunting place.

But when the sun rose, the drumming of a Peacock Tower greeted them. Such a meeting should not have happened, because warring towers avoided each other. But when Ephan questioned it, Psal's tower displayed a deep dislike for Dez.

"Apparently," Ephan told the others in the keening room, "in its desire to be rid of what it considers Psal's enemies, it has brought our longhouse face to face with a Peacock longhouse of four hundred armed Peacock warriors."

"Women, towers and studiers!" Connell yelled.

Dez glared at Psal's eimi suspiciously. "But it…'apparently' believes Psal will be spared?"

Ephan shrugged. "Psal, Maharai, and me. 'Apparently.'"

"The deceptions of the Firstborn are…" Jeejo began but Dez interrupted him.

"Challenge the Firstborn later. If we live. But now…our weapons are few and the Peacock warriors are well-armed."

The meadow echoed with the stamping feet and war chants of Peacock warriors. Outside, a Peacock Clan chief was calling the Wheel Clan warriors to the battle. Torches surrounded Psal's longhouse and more than two hundred warriors waved clubs and spears.

Galef said, "We're dead men."

As Dez and the others hurried to the armory, Steen said to Danu, "The Voca are our allies and they have accomplished the daytime keen. She's your mother, is she not? Call her and have her defend us."

"I have told you!" Danu shouted. "She is not my mother." This time his words seemed sincere.

"We're dead men," Galef said again and shot Psal, Ephan, and the tower an angry glare.

A battle had been suddenly thrust upon Psal, who was by no means adept at directing battles. "Dez will be our commander," he shouted to the others, the words almost sticking in his throat. "Payton will command from within the longhouse, Meeka will direct defense of the longhouse. Jeejo will command from the ramparts. And Danu will direct the women."

As Dez began to give commands, and Ephan and Psal tried to call the Voca Queen, Maharai grabbed Tsbosso's staff. Then, quickly opening the longhouse's entrance latch, she called out to the Peacock Clan chief.

"Great Chief," she said. "Why do you prepare to battle against us?"

Psal and Ephan came running to her side. Too late to close the door now, the rest of Psal's eimi stood, armed, behind them. A short man with feathered headgear approached, and Maharai raised Tsbosso's staff high.

"Because we're at war with your people," he said. "Is that not obvious?"

His voice. He has the same gentle, strong voice of my grandfather.

"I'm Okoa, Chief of the North Wind Peacock Clan," the chief continued, "and your longhouse is a Wheel Clan longhouse. Are you of the Wheel Clan? Or is this a failed Wheel Clan tower you found and repaired?"

"We are a Wheel Clan longhouse," Maharai answered him. "But a chief named Tsbosso gave my husband this staff to lean upon. He made an oath to my husband that it would guarantee safety should we meet a Peacock Clan."

Chief Okoa extended his hand and took the staff. Examining it slowly, he asked, "Why did you speak the truth just now?"

"Because I belong to the Peacock Clan and honor truth," she answered. "Because it would be futile to lie about the history of our tower. Because we are a small clan and could not triumph over you."

Chief Okoa turned the staff over, pausing several times to read its markings or to laugh heartily at some joke written on it. He spoke to Psal. "I do not like talking to women. Especially young girls, you two who stand beside her, are you the chiefs of this longhouse?"

Psal nodded. "I am chief, here."

He indicated the staff. "And are you the Prince Psal Tsbosso writes of?"

"Prince Psal, Nahas' son, yes."

"So you're Psal? You're taller than I expected. Renowned studier, because of you, some say the Wheel Clan king has a heart. Is that true? Does Nahas have a heart?"

Psal limped forward. "He has, I think."

"A heart that will be much grieved if he loses his Firstborn son, no doubt." Chief Okoa craned his head to look inside the longhouse. "Prince Psal, you've placed me in a bad situation. Not you, but this staff. And those others inside." The chief of the North Wind Peacock Clan approached the longhouse, placed his hand on Psal's shoulder and entered. "It is an elegant longhouse," He looked about the gathering room. "Strangely made."

"My father made it for me, Chief Okoa," Psal answered. "For my leg. For my hip."

"You understand my problem, don't you, my boy? To have the son of the Wheel Clan king here in my grasp! The Wheel Clan king would give much for his son, many regions. But, perhaps it is your lucky day. Many of my fellow chiefs would like the king's head among their trophies. But I am sick of war. I ventured here to rest after my last battle, and imagine my surprise when your longhouse materialized before me. Truly, my boy, I wish we had never met. For I am bound to treat you as an enemy." He examined the staff again. "But this staff declares you're Tsbosso's friend. He writes here that you are his son, and has vowed to protect you."

"When not traveling with the Wintersea Master, I was companion to his son," Psal said, "And I almost married his daughter."

"Moonlight?" the chief asked, looking impressed.

"No, Cassia."

"Ah!" The chief smiled. "She is lovely as well, a good mother, and a kind heart. But Moonlight was lovelier."

"'Was?'" Psal asked. "Has she died?"

"We are talking of your death, my boy. You should be concerned with that." The chief turned about and walked out of the longhouse, carrying the staff. "This is a complex situation and I do not want to offend against Tsbosso's oath. I must ponder this."

Maharai shouted after him, "We are promised safety, Great Chief. Tsbosso's staff declares this."

The North Wind clan chief laughed, as one laughs at a foolish child. "Tsbosso gave your husband the staff before the war began. The oath is probably dead now. Perhaps the Creator will overlook the oath, if I killed your husband. Yet one must be careful. I, myself, have lost many sons in this war, but none were slaughtered by Nahas. A good thing. If it were otherwise, I would most certainly kill your husband." The chief read the staff again, laughed at some joke written on it. "What am I to do? What am I to do? Great Creator, what am I to do? I shall have to speak with my studiers about this."

So Chief Okoa left them and began walking around the longhouse, his studiers with him.

Many of those in Psal's marriage tribe moved from window to window, watching Chief Okoa. Others prepared their weapons, but most remained in the gathering room, pacing.

"Do you think he'll kill us?" Connell asked Psal.

"He will not," Maharai answered.

"The Peacock Clan chiefs are honorable men who respect the Creator," Psal added. "They do not take oaths lightly. They believe words carry life and sound. For them, one cannot sin against life and words and expect a good life because words created life and words hold the world together."

"Firstborn," Steen said, "We are at war. What do oaths and old beliefs matter?"

"They matter to the Peacock Clan," Psal replied. "They are a honorable people."

"You call these murderers 'honorable?'" Dez entered and threw a lance to Meeka. "We stand here waiting waiting. Are we so powerless that we wait to be slaughtered like sheep?"

"Debate me another time," Psal retorted. "But now, Commander of my armies, trust me. Maharai has chosen a wise course." He looked toward the keening room. "Perhaps it was the only course because as yet the Voca Queen has not arrived to help us."

"So, the Voca Queen is on her way?" Jeejo asked.

"I do not know. Ephan is still attempting to contact her. Our tower was agreeable to it. But, we don't understand the day keen or how long it takes to set the crystals or to direct the tower to the region. Perhaps, even now, she hurries to our aid, but…"

"Firstborn!" The voice of Chief Okoa called the Wheel Clan warriors outside. "I cannot kill you."

Psal's shoulders relaxed. "I am glad to hear this—"

"But I will take your tower and all in your longhouse."

"'All?' Do you mean…" Psal indicated his marriage tribe. "They are my brothers."

"Do not push the privilege too far, my boy. The others must die. But you…and your wife…and if there is another husband she is bound to… take cloaken and set yourselves adrift. You're a studier. You will find yourself at home soon enough. But your blood will not be on my hands." He looked up at the sky. "When the shadows lie eastward, we will destroy these brothers of yours and burn your longhouse. Then we will take your tower."

The chief ordered his warriors to stand aside and wait while Psal related the news to his marriage tribe.

"So you will leave us to die?" Dez shouted.

"Him and his oaths!" Lilea yelled.

Why do they always shout? Psal looked out the window. "The Voca Queen must come. She must. But if not, I will not forsake my marriage tribe."

"How great a fighter you will be against this vast army! You with your damaged leg!" Dez snarled.

But Meeka said, "If the Firstborn wishes to fight and die with us, it is a noble thing. He could have escaped but he has chosen to die well, with and for his people. But perhaps we shall not die. The world is full of strange victories, is it not?"

So they armed themselves, and as the Peacock Clan chanted its war chants, Ephan remained in the keening room.

"Why does that pale one delay himself in towers?" Galef asked. "If the Voca Queen is coming, he should tell us. At least, we would fight with hope."

When the sun's shadows lay eastward on the ground, the Peacock Chief and his warriors sounded their horns. But as the Wheel Clan warriors took their places, there came a buzzing sound, like that of locusts. Maharai looked out the window. All around the longhouse the sky shimmered. In that great desert other Voca longhouses suddenly appeared as far as the eye could see, materializing in the sun. Longhouse doors opened and girls armed with lances advanced and surrounded the Peacock longhouse.

"I have longed to meet this great queen," Connell sounded awestruck. "And now, what an entrance!"

From one of the longhouses, a woman approached and called to Psal. "King's Firstborn, we meet again."

"Chief Tamira." Psal grasped Maharai's hand tighter, walked forward and bowed

The Voca chief beckoned to Ephan as if they were old friends. "And King's Favorite, you called for me?"

"I did," Ephan said. "We were in trouble, as you can see. And although I feared calling the great Queen herself, I remembered that this tower knew your tower song."

"Indeed. This tower should've been ours. But do not fear our Great Queen. I relayed your tower song to her and she sent this great army for your sake." She glanced at Maharai. "I heard you and Psal married the same girl. Is that the girl beside you?"

"She is."

Behind the Voca chief, the Peacock longhouse seemed to melt in the sun. "I will send them to the dark climes for a few days." Chief Tamira turned to leave. "Nevertheless, it is a bad time to go on marriage journeys. Return home. Who knows if we shall meet again?"

"One word with you, Great Chief." Ephan hurried toward her.

"Certainly, King's Favorite." Chief Tamira turned, bowed to Psal, then directed Ephan to follow her to her longhouse.

They spoke long together and some time after the Peacock Clan disappeared, Ephan walked back to Psal's longhouse. A little girl dressed in the garb of the Voca women stood at the entrance of the Voca longhouse watching him. Suddenly, Psal's tower whistled a tune of recognition. *Ah!* Psal thought, *the girl we saved two years earlier, the girl we had to give away.*

As they watched Chief Tamira's tower disappear, Connell said, "It is a strange thing to keen in the daytime! And did you see? They overrode the Peacock keen and sent them away with the daykeen! I have seen a great thing today!" He laughed. "Not that I would risk my life to see it again. But tell me, Studier Cloud, what did you two speak of so privately, King's Favorite?"

Ephan smiled shyly. "I asked her about their Great Queen."

"Their Great Queen?" Dez repeated. "And what did the chief say… about their Great Queen?"

Ephan blushed. "She said Queen Ezbel would like me."

Dez wrinkled his brow. "Queen Ezbel would 'like' you?"

"Yes."

"Ephan likes old woman," Psal said. "Bedding the Voca Queen is one of his great goals."

"It is not!" Ephan shouted, blushing.

"How strange you are, Ephan!" Galef said. "Why didn't you go with them then, if the queen 'would like' you? Meet the old girl, have your fill of her, then return here."

"I could not leave my eimi," Ephan answered.

"Come and study the crystals," Psal grasped Ephan's hand and dragged him toward the keening room. "Our tower is keening homeward. Do you hear it? Perhaps…we could…see…how this daykeen works."

So the marriage journey of Psal's eimi was cut short, and they returned to the Nahas longhouse alive. Like prisoners returning to a dungeon, but like deliverers as well, intent on saving their people.

PART V

NIGHT-TOSSED

CHAPTER 36

RETURN TO THE NAHAS LONGHOUSE

Psal had tasted freedom and peace again during his marital journey. When he returned to the royal longhouse in the ninth month of the year, he had to turn his mind again to death and the smell of corpses. He reminded himself that his life's purpose lay in saving his clan during the time of failing towers. Nahas would have to listen.

When they arrived in front of the royal longhouse, the sun had reached its height. Immediately, the king called the marriage tribe—all except Psal's eimi—into his chambers and pulled the doors shut. During that time, Psal and his eimi walked through the longhouse. A strange sensation…one of powerful, cruel, orderly perfection sent a shiver down his spine. Wherever they went, no spoken word of welcome greeted them; all but Daris, the comfort women, and the Iden women turned their faces from them.

In the residential corridor, Psal noticed Daris now walked with a limp.

Psal returned with the boy to the pharma room. "Has something happened to you?" he asked Daris. "You seem much changed."

"It is nothing, Chief Studier," Daris answered.

"If you will not tell me, I will not ask. But tell me, the others in the longhouse have not greeted us warmly. A strange thing for a Firstborn returning from his marriage journey. Has something happened in the longhouse?"

"You will discover the accusations soon enough, Chief Studier," Daris said.

"Accusations?" Psal asked and glanced up as Ephan entered.

"But, however they deride you," Daris continued, "remember this. Weak though we studiers are, weak though you are and have been, how powerful has your influence been! How powerful your absence as well. Do you understand?"

"You speak as one preparing me for death," Ephan said. "And what are these accusations?"

Daris turned to Ephan, then pointed in the direction of the king's door. "Let the accusers tell their accusations in their own words. But know that Lan and I have already been punished. And the absence of its chief damaged ones has affected the king's longhouse greatly."

Psal exchanged a glance with Ephan. "Where is Lan?" he asked Daris.

"He was speaking with the stewards in their longhouse," Daris said. "But when you arrived, the king sent Gaal and Cyrt to him. Excuse me, Chief Studier, I have much work to attend to." He bowed, then limped toward the gathering room.

"He has grown sadder," Psal said. "Sadness was never in him."

Ephan looked toward the corridor. "This strange silence bodes us ill. Perhaps we should not have returned."

"How could we not return?" Psal asked him. "Who is there to protect us—or those who help us—from the anger of the Wheel Clan? And the towers are failing. Should I forget my responsibility to this cruel clan?"

So they worked together, Psal and Ephan, mixing pharma. All day it was evident all was not well. When the sun began to set, Netophah appeared at the Chief Studier's room. He had greeted them once upon their arrival, then had joined his father and the rest of the marriage tribe.

"Father wishes to speak to you," His tone hinted at coming rebukes.

The bound three followed Netophah into the king's chamber and the doors were closed behind them as they stood facing the king and the Wheel Clan Heir.

"The others have told me about your journey," Nahas said, his voice calm, searching. "I would like to hear your opinion of your journey."

Ephan and Maharai remained silent while Psal spoke, telling the king and Netophah of the Gleaners, of the Sailing Clan, of his visit to the Falconer King, of their journey to the dark climes, of failing towers. Then the king said, "Psal, you've spoken as a studier. Speak now as a Firstborn would."

"I would only say what I have already spoken. I am neither one nor the other, but both."

The king then gave them his judgment: Psal was not to become a chief. Disappointed but not surprised, Psal bowed and turned to leave, but then Nahas called Seagen into the room.

Seagen entered with tracking parchments in his hand.

"I wish you to explain a certain matter to me," the king said.

Psal glanced at the parchments. "I will try, Father."

"Seagen has told me that at those times when we defeated Peacock warriors in battles, their women were returned in their broken towers to Tsbosso's home region? Do you know anything of this?"

"I know nothing of this, Father," Psal said. *So this is the accusation Daris hinted at?*

The king mumbled something under his breath and shook his head. "Of late, you have become a liar, Firstborn."

"I do not lie, Father."

"Ephan, do you know anything of this?"

"I know nothing of it, Nahas," Ephan answered.

"You too?" The king laughed. "So this Peacock wife of yours has taught you both how to lie? And I am now faced with a conspiracy?"

"We have not lied, Nahas," Ephan insisted.

"Is it because you fear for your wife's life?" the king asked them. "In my experience, that is often why men lie."

"We know nothing of this, Father," Psal said. "Do you wish us to lie and say we do?"

"Perhaps you should hazard a try." The thinly-concealed contempt in Netophah's voice surprised Psal.

"Perhaps the Peacock women are now being taught how to keen their towers," Psal ventured.

"Perhaps," Ephan added, "the Peacock Clan chiefs thought it best to teach their women keening skills. War necessitates much."

"'War necessitates much?'" The king's voice dripped sarcasm. "Is that your answer?"

Seagen cupped his hand over the king's ear, whispering while pointing at the parchment.

"Seagen tells me that it is a strange thing that all these Peacock towers were returned to Tsbosso's region," the king said. "A 'strange thing.' Do you hear that, Firstborn?"

A stupid error. Psal edged away from the king and prepared for a blow.

And Ephan said, "There are many strange things in the world, Nahas."

"The Peacock longhouses come from many sub-clans." Netophah looked through the window. "Yet they all return to Tsbosso's home region? Why? Did these women want to join Tsbosso's harem?"

Psal drew a long, slow breath. "It's possible, Father, that that is the only region the women know how to keen to."

"Which is more possible, Firstborn? Or more 'strange,' Ephan?" Netophah asked. "That the women were taught how to keen? Or that they wanted to join Tsbosso's harem?" He stood before Ephan. "You're smirking, Ephan. Do you find this amusing? You've betrayed your people."

"I do not find it amusing at all," Ephan said.

"The keening of the damaged Peacock towers to Tsbosso's region ended when your eimi went on your marriage journey!" The king's face grew red. "Have you studiers no loyalty to your clan? When Rain told me she suspected you were undermining our efforts, I didn't believe her. I should have. You have always seemed like one who would deceive your people." The king looked at Ephan. "But I thought Ephan had more sense, more loyalty."

"In many things I disappoint you, Nahas," Ephan began, but the rest of his statement was knocked down his throat by the king's hand.

A blow to Psal's stomach quickly followed. Psal's knee buckled; he almost toppled onto the floor.

"Maharai," Netophah said, speaking to her in the Wheel Clan tongue, "did you tell your husbands to send your Peacock sisters home?"

"I am unsure of what you're asking, Netophah," she answered in the Peacock tongue. "My knowledge of your language is not good."

"Enough, Maharai!" The king shouted in the Wheel Clan language.

"Father," she said, in the Wheel Clan tongue. "I knew nothing of this. And yet, now that I know of it, I'm glad my husbands did this…if indeed they did do it. Tsbosso will think that you were merciful."

"Like my former wife, you always have a good answer," the king said.

"Perhaps she herself was the instigator?" Netophah said.

"I doubt it," Seagen said. "The parchments show their scheme began long before Psal decided he wanted her as a wife."

The king picked up the royal goblet and threw it against the wall. The sound echoed through the room. "My studiers and one of my best warriors involved in a conspiracy against me! I've already punished Daris and Lan, but—"

"You should not have punished them," Ephan interrupted him. "They're guiltless in this. Would Lan not have forbidden us from saving the women if he had known?"

The king pushed Ephan into a nearby wall. "How subtle you are, Ephan!"

Netophah pushed Psal aside. "Lan should have told the king of the Firstborn's actions."

Lebo appeared at the door. "Go, all three of you. Now, children! Go! Before the king's anger boils over again."

Psal's eimi fled the room like robbers caught in the middle of their thieving.

When they returned to their room, Psal called Daris to his room. "How were you and Lan punished?" he asked.

"We were anchored six days in the cold clime," Daris answered.

"But…" Ephan stumbled through his words. "A child…a child… in…" He hugged Daris close. "He should not have done so."

"That I cannot speak of." Tears fell from Daris' eyes. "Yet I know I would not have been harmed if you had been here."

"Nahas punishes those we love because he cannot punish us," Ephan said. "He knew we would survive in the dark cold climes, or we would throw ourselves into the night. But he understood that seeing those we love punished would cause us much hurt, and make us fear leaving this cage he's bound us in. My friend, and my wife, we should not have returned."

Psal looked through the window into the darkness. "Where is Lan?" he asked. "Has he not returned from speaking with the stewards?"

"He returned when you were speaking to the king," Daris answered, "but left again with Cyrt."

Psal squeezed the boy's shoulder. "When Lan returns, call me. I wish to speak to him…even if he's angry with me. Do you understand?"

"I understand, Firstborn."

But third moon rose and although Cyrt had returned, Lan was still missing from the longhouse.

"Lan has not returned," Ephan called downstairs after the count was taken.

Nahas called up to the tower stairwell. "Studiers, the night is fast approaching, and third moon is almost at its height. Close the doors."

Ephan shouted back, "There's still time for me to seek him and to bring him back."

"The boy is strong and well able to take care of himself," Nahas answered. "He's a studier's son. If the night takes him, he'll return to us."

"Lan's skill in keening is not as expert as ours," Psal said, hobbling down the tower stairs. "What if he's fallen or is in danger? Let Ephan look for him."

"Ephan will stay here," the king said, firmly.

"Is this some scheme to punish him more?" Psal asked.

"Ephan will stay here!" Netophah shouted. "The conversation is ended."

The two studiers nodded their assent and allowed the longhouse doors to be closed. Then they hastened to their marriage chamber. There, Psal opened the shutters and the windows.

"Ephan," he said, "run fast. Find Lan. Take a cloaken. You may bring him home before third moon rises. But if not, the cloaken will keep you together. Go and return safely with our friend."

Psal and Maharai placed the leather cloaken across Ephan's shoulders and helped him climb out their window.

"Lan and I will return safely to you," Ephan reassured them.

"I know your skills," Maharai said. "But be careful and don't let the Voca find you."

"The Voca won't harm me." Ephan slipped through the window. "I fear Nahas more than I fear the great Queen Ezbel. Do you not see that he wants Lan to be lost? Farewell, then. Who knows when we will meet each other again?"

But neither Ephan nor Lan returned that night and the longhouse continued on its way without them. All that night, Psal lay awake. *Lan possibly harmed. By Cyrt. At Father's bidding. And the little one's foot and body blasted by the cold. Why fight? There is no justice. Ephan, wherever you might be, return with Lan. Both of you, return safely. And when you are safely returned, we will all depart this longhouse. What do I care about failing towers?*

In the morning, Nahas learned Psal's eimi had defied him. He ordered the stewards to keen one of the prison longhouses to meet the royal longhouse the next dawn. The stewards complied. The next day it stood before the royal longhouse.

Because of the rescued Peacock women, the king had begun to nurse a suspicion about his studiers and stewards, for—he said—"They helped the Firstborn deceive me." Therefore, when the stewards sent the prison longhouse, the king commanded Seagen, Gaal, and Cyrt to examine it.

"The tower is not as faint as it should be," Seagen reported to the king in front of the hearth. "Towers anchored in the dark climes are usually solitary and suicidal, but this one sings. Moreover, I searched the walls and compartments of this ancient longhouse. The stewards have hidden crystals, keening branches, cloakens, and much wood and candles. This is no prison they've prepared for your son. Nahas, your Firstborn has conspired with the studiers and stewards to make his exile a luxurious one."

"I have not conspired against you," Psal answered.

The king responded only to Seagen. "Captain, have all such items removed from the tower at once."

Seagen did as the king commanded and Maharai and Psal were cast into the longhouse, and anchored in the dark cold climes.

"I have been too patient with you for too long," the king said, as the heavy door of the prison was closed. "Perhaps a sojourn of forty-nine days in the dark cold climes will break this will of yours."

"And what if I do not stay there?" Psal shouted through the window at Nahas.

"You are damaged, my boy," the king answered. "One such as you should not choose to be night-tossed. Or will you destroy your life to gain freedom?"

"If he fled the prison," Seagen said, "he would soon return here, carried in the arms of some pitying clan who could not withstand his whining."

"That I would not do," Psal answered.

"Firstborn," the king advised, "even if you would risk your health to the night, do not be so foolish as to cause your wife to be night-tossed. No, I do not think you will endanger your wife. For her sake, you will remain in that cold darkness. Farewell, Firstborn. Who knows when we will meet each other again?"

CHAPTER 37

NIGHT-TOSSED

Thus it was, in the second day of the tenth month, Psal found himself in the dark climes. He could have survived the dark cold climes alone, or he could have thrown himself out into the night and trust that it would bring him to pleasant places, but Maharai was with him and he did not want to subject her to that harshness. Yet the continued darkness and the cold so oppressed Maharai that she pleaded continually that they trust their bodies and souls to the night.

At last on their sixth night in the darkness, as they lay together near the hearth, Maharai said, "If we stay here any longer, I will die or kill myself."

They lay under blankets, piled high. The flickering fire of the hearth and the dim candlelight of the hearth highlighted her distress. "This longhouse has neither cloaken, wood, nor leather," he told her. "But—"

"But? Tell me, Psallo! Because, if I remain here, I will give up all hope of living. Far from my mother, my sisters, I—"

"A cloaken could be made," he said, indicating the blankets piled high above them. "These blankets could be bound and wound together. But I warn you, although the cloaken will prevent the night from separating us, because it's made of cloth and not of leather or wood, the night will still unmake us."

"But all will be safe if we abide under the same cloaken?"

He nodded. "But…it is very unpleasant to feel one's self being unmade."

"I can endure anything if you are by my side."

"Also, my wife, know, that if we cast ourselves upon the mercies of the night, we must return here by the forty-ninth night. Or Nahas might do us further harm. Also, know that if you intend that we cast ourselves away from the longhouse forever, we might never be reconciled to your mother."

"I cannot stay here," Maharai answered. "And, if it is His will, the Ever-Present One will guide me to my mother. But, if not, we will return to this prison in time. The Creator will protect us."

"It is not wise to do this," Psal warned. "It is not safe for young ones like us to be alone in the world."

But she would not hear. So they wrought a cloaken from their blankets and bound themselves to each other, to it, and to Psal's staff and two days later, they jumped into the night, outcasts.

The cloaken, such as it was, prevented the night from separating them. But not being made of wood or leather, it did not protect them from the nightly unmaking. It had been long since Psal had felt himself being unmade by the night. His right hand, which grasped Tsbosso's staff tightly, seemed to freeze one moment, then burn hot the next. *Nevertheless,* he thought, *the cloaken keeps us together.* He had endured the unmaking before, a trial placed upon him by the old master of the Wintersea. Ephan had been at his side then. So he had not feared being neither here not there, neither whole nor scattered, yourself and yet not truly yourself. A fellow studier was at his side. But Maharai knew no studier's skills. *Both our lives depend on me. On me alone. If she is lost, she cannot return to me.* Under the cloaken, his left hand held hers tightly.

When day broke, his hand still grasped hers. He had hoped to find himself in a warm meadow or a sandy plain, but he was cold, freezing. *In a cold clime.* Through the narrow slit of the cloaken's opening, he saw whiteness. They had been thrown into the bright snows of the Wintersea. *I know this place. Nevertheless, I do not wish to be here.* They were on an ice floe, as large as a Falconer longhouse, but larger ones were squeezing, pressing into it, quaking it, and all were being crushed under a heavy snow.

Snow on ice. He held Maharai close.

"Maharai," he whispered, keeping his voice even. "Wake. Wake. Return to yourself."

"Where are we?" She shivered inside the heavy woolen blanket.

"We are on a floe that is being pounded by a rush of smaller ones. Here, they pile on top of each other, breaking, collapsing."

"I feel the movement."

He nodded. "It is a swift river, and this patch of ice will not remain intact."

He spoke truly. A large crack had begun on one side of the floe, and the swiftly-moving sea threatened to make the break ever wider. All the time, the ice around them rumbled, pushed and heaved higher and higher, making momentary ice cliffs that would suddenly come crashing down, grating, screeching, and gurgling.

We should not have left the dark cold climes. He rose, lifting Maharai. They stood bonded by the cloaken as ice chipped away at their temporary home. They stood there long, until Psal's senses heard a bird song, smelled frozen mud and wood under ice. Someplace, near, an ice cavern existed, with rotting wood inside, enough for a songbird to nest in.

He squinted into the dawn and looked far, far, far in all directions. To his right, something loomed: either a mountain of snow or a structure made of ice. He had seen such formations before, a combination of natural and human efforts. As part of the landscape, they existed unmoving in many regions. Humans often inhabited them. They could shelter there from the wind and snow.

The wind whipped at him, the frosty chill constricted his throat. His leg and stomach hurt. He pushed against pain and shouted. "Maharai. On my shoulder! Over there, look! We'll swim through the watery flow and find some entry."

Numb, his hand grasped her fingers tighter, and lifted them indicating a distance across the rushing waves. Shivering, she nodded.

The freezing water chilled, stabbed. Cold and shivering, they reached the ancient structure and found entry. To their joy, the former inhabitants of that abode had left behind animal skins and furs. Psal and Maharai wrapped themselves in these and sat together looking about the gloomy ice-mortared structure. Brittle tools—poles of wood, knives of iron and Falconer bronze, and slabs of stone—lay scattered on the icy floor. But food was nowhere to be found, unless they considered the ice reptiles living in a junctures where the ice cavern and the rotting wood met. Of these reptiles Psal caught two, and after removing their liver and stomach, they ate.

When night came, Psal said, "Come my wife, we must throw ourselves onto the mercies of the night again." He tried to smile. "The chance is great that any other place is better than this."

She took his hand and once again, taking the cloaken, they went out into the dark. Again, Psal felt his body dissolving from one region into another, felt himself being unmade and being transported. But he was comforted; Maharai was at his side. When morning came, it seemed that the only thing remaining of him was pain: old pain with which he was well-acquainted and new pain he had hitherfore not dreamed of.

The night had tossed them into a thorny field, a place of strange berries with sharp pricks. He attempted to rise, but the cold had exacerbated the hip pain. He yearned for Emon, Rangi, and Tomah, anything to free his mind, but saw only berries. He and Maharai ate, but soon their winter-chapped lips burned from the berries' tartness. Immediately outside the cloaken were thorns and nettles of the berry patch. Beyond that, a mountain stream rippled. Beyond the stream, cliffs, looming. If Cliff Dwellers lived there, they might be persuaded to help. But the thorn brushes rose also higher in that direction. The pain in Psal's hip was so great he could only drag himself along the ground. *Unless I lean on Maharai. Why have I brought her into this world to cast all my care on her?* He had a vain hope of finding an abandoned tower. *But to return to the Nahas longhouse? Or to the dark clime?*

"May I lean on you as we move toward water?" he asked Maharai. "I've nothing to trade, but if Cliff Dwellers live nearby, they might provide us with shelter."

Leaning on her shoulder and his staff, they passed through the briars and found the water, a muddied stream. The cliff showed no sign of habitation. So they sat near the stream, waiting for the night. Night came again and morning brought them to a desert region.

Now all was brown sand and sparse shrubbery, with fierce reptiles and wild cats. In pain still, Psal worried for Maharai. Although she had honed her skills in Peacock domestication science, she had no flute with her. Nor was his staff a formidable weapon against such creatures. While it was true that he understood what berries to eat, how to eat grubs without ingesting the parasites that lived in them, how to hear living towers, what herbs to use to repel fierce animals, he could not walk in the heat of the sun, and a young girl clung to his side! Moreover, outlaw bands abounded in the untethered world outside the longhouse. When Psal found a weeping, damaged Wheel Clan newborn, he despaired. The child lay dying and—if no animal ate it—would linger several more days, being tossed night by night; he strangled it. For the rest of the day, he thought only of the child.

The night tossed them here, there, to cold regions, to regions blazing hot, to seas, to grasslands, to sandy deserts. One morning they woke to find themselves in a wooded area. An abandoned tower-hut stood nearby. Its tower sang weakly, but Psal felt it could be tuned. All morning they aimed for it, the roars of the wild cats and the shrieks of the dying animals echoing through the forest as Psal limp along, leaning on Maharai's shoulder. When the sun was lowering in the sky, they reached its doors. They found it foul-smelling and stained with blood. Fearful of disease, Psal told Maharai, "The Wintersea Master warns against diseases hidden in the blood. We should not stay here. It might be the former inhabitants were ill."

Again the night, again the strangeness of being unmade, but in the morning they arrived in another wood. Leaving Maharai asleep, Psal limped up a nearby hill and looked in the ten directions. To his east, not too far away, lay a little hut without a tower. To the west, not too far away, lay a tower with a longhouse. He waited. Before the sun rose high, a family of the Grassrope Clan exited the longhouse. Seven men and three women. He looked down at Maharai; she would not be safe with such a clan. When he descended, he told her what he saw.

"In the east lies a hut. It seems empty. We'll continue to be tossed, but it could be a pleasant home until we find a better."

They walked there, eating whatever they found along the way. When they found and explored the little hut, Maharai said, "It is cozy. Perfect for two. This will be our home until we find my mother."

"You're asking for an impossible thing," Psal said. "This hut has no tower, and the chance is great that we could ever—no, not in a thousand years—find your mother if we remained here."

"I trust the Creator to make the impossible happen," she said. "Is he not as present with my mother as he is with me? Why should he not bring us together?"

They abode in the hut many days, being tossed about but together and free. Some days the night brought them to regions where sand abounded, some days to swamplands. Some days there were trees to climb. Some days only ice and snow. Several times, they were flung to the cold dark climes. But Psal had prepared grassy mats to sleep on, and their store of foods had increased. Still, exacerbated by cold or heat, Psal's hip continued to betray him. He longed for the Emon in the royal longhouse, for the comfort of his clan.

Yet, at the same time, he often thought, *I like this freedom and this randomness. The planet's troubles no longer concern me. If the towers fail, what does it matter? Whether tossed into verdant forests or harsh desert or watery swamp, humans can learn to be content. Perhaps such solitariness is the future of all the people of Odunao. Perhaps it is best for man to live alone.*

But Maharai was always looking for an empty longhouse with a tower that she may find her mother. One day she heard one.

"Do you hear it?" she asked.

Psal lifted himself up from the little grass mat on which they slept. "Yes," he said, wondering if Ephan had taught her how to hear towers. "I hear it. But it is not abandoned. And the sounds of it—its inhabitants are too few." He indicated the little gourd bowls and cups they had created, the drying meats hung about its walls. "Have we not made this little place a home for these many days? Why leave it? Let us wait until we find a towerless longhouse with kind people who will take us into their hearts. Then we will leave this place. But this…no, my wife! Let us avoid towers. The Voca and outlaw longhouses will find us. And Nahas as well."

She began packing two baskets. "Have you forgotten that Ephan will be punished if we do not return? Or that you must become Wheel Clan chief and save the towers?"

"You wish to return to Nahas?"

"I have not told you all my thoughts because you liked the freedom of this life, but I have been thinking. I will not find my mother if I do live in a longhouse without a tower. And you continually say that even if we find a tower, we will have to find crystals for it and teach it to keen for my mother's tower. 'Many days,' you said. So let us ask these strangers to return us to our prison. Look now, the time of our punishment is almost over. What will Nahas do if he lifts the anchor of our prison and finds us absent?" She picked up the basket. "Whether you come with me, or whether you stay here, I am off to this tower."

So they bade goodbye to their hut and he followed her, all the while pleading that she change her course and return to their unimportant little home. At last they came to the abandoned longhouse. Inside, they found its floor bloodied and its grain rooms destroyed.

"Didn't you say this tower was not abandoned?" Maharai asked.

"It was not. When we heard it. It is the Voca's work."

"Bloody or not, I will remain here," Maharai said. "And you will use it to keen for my mother or to return us to the prison longhouse. Either way, you must find my mother."

So they made the new longhouse their home.

Psal set to repairing the main keening tree, replacing its broken keening branches with branches from the listening and the speaking branches. It worked well but not perfectly; he could not hear the songs of other towers, nor could he send messages to them, nor could he properly keen because most of its crystals were missing. But the longhouse was warm and he and Maharai were no longer victims of the night.

They continued in that longhouse until one day, as Psal skinned some rodents in a dry grassy terrain, a Voca longhouse materialized before them.

The chief was a tall woman with tan skin and dark green eyes. She strode toward the fire-pit he had made. Beside her marched sixteen or more older women and some forty young girls.

"Young man," she said in the Wheel Clan language. "Put that rodent in a pot or on the fire, please. I do not like to see dead animals. It is evil to eat animals, oppressed as they are by humans. Fruits, grains, tubers, and vegetables suffice for me."

Psal's fingers tightened on the rodent.

"I'm Chief Alora of the Voca Clan,"

He bowed silently, watched as she warmed her hands at the fire-pit and looked behind him at the longhouse.

"It is long since I've seen one from the Wheel Clan alone." She studied his face. "And you're marked? Why? Did you displease your chief?"

She laughed. "You wear the clothes of a studier? Are you a studier? Or are those clothes borrowed or stolen?"

He lifted his pant leg to show his shriveled leg.

"Ah," She sighed. "A shame. I don't like men with flaws. It is a bad habit, I suppose, liking flawless men, flawless, pretty boys. But it is an ingrained one. But that mark of yours…is that why you are alone, Wheel Clan studier?" She sat on an old tree stump. "Has your king punished you, or have you been sent out for some evil purpose?"

"I'm not alone. If you have tracked my tower, you already know the path my tower has taken and who is inside."

Chief Alora leaned backward, looked at the sky. "Yes, your tower sings of a female presence." She raised her right hand and gestured to two young girls. "Denna, Elloni, search this longhouse."

Psal dropped the carcass and raced to block the entrance to the long-house.

"I'm Prince Psal," Psal said, "Son of King Nahas. You have no right—"

"Ah, Prince Psal! The Wheel Clan's Studier-Firstborn?" She smiled. "So it was you they anchored in the dark climes?"

"How did you know that?"

"We Voca know everything. You're the companion of the pretty one they call 'the king's favorite?' I would very much like to see him. I've heard he is quite lovely to look upon. Pretty and pale, a gentle boy, unlike the harsh men of your clan."

"He is not inside," Psal said.

"I know that." She turned to the tower and chided it, wagging her finger. "Not a very truthful tower, are you? You tried to hide the female presence? Was that an honorable thing to do?"

"It lacks crystals. It is often very confused." Psal eyed the young girls who lingered near the door. "The girlie inside is my wife. The king's favorite is part of my eimi, but he is lost and we are traveling night-tossed in this world, seeking him."

Anxiety, in her voice, on her face. "Why should Ephan be lost?" The Voca Chief asked. "You, hiding in the longhouse, Prince Psal's wife! Come out!"

"He made himself outcast to search for a lost warrior."

Maharai appeared, trembling. The Voca chief approached her and, gently, her right thumb traced the path of Maharai's lips and nose. "I had heard Ephan married a girl from an unallied Peacock Clan. And what is your name?" Her hands slid slowly down the front of Maharai's tunic, then rested on Maharai's right breast. "I like you as well."

"She's my wife," Psal said, pulling Maharai away. "You cannot have her."

The Voca chief shrugged, circled them. "Prince Psal, I am a woman who thinks too clearly and too much. True,"—she looked at Maharai—"I am a woman of passion as well. But my passions and my heart are ruled by thought and reason. Therefore, when I see or hear something that I do not understand, I will not rest until I understand it." She picked up the rodent and handed them to one of the smaller girls. "These little ones are as much children of the Creator as we are. See that they are honored with a good burial." She sat again on the old tree stump. "Now, tell me again why you are here. Nahas is clever! He's hoarded half of Odunao for himself and his clan. So I find myself wondering, because—as I say—I am a woman of thought and reason, 'Why have the only studiers in Nahas' longhouse been punished or sent away?' And remember, my tower is more faithful to me than it is to your tower. And much wiser, as well."

"You Voca know all things, Great Chief," Psal answered. "You must know that another studier tuned our tower while we were on our marriage journey. Father discovered our treachery."

The chief's dark green eyes twinkled. "Ah, yes, the Peacock Clan women you returned to Tsbosso's home region. I knew Nahas was not so merciful. So you and Ephan saved the women? But why is the King's Favorite lost?"

"Father was angry with his studiers and with those who helped his studiers," Maharai said. "He sent our friend out into the night. Ephan left to save him. When Nahas discovered Ephan was gone, he punished us."

"Ah, she speaks your language well!" A patient smile flickered on the chief's face. "She also explains things well. But women are good at explaining things." The Voca Chief clasped her hands and pressed her thumbs together. "So you sent yourself adrift into the night? Children, children! How stupid you are! And a studier too! The dark climes break spirits but it does not destroy bodies. You've thrown yourself into a cauldron of danger by trusting your life to the night. You do understand that I must return you to the royal longhouse, don't you?"

"Why? Our treaty says nothing of returning lost children."

"You are a humorous one, Prince Psal. But yes, you are children. Children should not be out in the world by themselves. Of course, Nahas may return you to the cold dark climes to finish your chastisement, but even that is not as hard a life as the one you've chosen for yourselves."

"No, Great Chief," Psal pleaded. "If you must return us to our people, return us again to the longhouse in the dark cold climes. Not to the king."

"That I cannot do, Prince Psal. I am no fool. I know you children, you male children. If I send you to the dark climes, you will cast yourselves onto the night again."

Psal thrust out his chin. "I am not returning there! The king…his warriors will mock me. You will bring us back as if we are lost stray sheep. Let us return to the dark climes. And let the king keen us home."

"Send me to my mother's longhouse then!" Maharai asked.

"Return home, Psal!" Then she spoke to Maharai, but eyed Psal. "Maharai, your mother is well. But I cannot send you to her longhouse. Firstborn, stop pouting. Do not challenge me. The king is not stupid. He knows you fled that prison. The little heart he has worries for you. I will therefore keen your longhouse to your father, and only to your father can you go. Farewell, then. Who knows when we will meet each other again?"

Chief Alora did exactly as she promised, tuning their tower by her tower's keen. All Psal's attempts to over-ride the keen were fruitless.

Inside the tower, Maharai said to Psal, "Perhaps it is best. I do not like to see you suffer. And you made me fear I would never see my mother again."

"I shall be mocked and humiliated," Psal said.

"Perhaps humiliation is better than being tossed about by the night."

Psal didn't think so. "You don't mind me being humiliated because it will bring you closer to your mother."

"I would not think of it that way," she said. "Humiliation one can bear. But…I do not want…" She paused. "It's a strange thing. Once again I have met the Voca, and although you declare them to be evil, I always find them pleasant enough."

"You would not find them half so pleasant if they were not your allies," Psal told her.

They were returned to Nahas by a daytime keen. Although all saw their arrival, only Daris, Indina, the Iden women, and the comfort women welcomed them. Ephan had not returned.

CHAPTER 38

A LOSS

Four days after they arrived, sometime at the end of the tenth month, Ephan was also returned to the royal longhouse by a Voca Chief. Psal, who was on the rampart, called down to him.

"Is Lan not with you?"

"He is in our Permanent Home," Ephan answered. "We will go to him but he will not come to us. And how is our wife? I thought of her many nights."

"She has longed for you too as well," Psal shouted back, then hurried to tell Maharai of Ephan's return.

How happy Psal was to have his eimi together again, but as they stood in the gathering room, surrounded by the warriors, Ephan whispered in Psal's ear. "I have returned only because of my eimi. And for that little one. My heart longs to leave this longhouse. But I will not leave it unless you two and Daris are at my side." Ephan approached the king. "I found Lan that same night I left. Blood flowed from a wound at his side. I will not surmise why he was wounded. I set up the cloaken immediately, because second night was fast coming. The next morning, many mornings, we found ourselves in strange regions. I found healing pharma but the wound was too deep." He glared at Cyrt. "Too deep. Always we listened for towers. Those towers we heard were too far away for me to carry him. Others were towers belonging to our enemies or to fierce outcasts. After many days, a Waymaker family in a towerless house found us."

"The Waymaker Clans have many healing herbs," Daris said. "Could they not heal him?"

"I have said the wound was deep." Ephan closed his eyes, choked back a sob. "Forgive me, Little One, I should allow my anger to fall on those who deserve it, not you. Then one day we happened upon a Voca longhouse."

"The Voca like you," Psal rubbed his friend's shoulder.

"They do, yes," Ephan looked at Nahas.

"And did you use your body as payment to the old girl?" Gaal asked.

"That I will not tell," Ephan answered. "Yet I will always remember their kindness to Lan as he died. After he died, they burned him in our pyres and called a failing tower and sent me here."

After Ephan finished speaking, Nahas and Netophah called Psal's eimi to the king's chamber.

"Did I not tell you to stay inside and not to go searching for Lan?" the king asked. "Why did you disobey me?"

"Because I feared for Lan and distrusted you," Ephan answered.

"This is not the first time this eimi has followed its own mind," Netophah said. "Such a thing cannot go unpunished."

Ephan laughed. "Have you been nursing this anger in your heart all this time?" he asked Netophah. "And you, Nahas, I heard you sent Storm and Maharai to the dark climes. Was that not enough? I assure you, seeing my friend's death was punishment enough. I will no longer challenge you, yet I understand quite clearly now why the Voca Queen hates you."

"I had hoped this eimi would become one of us." Nahas placed Maharai's hand into Netophah's. "But I see now that it is a vain hope. It is best that you three be parted. She is *your* wife now, Netophah. Not Psal's. Not Ephan's. Yours."

"What?" Psal and Ephan both asked at the same time.

Ephan's face reflected Psal's: surprise, hurt confusion.

Psal flung himself at his father, struck hard. But Ephan remained silent, watching Maharai.

"You cannot take my husbands from me!" Maharai pulled her hand from Netophah's.

"That is exactly what I have done," the king answered, and once again Netophah grasped her hand.

* * * *

Dragged inside Netophah's room, Maharai struggled with him. In the hallway, Psal called for her, his voice pleading. Ephan stood like one frozen in place. "Ephan," she called out, but Netophah held her tightly. She bit his hand and he let her go.

Psal's voice: angry and hurt, weepy, berated. The king's: distant. Both argued as they walked toward the hearth. Maharai raced toward them as Psal struck at Nahas, stumbling over the fermenting blood flour and clay pots filled with grain. Netophah caught Maharai's arm. She bit him again, hard. He loosened his hold. Meanwhile the Firstborn and the king fought. Several times they struggled on the floor, almost falling into the fire-pit. Psal reached for his dagger and Nahas knocked it from his hand. Psal's right hand groped for it until Cyrt kicked it away and Lebo lifted Psal from the floor.

Nahas stood and delivered a blow to the boy's face and stomach that left Psal tottering and clutching his weak hip.

"You are evil and worthless! Inhuman!" Psal yelled. Nahas struck him again. Clutching his side, Psal staggered to the door and fumbled with the latch.

Ephan and Lebo pulled him away.

"Casting yourself into the night will not benefit you! It will kill you!" Ephan said.

Psal ignored him until Maharai called out in the Wheel Clan language. "Psallo, you're my husband. Don't leave me!"

Her former husbands turned to look at her. Silent, they left the entrance door and ran past the warriors into the Chief Studier's room.

CHAPTER 39

MARRIAGE AND GRIEF

None spoke with Maharai for the first three days of her betrothal to Netophah. On the fourth day, Rain walked into her room and offered her a clay cup holding a reddish, viscous liquid. "What is it?" Maharai asked.

"A drink we give our young women. You're going to be Netophah's wife now. Our Nahas thought you should have it."

"It wasn't given to me when Psal and Ephan and I married."

"That is quite true, but Cyrt was a warrior, with no taint in him. Now you must sleep."

Maharai did not understand the old woman's words. But she took the drink. It was sweet like the rose jam the women often made. She was sleepy, suddenly so. She lay on her mat and slept soundly, dreaming of a tiny fish being battered by a red sea. When she woke there was a cramping in her side. It traveled up her torso and around her stomach then down her legs. Her whole body shivered and her stomach heaved. She sat up in her bed and felt an urge to push. Hastening, she grasped a chamber pot. Out came blood and water. For ten days she lay in bed, and only when she heard the Wheel Clan women speaking about the possibility that she would die "as well as the unborn child" did she realize what they had done to her.

The celebration of Netophah's marriage to Maharai is recorded in Psal's annals:

> The future king and his wife stood atop the rampart
> Golden they seemed, like the golden sun on a golden path.
> Behind them the standards of the Wheel Clan flew
> Below them, their subjects—sang and cheered.
>
> Once I had smiled to see her dressed as a chief's wife.
> But as she stood high above our gathered clans
> I thought: he has made her a queen.
>
> All power was his.
> To win her heart, perhaps, and cover her with the clan's glory.
> He was our Prince, the heir of all things yet so enslaved
> By love for the girl my father had given him.
> That morning, I saw tears falling from my brother's eyes.
> Tears of joy and amazement.

A future king admiring a future queen.
I saw his fearful joy and wept.

It was at that time that Psal and Ephan became enslaved to Tomah.

* * * *

My Prince, we have arrived at this place before. Again, I must tell you that Ephan and Psal were so grieved and enslaved to Tomah they rarely wrote in their annals—and what they wrote was deeply muddled. How, then, am I to describe the days after Maharai was taken from them? Earlier, when I spoke of Ephan's exploits, I used Seagen's annals. Now, I will use two other that were written at that time.

My prince, listen to them for they speak of the power of Tomah and of all such substances. As it is written in our proverbs: *Do not give your strength to such herbs. It is not for kings to take such herbs. It is not for princes to crave them. Give Tomah to those who are perishing and in anguish. Let them take it and forget their sorrows.*

The first is written in Mion's annals:

> The Eleventh month, the sixth day. Mion, studier to Chief Hokkan writes:
>
> What my eyes have seen! What my eyes now see!
>
> I arrived, along with the Hokkan Chief, at the Deep Tundra home region. Three other longhouses joined us. We were to bury the dead. It had been months since I saw the Firstborn and the Favorite, and because my heart is wholly woven with theirs and—of late—they have grown reticent, sending no whimsical message, gossip, or witticism through their tower, I thought fit to cross the meadow and visit them.
>
> My heart grieves even now as I recall the sights seen, the words heard, in the royal keening room.
>
> You who will read these annals in times to come: the great lights of our clan have dimmed. The hope of our damaged ones and the desire of all clans have destroyed themselves.
>
> When I entered the keening room, a gourd lay near their feet collecting their spittle and the chewed Tomah bark. Their clothes were covered with slime and mucus. None of which they regarded. The king entered and scornfully remarked that they smelled like old studiers and that they should refrain from destroying themselves with Tomah. They cared little for his counsel, his anger, the mockery of their clan, their humiliation or—it seems—their very lives.
>
> I am told by Seagen that they chew it to wake up, and to fall asleep, to endure the day and to put the day away, that—whether apart of together—they use the herb to quell their hurt and loss.
>
> I spoke to the Firstborn and to the Favorite, both of whom regarded me hazily through blood-shot eyes.

"Seagen speaks of a loss?" I asked them. "What loss is so great that you would destroy yourselves?"

"The king has taken our wife," the Firstborn told me. "I think continually of my eimi, and how we were taken from each other."

The Favorite, stumbling toward the sick room, stated merely, "Any other child they would have kept. But ours they did not allow to be born. And Nahas...that he should have lied to me. I am unable to push these sorrows from my mind. Even with Tomah."

I grasped the Favorite by the arm, and stood before him in the doorway. "King's Favorite," I pleaded, "the Damaged Ones depend on you and the Firstborn. King's Favorite, you have always been one who stood afar off, one who did not allow the troubles of this world to touch your heart—how can—"

"My heart was always touched, Mion," the Favorite said and pushed me out of the way. "Even when it seemed not to be. Because it had something it rested on. I could endure because...but now..." Then he staggered into the corridor.

"Farewell," I said, "Who knows when we will meet each other again?"

I had hoped this was the prophesied Firstborn-Studier who would save our world. I had hoped they were the two outcast-saviors. But now...all such hope must die. I fled the royal longhouse in great distress, grief-stricken. Later that day, I saw them again among the pyres. They were gazing steadfastly at the burning corpse of a child dressed in studier's black. When I approached, I saw that the child was Lyrenna's son, Daris.

"How..." I asked. Words almost failed me. I had always loved that wise little child.

"Tomah poisoning," The Firstborn answered. "He died yesterday."

"Tomah poisoning?" I asked. "You allowed—"

"The child imitated us," he said.

"We will join him soon enough," the Favorite said. Then he added, to the Firstborn. "You, perhaps, earlier than me. A boon that. I am tired of this world." Then he shouted to the sky, "Is this my life? Have I not been the Creator's friend? But this is the life you have made me to live?"

I hastened away from them, my heart broken, my hopes dashed.

And this, from the king's annals:

Ephan remains sullen, coming to my room only when called. Our old friendship is lost. If he speaks to me, he speaks only of his grief, about how I commanded the child of his eimi to be killed. It is as if he can think of nothing else.

Tomah has made Psal's illness worse. I have heard it termed "the selfish pharma" and now I understand. It allows no other drug in its presence. In his desire for Tomah, the Firstborn ignores Emon and all herbs that might ease his pain or extend his life. Perhaps I should not have taken their wife away, but even now it seems a small thing to them that they aided our enemies. No doubt their treachery will engender future strife. Already it is rumored through the towers: "The Firstborn of our clan betrayed his people." Who knows but others in our clan may attempt to take Netophah's crown? All my father's hope for a dynasty lost.

As for Netophah—wise though he is, he has fallen in love with his wife. It is exactly what I feared. I warned him the girl was subtle. A subtle queen is always a good thing—if one does not allow one's self to be deceived by her. But he dotes on her. I have sired three foolish sons.

CHAPTER 40

DISHONORED FORTRESSES

Maharai began building her blanket fortresses again, except now she built them as a wall between herself and Netophah. He watched as she built her towers and did not force her to lie with him, but he insisted she would not be returned to her husbands. So they lay together with blankets between them. She felt like a warrior with no friend or armor at her back, because during her marriage Ephan and Psal had protected her on all sides. She would look through the window at the dawning day and wish for the freedom of her marital longhouse or for her night-tossed days.

My Prince, for centuries, Netophah has been a favorite with storytellers. That is understandable, for Netophah, who was well-made, honorable, and nature-blessed should have had better luck with women. His mother was murdered by her co-queen. His second marriage of which so many sad songs have been sung—was a sacrifice for the higher good. And of course his marriage to Maharai—All declare that the beautiful, honored princes of the world are not always blessed with love. He had killed Maharai's brother. Trouble enough, but his father then removed her from her husbands. A worse fault, because the studiers were all Maharai's mind and heart could rest upon. Is it not comprehensible then that on the day he kicked aside her fortress of blankets and she saw her tower tumbling down, that this small thing pushed her grief past all hopefulness and caused his suffering? The hurt she felt when he violated her fortresses was not a thing Netophah could understand, but Maharai wrote this song at that time (or so the historians have stated):

> Sweet Ones, you are ever near
> but my heart must not look on you.
> When I lift my head
> and see your shadow in the sick rooms
> or hear your halting footsteps among the tower branches
> I must turn my heart and eyes and ears away.
> Desiring to shut away all others,
> I must steel my heart to live
> with those who seek to invade it.

I doubt Maharai had the skill at such a tender age to write about her heart in such classical Wheel Clan language, but that is the record, and the poem itself is old. We must, therefore, commit ourselves to believe it, because this poem explains what was to come next.

* * * *

Psal was in his bed when he heard the curtained screen in his doorway being pushed aside. Maharai. She touched him, her hands soft and smooth as a flower petal. He pulled her down to his blanket, wanting to make love with her. The intense sexual need surprised him. Their relationship had not been a passionate one, unlike that between her and Ephan.

He squeezed her shoulder tightly, struggled to rise from the bed. But Maharai was now his brother's wife—worse, the wife of a chief—so he reluctantly lay down. "My wife, my lost wife, you must go."

But she whispered to him, "Come with me."

"I cannot betray Netophah," he answered. "I want you as well, but where could we go in this prison and not be found out?"

"Husband," she said again, "Come and see."

"Return to my brother's bed, Maharai. If he wakes to find you missing—"

She took his right hand, tugged it gently, "Come!"

So Psal rose from his bed and followed her. He was surprised when she led him into Netophah's room. In the dark, Ephan stood in the corner beside Gidea, who held a lamp high. All that could be heard in the stillness was Netophah's sleepy, gasping breaths.

"Ephan? Gidea? What is this?"

Ephan said nothing. Gidea's face betrayed no emotion. Maharai stood before the window, gazing out at the moons. Psal's hands went clammy and he wiped them on the front of his tunic, then slowly crossed the room.

Kneeling, he held his hand before his brother's lips, then bent and sniffed Netophah's lips, then his palms. All the blood vessels of Netophah's body seemed to have burst all at once and his pale skin was now red with pin-pricks of blood. Netophah trembled and sweated as he slept. Psal's heart sank, and he struggled to breathe. The sickly-sweet odor of Rifik permeated the woolen blanket and all the bedding. But Netophah was no sickly horse being put to death; he was Psal's brother and the Wheel Clan heir. Psal looked at the others one by one.

"His life is in him? Rifik was all you gave him?"

"And Rangi." The smell of Tomah was so heavy around Ephan that even the similarly-enslaved Psal could detect it. "He will not die."

Maharai glared at Ephan. "You promised you would kill him. You promised me. You promised Gidea."

"Isn't it enough that he has become one of the damaged?" Ephan said.

"No," Gidea said. "It is not enough. You promised me he would die."

Ephan looked at Psal. "I could not kill the king's son."

Surely this was a dream. Psal looked at Netophah. No. "Curious," he said at last. "Not that I want my brother treacherously and cowardly murdered in his sleep, but it seems that if you were going to break your studier's vow and harm Netophah that you would have killed our Crown Prince outright and be done with it."

Ephan's answer was, "I could not harm you by killing your brother."

It was a subtle answer and not entirely true. Earlier, when I related Ephan's story, you saw his heart. You understood his anger that Nahas had kept his secret from him. Ria and Tanti had also been his sisters. And the two little ones...were they not also his very own brothers? How he would have rejoiced to know that he had true brothers, of his own flesh and blood, in that wretched longhouse! Yes, he had loved them, but he had loved them as the king's children. And they had loved him as well, but as a foundling adopted brother. And when they died, he had not known to grieve for them as his siblings. For this he could not forgive Nahas. But, herein lies the reason he could not kill Netophah: his little siblings in the Permanent Place would hear that he had killed their brother. They would hate him for it. This he did not wish. All this he did not tell Psal. Therefore Psal's anger against him grew steadily. Yet even then Psal could not rage against Ephan.

"Why choose a pharma like Rifik?" Psal asked. "It is not a weapon that hides itself. Won't Father's suspicion turn to us?"

"Let it turn to us," Ephan said. "I want it to turn to me. What can he do to us?"

"Perhaps my heart is not as bold as yours. Or perhaps you three are the sane ones. But I remember other kings who have killed their favorites. I do not feel so safe as you. Bring Molen bark."

Ephan didn't move.

"Molen will make his recovery easier."

Again, Ephan didn't move.

"Get it!" Psal ordered. "Now! Is it not enough that his body and face will be destroyed? Why should he awake in pain and wrackings? Get the Molen."

So Ephan left.

Psal spoke to Maharai. "After I leave, you must remain here and sleep beside him until morning." He glanced at Gidea. He could not bring himself to hate his eimi. But Gidea, yes, he could hate her. For she was the oldest of the three conspirators and he was sure it was she who had influenced them. "And Gidea must return to her room. The morning must not find us here. It will be hard for you to lie beside him but—"

"It will not be hard." The coldness of Maharai's voice felt familiar. She reminded him of his mother Hinis. "While he was healthy, he was dead to me. Why should his illness be any different?"

Psal closed his eyes then opened them again. "Because it is a hard thing to be relentlessly angry. It is difficult to see anyone suffer, even one's enemy."

After Psal had rubbed the numbing Molen pharma on Netophah's body, the conspirators returned to their rooms and Psal to his bed.

His friends seemed strange to him. Or perhaps only life seemed strange. The boy hardly knew what to make of the situation. He had always thought the anger of the weak harmless. He knew now he was wrong: Yet, it was not he—a raging studier who had no ability to hide his tears—who had poisoned Netophah. It was the quiet, steady, easygoing Ephan. It was the simple Maharai.

You, my boy, and I are wise. Moreover, we have had the benefit of hearing Psal's story told in our histories and by wondrous storytellers. We understand the questions raging in his heart as he lay looking at the ceiling. But at that moment, his heart struggled to understand, his mind could frame neither words nor thought.

"We are so young," he said to the Creator he did not believe in. "And our emotions overwhelm us." He rebuked and raged at the Creator for giving the young such terrifying anger, and such powerful loves.

He lay on his stomach crying softly. *May the morning never come. I hope in vain; the conspiracy cannot be undone.* He looked up through his tears to see the daymoon rising, and with its rising, Maharai's scream echoed through the longhouse.

"Help, help! Oh, help! Something has happened to Netophah."

Psal closed his eyes. *Maharai screams as if her heart would break. She has a remarkable ability to pretend. Now I will have to pretend as well. I can manage, for I learned the art of pretense after Cyrt attacked me.*

Footsteps raced past his room. His father's. There was a terrified tentativeness to them, as in the day Nahas entered the longhouse on the day of the Peacock Clan treachery. Psal rose from his bed just as Ephan's shouts rang out.

When Psal entered Netophah's room, Indina knelt by Netophah's side, and Kwin stood looking on, holding his wife's hand. The room reeked of urine and excrement; mucus and sweat flowed from Netophah's face. The white wool blanket on which he lay was now red with blood, yellow with urine. Maharai sat by his side, weeping. She had lain all night beside one she had tried to murder. Ephan wept also. Were they now no longer pretending? Perhaps now they truly grieved.

Then Maharai threw herself into Psal's arm. "Psallo, when I woke this morning, he was hot and wet at my side, sick of a fever. I turned to look and…" Her words trailed away into sobs.

* * * *

Netophah slowly recovered, his body growing more scarred and twisted. Maharai continued weeping, and Ephan retreated into silence. Psal felt himself alone. A poem, in the annals, authentic but whose authorship is unclear—Ephan's or Psal's, who knows?—goes as follows:

> *Another's sin taints me.*
> *And yet,*
> *And yet,*
> *In old age, I will return to my childhood pleasures.*
> *I will allow myself to meditate on your face again.*
> *I will dream of your nature-blessed strength and beauty*
> *And look forward to it in Our Permanent Home.*
> *For this girl, brother wounded brother.*
> *If she is returned to me,*
> *Should I regret the sin and yet enjoy the prize?*

As you know, the last line is a famous saying, spoken still among the inhabitants of Odunao. This is the origin of it.

Psal covered his face with his hands: *Even if my own hand did not touch the poison, I have not told the king what I know. Therefore I am as guilty as my eimi and as the fierce and bitter Gidea. Who will wash away this confusion and this sin?*

He returned to his rounds. Once again, the pharma rooms, the studiers' rooms, sick rooms, keening room, and the rampart were his only havens, but now Netophah lay ill and all in the longhouse suspected Psal.

On the eight or ninth night after Netophah's poisoning, the king spoke to Psal. "Can you and Ephan not heal him? With all your pharma, all your studies, is there no balm you may use to restore his face, bones, sinew, all?"

"We continually search for the answer, Father," Psal answered. "But—"

The king punched the wall hard. "That such an accident should happen to your brother!"

"It is sad, Father. Perhaps tainted water when he fed a wounded horse. It has happened before, I think. A studier accidentally poisoned with a surgical knife when he tended a sick animal."

Of course, such a thing had never happened. But the king nodded. He was pretending. The pretense had to be maintained.

CHAPTER 41

THE VOCA QUEEN'S SON

The day came when Netophah sat up in his bed. He rose with an old man's gait and an old man's blotched, scarred face. He looked like a debauched, old king of a Waymaker Clan. Nahas, who had stayed at his bed day and night, walked with him into the gathering room where all greeted Netophah's recovery with songs of joy.

Psal looked at his father. *The king has kept his patience until the recovery, for he needed our help. Now punishments will be meted out.*

Two days later, Nahas called Psal to his chambers.

"It is understandable that you would want to kill your brother," Nahas said. "But to actually contrive to accomplish the deed?"

"I…" Psal stammered, sweating. "I…"

"The effects of that poison are memorable," Nahas said. "Many here still remember how Netophah's mother Ruanna suffered at Hinis' treacherous hand." He turned scornful, disdainful eyes on Psal. "That the son should choose the same poison as the mother…it offends me. But, as they say, like mother, like son."

"Father," Psal said, "I did not poison my brother."

"If you could poison your brother, who can you not kill?" Nahas said.

"I told you. I did not poison him."

Nahas walked toward the window. "Perhaps it is true that it is not your body alone that is perverse. Your mind is also perverse. As your mother's was."

"I have never lied to you, Nahas," Psal retorted.

The king laughed. "Of course you have, Firstborn."

"I do not lie now. If I said I did not harm Netophah, you should believe me. And if Hinis' mind was so perverse, why did you mourn for her when Tsbosso killed her?"

His father looked at him like one studying a venomous insect crawling near one's boot. "The warriors would have understood if you had killed Maharai, a stranger to your clan, to keep her from your brother. Yes, they would have understood that. But your harmed your brother! How foolish my heart has been to love one like you! Now, that love is finished. Who could love one like you?"

Psal flung himself to the floor. "Father, no! Please, you must love me. Although you did not love my mother, please love me. Continue to love me, Father! Even a little. I did not—"

"Why should I love you? I cannot forgive your cruelty or re-make that foul mind of yours."

Psal clung to his father's tunic, but Nahas turned away.

"I understand how murderous thoughts can come to the heart of the young," the king continued. "After Hinis killed Ruanna, I lay in bed many nights scheming to murder her, not caring for the alliance between her clan and mine. She had killed my remaining brothers and my beloved wife, all to make me the sole king. She was hated by all. I told myself that if I killed her no one would challenge me. Yet I did not do it." His eyes held Psal's. "I could not kill one so close to me, one I had grown to love because she was the mother of my children. But you...how could you kill? What kind of viper have I brought to birth?"

"I am no viper, Father," Psal said, weeping. "Please continue to love me."

"Yes, you are indeed a viper, Psal," Nahas said. "And a stupid one, too. Did you not know the effects of this poison would be plain for all to see? Not only have I created a monster who poisons his brother, but I've created a fool."

At that moment, Cyrt, Gaal, Seagen, Lebo, and Ephan burst into the king's chamber.

"Forgive us, my king, for entering your room uninvited," Cyrt said. "We feared you would do the Firstborn great harm, and such harm in a time of war, with failing towers, is not a thing to be lightly done. The tower will not—"

The king spoke only to Ephan, "Cloud, you're not needed. Attend to your wounded." Ephan made no move to leave. "Ephan"—the king indicated the door—"Go. You are not needed here."

"I was the one who poisoned Netophah," Ephan said. "Therefore I *am* needed here."

All looked at Ephan in stunned silence. The king's face fell, and for a moment it seemed to Psal that his father was trying to rebuild a shattered world. "What? What did you say, Ephan?"

"I said it was I who poisoned Netophah. Therefore I am needed here. Storm knew nothing of it."

"Why have you done this?" The king moved toward Ephan.

"Gidea must've forced him," Lebo said. "A youth's mind in the hand of such a woman! He's been visiting her. No doubt she has poisoned his mind. Such things are bound to happen!"

"I have my own mind!" Ephan shouted. "Nahas, I know it surprises you that your 'favorite' and not Psal did it, but believe me. It was I."

Psal raced to stand between Ephan and the king. King's favorite or not, Ephan seemed utterly, stupidly, fearless of the danger that awaited him. Tomah must have affected Ephan's common sense.

"Ephan, is this true?" Seagen asked. "You threw away your integrity for that woman?"

Lebo called to an unseen warrior in the passageway. "Bring the woman Gidea here. She's responsible for this. She should be made outcast or killed for what she's done."

"Why should she be brought here?" Cyrt challenged Lebo.

"Do you excuse her treachery?" Seagen asked.

"There is no evidence that she is behind this," Cyrt said. "He visits her, yes. But what is that? She's a comfort woman. Why should he not visit her since the king has taken his wife away? But she has no power over him."

"True," Lebo said. "A Wheel Clan studier would not seek to destroy the heir of his clan for such a woman. And yet Lan was influenced by her daughter. I admit the world has gone senseless. I no longer understand what the great ones of our longhouse do."

"Nahas is the true culprit." Ephan said, coolly. "Separating hearts in the same way he separates regions. Separating families and friends. It is all the same to this heartless one who ordered Cyrt to murder Lan, and who took Maharai from me."

"Beware your pride, Ephan," Cyrt warned. "The world and the clan is the king's to turn as he wills."

"I am no lathe or inanimate thing to be turned as a king wills," Ephan said. "Who is he that we should obey him? The grandson of one who usurped our clan's rule? The king of a corrupt and cruel clan?"

"Enough, Ephan." The king's voice was coldly calm. "You've learned Psal's petulance, Ephan. And you've mastered it. Since the day of your betrothal, you allowed hatred to grow against me. And like Psal, you've nursed a studier's petty anger in your heart."

"Storm taught me none of this," Ephan said. "This anger is all my own. I am no king who has taught himself to have no heart—"

Nahas cut Ephan's words short by thrusting him hard against a nearby wall. "A true student of the master of the Wintersea," Nahas spat in Ephan's face.

Immediately Ephan spat back. He steadied himself. "A true son of my mother, rather."

The king wiped Ephan's spittle from his cheek.

Gaal's voice: "You've told him about his mother?"

Seagen's: "A stupid action, Nahas…if you did."

"Indeed, he is very like his mother," Cyrt added.

Psal looked from one to another, then at Ephan. Narena hated damaged children. Was that the mother Ephan was speaking of? Or did *true son of my mother* mean something else?

"Are you considering killing me, Nahas?" Ephan asked. "Or thinking of sending me into the night? Do what you will. You are nothing to me. Many nights we spoke together and I loved you as my own dear, adopted father. You saw my heart, saw how I longed for a mother, for father, for sister, for brother. Yet you never told me. Why didn't you tell me? I would have kept my own secret. But you hid the truth from me until you were forced to speak it. So send me away now. Why should I stay here and serve so fierce and lying and uncompassionate a king?"

"Keep silent, Ephan." Cyrt took Ephan's arm. "Do not ask the king for what he is even now well-disposed to grant."

With the exception of Lan, Nahas rarely made a warrior outcast, let alone a studier. But there were worst punishments: maimings, amputations.

"Ephan, be silent," Psal warned.

But Ephan said, "Nahas will not dare punish the son of the Voca Queen." He spat at Nahas again. "Would you, Nahas?"

Psal swallowed hard; *Did Ephan say Queen Ezbel was his mother?*

The king did not move. Outside his chamber, several women, Orian, and Satima stood in shocked silence.

Lebo hastened between Nahas and Ephan. "I've seen the death of two of your sons, Nahas. The death of your daughters. I will not see another of your children die."

"Even this ill-begotten one?" Nahas turned and struck Ephan again.

Psal stared. *My brother?*

Ephan rose. "How weak you are, Nahas! And how pitiful! To have sired two damaged ones!"

Nahas shook the pain out of his hand. "Too late I realized the traditions were right. A king should never allow his own damaged child to live. Such children breed bitterness and foment treachery, turning studiers and stewards against him. But I have sired two such traitors. And I am rewarded for my stupidity by one who destroys his brother and by another who protects the destroyer."

"Go quickly," Lebo pushed both Ephan and Psal out the door. "Go now, young ones. The king will forgive you in time. But for now, avoid him, lest he murder you in his anger."

They left the room immediately. In the gathering room, many who had not known the secret of Ephan's birth reacted with silence. Others argued against the king for deceiving them about Ephan's birth, or raged against Ephan for harming Netophah. Some women from the Waymaker Clans who had lost family to the Voca Queen hurled insults against Ephan for his mother's evil. Psal and Ephan could only retreat to the rampart.

"So…" Psal said when they stood in the watchtower, "you're my brother?"

"I am."

Psal nodded slowly, looked at the daymoon crossing the sun. "I understand now," he studied his friend's face. "But that you should—"

"Because he took our wife from us."

Psal's voice was empty, his soul tired. "Netophah had the gift, but it was Nahas who stole her from us. And what did Maharai's loss matter to you? You had a new woman at your side. Gidea had begun to like you. And you…"

"I love Maharai." Ephan walked outside the watchtower and leaned against the rampart. "You taught me to open my heart to her, and when I did, this king took her away from me. Worse, he killed our friends."

"I am sorry I made you open your heart," Psal said. "And yet, Nahas' death I could understand. People are always rising up against their chiefs. But Netophah, although he had our wife…he was—"

"He is a liar," Ephan walked toward the stairwell. "He knew the truth, as well. My truth. Nahas told me that on the day the war began he told Netophah all."

Psal limped slowly behind his brother. "Perhaps Netophah wished to tell you. Perhaps he awaited the appropriate time. After all, you didn't tell me when you found out this secret. Should I consider you a liar because you waited to tell me?"

Ephan turned. "I tried to tell you. That morning in our longhouse when I knelt before your dagger."

"Ah," Psal said, remembering. "Why didn't you? I would not have loved you any more or less because of it."

Ephan shook his head. "Do you not understand, Storm?"

"Understand what?"

Ephan was quiet for a moment. "I am older than you are, Brother. By a few months, yes. But older nevertheless."

Psal gasped. *Ephan is the true Firstborn of the Wheel Clan. I am only a second son, a damaged second son. Ephan—like Netophah—is surely a son of Nahas, whereas I am the son of a shared but hated wife.*

"I see. I understand. Yet Father and his captains kept my secret. You would have as well. You're not one to grasp for power."

"True, but you would not have kept your own secret. You might have harmed yourself." He smiled. "You rather like being Firstborn. How would you have lived with that truth?" He burst out laughing. "How strange it all is! How wonderfully the king has treated the damaged second son of his hated shared wife! And how cruel he was to his First-born, his so-called Favorite!"

Psal was silent. *Strange indeed.* He took his brother's arm and together they descended to the keening room. They found Maharai waiting for them.

"So, here we are, together again," Ephan said. "Do you think Nahas will return us to each other now?"

All three looked at each other. "All here avoid us," Psal said. "Perhaps we should avoid each other also. They will grow angry to see us still together."

Maharai touched Psal's hand. "So you don't hate me?"

Psal shook his head. "No. Nor Ephan either. But you must give me time. I desire, I long to touch you. But understand that those hands of yours have caused me much grief. Netophah allowed Nahas to punish Lan and Daris. Perhaps Netophah deserved some punishment as well. All this I understand. And yet"—he picked up his parchments. "I need some time to think."

"Try to love me again, Psallo," she said. "And Ephan as well. The Firstborn."

Psal half-smiled. "I did not say that I didn't love you. I only…I must learn to love you as you really are. Myself as well. I did not know my true place in this longhouse. I have not known you or myself, it seems. A tree, you see, has many parts. Even the best of trees. The leaves, the roots, the bark, the blossom, the seeds. The same essence in the leaf shows itself stronger in the bark or the roots. But sometimes the bark and roots hold more poison. I had not, had not seen all…all of my friend, all of my wife. Your actions surprised me, that's all."

He bowed to them, bowed low as captives bow to victors, and walked into the hallway. In his chamber later, he watched the region change before him. His mind turned on itself. *I have been a studier,* he told himself, *and yet, something so evident—Ephan being the king's son—has gone unnoticed. I am a pretense, someone who plays at knowing and yet who knows so little. Little things now come to mind, such little things—the shape of the toes, the rubbing of the forehead when angry—I should have perceived: the many similarities between Ephan and Netophah, between Ephan and Nahas, between Ephan and myself. My mind, you are no mind at all. My insight, how lacking in sight you are!* He lay on his sleeping mat looking at the Greater Light.

* * * *

As for Maharai, no stigma clung to her: she had played her part well, kneeling by Netophah day and night, weeping and tending to him. Long nights and long days she sat by his bed, stroking his forehead and his deformed body and scarred face. At first she did not pity him. When his pock-marked, half-paralyzed face looked at her or when he moved slowly about their room, his breathing halting and heavy, she would force tears to flow from her eyes. Then as days and night went by, tears came without force or guile. She found herself rising to hold him as his own trembling hands held onto her for support. Often he complained of cold when she was not cold, or of heat when no one else was hot. He was unable to control his body and his bowels. At that time, he would look at her so tenderly and so trustingly that she cried even more.

She could not pretend to comfort without actually falling into actual comforting. Yet Netophah had cut her brother's throat and so she could not quite love him. Neither could she hate him, and she hated herself for not hating him enough. As Netophah's strength returned—only a miracle from the Ever-Present One would return it to its proper state—Maharai would lead him to the hearth to eat with the others.

The day came when Netophah called Ephan and Psal to his room. When they entered, he directed them to shut the door behind them.

"Why, Ephan?" Netophah's voice was as weak as his almost-destroyed body.

Ephan looked out at the morning, distant.

"Brother, I asked you a question." Netophah directed Maharai to bring a chair for him to sit on. "I feared Psal, not you." His trembling hands grasped the chair she brought and he sat in it like an old man waiting for death. "I had thought this longhouse strange, being made as it was for Psal, but now I see the ease and comfort of it. Ephan, my brother, you have killed me. Yes, in many ways, I am dead." He was silent for a long time. "No wonder Father feared what you both could do."

"Father feared Ephan *and* me?" Psal asked. "I am no one. A peace child born of an alliance with a neutral clan. A second-born damaged son. What is that worth?"

"It is worth much, Firstborn," Netophah said. He beckoned to Maharai who came and stood beside him. "Ephan is the Voca Prince. And you... The Macaw Clan are a large neutral clan. And you are both studiers."

Psal lowered his gaze. No, he had not seen his worth.

Netophah leaned his head on Maharai's shoulder, then stood up. "It hurts to sit. It hurts to stand. It hurts to lie down. I am never at ease."

Ephan shrugged.

"Tell me, Firstborn," Netophah said. "I speak to Ephan. How long do you trust Nahas to keep Gidea alive?"

"Why do you think Gidea is guilty in this thing?" Psal asked.

"Punishment will not bring my life back, but someone must be punished for the Voca Prince's action, and all know Ephan has been speaking with her. You know our father. Perhaps you should send Gidea away to the Macaw Clan. Or send her to live with one of the Voca chiefs. Or to one of our steward houses. Because I assure you, the thought will come to Nahas to punish her. And on that night, neither Cyrt nor Ephan will be able to save her. And I, for my part, will not try to." He pointed to the door. "The conversation is finished."

"You have always been gracious, Wheel Clan Heir," Psal said and bowed.

"What has my graciousness gotten me?" Netophah answered.

So Psal and Ephan left the Crown Prince's chamber.

In the keening room, Ephan said, "Firstborn, we should heed the counsel of the Wheel Clan Crown Prince and send Gidea away. And yet, neither Maharai nor I wish to be without her."

"That I cannot do. The stewards love Netophah, and all believe Gidea caused you to hurt our brother. As for the Macaw Clan, they will not challenge Nahas by taking her. Your mother, perhaps?"

"I have not spoken to her. What about Ktwala? The child's birth nears. Ktwala will need one of her sisters to help her."

"Firstborn, love and bitterness have blinded your heart. Gidea has harmed Netophah. Do you think she will allow the child of Nahas to be born?"

So Psal did not immediately send Gidea away. It happened that not many days later, the king anchored the royal longhouse in the cold dark climes. There the studiers gathered Dama seeds, and as third moon rose high Gidea was dragged to the prison longhouse anchored there. She was bound there alone in the dark cold climes. As night took the royal longhouse from the region, Cyrt stood by a window looking out at Gidea's prison.

Near the hearth, Psal watched him. Perhaps Maharai's grief had affected him; he was not sure. But he approached Cyrt.

"Captain?"

Cyrt turned. "Firstborn?"

"No longer Firstborn."

"Though you resist the honor, it is yours. You will always be the Firstborn to those in the Wheel Clan." He looked again through the window. "The dark cold climes. A grievous place, horrible to endure. But who can turn the heart of a king once a decision has been made?"

Psal nodded. "Yet. Perhaps. Perhaps she will leave it and cast herself into the night."

Cyrt shook his head. "No, she will not. Have you not read our own histories, Firstborn? Many have been imprisoned in the dark climes. Few have escaped it by throwing themselves into the night. It is not the way of we humans to leave the sorrows we know for unknown ones." He looked again at Gidea's longhouse, a tear brimming at the corner of his eye.

CHAPTER 42

VISITORS

Battles passed, as well as burials and pyres. Ordinary events in war, but as the number of deaths increased, more towers failed across Odunao. This happened in all the clans, whether warring or neutral. They fell from Psal's charts like stars or outcasts disappearing into the night. The war within the royal longhouse continued, but only against the studiers. Although one can never leave the place of one's torment except that some great sorrow or rejection forces one out, Psal never hearkened to Ephan's voice to flee.

But one morning, toward the end of the twelfth month, Ephan said to Psal, "I am determined to leave this place," he said. "For me, this royal longhouse is the Constant Tower because it is constantly with me. But I will not fly into the night unless you come with me. And will we not be safe? The Voca Prince will be at your side. Who will war against my mother?"

Psal looked out over the rampart at the pyres and the distant orchards. "Many times you have asked me, and I would not leave this people in the midst of war and with towers failing on all sides. But now…yes… Seagen is knowledgeable enough. And even if he is not, I do long to be free from this place."

Ephan's apricot eyes lit up. "Brother, you surprise me! So…you are saying…we may leave at last?"

Psal nodded.

"Maharai will rejoice to hear this. She will rejoice to be reunited with her mother."

"Brother," Psal warned, not hiding his worry, "if we join Ktwala's tower, we will have returned to Nahas' wake."

"There are ways out of a wake," Ephan said and smiled.

Psal had not seen him smile in a long while. "Voca Prince, Firstborn, I will follow you and yet…remembering Renn's words…I curse myself that I will put aside the Firstborn's responsibility to his people, a duty assigned to me by birth. I had hoped to do much to bring honor to studiers…And now…must I forsake them in a time of failing towers?"

"One need not be in a Wheel Clan tower to save the world, Firstborn," Ephan answered. "Or do you, like all in the Wheel Clan, think that only the Wheel Clan can save the world?"

Psal half-smiled. "It is a proud belief we Wheel Clan have, is it not?"

"Perhaps you must forsake this people in order to help them later. Perhaps, if you continue here while the towers failed, the Wheel Clan would be no more."

"Perhaps. Why is the world so full of 'perhaps?'" Psal walked toward the rampart stair. "But how shall we escape? And when? If night comes and the king finds us missing, he will search for us til third night. And with this treacherous leg of mine and the worsening of my illness, how should I escape?"

"I will find a way," Ephan answered. "Let your mind not think of it."

But at daybreak the next morning, as Psal stood chewing Tomah with Ephan on the rampart, the Gleaners and Chief Amar re-appeared. Their tower had been extensively repaired and a larger dwelling—larger than a hut but by no means as large as a longhouse—had been built around it.

* * * *

On that very day, Ktwala dreamed that the Ever-Present One spoke to her:

"Ktwala, today, you must rise from your bed, difficult though it might seem. I have sent lions to lead you to a hidden cavern. Stay there with Gillan, Lian, and Tomo until I give you leave to return."

At daybreak, Gillan called to her. "At the entrance...seven lions. They kneel outside our longhouse door. How strange this is! Mother, did you call them?"

Ktwala pushed past pain and rose from her sleeping mat. Holding her heavy belly, she walked to the gathering room and looked through the window. "I dreamed the Ever-Present One spoke to me. And, look, here they are."

Tomo laughed. "And why should the Ever-Present One, who is so distant and so holy, speak to one of us?" he asked. "Is the wife of the Wheel Clan king now among the prophets?"

"Whether I am a prophet or not, I do not know, but these lions have been sent to lead us to a hidden cavern. Gather food and blankets. We will allow the cavern to protect us until—"

"But how do you know it was the Ever-Present One who spoke to you?" Tomo asked. "Did you not say that Samat deceived you? And why should you leave your longhouse? Is this not the same deception Samat spoke before? What if no cavern exists and we are left at the mercy of the night?"

Gillan nodded. "Mother," he said, "you are not well. Can you walk to these caverns—wherever they are? Will the journey not be too hard for you?"

Ktwala held her sack in her hand, but now she doubted her dream. She returned her sack to its place. "It is possible," she said, "that Samat is once again deceiving me."

"Stay here and rest," Tomo said. "We will hunt and return. And what harm can be done to you while these lions rest outside?"

So they left Ktwala in the longhouse, and Ktwala lay in a bed by the window in the gathering room.

But before the sun reached its height, when the daymoon shown brightly, women's voices called out to Ktwala. She rose from her bed and looked through her window to see a woman, pale and beautiful, stand before her, hair and skin as white as snow: Ezbel, the Voca Queen.

That pale one spoke: "Ktwala, we've come to help you at the time of life."

Ktwala held her belly, looked about for the protecting lions, saw none.

"Great Queen Ezbel," she said, "the child does not search for life yet."

"Not true," Ezbel answered her. "It will live if born now. And do not fear. Herbs we know, and their power. Neither you nor the child will be harmed."

Footsteps echoed through the longhouse. Ktwala turned. Twenty warriors with lances raced down the corridor into the gathering room.

"How have you entered?" she asked the one unlatching the heavy door.

"Windows were left open, Ktwala."

The Voca Queen entered, bowed to Ktwala. She extended her hand and touched Ktwala's round belly. "Ktwala, my sister, we have much in common. Mothers of the children of Nahas. I, too, bore his child. And would have kept it, had it been a girl. Ephan is his name."

Ktwala eyed the lances in the hands of the Voca warriors, eyed the Peacock lances leaning against the walls. "My Sister, Great Queen, I have met your son. A gentle boy."

"A noble prince, the Firstborn son of the King of the Wheel Clan, the Voca peace child. Once, at a truce festival, I saw my son. Young and bold, he was readying himself to keen to study the world. The more I hear of him, the more I like him. I am told he is a gentle and wise lad. Unlike other men."

"Great Queen, your words show you to have a mother's heart. Therefore, I ask you. Have you come to take my child? Is there not a truce between the Voca and the Wheel Clan king?"

The queen clapped her hands and several girls behind her stepped forward. "Nahas owes me a daughter.

Ktwala, I have seen from my tower. Your brothers are far beyond, hunting and killing, as men do. They will not return before my task is finished."

She called out a word in a language Ktwala did not understand and two Voca warriors stepped into the longhouse. These carried knives, cloths, pharma, and clay containers. The Voca Queen said another word and the warriors took hold of Ktwala, held her arms tight as she struggled, then put a cloth soaked in sickly-sweet pharma over her mouth. Sudden sleep descended, although Ktwala fought against it. Her body grew heavy, tumbled from her control and she fell asleep.

When she woke, her stomach was cut and the wound sewed together. Her dress and the floor were covered with blood; the child had been taken. Gillan was at her side, Lian too, weeping. She heard Tomo near the door, raging. She felt no physical pain. Only the pain of heartache, another child lost. She wept throughout the night, saying, "Why did I not listen to the Ever-Present One? Why did you tell me to doubt my heart?"

* * * *

Psal turned to Ephan. "We should have fled many days before this, for look, more cause for sorrow has come upon us. Those in this longhouse already think of us as traitors, and now these Gleaners arrive." He looked through his spyglass and his heart became weighed down with grief. "The old man is running toward us with arms open! My mind relives the day we met the Iden clan. Do you think the king will kill these Gleaners also?"

"I do not think he will," Ephan answered, hurrying down the rampart. "His guilt over the Iden murders claw his heart daily. The war has wearied him."

When Psal and Ephan entered the gathering room, the Gleaners Clan was already crowding into the longhouse entrance.

"Young Chief!" The old man hurried toward Psal and hugged him. "My ally and my brother." He slapped Ephan on the back. "And you too, Prince's Wife's Husband!"

When Maharai came rushing in, arms outstretched, he flourished her forehead and hands with kisses.

Nahas stood at the entrance to the gathering room watching, but Chief Amar pointed at him. "I know it. I know it," He shouted to Nahas in the Wheel Clan language. "You stand like a king. Therefore you must be Nahas. Come now, admit it. Are you not this one's Father?"

Nahas bowed slightly, then threw an impatient frown in Psal's direction. "So, you are Psal's ally?" he asked Chief Amar. "And…the night has tossed you here?"

Chief Amar approached the king. "Oh Great Chief, what can I say? We have met many clans. Clans as poor as we but generous. Clans rich in the world's goods but not inclined to share. We have—"

Psal hastened to interrupt. "This level three tower has accidentally crossed our path, Father," he said. "It is marvelously strange how these towers befriend each other."

"Marvelously strange," Nahas echoed, his voice sarcastic.

"And what do you expect from us?" Netophah asked, leaning on a staff.

"Our Brother, Prince Psal taught us how to repair our tower but he did not teach us how to properly keen our tower. If we knew this lore—"

"Nahas," Seagen warned, "these strangers might have been flung here by the warring Peacock Clans."

"Nonsense, nonsense!" Chief Amar said. "I would not betray my ally. And we have met no Peacock Tower. Search our tower song. See if we have met any!"

"Father," Psal said, "these are the small and unimportant people we allied ourselves to while on our marriage journey. A good and kind people, Father. People in whom there is no harm, Father."

Nahas spoke to Amar. "How came you to be here on the same day as we? Since you say you lack tower science."

"Their tower called to ours obviously," Ephan answered.

"Obviously." Nahas placed his arm around the shoulders of the Gleaners' Chief. "So you need some more tower science?"

"That and more," Amar answered. "We need axes and knives, new blankets, clothing and pharmas, seeds and perhaps some salted meat and fermented vegetables. And, of course, tower science. Great King, as we both know, it is the duty of the great clans to help the poorer ones. The Great Principles state that. And, we all know, your clan has stolen much of Odunao. Its best regions, its food, its rivers. We poor clans would not have to beg if you had not stolen so much."

Tomah had made Psal's heart numb, yet he found himself fearing for the Gleaners Clan.

The king said, "You are bold to speak to us in this manner, Chief Amar."

"I speak as one chief to another. Are we not equals? If you needed a thing from me, would I not give it?"

"You are little and lacking," the king said. "There is nothing you could give me."

"True, Great King. But, as I said, 'if' we had it, we would give it to you."

The king took Rain aside and spoke with her. Psal kept his gaze on them, keened his ear to listen. *I cannot discern their voices from the others in the gathering room,* Psal thought surprised. *Have I so shut my mind away from humans that I cannot hear far-off human voices? Or is it the Tomah?* The king and Rain returned and Nahas invited the Gleaners to feast with them. Chief Amar and his daughter sat at the king's table with the king's captains, stewards, and studiers.

"If only Amar would not talk so!" Psal whispered to Ephan.

"It is good that Nahas thinks him foolish and open-hearted," Ephan answered. "Then Nahas will assume Amar is incapable of withholding any truth from him."

So in silence they listened to Chief Amar ramble on. "Great Chief Nahas," he was saying, "Prince Psallo has been good to us. After he repaired our tower, he gave us the basic knowledge of tower keening. It helped very much." He smiled at Psal. "But now, little prince, I need to know more."

Psal flushed. "The tower science was rudimentary, Father."

"Rudimentary?" Netophah asked. "Yet he has the skill to meet our longhouse."

"We are a wise people," Amar said, laughing. "Teach one of our children to add today and tomorrow he surprises you with multiplication. Do you know we have discovered how to shadow keen? Not many know how to do that. Well, at least, they don't know how to do it well. That is how our tower found you. Yes, yes, we are a very wise people."

Seagen said to the king, "He knew our longhouse would be here. Not an easy feat."

"We even know how to do the daytime keen," Chief Amar added as he ate some fermented fruit. "It wasn't difficult to learn. Sometimes we travel back and forth between regions four or five times in a single day."

All looked at him in disbelief. "Are you always so full of boasting?" Nahas asked.

"I do not boast!" The old chief looked appropriately insulted. "What do you take me for? But you probably know this already. As you have said, we little clans can offer you very little."

"No, Amar, we do not know how to keen in the daytime," Ephan said. "None but the Voca know it."

Amar's eyes widened. "You don't? Oh my boy! Then I will tell you how it's done. Oh, it is so easy. No, no, not difficult at all." He burst out laughing. "After I've finished this lovely meal."

The chief's words caused a stir and soon Nahas, Netophah, and his captains were all whispering together. But none of them spoke to Psal or Ephan. As the meal drew on, Psal's fear grew. After some time, the Wheel Clan warriors rose from their meal.

But they stand about. Why do these warriors not leave? Is some evil planned against this chief and his people?

Psal sat, tense, looking from Ephan to Amar to Maharai to Nahas to Netophah. Then suddenly, Nahas raised his hands and throughout the gathering room, the Wheel Clan warriors unsheathed their daggers.

The meat in the mouths of the Gleaners fell onto their plates.

"We are murdered, my brothers!" Amar shouted. "We are destroyed and fallen into the hands of enemies we thought were allies!" He turned to Nahas. "Why destroy us?"

The children of the Gleaners Clan cried, the men brandished pronged eating utensils and knives—anything to use as a makeshift weapon while the Wheel Clan warriors threatened. The Gleaner women held their screaming children to their chests and rushed toward the entrance and the windows.

"It is because we are enemies," Nahas answered. "And you Peacock Clans are—"

"Enemies?" Amar asked, his voice shaking. "I am not at war with you, King Nahas! I would have known if I had declared war upon you. Weak as I am, why should I be so bold as to declare war on the great King Nahas? Surely we would not betray our allies, Prince Psal and his wife and his wife's husband." He made a sweeping gesture toward the Iden women. "And do I not see Peacock Clan women cooking and eating among us?"

"These women have become Wheel Clan wives," Netophah said. "They are no longer Peacock Clan women."

"If marriage is what brings an alliance, I have a daughter of marriage-able age." He pushed his daughter forward. "Let her marry one of you."

The girl was pretty with kind brown eyes, but Netophah said, "We do not want her."

Maharai and the Iden women now began chanting:

Will you kill these as well, Nahas?
Will you kill these as you killed our men, Nahas?

Netophah touched Maharai's shoulder. "This is what Tsbosso's clan did to our women," he told her. "What we did to your women, we learned from the Threshing Floor Clan. Amar is safe." Then he spoke to Amar in a loud voice, "We will not kill you, you Gleaners. But remember how your own people destroyed our women and value this alliance you have with my brothers."

Amar wiped sweat from his brow. "You must not joke like that, Wheel Clan Heir."

"Indeed, it is a cruel sort of game," Maharai said, glaring at Netophah.

Relieved but angry, the Iden women threw plates of food at Nahas and their Wheel Clan husbands, causing the Wheel Clan men to laugh.

When the joke had been played out, Ephan turned to the king. "Nahas, these Gleaners say they have discovered the daytime keen. Let us see their skill."

"The boasting of fools," Seagen said, dismissively. "Years and years the daytime keen has been studied and so far no one—Ezbel excepted—has discovered its secret."

"And yet," Lebo said, "let us see them try. The ancient ones used to say that innocence and ignorance often falls into paths the wise never find."

Cyrt nodded. "True. And if they have learned this skill, and if they teach us, the victory in this war will be the Wheel Clan's."

"I do not think they know any such thing," Psal told the king. "Or why would they have arrived with the morning?"

"The daytime keen is not so complicated, but this region is a large one," the chief said. "Daykeening one longhouse is one thing, Daykeening to meet another longhouse—well, that is entirely different! One has to call to the crystals and branches in the other longhouse. One must not arrive too close or too far away. It is really quite a delicate matter."

Psal sighed. "I'm sure it is."

But the captains and steward convinced the king that, however foolish the notion seemed, the matter should be looked into. After he had finished eating, the Gleaners' Chief declared the best way to teach their discovery would be to have the studiers see for themselves. Then, taking Maharai by the arm, he smiled his wide and toothless smile. "Come now, little princess! I will repay your husbands' kindness to me."

So Psal led Amar and the others to the royal keening room. The king directed Seagen and Gaal to join Psal and Ephan in the tower's base. But the tower dimmed when Seagen and Gaal entered.

"Since the day your sons returned," Seagen said, fuming, "this tower has developed a grudge against me."

"Why?" Chief Amar asked. "Why does this tower dislike you?"

But Ephan said, "Let it be so even now. If the tower resists all but Storm and me, it will not cooperate." He shrugged, then added, "Although I doubt Chief Amar knows the daykeen."

Gaal laughed, tousled Ephan's hair. "How arrogant you studiers are! I will rejoice to see this non-studier prove you wrong!"

"Come away," the king said. "Let them learn at this great master's feet."

So Gaal and the others left Amar, Maharai, and the king's sons in the keening room.

After Chief Amar finished setting the crystals, he handed Maharai several crystals and Ephan two keening branches. "Maharai," he said, "you must walk outside and stand between the two longhouses. Ephan, you must remain here. Prince Psallo, lean on your staff and follow me to my longhouse."

Psal rolled his eyes. "Never have I seen so complicated a keen!"

"You will see greater things than this hereafter," Ephan said.

CHAPTER 43

THE JOINING OF THE GLEANER AND
THE IDEN LONGHOUSES

So, under the curious and doubting eyes of the Wheel Clan, Psal and Maharai walked to the Gleaners longhouse-hut. Maharai stopped half-way between thee royal and the Gleaners longhouses, but Psal followed the aged chief inside. Moments later, Maharai, Psal, and Ephan were all together in the Gleaners longhouse, watching the terrain change around them, merging into a region Psal recognized from fourteen days earlier.

"Maharai?" Psal asked, mouth agape as Maharai's unmade form re-made itself before his eyes. "But how?"

Fully materialized, she fell weakly into his arms.

Then Ephan stood beside him. "I have never dreamed of such!" Psal shouted. "Were you not in the royal keening room? And Maharai... wasn't she outside in the meadow, standing between both longhouses?"

Around him, Chief Amar and the Gleaners—which consisted of about forty people, fifteen of them women, fourteen children—all sang Pea-cock songs of victory praising the escape of Psal, Ephan, and Maharai.

Ephan tapped his studier's pouch hanging about his right shoulder. "We have escaped."

Psal looked at him. "Escaped? Are we... Can it be the—"

"The Gleaners don't know how to do the daytime keen," Ephan said grinning.

"Well, of course not!" Psal laughed, hugging his friend. "But...how?"

"But I do."

Psal hugged Maharai closely, awaited her awakening from the un-making. "Since when?"

"Since I was outcast with Lan. When I told the Voca chief why we had been made outcast, the old girl pitied me and told me the secret of the daykeen. And since then, I have discovered more. More than the Voca even know."

"But you didn't tell Nahas..."

Ephan shrugged. "Would you tell a secret to one who had lied to you your whole life long?"

"You didn't tell *me*."

"I promised her I would tell no one and would not use it unless it was necessary to save my own life. And the lives of those in my eimi. Moreover, the Voca Queen who has loved me all these years has helped us and will help us. As for the royal longhouse, tonight it will be night-tossed. For several days, it will be unable to recognize or track us. Unable to keen us from afar." He showed Psal several keening crystals in his pouch. "Yes, the keening crystals. The spare ones as well. Others I moved to different sockets or scattered throughout the royal longhouse during the night."

"So…until they find the scattered crystals or get new ones…"

Ephan grinned. "They will be as all poor clans are!"

"So…but…didn't you say you had not yet met your mother?"

"Not yet. But today, I will." He looked about the room like one bidding indifferent farewell to his past. "Soon—this very day!—I will meet my mother. And Maharai—she will be reunited with her mother as well. A wondrous day for our eimi, is it not?"

Psal looked out at the Iden longhouse and the pyres and burial ground. "And I will have lost my father."

"Will we see my mother today?" Maharai asked, her voice weak nad slow, like one rising from a dream.

Psal looked at her. "Are you well?" he asked tenderly.

Ephan hugged his wife, squeezed her tightly. "And now, Maharai, how does it feel to be keened and transported without being inside a longhouse."

"It is not a thing I would always do," she answered.

Ephan looked about at the tiny little longhouse and laughed. Then, with a giddiness Psal had never before seen, he rubbed Chief Amar's balding head. "Brave Chief, I wasn't sure you heard our call or that you would do this for us."

"I would do anything for you and Chief Psallo," Amar answered. "I owe you boys. We have traveled safely from Wheel Clan orchard to fenced fields, meeting neither the Voca nor any other clan. Your stewards and studiers have treated us most kindly because of the alliance."

"But Ephan," Psal said, "Firstborn! Why did you not tell me? And you, Amar, how well you played your game!"

"It is easy to play the idiot when a king expects very little of you," Ephan answered.

"Indeed!" Psal laughed. "Indeed."

"But," the old chief said, "by nightfall, they will begin to wonder why we have not returned. Neither your nor we will be safe from King Nahas or his chiefs."

"We will be safe, Great Chief," Ephan said. "The Gleaners will leave their hut and travel with us in the Iden longhouse. Nahas will not be able to follow until he replaces the crystals. He can neither keen his vessel nor communicate with other Wheel Clan chiefs. By then, all will be safely with the Voca Queen, Queen Ezbel, my mother."

* * * *

The sickening odor of decomposing Peacock bodies seeped through the door, windows, and cracks of the tiny Gleaner house when it materialized at the battle field where Ktwala's longhouse rested. Maharai was already at the door, her hand on the latch. "Its markings are different, but my heart recognizes my old home."

She ran outside. Rushing over bloodied and broken bodies, she reached the Iden longhouse and banged hard on the door, but no one appeared. She walked to a nearby window and peered between the slats of the shutters. The window opened and two men looked out. The older one had fierce, angry eyes and looked like one from the Grassrope clan. The younger one, who seemed only a few years older than Psal, had kinder eyes, one arm, and long blond hair. A child stood near them crying, his eyes red. All wore tunics with the Iden cloth pattern. They looked past her at Psal and Ephan racing toward her.

"Open the door," Maharai begged. "I want to see my mother. Is she within?"

The one-armed one looked at the dark one, then asked Maharai. "Are you…"

"Maharai. My mother is Ktwala. Let me in."

"Have you escaped?" the dark one asked. "And who are these with you?"

"My husbands," Maharai answered. She ran to the door and banged harder. "We've escaped from the Wheel Clan king. Open the door."

The door opened as the Gleaners, Ephan, and Psal arrived. The young child inside grasped Maharai's hand but the man from the Grassrope clan said to Psal, "Are you the king's son, the lame studier? The one who sends parchments?"

Psal nodded. "And you must be Tomo, and the other Gillan, and the other Lian."

Tomo glanced in Ephan's direction then stepped aside. "So the Wheel Clan's two studiers have escaped?" He gestured them toward the corridor where Maharai now ran. "Your king should guard his wife better."

Psal hastened his dragging steps. "Has something happened?"

"She's in her room," he said. "Dying. At the hand of the Voca Queen."

Psal and Ephan hurried into the room where Ktwala lay, curled up on a sleeping mat. Maharai was beside her, holding her right hand. "Help her!" Maharai shouted to her husbands.

Psal leaned over Ktwala. "Mother, I'm here."

She stirred and held out her left arm, looked past him at Ephan, then at the Gleaner Clan.

"The Voca Queen herself came," Ktwala murmured. "She has taken Nahas' daughter."

Maharai lifted the blanket. A large wound stretched from Ktwala's right side to her left. "Ephan, the Voca Queen helped us with one hand and destroyed us with the other."

"She's exacted a great price for helping me." Ephan turned to the Gleaners. "Is there in your longhouse any child-birth pharma?"

A woman named Kereth stepped forward.

"You know what herbs to look for?" he asked her.

The woman nodded.

"She will live. But give her what comfort you can." Ephan looked at the wound again, frowned. "As for the child, I will go to the Voca Queen and ask—"

"You're asking help of the one who wounded her?" Tomo yelled.

"I did not know her intention," Ephan replied. "But she will speak to me."

"Who are you that she should she listen to you?" Gillan asked. "She told us you Wheel Clan have a truce with the Voca. Yet she broke it."

"I am her son. She will listen to me."

Gillan and Tomo looked at him, speechless. If he had said he was Samat himself, they could not have been more silent.

After removing a sliver of Tomah bark from his studier's pouch and giving half of it to Psal, Ephan set the Iden tower for a daytime keen to the Voca Queen's home region.

CHAPTER 44

THE VOCA QUEEN

The Great Mesa was still visible through the heat-hazy sky and shimmering sand. The queen's longhouse stood before them. On either side of the central longhouse and tower, its corridors spread like great eagle's wings attempting to encircle the ancient relic in the distance. Psal's eimi approached the Voca Queen's longhouse, but the others remained near the Iden longhouse.

Ephan walks like a prince. Psal glanced at his brother, walking beside him. *And indeed that is what he is.*

Two females dressed in tan tunics stepped from the queen's longhouse. One was a young girl about eleven years of age and dark. The other, a woman with features of the Western Mound Dwellers. Both held lances, the tips aimed toward the visitors.

Psal squeezed Maharai's hand tightly. "Don't be afraid, Maharai. And restrain your anger. Don't speak to her unless she speaks to you. She's powerful. Ruthless as well. Very like Nahas. But Ephan has said she loves him. For Ephan's sake she may return the child."

When Psal entered the great queen's longhouse, his mouth fell open. Not since the festival truce had Psal seen the children of so many clans in one place. The longhouse bloomed with little girls. Queen Ezbel sat in the middle of the gathering room looking at the children. *Ephan and his mother share the same love of children. But these children! How many were born of Voca women? How many were ripped from the wombs of women across Odunao? All across our planet, the mothers of most of these children are probably dead or grieving their loss.* Some of the younger girls approached the eimi, but others, older, hurried from them and hid behind the queen's great throne. *Apparently, she has taught her daughters to hate all men.*

Ephan called out, "Great Queen, Dear Mother. I have been told that you are my mother."

"Come closer." She squinted. "My eyes are failing. It is the way of this illness."

Ephan walked toward her, but Psal and Maharai lingered.

The queen rose and stepped down from her throne. Carefully, slowly, she studied Ephan.

"Ephan, Child of Nahas, Great Firstborn, King's Favorite, Cloud. You are known by many names. All of which I know."

Ephan's voice faltered. "All of them, Mother?"

"*All,* my son." She raised a hand, removed the glass-wired crystals from his eyes. "My son, what are these?" She placed them over her own eyes. "Oh, how delightful! I can see your face more clearly. So this is what you look like? How beautiful you are, my son!"

Ephan laughed, blushed. "I have been told I am too beautiful, Mother."

She removed the crystals. "Did you make these?"

"I did, Mother, but…"

"A wondrous thing, a wondrous thing! To see clearly!"

"I am honored, Mother. They are indeed useful, yet…" He paused. "Mother, I have come to speak of Ktwala's daughter."

The queen bowed. "I met you once. Do you remember? How bold you looked! And yet how helpless, as you readied yourself to study with the Master of the Wintersea. My heart ached to hold you. Lebo had told me that you were a gentle lad, loving and tender, and not like other men."

"It is strange to find myself loved by a mother, Great Queen, but I wish to speak of Ktwala."

She smiled, looked behind him, squinted. "Who are these with you, King's Favorite? Your friend, is it? He, too, has grown. And the girl… your wife?"

"Yes, Mother. This is the eimi the Ever-Present One has given me."

"Not Nahas? Not life or happenstance? You believe the Silent One gave you your friends? You believe in Her then? How like me you are, my boy! I believe in Her as well."

"'Her,' Mother?" Ephan asked.

"Why should the Ever-Present One not be a woman, my son?" She took his arm. "You have been raised far from me, and lived among those who treat women harshly, yet I am told you have developed a true heart. You do not fit in with your own people."

"Mother," Ephan said, "you do not fit with your own people either. For here you stand loving one who is a man."

She hugged his neck and laughed. "True, my son."

Tears flowed down Ephan's cheeks. Psal stood transfixed by the sight, but Maharai shouted, "Enough of this! I want my sister! I want my mother made well with your pharma. Ephan has been trying to speak to you of my mother, and you have ignored him these three times. You are reunited with your son. My mother wishes to be reunited with her daughter. Do you hear me?"

The Voca Queen glanced at Maharai. "And you are Ktwala's stolen daughter?"

"Yes! And you have broken the Wheel Clan truce by taking Nahas' daughter."

"Mother," Ephan said, "I have long wanted to meet you, but before we speak as mother and son...you should return Ktwala's child to her. And yes, since a truce exists between the Voca and the Wheel Clan, you should not have taken Nahas' child."

Ezbel frowned. The same suspicion Psal had seen in Nahas now shone from the queen's eyes. "Is that why you're here, Ephan? To take the child? Or is this some ploy created by Nahas to steal the secret of the daytime keen?"

"Mother, it is no ploy. Since the day I discovered the circumstances of my birth, I intended to come to you. But your theft of Ktwala's child has harmed our reunion."

"My son, it is hardly theft. Nahas owed me a daughter. I gave birth to a son instead. Ktwala's daughter is the daughter Nahas owed me. That is also part of the truce."

"My sister is not your daughter!" Maharai shouted. The girls near Ezbel's throne raised their lances.

Psal pulled Maharai aside. "You must not challenge her," he whispered. "Choose better battles. Isn't your husband fighting your cause even now? Let him."

"Little Princess," the queen said. "I tended to your mother's wounds. Is her life not enough?"

"Tell me, Mother," Ephan said, "why did you choose today to take the child? You did a treacherous thing, betraying your son."

The queen returned to her throne, sat and leaned back. "Long before you told me you wished to escape Nahas, I watched that longhouse. When you told us you would cause the Nahas longhouse to become night-tossed—and thus unable to track towers—it seemed the right time, because the child was due anyway."

"I was the cause of Ktwala's great harm, then?" He asked.

"Don't blame yourself. I would've taken the child in any case."

"Mother!" Ephan said firmly. "Give me the child."

"And why should I?" How cold her voice was!

"Because the son you love wishes it."

The Great Queen was silent for a moment. "Well, then, take the child! I have...you have humiliated Nahas. To live to see this...to return the child is not a sacrifice. Yes, yes, you may take the child. But know you owe me a great deal."

How cruel our parents have been! Psal thought. *And yet, what scheme does she have in mind?*

Queen Ezbel brought the eimi to a room full of newborn children, about eight in all. Five women lay there, Voca girl children attending to them. Only one of the women wore the Voca tunic. A newborn boy lay on the ground crying, his umbilical cord uncut. Maharai walked toward the child.

"Do you want him?" The Voca Queen asked. "Take him also if you wish. It is the child of one of my chieftains. She has no need of it." Ezbel moved to a small cradle separated from the others. Inside it lay an infant. "Here is Ktwala's daughter. Your sister, my son's sister. A lovely thing."

"Is that truly she?" Psal asked.

"Do you not trust me, Fated One?"

"No, Queen Ezbel. I do not. I have been trained to believe you're a deceiver."

"That is the child which Ktwala bore, the one who belongs to Nahas." Then quite suddenly she turned to Ephan. "My son, Tomah is a deadly herb. You and your friend reek of it. If you wish to live, purge yourself of it."

"We are battling our enslavement to it," Ephan said. "But it is a pharma that does not easily release it's grip." He smiled. "It is strange to have a mother standing before me, wishing me well."

Psal lifted the boy from the ground, while Maharai took Ktwala's daughter. They brought both children to the Iden longhouse.

* * * *

As Maharai gave the child to her mother, Psal remarked, "So this is Nahas' new daughter?"

Ktwala touched the silky smoothness of her daughter's hair and skin. "Not Nahas' daughter, but mine. And this boy will be a replacement for Ouis, whom the Wheel Clan king slew." She opened wide her arms to Psal's eimi. "You are my daughter's husbands, my sons. But Nahas is not my husband."

Thus the Iden clan grew. For the Gleaners were also added to it.

* * * *

During the next three days Ephan spoke often with his mother. But on the fourth day, Queen Ezbel called both Ephan and Psal to her throne room.

"Nahas once again controls his longhouse," She handed them some parchments. "Do you intend to continually flee Nahas and the Wheel Clan? For he will surely try to find and punish you. I will protect you, but you must do a certain thing for me."

"What will you have me do, Mother?" Ephan asked.

"Have you heard of the Constant Tower?"

Psal frowned, rolled his eyes.

"Why do you frown, Chief Studier?" the queen asked. "Do you not believe what the clans believe, that humanity diverged from a great tower and the forefathers of each tribe took a piece of the original tower with them in order to remember their common humanity?"

"No, I do not believe that. Nor do I believe the Ever-Present One dispersed our forefathers. The world has always been as it is. There was no great sin at the beginning and no great curse. Only the superstitious believe such things."

"So you think me a fool?" she asked.

"I think there are better things a mind such as yours should be searching into."

"Nevertheless, I have seen this tower that only the superstitious believe in."

"Why haven't you begun to rule the world, then?" Psal asked.

"Because I cannot hear its song, unbelieving Studier. I am told by those who have heard it that it has a beautiful, lovely song. You can cast it off as some dream of weak humans, but I agree with those who think it's a literal tower. Or do you not wish to save the failing towers?"

Psal glanced at the parchments. They bore the same co-ordinances as Antun's tower. "Ah me!" he said. "We have seen this place before. There is nothing there."

"Go yet again, Chief Studier. If it's the true Constant Tower, it will make itself known to you, because you are the Fated one."

The delusions that abound even in intelligent minds! Psal thought. "If it wanted to make itself known to me, it should have done so when our tower tossed us there. Why should it do so now? And why am I the Fated One?"

"You are the only Studier-Firstborn Prince whom the Wheel Clan has allowed to live," she answered. "True, other Damaged Firstborns exist among the scattered clans, but the world does not revolve around the scattered clans. It revolves around the Wheel Clan. I shall not wait another one hundred years for a Damaged Wheel Clan Firstborn, and I doubt the towers will last another hundred years."

Psal laughed. "Even you think the Wheel Clan..."

"You owe me this, for I freed you from Nahas. I returned Ktwala's child to you. And now I have changed the settings of the Iden tower to prevent Nahas from finding it."

"How wise a mother I have!" Ephan's eyes lit up with admiration. "This hiding skill is one not fully understood or developed among the Wheel Clan studiers!"

How he worships this woman! Psal thought. "When did you change the settings?" he asked Ezbel. "And why?"

"Because I do not wish the king to trouble you when you search out the Constant Tower," she answered.

"I had not yet agreed to search out a Constant Tower," Psal answered, annoyed to be pulled into Ezbel's obsessive delusion.

"Nevertheless, you will do it," she replied. "Because you are the Fated One of Prophecy."

"Is that all you require of us, Mother?" Ephan asked.

"I ask only that when you rule this world, you prepare cities of refuge for women who need to escape the keen of their husbands, that you make the world safe for women who wish to flee the world of men."

"I can easily promise that," Psal answered, "because there is no such tower. Nor do I wish to become a king over this world."

CHAPTER 45

THE CONSTANT TOWER

"I want to see!" The first words Ephan spoke when the Iden long-house materialized across the field from the supposed Constant tower. He spoke not to Psal but to the Creator, adding, "I was wrong to ask for blindness. Whatever the truth is, I wish to know it. In all its beauty, in all its ugliness."

Although they had used the daykeen, the area around the tower was black as night, the area heavy with mist. Psal could see neither the ground before him, nor the sky around him. He sighed, sighed again, sighed continually, and thought of the deceptive mound of twigs, branches, and dead men's bones that had fooled Ephan and Daris months earlier. "Why are we wasting our time in this dark wood when towers are failing? It is as dark as the dark climes, and not nearly as interesting."

Ephan laughed. "It is not so dark as that. The light shines brightly, and past the trees in the clearing where the tower stands, the light shines even brighter."

He raced ahead through the mist toward the tower while Psal limped behind, leaning on his staff, and held his arm aloft in the darkness to prevent himself from stumbling.

"Does that mother of yours truly expect us to trust our feet to an unstable pile of— *No wonder Ezbel has not examined it. She fears dying.* "Slow your pace. This darkness. How black it is! Yet you run? The blind leads! If you fall and I stumble over you—"

"It is not dark!" Ephan shouted back. His voice sounded a long distant away. "It is well-lit. I can see quite clearly."

"Ephan, have you arrived at the tower? In this darkness?" *Did Ephan say it was well-lit?*

"Storm, do you see?" Ephan shouted; fear edged his voice. "Do you see? Is it true, then, Brother? Can you really not see?"

Psal did not answer. *Ephan is as blind as...*

"Follow my voice!" Ephan shouted. His fear had grown. "I am here. Come! Come!"

Confused that one with weak eyesight had not stumbled in the way, Psal continued walking, tripping occasionally along the dark path, Ephan's voice his only guide. But then Ephan's hand grasped him. He stopped, spoke in his friend's direction, looked about.

"You can see? In this darkness?" Psal asked the faint shadow beside him.

"The tower is lit, Brother." Ephan sounded as if unsure whether it was Psal or himself who had gone mad. "It is brightness all the path around. Its song rises bright and loud, guiding all here."

Madness. I see no tower. And yet, blind though he is, he has not stumbled. "Why were you afraid just now?"

"The Unfleshed Ones surround this place," Ephan said. "Samat himself stands before us, sword drawn."

"So you're seeing Samat now?" Psal groaned. "Impressive. Regal company. You are a queen's son. Why should you see mere minions now?" He held onto Ephan's arm. "Samat aside, lead me to this tower that only you can see. Then we can depart this unsettling place."

"I tell you, Psal! He stands before us…before it…barring our way. With sword drawn."

Psal sighed. "Samat has chosen to battle those who have no skill in fighting?"

"Why must you mock?" Ephan shook off Psal's arm. The sound of his pacing footfalls increased or decreased as he walked ahead of Psal, then returned. At last, he stood again beside Psal. "I will tell you what I see. And you will have to cast aside the strongholds and fortresses in your mind. Can you put aside your resolve to consider all I say mere ramblings?"

"I have no wish to…"

"Brother!" Ephan shouted. "I am Firstborn, am I not? I order you to listen to me."

Psal scowled. "You're using an accident of birth to force me to obey you?"

"It was necessary."

"I will listen to the Firstborn's ramblings," Psal said, "Anything to complete that evil queen's request. The evil queen whom you have so easily forgiven all her sins."

"We all must forgive," Ephan said. "Or how can we overcome Samat? Have you no sins that need forgiving? Have you not forgiven my sins and our father's sins?"

"I have no wish to speak of it. Just tell me what you see."

"Imagine then, the crystal column of this tower as a mirror."

"I will try."

"Perhaps you should close your eyes, that the physical truth does not blind you."

"It hardly matters. I cannot see with them open."

"Brother!"

Psal closed his eyes, sighed. "The foolish things I have done—"

"Brother, the Unfleshed Ones are watching us. There is no time for—"

"Yes, yes. The Unfleshed Ones and Samat's drawn sword. So you say. Go on."

"The crystal is full of light. It is light itself. This light is the very word of the Creator. It is like a mirror. When I look into it, I see the Creator's view of things. I see myself. I see the workings of the Unfleshed Ones."

Psal snorted. "I am imagining it. But I do not believe it."

"For now, imagining it is enough. Do not lean on your own understanding. Remember what I saw the last time. Crystal mirror river. Marble parchment."

"Yes, yes, I remember. White parchment, made of rock."

"You remember?"

"How could I not? I'm a studier, after all."

"So you remember the horizontal and vertical red intersecting lines?"

"Yes, unfortunately. 'Blood red,' I remember you called them."

"Trust me then. This tower joins the word, the blood, the light. It is a Book that has existed since before the beginning of time. It is the Creator's Book. It is the mirror. It is the door. They are all one. Do you understand?"

"I will try to understand," Psal answered. "But this is quick study you demand of me."

He looked deeply and in the darkness of his closed eyes, he saw Ephan. As if his eyes were opened, as if they stood together under a bright sun. But Ephan's hair appeared darker, redder, and his skin not so pale. Psal turned from looking at his brother toward the tower. He saw it, exactly as Ephan had described it. *Curious,* he thought, and opened his eyes. But his opened eyes saw darkness only. He closed his eyes again. Again, there stood Ephan with the tower.

"I see it," he admitted. "But I...I still do not understand."

"Do you see the Unfleshed Ones? Ephan asked.

Psal searched the scene that played behind his eyelids. "I see them." *How strange.* He saw one like a worm regally dressed. A snort escaped. *Is that Samat?* "I see the pretender as well. How fascinating! And to think I thought you mad!"

"We will have to battle them."

"Now that is madness." Psal opened his eyes. "Did you see his sword? I wonder what metal it is. Nahas would...Oh, how strange this spiritual world is!"

"Look to the tower," Ephan said.

"I am looking."

"Do you see the words? Do you see that they are light?"

"I see them."

"Each light is a sword, a spirit sword. Do you see it?"

Ah!!! Yes, yes, I do see! "Two-edged?"

"Yes. Be careful how you yield it."

"Yield it?" Psal was puzzled. "The sword light is on the tower."

"Reach up and grasp their light!" Ephan said. "The sword will become yours."

Psal felt Ephan's hand on his shoulder.

"Open your eyes!" Ephan commanded. "The Firstborn wills it."

Psal opened his eyes.

"What do you see?" Ephan asked.

"Darkness. Darkness only. No tower. I don't even see you."

Ephan sighed. "I had thought…Well, we can't have you fighting with your eyes closed, can we? Can you remember the truth, even with your physical eyes opened?"

"The memory of the tower and the words fade," Psal answered. "It is like a mirror and when I walk away from it, I forget what it looks like, what I look like, what I am."

"Hold to the vision you have seen," Ephan said, "Do not forget."

"I cannot promise to always remember," Psal admitted. "The image of this realm fades so quickly when I turn from focusing on this tower."

Again Ephan paced. This time, however, Psal watched him with closed eyes. In the chambers of his imagery, he saw his friend pacing, advancing toward then retreating from the tower. Then suddenly, Ephan leaped with his arm raised. A word came like living light from the tower and landed in his hand, like the hilt of a sword.

Psal opened his eyes. "What…what did you just do?" he stammered.

"The Creator has sent his word to open your eyes. Close your eyes again."

Psal closed his eyes. But the sword was nowhere to be seen. Instead, the sword seemed to have become a book in his hand.

"Eat this book," Ephan said.

"Eat it?" Psal would have balked, but he had journeyed too far into the spiritual sight to distrust Ephan. "I've had to eat my own words before, but never the Creator's words. These are the Creator's words, are they not?"

In the vision behind Psal's closed eyes, Ephan nodded. "They are. They will be sweet in your mouth and…very sour in your stomach. Like fire and nausea."

"How do you know this?" Psal asked, opening his eyes.

"Shut them!" Ephan commanded.

Psal immediately closed his eyes.

"The Creator told me," Ephan said.

So Psal took the book and ate, eyes closed. "How sweet it is!" he said. But as it entered his stomach, he grew nauseated. He began to retch. "This world, my own self, how disgusting our sins are in the Creator's sight!"

Ephan laughed. "You believe in a Creator now?"

Psal did not answer. He was suddenly aware that he had never believed in the irrational, and here it suddenly was: belief in a Creator.

"Open your eyes," Ephan ordered.

Psal opened his eyes. Disappointed, he said, "I still see nothing."

"It is no matter," Ephan said. "Your spirit is stronger now. The book has strengthened it."

"I suppose," Psal said, not sure if his spirit was strong enough to battle Samat.

Then—he knew but could not tell how he knew—Psal knew that he too held a double-edged sword. *But it's in my mouth?* He laughed. "Do you see a sword in my mouth?" he asked Ephan.

"I see it clearly," Ephan answered. "Do you see mine?"

Psal laughed. "Strange as it might be, I see it. I do. Quite clearly. But how strong are our word swords compared to those Samat and his clan carries?"

"Samat's swords are fiery darts of deception," Ephan said. "Did he not deceive you about the tower the last time we arrived here?"

Psal nodded. "And yet, forgive me, Brother, there is so much to think of. I cannot battle until I have it resolved in my mind."

Ephan looked up toward the Unfleshed Ones and toward the tower, sighed. "Not all questions can be answered but ask on."

"If the Creator created the darkness because the peoples of Odunao were evil, and if he created the towers that their light might guide us to him, why then should the Unfleshed Ones resist us? And why should the Creator allow the towers to fail?"

"Because the Creator made one true tower. All others call to it, imitate it, but only the Constant Tower abides forever. Time was when the Creator allowed our confusion, but now all false towers must fall away. The Unfleshed Ones do not desire this. They want us warring against each other and against the Creator."

"So, while I thought myself wise, I was deceived?" Psal asked. "I understand now."

"To battle then." Ephan cast Tsbosso's staff aside. "You cannot depend on this."

Psal put it aside but as he did, his leg give way under him. Fever and trembling overtook him. It seemed to him that death was working powerfully in him and that he would die in that darkness.

"I cannot go on," he told Ephan and fell to the ground. "I know suddenly that I will die if I continue."

"This is Samat's deception." Ephan sat beside him. He pointed to the tower. "The tower is near enough. Only walk toward it, not turning aside."

Psal could not see the tower. He knew where it stood, knew the Creator was more powerful than Samat, yet…"What am I, a Damaged One, that the Creator should use me?" he asked. "How deluded I have been!"

Then, although the day had been clear, a great storm arose. Psal felt himself being blown across the field. "Now I am farther away than I was previously," he shouted to Ephan.

"Endure," Ephan pleaded somewhere ahead of him. "Endure a little more and continue the walk with me. Look! It is near. We must resist Samat and he will flee from us."

Psal attempted to rise. But now Fiery daggers plunged into his back and side. "The pain, Brother!" he yelled, panicked. "Like fire-arrows piercing my skin. It pushes at me. I will not live to make it to the tower."

Ephan shouted to him. "You have survived much more than this, Brother! Did you not walk in the cold dark of the cold climes? Yet you lived! Did you not survive Dez's mockery? What is Samat to Dez? Did you not survive being night-tossed? What is this little walk? Have you not endured the royal longhouse? Come! Advance! Move by the light of the sword in your mouth. Speak into the darkness!"

And yet, to Psal, the walk to the tower seemed to be more burdensome than any other ordeal he had endured. Moreover, he grew fearful. *What shall I say? How do I use this light?* He advanced, stumbling. Sometimes the way seemed like light about him, sometimes he forgot himself, forgot the light, forgot the tower, and saw only darkness. At those times, he pleaded, wept. "I shall not endure."

Ephan had his own battles as he raced toward the tower. "Endure, Brother!" he shouted back at Psal. "Do you not feel something on your head?"

Psal calmed himself. *Yes, yes, something does cover my head.* "What is it?"

"It is a helmet of hope!" Ephan answered. "The Creator has placed an armor before you. Put it on! It is impossible that Samat can fight against it. Look about for a shield as well. It is the shield of faith. With it, you can conquer. The word of truth is in your mouth as a sword. With the Creator no word is impossible because His words are living, alive, active, and two-edged. Brother, you must believe you will make it to the tower."

"And yet," Psal shouted, "who am I that I should make it to this tower?" The shield lay at hand, a transparent thing it was made up of light and words from the tower. He grasped it. "But what use is this feeble thing against these monstrous beings in my path? I am powerless against them. And this shield as well. Such a frail thing! Won't it be broken in my hand?"

As he spoke, he saw a dark sword come from his mouth. The sword flew into the hand of one of Samat's minions. "I am weak," he said aloud. Another dark sword flew from his mouth into the hand of another of the Unfleshed Ones.

Ah, Psal thought, *When I speak words of doubt and despair, I give my enemy swords they may use against me.* He shouted to Ephan. "What new wisdom is this!" And began to laugh against the pain.

"Let the weak say 'I am strong!'" Ephan shouted back. "No good word from your mouth will fall to the ground. Do not whine, do not complain, do not murmur. Only walk and speak words of power."

It was not in Psal not to complain. Yet, he knew. In order to conquer, his mouth must be silent, and he must only speak the Creator's words.

As he contemplated this, one of the Unfleshed Ones—in appearance human, and yet with the claws and teeth of a beast—sprung out of the darkness and clung to him. Its claws embedded in his back and neck, it tore at his back like an outlaw seeking to find entrance in a longhouse door before night fell.

In an instant, Psal was on the ground, the wicked thing wrestling against him and the shield cast off from him.

"I am destroyed!" Psal called out. And as he did so, a dark sword sprung from his mouth into the hand of his enemy.

The Creature smiled. "Thou art vanquished!" it snarled.

Momentarily, Psal agreed. "Yes, I am destroyed."

But he remembered the shield and the cap he wore. What magic lay in them he did not know; he only knew that he was told they had some power.

The Creature's power apparently lay in the imagination, for as its hands grasped Psal, visions of death and loss assailed the Firstborn. Again, he felt the sickening power of hopelessness and despair. Again, all he dreaded of his future, all he hated of his past, loomed large in his mind.

I must remove my studier's cap, he thought. Thus he forced himself to think of the helmet of hope he wore. Now images of health and restoration lined the path ahead of him. He saw himself advancing the path to the tower. Such images! He had never dreamed of health. All his life he had known only sickness, but now the promise was that with each step a light would guide him on the path toward a health he had hitherfore never known. *Is it possible? Is it possible? That I could walk as others walk? That I could live a long life and not die?* He felt the Creature's grip loosen, then release. Yet it stalked him and now as he looked up in the darkness, he sensed other creatures of that darkness were preparing to aim their fire arrows at him.

The shield! But what can it do? What power does it have against such arrows?

All about him, fire arrows flew, each hitting their mark. He had been wounded once in a journey with the Wintersea Master. He had slipped on ice and fallen against a jagged rock. The present wounds reminded him of that, but far worse. The spirit arrows lodged in his heart, and with each strike, his heart felt like a longhouse under fire. His heart burned with the insults and taunts he had received.

The shield! What can it do? What does it do?

But now, instead of disregarding it, he reached for it. As he did so, the shield grew larger, like a plant suddenly shooting up in one day, and it immediately surrounded him. As it did so the creatures retreated. They still aimed their fire arrows, but now the arrows could not reach him.

He continued walking. As he walked, he felt like one with a living armor, like one in a state of flux. For at one moment, the cap he wore was his own studier's cap, and the next, the helmet of hope would return. Also, the shield sometimes returned to its normal size and sometimes looked large. He looked up to the tower and saw words streaming from it. Wonderful words of life, light, and love. *I must speak words from the light,* he reminded himself. And as he did so, the helmet remained and the shield grew.

My prince, this is not like the human battles you have studied. It is certainly not like the tales told of Netophah's battles. For it is a tale of studiers, sickly and damaged, who spent their days between charts and pharma, a tale of spiritual warfare. Yet it was the greatest battle ever fought on Odunao, and it was fought by weakly ones like yourself. Shall I tell you of the many fiery darts Samat's army threw at our studiers? Shall I speak of their faith which shielded them and the helmet of hope which encouraged them as they moved forward? My boy, you have heard all my stories. Do I not always speak of faith in the Creator and His words?

Shall I speak of the many vain and fearful images the Unfleshed Ones caused to rise before the mind of Prince Psal? Shall I speak of how, with the spirit sword from the Creator, Psal cast down and slashed at those vain imaginings? My boy, if I were to tell you all that was sent to conform his mind to fear and doubt, there would not be time enough to hear such tales! I will say only that the boy suddenly knew himself a true prince with authority against those wicked ones—better, with authority against his own mind. No longer was his mind like an unclosed longhouse into which marauders could enter at will, but he diligently renewed his mind and was transformed into a warrior. The battle lasted long, however. And if any had happened upon the path, they would have thought the studiers mad, for they seemed to be fools beating against the air. But Psal and Ephan endured and at last they set their feet upon the steps of the tower.

When they entered the Constant Tower, Ephan immediately began climbing. Like all towers, it had both internal and external steps. But is anything promised to those who scale and examine God's word from the outside only?

I have already told you Ephan's story. And this is Psal's.

The climb was difficult for him. He had endured the assailing images Samat had laid on his mind to bind it. But he was still weak. When he put his left leg on the lowest stair, he found the ratio of the tower's rise to its run troublesome. His mind struggled to accept this new ratio, but after a while he lost his own measure and accepted the tower's. Instinctively, his feet began to understand the tower's rhythm and meter. Ephan already seemed to become one with the tower's music and had raced ahead, out of sight upward to the watchtower.

"What do you see?" Psal called as he neared the top.

Ephan didn't answer.

"What are you seeing?" Psal asked again.

"The Creator," Ephan now answered.

"With your human eyes?"

Ephan didn't answer, and Psal stopped. He sagged against the wall. A new thought arose: *How can I hazard my life on this staircase of branches and air?*

It is Samat, he told himself. *As always, he wishes to dissuade us from the Creator. I have seen this tower in my mind's eye, and it is no man-made thing built up by foolish old men. It is truth itself. I believe. I believe.*

This he continued to repeat to himself until Ephan came running down.

"Ephan?" Psal looked at his brother, his mouth opened in surprise.

Ephan's weak eyes were not jittery nor apricot-colored but jade green. His skin and hair were no longer white, but his skin was a healthy tan, his hair light brown.

Why could Psal smell Tomah? He had not smelled it for ages. It lingered on Ephan's breath and in his own sweat. The scent grew stronger, then all at once it was gone.

"What is He like, the Creator?"

"A consuming fire," Ephan said, "Living Water, the Greater Light. The perpetual, eternally studied, yet eternally incomprehensible."

Fearsome indeed. "I do not wish to see Him."

"He wants all to come. He is not so fearsome as that."

Psal resumed the climb. *Meeting the Creator will mean putting aside all I believe about the world, but my heart assents to this climb. Some unseen but lovingly persistent Force urges me along. And yet, I still hear no song. Why did Ephan and Daris—good, pure little soul—hear a song?*

He listened. *The wind is blowing in the moss in the trees. Insects buzzing.* He listened to all the communal harmony being sung by the living creatures of the earth. *I still do not hear the Creator. Ah, the songs of inanimate things: rocks, metal, the moons, the sun.* But, again, he did not hear the Creator. Then he heard one solitary sound, like the chirping of a tiny insect. He keened his ears, searched all the directions. At last he found the insect. It was crawling near the bottom step of the tower stair. He closed his eyes, imagined it, heard these words spoken in the center of his being:

"It is a tiny thing unique among all the other created speaking things. Many-colored. It is something you might have brought to Ephan on exploration days."

He stopped short. Had the Creator just spoken to him? *And what a strange thing to discourse on.*

He looked down the stairs at Ephan. "I'm afraid. For I am like an insect in the eyes of this Being Who has created all this universe."

"He loves you even so."

"Brother," Psal shouted back to Ephan. "What good things would I not do for Him if the Ever-Present One truly exists!"

He limped upward. *Yet, it is not as if I have climbed this tower. Not by my own might or by my own power but by the Creator's own will.* Soon, he was on the tower's rampart.

"Speak, My Maker, for your servant is listening."

No voice answered him.

He waited, looked toward the north.

There he saw—but not with human eyes, in the far distance all that was occurring in Nahas longhouse. He saw Nahas plainly, as if his father stood a mere hand's breadth away from him. Then, like a living scroll, the small and large events that had brought him to stand inside the Constant Tower, his life unfolded before him.

Then the many regions of Odunao rose before his eyes. Whether through his mind's eye or with his physical eye, he was not sure. He saw the fire pits of the Wheel Clan longhouses, their wading lakes, their corralled fields. Oh, how fertile and bountiful their regions were! And then he saw other clans, clans very much like the Gleaners when he had met them, tossed by the night, poor and hungry, with bloated stomachs who lingered outside fenced fields. Everywhere he saw…failing towers and warfare. Then he saw Ktwala. She stood among the poor clans, and among the rich ones. She stood with the Wheel Clan, and with the Peacock Clans. In all he saw, Ktwala was always present.

Is she to be the reconciler? Is that why she is with both poor and rich, enemy and ally? He looked toward the stairwell. *Nevertheless, I must do something to help these people. Or how will I redeem myself? But how will I do it?* "Ephan!" he shouted.

Ephan did not answer.

But something, Someone, did. It sang to Psal of the universe, and of his purpose in it. Then the needles of evergreens and ferns lying low in the meadow joined in praises of the Creator. At the same time, all Psal's past sins rose before his eyes; *What would I not give to show Lan and Antun the love I should have shown them when they were alive? And my sisters and brothers, how they loved me! And my mother! How can I return love to one whom I owed love, even if she did not love me?* Like daggers, his sins pricked his heart. *I have lived a lie. All my life I have not loved as I should have loved.*

The voice answered him. Not with words, but with an idea: *The joy of giving is eternal. In your Permanent Home, you will be able to give wonderful joys to all you love.*

Psal thought again of the insect and the tiny pattern on its back. What a beautiful small thing it was. Had the Creator spent so much time embroidering such a little thing? He thought of all the beetles he had seen in his explorations. "Creator," he said, "you have an inordinate love of beetles."

They are created for joy, as you are. I am that joy. There is no other joy but joy in me.

"And yet we rarely have joy," he answered. "We are created to believe and yet how difficult is it for us to believe in you."

He turned to the circular stairwell. He blinked: the tower walls looked like parchments, the dark and light specks on it like notations. Stranger, the walls of the tower seemed alive: living parchment. The notations started at the base of the tower and reached to its top. Like music, the ancient Scripture sang to his heart.

The parchment walls of the tower—the songs, the notations, the rhythms of lost, abandoned, and failing towers, were suddenly all written on his heart. *I have not loved the Creator with my whole heart. I have not loved my neighbor as myself.* Overwhelmed, he stood looking and waiting. More would come. But not yet. He must leave, yet he feared the descent into normal life. I will become blind again. I know it. When I am far from this tower, I will become blind again.

He bowed, then started down. When he was halfway, he saw Ephan at the bottom. The Firstborn's hair now had a reddish cast, almost as dark as the king's.

"Psal!" Ephan called. "You're not limping!"

It was true. His leg, knee, hip, stomach! There was no ache, no fatigue, no nausea, no fever. All his life he had never known such peace within his body. The tower that pulled him upward was now returning him to the world as a healed, whole person. They raced across the brightly-lit path toward the Iden longhouse.

* * * *

The sons of Nahas raced into the Iden longhouse, leaping and laughing.

"Mother," Psal shouted. "Wife! Brothers! Come and see."

Ktwala turned her eyes from her nursing. "What has happened to you?"

"Mother," Psal shouted, "look at my leg."

Ephan said, "King's Wife, look at me as well."

"A strange sight!" she said.

"A strange sight, in truth!" Chief Amar agreed.

"Mother," Psal said, "the wonders I have seen today."

"You yourselves are walking wonders," Gillan studied them closely.

Inside the Iden longhouse, the two studiers told all they had seen and done, of their battle with Samat and the Unfleshed Ones. Maharai, Chief Amar, and the others listened with mouths and hearts opened to the wonders they related. But when he finished Psal spoke to Ktwala, to Ktwala who gently rocked her restored daughter and her adopted son.

"Mother, come to me to see the Creator. Come and be healed. The tower has asked for you."

"I?" She laughed. "I have never had a tower call me. Do towers often do this?"

"Sometimes. But this…Mother, are you not sick of war and corpses? Of brothers, sisters and little ones lost in the night?"

She held the children tightly. "I am."

"Mother, I think the tower has told me that you were born to save the future generations from the night."

She raised a cynical brow. "You think this?"

"I do, Mother. In the future, all will praise your name."

"That I doubt...and yet...I also have seen strange things." She raised herself from her bed. "You spoke of Samat? If he battled you, will he not also battle me?"

"I do not think he will." Ephan drew near. "Your eyes have been opened. And you have endured much already." He smiled his half-smile. "The Creator told me that."

She placed the newborn babies in their beds and, holding her belly with her right hand, supported by Lian, she walked into the Constant Tower, answering its call.

As she entered, the boy's tongue was loosened and he ran to the top of the tower, singing.

"What do you ask me to do?" she asked from the bottom of the tower. The Creator answered her.

Only that you should rule this great world with Nahas at your side. A Peacock Clan queen, a Wheel Clan warrior.

She stumbled back to the tower wall. "Nahas and his treachery caused me much grief,"

Be as a living sacrifice, like Jefta's Daughter, and Esta, whose self-sacrifice to a harsh king brought life and freedom to others.

Then she climbed the stairs, her wound healing as she climbed. Atop its ramparts, she held Lian tightly and looked into the night. Far in the distance, she saw the Wheel Clan longhouse. She saw Nahas.

She saw him as he was after the slaughter of her people. In his chamber he sat, slumped against a wall, his arms on his knees. Blood-stained clothes lay in a crumpled pile on the woven carpet. Blood pooled into the woolen rug. He did not wipe it away. It rose, like a tide, surrounded him, waters to swim in. He spoke: "The rip of Iden flesh should have healed my soul, should have been balm for the grave wound caused by the loss of my little ones. But war cannot heal any of our souls. And Ephan spoke truly: I have allowed Samat and his Unfleshed Ones to seduce me."

The spirits of her brothers called to her. The outcasts, too, from all the clans lost to the night, wandering alone. It was for them she had seen blood, death, pyres, and suffering outcasts. Could she become queen of all the world for their sakes? Could she put away her bitterness against one for the good of all?

The tower sang to her: *The Peacock Clan and the Wheel Clan must become one, the princesses of the Peacock Clan joining in marriage to*

the Wheel Clan princes. You must be queen and must teach the Odunaon
clans how to conquer the Unfleshed Ones.

Last of all, she saw a warrior—the same stout Wheel Clan warrior she had seen in her dreams. He climbed a hillside, alone, a rope in his hand. He advanced on a tree, threw the rope over a strong branch, and hung himself. He struggled for air, his body swung and his bowels emptied, staining his Wheel Clan leggings and tunic. After he died, she waited for the vision to end. But it did not. Only after the Unfleshed Ones fled his body did the image fade.

"That the Ever-Present One should consider my life so important. Such knowledge is too high for me. It is high. I cannot attain it."

CHAPTER 46

THE TRUCE MEETING

When Psal and Ephan returned to the Voca Queen, they told her all they saw, how they had met the Creator there, that healing was within the tower, that soon towers would fail all over Odunao. She listened to them, but who can tell what she heard, for she looked upon them with such shock, amazement, and fear because of all the change that had occurred in their bodies.

"It is time to meet Nahas," Ephan told her. "The war must end. But if I bring the Peacock and the Wheel Clan together, they will murder each other."

"I will help you," the queen said. "So this is the work of the Constant Tower?"

"And what will you ask for your help?" Psal asked. "I have heard that you wish to rule the world. If we ally ourselves to you, will you not murder again?"

"I killed because I was at war," she answered. "In the search for power and vengeance, all have murdered. Have Wheel Clan studiers not aborted innocents and led to the deaths of their mothers? I sought to empower and free women. How then was I wrong?" She straightened herself on her throne. "I see no need for vengeance."

"I must admit your lack of blood-thirst surprises me, Mother." Ephan said. "Would the oppressed not attempt to destroy those who had oppressed them?"

"My son, do you not understand? I may be wise, but the wisdom of this world is passing away. What use is all my tower knowledge if the world will no longer use towers?"

That night, Psal and Ephan sent word to the Wheel Clan studiers and to many of the king's stewards, asking their allegiance to the "two Firstborns" of the Wheel Clan. The major part agreed to do whatever the Firstborns desired.

* * * *

The next morning the queen called for eight Voca longhouses. They appeared immediately, flanking her royal home, two on either side. From these poured forth girls and women from aged to very young, all bearing lances. These stood in eight ranks, four facing east, four facing west.

When Chief Amar saw such a display of power he exclaimed, "I would not have that woman for my enemy. Not for the world."

"Nor I," Tomo said.

"Nor I," Ephan said. "How powerful the weak and damaged can be!"

Outside, the Nahas and Tsbosso longhouses began to materialize; Ezbel's daytime keen bringing both longhouses directly across from each other. When the keen finished, the warriors of each longhouse immediately rushed out, lances raised. The eight ranks of female warriors stood between them.

Chief Tamira called both Nahas and Tsbosso. "Do not fear. Those who were not in your longhouse when we keened you here will see you later tonight. But now you must create a truce to end this war."

Both Nahas and Tsbosso looked on at the Voca in anger and amazement. Soon the chiefs, their captains, and stewards of both longhouses proceeded toward the entrance of the Iden longhouse where Psal stood. *How empty my heart feels, seeing Nahas and Tsbosso approach this longhouse!* Psal thought. *Before my chest would have tightened, my blood would have run cold, my armpits would be drenched in sweat at the thought of speaking to this father of mine. And this Tsbosso who murdered my mother, brothers, and sisters! Have I grown numb to these two fathers who betrayed me? Or has the tower healed my heart?*

In the council that followed, Psal directed his words to Nahas and Tsbosso. "The war must end."

"You have the power to end it obviously," Nahas seemed transfixed by Ephan's face and Psal's leg. "End it, then."

"I have no power over human will," Psal said.

"This is what I feared," Tsbosso struck the table with his shoe. "The Wheel Clan will take what we have. Is that why you brought us here? To turn the world over to your Father and his greedy clan whose eyes are on all they see?"

"I will create a new world, Great Chief, which neither of you will own."

"Neither of us?" Nahas asked. "Do you mean to give it to Ezbel, then? Does Ephan's anger know no bounds?"

"Nahas, listen to me," Psal said. "Ezbel's desires are not being considered here. Only know that many of your studiers and your stewards are already in league with me. They do as I will. They will follow where I lead."

"My stewards? Follow you? Do you hate me so much, to subvert my kingdom? To steal it from me?"

"Long, long, have your studiers and stewards lived under the Wheel Clan traditions. We weak and damaged ones, Father, no longer want to be treated like the dirt under your feet. And I do not hate you, Nahas. But this world is not yours to do with as you will. Ephan and I have done only what was required of us. We were made for this time by the Creator."

"Are you saying you were created by the Creator to destroy our people?" Cyrt attempted to lunge at Psal, but the Voca Queen's guards turned their lances toward him. "Because the tower has done some trick of healing, he believes? Do you wish to take rejected, damaged ones and turn the world upside down?"

Then Gaal said, "Two Firstborns, do you truly desire to give all our lands to those who did nothing to reclaim them from wildness? Our orchards? Our longhouses? Our stables? Our barns? Surely you owe something to your own people?"

Before Psal could answer, Cyrt said, "I will not live in peace with these Peacock Clans. And it would be better for me to die than to be ruled by Damaged Ones." He rose from the table, then turned to Tsbosso. "Tsbosso, tomorrow our longhouses will do battle in the Dry Plain."

He walked out the door and Nahas and Tsbosso followed him. All returned to their longhouses with angry curses on their lips. By third moon rise, it was evident that there would be no truce.

That night, Psal sent the same song to all the Wheel Clan studiers and stewards. But not only to them. He over-rode the towers of the Peacock Clans and all the clans of Odunao. All longhouses—except the Constant Tower, the Voca Tower, and the Iden tower—became night-tossed.

For forty-nine days, Psal sat in the Iden longhouse while the great clans were swept along, unable to contact other clans or those longhouses within their own clan. Then on the fiftieth day, he said to Ephan, "This is the Day the Creator Made. The clans now understand their powerlessness. The Jubilee has come."

He sent a message to all the towers and longhouses of Odunao, calling them to the Meadow of the Constant Tower. "Tomorrow," he wrote, "the power of night will be broken. At midday we will keen you to this pleasant land. As for those who do not wish to live among their clans, you leave your longhouses. We will not bring you here. You will remain where the day and night have found you and create your new lives there."

He was not sure if the studiers of some of the clans believed him. Certainly, if he was in their place, he would not have believed the ancient prophecies had come true and some damaged Firstborn from a far-off clan had been appointed by the Creator to overcome the power of darkness.

When day dawned, all the peoples of Odunao—even those without towers and longhouses, even those who had left their longhouses—were gathered in the meadows, a spontaneous city stretching far and wide around the Constant Tower.

Anger and confusion reigned at first, but as friend greeted long-lost friend, and family called to family, joy rose in all hearts. People stood on ramparts, calling out, seeking and searching for lost sons and daughters, lost mothers and fathers, lost wives and husbands. Sumra was there, Gillan's sisters, the brothers of the Grassrope outcast, Tzaddi, Cassia, Moonlight, all. Lost spouses, children, clans all found each other. All who entered the Constant Tower were suddenly healed of all their ailments. Whether king's son or outcast, all left the tower praising the Creator for reconciling them to Himself. All the while, Psal and Ephan stood on its rampart.

* * * *

Inside the Iden longhouse, Ktwala stood at the window. Netophah and a wounded Wheel Clan warrior left the Constant Tower, laughing and running toward the royal longhouse. The Creator's command to Ktwala had been difficult to hear. And yet she understood that the sacrifice of forgiveness was necessary. Her life, her continued marriage to Nahas was necessary. She had seen the aims of the Unfleshed Ones, had understood how they used and amplified human evil.

She lifted Nahas' daughter from the wooden crib and walked outside toward the royal longhouse. Her Iden sisters had seen her approaching and ran toward her, rejoicing and enfolding her in their arms. All praised the Ever-Present One for returning Gidea, Tolika, and Ktwala to them.

Nahas stood nearby, unspeaking. She walked to him. What could words do? She only extended her hands to him and hugged him. His arms enfolded her and their daughter. Together, in pained silence, they walked to the royal chamber. After Nahas closed the door behind him, they sat on the floor facing each other. For a long while, they did not speak. Not one word. Only bitter tears flowed til after long weeping, unspoken mutual forgiveness staunched their flow.

* * * *

On the rampart, Psal took Maharai by the hand. "The world will not be what it has always been. The Creator has made all things new."

Only one sorrow marred the joy of that day: Cyrt, Nahas' mighty warrior, had walked to a hillside and hung himself. In days to come, the king would mourn him.

As for the Voca Queen, before the sun began to set, she met Ephan at the top of the tower stairs.

"From here," she said, "we will map the world and give the clans the lands for their inheritance." She called out to Psal. "Psal, why do you and your brother stand looking out at the sky? You must declare your kingship. The world must be ruled in fairness or once again, the weak will be oppressed."

Ephan kissed her cheek and pulled her close, whispered. "Forgive me, Mother. I have no desire to rule kingdoms. Let kingdoms and clans form as they will without interference from me."

"All these people," she replied, "will make you and your descendants king in spite of all you desire. Psal, too. It is the way of the world. Already all the studiers and stewards of the Wheel Clan have withstood their king for your sakes, and are guarding you against the king's anger. What do you think the people of this world will do when you show them that the darkness has been conquered? They will make you kings."

Psal called from the tower's ramparts, his voice floating on the wind, carried to all the gathered peoples and clans. "Peace will reign among the clans, and nevermore will separation or the night rule over us."

When the people heard this, they all laughed. It was one thing to keen all humanity to the Meadows. It was quite another to conquer the night. They could not believe.

So Psal waited. When third moon began rising, the people raced to their towered longhouses and huts, as they had always done.

That night Maharai and the women of the Gleaners Clan drummed and danced under the uncovered sky, because they knew the Creator had covered them with his own cloaken. All of Odunao waited for the night to bear their longhouses away. But when third moon rose high in the sky and the truth could no longer be denied, longhouse doors opened. Heads peeked out. Soon other food was brought out and the air grew festive with song and dance. The people at last understood that the curse had been removed and that they had been reconciled to their forgiving Creator. They danced and sang long into the night.

It was called the Night of Watching Stars. On that night, three things were celebrated: The end of the war, the reconciliation with the Creator, and the destruction of the power of the night.

That was when your ancestors' great dynasty began, for although Psal did not wish for a kingdom, a kingdom was now his. And because the clans were fearful more warfare would arise, marriage alliances were made. But you know already how the reconciliation came about: Psal, the second son of King Nahas, married Cassia, Tsbosso's second daughter; Netophah, the youngest son, wedded Moonlight, the youngest of Tsbosso's daughters; and Ephan, Nahas' Firstborn son, was wedded to Tzaddi. And because Ephan was also the son of the great Queen Ezbel, peace reigned also between the Peacock Clans and the Voca. Maharai was their great queen, beloved and shared wife of Nahas' three sons.

Our ancestors lived together in peace around the Tower until the place became too small for them. After that, the clans spread across the planet and forgot the location and power of the true Tower. Once again, the Unfleshed Ones brought confusion. But the people of Odunao have never forgotten the Night of Watching Stars and the two sons of King Nahas, whose task it had been to return the night.

* * * *

What? Oh my boy, you are tiring me out. Already I've told you Ephan's story and Psal's. And now you wish me to speak of Netophah? Well then…I will speak of Netophah. But first, let us recite Maharai's elegy, written after Psal's death. The poem is widely-read, even to this day:

> *The Cloud disperses*
> *The Storm breaks*
> *And I am alone.*

Now, in the old days, there was no law on Odunao, and hearts were divided, especially the heart of a boy named Netophah. See then: Netophah, a boy nature-blessed, a prince of all the Wheel Clans, but primarily a boy…

THE END

GLOSSARY

TOWER SCIENCE

Level One Towers—Towers inhabited by those who are knowledgeable in tower science, region mapping, notation, and keening. These towers generally are inhabited by clans such as the Wheel Clan, the Waymaker Clan, the Falconer Clan, the Macaw Clan, the Voca Clan and the Peacock Clan. These clans are often explorers, conquerors, or marauders.

Level Two Towers—Towers inhabited by people with limited tower science. These towers usually are keened to travel from known region to known region.

Level Three Towers—Also called night-tossed towers. Inhabited by people who know nothing about tower science.

Level Four Towers—Towers that are abandoned, damaged, and possibly irreparable.

Un-towered Longhouses—Longhouses that have no towers attached to them.

THE CLANS

Only tightly-affiliated clans such as the Wheel Clan, The Voca, the Waymaker Clan, the Waymaker Clan, and the Voca are ruled wholly by one Ruler. A sub-clan is often called after the chief of its longhouse. The Wheel Clan sub-clans are all ruled by King Nahas.

The Waymaker Clan—A pale-skinned clan with crescent-shaped eyes, known for their expedience and skill in tower science. Unified, they often inter-marry with the Wheel Clan.

The Grassrope Clan—A scattered loosely-affiliated clan of dark-haired, green-eyed people, they are prone to in-fighting.

The Macaw Clan—Distantly related to the Peacock Clan, they are allied to many clans through inter-marriage. Generous in everything except their knowledge of the towers, they are neutral in all wars and are often used as reconciliators during truce-meetings.

The Wheel Clan—A fair-haired, pale-eyed clan. They are the most technologically advanced of all Odunao clans, because they're so unified. They share their tower science only among themselves. Because of their skill and knowledge, they own much of Odunao's resources.

The Peacock Clans—A commonwealth of loosely affiliated dark-skinned tribes. However, they lack the unity of clans such as the Wheel Clan or the Voca, and each sub-clan tends to keep its knowledge of the towers to itself. Because the Wheel Clan owns and hoards so much of the planet's resources, the Peacock Clan has waged war against them.

The Voca Clan—An all-female clan, at war with all male-ruled clans. They add to their population by stealing women and young girls from other clans. They have a truce with the Wheel Clan.

THE SEASONS

For those who have no power to steer their towers, seasons come in a fairly routine way. By its own internal clock, a tower transports itself periodically to a new clime. The nightly changes still continue to occur but now the changes take place in a particular clime until the next clime change occurs.

The planet of Odunao has no true seasonal changes. However, there are geographic areas which are permanently cold, cool, warm, or hot. These areas are called Cool Climes, Desert Climes, Mist Climes, Cold Climes, Cold Dark Climes, and Dark Climes.

Since each tower has its own internal rhythms, and their own patterns, the "climes" don't occur in the same pattern with every longhouse. Thus, one tower may travel to a cool clime, while another is in a warm clime. Knowledgeable clans can plan to meet in a particular clime because for those with the knowledge of tower science, the clime changes have no power.

MAJOR HERBS USED BY WHEEL CLAN STUDIERS

Caftay Beans—a bean used by the Wheel Clan, often fermented

Dama seeds—a grain used as an antibiotic

Dovi—an herb that can be a gentle sedative or a harsh poison depending on whether seeds, roots, leaves, are used, and depending on the potency

Emon—An herb used as a mental sedative, numbing agent or a painkiller. Also called the studier's herb because they often smell like it, using it on their patients or on themselves.

Gorek—an herb used as a purgative and anti-parasitic

Kepbu—a berry, principally used for women

Mirta berries—a tart/sweet berry used to make medicines more palatable

Naro—a plant used for grain, spice, and dyeing

Pida—an herb used to prevent infection
Ramsa—a toxic mushroom
Rifik—a drug which can also be used as a poison
Rangi—a root used as a sedative
Tomah—an addictive herb, often abused by studiers
Yisin—a grain used by the clans in cooking